The wife of a succes[...]
Elizabeth Walker li[...]
Pennines. She combines writing with keeping live-
stock and has written nine previous novels, including
Voyage, *Rowan's Mill*, *The Court*, *Conquest* and
Hallmark, all available from Headline. She is an
internationally established bestselling author.

Praise for her previous novels:

'A wonderful, romantic read' *Annabel*
'A memorable book and refreshingly different' *Woman's World*
'The perfect holiday read' *Me* Magazine

Also by Elizabeth Walker

Child of Shadows

Elizabeth Walker

HEADLINE

First published in 1994
by HEADLINE BOOK PUBLISHING

First published in paperback in 1994
by HEADLINE BOOK PUBLISHING

10 9 8 7 6 5 4 3 2 1

ISBN 0 7472 4476 6

Typeset by Keyboard Services, Luton

Printed and bound in Great Britain by
Cox & Wyman Ltd, Reading, Berks

HEADLINE BOOK PUBLISHING
A division of Hodder Headline PLC
338 Euston Road
London NW1 3BH

To Rupert,
a good dog and a good friend

BOOK ONE

BOOK ONE

Chapter One

The wind travelled the wide, flat fields like a conqueror. Nothing dared stand in its way. It tore at the washing on the line, ripping it down and tossing it in the mud, for her mother to gather up, wearily, and do again. It dragged tiles from the farmhouse roof, great slabs of rich red clay, and smashed them on the cobbles, sending the hens squawking. Now and then, enraged by some nameless insult, it uprooted a tree, to leave the poplars on the long avenue as gap-toothed as an old woman's smile.

At its worst, the wind put everyone in a terrible bad temper. Madame Girand swore at her husband and slapped her sons, and was not above giving Lori's mother a jab in the ribs, because the cream had curdled in the churn. 'Really, Mademoiselle! After all this time I should have thought you had learned to make butter!'

Lori hugged her mother's skirts, listening to the necessary apology. Everyone knew that when the wind came from the east the cows turned their tails to it and the butter wouldn't churn. She put her finger in her mouth, sucking for comfort.

'It's all right, Lori. Don't worry.' Her mother's soft voice, speaking their own special language, her warm and tender smile. And Lori knew, with absolute certainty, that her mother would keep her from harm.

Because her mother was always there. She hadn't known a time when she was absent, could not believe there would ever be such a time. When she woke in the morning she didn't even have to open her eyes to know that her mother was there; the bed smelled of lavender and soap, cutting across the sour tang of Lori's own urine. How good it was to be freed from the wet folds of her nappy, to be washed and made fresh again.

3

'You should beat that child. She's too old to be wetting at night.'

'She's only two, Madame.'

'She's almost three! You should put her out of your bed. Put her out and find a decent man to sleep with. One that'll marry you this time.' But Lori's mother only gathered her child up and took her out to the cows, blue-grey in the morning, up to their knees in straw.

They smelled so rich, the cows; of dung and grain and grass. Lori used to watch as her mother worked, listening to the slop and suck of the washing bucket, the slap of a cow's wet tail. The byre was warm in winter, the great bodies quietly steaming, while the cats prowled restlessly. Sometimes a hen would perch on a door and watch Lori with its hard, black eye, a giant bird, all feathers and sharp beak. Lori didn't like the hens very much.

So she played with the kittens while her mother milked, watching her move from beast to beast, each pail taken as it was full by Monsieur Girand or one of his big, ugly sons. At least, they seemed ugly to Lori, tall as trees, rough-voiced, smelling of dung. Sometimes, when there was no one else there, Jean went into the stall with Lori's mother and wouldn't let her come out. The talk was quick, low and angry. Lori would start to wail.

'Can't you shut the brat up? Jesus, why do you keep her?'

'I'd rather have ten of her than one of you. Hush, Lori. Mummy's all right.' And so was Lori. Held in her mother's arms, not even Jean could alarm her.

The spring came, and with it a flush of milk. Jean was with the cows every day. Lori played in the sunshine with a new litter of kittens, and she loved the black one best. She was holding it the day her mother came flying from the barn and snatched her up. The kitten put out its claws and Lori shrieked.

'Oh, little one. Oh, I'm sorry. It's just a scratch.'

Jean loomed over them, sending the kittens scurrying. 'Look, there's no need for all this. If I got you in the family way I'd take care of you.'

Some of the stiffness eased from her mother's body. 'Would you? Really, Jean?'

'You know I would. I'm not the man to let you down. Come

4

on. The kid's had your titties long enough. Let a man get his hands on them for a change.'

Her mother blushed and put Lori down again, and went back to her milking. When Lori tried to follow Jean pushed her away.

Later, in the summer evenings, with the swallows darting over the meadows and the fields deep in corn, Lori's mother put her child to bed and went walking with Jean. Sometimes, when she returned, her skirt was damp from the grass. She might bring fruit though, that she called greengages and Jean called *reine-claudes*, from an orchard at a ruined farm nearby. They were sour, because the tree had gone back to the wild, her mother said. Everything had gone back in the war. Lori wondered if that was why Luc, Jean's brother, stayed in the house and scowled.

Summer changed to autumn, and with winter came the snow. The fields looked flatter still, white as they were with just the trees and the vines poking through. Crows flapped like great black dusters as you passed, and Lori's mother didn't walk with Jean any more. She worked at the washing and the butter until her hands turned blue with cold, and at Christmas Jean tramped into the village carrying a load of mistletoe and brought back a plump baker's daughter. He took her into the barn and when Lori stood at the door and watched them he cursed and chased her away.

So the next summer it was Luc who took Lori's mother into the fields. Lori, older now, knelt up in bed and watched from the window, hating Jean and Luc and the baker's daughter, and most of all Madame Girand, for saying to Lori's mother, 'You've got a roof, haven't you? What else do you expect with a bastard child?'

'I'm still a human being! The girl had no right to speak to me like that, and Jean to stand and let her. I still deserve some respect!'

Madame Girand put down her kitchen knife and gave the young woman an unyielding stare. 'What did you expect? You're nothing. You're nobody. A fool. Be grateful Luc doesn't mind his brother's leavings. You're lucky I don't put you from the door.'

The year began slipping away. The swallows were gone, the grain lay heaped in the barn, the mice ran scuttling along the

5

rafters, now and then falling into the vat of plum brandy to swim for a minute and then drown. Lori's mother didn't seem to mind the mice. She went into the loft now with Luc and the winter apples, while Lori stood below, listening as the mice ran, as Luc groaned, as her mother gasped. Then they talked a lot and Luc came rushing down the ladder, his ugly face all fierce and white. Lori hid in the corner.

When she came down and saw her, Lori's mother picked her up and hugged her tight. And instead of the warmth that she and her mother shared, Lori felt the first beginnings of a mutual fear. Now that Jean didn't like them, now that Luc was growing cold, they weren't safe here any more.

'Oh, Lori. Why won't it come right? What am I going to do?'

On Sunday they went to church and prayed, although the women of the village always stared and muttered when they walked past. The houses were huddled together like cows at a gate, all different shades of cracked and peeling paint. The roofs tumbled together, some thatch, some tile, while above it all stood the church, grey and forbidding. Inside it was dark and smelled strange. The light was blue and gold, falling from the candles like coloured stars. But no one looked kindly on them. 'It's not the right sort of church,' whispered her mother, 'that's the trouble. I'm not one of them!'

But Lori had always known they were different. They had two languages, one for each other and one for the rest. They had no family, and living as they did no friends, while all these people had cows and houses and people to talk to in the street. Lori and her mother had just the one room in a house that was not theirs. They had no one they could call a friend. And with snow on the wind, the ever-present wind, Lori had no winter shoes.

Her mother spoke to Madame Girand, and went out into the fields, digging turnips. It was too cold for Lori in the fields, she said, 'And too cold for you!' cried Lori. But her mother went just the same, for the francs she would earn, leaving Lori in their room, because she was not welcome in the cosy farm kitchen. Keeping warm in bed, she looked through a book her mother read to her, about rabbits and hedgehogs that wore clothes and spoke, not like French rabbits at all.

On the first day, Lori's mother came home and went straight

to work with the cows. Luc went out to see her and then to see his mother, and he shouted and banged doors. On the second day, when she got up Lori's mother's clothes weren't dry, but she put them on anyway. Lori had eaten nothing the day before, so her mother said, 'You're to go in the kitchen when the men come in. Ask Luc for some bread.'

But Lori knew Luc didn't like her. She didn't go.

That night her mother had a cough. Luc shouted even more, and Jean shouted at Luc, and Madam Girand screamed, 'All this fuss over a stupid English bitch.' Lori's mother fetched bread and some cassoulet for Lori, thick with wine and strong fat bacon, but ate nothing herself. It was good too. Lori gobbled it down.

On the third day the wind came up, and drove the rain across the fields like a million icy arrows. Sometimes it turned to snow, only enough to fill the furrows of the ploughed fields, leaving them striped like an old bedspread. That night when Lori's mother came home, her shoes cracked and full of snow, she went straight to bed and lay shivering all night long, although Lori did her best to warm her. She lay against her mother's icy back, putting her little hands against the knobs of her mother's spine. She was very frightened. She longed for her mother to lie still.

In the morning the shivering had stopped, and Lori thought her mother must be well. She was so peaceful and quiet. She didn't wake, even for milking, and Lori got out her book and looked at the pictures, so her mother would have enough rest. But then up came Madame Girand, cross as two sticks, and Lori thought she should have woken her mother and not let Madame Girand get angry.

When Madame leaned over the bed she screamed, which frightened Lori a lot, and Monsieur came running, and Jean, and everyone said, 'Mon Dieu' and crossed themselves. When Luc came in from the barn, his hands wet from the milking, he stood at the foot of the bed and made sobbing noises, as if he was crying, with his face twisted up, but no tears.

'You killed her! You killed her, you hard-hearted cow!'

'She was weak from the start. I told you she was no use.'

'She was perfect. You killed her. My God, I shall never forgive you!'

7

Lori stared down at her picture book. The rabbit stared back at her, and she looked away, at her mother, although she looked quite different from ever before. She smelled of mud and turnips and cold.

Lori's early morning hunger seemed to settle like snow deep inside her. She thought of yesterday's meal. She should have shared it with her mother and not eaten greedily herself. Who would feed her now? Who would comfort her? Where was her mother gone? Sobs began to bubble up within her, like milk on the fire. The book was spattered with tears.

'Get the child out of here,' said Madame Girand angrily. Jean picked her up and carted her down the stairs.

'No! No!' screamed Lori, kicking him as hard as she could.

'Stop that, you idiot!' He shook her, like a dog, and Lori wet on him.

When Madame Girand came down Jean said, 'The stinking brat wet on me,' and his mother said, 'She's spoiled rotten. I don't know what we'll do with her. Little bastard.'

The space inside Lori grew colder and colder still. Her sobs turned to shivers. No one noticed. She didn't expect them to. She knew they didn't like her. A great agony of tears seemed to lodge where her heart should be, because Lori knew that her mother would never come back. She was alone. There was no one to love her any more.

Lori sometimes wondered if her mother's death had ended her life too. She wasn't living now. Days passed, admittedly, one following on another; food was eaten, work was done, but inside herself there was nothing. Even her tears ceased to fall. Sometimes, at night, sleeping now in a room under the roof, close to the cold empty sky, she dreamed that she wept. Exquisite, blessed solace, easing the anguish of her heart. But her cheeks were dry when she woke.

At first Madame Girand talked of sending her to an orphanage. But they lived very far from town, and no one was prepared to exert themselves on Lori's behalf, even to be rid of her. Then, after a month or two, Luc walked out. Madame Girand, stricken and vengeful at one and the same time, brandished a boning knife at Lori and said, 'It's your fault, you brat! You and your bitch of a mother. Take that look off your stupid face. You haven't the sense you were born with.'

The child gaped at her, expecting at any moment to be slit like the chicken on the table, from gizzard to crop. Her mouth opened and closed in a silent plea for mercy. But she knew Madame wouldn't spare her. To her surprise, the woman turned away.

'Curse that you are. Your mother, then Luc – you'll be the death of me one day. You're a child of hell.'

After a while, in the silent kitchen, Lori took up her scrubbing brush and began to rub it on the table. The chicken blood was sticky and would not come off. When Madame saw, and yelled at her with her usual spite, Lori felt a strange sense of relief.

Months passed, marked by the endless rhythm of the farm. In spring, Lori went into the fields with Jean or Monsieur, leading the horse in the furrow. All the good horses had gone in what they called the Great War, finished only three years ago, so they had a beast that couldn't walk straight unless someone led it and turned it and backed it up. It did as Lori wanted, though, towering hugely above her, its mane a tangled mass of blond hair over a shiny red coat. It only shied when they passed the blown-up horse, all bleached bones and grinning teeth. In the war, a shell had fallen here and the horse had stepped on it a month later and been killed. Monsieur said it wasn't as bad as some places. There, the plough turned daily on the bones of men.

In the hot, sultry summer days Lori struggled with heavy pails of milk, skimming cream and churning butter, pressing hard cheese and squeezing soft, her little hands raw from muslin soaked in whey. The dairy was next to the cowshed, so dark that it hurt to look at the patch of sunlight by the door. It was like thinking of her mother; an intensity of warmth that hurt when you weren't inside it. Sometimes, Lori would close her eyes and listen to the summer sounds outside, trapped in her dark, milk-smelling world.

In the autumn came the nuts, shelled and soaked in the first pressings of the grapes, to be sold in jars at the market. Now that the war was ended there was money to be made. The year brought truffles too, for which Monsieur hunted in the woods, his old dog mad with the scent of them. Lori sometimes carried

9

the bag, struggling through the trees, excited by the yapping of the dog but dreading that someone should hear it and find the truffles first. They were like great earthy stones, once as big as Monsieur's head. He was delighted and clapped his hands and rewarded himself with a sip from his bottle. Lori simply sighed and thought how heavy it would be to carry home.

The truffles too went to market, and sold for much money. All the same, now and then when Monsieur was not looking, Madame took a tiny piece of one and fried it in butter for herself and Jean, and sometimes she made a stuffing with little nuggets of truffle amongst the suet and herbs. Lori never had any though. She expected none.

Towards the end of October, on a still, misty day when the empty fields were light and clear and the sky without colour, a priest came cycling down the avenue to the farm. They could see him turn off the road and come pedalling up through the poplars, flashing in and out of vision as he passed behind each tree. Madame went outside. Now that he was nearer they could see not only his wide hat but his soutane, riding up over his bicycling, muscular knees. So it was the young priest. The new one.

'What does he want?' Her hands redolent of the stuffing she had been mixing, Madame wiped them vigorously on her apron. 'He comes in the truffle season, of course! Thinks we're rolling in it. Young vulture. Priests flap out of the trees the moment they smell money. He'll get nothing from me.'

Lori shielded her eyes against the pale sky and tried to see. She felt afraid. No one ever came to the house except the carter, once a month or so. No one ever flashed between the poplars with such purpose and energy. No wonder Madame was cross.

He was a broad-shouldered young fellow with a smile that resisted even Madame's attempts to extinguish it. She ushered him into the salon, a cold, unused room with a polished wood floor and high chairs. Lori had never entered it, not even to clean. She stayed in the kitchen, stirring the mix as Madame had said, wondering if perhaps the young man didn't know about Madame. If he had known he would surely never have come.

Her arm began to ache. The stuffing was heavy with good things, full of herbs, the last of the year, picked that day and crushed. Lori breathed deep of the scent until she was dizzy. It

10

wasn't fair that she never had truffles, after all the walking and the carrying that she did. Not to mention the nettle stings. Would Madame notice if she ate some? Madame always noticed. But not even fear could combat this temptation. Lori reached in and crammed a handful of the mixture into her mouth. Truffles! The divine, forbidden food.

'Lori!' The child froze. 'Lori, come here!'

Madame was at the door. The stuffing set in Lori's mouth, unchewed, unswallowable. Surely Madame didn't want her in the salon? But Madame did.

'Hello, Lori.' The priest put out his hand for her to take. Lori, watching Madame from the corner of her eye, stayed still. The priest withdrew his hand.

'How old are you?'

It was impossible to say. Quite apart from the stuffing, Lori didn't know. 'Madame?' The priest looked enquiring.

She shrugged. 'As you see, she's an idiot. We keep her out of charity. Her mother was a servant here, a slut of a girl. We do what we can with the child.'

'I never see her in church. We must all walk with God.'

'Her mother was a Protestant. Her dying wish – her own faith—'

Madame crossed herself devoutly.

'And she doesn't go to school.'

Madame bridled. 'You would send an idiot to school?'

The priest looked again at Lori. He leaned down to her, not unkindly. His front teeth were twisted. If he'd been a hen they'd have wrung his neck. He said, 'Would you like to go to school?'

Lori's mind raced. The priest was so clean. The stuffing must soon choke her. How odd Madame seemed with her mouth pursed up under her big, bulbous nose. But she thought nothing of liking or not liking school. Whatever school might be, she knew Madame would never let her go.

The priest sighed and stood up. 'If you cannot at least clothe her decently, Madame, then she must go to the orphanage.'

Colour flooded into Madame's cheeks. 'You would have me put good clothes on an idiot?'

'I would have you feed and clothe her adequately. Or leave it to others to do so.'

They each assessed the other. Young, energetic priests were

always the worst, thought Madame. Much better when the years had depressed them. For the time being, at least, she must make a concession.

'Perhaps I could find her something,' she said grudgingly. 'Of course she eats well – nothing but the best – enough for a full-grown man—'

'Indeed. Dress her in something warm, Madame. She looks half frozen. May Christ and the Virgin be with you.'

When he had gone, creaking away on his bicycle, Madame turned to Lori. 'Right little troublemaker you are. At least you had the sense to keep a still tongue. Just remember, they beat you at school. Twice as bad as Jean.'

Lori wondered if that might be true. Surely not. If anyone hit her twice as hard as Jean she would break up into pieces and be dead. Her bones would be in bits, like the blown-up horse. Her head would be cracked like an egg, and just as runny.

Surprisingly, though, Madame did find her some clothes. There was an old jacket, with the arms cut off, the hem skimming Lori's ankles. There was a hat too, huge and unwieldy, which Lori crammed over her stringy hair when she walked with the horse in the rain. And some shoes appeared, ugly and cumbersome, but better by far than the outgrown sandals that had been her lot up to now. She wriggled her toes in them, luxuriating in space. But when she tried to run she tripped and fell over her feet. Not that she ran very often. The long days with the horse, knee deep in mud or buttercups, depending on the season, left her too weary for anything but sleep.

Lori was clad in her amazing clothes when the priest next came. He got off his bicycle, holding a large brown parcel, and stood looking down at her, an odd expression on his face. 'Hello, Lori.'

She smiled at him. Thanks to him she had a coat and hat and shoes. 'I brought you some more clothes. Pretty ones.'

She looked at him dubiously. What did he mean? In her small world clothes were not pretty. They were thick or they were thin, they were small or they were big, but as for prettiness – the word was irrelevant. It didn't apply to clothes.

'You like pretty clothes, don't you?'

Suddenly, as if rushing out of the emptiness of the past, a

12

memory came to her. Her mother's lavender-scented night-dress. To close your fingers on it was to catch hold of a cobweb. To have it again – to touch it again – she nodded, violently.

'Of course you do. Let's see what we have here, shall we?' He put the parcel on the grass and began to unfasten it, and Lori felt a great rush of excitement. What would she see in the parcel? Was it truly for her?

Just then Madame came out.

'I saw you arrive, Father. You will take a glass of wine. Lori, go and play with Monsieur, as you always do.'

She meant go and see to the horse. But the priest said, 'Perhaps Lori could stay, Madame? I have some clothes for her.'

'Indeed. You are too kind.'

Lori, Madame and the priest all went into the salon. The priest patted one of the high wooden chairs, meaning that Lori should sit down. Madame shot her a look. Lori stood. The priest, opening his parcel, spread out a little girl's skirt in white cotton, bordered at its edge in blue. 'See, Lori. The blue matches your eyes.'

'The child's eyes are without colour. Blue, indeed!'

'They are certainly very unusual eyes. But the blue will reflect in them. With a little care and a little tending she could be attractive. Imagine that black hair, tied up in a ribbon.'

Madame let out a sound somewhere between a growl and a groan. 'And what use is all this? She was the ruin of her mother and she'll be the ruin of me! Don't you think life's hard enough, trying to build something after that damned war? I took the brat in, as was my duty, and now you want my days spent washing her clothes and combing her hair and waiting on her hand and foot! Take her then! Take her! The orphanage can have her!' She cast her arms wide in a grand gesture, leaving her bosoms to heave and wobble like unset caramel. Lori's heart began to pound in her chest. What would happen now?

But Madame had called the young priest's bluff. Lori's life here, however unsatisfactory, had to be better than the orphanage. There, under the unyielding supervision of nuns, four hundred children were subjected to stark and impoverished conditions. With numbers swelled dramatically by the war and its aftermath, there was neither the will nor the resources to care for them. Within the ranks of the children were incipient thieves, gangsters and torturers, practising their skills in the corners and the passageways and the dormitories, preying on their fellow unfortunates. Wars left such children like flotsam on a beach.

He looked at the young girl in front of him. He had chosen to help her because in this one instance help was possible, when for those others it was not. She was so frail, so silent. If, through his tactlessness, she was sent to the orphanage, he would never forgive himself. 'You – you misunderstand me, Madame,' he said soothingly. 'I speak often to others of your Christian charity. You will most certainly be blessed in heaven for your good works and kindness to this child of God.'

'I do what I can – a poor family, much distressed—'

'It is only that I hoped you would bring the child to church soon. As an example. To others less charitable than yourself.'

Madame's nose seemed to twitch, like a pig sensing apples.

'Indeed? These clothes are to take the child to church? As I said to you, her mother was a Protestant, God rest her soul.'

The priest took her hand and patted it. 'We can bring her to the true faith, Madame. To be one in Christ.'

'You'll speak of me from the pulpit? Before them all?' She wouldn't give in for less.

'Madame – Madame, of course.'

Lori stared at the blue edge of the skirt. It was slightly frayed. The priest and Madame droned on and on, and she thought of wearing the skirt and going to church. She wouldn't go to the orphanage, she had realised that much. Madame was pretending. She should have known. Who else would lead the horse and scrub the table and catch the chickens? She sighed, weighed down by the labour that lay in front of her, more each day, harder each day. But a flicker of hope sustained her. She might one day get to wear the pretty skirt.

The day came at Christmas. The household never celebrated much, except to make more and more food. Hams, and galantines, and pies and pâtés and mousses; sauces and dressings and garlic butter; puddings and tartelettes, and dramatic, dangerous soufflés. This year, especially, Madame was hoping Luc would come home. But as the days passed and he remained absent, despite the groaning table, her mood darkened. She took to mumbling to herself in the kitchen. 'Won't come now that bitch is dead. Good-looking boy like that could have had anyone. Could have had money. All the fault of the other! Ought to come back and show them. Ought to come back and let them see what a fine man he's become.' She brightened visibly, pausing in her pounding of dough for walnut bread with olives. 'That's what he's waiting for. He's going to come back in style!'

The thought inspired her so much that she decided it was time to take the priest up on his promise now, rather than waiting until Luc came home. After all, then she would have an embarrassment of riches. If Lori could provide a little social credit now, when she needed it, then there was no reason to wait.

She filled the small tin bath from the copper by the fire and threw in a good handful of washing soda. Then she grabbed her victim. 'Come along, brat! In you go!'

For the first time in her life, Lori resisted Madame. Faced with the steaming cauldron, flecked with pinnacles of white foam, she fought like a tiger. Madame struggled with her, stripping an arm from its coat, a foot from its stinking threadbare sock. Lori's toes flexed madly, as if they would leave her body and fly away and be free.

Jean came in. When he saw the struggle he began to laugh.

'You'll stop that!' gasped Madame. 'Grab hold and help me. She's a hell-child all right.'

'Put her in that tub and you'll boil the skin off her,' remarked Jean.

Madame snorted and stuck a hand in the water. She pulled back smartly and cursed. Jean went to fetch a pail and slopped some cold in as well. The child, naked and wriggling, was held up.

'God, but she stinks! The priest should wash her, since he wants her clean.'

'Looks like a snail without a shell. We should eat her. Boil her up and eat her. Let's do that, Maman!' Jean leered at Lori. Transfixed with terror, she stayed still for the second it took to plunge her into the tub.

Like dipping sheep, Madame put her in and held her down. Lori's arms and legs began to windmill, sending water and suds

15

flying. At last, when she was sure she must drown, Madame released the pressure on her head. Lori popped up, coughing and blowing.

'Not much has come off,' said Jean.

'She'll have to be scrubbed.'

'I'll do it.'

Lori watched dubiously as Jean approached with the brush. It had hard brown bristles and instinctively she flinched away. He was grinning, making menacing noises, like a wild beast. She flung out an arm to fend him off, and he grabbed her. The brush came roughly across her tender skin.

It left a hard, red trail. At every stroke she squealed, but after a while the bristles softened in the water, and she began to squeal less. Jean was grinning, enjoying himself. Suddenly he pulled her arms wide and raked the brush across her narrow little chest. Her nipples, no more than pink dots, turned dark. He laughed and poked the brush, left right, left right. She tried to cover herself but he pushed her arms aside. When she looked up she saw that his tongue was gripped by his teeth.

'Haven't you finished with her yet?'

'She's filthy.'

The brush moved lower into the water. Lori tensed, waiting for the pain, but it wasn't the brush that touched her. Jean's big, horny hand pushed between her legs, digging, probing, rubbing. His big glistening face loomed over her, eyes, skin, teeth. Below the water a finger pushed between her infant folds. She screamed, and Jean jerked back.

'It's the best I can do,' he said briskly, getting to his feet. 'Likes being dirty, she does.'

'Dirty little bastard,' said Madame automatically. 'There's not many would take her in. When I sit in that church with her that priest's going to swallow his Bible, so he is.'

Lori climbed awkwardly from the tub, its edge cutting into the soft flesh of her thigh. The tingling of her skin was not unpleasant. She hurt though, from Jean's finger. She could tell he had liked to do that, just as she could tell that he liked to beat her, or imagine she had done something wrong so he could take away her food. Her hair, full of suds still, hung in rat's tails over her skinny shoulders.

'God, but she's ugly,' said Jean.

The next day Madame dressed her in the blue and white skirt. She dragged a comb painfully through the tangled hair, and tied it up with a ribbon. She found an old wool shawl for Lori to wrap around her shoulders, over her thin little vest.

To Lori's surprise, Monsieur took notice. 'Put her in a coat,' he instructed. 'The child's going to freeze.'

'Then freeze she must,' said Madame. 'Looks twice the size in that coat. Don't want people thinking she's any use to us.'

Gripping Lori tightly by the hand, she marched her briskly down the avenue. Frost had turned the grass stiff as straw, and the crows sat in the poplars, hunched and silent. When they reached the road they waited, and sure enough a cart came along and gave them a lift.

'Don't often see you in church, Madame,' said the driver incautiously.

'Don't often see you sober,' she retorted. 'Keep your eyes on the road, Flaubert.'

They were silent the rest of the way. Lori, in her thin vest, began to shiver.

The village seemed full of people. Lori had forgotten there were so many people in the world. She stumbled in her heavy shoes, trying to keep up with Madame and not be lost. Fine flakes of snow were drifting on the wind, and women wore hats of glossy fur, gathered about their faces. 'Look at that poor child!' they said to each other. 'Summer clothes at Christmas. She'll freeze to death.'

Madame's face darkened. Although it was not yet time for the service she took hold of Lori and flung her into the church.

It seemed no warmer inside. Unseen breezes fluttered the candles and threatened to put them out. Lori remembered lighting candles with her mother and at once closed her mind. The pain lingered though, reminding her. She was learning to hate remembering.

Madame was looking around constantly, and only settled when she saw the young priest. He was kneeling at the old peasant crib, putting the final touches to the setting. Candles framed him, giving his face a certain holiness it never had by the light of day. Madame pursed her lips as if to spit, but even she gave pause. The little manger scene, the colours once garish but now dulled to rose and ochre and old gold, seemed to bring the

17

reality of the farm and the cowbyre into this other world.

The nativity had been in the village for as long as anyone could remember. Each carved and painted figure, no more than nine inches high, bore an odd similarity to the villagers themselves, with big noses, craggy cheeks and inquisitive eyes. No one could look at them without a smile. The Christ child was no baby though, he was a perfect little man, his hands raised in blessing. He lay in his crib, with beechwood cows and sheep looking reverently upon him. Lori, fascinated, put her fingers in her mouth.

Madame waved, making sure the priest saw her. 'Father! As you see, we have come.'

Did she imagine a tightness in his smile? He came over at once. 'Madame, how good of you. And to bring little Lori. Looking so—' He hesitated. The child looked frozen. 'Looking so fine.'

'So. You'll speak about us, then. Tell everyone.'

'Madame – indeed, Madame. Lori, come and see the crib.'

He put out his hand, smiling at her. 'She'll break it up and then you'll be sorry,' said Madame, but the priest did not withdraw. And Lori did so want to see the crib. She slipped from her seat and ran up the aisle, her shoes so big that they clattered on the stones. The priest followed quite slowly, although people were hissing with alarm. The idiot child was going to break the crib – the precious crib!

But Lori did not touch it at all. She knelt on the stones and stared in awe at the little people with faces she knew. The big man might have been Monsieur, the smaller one the priest himself, and the lady – why, the lady was so lovely.

'Do you like it, Lori? Can you see the infant Christ?'

Pointing an unerring finger to the Virgin, Lori said, 'I can see my mother.'

The young priest gave an inspired sermon that day. He talked of God's power and wisdom, in entrusting a precious soul to Madame Girand.

'This child has no learning, and before today, no speech. And yet, with my own senses, I saw her this day point to the Virgin and call her Mother. A miracle? Yes. Given to us this Christmas Day.'

Chapter Two

The miracle did not entirely convince everyone in the village. There were those who distinctly remembered Lori chattering to her mother before she died. There were others who considered a young priest in an obscure church to have rather too much to gain from a miraculous happening. But for the rest, weary of hardship and grim reality, that a small idiot child should be blessed by the Virgin in their very midst was a beacon of hope.

Although the priest kept his attention firmly on the Virgin and less on the object of her grace, others were less discriminating. Little pilgrimages began to the farm. At first it was only two or three of the curious, but soon the truly devout began to come. They required only that they should see the little girl with her strange pale eyes, and hear her speak. Madame made sure she spoke all right. 'All you need say is, "I pray each day to the Blessed Virgin, my Mother,"' she instructed. 'Nothing else. And none of that grinning you were doing last week. You keep a straight face, or else.' She wasn't going to have Lori acting the star. She was a bit part player, while Madame held centre stage.

At first they brought Lori presents of toys or clothes, but Madame soon let it be known that money would be better. Naturally, Lori saw none of it. Nowadays she spent her Sundays in a plain black dress, reciting her lines two or three times a day and being kissed and hugged by strangers, while Madame told them all of the struggle it had been to rear such an unpromising specimen. Since the rest of Lori's life was quite unchanged, she might have been forgiven for wishing she'd never gone to church in the first place, except that Madame was different. Now Lori was a valuable commodity. The beatings were less, the food was more. In fact, if it hadn't been for Jean, Lori might have been happy.

He came to her room at night. She would hear him creeping

up the stairs, smelling of plum brandy and strong cigarettes. At first she only woke when he opened her door, but soon she could sense the second his foot touched the stair. She lay beneath her covers, holding herself rigid, as if she could make her body stone and repel him. Jean didn't say anything. He never spoke at all, not even to threaten her. They both knew what would happen if she told.

There seemed to be no escape anywhere. By day there was Madame, less anxious now to send her charge into the fields. By night there was Jean, and even if he did not come she was haunted by the thought that he might. After a month or two, Lori's regular Sunday visitors began to remark darkly that the child looked as if she was not long for this world. 'Mark my words. Eyes bigger than her face, skin so pale you can see through it. The Virgin's taking her home, that she is.'

The rumour brought a resurgence of pilgrims. They gasped at Lori's deathly appearance, and held her hands up to the light. 'Do you feed her well, Madame?'

'The bread of heaven is all she will eat,' said Madame, folding her hands devoutly. But even she noticed the child's skinny legs. She said to Jean, 'The brat's going to die on us, just when she's getting to be of some use!'

They were amazed one Sunday when a motorcar appeared in the avenue, driving cautiously over the ruts. All the same the horse, terrified, bolted across the fields, towing the cart, and a herd of cows stampeded through a fence. Madame crossed herself and took off her apron. 'Now we're getting somewhere. It's the gentry.'

Lori, forbidden to come out to greet visitors in case she appeared less than ethereal, peered from the window. The motorcar stopped at the door, smoking and roaring, until someone choked it into silence. The hens, idiot brave, as usual, began pecking around its wheels. Unmoved by the commotion, a beautiful lady closed her parasol, lifted the veil of her hat, and descended.

'My God, Gerard, I never thought we'd make it. You didn't tell me the country was full of shell craters.'

'Only potholes, Sophie. I'm sure we can show you shell craters, if you wish. Good day, Madame. We've come to see your little saint.'

Standing amidst the hens, the car smoking and gurgling behind them, it seemed as if they had descended from heaven themselves. Lori knelt up at the window to get a better view. The man wore a little round hat, a tight brown suit and a flower in his buttonhole. What's more, instead of a beard, like Monsieur, or three days' whiskers, like Jean, he had a neat and well-trimmed moustache. But the lady – oh, the lady! If her cheeks were red, her lips were redder. Her curls, under her feathered hat, were fat and golden. Her parasol was blue, trimmed with white lace, matching her dress exactly. Beneath the dress, the focus of both Lori's and Madame's amazed attention, were two neat little feet and two dear little shoes, topped with diamanté buckles.

Madame, overcome, bobbed an approximation of a curtsey. 'Good day. I didn't expect – I didn't imagine—' She pulled herself together. 'It's twenty francs to see the child.'

Gerard sighed. 'I see the rogues don't all live in Paris. We'll give you two, Madame. If we're satisfied you can expect further custom. If we're not I'll speak to my cousin the cardinal. Hurry up now, where is the child?'

'Two francs each,' said Madame, trying to keep the wind in her sails.

'Oh, very well!'

He tossed the money over and stood waiting. When he realised Madame wished them to enter he said to Sophie, 'Good God. She expects us to go in. The place looks vile.'

'Getting very particular in your old age, Gerard. I used to live in a place worse than this. Come on, will you! I'm sick of hanging about.' Sweeping Madame aside with a swish of her satin skirt she entered the house. After the sun outside it seemed very gloomy. The flagged floors held a heavy chill. Lori, almost invisible in her black dress, stood at the salon door.

'Help! My God, Gerard, I thought it was a ghost! No one said she was so small. And thin! My dear, you're just a baby, and so thin!'

She knelt at Lori's side. The child was at once enveloped in perfume, like a thousand delicious flowers. 'You smell so good,' she said, sniffing the lady's hat, hair, everything.

'Do I, darling? Come and talk to me. Come and tell me everything that's happened in your life.'

Lori, seeing Madame gimlet-eyed in the hall, said, 'I pray every day to the Blessed Virgin, my mother.'

'But who is your real mother? You know that, don't you?'

Parroting, Lori repeated her set phrase. Raising her eyes skywards, Sophie propelled her into the room, excluding Madame.

Gerard kicked the door shut and leaned on it. Sophie whisked Lori to a chair. 'I'm sure you do a lot of praying, sweetheart. I would if that harridan had me in her charge. Did you see the Virgin? Did she talk to you?'

With such an unusual visitor, Lori's restraint slackened. 'I'm not supposed to say.'

'Why not? Does big fat Madame get cross?'

Lori put shocked hands over her mouth. She nodded fiercely.

'Looks a right old battle-axe,' said Gerard. 'Does she keep you locked up?'

'Only on Sundays,' said Lori.

Sophie picked up the child's work-roughened hand. 'What about the rest of the week? Works you hard, does she? Cooking and scrubbing and in the fields? Why don't you go to school?'

'Madame says I wouldn't like it. She says they'd beat me. Every day.'

Sophie was silent for a moment. Then she said, 'And how often are you beaten now, my dear? Don't answer. I can guess.'

She got up, fighting tears, one gloved hand pressed to her mouth. 'She could be me,' she said rapidly to Gerard. 'Just like me. Poor little devil!'

'You didn't have to come, you know.'

'What else is there to do around here?'

'Ye gods, Sophie, what else did you expect?'

She glanced back at Lori's puzzled face. 'Not her.'

They left as rapidly as they came. 'What did you say to her?' demanded Madame, giving Lori a clip round the ear. 'She was crying. What did you say to make her cry?'

'Only about the Virgin – I promise, Madame, only that!'

Lori thought all day about her visitors. Even when Jean came up the stairs that night, she kept thinking about them, remembering Sophie's pink and white face, her golden rolls of hair. She remembered so hard she almost smelled Sophie's scent, instead of the sweaty, sticky, sour stench of Jean. She thought, unusually, that she was glad Jean had been. At least now she knew he wouldn't come again before morning. She could lie all night and remember.

But the next day, to everyone's surprise, Sophie called once more. This time there was no motorcar, merely a pony and trap, and Gerard had been replaced by Flaubert, grinning and smirking at them all.

'What are you doing, bringing visitors on a Monday?' demanded Madame, accosting Flaubert. 'We don't receive on a Monday!'

'I'm sure you can make an exception,' said Sophie, descending gracefully from the trap. Today she was wearing peach, her skirt lifted at the side to reveal a length of silk stocking. Jean, watching from the barn, grinned. 'Ten francs, Madame,' said Sophie. 'I wish to talk to Lori.'

They haggled for a while. Lori, carrying pails from the cowshed, was suddenly aware that Madame and Sophie were bearing down on her. 'I'll wash her and dress her,' declared Madame, determined at least to get her out of Monsieur's old jacket, not to mention frighten her enough to keep her quiet.

'She'll do as she is, thank you,' countered Sophie. The lighter by several stone, she reached Lori first and rested a proprietorial hand on her shoulder. 'Come walking with me, Lori. That big man over there can carry this heavy pail. He doesn't seem to have anything else to do. Come along, my dear.' Madame's little black eyes malevolently watched them go.

They walked in silence through the fields. Young wheat was springing into growth, and birds fluttered along the hedgerows. Pink and yellow wild flowers dotted the banks and bushes. Sophie took off her hat.

'Do you like to live here, Lori?' she asked. 'It's very pretty.'

Lori considered. 'Where else would I live? In the village?'

'There are lots of other places. Madame works you very hard.'

Lori nodded.

They walked on through the meadow, and one of the old cows ambled up to them and waved her horns. Lori shooed her away with a fierce wave of her tattered skirt. Sophie said, 'Look at your legs! All covered in bruises. Poor Lori.'

Lori said nothing. Instead, she parted the grass to show Sophie the bones of the blown-up horse, and pointed to the tree

23

where the herons nested most years. When they reached the river Sophie sat down on a log. 'Here, Lori. I brought you some bonbons.'

They were wrapped in silver paper in a striped bag. 'For me?' Lori clasped her hands in delight. Then a thought came to her. 'Madame mustn't know.'

'Eat them all. Then Madame won't know. Quick, now.'

Lori stuffed herself. She was so anxious that all should be hers she didn't finish one sweet before forcing another into her mouth. So when Sophie said, 'Now tell me. About the Virgin. Did she really speak to you?' Lori's teeth were stuck together. So Sophie laughed and they walked on down the riverbank, and Sophie got her lovely stockings wet. But she didn't seem to mind.

The next day Sophie came yet again. Madame purred with delight when she saw the cart rumbling up the avenue.

'What the devil does she want?' demanded Jean angrily. 'Why don't she keep away?'

'Society ladies take fancies,' said Madame. 'They need their little interests. She's from Paris, you know what they're like. I'll charge fifteen francs today, that's twenty-nine since Sunday. Better than working for a living.'

But Lori scrambled from the house before Madame could begin her negotiations. Madame stuck out a foot and tripped her, and then advanced smiling towards Sophie. Lori got up, stoically dusting off her grazed knees. She knew better than to cry.

No sooner were they away from the house than Sophie turned and said to Lori furiously, 'That woman! To make you fall like that! We'll bathe your knees, darling, straight away.'

'They're all right,' said Lori, bewildered.

'Don't they hurt you?'

'Yes.'

'Well. We must bathe them.'

The knees were soon done. But Sophie began to explore Lori's bumps and bruises. 'What's this, sweetheart? And this?'

Marks where the buckets chafed her, weals where the plough lines cut her flesh. Dark, heavy bruising on her thighs. Lori pinned her legs together, a flush rising like a tide. 'How did these come here, Lori?' The little girl started to cry.

24

The exploration continued. Gently, expectantly, Sophie eased Lori's bony little shoulder from her dress. There, stark against white skin, was a circle of bruised, half-healed punctures. 'How did this come here, my dear?' The child hunched her shoulder away but carefully, gently, Sophie fingered her skin.

'Don't worry, my darling,' she whispered. 'I know. I understand.'

Suddenly Lori turned and said fiercely to Sophie, 'I wish you were always here! I wish this was always!'

Sophie's face had an odd, stiff expression.

Madame was quite unprepared for what took place. She had never known anything like it. Suddenly, on a bright spring day full of promise, disaster. Flaubert, bearing in his trap a gendarme from the town, the priest on his bicycle, and the wench and her loverboy, all at once. Sophie, in black this time, her hat a drift of feathers, was implacable.

'The child's abused, Father. Her clothes, her food, her schooling – and bruises. You know what I mean.'

The priest, bemused, said, 'She's beaten, you mean? I know Madame's firm, but the child is an orphan—'

'Not her, although she's bad enough. Him.' Sophie lifted an accusing finger. Jean, gaping like a fish, stood stockstill by the barn.

Madame erupted in loud fury. 'He never touches the child! Why, he dotes on her. Nothing's too much trouble, he'll even put her in the bath.'

'I bet he does!' said Sophie cynically. 'Men like him just love to get their filthy paws on little girls. They like naked little girls best of all!'

There was a shocked silence. Jean melted away into the shadows of the barn. The priest murmured, 'Perhaps you're a little overwrought? To suggest such a thing – Monsieur is a respected member of our community—'

Sophie laughed cynically. 'Is that why he's run for cover? Look, Father, you and I both know the life this child leads. No better than a slave. The Virgin blessed her, and brought me here for a purpose. It's my duty to take the child away.'

Madame exploded. 'Take her away? Take her away? I spend

my life caring for her, without her I'm nothing! This woman's insane, Father, we love the little one like the Baby Jesus Himself! Her mother gave her into my care. "Take her, Madame," she said, with her dying breath. "Take her and love her as I know you will." A deathbed promise, Father, that's what I gave. I'll not break it now.'

Flaubert, in a sepulchral voice said, 'Bit bloody difficult to hear all that. Child's mother died in her sleep, unexpected.'

'Who asked you?' flared Madame viciously. 'You and your fat mouth! Shut it or I'll shut it with my fist!'

'Keep the kid well choked, I'll say that for you,' went on Flaubert. 'Never says a word you don't allow. We've all seen the way you treat her. Rags, winter and summer. And the bruises! My God. You only took her mother in because she was so damned grateful for a roof that she'd work herself to death. But she didn't leave her kid to you. That she didn't.'

The gendarme, pencil poised, was trying to make sense of this. 'So the child was not left in Madame's guardianship? Is this true?'

'Flaubert's a lying bastard,' asserted Madame. 'I was left as the child's guardian. I swear.'

'You have papers?'

'Papers?' Madame's big hands fluttered uncertainly. 'Papers?'

The gendarme sighed. 'Where is the child?'

Lori's appearance, in an apron of sacking, her feet bare, did nothing to enhance Madame's case. But she bent to her and cooed affectingly, 'Why have you dressed up like that, sweeting? Were you playing?'

Instinctively Lori flinched away.

'You see the child's scared of her,' said Gerard dispassionately. 'I shall offer the woman money. Then she'll let her go.'

'You think you can buy my little treasure?' wailed Madame.

Sophie snorted. 'Be grateful we don't imprison you. Fifty francs.'

Madame's jaw worked. She was reluctant to haggle in front of everyone. Flaubert was grinning, the gendarme was looking grim, while the priest gazed at Lori as if she was a corpse he was going to bury. Well, she would be soon. Anyone looking at her could see she was going to die. That cough she had – the brat was in all likelihood consumptive and would infect them all. Best she was gone.

'A hundred,' she muttered. 'It cost me a fortune to clothe her.'

'You never spent a sou!' Sophie's colour was high, she seemed on the verge of tears. 'Give her seventy-five, Gerard, and let's go. I can't bear this place another minute.'

It was over so quickly. Crammed into the trap between Sophie and Gerard, Lori was hopelessly bewildered. 'You'll be sorry,' called Madame. 'You'll soon find what she's like. Don't bring her back to me in a hurry.'

Lori was suddenly terrified. She didn't care about Jean, she didn't care about anything, only let her stay. What would she do if she was not here? She knew nothing and nobody. Even her little book was left behind. She started to cry and Sophie put her arms about her, soothing and clucking. In the avenue they passed Monsieur, standing with the plough horse, watching them. If Lori loved anyone she loved these two. 'Monsieur! Monsieur!' she called out. But he stood quite still, saying nothing, the spring breeze stirring the thin grey hair on his head.

Chapter Three

It was the train that frightened Lori most. Were it not for Sophie she would have run, back to the fields, back to Monsieur, even to Madame. Crowds of people chattered and laughed and waved, as if the monster didn't matter, for all its hot, steamy breath. Men, looking small as children, came and went through the steaming clouds, as if the monster ate them and then spat them out again. Who knew how many never came out at all? Lori clung to her fragile security. One small hand held on to Sophie's, the other was clamped tight in the satin of Sophie's skirt, hampering her walk.

Gerard was embarrassed. 'Get her off, Sophie. People are looking.'

'Let them. It's only a train, Lori darling. Like a big motor-car. You didn't mind the car and you won't mind this.'

But she had gone to the car from the trap, and she knew where the trap had come from. Now, at the train, she realised suddenly she had no way of knowing how to get back to the farm. Try as she might she had forgotten all the twists and turns. What would she do without Sophie? She would be utterly lost. She held even tighter.

'For God's sake! People think she's a half-wit.'

'So what? Shut up, Gerard, and find us a seat.'

It was better, on the train. It smelled of polish and strong tobacco, and the windows had blinds pulled by little silk tassels. But it seemed to Lori that everyone was looking at her. Ladies in big hats and men with moustaches, and everybody dressed as if for church. She squirmed in her seat, and the red plush fabric made her legs itch. She moved surreptitiously to scratch them.

'Is she an orphan, Madame? A relative?' A woman leaned across, her large face white with powder.

28

'An orphan, only. I'm taking her to Paris. The war—'

'Ah, yes. A million bastards. You're too good. She'll need watching, though. They're bred deceitful. Did you know the parents at all?'

Sophie shook her head. A murmur ran round the carriage.

'Rather you than me,' said a man lugubriously, putting on his spectacles and raising his newspaper. 'Animals, the lot of them. They all go the same way, it's in the blood. You wait and see.'

Lori saw that Gerard had gone very red. He sat bolt upright, staring out of the window, and she knew he was ashamed to be with her. Was she an animal? She looked down at her hands with their broken and bitten nails, at her dirty, scarred legs, at her feet in their broken shoes. He was right to be ashamed. She had been nothing on the farm, less than a good cow, but here, in the world, she was like a beetle in a pile of clean linen.

It was dark when they arrived. The rhythm of the journey was turned in an instant into a turmoil of banging and shouting. Lori had been asleep, and almost fell down the steps of the train. 'Help her, Gerard!'

'Like hell I will! You're the one who wanted her. What do you mean to do now? You can't take her to St Fauberg!'

'Why not? She won't bother anyone. Albert's still away, and besides, he doesn't come in the day. At night she'll be asleep. He won't even know about her.'

'He will if I tell him.'

Sophie stopped abruptly in her passage across the concourse. Everything was lit with a strange yellow light, making everyone seem different. 'Would you do that, Gerard? Would you do that to me?'

For a moment he said nothing. Then he shrugged. 'Just don't get me involved. If he finds out, I won't take the blame. It's your funeral, not mine.'

Sophie flashed him a look. 'I don't intend to get buried.'

Lori, tired beyond thinking, fastened her free hand into the mangled folds of Sophie's skirt and hung on.

The apartment in the Rue St Fauberg had three bedrooms, a large salon, kitchen, bathroom and small balcony. To the educated eye it was ordinary, the frills failing to hide much that was shabby, a silk hanging thrown over the sofa where the stuffing threatened to come out. But, waking in a narrow bed, Lori was impressed. She saw luxury, from the popping gas jets on the badly papered walls to the scalding stream of rusty water in the bathroom.

She moved cautiously from room to room, expecting at any moment to be recalled or slapped. But Sophie stayed in her room, propped up in bed on lace pillows, sorting through letters and bills. From time to time she dipped bread in a cup of chocolate and munched, enjoying herself. The child wasn't so difficult. It was pleasant, knowing oneself to be charitable. She would be Sophie's talisman, her buttress against misfortune, God's hostage. But perhaps the child was hungry too.

Sophie held out her half-finished cup and a piece of bread. 'Here. Have some. It's good.'

Lori ran across the room, snatched the food and stuffed it into her mouth. She was like a starving animal, like a wild thing, like – a beast. Sophie reeled back, watching the child cram her mouth until it would take no more, until it was too full even to chew. Bread was swallowed in great gargling lumps, while crumbs and dribbles of chocolate made their way uninvited on to Sophie's white bedspread. As soon as anything was swallowed more was grabbed, until at last Sophie put out a shaking hand. 'Lori. That's enough.' The child was instantly still.

Sophie found that her heart was beating quickly. She felt frightened suddenly, as if a pet dog had shown teeth. How did she begin to change this? What could she say? Even the child's obedience had to be corrected. She was almost servile. The words of the night before came back to her. 'Deceitful. Animals. It's in the blood.'

She got up and went to the door, standing to look at the child. She was so strange. Her head with her tousle of black hair seemed too large for her body. Her eyes, so oddly colourless, as if you might look into them and see everything that was there. The little, sour unpleasantnesses of her body, from her bitten nails to her crusted lips and disgusting running nose. It hadn't seemed so bad in the country. In the country everything was disgusting; if you wished to spend time there you must simply close your mind. But now, in Paris, Sophie's mind was open again. What had she done?

She went slowly into the kitchen. She tried to recapture her mood of a day or so before, by the river. The child had seemed attractive then, a fragile bird, pathetic, needing her. The slightly bestial air that now seemed so repellent had been nowhere to be seen.

In that moment Sophie's enthusiasm guttered like a candle. Why had she taken the child on? It had been a whim of the moment, a desire to get the better of the harridan who had her in her care. And she liked the picture she made, the elegant town lady, impressing the priest with her kindness.

There should have been a Sophie in her own life, she thought wildly. She had rescued Lori as she wished to have been rescued herself, only to find she had been living in a fantasy. Lori was a savage.

She pulled herself together. If this failed, how Gerard would gloat! He would mock another of Sophie's stupidities. And this was a child like any other, and could be taught how to behave. She went to the little pine table and began to lay it with cloth, plate, knife and spoon. She set out chocolate, bread and butter. Then she called the little girl. 'Lori. Come and learn how to eat.'

The child stood in the doorway, looking from the neat table to Sophie's set face. The skinny legs, protruding from an old shirt, looked inhuman, alien. Sophie felt a sudden shiver of revulsion.

'Come, Lori,' she said again. 'You must learn to eat nicely.'

The child, sensitive to every nuance of Sophie's voice, felt the sudden chill. What had she done wrong? What must she do to put it right? She went to the table and looked at the food. She glanced up at Sophie. 'I won't eat if you don't wish it,' she said humbly.

'Everyone has to eat, Lori. We eat to live.'

'I won't eat if you don't want me to.'

The woman closed her eyes for a moment. A sudden rush of heat seemed to run through her, a blush of shame and anguish. Perhaps the child was a saint after all. And she was Sophie's creature, so much her own that if she wished it the child would willingly die. Weakly, almost plaintively, she said, 'I only want you to eat properly, Lori. Like a lady. Watch.'

She sat at the table, breaking and buttering the bread with exaggerated daintiness, using her best and most affected manners. She lifted the cup and sipped chocolate, dabbing at her lips as if her napkin were finest linen, and not a mere square

31

of darned cotton. She smiled and gestured and pretended to make conversation, and in Lori's eyes the room was filled with people – town people. The people on the train.

'Now, Lori. Your turn.'

The little girl sat at the table. She twisted and turned her head, parodying Sophie's manners. She nibbled bread, and sipped chocolate, she simpered and smiled. She was entirely Sophie, with all her little vulgarities, all her pretended grandeur. Nothing was missed.

In a stunned voice Sophie said, 'Is that how I did it, Lori?'

Lori nodded emphatically. 'Was it right? Was it what you wanted?'

Of course, the child was imitating badly. Sophie said, 'Yes, darling. It was.'

As the day began, so the week went on. Only gradually did Sophie begin to see the enormity of her task. Lori was obedient, utterly obedient. It was as if she had no inner compulsions at all, and was under the command of others in every moment of her waking life. If she was told to copy, then she did so, including every sneeze, every foible, every mishap. An irritable request for quiet meant utter silence, a plea for a smile resulted in a terrible, immobile grin. She was a tyrant's dream, thought Sophie. Lori's mind was like smooth sand, washed by waves, and yesterday's footprints could be entirely erased and a new design tried, just as you pleased. Whatever thoughts went on behind those pale, glassy eyes, were secret. Lori said what others wished to hear.

By Saturday Sophie was exhausted. She had shown Lori how to eat, how to walk, how to dress, how to wash, how to comb her hair, how to use the bathroom, how to sit, how to lie – in short, how to live as Sophie lived, in Sophie's world. But Lori had not performed one spontaneous action. She observed, she was commanded, she reproduced.

When Gerard called that night, Sophie was hysterical. 'She's a doll! A lifesize doll. Is she an idiot, Gerard? Some kind of special idiot, that does as it's told. Was she like this before and I didn't see?'

'You saw what you wished to see,' said Gerard, flinging himself down. 'The girl's stupid but not an idiot. She can do as she's told.'

'I want more for her than that. I thought – I intended—'

In a bored voice Gerard said, 'Didn't I tell you? Didn't I say?'

'What did you say? Only that I was to leave her. She was being tortured, Gerard!'

'And now you are being tortured. The world is a cruel place, my darling. I admit, the child was a very sorry sight. But you're going to be sorrier. Mark my words.'

Sophie said nothing. Lori, standing at the ill-fitting door of her room, watched them through a crack. She didn't understand Sophie and Gerard. At one moment Sophie was in charge, and the next the roles were changed. Gerard got up and poured Sophie some wine. He said, 'By the way, I came to tell you. Albert's back in town.'

'He's not coming, is he? Not tonight? I'm worn out.'

'Tomorrow.'

There was a silence. Sophie looked up at Gerard standing above her, in his tight, narrow suit. Lori drew in her breath. She knew this sort of silence. As she watched, Gerard reached out and touched Sophie's knee, under the soft skirt. She heard Sophie's low, slurring whisper. 'I'm worn out. Didn't you understand?'

'I'm only asking you to open your legs. Come on, if Albert makes a fuss about the kid I'll speak up for you.'

'Just make sure you do.'

Sophie leaned back in the big chair, her knees spread wide. Lori could see the tops of her stockings, bordered with ragged lace. Gerard was pulling at his trousers, letting his stick go free. Lori was surprised to see it, Gerard didn't look like a man who had one. His trousers were too tight. But he came down on Sophie, pushing the stick up between her knees, his hands on her dress, pressing on her bosom. And Sophie was groaning, a low moan, as Gerard's bottom in those trousers worked in and out. Watching, Lori wrapped her legs one around the other. She hadn't known that Sophie submitted to this too. She wondered if Gerard would want to do it to her, as well as to Sophie. Gerard didn't like her, that much was plain, but in Lori's mind that made it all the more probable. This was something men did to girls whether they liked them or not. Suddenly terrified, Lori ran to her bed and hid.

* * *

33

Sophie was distracted the next day. Lori tried to be as small as possible, in the hope that she wouldn't be in the way. In the afternoon, when Sophie found the child squeezed between the bed and the wall, she was overcome with remorse. 'Come out of there, sweeting! I've been cruel to you today. Come out and let me hug you.'

They sat together by the fire. Suddenly Sophie was full of promises. 'Tomorrow we'll go shopping and buy you clothes. Won't you be beautiful? And I shall teach you to read. Will you like that? Everyone will see how pretty you are and how well you read and they'll say, "Sophie, you've been so clever and kind!" I shall like that and so will you. Will you, Lori? Will you?'

'Yes,' said Lori dutifully.

She felt Sophie draw slightly away from her. She heard her sigh.

Lori was sent to bed early that night. Sophie gave her a magazine to look at, with pictures of ladies in long dresses. 'Don't you just love this one?' said Sophie, pointing to a dress with a feather boa. 'Wouldn't I look adorable in that? All the men would want to get their hands on me. Ah, well, I'll just have to make do with Albert.'

She was drinking wine, wandering about the flat with a glass always in hand. She was wearing a négligée, caught between her breasts with an artificial rose, with nothing underneath but her round, pink body. Lori thought she looked beautiful.

When the doorbell rang, Sophie put her finger to her lips. 'No noise at all. He mustn't know you're here.' Lori nodded fiercely, but as soon as Sophie was gone from the room she slipped from bed and peeped through the door crack. A small, fat man in a grey waistcoat had come in.

'Sophie. You are well? Better?'

All of a sudden Sophie seemed nervous. 'Yes, thank you. I – I missed you. Are you well?'

'Perfectly. Do you have cognac?'

'Of course. Your favourite.'

She fussed round him, anxious, trying to please. As he sipped his drink, he said, 'Gerard gave me the bills. You've been extravagant, Sophie.'

She drew in her breath. 'Really? Just a few things – just to live – and some clothes you might like. This is new—'

'Yes. It's good.'

Perhaps the brandy was soothing him. Sophie was laughing too much, answering each of Albert's comments with a shrill giggle. He settled himself in the high-backed chair, sipping his cognac, watching Sophie flit nervously about the room. Then he gestured with his fingers.

'Sophie.'

She came towards him at once, kneeling before him in his chair. Reaching out with slow deliberation, he twitched the flower from her dress. Her breasts, large and rosy, tumbled free. Obedient, without command, she moved to offer them to his lips and knelt there, eyes tight shut, as he pulled and dragged at her. 'Albert – you're hurting me.'

'Be quiet, Sophie.'

'You aren't kind—'

'I'm too kind. I won't be taken for a rich fool. Come into the bedroom.'

Lori crept from her room to listen. Once, and only once, she heard Sophie cry out.

It was very late when Lori awoke. There were voices again beyond her door, but this time, when she crept to her vantage point, Albert was gone. Instead there was a man with a beard, and Sophie was arguing and taking off her coat. 'If you haven't got it, you can go right now. I'm not wasting my time. Either you pay or get out.'

'I'll pay after.'

'Like hell you will! You agreed!'

'Does the concierge know what kind of girl you are?'

'Bastard! Pig!'

'That's rich, coming from a whore. Come on, let's do it.'

'Pay first or nothing!'

He shot out a hand and caught Sophie a crack round the jaw. She fell and lay on the thin carpet, and then, as she saw him coming again, scrambled behind a chair. The man began to unfasten his belt.

'I'll get my friends to you,' muttered Sophie.

'Will you now? Shut your mouth, bitch.' He drew back his leg to kick.

'No! No! Leave her alone!' A small, furious body hurtled

across the room. It cannoned into the man's legs and hung there.

'Get the cat off! Get it off, damn you! Jesus! She bit me.'

'Lori! Lori, no!'

Lori hung on, all nails, teeth and loyalty. No one should hit Sophie. No one!

Feet sounded on the stairs, there were voices, someone was hammering on the door. 'Mademoiselle! Mademoiselle, what's happening?'

'Oh God! Lori—'

The man wrenched himself free, leaving Lori crouched speechless on the floor. Barging past the concierge, he was suddenly no more than footsteps running away down the street. Sophie staggered upright, pinning on the travesty of a smile. 'My cousin, Madame. Drunk. I'm so sorry.'

The concierge took in everything with one grim, world-weary stare. 'A satin dress, Mademoiselle? So late at night?'

Sophie's hands fluttered up and down. 'What can I say? The opera—'

'I'll have you know this is a respectable house.'

Sophie reached for her purse. 'I'm sorry, Madame. So sorry.' She offered the note. After a moment it was taken.

'Just make sure it doesn't happen again.'

Her footsteps marched righteously down the stairs. As they faded, Sophie gathered Lori into her arms. 'You shouldn't have done that, sweeting. It doesn't matter if they hit me. They just have to pay.'

'He wasn't going to pay.'

'Oh! You were listening, were you? Well, he might have paid. You can never tell with that sort. He didn't hit me hard.'

'Your face is blue.'

Sophie sighed, and wiped her hand across her eyes. 'Is it? I'll have to paint it. Oh God, Lori, what's Albert going to say? It's his fault anyway, the mean bastard. Why don't rich young men ever want a whore?'

She got up and went wearily into the bathroom, leaving her dress in a heap on the floor. She inspected herself in the cloudy mirror.

'Christ, will you look at me? Blue chin, tits chewed up, and it hurts to sit down. If I go on like this I'll be a wreck in five years. Like the old cats under the bridge, doing it for a bottle. I want a

36

rich man. I want a young man! Why can't Gerard get rich?'

She went to the cognac and poured herself a glass, and then another. After a while she began to snivel, tears stinging her sore breasts. Lori went and fetched a quilt from Sophie's bed, and spread it round her as best she could. Sophie said drunkenly, 'You're a good kid. You know what it's like. Got to give them what they want, or else. Damn Albert!' Lori curled up beside her as Sophie cried herself to sleep.

Somehow Sophie smoothed Albert down. It cost her, though. Suddenly there was less food on the table, and the clothes she bought for Lori were second hand, from the stalls in Les Halles. But to Lori they seemed glorious. No clothes in her life ever pleased her as these did. There was a blue serge skirt and jacket, with a matching hat, and little black shoes only a size too big. Sophie said, 'You must curtsey to your betters, Lori, like this.' And Lori dipped as Sophie did, tilting her head coquettishly, just like her.

Seeing herself in the bathroom mirror, Lori was very pleased. The tangled mass of hair was now a neat, shining bob, on which her hat perched insecurely. The grey look of her skin, the result of dirt and under-feeding, had given way to pale translucence, with barely the tinge of colour. Her legs in their black socks had some shape to them now, and then the shoes – her wonderful shoes! If a speck of mud marked their blackness, Lori wouldn't rest until they were clean. In this one thing she was determined; she adored her shoes.

One evening, when Albert was expected, Gerard called. Sophie was surprised. She had lit candles and was wearing only a robe. As she let him in she called to Lori, 'You can come out, sweetheart. It's only Gerard.' And then, to him, 'Can't Albert come?'

'He has a business meeting. He told me to let you know.' He tossed his hat on to a chair, and stood very close to Sophie, looking down.

She said, 'You've been drinking.'

'So have you.'

She laughed. 'And who can blame me, having to face Albert thumping away half the night? But now I don't. I've got the message.'

She turned away, but he caught her arm. 'Why don't we amuse ourselves?'

Sophie said, 'A nice thought, my dear, but not very profitable. I've a better idea. Why don't you take me to a café and let me see what I can pick up? Unless, of course, you want to pay?'

'Sophie!'

She flared at him, 'It's about time I stopped giving it to you free! What do you think I am, an idiot? You don't take me out, you don't buy me presents, but you think you can come and do it whenever it suits. You've got someone else. Since the holiday, there's someone else.'

'No!'

'Liar! Get out of here. Get out!'

She aimed a fist at him, but Gerard grabbed her. They wrestled, but it was no match. Gerard's wiry strength pushed her arms down and back, twisting until she was trembling with pain. He said, 'Now, Sophie. What now?'

'Don't hurt me. Please.'

'Then behave yourself.'

He let her go. As he stood away from her, Sophie fell towards him, sobbing, 'There isn't anyone, is there? I didn't mean it, I swear I didn't. You don't have to go.' She fawned on him, trying to kiss him even as he turned his head away. Her robe was open, he could see she was naked, and at that moment the door opened and Albert was there.

Sophie fell into a chair, giggling hysterically. Albert said, 'My nephew. My nephew. And whose is this child?'

Gerard said, 'It isn't as it seems, Uncle. She forced herself – the child's hers—'

'Hers? I've been keeping her bastard?'

Sophie's laughter shrieked again. 'Why not tell him it's his, Gerard?' she demanded, tears pouring down her face. 'Just another of your lies!'

'Of course it's not mine. Shut up, woman! Shut up!' Albert dealt Sophie a cruel blow across the face. But it was Lori who screamed and went on screaming as the concierge, breathless from the stairs, stood in the doorway and said, 'It's the last straw, Mademoiselle. You're out.'

Chapter Four

Lori was wearing her blue jacket and skirt. Her hat was perched squarely on her head and her shoes were as shiny as could be. She stood beside Sophie, utterly serious, staring fixedly at the woman they had come to see.

Madame Bonacieux was imposing, large without being fat. She had a bolster of yellow hair, piled up on a solid head balanced on a pillar of a neck. Even her fingers were thick, like railings encased in diamonds, and she drummed them on one firm knee.

Sophie was finishing her tale. 'His nephew loved me, Madame. He would have married me, I know, but the money—'

'Yes, yes.' Madame waved an impatient hand. 'You girls are all the same. You won't be told. The rules are as before. I take you but not the child.'

'Madame, she has nowhere else to go. I rescued her from the country. A terrible place, worked to death, and an orphan—'

'Put her in the orphanage, then. You can't keep yourself, let alone a child. And this isn't a place for children.'

Lori let out a strangled gasp. Sophie said, 'She understands, Madame! See how clever she is. She can do anything, can't you, Lori? Madame – I was in an orphanage. It's where I began.'

Unmoved, Madame Bonacieux said, 'I never take a girl's children. Think, Sophie! What would be the result? No child should watch its mother at her work. Time enough to know how men behave.'

Grim, resigned, Sophie said, 'She knows already.'

'What?'

'In the country. A great brute of a man had her. I bought her for seventy-five francs, like a little slave. She isn't stupid, Madame, truly. She can't read or write but she knows about me. All the time, with Albert, and sometimes Gerard, and the others

39

– she keeps out of the way, she's very good.'

Madame looked from Lori's pale face to Sophie's flushed one. She said to the child, 'Is this true? Or another of Sophie's tales?'

As she watched a tide of crimson suffused the ice-pale cheeks. Lori hung her head. 'I want to stay with Sophie,' she whispered.

Madame shrugged massively. 'The child's ruined already. What is there to lose?'

So began Lori's time at the brothel. There wasn't much to bring from the flat except clothes and linen. The silk cover from the sofa was promoted to Lori's bed, high up under the roof. There was a view of the Seine, a silver ribbon, and the glorious skyline of the city.

Sophie peeped from the window, in one of her abrupt changes of mood, suddenly excited, suddenly optimistic. 'Look, Lori, you can see all of Paris from here. You're as high as a bird. I know most of the girls still. No more dull days. It's going to be fun again. And in the evenings – Lori, in the evenings you stay here.'

The little girl nodded. She understood.

They went downstairs for Lori to be introduced. The house seemed very big and very grand, with huge gilded mirrors at every turn of the stair. The walls were a dark, thick yellow, on which were painted amazing scenes. Men and women writhed together, lashed each other and strapped each other down, managing nonetheless to smile. Lori goggled openly and Sophie said, 'Don't you look at those! They're disgusting. Madame should have them painted out.'

Everyone was waiting in the salon. It was a huge room, lined with sofas, the windows curtained so thickly that lights had to burn even in the day. About a dozen women sat round, in beautiful dresses of silk and lace, turning their heads now and then to catch sight of themselves in a glass. Lori, who had always thought Sophie the most beautiful thing she had ever seen, was amazed. Next to these, Sophie seemed over-coloured and badly dressed.

The women rose in a body, a fluttering, sweet-scented cloud.

'Sophie! She's gorgeous, where did you find her? Those eyes, that hair! I shall buy her a dress. Two dresses. I'll put a ribbon in her hair.'

Sophie said hastily, 'Really, she doesn't need anything. I'll buy it.'

'Where did you get her terrible jacket? Les Halles? And the shoes don't fit. I'd better take her in hand.' Marie clicked across the floor on her own expensive high heels, jutting a hip or a shoulder like a model.

'I'll take care of her. Really,' said Sophie again.

Zelma, tall and slender, said, 'Worried that we'll steal her? We didn't steal Albert, and don't you wish we had? You wouldn't be broke, that's for sure.'

'Don't be unkind to Sophie!' Little Mathilde, a large-eyed and lustrous blonde, went to embrace her. 'He always was a skinflint. Look at this cheap satin! We'll have to dress you too, Sophie. Can't have you letting us down.'

It was their revenge. When Sophie left, for a man of her own, they had all envied her. Her ignominious return both justified and enraged them, proving as it did that there was no future for them but this. So they scratched her a little, and Sophie let them. She knew the rites of the pack.

After a while, when the jokes about Albert had been exhausted, Zelma stretched out along a sofa. 'So, what's to happen to the little one?' she demanded. 'What about school?'

Marie tossed her head. 'I'm sure we can teach her what a girl needs to know.'

They all laughed, but Zelma persisted. 'She has to go to school! She can't grow up a savage. Can you read, little one? Sophie, have you taught her to read?'

Sophie coloured. 'Not yet. There wasn't time. But she's clever, she learns anything I teach.'

'Except you don't teach,' said Zelma ironically. 'Mademoiselle Promise a Lot, that's you. Do you know how old she is? Five – six? She's small for her age; she may be older. What's her real name?'

Sophie looked blank. Lori, wishing to help, piped up, 'Lori. That's my name.'

Zelma looked down at her. 'That is your little name. Have you no other names? Who was your mother?'

Lori blinked. The memory of her mother, once so clear that to experience it was like swallowing a knife, had receded into mist.

41

'She was Mummy,' she said slowly.

'Mummy? Mummy, you say? Was she English?'

The grey eyes gazed up at her. 'I don't know.'

'Do you know English words? Er—' Zelma sought for some '—cat. Dog. Mouse.'

Lori thought for a moment. She knew those words. Then she recited:

'Oranges and Lemons, The Bells of St Clement's,
I owe you five farthings, Says the Bells of St Martin's.'

'My God!' Zelma looked about her. 'The child's English. She can speak it. Well, that settles it, Sophie. School, at once.'

Lori felt herself go cold. School was terrible, they said. It was a terrible place. She wanted to stay here, in the warm, with Sophie and these lovely ladies. They'd buy her dresses and shoes, and put ribbons in her hair. She didn't want to go to school.

To Lori's relief no more was said about it for some days. Instead her time was filled by one or other of the girls taking her shopping, marching her briskly through the busy streets. Lori was at first frightened and then entranced. So many people, so much life! The artists by the river seemed to know Sophie and her friends; they called out to them, not unkindly. And sometimes the girls would stop and talk for a minute or two. Lori stood and watched the cars, roaring and hooting, and the pigeons, rising in clouds, and smelled good strong coffee and hot bread. A little knob inside her seemed to twist, making her insides tight and hot. The feeling made her want to jump and run, but she didn't know why. Perhaps it was Paris, everyone was busy in Paris. But the knob twisted to its tightest when she was walking with Sophie and everyone was smiling. Lori felt her own face stretching and moving, she couldn't help it. She too had to smile.

They bought her dresses and skirts, and even shoes. Lori didn't like her new shoes. She loved her old black ones, bright as a bird's eye, and had no time for the sensible brown buttons that Marie preferred. In fact, she loved all her old clothes more than the new. They even put blue ribbons in her hair, when she longed quite desperately for red. Now when she looked at herself in the glass at the head of the stairs she saw a dull little girl, her hair tied firmly into plaits with the hated navy blue bows.

She went to Sophie. 'I want red bows. For my hair. Like before.'

Sophie, lying on her bed reading a novel and eating sweets, absently stroked Lori's cheek. 'Yes, darling, but not for school. They won't take you if they know where you come from. Zelma says you've got to look respectable.'

Lori didn't understand. She only knew that other little girls wore reds and greens and yellows, and wore their hair in curls right down their backs. She saw them in the street and from her window. But she had a grey skirt and button shoes and the hated navy blue ribbons.

She said again to Sophie, 'I want red bows. Like before.'

Sophie put down her book. It wasn't as if the child was even going to school yet. She giggled and got out the red bows.

Marie was the one who noticed. She went to Zelma, who confronted Sophie on the stairs, just before they opened that night. Sophie was in Albert's négligée, in marked contrast to Zelma, who was in full evening dress. 'Do you have to try so hard to bring up another whore?' demanded Zelma, bosom heaving magnificently, lifting her skirts as she swept towards the sinner. 'The child has to be clothed decently! Marie has done what you could not, and does she get any thanks? No. You change the child's ribbons. We know what you mean by it.'

'It was only because she asked—' said Sophie feebly.

'How can children know what they ask? It's always the same with you, Sophie, never any thought! Left to you, she'll come to nothing.'

Sophie had been meek long enough. 'Left to you she'll be miserable!' she flared. 'You're jealous, that's all. Two of your men asked for me last night. You may be clever and you may dress well, but you're no damn' good in bed!'

'How good are you, may I ask? Albert set you up in a rented apartment at the cheap end of St Fauberg, but he still came here. Oh, yes. And his nephew. Let me tell you, I know just how to make them come back for more!'

Sophie drew in her breath and stood there. She wanted to hit

43

Zelma. She wanted to kill her. But suddenly Madame Bonacieux was there. 'I hope my girls aren't fighting?' she asked menacingly. 'If you fight over the child she'll have to go.'

Sophie shuddered. 'Zelma – Zelma was telling me about Albert, Madame. My – the man who took me away.'

Madame said, 'Zelma knows nothing of him. He had Mathilde twice.'

'And – and his nephew? Gerard?'

'Him!' Madame snorted. 'He wanted what he couldn't afford. Get to the salon, both of you. Our clients are waiting.'

Sophie went first, but Zelma, as she passed Madame, stopped to say furiously, 'Why do you take her part? The girl's a fool and always has been. She's bringing the kid up to be a tart.'

Madame shrugged. 'What else is she going to be? Get to work, Zelma. Monsieur le Comte is asking for you. Anger does you good, you look well.'

Later, Madame stood at the door of the salon and surveyed the scene. Sophie was dishevelled and drunk. If the girl wasn't so popular Madame wouldn't keep her a day, she had no idea of business. Zelma was still talking with her aristocrat, but that was all right. He had paid for the night, and enjoyed the salon with its comings and goings. Mathilde was upstairs with a soldier, and some of them could be rough. It was the trenches, no one forgot. But Mathilde had had him before and he was no trouble. As for Marie ... Madame frowned. Something was lacking there. A beautiful girl, but not popular. No one ever asked for her twice.

She signalled, and Marie came over. 'Go and change into a négligée. We're a whorehouse, not a fashion shop.'

'I suppose you want me to look like Sophie!'

'Men ask for her. She takes too long, that's all. And you've only had one tonight.'

'It's a bad night. Slow.'

'So make it quicker!'

Marie went reluctantly to change. Two men were at Sophie now, and she was letting them fondle her breasts. Ye gods, thought Madame, the girl behaves as if they were asking to marry her. She went across. 'Gentlemen, if you would like Mademoiselle's company that can be arranged. Together if you

44

wish – for a consideration. But please, not in my salon.'

'Together, Madame?' Sophie blinked in amazement.

'What a brilliant idea,' said one of the men. 'What do you think, Jacques?'

'Splendid.'

Madame bowed and withdrew.

Sophie hurried after her, pulling her négligée across her breasts. 'Please, Madame – I can't do two at once. I've never done that.'

Madame eyed her dispassionately. 'You're not a novice, Sophie. You'll get a good tip. You've got till three.'

'But, Madame—'

Madame's large head swung her way again. 'I took you back, Sophie. You and the child. Now, do as I bid.'

Later, Madame patrolled the corridors. Every room had its spy hole, and she looked in each. Zelma was still talking to the aristocrat; he talked more than he screwed. Marie had a disappointed old man and was lying bored and listless on the bed. As for Sophie ... Madame chuckled as she slid back the panel. What a good thing she'd taken the girl back, she thought. She was strong, she could manage this. It could become a speciality, a little extra, offered to the jaded palates of friends. Madame moved on.

Lori was awake early the next morning. She got up and crept downstairs, shivering a little in her new nightdress. The house was silent, and smelled strongly of cigarettes. Just then, a door opened and a man came out. 'Good God,' he said. 'What are you doing here?' Lori scuttled away.

A moment later, Zelma appeared, yawning capaciously. When she caught sight of Lori, she said, 'You should be dressed. It's school today.'

Lori's mouth opened and shut. She began to sidle off to Sophie's room, but Zelma said, 'You can forget going to see her. She'll be sleeping late this morning. And if you want to know what's what in this world, don't listen to Sophie. She knows nothing and never did.'

Lori was dressed within the hour. She sat in the kitchen, at the long table, trying to force down a croissant and milk. The food was good, but Lori couldn't eat it, however much the cook cajoled. She sat watching the maids bustle about, ironing linen, brewing coffee. Madame was strict with her staff, there was no idling here. Not so bad as the farm, though. And surely not so bad as school. Lori felt sick again. How she wished Sophie was here.

Marie came in, stretching. She was wearing a blue nightdress trimmed with Brussels lace. 'God, what a night. Useless, all of them. The child's hair needs brushing.'

'Then brush it,' said Zelma, looking over her shoulder to check that the seams of her stockings were straight. Marie sighed and began work on Lori's hair. The plaits were exact and uncomfortable, tied at top and bottom with neat navy bows. Madame came in, leatherbound accounts book in hand, casting her cold eye over everything. 'Get that child on her way,' she commanded. 'Half the morning's gone!'

Lori dragged her way down the street, running her fingers along the iron railings of the houses they passed. Zelma was brisk, rattling along in her sober serge suit, a hat cutting across her brows. 'Now, Lori,' she said, gathering her up firmly, 'remember. You're an orphan and you live with your aunt. Aunt Zelma, that's me. Not a word about Madame Bonacieux, and not a peep about Sophie. Otherwise they'll send you home. Now, what do you say.'

'Yes, Zelma.'

'Yes, Aunt Zelma, if you please. We're here.'

She dragged Lori through a gate into a small courtyard, from which steps led up to a house. There were children in the courtyard, all of them dressed more brightly than Lori. One even had red bows. Lori's heart sank lower and lower. The children looked strange and dangerous. She had no wish to be left here.

Zelma swept into the house. It was quiet, with pale walls and a dark wood floor. Zelma hesitated for a moment, then drew herself up and rapped authoritatively on a door. After a long moment a voice commanded them to enter. The muscles in Zelma's cheeks suddenly went taut. Grasping the handle like a weapon, she opened the door and went in.

A small grey lady was seated at a desk. 'Bonjour, Madame,' began Zelma. 'My niece, half English, I wish her to begin school. Can she start today?'

'You wish to enrol a child at our school?'

'Yes. Yes, I do.'

'But, Madame – our children are registered at birth. We don't take children from the street.'

Zelma bridled. 'From the street! I beg your pardon, Madame. This is a respectable child, from a respectable family!'

The grey woman looked taken aback. 'I only meant – we don't enrol casually. Obviously this child – I mean to say, our children are recommended. From families known to us.'

'Oh. Oh, I see.'

The wind had gone from Zelma's sails. For a wonderful moment Lori thought she might be free. She could spend her days with Sophie and the girls, running their errands, putting cream on their hands, getting them drinks when they were tired. She did not want school and school did not want her. Hurrah!

But the woman turned to Lori and said, 'I take it you speak English?'

For a moment the child was struck dumb. It was so hard to believe that others understood the special language. But Zelma was looking at her in an agony of suspense. 'Yes,' said Lori.

'There you are!' declared Zelma. 'She speaks it. Two languages, at her age.'

'What is her age?' asked the lady. 'Five? Six?'

'Six. And would you believe it, her birthday's on Christmas Day!'

'Indeed.' The lady opened a huge book, bigger even than Madame's accounts book, bigger than any Lori had ever seen. She scanned the pages. 'As it happens we do have a vacancy. And the child is bilingual – that is good. But we would need a recommendation. One of our parents – one of our governing body, perhaps?'

Zelma, mouthing helplessly, said, 'But I wanted her to start today. The formalities can wait, can't they?'

'I regret, Madame. No.'

She was waiting for them to leave. Lori began to drag at Zelma's hand, urging her to the door. But at that moment there was a knock. A gentleman entered, holding the hand of another little girl. In contrast to Lori's tame sobriety, this one wore a dress made entirely of frills.

Both the man and Zelma gasped. Then Zelma spluttered,

'Monsieur le Comte! How good to see you again.'

'Madame – Madame. Indeed. You look – very well. Much – refreshed.'

'And you. And you.'

He looked down at Lori. 'I do believe I've seen this child before.'

'My niece.'

'Ah.' He gestured to his frilly charge. 'My daughter. But I intruded. You were talking to Madame la Directrice.'

Zelma rested a gloved hand on his arm. 'Perhaps you can help, sir. Madame needs a recommendation to take my niece into the school. Had I known your daughter attended I'd have spoken to you before, but this is a stroke of luck, is it not? You can give Madame the recommendation.'

'For your – niece – to attend school with my daughter?'

'Indeed.'

Lori looked from one to the other. Zelma's eyes were full of entreaty. In that moment, in that brief second, Lori knew that this was far more important than school. If Zelma was refused she would be deeply ashamed. And he didn't speak. Zelma's colour began to come up, but before she could say a word the man said, 'Of course! I'm sure – yes, of course, Madame. I can of course recommend her.'

It was going to be all right. Much as Lori hated the thought of school, she knew she couldn't have borne to have the man say no.

Zelma turned back to the desk. 'So,' she said happily, 'that's settled. You have your recommendation.'

'We haven't discussed fees.'

Zelma said airily, 'If this gentleman can afford it then surely so can I. What else? I don't want to waste any more time. I wish her to begin class.'

Lori's heart began to lurch against her ribs. It was going to happen. It really was.

'Well—' The woman appeared momentarily nonplussed. 'All that remains is to register, of course. I need the child's name.'

'Her name?' Zelma swallowed. 'Of course. Her name.'

She looked down at Lori. The child's huge grey eyes stared back. What name could she give to this thin little waif, without parents, without history? She was English and she was French, so she must have a name that took both parts. And a name perhaps that reflected what she was. 'Laura,' said Zelma thoughtfully. 'Laura Perdu.'

'Perdu as in lost?' enquired Madame.

'That's how you say it,' said Zelma. 'But it's spelled a little differently. O U X at the end. Laura Perdoux.'

Chapter Five

The frilly child was called Anabel. She had been at the school for three months and knew everything, and she had a cold and had permission not to play out. Lori didn't play out, either. She was to do extra work on her letters, and besides, she had no apron. All the other children had them, but Lori had not.

When they were alone together, Anabel said, 'How does my father know your aunt? I've never seen her before.'

Lori, struggling with a pencil gripped in vicelike fingers, muttered, 'I don't know.'

'Oh yes you do. Does she work in a shop? She looks as if she does. Smart.'

Lori looked up. Anabel was tall and well made, with bright eyes and rosy cheeks. Next to her Lori felt pale and weak, like a bad tisane.

'It isn't a shop,' she said carefully. 'We live in a big house. Very big. I've got a room right at the top.'

'Your nursery,' said Anabel, understanding at once. 'Who looks after you?'

'Sophie,' said Lori. 'She's good and kind.'

'I have Brunhild. She's stupid.'

Anabel flopped down energetically in the seat next to Lori's. 'You're going to be my friend,' she announced. 'I shall come to your house and you shall come to mine. You can ride my pony. Do you have a pony?'

'Yes,' said Lori, thinking of the horse at the farm.

Anabel sighed happily. 'Are you as rich as we are, then? We've got a château in the country with twenty bedrooms.'

'Our house has more than that,' said Lori, wrinkling her brow. There were floors and floors of bedrooms.

Anabel looked a little crestfallen. Then, suspiciously, she said, 'I'll count them when I come.'

Zelma came to collect her in the early afternoon. Lori was very tired. As she trudged down the steps into the golden autumn day she was more tired than after a day at the plough. 'I have to have an apron,' she said wearily to Zelma. 'Mam'selle says I have to practise letters at home. I need a satchel. And Anabel wants to come to tea.'

Zelma's grip tightened on her hand. 'Anabel de Montauban? I saw her this morning.'

Lori nodded distractedly. 'She says I've got to be her friend.'

Zelma said nothing, but hurried down the street, quite forgetting to cultivate an elegant gait. Lori trotted at her side, clutching her letter card, realising that she had once again done wrong. But it couldn't be helped. Lori had been claimed by a stronger soul, and reacted as always in her short life: passively.

They came to the house in the Rue de Claret. Zelma rushed to the salon, where everyone lay around, gossiping and looking through magazines. 'It's all up!' she declared dramatically. 'One day and it's finished. Anabel de Montauban says she is coming to tea.'

There was a stunned silence. Sophie, on a chaise longue, giggled, and Zelma rounded on her. 'Is that all you can do, laugh? It's all going to be for nothing.'

Marie sat up. 'Say there's illness in the house. She can't come.'

'She'll come. If not this week, then next. Such a good Burgundian family! And even the nurse will know what we are.' Zelma collapsed on to a chair and hid her face in her soberly gloved hands.

Sophie stood up. 'You're the one who chose the snob school,' she said viciously. 'You wanted to pretend to be Madame la Comtesse. The kid looks worn out. Go and get some milk, Lori, and a tarte.'

'I have to do my letters.'

'I wouldn't worry too much about that. When Monsieur le Comte's nurse tells Monsieur le Comte's wife who Monsieur le Comte's daughter has been consorting with, you won't be doing letters or anything else at that school.' Then, seeing Lori's bewildered expression, she enveloped her in an embrace. 'Don't worry, darling. Who cares about school?'

'I do!' shrieked Zelma. 'The poor kid's got enough problems

51

without losing out on an education! I won't have it go wrong now. I won't!'

'Ladies.'

Madame Bonacieux stood in the doorway. 'More arguments?' She scanned them with a cold and considering eye.

'Not at all, Madame,' muttered everyone. Except Zelma. 'Please, Madame,' she began, getting up and going towards her. 'Please. Anabel de Montauban wants to come home with Lori for tea. She has a nurse and the nurse would see at once – or her mother might bring her. This house, in this district – there would be an outcry. Monsieur le Comte might be embarrassed. I don't know what to do.'

An unusual expression crossed Madame's face. It was a grin. 'A dilemma indeed. What a pity we can't entertain the daughter of one of our oldest families in the surroundings which her father enjoys so often. We cannot, of course. But, Zelma, you're making too much of it. There's a simple story. The child's grandmother is very old and must not be disturbed. You must take her friends to a café, and give them chocolate, and afterwards they can play in the park. *Voilà*.'

Zelma's face lit up with relief. Marie crossed herself. But Sophie said, 'Lori can't lie all the time. She's a child. You're asking her to live a lie.'

'She'll get used to it,' said Madame. 'At that school, she must.' As she turned to go, she said, 'Some sailors are in town. Pierre is bringing them here at five. Be ready, please.'

There was a general groan. 'Sailors,' muttered Marie. 'They'll all have the clap. Watch yourself, Sophie, I know what you're like. A few drinks down you and you forget everything.'

'You can knock on the door and remind me,' said Sophie nastily. 'You won't have anything else to do.'

Mathilde stretched luxuriantly. 'There's one good thing about sailors,' she commented. 'It's over in a blink. They'll be gone by midnight. All those months at sea, thinking about nothing else, and then – phut!'

'As long as they phut into a *préservatif*,' said Zelma. 'Come, Lori, your letters.'

The house was full of noise that evening. It rose in waves up the stairwell, as doors below opened and shut. Lori sat outside her room, looking down through the banister rails, watching everyone come and go, seeing Madame instructing, ordering, deciding. Like the conductor of an orchestra, making no music herself but in charge of every sound. No one entered of whom she did not approve, no food left the kitchen without her approval, no doorman slid out into the street for a smoke without Madame's eagle eye noting the fact.

Hauling in one miscreant, Lori heard her say, 'You are employed to protect this house and the girls who work here. Not to enjoy cheap tobacco and free sex. Do your job or get out, I've had enough of you.'

The man whispered, 'Yes, Madame,' and scuttled out of Lori's line of sight. Now Sophie was in the hall, with a sailor, so drunk he needed help up the stairs. Mostly the girls liked to go in front. They walked in a special way, sliding their legs one in front of the other, undulating their backsides. They said it made the men keen and they were quicker.

Sophie disappeared into a room, dropping the customer with a thud on the floor. So the sailors weren't any good, thought Lori dispassionately. Now Marie was coming, looking back to encourage the man with a smile. He paused, swayed, and collapsed in a heap on the stairs. In a flash she had his wallet, the notes were out, the wallet back and he was being helped to his feet and urged on. Lori wasn't surprised. Mathilde had a bowlful of cufflinks and tiepins, and when the bowl was full she took them to the jeweller and sold them. And now and then Zelma took watches, although that was dangerous because sometimes men came back sober and demanded them.

Lori's nightdress was thin and she was cold. She slipped from the landing back to bed and lay kicking under the covers. That always warmed her up. She felt different tonight – almost unhappy. Sophie had been too busy for her, the letters had been hard and Mademoiselle impatient, and the days ahead seemed full of challenge. She had a friend. What did you do with a friend?

Lori felt daunted by the task ahead of her. If she was to succeed in this new world, she must learn everything, do everything, become everything that was wanted. Sophie, Zelma, Anabel, Mademoiselle, everyone wanted something different. Lori knew she must satisfy them, because if she did not – the farm came back to her. She shuddered, but not with cold. If she had to go back to the farm, better by far she had never known kindness.

The days assumed a pattern, and within that pattern lay Lori's happiness. She learned to read, English as well as French, and to do mathematics of a sort. She was poor at figures and Mademoiselle sometimes called her out of the class and made her stand and admit her failure. But others were worse, although not Anabel, who was good at everything, even sewing. Lori laboured for hours at her hemming, and pleased Mam'selle, but when she took it home Zelma said scathingly, 'Do they call this education?' and went to see Madame la Directrice. After that they did poetry instead.

When school was ended, twice a week Lori and Anabel went to a café with Zelma – Anabel's nurse waited in the park – or to Anabel's house. It was a smart and glossy town house, with gilded chairs in the salon on which the girls were not permitted to sit. There were no paintings though, on the stairs, or at least none of interest. 'Just ancestors and things,' said Anabel. Lori wondered if she would prefer ancestors at the Rue de Claret. Probably not.

On fine days they took turns to ride the pony, trotting along the tan in the park, surrounded by nursemaids and their charges. Anabel wished aloud that Lori's grandmother was well, so they could ride Lori's pony too. They could ride a long way then, past the military band. Perhaps the pony could be brought over to Anabel's and they could ride together? The pony was too old, announced Lori. Older even than her grandmother. He'd probably die soon too.

But the eating was so difficult! All the manners she had learned with Sophie had to be unlearned for Zelma. Seated in the tall, mirrored cafés Sophie giggled and hiccupped behind her hand, while Zelma merely scanned the room authoritatively. Sophie fluttered at any man within reach; Zelma challenged them behind cup and saucer, and ate with no trace of Sophie's greed.

On one never-to-be-forgotten day, the nurse was absent. Instead Anabel's mother joined the tea party, Madame La Comtesse, when only the night before Lori had seen Monsieur le

Comte embrace Zelma passionately in the hall, putting his hands inside her dress while she grasped fistfuls of his hair. He was darker than Anabel, and her mother was fairer still. She was small and pretty, and wore a coat with a becoming fur collar and a matching fur hat. She shook elegant, beautiful Zelma gently by the hand and said, 'Anabel talks so much of you. She says what a lady you are, and I thought we should be friends.'

Zelma was stiffly gracious. She offered cakes and made conversation well enough to deceive everyone except Lori, who could see her toes curling within her shoes. So Lori chattered like a magpie, filling the silences with rubbish and making Anabel's mother laugh. She couldn't eat, though. Both she and Zelma left their cake in a mess on the plate, and smiled and said they were too, too delighted to have come.

At last it was over. They walked home in silence, until, safe within the house, Zelma let out a sudden howl of pain and fury. 'How could he let it happen? How dare he? It demeans us both. Madame la Comtesse and her husband's whore. Oh, I'm so ashamed.'

Sophie and Marie said nothing. After a while, Marie got up to make one of her tisanes. In an hour or so Zelma stopped sobbing.

But that night, when Sophie put her to bed, Lori asked what she was to do. 'Tell your friend that Zelma's shy,' said Sophie, whisking Lori's vest over her head. 'It's a problem with her. She doesn't go out much in company. And don't talk about it to Zelma. She won't want everyone to know.'

But everyone in Lori's world seemed to know. Monsieur le Comte, when he was told, laughed and laughed and laughed.

Anabel sat on a wall, kicking the heels of her shoes. Almost twelve years old, rounding with the beginnings of puberty, she nonetheless retained much of the little girl. Perhaps, like her mother, she would always do so, although she could follow her father with his clean jaw and firm stare. She wasn't yet pretty.

Lori was different. Not pretty, not in the least, but already someone you would notice. Her hair was good, black and abundant, and her pale eyes gave her an unworldly appearance, as if she might be handmaiden to an oracle or something equally odd. She had long, slender arms and legs, but her body lacked any curves at all. Her new, young breasts pushed at her school apron as if someone had stuffed apples down her blouse.

'What will happen when your grandmother dies?' asked Anabel.

Lori shrugged. 'I don't know. Perhaps Zelma will run things her way.'

'Does she stay in bed all the time?'

Lori thought of Madame Bonacieux. 'Only on Sunday mornings. She takes care of everything in the house, the maids, everyone. All the tradesmen have to talk to her once a week, and they're ever so scared. If there's an argument or anything she comes in and everyone's quiet. She's very strict.'

'Will she leave you any money?'

'I don't know.' Lori grinned at her friend. 'She might have spent it all.'

As Lori had intended, Anabel changed the subject. Monsieur le Comte's extravagance was getting out of hand. Nowadays it wasn't unusual for Anabel's mother to be found sobbing into her morning coffee, and her father nowhere to be seen. Lori knew exactly where he was; with Zelma.

'Men are very strange,' she said thoughtfully, as they paced the little courtyard. She could remember when it had seemed vast. Not long ago.

'Men are mad,' said Anabel. 'Maman says so. She says nothing makes them happy.'

'Except women,' said Lori. 'But even then, not for long.' Sophie's lasted barely half an hour. And even Zelma couldn't keep Monsieur for longer than a night.

Anabel's colour rose, and Lori knew she should retreat from this conversation. It was just that sometimes she longed to say what she was thinking, to allow Anabel a glimpse of the world in which she lived so much of her life; a world of which she could never, ever speak. She shouldn't have spoken now.

But even as she prepared to abandon the subject, Anabel took it up. 'You mean – like dogs, don't you? In the park. Men and women.'

'People do it face to face,' said Lori matter-of-factly.

'But not like that. Not—'

And suddenly Lori needed to say, needed to shock. 'Yes,' she said. 'It's the same. The man puts it in the woman. He doesn't mind if it hurts her or anything, he just does it. Of course, women don't like it, and if they can they won't let them. So there are special women for men to do it to. When their wives won't.'

'Special women?' Anabel's eyes were saucers. 'But there can't be any woman who'd want that!'

Lori flapped her hand. 'Of course they don't want it. Nobody wants it but the men. The women get paid. And they do things to make sure they don't have a baby.'

'What things?'

But Lori had said enough. She shrugged. 'Things.'

Anabel's eyes were wet. She turned away, and Lori felt a strong shaft of pleasure. Her two worlds, so separate, so different, had touched. Anabel adored her handsome father. It was time she knew what he did, what all men did. In an odd way it made Lori feel less alone.

Going home with Zelma, past the big stores with their glamorous windows, through the sidestreets of shops with flats above, entering the maze of ambiguous byways that led to the Rue de Claret, Lori said suddenly, 'Why don't you work in a shop or a library?'

Zelma glanced at her. She had wondered how long it would be before Lori began asking questions. She had expected them before now. 'Not enough money,' she said simply.

'Even so. You wouldn't have to live with Madame Bonacieux. And Monsieur le Comte wouldn't—'

'Monsieur le Comte would!' snapped Zelma. She pulled her fur tippet around her shoulders. She often wore fur since she knew that his wife did also. 'He isn't happy at home. How can he be? He married a fool. Good family, of course, he must have that. But a fool. She hasn't even given him a son.'

Lori persisted. 'But if you worked in a library, you wouldn't have to do it. You know. The business. You could say no.'

They were passing a bookshop, one that Zelma sometimes used, and the dusty proprietor bobbed up and down when he saw them. But Zelma was oblivious. She turned and met Lori's eyes, almost level with her own. 'I would do it with him for nothing. He's a wonderful man, Lori. Intelligent. Sophisticated. Handsome. I've had hundreds of men in my time, but when I'm with him I'm a virgin again. He married that fool – and it should have been me.'

That evening, Lori pondered. When she went to sit with Sophie while she dressed, as she often did, she said, 'Is Zelma in love with Monsieur?'

Sophie chuckled. 'Only just realised, have you? She's mad for him.'

'But he's just like them all. Just the same.'

Sophie put down her rouge brush and reached for a glass of wine. 'They're all different, sweeting. We say they're not but we don't mean it. Some you hate, they make your flesh creep, just by being what they are. And some – well, if you weren't a businesswoman, you'd do it for nothing. You'll learn, sweeting. One day.' She tossed Lori a bonbon and went back to her powdering.

When Monsieur le Comte next came, Lori sat on the landing and watched. Was he different from the others? Well dressed, certainly, but no more so than the lawyers and doctors who called. She thought he looked tired, with lines carving his cheeks into long rectangles. But next to him, Zelma looked beautiful.

As she greeted him in the hall, creamy shoulders rising from green shot silk, Sophie came by. Lori saw her face, saw the effect on her of Zelma's beauty. She caught drunkenly at the newel post of the stairs, and swept an exaggerated curtsey. 'Monsieur le Comte,' she said gushingly. 'Do let me have the pleasure sometime.'

There was a moment of tense silence. Zelma stood frozen; any other customer and she would have hit out then and there, but not in front of him.

'My dear, the pleasure would be all mine,' murmured Monsieur, making a mock bow.

'Go to the salon, Sophie,' said Zelma tightly. 'If you're sober enough to find it.'

Sophie put her hands to her hips. 'Oh, I'm such a bad girl, aren't I, Zelma? You know, sir, you ought to bring a friend. I specialise in doubles. I could teach you a lot.' She strolled across the floor, the lace of her négligée torn and dirty, pulled across breasts and hips no longer firm.

Monsieur said, 'Perhaps I'll take you up on that,' and Sophie giggled.

* * *

58

There had never been such a row in the house. Just after six in the morning, when Monsieur had at last gone home, Zelma burst into Sophie's room and dragged her from bed by the hair. The screams woke Lori, who leaped from bed and down the stairs. Girls were opening doors and wandering down the hall, and the odd late client was pulling on clothes and making for the street. Suddenly Sophie and Zelma burst into view.

'You bitch! You animal!' Zelma was shrieking. Sophie's squeals were high and desperate, like a rabbit caught by a fox, thought Lori.

'Don't, Zelma. Don't!' she yelled. But Zelma kicked and punched.

Her foot landed in Sophie's back. 'Drunken cow!' she yelled as Sophie sprawled on the floor, and lay for a second, winded. She looked ghastly, thought Lori. She wasn't strong, Zelma would kill her! But before she could rush to intervene, Sophie suddenly wriggled across the floor, grabbed an iron doorstop and threw it. The missile passed Zelma, flew over the banister and down to the hall below, curling almost lazily around the chain of the crystal chandelier. A collective shriek rose from the watching women as the doorstop crashed into glass and candles, sending them cascading on to polished floor and precious rug.

Sophie let out shriek after shriek of laughter, slumped down against the wall. One of Zelma's fingernails had scored a deep cleft down her cheek. There was no sound but Sophie's laughter, and the diminishing tinkle of broken glass. No one dared even to speak.

Far below, the door to Madame's room opened. One of the girls yelped, 'Mon Dieu! She'll kill us all!' and ran to hide in her room. Madame Bonacieux stood in the hall and looked up. She wore a dressing gown massively encrusted with brocade. Under her gaze, one by one the women melted away. Lori, in an agony of loyalty, longing to hide from that relentless gaze, went to cling to Sophie's feebly waving hand.

'Oh, Lori,' whispered Sophie between giggles. 'What now?'

Madame said, 'Sophie. Zelma. Go to your rooms.'

Whitefaced, Zelma muttered, 'Yes, Madame. My apologies, Madame.'

Sophie, with Lori's aid, lurched to her feet. 'Stupid cow,' she muttered audibly. Lori helped her away.

Lori stayed home that day. She took Sophie coffee and later brandy. She bathed her scratches and the huge bruise on her back. 'How do you like Zelma now?' Sophie demanded. 'She started it.'

'You tried it on with Monsieur,' said Lori laconically, and Sophie gave a surprised grunt of laughter.

'You're coming out of your shell. And what if I did? He's a man, isn't he? He fancies me, I can tell. And he's stuck with bloody Zelma, because she takes half price and it's all he can afford. Or says he can. And Madame gets what he does pay, so she's doing it for nothing. What kind of whore is that?'

Lori sat and stared at Sophie without speaking. Suddenly Sophie said, 'Gerard was right. I shouldn't have taken you from the farm. I shouldn't have brought you here. What sort of life is this for a child? Look at you. You know everything.'

Lori said, 'I'm glad you took me. I'll always be glad.'

Sophie turned her scarred face to the pillow. 'But it's Zelma you love nowadays. Poor old Sophie's just a drunken cow Madame keeps for the men who like a bit of rough.'

Lori drew in her breath, and it lodged in her chest like a stone. 'You must know I love you best, Sophie!' she burst out. 'It's just that – Zelma knows about school and things. I still love you best. I always will. If you didn't get drunk—'

'What? Would you love me more?' Sophie looked at her. Resigned. Bitter. Weary.

'No,' said Lori softly. 'I wouldn't worry so. That's all.'

'Oh, God.' Sophie turned away, smothering unlooked for tears. She put out an arm and drew Lori close. 'Come and cuddle me, darling. Cuddle little Sophie, who rescued you from that filthy man and his mad mother. If it wasn't for you I'd still be with Albert. I'd have married Gerard. I would, you know.'

She smelled of sweat and drink. It was repulsive, but Lori closed her mind and thought only that this was Sophie, dear Sophie. The others looked down on her, despised her almost, but then they didn't understand. Sophie wasn't cautious, or even sensible, but she was warm. Lori clung to that warmth, and always would.

Sophie's mood, mercurial as ever, ballooned upwards. She patted the bed, for Lori to lie down too, and she clanked the brandy bottle against the glass. 'What a nice day this is! I shan't work tonight, I'm such a mess. Why don't we have some bonbons, Lori darling? We had bonbons by the river when I first saw you. You ate the lot. God, but you were a funny kid. Do anything I said, absolutely anything. Scared me, actually. Like a doll. And here you are, almost grown up, and still so odd-looking. Except now you've got tits. Aren't you glad old Sophie saved you? Good old Sophie?'

Lori stood by the bed. 'Of course I am. Shall I get the bonbons, Sophie?'

'Silly me! Someone must, I suppose. Yes, darling, you do that. And then we'll be cosy, all day. The two of us. Like it used to be.'

She guzzled again at her glass.

Outside in the hall, Lori felt the tears come. Perhaps Pierre would go for the bonbons? Everything was so awful suddenly. Madame wouldn't put up with scenes like this morning's, Lori knew that as she knew her alphabet. Something would be done. And Sophie was so little regarded. In the complex hierarchy of the Rue de Claret, she was indisputably on the lowest rung; even the new girls, who knew nothing, looked down on her. Even Marie, who never did much business, was regarded more highly, because curious women, driving past, would see her at a window and be impressed by the beauty of the whores.

Madame Bonacieux was coming up the stairs. Lori felt sudden alarm; she never saw girls in their rooms but always in her study. She looked back to Sophie's door – she had to know what was to happen. In an instant she was gone from the landing, and no one was there.

Madame, breathing heavily from the climb, paused to regain her composure. Then she advanced heavily towards Sophie's room, extending her large hand to knock.

'Who is it?' came the slurred enquiry.

'It is Madame.'

The door opened and closed once again. Lori, hidden in one of the curtained alcoves which gave access to each and every room in the place, slid the panel aside to watch and listen.

Sophie made no move to tidy herself. She lay on the bed, her robe crumpled as always, stained with coffee and brandy and tears. Madame sat down on the small bedroom chair, overflowing it on either side. She looked at Sophie with dispassionate,

Olympian judgment. 'You are always drunk. Even now.'

Sophie said nothing. After a moment Madame went on, 'Zelma has apologised and offered to pay half the repairs. I have heard nothing from you.'

Sophie shrugged. 'She attacked me. It was her bloody fault.'

'Because you propositioned Monsieur le Comte. You know the house rule. You do not approach another girl's customer. Under any circumstances.'

'I can't afford to pay for that chandelier!'

'Because you spend your money on drink.'

'No! On Lori. And – and everything.' Sophie put a hand in bewilderment to her head. She never knew where her money went. The truth of it was that she was too drunk to steal from the men and too easygoing to demand cash for extras.

Madame sighed. She always disliked these occasions, when a girl had at last sunk below the standards of her house. It happened, sometimes through age, often through drink or drugs, sometimes because the life unhinged their minds and they no longer worked well. It took a strange sort of woman to maintain standards year after year. The ones who did, Mathilde, Marie, Zelma, were valuable.

'It's time for you to leave,' she said firmly.

Sophie flopped angrily against the pillows. 'All right! I apologise. I'll find the money somehow.'

'It's too late for that, Sophie. I shall rent a room for you, to which you will go this afternoon. Somewhere you can work from. It shouldn't be hard. I'll throw in a month's rent and a hundred francs.'

The brandy fumes still clouded Sophie's understanding. 'Come off it! Who else will you get to do the doubles? I've got regulars. They only come because of me.'

'I shall give them your address. Times have changed, I fear. After the war, we had to take what we could, anyone who could pay. Now – well, things are better. We discriminate.'

'And my sort aren't good enough for you? Is that what you mean?'

Sophie struggled up on the bed. From Lori's spyhole she seemed huge and flabby, a scarred, used, desperate woman. Lori's heart ached for her. 'I didn't ask for that sort! You were the one who told me to get on with it. My God, there's nothing I haven't done, and you throw me out because of it! Do you wonder I drink? Does it surprise you? Wouldn't you drink if two filthy peasants were going to stick you every way they could?'

Implacable, Madame said, 'May I remind you that this was a life you chose? You begged me to take you back. You and the child.'

There was a pause in Sophie's breathless sobs. 'What will you do? Throw her out too?'

'No. There's no need. All the girls help with her clothes and education. You said she was intelligent and so it has proved. She can stay.'

Lori put her fist to her mouth, experiencing a rush of wild relief. She could stay! But almost at once she was ashamed. She didn't understand herself. How could she feel glad when Sophie was cast out? She'd be on the streets.

They all saw them, the wretched, hopeless ones. Lori looked out for them, clustered on corners, too old, too young, all desperate. Some of the girls had been like them once. All feared that this was where they would end. The police hounded them, the customers robbed them, the thugs took them into alleys and beat them up. The only hope was a pimp and they didn't bother with Sophie's sort. She was on the slide.

Lori waited until Madame was again downstairs. The house was very quiet, and the corridors deserted, as if everyone knew what was happening and kept well away, lest they too should suffer. Lori slipped into Sophie's room. The woman was sobbing, dry-eyed. 'I'm done for,' she said to Lori, her voice weak and surprised. 'The old cow's done for me.'

'No! It doesn't have to be like that. Get a job in a shop. A library.' Even as she said the words, Lori's voice lost its conviction. Sophie in a library? And what kind of shop would employ this bedraggled wreck?

Sophie went on as if she hadn't heard. 'I hate the rain! And the snow – that's the worst. You know who she'll send me, don't you? The rejects. The ones they don't let in. Good enough for Sophie but not for her!'

'You'll have your regulars still,' ventured Lori.

'Yes. Yes, so I will.' Sophie sat up and smiled tremulously. 'Not so bad then, Lori love. You can stay. I know you want to come with me, but it's best you don't. School and everything. You've got so grand. You'll come and see me often, won't you? I can't come here.'

'I'll come all the time,' said Lori desperately. 'I'll bring you things.'

'Will you? That's a good girl.'

She got up and went to the mirror, surveying her wrecked face. 'My God, I'm a sight today. Best not let everyone see me like this. I haven't dressed up in ages, so it's time I did. They can see what they're losing. Be damned to them!'

At four in the afternoon, just as the short winter day was ending, Sophie left the house. No one but Lori said farewell, but at all the upper windows women stood and watched her go; dumpy, over-coloured, her scratched face caked with make-up, but still with some vestige of spirit, she lifted an arm to summon a passing taxi. It stopped, showering her skirts with mud, but Sophie took no notice. She made her exit with style.

Chapter Six

The winter was hard that year and snow fell often. Lori went to see Sophie every day, until Sophie said she couldn't work with Lori always there. After that she visited on Mondays after school, slipping out of the house and walking across town. It was very cold. Lori's hands in their good gloves were blue, and she imagined Sophie, on the street. She'd never kept a pair of gloves for a whole week.

Sophie made an effort on Mondays. The shabby room at the top of a sour-smelling flight of stairs was almost tidy. But Lori saw the heaps of clothes under the chairs, heard the clank of bottles when Sophie sat on the bed. She unloaded her own gifts. Wine, bonbons, money. 'From Zelma,' Lori explained. 'She had a good week.'

'Her? Take it back. I don't need her charity.'

Lori left it, of course. Because Sophie did.

Once or twice the door was locked, and although no one answered when she knocked, Lori was sure Sophie was inside. She was drunk, or a man was there perhaps. She pushed the money under the door and left the parcels outside it and then, when she was at the foot of the stairs, stood in the shadows and waited until she heard the door open. That was all right, then. She ran hectically home.

The other girls were especially kind just then. Lori hated their sympathy, hated needing it. She would never have taken their gifts if only she had money. But she had nothing but their charity. Everything that she took now seemed to be undeserved. After all, what did she do but serve as a pet, useless, in the way, to be doted on when required.

Somehow while Sophie was around she hadn't noticed it so. The girls were naturally generous. But suddenly she seemed to have grown up. As a child she could take without thinking, without knowing what it cost. But now she knew how many minutes it took to earn ten francs, how many soldiers to earn a hundred. And her mind turned to Sophie and what she must do. No Pierre now to matter-of-factly chuck out the rough ones. No Madame to look a man up and down and say, 'No, Monsieur. We regret. We don't take your kind.'

The snow came hard in February. The school was closed, and Lori sat in the salon looking out. There would be no customers in weather like this. The roads were clogged with trucks and cars, while the horse-drawn wagons, the few that remained, for once did best. The girls went into the kitchen to cook; Heloise was making her special fondue. Even though Madame employed an excellent chef, the girls loved to make the foods of their childhood. Sometimes they were strong peasant dishes, full of meat and red wine, and sometimes there were delicate pastries of much finer parentage. Lori thought of the fondue with relish.

A man was walking quickly down the street, in spite of the snow. Tall, in a fine wool coat. Lori watched for a moment, and then scrambled back from the window. Monsieur le Comte.

'Zelma,' she called urgently through the kitchen door. 'Zelma, Monsieur's here!'

'Oh my God! Lori, look after him while I get changed.' Zelma ran frantically upstairs. No man liked his whore to look like his wife, floury hands, messy hair and a dull dress. Lori went reluctantly back to the salon.

'Monsieur.'

He looked at her with surprise and a little embarrassment. 'Hello. Laura, isn't it?'

'Yes. Can I offer you some wine? Zelma won't be a moment.'

'Wine – yes, I'd like some wine.'

He sat down rather recklessly in a flimsy chair, and then got up again almost at once. He looked ill, thought Lori. The colour had receded from his skin, leaving odd blotches on his cheeks and forehead. There was a brown stain on the cuff of his shirt. She poured him the wine and he took the glass and paced the room, turning suddenly and saying, 'Do you like it here? I mean – for a child it's very odd.'

Lori shrugged. 'I'm used to it. It's a life.'

'But you've never told Anabel? About—' He hesitated. Lori

waited, although she knew what he meant. 'About me?' He finished awkwardly.

'I never talk about my life here,' said Lori. 'Anabel wouldn't understand.'

'And you do?'

Lori nodded. 'Yes.'

He sat down again and chuckled to himself. 'Well, well, well. A woman of the world, at twelve. Perhaps all children should be brought up in bordellos. What will you do when you grow up?' He smiled at her suddenly.

She wondered uneasily what she looked like, if to him she looked as tall and shapeless as she felt. 'I might work in a shop,' she said. 'Or a library. I could be a housekeeper, perhaps. Madame shows me how to manage.'

'Why not work here?'

There was something unpleasant in the way he looked at her. Some assessment, some consideration of her worth. She might dress with restraint, she might talk, learn, play just as Anabel did, but that was as far as it went. Anabel, the aristocrat, was true metal. Lori, the foundling, was base.

'I won't work here,' she said falteringly.

'Are you sure? Look at you, growing up so fast – developing.'

Lori's cheeks flamed. She turned to run from the room but he moved in front of her. 'Please – please don't go,' he said urgently. 'My apologies. I didn't mean to upset you.'

'Yes, you did.'

'Don't you know young ladies aren't supposed to tell the truth?'

'I haven't told the truth about you. That's enough, isn't it?'

He laughed, a little shakily. 'I sometimes wonder what would have happened if you had. Sometimes – I almost wish you had.'

Lori didn't know what he meant. He reached out and touched her hair, hanging in carefully curled ringlets on her shoulders. 'This is beautiful,' he murmured. 'So young, so alive.' He crushed the curl between his fingers. Lori felt a charge run through her, as if her hair was an extension of her skin. He smelled of wine and cheroots and toilet water. Every beat of her heart sent racing blood to each excited nerve. Her breasts, those hated embarrassments, seemed suddenly hot and heavy. She pulled away, utterly shocked.

67

'Pour me some more wine,' he said.

Zelma came rustling down the hall. She was in a taffeta evening dress, black as night, her bosom surging from a sea of ruffles. She was smiling, her colour very high. 'You took me by surprise, Monsieur,' she said, extending her hand. 'I wasn't ready for you.'

He took her hand and held it for a moment. 'I was asking this child if she'll become a whore.'

Zelma blinked. Then she said smoothly, 'Who can tell what will happen? Go upstairs, Lori.'

But he said, 'No, no, let her stay. It's so piquant, something fresh amongst the jaded hags.'

A look of horror passed between Zelma and Lori. He was drunk or mad. Monsieur had never been rude before. 'Perhaps you and I should go upstairs,' said Zelma gently. 'We can talk about what has upset you. For you are upset, I can see.'

'Can you?' He stood looking down at her for a moment. Then his face contorted. 'It takes a woman like you to see it.' Zelma pulled at his arm, to lead him away, but he turned to Lori and said, 'You should work here. Start work at once, with as many as you can get. The world's full of good women. Mealy-mouthed cows, the lot of them! And see how I love my whore.' He reached for Zelma, and buried his face in the valley between her breasts. She let out a guttural sob and put her hands in his hair. For a second, until she recovered herself, she looked ecstatic. Then she murmured, 'Come, Charles.' Like a lamb, he went.

In the kitchen they were raucous. 'His wife's found him out,' said Heloise. 'They always go funny when that happens.'

'What d'you bet he's got the clap?' said Françoise. 'His sort are always at it, the dirtier the better.'

Lori said, 'I hope Zelma watches out, then,' and Heloise guffawed.

'What would you know about it, chicken? Been at the peepholes, have you?'

'No,' said Lori, but a telltale tide of red rose up from her neck. They all roared with mirth.

The fondue was very good. At the last moment Heloise threw a handful of tarragon into the oil and the meat was wonderfully scented. The girls sat around the table, gossiping about this or that client. The brothel was going up in the world just then, frequented by several politicians. Madame was going to hire a band for Saturday nights and have dancing. 'I don't know all the new dances,' complained Marie, patting her hair and thinking how well dancing would show off her figure.

'Madame's going to get a dancing teacher,' said Mathilde. 'Personally, I can't be bothered.'

Heloise patted her cheek. 'Time you retired, love. You must have a bit put by. Hire a few girls, get a place of your own.'

'I'd have to leave Paris. You know Madame, can't stand competition. She pays the cops a fortune to leave us alone. It wouldn't cost a lot more to have them crawling all over my place. In the provinces, perhaps. One day soon.' Mathilde brooded on the future.

Lori wondered how old she was. Forty? Fifty? In soft light, with her hair dyed and her face made-up, she could easily pass for thirty, but not here. Yet there was still something attractive about her straightforward, knowing, understanding gaze. Mathilde had seen everything, knew everything, and still found the world to her taste. Perhaps that was why the men still came; despite their thieving, these might be the only truly honest women in Paris.

'I shall start a dress shop,' said Marie, holding up her hand and twirling it, as if she saw it clothed in a long kid glove.

'I thought you were in one already,' said Heloise. 'You never sell anything else.'

Everyone laughed, including Marie. They were living well and could afford to be generous. As times grew better Madame was turning the place into more of an exclusive club than a simple brothel, and the girls were gaining in self-esteem. They began to talk of fashions, and Marie, as the acknowledged expert, held court.

They fell into deep discussion of hemlines. Did short skirts encourage men or show them everything for free? Lori, bored, got up and wandered to the window. It was still snowing. Across the street a man was clearing the pavement with a shovel, but in only a minute it was white again. She felt lonely suddenly. She wanted to talk to Sophie, and failing her, to Zelma. Why had Monsieur been so odd?

Something cracked. The noise was so loud and so unexpected that everyone stopped talking and stared at each other. 'Did something break?' asked Lori in bewilderment.

Mathilde, suddenly white, said, 'My God, that was a gun.'

They ran in a body into the hall. Madame Bonacieux was there, massively calm. 'Who is upstairs?' she demanded.

'Zelma, Madame. With Monsieur le Comte.'

'Zelma!' Lori was galvanized by terror. She flew past Madame and up the stairs.

'Do not go in that room!' Madame's voice was like a whip. But she was coming so slowly up the stairs. Lori reached a desperate hand for the doorknob. She wanted to see, and yet dreaded that she should. Let it not be Zelma, she prayed. Not Zelma.

Zelma sat in the middle of the floor. She was naked but for her stockings. Across her lap, wearing nothing at all, lay Monsieur. Where his head had been, his dark, attractive face, there was mashed and bloody pulp.

Madame, breathless at Lori's shoulder, said, 'Get away from here, child. Tell Pierre to call the police.'

It smelled like the farm, when they slaughtered a pig. Zelma was rocking backwards and forwards, beginning a long, low moan. Her breasts dabbled in the blood where the face should be. Her stomach contracting in horror, yet her throat closed against the vomit, Lori fled down the stairs.

They took the body away in the middle of the night, and Zelma went the next morning. Hospital, Madame said, but anyone could see that Zelma was mad. She had fought them when they tried to move her, until in the end the police dragged her away screaming. She wouldn't wash, or speak, but simply rocked and moaned, on and on.

One of the police told them Monsieur was ruined, and that was why. 'He's not the only one,' the man said. 'If you ask me, thing don't look so good. The country's in a mess, a man can't earn an honest wage no more.'

Madame took the hint and offered money. But, pay though she might, the news got out. Reporters stalked the street outside the house, and someone, Heloise probably, talked. Monsieur le Comte had killed himself in naked embrace with his whore, one Zelma Legrand.

Lori didn't know what to do. The snow had stopped, and people had heaped it up in muddy piles all over the city, so she could go to school again. School? Lori could hardly imagine being there. This was so real, so horrible, and that so remote. English grammar with Mademoiselle; singing lessons. But she knew she had to go. If Zelma came back and found she had stayed at home she'd be very angry.

It seemed strange setting out on her own. The journey felt purposeless, the faces of people seemed to look at her oddly, as if what had happened showed on her skin. When she was only halfway there Lori felt engulfed by a terrible panic, as if she was disappearing, dissolving into blood that would sink into the ground to leave nothing but a stain. The stain in Zelma's room had leaked even into the room below. So much blood.

She leaned against a tree, breathing hard. If only Sophie were here. When she was, nothing seemed so bad; there was always a joke, a vulgar comment. Sophie believed in good luck, believed it deep down, when all sense denied it. Her very presence would defeat this horrible despair. Lori felt bile rise in her throat. She so needed Sophie's foolish, misplaced optimism.

After a moment she collected herself. This wasn't so bad. Not so bad as the day her mother died, certainly. But worse than the day she left the farm. Tomorrow would be different, that was the way of things. Monsieur le Comte would never have killed himself if he had understood that however bad things were, you had only to wait until tomorrow.

She went on to school, past the shabby houses, past the shops, into the neat respectable streets. In through the gate, her footsteps steady now, across the snowy courtyard where little children ran and laughed. Anabel was waiting in the hall, and Lori beamed with sudden relief. Anabel. She hadn't thought to see her today. They could stand together, united in the face of this disaster. 'I thought you'd be at home. I'm so glad to see you. How are you, how's your mother?'

'I hate you.'

Lori fell back, amazed. Anabel's soft face was a mask of loathing.

'I don't understand,' said Lori. But she did. She did. She felt the cold of the day returning. She was cold as death.

'You knew what she was! You knew what they did. When you

told me about those women I didn't understand, but now I do. You came to my house and my mother was kind to you!'

Lori licked her lips. 'There wasn't anything I could have done,' she whispered.

'We're ruined because of you. He spent all our money on – on her. We won't have anything left. We shall be poor.'

'He didn't spend money on her,' Lori muttered.

'Don't lie to me! No more lies, not now. It was you and her. Together.'

Was there any point in denial? It was only nibbling at the edges of truth. She said, 'Will you still come to school?'

'I only came today to tell you how awful you are. A traitor, not a friend.'

Lori stood with her head bowed. She felt a consuming guilt, for Sophie, for Zelma, Anabel, even for Monsieur, who had touched her hair and then shot himself. It was all her fault! Her rational mind made a feeble show of resistance. 'It wouldn't have helped, would it? If I'd told?'

Anabel said, 'I don't know. But we'd have known. We could have gone away.'

She was going away now. If Lori had told, she would have gone sooner. Her friend. Her only friend. She stood on the steps and watched Anabel walk across the courtyard, her gait stiff and unnatural. Lori longed to call to her, knew that Anabel too must long for this day to be normal; ordinary.

Anabel crossed the courtyard to the gate. A woman bent to kiss her; a warrior returned. It was Madame la Comtesse. Lori must have passed her on her way in, wrapped in a dark fur coat. She wanted to run, wanted to say, 'It wasn't my doing! Please believe me. There wasn't anything I could have done!'

Just then a hand touched her shoulder. 'Laura. I have to talk to you. Please come this way.'

Ten minutes later Lori too stood beyond the gates. But she walked home alone.

The house was raided the next Saturday. Madame Bonacieux was furious, but no amount of rage prevented her from being hustled off. She returned the following day, still smouldering. A mood of gloom descended over the place. There'd be no more politicians, that was for sure.

Lori felt useless and in the way. Without Sophie or Zelma she had no champion left. The other girls liked and indulged her, but she felt still more like a dog. They didn't care that she no longer went to school, that she mooched around the house all day aimlessly. But they complained when boredom drove her to play ball upstairs, banging hour after hour against a wall. And the night she walked into the salon for a book, just as if there were no customers there, nearly caused her to be lynched.

'Two of them left at once,' complained Heloise. 'Thought they'd got the address wrong.'

'Mine kept asking for the schoolgirl,' said Françoise. 'I'll have to get a pinafore and socks.'

Madame, listening as always, looked inscrutable.

She called Lori to the study next day. The girl was uneasy. Ever since Zelma went she had known herself to be on borrowed time. Sophie said she was imagining things, but that was just Sophie. Lori knew Madame's ways, her inexorable progress from problem to solution. This was entirely expected.

She stood on the worn square of carpet in the centre of the room, clenching and unclenching her fists.

'Are you nervous?' asked Madame.

'No,' Lori lied. Then she plucked up her courage. 'Madame – do you know where Zelma has gone? Could I visit her?'

'She's in hospital. Mental hospital. No visitors.'

'But—'

'Yes?' The hard, blue stare. Lori subsided.

Madame continued to look at her. She seemed to be noticing Lori for the very first time. After a few minutes she lumbered to her feet and walked around the girl. When she had viewed her from all possible angles, she said comfortably, 'Now. Take off your clothes. I want to look at you.'

Lori went suddenly cold. She licked her lips. 'Please, Madame,' she managed. 'Please, Madame, no.'

The old woman came close to her and tipped her chin with her large fingers. 'I took you for Sophie and I kept you for Zelma,' she said. 'Now there's no reason for you to stay. You can go to Sophie if you wish, or wherever.'

'Sophie wouldn't want me. She can't keep me.' She looked into those pebbles of eyes. 'You don't understand, Madame. The men. I couldn't—'

73

'Don't be foolish. A man hurt you as a child, but you can still enjoy pleasure as a woman. Most you won't enjoy, it's business, no more than that. Some will be different. They'll excite you. You're young, I won't expect too much. One now and then, to begin with.'

She began to unfasten the buttons on Lori's tunic. Lori raised a hand to stop her, and Madame slapped her. 'Be still. I haven't time to waste. Now, the rest.'

Lori wasn't physically very shy. The girls lived openly, dressing and undressing in front of each other, and so had Lori, until her breasts began. It was those she was shy of. When the schoolgirl vest had been discarded she stood with her arms crossed from shoulder to shoulder.

'Arms out. Quickly now.'

Lori hated her. But she extended her arms and stood naked. Madame poked an exploratory finger at the flesh of her buttocks, and tweaked the skin of her upper arm. When she jabbed at a breast, Lori gasped.

Madame chuckled. 'You're young, that's the best that can be said,' she remarked. 'Your shape's not good. Thin enough but no waist and too much back. I'll get Marie to look.'

She rang a bell and to Lori's relief Marie came in. She waited, expecting disapproval and disbelief. Of course Lori could not work. She was a child still. She was different. But Marie stood and swung on her stylish heel. 'She may develop,' she commented.

'But for now?' urged Madame. 'No hips and no bum. And her tits look as if they've been stuck on.'

'Lots of men like the girlish look.' Marie pinched the flesh beneath Lori's arm, pushing it forward to see if it enlarged her breasts. 'We can make her look bigger,' she remarked. 'We can disguise the waist. A little make-up for her face, lashes and brows and nothing else. We don't want her to look like a tart!'

She and Madame laughed. Marie patted Lori on the backside. 'You'll look a treat, dear. Run along and talk to Heloise. She'll tell you what to do.'

Lori blinked. 'Do?'

'About the men! Don't want to get the clap or have a baby, do you? Remember Janine, last year?'

74

Lori nodded.

That night she couldn't sleep. She lay and listened to the dark, to the sounds of the old house sighing. Tonight they sounded like Jean, climbing the stair. She tried to imagine him clearly, but the years had blurred everything. Everything except the horror of his body on hers, the smell of him, the pain. She had said to Heloise that day, in the middle of being told about washing and rubber. 'Aren't you ever frightened of them?'

'Not here I'm not,' she had said. 'Why do you think Madame keeps Pierre? It's on the streets you've got to worry. Some of them don't think twice about knocking you about.'

Jean had never thought twice. She doubted that Monsieur le Comte had either. But if he was to come to her – if he had done more than touch her hair – a great blush ascended from groin to scalp.

The next day Marie brought her clothes. She was to wear a brassiere under a white blouse. It was a vicious contraption, with wires pushing her breasts up and together. The blouse was buttoned low, giving Lori a cleavage she had never before possessed. As for her waist, it was disguised in a slim grey skirt which came to just below her breasts, and on her feet she had neat black shoes.

'I had shoes like this once before,' said Lori suddenly. 'When I first came.'

'The stuff you had then,' said Marie. 'It smelled of dead bodies. But that's Sophie for you.'

Lori hadn't taken Sophie anything worth having for weeks. Since Zelma stopped giving her things. Lori knew she was living on soup and yesterday's bread. She said, 'Will Madame pay me?'

Marie nodded, her mouth full of pins. 'You should do well,' she mumbled.

But it was Saturday before anything happened. Lori was in a ferment of anxiety, unable to read or sleep, growing daily more fraught. When Madame summoned her again to the study she felt sudden relief, sure that she had thought better of her scheme. Perhaps Lori was to go back to school? But Marie stopped her running down the stairs. 'Go and change,' she said. 'Put on your things.'

It took time. Her fingers were stiff and cold. In the end Marie came in and hurried her, brushing her hair in a long black drift down her back. Lori looked at herself in the glass. A stranger stared back at her, a child in a child's clothes, but unnaturally voluptuous. Her eyes, fringed and edged in black, were themselves like panes of glass.

'Wonderful,' said Marie. 'Don't look so worried, pet.'

But her tongue was stiff with fright. She tried to swallow on her way downstairs, and almost choked. The hall was very quiet. Did everyone know? If she ran from the house now, if she ran to Sophie, what then? She let out a sound that was almost a sob, and opened the study door.

Madame grunted. 'You took your time. This is Laura, Monsieur.'

She didn't look at him. She couldn't. She sensed someone approaching from behind, felt hands brushing her shoulders, light as a breath.

In English, a voice said, 'Wonderful. She's divine.'

'She speaks English,' said Madame. 'She's not a virgin, a man had her as a child, but she's as good as. I charge as such. And in this house we insist on washing and the use of the *préservatif*.'

He laughed. 'Ah! The famous French letter.'

Sardonically Madame said, 'We call it the *coup Anglais*. Come, Laura.'

Still she didn't look at the man. She followed Madame up the stairs, her own legs almost as ponderous, to one of the rooms on the first floor. Each girl had a room to work in, although she could use her bedroom if she wished. Some did, for their special men. Lori knew she would never let a man in her room, to look at her private things. She would never let any man have anything that mattered. This was business, no more than that.

There was a rustling in the hall. 'Good luck, chérie! Enjoy yourself!'

No one was going to save her. Everyone thought this was something she should do. Madame stood beside an open door, and gestured to Lori to go in. This was inevitable, then. She must.

The room was large, with a double bed and many pillows. Every wall was hung with mirrors, and behind one was a small bathroom. Without looking, Lori knew the man was an inch behind her. Was this what he expected? Why had he asked for her?

Madame said, 'You have two hours. Then someone will knock.'

'Yes,' said the man. 'Er – thank you.'

The door closed softly. They were alone. Lori went to the heavily curtained window and moved the net aside to see out. The windows in this part of the house looked on to blank brick walls. A tree would have helped, thought Lori desperately, something natural, something green. At the farm, she used to think of the wisteria, hanging like a curtain over the barn roof, its flowers like heavy pieces of sky.

'Excuse me.'

She jumped. He spoke in English, but that wasn't the surprise. Like Jean, she hadn't thought he would speak at all.

'Excuse me,' he said again. 'I wanted to ask you—'

'Yes?'

'What does she want me to wash?'

Lori gritted her teeth. She must face him, it seemed. She clasped her hands and turned round. And she was amazed! She had expected a man and this was – he was just a boy! Tall, slender, in an English suit of some sort. He couldn't be more than seventeen. His hair was bright gold and fell forward in a slide over bright blue eyes. What's more, he was blushing.

She said wonderingly, 'Don't you know?'

'No. I've never been to a place like this before. I was here on holiday, and – Parisian brothel and all that.'

'Are you a virgin?' God forbid that they were both new to this.

'Er – not actually, no. A friend of my mother's. Last summer. You needn't worry, I know what I'm about.'

Lori watched him blank-faced. He grinned at her, and she realised that despite everything, he was enjoying himself. When he went home he would tell his friends what had happened, about Madame, the house, about her. She felt her stomach twist at the thought, and at once smothered it in practicalities. She knew already that in this business it didn't do to think. 'You wash your – parts,' she said abruptly. 'There's a bowl with blue water in it.'

He went to look. 'Oh my God! Won't make it fall off, will it?

Bit of a waste of time if it does. By the way, you speak jolly good English. Hardly a trace of accent.'

'Thank you.'

She sat on the bed. Sounds of splashing came from the bathroom, and a few moments later he emerged, carrying his trousers. Lori's eyes were drawn at once to his groin, but his shirt tails hung down and concealed him. She felt a growing sense of unreality.

'You don't mind doing this, do you?' he asked suddenly. 'The old bat isn't forcing you or anything?'

She felt like laughing in his face. Why else would she be doing it? It wasn't as if she wanted to have him, him or anyone. 'Do you want me to undress?' she asked stiffly, and he nodded.

Marie had told her the sequence. Skirt and underskirt, then panties. Blouse, brassiere, leave shoes and stockings on. 'Wander about like that for a bit and you won't have any trouble,' she advised. But when she began to unbutton her blouse he said, 'Doesn't it embarrass you? To have me see you like this?'

'No,' said Lori, her insides tense with shame.

'Well – could you leave your top things on? All of this is pretty exciting, you know.'

'Don't you want to be excited?'

'Well – yes. But not too much, you know. Not at first.'

He came towards her, throwing off his shirt. The sight of him appalled her. Revolted her. Smooth white skin, with a fuzz of pale hair across his chest, shoulders not yet fleshed with adult muscle. And – that. Once she had seen it, she couldn't stop looking. It was huge, she had forgotten how big it could be. She fell back on the bed, watching with horror as he wrestled with the rubber protection. Seeing her face, he said, 'I'd kiss you, but – I didn't think prostitutes liked it.'

'They don't,' said Lori. She wanted as little contact as possible with this man – this boy.

'All right then. Look, I'll try not to hurt.'

She lay back and he came down on top of her. The remembered sensation. Instinctively she held her breath, but when she was forced to breathe there was no stench of Jean; just the smell of clean skin, and the subtle tang of maleness. His hand touched her between her legs. She moaned in misery and he thought she was enjoying it, and laughed. 'You French girls are all the same.'

He lifted himself up and pushed into her. She lay very still, expecting pain, feeling only that she was invaded. He said, 'My God, you're fantastic. Tight as a drum. I knew it was all an act. You must be twenty at least. I bet you've had hundreds of men.'

He began to move in and out of her unresponsive body, pulling himself up on his elbows to look down into her face. 'God, but you're lovely,' he whispered, and fumbled for her breasts in the heavy brassiere, gripping her in vice-like fingers, putting his face into her neck to lick and suck. Now he was hurting her, battering at her body, just like Jean. He was so strong, so hard, at every thrust she groaned. Suddenly he reared up from her, his face in a rictus of pleasure, his body pulsating. Then he subsided, panting, grinning, his eyes tinged red. Lori rolled out from under him, staggered into the hall and was sick.

Madame Bonacieux and Marie were breakfasting together. 'I don't often make mistakes,' said Madame. 'I thought she'd like a clean young boy.'

Marie bit into a croissant. 'What did she say he did?'

'Nothing unusual. No finesse, of course, but you don't expect that at his age.'

'How long was he in there?'

'About ten minutes.'

Marie lifted her shoulders in a shrug. 'Well, Madame. There you are. He mated her like a cow.'

Madame's jaws moved steadily as she ate. She took more coffee and some English jam. She usually liked things English, although that young man had annoyed her. He had called her a fraud and a cheat, and threatened to have her closed down for using sick girls. She had been obliged to tell him that he could be arrested for seducing a minor, since Lori was not yet thirteen. He'd been thrown on the street, his pants flying after him.

But what to do with the girl? She'd been hysterical, claiming that he bit her and smothered her, although it seemed he had done no such thing. 'Boys are always rough,' said Marie thoughtfully. 'She needs an older man. What a pity Monsieur le Comte went and killed himself.'

Madame grinned, but it soon faded. That episode had been

no laughing matter. 'We get so few good lovers here,' she said petulantly.

'They don't need to pay,' said Marie, and this time Madame laughed out loud.

Chapter Seven

Standing outside the study, rigged up as before, Lori was shaking with terror. Each time she lifted her fist to knock it was as if some invisible force prevented her. Wild schemes kept flitting across her mind; she could run away, to Sophie, to the orphanage, even back to the farm. But she knew, she more than anyone, that girls on their own only earned their bread one way. She would run from one nightmare to another.

'Where is that child?' The door opened and Madame was there. Lori swallowed audibly. Madame gave her a look that would have frozen hell and stood aside to let her enter. In Madame's large armchair, sipping a glass of cognac, was a grey-haired old man.

He stood up as she entered, and smiled down at her. 'Hello, my dear. Laura, isn't it? Please don't look so frightened. Really, you've nothing to fear.'

He extended his hand and she took it. He wasn't one, then. A customer. He might run a school or a shop in which she might work. Lori's imagination took wing, carrying her off to a golden future.

'You see the state she's in,' said Madame laconically.

'I can see only a lovely young lady,' said the visitor. 'Have you a coat, my dear, and some boots? I thought we might go shopping.'

His name was Henri. He seemed to Lori very old, although he was only around forty-five. He had a short little beard on the point of his chin, streaked grey like his hair, and small bright blue eyes submerged in creases when he smiled. He treated Lori with absolute punctiliousness, as if she were a very great lady, opening doors, holding her chair in cafés, buying her flowers. They shopped for chocolates and gloves, and he helped her choose stockings, rejecting the workaday items with silk bottoms and woollen tops for delicious confections with lace flowers from heel to thigh. 'Don't let anyone see us,' he whispered conspiratorially. 'I'm not sure it's proper for a gentleman of my age to buy a young lady stockings.'

Lori giggled into her hand.

They returned in the early evening and he bade her farewell in the hall. Mathilde was walking by, and to Lori's surprise she stopped.

'Darling Henri! How delightful.'

'Mathilde. I'm enchanted. It's been too long.'

They embraced and Mathilde said, 'How is Mona these days?'

He made a face. 'A little unwell. Not too bad. We wait for the spring.'

'Don't we all? Are you taking care of our little Lori? That's kind. She's a good girl.'

'A charming young lady,' said Henri.

He took his leave with only a kiss on Lori's fingers. She was bemused. What was this for?

The next morning, Lori waited for Mathilde. She had been busy the night before, two of her regulars, and she breakfasted late. She came down around noon, hair dishevelled, face shiny with cream, to take coffee and brioche. She could be any tired housewife, thought Lori. She sat opposite at the table. 'I didn't know you knew Henri?'

Mathilde stretched her well-fleshed legs. 'He's an old customer. Used to visit a lot a few years back. Fell for one of our girls, a Chinese called Mona, very young, and in the end he bought her from Madame. He's got a wife somewhere, I think, but he spends his time with Mona. He bought her an apartment. In a good area too. But she's ill. Consumption. Probably had it when she came to us, she'd been around. He's a dear man, Henri, to stay with her.'

'He must love her, then.'

Mathilde reached out and took Lori's face in her plump hands. 'It happens, chicken. In all of this, don't forget. It happens.'

That afternoon Henri came again. Lori, sure now that all was well, bounced downstairs to see him in her pinafore, lifting it to show off her new stockings.

'What legs! My dear, you'll be the talk of Paris!'

'Are we going out? Shall I get my coat?'

'But certainly! Wrap up well, we'll go on the river.'

When she had gone Madame, sardonic at his elbow, said, 'You'll catch your death and nothing else.'

He stroked his beard. 'You think so? Wait and see.'

It was very cold on the river. They sat in the open, the wind making their eyes stream, with Paris like a picture drawn on the crystal air. Domes and spires, towers and arches, it seemed a fairy citadel.

'So beautiful,' mused Henri. 'It's hard to think so much that is ugly lives there.'

Lori shivered. She thought of Sophie's apartment, the women of the dingy streets, of Monsieur le Comte dead and smashed, and Zelma moaning. She thought of the boy's face, hanging above her. She shivered again.

It was as if Henri knew what she was thinking. He said, 'Ugliness and beauty, side by side. If we look only at the ugliness we let ourselves down, you know. We must raise our eyes and our spirits to see what is good.'

'There isn't anything,' said Lori simply.

Henri turned an amazed face to her. 'How can you say that? When Paris is spread before you in all its difficult, complex splendour? When you have your health and your beauty, not to mention your lovely new stockings? When we shall go shortly and eat cakes and drink chocolate, and think how good it is not to be cold any more?'

Lori dropped her eyes. 'Those things aren't important.'

'And what is, little one?'

She sighed. 'What's to happen. To me. Madame isn't patient, you see. Everything has to pay, to be good value. She permits nothing that isn't – productive. I have to work. If I don't I must leave, and there's nowhere for me to go. Besides—' she faltered, and Henri finished the thought for her.

'Besides, you are at home there. You don't really wish to go.'

'It's all I know.' Then, distraught, she burst out, 'But I can't do it! I can't! It's impossible!'

She might have been crying, but the wind's tears disguised any others. He took her gloved hand and held it in his own.

83

'Now, my dear,' he said. 'We must talk about this. I know from Madame all that's happened. A man when you were very small, and a boy who knew nothing. A lot of pain and a lot of fear. And no doubt the girls have filled your ears with stories of men quite unnaturally big, and men who were so rough they feared for their lives, and men who smelled so bad they had to lie with a perfume bottle up their noses!'

Lori giggled and Henri went on, 'They exaggerate to impress you, my dear. And what are we talking about? The act of love, the joining of man and woman for pleasure. The man enjoys quickly, the woman slowly. Like a dance. And as dancing must be learned, so with this.'

'I shall never like it,' said Lori desperately. 'Whatever you say!'

He sighed. 'Then what is to happen? You see, my dear, you have to live. If a girl is good at – dancing – she can live well. Don't you see how some of the girls at Madame's have much more than some others? Zelma, for example. An intelligent, educated woman with a few selected men. Men paid a great deal for Zelma, much more than the rest. And until her tragedy, she was happy.'

'What about Sophie?' asked Lori. 'She had lots of men too.'

'But what sort of men? Unpleasant ones who wanted a woman, no more than that. Sophie should have learned from Zelma, you see. Because, my dear, the act of love can be very brief and nasty. And it can be superb, a night of pleasure and delight. For both.'

The boat was puffing back to the quay. Sailors with thick arms and legs were shouting and tossing ropes. In a while they'd go down into town and pay a few francs for a woman. A woman like Sophie. Lori shuddered.

Henri said, 'I know girls from Madame's who have their own apartments, and entertain men of their choice in the greatest discretion and luxury. Remember Lilian? She has a motor car and four fur coats. And her gentlemen friends – and I assure you they are gentlemen – plead to be allowed to come and see her. She has learned to be good at her job.'

Lori stood up, ready to leave the boat. Henri remained seated, looking at her quizzically from beneath the brim of his hat. She was aware of the beating of her heart.

'Is it hard to learn?' she asked.

He shook his head. 'Not at all.'

'I don't know who would teach me.'

He stood up, the image of a well-bred, respectable man. 'Would it revolt you too much to take lessons from a very old man like me? I promise we shall both discover pleasure.'

He helped her from the boat with a hand beneath her elbow, and they linked arms to slither through the half-melted snow. But they did not go back to Madame's. Instead he took her to an hotel, huge, imposing, defended by ranks of uniformed commissionaires. 'Don't worry,' assured Henri as she shrank back from the marbled hall. 'They know me here.' And a chorus of 'Good days' followed them across the glittering foyer and along the carpeted halls. Henri stopped a waiter and ordered chocolate and cakes. 'In my room, if you please. We've been on the river and are quite frozen.'

'At once, Monsieur.'

Was he really staying here? Lori was very impressed. His room was large and opulent, with gilded sofas and a huge curtained bed. A large fire burned, and they took off their hats and coats and shook themselves like dogs. Henri made a game of it, and Lori laughed. When the chocolate arrived it was heaped with whipped cream, dissolving in the heat from the mugs. She sat by the fire, keeping her mind on the moment, shutting out all thoughts of what was to come. But pictures kept flashing into her head; the boy and his nakedness; his face when it was done.

When they were warm and full, Henri came and sat on the sofa next to her. 'Now,' he said. 'It is time to stop worrying. I'm here to make you happy, no more than that.'

'Shall I take my clothes off?'

'I don't think that's necessary, do you?'

'But I thought—'

'Don't think, my dear. Just feel.'

He took her hand, still with its childish nails, and put it to his mouth. He seemed to breathe on her fingers, to touch them so lightly that butterfly wings of sensation ran up her arm. Gradually, so gradually that he seemed barely to move at all, he moved up her arm. It was hypnotic. Lori slid down on the sofa, her eyes half closed, the sleeve of her blouse bunched at her shoulder.

85

She hadn't been touched so gently since early childhood. Sophie's hugs were rough and warm, there was none of this delicate sensuality. Some well of emotion began in her, as if she was sliding back into trust and dependence. There was no way she could know the extent of her own loneliness; so great that she must have whatever this kind old man had to offer, and would give him whatever he wanted in return.

The blouse was preventing him touching her neck. Lori began to wish he would touch her there. She said, 'I'll take off my blouse.'

'Do you want to? I won't look.'

She slid the straps of her pinafore down and took off blouse and vest, before pulling up her pinafore once again. 'There.'

'Indeed. What beautiful skin you have.' He stroked his fingers from one shoulder to the other, caressing the hollows of her throat. Lori let her head fall back a little, and he ran his thumb from the point of her chin to the edge of her pinafore. He did it again and again, and each time as he stopped her eyelids fluttered.

She was breathing more quickly. Was it time? While one hand still stroked, the other slipped the buttons of the pinafore straps out of their holes. Her young breasts came into view, soft still, without definition. This time his thumb moved down into the valley of her breasts and travelled on, marking the lower edge of each mound. Her nipples suddenly hardened into berries.

Lori was experiencing an odd mixture of warmth and excitement. Her eyes were closed and her head was full of nothing but the touch of fingers on her skin, going on and on. Now he had both palms on her naked ribs and was easing her skin upwards, moving her breasts without touching them. But she wanted them touched. She wanted it more and more. Her eyes half opened, and he was smiling at her, gently. Her nipples were hurting her, as if they were burning, and he seemed to know. Taking each between finger and thumb, he rolled them like beads.

Her pleasure was exquisite. It was as if he had touched a string that connected from her breasts to some centre of ecstasy in belly and groin. She fell back across the sofa, and let out a long moan, and in that instant he brought his thigh across her, pressing between her legs. The weight of him alarmed her. Some part of her mind urged her to escape. But her body was in thrall to his hands on her nipples, to the steady, rubbing pressure that was fire and wetness combined. She began to be frightened, something terrible was going to happen to her, her body would burst! She could feel the explosion start, feel it building, and he must go on, he must! The fire engulfed her, scorching each nerve in her body, gripping her womb. For a moment she was lost to herself. It was done.

She opened her eyes to see him watching her. He was smiling. 'Did you like that?'

She nodded bemusedly. She was still burning, still on fire. He said, 'You see how easy it was? Now perhaps you can understand why men desire women. By entering a woman, they feel as you felt then.'

'Yes.' She could see now. Anyone would desire that. She said, 'But customers won't make me feel that way.'

'How do you know? You're not ready for customers yet. I shall teach you how to please them and yourself. But not today.'

She began to look forward to her afternoons. They usually went to the zoo first, and sometimes to a gallery when he would take as much trouble over explaining art as he did over her sexual education. He never seemed in any hurry, over this or anything else. He seemed to take pleasure in every aspect of her company.

Once they went to a theatre matinée, and afterwards, going to the hotel, Lori was in a mood of transcendant joy. That was the day she fully experienced him. She always thought of it as the day she truly became a woman.

He taught her everything; patience, caution, humour. His body was lean and pleasant; she became so intimate with him that nothing was ever an indignity. She discovered the pleasure of kisses where she had never thought kisses should be, the delight of a little judicious pain. But he warned her too. 'You have discovered what love can be. Don't let it be less than this just because you give it for money. Not many women can love as you, Laura. It's a great gift. Don't let drink or drugs – or love, indeed – lead you into foolishness. Take care, my dear. Value yourself.'

She adored him, she was lost in happiness. Suddenly she began to blossom, her figure improved, her skin. She took an interest in the fashion papers that fascinated Marie, and the older woman said, 'You're right. That evening dress would suit you. I'll run something up.'

A month went by. The snow was starting to thaw, and crocuses began pushing their way through icy earth in the parks. A few cafés began to put out tables once again and on a fine spring day there was the scent of hyacinths. That was the day Henri said, 'We must say goodbye, Laura. I'm leaving Paris.'

She looked at him in horror. That Henri should go – she couldn't bear not to have him. He was the best, the most perfect man in all the world. 'I'll come too,' she said urgently. 'I'll sneak out of the house and come to you.'

He looked down at her sadly. 'That wouldn't be right. I'm sure you know, I've got someone of my own.'

'I thought she was ill. That she was dying. I thought—'

'My dear.' He took her hand and pulled it through his arm, beginning to pace the wide walkway under the trees. 'It's very easy to fall in love with someone who gives you pleasure. You'll find half your customers in love with you. True love is different, it's a meeting of mind as well as body. Mona and I had that once. Now she's ill and I care for her. We're going to have spring in the country. But you have my gratitude, Laura. You think I gave you everything, when you brightened my own dark winter.'

He stood and faced her, and even through her tears Lori felt reluctant admiration. He was good at everything, even saying goodbye. With a sudden flash of insight she realised he had said it many times before, that everything he had done with her had been done before.

'Have you trained many girls?' she asked shrilly. 'Does Madame pay you?'

He chuckled and put his hand to his beard. 'Oh, Laura. You are a bright girl. Not all harlots are women, my dear. And not all beautiful women know as much as the harlot. Each of us uses what we have. And one last lesson, chérie – don't despise people. Everyone does what they must. It's far, far better to try and understand.'

But Lori was suddenly bereft. She flung herself on him and began to sob, and he patted her shoulder and soothed her. He was expert, in this as in everything, and when she was calm he took her shopping. First he bought her a lace négligée of exquisite workmanship. Then he bought her a ring. It was a gold band in which tiny diamonds had been inserted, like currants in a cake. It fitted Lori's little finger.

'In case you forget me,' he said.

Lori said fervently, 'I won't. Ever.'

He took her hands. 'Remember me when you're an old, old lady and I am in my grave. Give me a little time then, my sweet.' He bent down and kissed her cheek.

That night, Madame summoned her to the study. 'Now,' she said, ignoring the marks of tears on Lori's face, 'are you ready to begin?'

Lori took a deep breath. 'I'm not sure, Madame.'

'There's nothing to be sure about. You work or you go. And I warn you, life's hard for everyone just now. There's no easy money.'

'I know that, Madame.' She looked the older woman in the face. 'I mean to work. But Henri said – I don't want to be like Sophie. No short times.'

Madame snorted. 'You prove you're worth special treatment before you ask for it, my girl! Henri's an old flatterer. What you know about men could be written on the head of a matchstick, don't deceive yourself.'

Lori said nothing. Madame's mouth was a rigid line beneath her bulbous nose. But then she said, 'As it happens there are one or two gentlemen who might pay for all night. Just make absolutely sure that you behave. I warn you, another fiasco like last time and you're out!'

Lori fled from the room. What would she have done if Madame had said she must work the salon, taking whatever turned up? She felt a frisson of panic. It still might come to that. She wasn't safe. But even as she sat on her bed, forming hopeless plans that she knew would come to nothing, there was a knock on her door. One of the girls put her head round. 'Customer, Lori. Madame says to wait in the blue room, she'll send him up.'

She didn't move for several minutes. All the old panic began again, making her sweat and shake. But she had to go. She'd asked for selected customers, after all.

She got off the bed and went to the mirror. She looked very pale, her hair black and dense. She undressed, noting the figure faults that drew Marie's criticism, the wide shoulders, the well-spaced breasts, the waist which for all its leanness was unfashionably thick. She pulled on the négligée Henri had bought her. It was a deep, singing blue, the colour which he said reflected in her eyes. The ribbons tied tightly beneath her breasts, forcing them to bulge against the lace. She reached up to fluff her hair into a thick mane, and her skirt swung open provocatively. She was ready.

The blue room was already furnished with a bottle of champagne and two glasses. An important customer, then. Lori looked thoughtfully at the ice in the bucket. Then she settled on the bed.

A moment later the door opened, and a tall, balding, rather portly man was ushered into the room. A gold watch chain spanned his waistcoat and his shoes were the very best leather. Definitely a man of importance. He stood staring at the girl on the bed.

'Hello,' said Lori. 'My name's Laura.'

He pulled out a handkerchief and mopped his brow. 'Er – I'm George. I wonder if there's been some mistake? Aren't you too young?'

'Didn't you want someone young?'

'Well, yes – but usually it's some tart pretending, you know.'

'You don't have to worry. I know what to do. You can ask for what you'd like.'

'What – what might I like?'

He was less sure of himself than she. Perhaps he liked young girls because they intimidated him less, their ignorance masking his inadequacy. Lori swung her legs to the floor and stood up, knowing that her gown was falling open. Sweat started on his brow again, and he mopped once more. He was unbearably tense. She opened the champagne, twisting the bottle expertly, as she had often done for Zelma's important lovers. George drank his greedily, but she barely sipped at her glass. She didn't like champagne.

She said, 'Why don't I undress you?'

'I'm not sure – if you think—'

'It might be nice.'

She took the collar of his coat and eased him out of it. □□ hung it up with much swishing of skirts. Then she pushed him back to the bed, half kneeling across him to unfasten his shirt. His eyes were fixed on the bush of hair between her legs and his podgy fingers slowly reached out to touch. She ran her hands across his naked chest, feeling him fumbling clumsily, as if he didn't know what a woman was like. She bent her head and licked his nipples very quickly, then reached to take his hand. She felt powerful, in a way she never had with Henri. That in itself was arousing.

'Touch me at the front,' she murmured. 'Women like that. Are you married?'

'Er – yes.'

'Put your fingers inside me and then touch where I said. Not so hard – oh yes, that's good. Oh George, I like that.'

She licked his nipples again, her hands busy with his trousers. His pelvis was thrusting up at her, he was grinning like an idiot. She rolled off and said, 'Now you must wash, George.'

He went like a lamb and came back naked, a towel held before him. Lori liked such delicacy. She decided to be kind. She put the champagne bucket next to the bed and sat against the pillows, her knees raised and apart. 'Have some more champagne,' she said.

He drank another glass. Lori closed her eyes, as if she was dozing, only to feel his hand stealing shyly between her thighs. Clearly his wife never let him touch. Poor George was consumed by curious desire.

'You excite me very much,' she whispered truthfully. But it wasn't George's inept hands that pleased her. It was her own power and confidence. Why had she been frightened of what he might do? If she wanted she could make him beg.

She eased down underneath him, neatly sheathing him in rubber. Henri had made her practise that twenty times. George was saying, 'I'm sorry, but I must – I simply must—'

'Just wait a little.' He would take nothing that was hers to give. She lifted herself up, pressing her opening against his soft belly. She rubbed herself, letting her head fall back as if moved by passion. Then she slid down on to him. There. They were connected.

He began thrusting at once, grunting with eagerness, and

Lori reached out to the champagne bucket. She took a handful of ice, waiting as the blubbery body on top of her reached its peak. Just as the end came, she put the ice to George's scrotum. His mouth opened, his eyes gaped and he let out a cry of ecstasy. The girl beneath him, task completed, writhed briefly against the pillows. Her job was done.

Madame sat in her study, looking at the man before her. He was important, she gathered, something in government, but he meant nothing to her. The men she had seen in her time – thousands.

'So. You want Laura?'

'Yes, Madame. I understand she's very special, very fresh. Everyone says—'

'Not everyone, Monsieur. A selected few. Laura is our best girl, you understand. She has to be persuaded to take a new client. Her list is very full.'

'How much does it cost?'

Madame rapped, 'Ten thousand francs introductory fee and then payment on the night. It depends what you have. Laura decides. You arrive at eight and leave at two, no later. We could fit you in—' she scanned a diary '—June the twelfth.' She gave him her bulldog stare. 'You must realise if Laura takes a dislike to you, then that's that. You'll be asked to leave. No refund.'

He blinked in amazement and Madame felt a flicker of genuine mirth. These men. The way they behaved. The higher the price of something the more they wanted it, or thought they did. Who would have imagined six months ago that a silly child could become a phenomenon? She was the most spectacular girl Madame had ever had, combining innocence with the utmost sophistication. She wasn't the first for that, of course, although innocence didn't last long in this game. What might be unique, and was in Madame's experience, was the girl's insistence on consideration by the men. She wasn't a prostitute giving what was paid for, she was a participant in mutual, shared desire.

The man booked his date and paid his fee. Madame put two thousand francs on one side for Lori and pocketed the rest. It was fair, she knew the girl took money from her partners herself. Usually Madame came down on such transactions like a ton of bricks, but in Lori's case she was hamstrung by admiration; after paying so much, it was incredible the girl could extract more. But she could.

She saw Lori later in the day. The girl was going shopping with Marie, and stood in the hall, straightening her hat. She was immaculately dressed in a narrow black coat and skirt, the hemline resting just above neat black boots. Her hat fitted close around her face, encircled by a curling grey feather. She looked unimaginably expensive.

'June the twelfth, Laura,' said Madame. 'A new one. Nothing special, but a member of the government. I thought it would help your reputation.'

'Or your bank balance,' said Lori rudely.

Madame said nothing, and Lori felt full of triumph. Why had she been frightened of Madame all these years? Now she was standing up to her it was all easy.

She picked up her purse and made for the door. Marie was waiting on the step, taking the opportunity to stand in full view of some tourists opposite, who were gawping at the house of ill repute. 'I hope you told him he might not pass muster,' said Lori loftily, as she too stepped out to stand beside Marie. 'I don't care how important he is, if his breath smells he's out.'

'I told him,' said Madame.

Lori gave her a gracious nod. 'Thank you, Madame.'

As they walked down the street, Marie said, 'One of these days she'll put you back in your place, you know. If you realise what's good for you don't tweak Madame's nose. She'll remember.'

'She can't do a thing to me. I earn too much,' said Lori, full of childish self-importance. Marie, who had seen girls come and seen them go, said nothing.

They shopped for anything that took their fancy; presents for Sophie, shoes, bags, feather boas. Lori liked feathers, she liked to tickle the men with them and make them sneeze. As she and Marie strolled and giggled, now and then people nudged each other and whispered. Lori felt exhilarated. People were admiring their beauty.

They went for coffee in a chic café, and Lori opened her coat to show the beading on her dress and the elegant turn of her silk-clad ankle. A couple of old guard aristocrats, distinguished by their thin, patrician faces, sat at a nearby table. The older woman turned to the younger and said, 'My dear, do let's go, they're letting harlots in. I really can't bear to have the creatures sniggering and leering as I take my tisane.'

Her companion nodded and they got to their feet. She said, 'You can always tell, can't you? Like farmyard hens dressed up as birds of paradise.'

They walked away and spoke to the manager, no doubt dripping their poison. Lori felt her pleasure in the day drain quietly away. She turned and said to Marie, 'Do we really look different?'

'Different to them, I hope,' said Marie. 'We're prettier, that's all. And better dressed. And, of course, we look at the men.'

'I don't,' said Lori.

Marie lifted an elegant shoulder. 'Too young, my dear, and too sheltered. You've never had to struggle for trade. If you had, you'd know a customer when you see one.'

Their cakes and coffee arrived. Lori tried to eat, but the food seemed to stick in her throat. She wasn't like Sophie, or Marie, or Mathilde, she thought helplessly. She wasn't a whore like any other. She was young and desirable, men paid thousands of francs for just a few hours of her company. Even so, the manager was glancing across at them, making sure that none of the waiters guided anyone to the tables nearby. Expensive she might be, but in some circles she was no better than a woman of the streets. If she sold hats or dresses or badly painted china she'd be accorded some measure of respect. But selling herself, she was despised.

As they signalled for the bill, the manager came across. 'Mesdames,' he murmured discreetly. 'Please, there will be no charge. But there've been complaints. Be good enough not to call here again.'

Marie said, 'My niece and I are merely in town to shop. What possible complaint could there be?'

'Nonetheless, Madame. There are other cafés more suitable for ladies from the Rue de Claret.'

Marie swept haughtily from the shop, Lori trotting unhappily in her wake. It was like school again, the taint clinging like the smell of rancid meat. Her thin shell of sophisticated poise was falling about her minute by minute. As they hurried down the street, anxious to escape the scene of their humiliation, a man coming towards them crossed over with haste. Lori recognised him as one of her regulars. Last time, he'd called her his queen. Yet he wouldn't tip his hat to her in the street.

'Now,' said Marie, once they were safely around the next corner, 'let's go to one of the couture houses and look at the designs. They don't dare turn up their noses, we spend too much.'

'I – I think I'd rather go home,' said Lori. Her spirits, this morning so buoyant, were plunging to the depths.

'What will you do there?' asked Marie.

Lori shrugged. 'Read, perhaps. I don't know.'

'Young girls!' snorted Marie. 'So moody. You go home, I've had more than enough days within those four walls. God, but the house is boring just now. Nothing going on.'

They parted, and Lori watched her stroll down the street, as elegant and fashionable as anyone in Paris, and yet stared at with curiosity by lots of passersby. They couldn't all know who she was. There must be some aura that hung about women like Marie, women like – women like herself. Suddenly, for all her fine clothes, Lori felt branded.

Chapter Eight

As Marie said, it was boring during the day. Lori sat at the window and watched the passersby, voyeurs mostly, and women from the other houses in the street. She knew most of them by sight, but fancied now that she could see something different about them. Their walk – or as Marie said, the way they looked at people? Perhaps once you had done such work there was no way you could keep it secret. That was why girls always went back to the streets.

It was weeks since she had visited Sophie. Lately she had just sent money. She sat gloomily in the window, thinking of the early days in Sophie's apartment. Imagine, foisting an orphan on a lover! She giggled. It was so like Sophie, optimistic, foolhardy Sophie.

Suddenly she felt a sense of urgency. Why was she sitting here, wallowing in money, pitying herself, when Sophie was lonely and miserable across town? She went to her room and fetched the things she had bought her, lace handkerchiefs and warm scarves, and ran to the kitchen to demand patisserie and carved ham. Money wasn't everything, after all, and there were things Sophie would never buy for herself. And there were some things she would. Lori added the obligatory bottles of wine.

Travelling across Paris, she noticed suddenly how shabby everything seemed. Some of the gloss seemed to have gone from Paris lately. It didn't show in the centre, nor even the Rue de Claret, but here, in the sprawling suburbs, the roads were broken and the drains full. Had it always been like this? High fashion was nowhere to be seen, and instead people hurried by in old coats and battered hats. Two girls were working on a corner, hands on hips, looking boldly around. Lori shrank back in the cab.

She walked the length of Sophie's street, passing little shops selling everything from bread to old clothes. 'You're doing well for yourself, chicken!' called out one shopkeeper. So even here she could not pass for an elegant lady of fashion. She increased her pace until she came to Sophie's door. At least here things had improved; the building seemed cleaner than she remembered, the stairs less sour. Lori knocked and at once a woman answered, neat and clean in an apron.

'Yes?'

'I – I was looking for Sophie.'

'Oh.' The woman drew back. 'She's gone. Moved out. Thrown out, I should say. And I don't know where she's gone, as I tell the men every night. Disgusting, I call it.' The woman paused in her tirade and scanned Lori reflectively. 'You're one too, aren't you? I can always tell. Get out of here. Get out of here, I say!'

She gave Lori a push. She nearly fell backwards down the narrow stairs, clinging to her basket with no free hand. The woman said, 'Serves you right. Nasty little tart dressed up in all your finery. I know where the money comes from. Disgusting!'

Lori turned and fled down the stairs. At the bottom she stood, heart pounding. People always changed when they knew what you were. The knowledge seemed to place them on a pinnacle of respectability, from which they could throw stones at whoever was beneath. She might be above those street corner girls, above Sophie, but as far as that stiff-faced, mean-mouthed woman was concerned, she was still in the gutter.

She closed her eyes, gathering herself, as she always did before she saw her clients. She needed to be strong and calm, to be in control. But her heart still pounded, tears still threatened. And where was Sophie?

She went to the baker's further down the street. A small man was working in the back, arms like pistons in the dough. The smell of yeast was almost overpowering, like the scent of the herb garden on a hot day at the farm, so strong it almost smothered your breath. The baker came out to her. He was a Jew.

She said, 'I was looking for Sophie. Perhaps you know her – blonde, she wears bright clothes. She works – she works around here.'

97

The baker looked at her quizzically. 'I know who you mean. Thrown out of her flat, wasn't she?'

Lori nodded. 'I brought her some things. I don't know where to find her – did she go away?'

'Only a street or two. She came in here, and I sent her to the Rue d'Orléans. Don't know if she took a room, though.'

'Thank you. Thank you very much.'

As she turned to go he said, 'Take some bread, why don't you? I can spare it.'

She had enough in her basket, but it would be churlish to refuse. She said, 'You're very kind. So many people aren't.'

'Don't tell me such things! I know, who better? Some nights when the boys come down here, they can't decide what to do first, throw stones at the girls or my windows. I said to Sophie, just be thankful you're not a Jew.'

Lori left and went off down the street. The old man's kindness had strengthened her. But when she found the Rue d'Orléans, she was at once taken aback. She'd sent Sophie money, there was no reason for her to come here! Tall, crumbling houses, dotted with unwholesome shops, their windows full of the corpses of last year's flies. Women were everywhere, in the windows, the doorways, clustered around lamp posts smoking and talking. Women with pockmarks, women with teeth missing, fat ones, thin ones, some reeling drunk. Many bore telltale knife scars across one cheek, the mark of the disgruntled pimp.

She went up to three tarts on a corner. 'I'm looking for Sophie,' she said hesitantly. 'Blonde. She wears bright things—'

One of the women said, 'Working girl, are you? What are you paying?'

'I just want to see if she's all right,' said Lori nervously.

'Fifty francs. You could afford ten times that by the look of you.'

'Twenty,' said another, rubbing grimy fingers on Lori's coat. 'Who takes care of you, little one?'

'I'll give you twenty francs,' said Lori.

'Christ, she's tight as a Jew! No go, sweetheart.'

'All right then! Fifty. I've got to know where she is.'

The women encircled Lori like witches, discussing her

openly. 'She's never the daughter, much too dark. Wonder who she works for. Does the posh trade, I expect, the ones who like a bit of young flesh from the president down. Make the most of it, love, you'll be here with us soon enough.'

She fumbled in her pocket for the money, not daring to bring her purse into the open. Standing so close she could smell them, a mixture of sweat and garlic and cheap perfume that turned her stomach. She brought out the notes and the women grabbed. 'It's mine! Damn your eyes, it's mine!'

'Tell me where she is,' said Lori desperately. She should have made them tell first, that was plain.

'Wouldn't you like to know?' leered one, but another said, 'Brown building, just down there. Top floor. Mind out for the rats.'

'And she doesn't mean human ones!'

She had escaped! She walked quickly away, her basket almost breaking her arm by now. Two young men sat at a window, smoking and drinking wine. They leaned out to yell at her: 'Hey, you! Lost your way, have you? Come on, let's warm you up.'

She hurried on, her eyes fixed on the building ahead.

The steps were piled high with stinking rubbish. What had Sophie done with the money she sent her? Drunk it, lost it, had it stolen? Knowing Sophie, anything was possible. She picked her way through ordure, watching the rats scurry. They didn't scare her too much; on the farm they had leaped out of the corn stacks sometimes, and run across her hands. The floor of the hall was swimming in water from a leak somewhere. She tiptoed across and up the stairs, hearing doors open as she passed. No one spoke. She kept on up the stairs, her gloved hand clutching the rickety handrail, wondering if she would be killed for her money. Anything was possible in a place like this. But she reached the top unscathed. At the very top a door was closed. Her knock went unanswered.

She turned the handle and it gave. 'Sophie?' she called. 'Sophie, it's me, Lori.'

No reply. The floor was covered in newspapers, the walls in peeling paint. There was a figure on the lumpy bed. When Lori went across she thought for a moment that Sophie was dead.

'Sophie? My God, Sophie!'

The figure stirred. It coughed, a racking, terrible sound. Lori touched the forehead beneath the yellow hair, dirty now, and streaked with grey. Sophie was burning, but her hands were ice cold. The eyes opened slowly.

'Lori. You shouldn't be here.'

'I was worried. I brought you some things.'

'All I need's a coffin.'

Lori's heart crashed against her ribs. 'But you're not dying! What's the matter with you? It's just the *grippe*.'

Sophie laughed and her lungs rattled. 'Got any wine?'

It was dark when Lori left. Sophie was asleep, her bed straightened, her chamber pot emptied, her rubbish piled up with the rest. She had eaten a little and drunk a lot, taking rattling breaths between pulls at her glass. Separated from the night only by a roof of cracked tiles, the room was icy. Perhaps Sophie would really die.

Lori picked her way down the steps and into the street. Light spilled from many windows, masking the dirt and hinting at warmth. Men were walking up and down, and cabs were stopping.

'Look at the pretty thing!' a familiar voice called. One of the three crones she had asked the way. 'Why don't you join us, love? Show us all how it's done!'

The women swaggered across the street towards her. Lori turned and fled, waving frantically at a cab. 'Taxi! Taxi!' A car drew up. She fell inside. She was safe. The women were gone.

She was working that night, but failed to give her best. The client was difficult, and at one point flung her roughly on the bed. 'I'm paying you to concentrate, damn it!'

'Don't you do that to me!' Lori had been bullied once too often that day. She tried to reach for the alarm which would instantly have the man removed, but he caught her arms and held her down, covering her with his body. He grinned and she spat in his face. 'God, but you're wonderful,' he said.

She went to see Madame next morning, to demand that he be struck off her list. 'He was unpleasant,' she said stiffly. 'And rough. He tried to avoid using the *préservatif*. I don't want him again.'

'We'll ban him for three months,' said Madame soothingly.

'I don't want him again, ever!'

Madame shrugged. 'In three months, who knows? You may be out of fashion. You may be glad of him.'

'Of a brute like that?'

'Certainly.'

Madame met Lori's eye with her usual uncompromising stare. Lori was the first to look away. She said, 'Madame – I went to see Sophie yesterday. She's in trouble.'

'Women like her always are. She drinks too much.'

'But she's ill, Madame! Coughing, can't breathe – in this terrible place.'

'To which you should not have gone. You could become ill yourself, and infect a customer. I can't afford it, not since that business with Zelma. We've got to be clean! You're not to go again, I forbid it.'

'But I have to go. Or Sophie must come here, and be cared for. Please, Madame. There's room, and I'd do everything, I promise!'

Madame looked at her thoughtfully. What would it cost to put Sophie in a nursing home for a bit? Times were hard and getting harder; she knew how lucky she was to have a star like Lori in the place. The girl wouldn't last, of course, none of them did. But if it kept Lori happy . . . She said, 'I'll see about a place. Not here. Somewhere she can be properly nursed.'

Lori bent her head. Gratitude welled up in her. 'Oh, thank you, Madame,' she said tearfully. 'I'll pay what it costs. You can take it from my money.'

Madame's rocklike face betrayed no hint of surprise. Well, if the girl was prepared to pay why had she come to her in the first place? She was a child still, that was obvious. What a good plan this was turning out to be. With Lori paying for a nursing home she'd have little left to set up on her own. That was always Madame's fear – that a good girl would suddenly depart. She could threaten them, of course, and send the heavies round to beat them up, but that wasn't her way. It was the reason she kept her girls as long as she did.

But Lori still stood, twisting her fingers together. 'Might Pierre come with me to fetch her, Madame? It's a rough area.'

Madame Bonacieux chuckled. God, the girl was naive! Madame herself had worked the docks at Marseilles for more years than she cared to remember. She had seen the women there tear a man into pieces and throw him off the quay. How long ago that seemed! And in the end she'd grown accustomed. There was nothing could frighten her now, certainly not a few raucous whores. She got ponderously to her feet.

'Tell Pierre to get the auto. I shall come too.'

Madame's car was long, black and elaborate. Lace curtains hung at the rear windows and small walnut tables with brass edging permitted her to rest her glass of Pernod during a journey. Lori felt ill at the thought of this vehicle in the Rue d'Orléans but Madame was unperturbed. This was a rare outing for her, and she dressed accordingly, in black fur and a high black hat trimmed with feathers.

Lori said anxiously, 'There may be vermin, Madame.'

And for once Madame smiled. 'A few fleas don't concern me, child. Besides, my furs are stored in camphor, which the creatures can't abide.'

Neither could Lori, unfortunately. In the confines of the car, the smell was suffocating.

Pierre drove badly. They made their way into the street in a series of jerks. At once the women started to gather, and someone threw a tomato which landed soggily against the window glass. Lori choked back a shriek and Madame said, 'Relax. What's a few tomatoes? For them, we're an amusement in a life of bitterness.'

If Madame was feeling sympathy, it was soon suppressed. When they drew up outside the crumbling brown house they were at once surrounded. Madame alighted from the car, gathering her furs about her, supporting herself on an elegant malacca cane.

A snotty boy threw a cabbage. It struck Madame's hat, knocking it askew, and suddenly she was after him. The cane came down with a crack across his shoulders, sending the kid sprawling in the mire.

Madame centred her hat on her head once again. 'Bloody kids,' she said, looking balefully round. 'Go up, Pierre, and fetch her. I shall stay with the car.'

She positioned herself by the bonnet, fixing the shuffling

crowds with her implacable gaze. Someone whispered her name; it was passed from mouth to mouth. 'Madame Bonacieux – the Rue de Claret – she's had more men than I've had hot dinners – it was one of her girls yesterday.'

One of the women, drunk, lurched up to her. 'Tell us, Madame, what's the secret of your success?'

Madame eyed her coldly. 'Keeping clear of women without the sense to avoid drink, opium and the clap. Which rules you out on all counts, you old hen.'

Laughter erupted as the woman pushed her way back through the crowd, muttering, 'Bitch. Bitch!'

A pimp sauntered up. He was dark and quite good-looking, wearing a lot of gold. 'We should do business,' he murmured. 'I can get you girls. Clean young virgins, just as you like.'

At that moment Lori came down the steps, neat and expensive in crocodile shoes and a fur-trimmed coat. Madame caught her by the arm.

'Look at her,' she said aggressively. 'Just look! When you can get girls like this, then you may speak to me. Whore she may be, but this girl's an artiste!'

'Does it swinging from a trapeze, does she?' enquired a laconic voice.

Pierre was carrying Sophie down the steps. 'Put her in, put her in,' rapped Madame. 'Cover the seat first.'

Lori rushed to do as she was told. Sophie was coughing and trying to talk, sprawling on the wide back seat with bare legs struggling like twigs from the blanket. Madame took her seat beside Pierre, leaving Lori with the patient. Looking at those legs, stained and bitten, she felt her throat close. Beautiful Sophie, come to this.

The people were crowding round the car, making departure impossible. 'Start,' said Madame. 'Drive on, drive over them. No one here's got much to live for.'

Pierre let in the clutch and the car jerked forward. They lurched back the way they had come, scattering people like sheep. Sophie burst into guttural coughing.

Sophie was admitted to a nursing home run by nuns. From the first they looked down their thin noses at her, obliged by their calling to despise her and care for her in equal measure. They moved like wraiths through the clean, white corridors, conveying with barely a sniff what they thought of this creature God had wished upon them. Lori burned with rage on Sophie's behalf. It was so easy to sneer! How would they have fared out on the streets?

But they were good nurses. Sophie had a bed in a long, scrubbed ward and when she was well enough would be able to sit and look out on the immaculate garden.

'She will get well, won't she?' asked Lori nervously of the sister in charge.

'We leave that up to God. Let's hope He can trouble Himself with her. Street women are all the same.' She reached into Sophie's ragged nightdress and pulled out a string of rosary beads. She snorted. 'No doubt this one thinks she's a good Catholic!'

Lori bit her lip. It was impossible to explain that Sophie, beneath everything, was good. The nun gave Lori an assessing stare.

'You're one of them, aren't you? I can always tell. Let this be a lesson, my girl. Expensive shoes or not, sooner or later you all come to this. Fornication is a sin!'

'I'd rather fornicate than starve,' said Madame from the doorway. 'And so would you if it came to it. Do yourself a favour and pray that it never does. I'm sure God will listen. He's bound to put you before a woman of the streets. That's right, isn't it?'

'God listens to all prayers,' said the nun stiffly.

'But he only answers the ones you can pay for,' retorted Madame. 'Come, Lori.'

On the way home she said, 'You're not to pay any attention to that vulture. Born rich, she was. They all were. Being nuns, of course, they play at poverty, but they don't go hungry. Even in the war, when people were starving, the nuns fed well.'

'Yes,' said Lori dully.

'As for you going on the slide – not if you're careful, you won't. Save your money. Don't let men run you. Keep clear of the drink. It's hard for a girl, I admit that, but while you're with me, you're safe.'

And so it seemed. Beyond the walls of the house in the Rue de Claret there was nothing but shame and danger. Only there was she loved and admired. Lori began to hate going out, even to visit Sophie. Especially to visit Sophie. Scrubbed and pallid in her hospital gown, bullied by the nuns, she seemed colourless and diminished. She wheezed as she spoke.

'When I get better they're going to put me in a home,' she said throatily. 'That's what they like to do, pen us all up together. They've got another think coming! Still some life in the old girl yet. I'll find someone. Someone like Gerard. Get married. What do you think of that?'

Tears closed Lori's throat. There was nothing for Sophie but the home, and nothing for her but night after night in the Rue de Claret. It was all planned, hopeless, inevitable. She felt a deepening despair.

Summer came, and the people of Paris were like torpid fish. They moved slowly around the streets, waiting for the chance to flash away to the sea and the country. One by one, Lori's bookings fizzled out. She had nothing to do but sit at an open window by day, and toss in the heat by night. The other girls urged her to walk with them in the park, or shop, but she always refused. Suddenly she couldn't bear to be stared at. The looks people gave her felt like knives digging into her flesh. There she goes, people were thinking. There goes the whore.

Madame summoned her to the study one evening. Lori was wearing a cream dress in soft cotton. A breeze from the window smelled of dust and tired leaves. She pushed her mane of hair back from her damp forehead.

'Yes, Madame?'

'A new client, Lori. I don't know him, but he comes recommended. In diamonds or some such. He wants tonight.'

'Oh.' Normally she wouldn't consider it. But business had been slack lately, and each week Madame took the money for Sophie's care. 'Have you seen him?'

Madame nodded. 'Big and blond. No problem there. Be ready for eight.'

Lori went to the room and made her preparations; sweet oils for massage, wine, ice, silk scarves to tie wrists and ankles to the bed. Some men loved that, others hated it, just as some found pleasure in pain. She opened the window to let the evening air drift where it would; and a memory came to her. The farm, and the sweet scent of honeysuckle carried on a warm east wind.

The client arrived promptly, and was shown to the room. Lori was wearing high heels, stockings and suspenders beneath a sheer robe. She had brushed her hair into a solid mane of black, long enough to sit on, long enough to hide her when she was naked. Tonight she touched her nipples with dark rouge, and thought ruefully of Henri. She had learned a lot since him.

The man said, 'I thought the old trout was rooking me, but I think she's done me proud. You look tremendous.'

His French was heavily accented. She couldn't place him. Perhaps he was Dutch or even Russian? She said, 'What shall I call you?'

'Nothing.'

That surprised her. She wasn't used to men who wouldn't even give her a name, albeit a false one. 'What sort of thing did you want?' she asked tentatively.

'You'll see.' He was throwing off his clothes.

Lori moved to the bathroom and pushed open the door, saying firmly, 'It's a house rule to wash your private parts and use the *préservatif*. Please. You must do that at once.'

'Must I?' He came towards her, his eyes very light, as if a candle was behind them.

Suddenly, inexplicably, Lori felt terror. She lunged for the alarm, but an iron hand snapped around her wrist. She opened her mouth to scream, but a handkerchief, one of her own silk handkerchiefs, was stuffed in her mouth. He flung her on her back on the bed.

His body came down on hers, already thrusting, searching. She was sure he had the clap. She writhed and pushed, clawing at his shoulders. He pulled back, hit her viciously across the face, and dragged her legs apart. She lay, half-stunned, while he violated her.

She thought he might go then. She lay quite still under him, assessing the situation. Her head was throbbing, and her jaw grated as if it was cracked. As soon as he went she would summon Madame and do what she could to stem the infection inside her. It was a minute, perhaps two, since he had finished. But the man lay on her still. She tried to spit out the gag to scream, but he put his thumb on it and forced it half down her throat. Her vision went red, she could hardly breathe, and suddenly he knelt up and rolled her over. Her hands were free, she could claw at the gag, but even as she sucked in lifegiving air he drove into her.

The pain made her lose her breath. She reared up against him and he grabbed at her breasts, viciously kneading her. The beginnings of a scream broke free, and he sank a hand into her hair, holding her arched towards him like a bow, ready to break her back. She was motionless, anguished. He was going to kill her, she knew. He bent her back and back, his breath like hot wind on her shoulders, his body a sword cutting her in two. But his climax came. He let her go, pushing her forward on to the bed, leaving a trail of blood as he withdrew from her.

He left her lying there. 'Now you know what a whore's for,' he said casually. 'Tonight you satisfied a real man.'

Lori couldn't work for two months. Madame was matter-of-fact. These things happened, it was the way. The girls, outwardly sympathetic, were nonetheless pleased. Lori's success had been their failure. It was good to see her brought low. Everybody but Sophie seemed to smile behind their hands. But then, ill and defeated as she was, Sophie understood.

At first Lori's fractured jaw meant that she could only drink through a straw, and eating was out of the question. She lost pounds in weight, and lay in bed, listless. Madame summoned doctors, who gave her pills to swallow, to ward off whatever germs the man might have carried. But there was one infection they couldn't prevent: Lori was pregnant.

She didn't know what to do. At first she thought she was imagining things, but soon she was ill in the mornings and her breasts oozed tiny drops of fluid. Suddenly she hated herself, hated the thing inside her, planted by an enemy. If this child was born to her, looking at her with its father's eyes, she would rather die.

She went to Madame and told her. The woman listened without a word. Then she nodded. 'It happens. You're not the first. I shall see to it.'

'I won't have it. I won't.'

'Naturally. As you wish.'

That afternoon, Lori was taken in the car to a doctor. That evening, half dead from haemorrhage, she was taken by ambulance to hospital.

Chapter Nine

A dark young girl sat in the last thin sun of the year. There was a book on her knee, but she didn't read it, and a glass at her side from which she never drank. After a long time, when the sun was sliding away behind the hills, she got up and went slowly into the inn. The day was over.

One of the farmhands, coming home from work, wondered about her, as he did every day. The girl wasn't pretty, not in the usual way that is, but she attracted him. She seemed so quiet, so self-contained, as if she was looking out at the world from behind glass. She'd been in trouble, most like. Girls like that often came here.

He went to the inn later that night, hoping to see her. She was sitting in the corner, doing some of the mending, her head bent to her work. He stared at her, and she looked up. Her eyes were like clouds, he thought, and smiled. She didn't smile back. Instead, she got up and left the room.

Alone in her bedroom, Lori paced up and down. Damn that farmboy. Damn all the men who drove her from the bar night after night. They all knew why she was here. It was why Sophie had come to the country, all those years before. She could see it now. She and Sophie were treading the same path, making the same miserable, inevitable descent. She too would end her days taking anyone who'd have her for anything they cared to give. You began high and sank to the depths, to end in destitution. So where was the point in going on?

She was sixteen years old. Educated, after a fashion. A prostitute. To go on with her life meant returning to Madame's, to the endless procession of men. But she couldn't bear to be alone with a stranger now. The mere thought of it made her gag, made the muscles in her belly contract with fear. She would disgrace herself and be thrown out.

Perhaps she could tell Madame she would only take men she knew, she thought desperately. But of course that was foolish. Men tired of a girl, they moved on. And she could not bear Madame's cure for a girl's fears, that of Pierre at the peephole. She would never submit to that. She had submitted to everything else, a voice seemed to whisper. Every little step is always a step down.

She went to the window and looked out. How far would she fall? Ten feet perhaps. Not enough. If she truly wanted to die she should do it in Paris, from a bridge; they fished bodies from the Seine every night. Boathooks in bloated, dead flesh. She thought of the moment before the jump, imagined the seconds, holding on, gripping tight with fingers that didn't want to die. People shouting, they were bound to see. You had to hurry if you meant it. The terrible, rushing passage through the air to plunge into icy water, the urge to swim, to breathe, overpowering all else. She knew how to swim a little. She might not drown after all.

The room was crowding in on her. She pulled on a jacket and ran downstairs, and the waiter stopped her in the hall and said, 'You should take care. The men have been talking about you. Best if you stay inside.'

'What have they been saying?'

He shrugged. As if she didn't know. Wherever she went, she couldn't get away!

She went back upstairs and lay on the bed. Gradually her restlessness drained away. Her thoughts meandered, moving towards sleep. Odd fantasies drifted through her mind; she saw the misty, half-forgotten face of her mother. She began to construct it more firmly, to fill in the gaps. The face wasn't one she remembered.

It would have been better if she had been disposed of, just as her own incubus had been swept away. Her mother had died because of her, and now look; her life was a sad, weary trudge down a path walked by many before her. Perhaps she could do as her mother did, she thought, and get a job on a farm. Or in a shop. Or a library. But she wouldn't earn enough, not enough certainly to keep Sophie. Who would keep Sophie if she was dead?

Her thoughts ran round and round. Some girls got out of this business. They married, usually, or like Madame, set up an establishment of their own. None of Lori's clients had shown any urge to marry her, they were mostly married already. That was the trick: to find a kind old man who liked the spice of corruption and sell it to him for a wedding ring. Then there could be children – although Lori wasn't now sure she would ever have children. The doctor at the hospital had said, 'We don't often discover what happens to you girls. But I doubt you'll be a mother, Mademoiselle.'

Had he expected tears? What were children to a girl like her? But then, suppose she did get married? Time enough to worry about children later. They weren't something to marry for. She imagined her life as a married woman, respectable, assured. She could see herself opening the door to guests, welcoming them as a woman should. Suppose one day she opened the door to a man who had been a client? Her fantasy shrivelled.

She must live outside Paris, then, perhaps outside France. She'd had very few foreign clients, except the last, and, coincidentally, the first. The English boy.

She thought of him with a wry smile. How foolish she had been; they had been foolish together, two children knowing nothing. His exciting adventure had turned into riproaring farce, sending him half-dressed and red as a beetroot out into the night. She chuckled. What a way to go.

Who would think that she could look on that Englishman almost with affection? He hadn't been unkind. And her mother had been English. She thought of what she knew of England; all that came to mind was the picture book she used to have, with the rabbits and hedgehogs wearing clothes. She giggled to herself. She supposed that even in England that wasn't likely. But a country that produced something so charming for the amusement of little children must surely be a kind and gentle place.

Vague plans began to form in her mind. If she travelled to England – could she get papers? – she might find work as a waitress perhaps, or in an hotel. She could put some money by and in time open a shop, a dress shop, full of pretty things. One day, when all this was long past and long forgotten, someone might want to marry her. A kind old man. All the knowing glances, all the whispers, would be left behind once and for all. She could start again. She could be free.

Madame said, 'But what about Sophie? She depends on you.'

'I've got savings. Enough for a few months. Then I'll send more.'

'There's only one way for a girl like you to earn. Mark my words, you'll be back at it. I thought at least you were a girl of sense!'

Clearly, Madame was upset. After all the trouble she had taken over Lori, to have the girl up and leave after a scant two years, two of the best years Madame had ever known. She had thought at least that Sophie would keep the girl here. But that was the trouble with this game, you could never depend on anyone! 'After all I've done for you,' she said in aggrieved tones. 'Years of support. Months of training. And the medical bills. God knows it's cost thousands!'

'I'm sorry, Madame. Truly.'

Madame opened her mouth to give vent to a tirade. At the last moment she remembered herself. It was bad business to make enemies. Not many girls left and never came back. This England thing was a young girl's adventure, no more than that. In the end, Lori would come home.

'I'll visit Sophie for you,' she said unctuously, knowing she would not.

'That's very kind, Madame. Her chest's still bad.'

'Is it?' Madame tried a cough or two herself, in search of sympathy. 'Write to me. Tell me where you are.' And suddenly, for once in her hard-bitten life unable to think of anything else to say, she burst out, 'In the name of the Virgin, take care of yourself, child!'

BOOK TWO

Chapter One

The fat little boat heaved and rocked on a lumpy grey sea. Laura
Perdoux sat hunched in a corner of the lounge, a handkerchief
pressed to her mouth. All around were figures in various states
of distress, and now and then a steward came by, handing out
paper bags. This was hell, thought Laura, feeling the boat slip
and slide down a wave and crash headlong into another. Why
hadn't she killed herself in Paris rather than die like this?

If she stayed there any longer she'd be sick again, and she had
nothing further to give. She got up, pushing hurriedly past the
groaning bodies to rush up the stairs and out on to the deck.
Thank God. Thank the merciful God. Fresh air.

Someone said, 'Don't stay there, Miss. You'll end up in the
briny. If you sit in the lee of the bridge, you should be safe.'

'*Merci* – I mean, thank you.' She slithered across the
streaming deck. There was a seat where he had pointed,
sheltered on the one side by the bridge and on the other by a
lifeboat. Two men were there already, muffled up in dark coats
and hats crammed down against the wind. She hesitated.
Strange men alarmed her. But just then a wave threw the little
boat sideways and she ran to the seat in a panic.

Both men stood up and touched their hats. The boat was
heeling wildly and they were showered in torrents of spray. At
any moment Laura expected to see the men slide off into the sea.
'Sit down! Please, sit down!' she wailed.

'Can I fetch you a rug?' asked one man.

'No! I mean – please, sit down. You're going to be drowned if
you don't.'

They both sat down once more. A tense silence developed,
and Laura began to wish she hadn't come. But it was better up
here. Her stomach no longer seemed the most important thing
in the world.

The relief made her talkative. She said, 'The cabin was dreadful. Everyone was so sick.'

'Always the way on these trips. Bad today, though. We'll be lucky to make Dover.'

'Do you mean – do you think we'll be shipwrecked?' Her eyes were like saucers beneath the bedraggled feathers of her unsuitable hat.

'No! Not at all – I'm so sorry, I didn't mean to alarm you. It's just that we might have to land at Folkestone. Better harbour, you see.'

'Oh.' She felt foolish. 'Is Folkestone far from London?'

'Not especially, no. Forgive my curiosity, but I thought you were British. Your accent—'

'Yes. But I've lived in France all my life. My papers are French.'

'Oh! Well, I'm sorry the old country's making things so difficult for you. No way to greet a lady, this.'

She felt a warm glow beginning in the emptiness of her stomach. They thought her English, and a lady. If only she wasn't wearing this terrible hat, from which the wind was stripping all but the stems of the feathers, she'd be content. Just then the boat ploughed into the trough of a wave, and the crest broke over them, drenching her to the skin. Without a word her two companions took an arm each and escorted her back inside. The deck was no place for a lady.

She landed at Folkestone more dead than alive. On the cramped and crowded boat there had been nowhere to dry her coat, and she was cold to the bone. On land the storm was no more than grey skies and heavy rain, turning the little town into a dismal and colourless place. She walked away from the quay towards the clusters of little houses, longing for food, rest and warmth.

'Excuse me.' She stopped a woman hurrying by with a basket full of shopping. 'Excuse me, is there anywhere I could stay? The ferry – they say I can't get to London until tomorrow.'

'Bad crossing, was it, love? You look green as grass. Mrs Tompkins'll put you up, first on the left. You'll see the sign.'

'Thank you.'

She trudged on, her feet squelching in their sodden shoes.

Perhaps it would have been better if she'd accepted when her two protectors offered to find her an hotel. But they might have thought – it might have been that they wanted something else. Nothing like that was going to happen to her now. She was different.

The sign in Mrs Tompkins' window read 'Vacancies. BB & EM'. Laura had no idea what it might mean, but rang the bell just the same. She was in no mood to quibble. A small, plump lady answered and beamed at her. 'My, my, you are in a state. I knew I'd get some orphans of the storm tonight. In you come, hot tea and toast for you, and don't say you couldn't touch a thing. It's the best cure I know for the greens.'

She was propelled indoors to a room where a little man in braces was sitting reading the paper in front of the fire. He was expelled at once to the kitchen with instructions to put the kettle on, while Laura was forcibly removed from her wet things. 'I'll find you a dressing gown, love, no need to unpack. Sent a wire, have you? They'll be worried sick at Dover.'

'I wasn't being met.'

'What? Young girl like you?' Mrs Tompkins tutted her disapproval.

The tea was strong enough to pickle an ox. Laura sipped and made a face, whereupon Mrs Tompkins ladled sugar into the murky depths, which Laura thought disgusting. Next came dinner, of overcooked beef and soggy vegetables, followed by suet pudding and custard. Not one mouthful did Laura enjoy. She looked in vain for her wineglass, used as she was to wine at every meal, but no sooner were the plates cleared than out came the tea again.

'You'll need a really good breakfast in the morning,' said Mrs Tompkins. 'I can see your appetite's still a bit down. Will you listen to that rain!'

Water was slashing against the windows and running gurgling down the street. In her room, looking out across black wet rooftops, Laura felt comforted and dismayed, both at the same time. The kindness of strangers seemed only to highlight her isolation in a place of rain and greyness and bad food. No wonder her mother lived in France, she thought, rubbing at the window with a finger. Now, at a distance, she remembered only sunshine. A policeman was standing beneath a streetlamp, rain streaming from his cape. After a moment he walked ponderously on.

She left in the morning and caught the train to London. Her stomach was churning again, this time under the strain of the breakfast Mrs Tompkins had cooked. The soaking of the day before had left its mark on her coat in a series of faint stains in the dark cloth. She had another in her bag, but that was lighter, a summer garment. Her hat, with its jaunty feathers, was wrecked. She pulled the feathers off and pinned a brooch in their place. It would do, for now.

The train seemed very slow. A fellow passenger, glancing at her, said, 'Going to London, are you? Should have caught the express.' She felt a fool, a foreigner in a foreign land. As the man left he tossed her his newspaper. 'Here. Help to pass the time.'

She scanned the columns with mild interest, which soon turned to fascination. Great things were afoot: the King of Jugoslavia had been assassinated in Marseilles. There was a picture of his widow, swathed in black. More poignantly, there was a photograph of his son, the boy King Peter, serious-faced, dressed up like a grown man, leaving Victoria Station – perhaps the very station at which she was about to alight. It was a year of change, the papers said. 1934 would long be remembered.

France was in furore, of course, and other nations were making portentous comments: Mussolini in Italy declared sorrow, admiration and respect; the Germans said the whole of Europe would be destabilized; the Spanish didn't say much, they were in the middle of a rebellion; while the British Home Secretary – why him she didn't know – said that Fascism and Communism were both things they could well do without in this country.

She lost interest and turned the pages. It was just the usual squabbling, seen from a different angle in the British press. The Germans had a new type of battleship which was visiting Britain, there were dozens of new cars at a motor show, and a jockey, Gordon Richards, won four races in one day. What's more, one of the Royal dukes was getting married, and the BBC was to broadcast the ceremony on radio. There were to be three wedding cakes. She put down the newspaper, and thought how wonderful it must be to be marrying a duke.

When at last the train puffed into London, she hurried with

118

the rest into the street. The rain had stopped, and people everywhere were furling umbrellas. A line of cabs was standing at the kerb and she walked up to one, but a man further down yelled, 'Here! Get to the back of the queue.' She couldn't understand why, there were more cabs than people waiting. 'It won't matter if I take this one,' she said, and the man snapped, 'Not to you, it won't. Bloody cheek.'

She got her cab eventually. The driver said, 'All right, Miss, I'm all yours. Where to?'

'Er—' She floundered for words. 'I don't really know. You see, I've come from France. I need somewhere to stay, just a room. And I need a job. In a shop or something. Perhaps a library.'

The cab driver snorted. 'You'll be lucky. No jobs anywhere right now. Didn't they tell you that in France?'

She shook her head. 'But I'm sure I'll find something. Once I've somewhere to stay.'

He took her to South Kensington. It was an area of heavy respectability, infested with nannies walking their infant charges to the park. 'Now you could try that,' said the cabbie. 'Domestic work. No one can get staff nowadays. You can live in, too.'

'You mean – be a maid?' She was shocked. As one of Madame's girls she employed maids, she didn't become one.

'Better than going hungry,' said the man. 'Look, I'll drop you here. Lots of these houses let rooms. If you change your mind about work, there's an agency in that place on the corner. Up two flights, you can't miss it. Best of luck.'

Laura tossed her head as he drove away. As if she'd be anybody's maid! With her dress sense – which she had never thought remarkable until now, amongst the drab Londoners – and her languages, and her manners, and her absolute determination to work harder than anyone had ever worked before, she was sure she'd be snapped up.

Three days later she climbed the two flights of stairs to the domestic agency.

'We do normally expect references – although in your case, I do understand the difficulty. The lack of experience, though . . .'

'I'm very good at hair,' said Laura desperately.

'Hair? I'm sorry, I don't understand.'

'Doing hair. If a lady wanted a maid—'

'A personal maid, do you mean? We only ever send our very best girls for those positions.'

Laura was humbled. Apparently she wasn't even good enough to be a maid. But the woman was rifling through the cards in her index. 'I do have one position that might be suitable – they are quite desperate. But I warn you, it's a very – well – raffish household.'

Laura blinked. She didn't know the word. But she said, 'If you think I could do it, though – I would like to get something at once. London's very expensive.'

'Indeed.'

The woman tapped a finger against her teeth for a moment, considering. Then she picked up a pen and wrote a note in a flourishing hand, blotting it, holding the paper and then sealing it with wax. 'Take this with you. And remember, if anything should occur which isn't to your taste, you can always return here and I'll try and find somewhere else. There's always kitchen work, of course.'

'Of course. Thank you. Good – goodbye.'

She took the note and hurried down the stairs and into the street. The urge to burst into hysterical giggles was almost overpowering. Was she being sent to a brothel? Was that what 'raffish' meant? She flagged down a cab and gave the address, watching carefully to see the reaction. There was none. What then was the fuss all about?

The house was in Grace Square, a part of London that in prosperous times might have been fashionable. Laura looked up at the blank faces of the houses, at the fenced-in greenery – or what passed for greenery – in the centre of the square. Her letter was addressed to Number 35 at the end of the terrace. It looked no different from any other house. She went to knock.

A maid opened the door. 'I've come about the job,' said Laura. 'The agency sent me.'

'Oh. Right. I'll tell Miss.'

Laura was ushered into a small, cold room. A few moments later a woman tripped down the hall on audible high heels and hurried in.

'Hello!' she said breathlessly. 'You're Laura, are you? I'm

Miss Monk, Gloria Monk. My sister Evelyn ought to be here too but she's gone racing. You look frightfully suitable, do you want the job?'

'Er – what do I have to do?'

'Well, the usual, you know. You have a room in the basement next to Jane and Susan, they bother with the house. The salary's what the agency recommends, they're absolute martinets. And you look after us. Clothes and so on. You've no idea what a bore it is having no one. We can't get a soul to stay a minute, heaven knows why. Do say you'll come.'

Laura looked assessingly at Gloria's clothes. They were silk and in a mess, the skirt creased and beads missing from the fringe. This at least was something she could do. And she hated her little rented room. She nodded.

It was soon very clear why Gloria and Evelyn Monk had trouble keeping staff. They paid the minimum, from which they deducted the cost of an expensive uniform – brown, which suited Laura not at all – before work had even begun. And they were the untidiest, messiest, most undisciplined and inconsiderate pair she had ever known.

They never hung up what they could drop, and they never dropped twice in the same place. They demanded food in their bedrooms, and put plates coated in jam on piles of clean underwear. They lit cigarettes and failed to put them out, so that twice Laura was forced to pour coffee on small fires. And they changed their clothes up to five times a day.

Jane and Susan were friendly, but mocking. 'You'll not last five minutes,' said Jane the cook. 'None of them do. And those girls are no better than they should be. The men we've seen here!'

'Lovers, you mean?' asked Laura.

'Well – not exactly. Trust you to think of that, it must be the French in you. Boyfriends, like. A different one every five minutes.'

'Why don't they get married?' Laura picked up her mending, an arduous task sewing on more of the disappearing beads.

'Can't get anyone to ask them,' said Susan. 'They try hard enough, though. Trouble is, men are as slippery as fish.'

'You're right there,' said Jane. 'Bloody eels, the lot of them.'

Laura became used to rising before dawn to help Evelyn get ready for riding in the park, and staying up until three to assist Gloria when she returned from a party or a club, and taking herself off discreetly when one of the elusive men did in fact pass an hour in the bedroom. But the girls were never grateful. 'Really, Laura, I thought I told you I wanted my ivory dress?'

'It was dirty, Miss, I had to wash it.'

'Don't wash anything without my express permission. Please. Try for a little common sense.'

But if anything was found unwashed the response was, 'Laura! Surely it isn't beyond everything to expect you to wash something now and then? I wanted to wear this today.'

'But, Miss, you said—'

'Laura, have a little common sense, please.'

She began using the afternoons to look for another job. At first she tried some small hotels, lacking the courage to approach any of the glamorous ones. None of them wanted anything more than a chambermaid, and paid less than she was getting now. It was very hard to manage, sending money for Sophie each month.

She thought of Sophie often. When she left, she had gone to the hospital and tried to explain, but in that starched white world, with Sophie no more than a stain of brassy curls on the pillow, the words died in her throat. All the same, Sophie understood.

'Don't you worry about me, sweet,' she said. 'Sophie'll be all right. Just you make something of yourself.'

'I won't forget you,' burst out Lori. 'I'll come back. And I'll send money, I promise – I'll write.'

Sophie's hand, so pale, so thin, had patted her. 'Don't expect me to write back. I'm no use at writing. You're a good girl. You always were. Don't you worry about me.'

But of course she worried. Sometimes she woke in the night, thinking that Sophie might have died. Although surely Madame would tell her if that happened. Or perhaps the nuns – she had made sure they had her address. It was more likely that Sophie was well on the way to recovery. If only that recovery wasn't quite so expensive!

At last, after weeks of silence, she wrote a letter to Madame:

'Do let me know when Sophie can leave hospital. She's been there so long and the bills are very large.'

Almost by return Madame wrote to say that Sophie was transferred into a home where she could live out her days in peace. It cost as much as the hospital, if not more, but at least Sophie was happy. She was still very weak, wrote Madame, and to add to her physical problems, the poor woman was becoming bewildered.

Laura was stabbed with guilt. Should she have stayed? If she had, what could she have done? Poor Sophie. Poor dear Sophie. How could she have begrudged a little cash? The least she could do was provide for her, as Sophie had provided when Laura had nothing at all. So each month she sent the money, always enclosing a little note to which Sophie never replied.

She had to have more money. Perhaps shops paid better. She went to the big department stores in Kensington High Street. She could see herself working on the perfume counter, or even selling dresses. They made her fill in long application forms and promised they would write. She was encouraged at first, but when she heard nothing after a week her spirits fell again. What would she do if this was the only job she could have?

Her plans seemed very foolish now. She had imagined a fresh start, moving steadily up the ladder towards prosperity and respect. But in England, everything seemed fixed and unchanging. Pleasure was enjoyed by people such as her employers, and they alone were entitled to it. Perhaps they alone could afford it. Scarce jobs meant low wages, there was no money for fun.

Maids had the worst of all worlds. Serving their wilful employers, they were isolated from life, meeting no one but the odd delivery boy. Jane and Susan looked forward only to weekends off, when they could go home. For Laura, there was nothing but the occasional free afternoon.

Sometimes she walked out of the square to watch people driving by in buses. Where were they all going? Somewhere exciting, surely. This part of London was drab and dull, but there must be light and gaiety somewhere. And if not that, then homes full of warmth, where they were happy. But the blank, strange faces gave nothing away. Wherever these people were going, she could not go with them. She felt her life dissolving into failure and emptiness.

123

One evening both Gloria and Evelyn were going to a private house for dinner, and then to a nightclub later on. Evelyn was being difficult. 'I told you I wanted the black dress, Laura. Why did you send it to be cleaned? I can't possibly go to dinner at the Baldwins' in silver grey!'

'Why not, Miss?'

'Laura! Don't be rude.' Evelyn glared ferociously and lit herself a cigarette. Lighted ash fell on a pair of silk stockings and shrivelled a hole. 'Now look what you've done!' shrieked Evelyn, taking the flesh of Laura's arm in her fingers and pinching viciously.

Tears of surprise and rage flooded Laura's eyes. She blinked hard and Evelyn said, 'Don't you dare snivel. You deserved it. If I must wear the silver grey you can come to the Baldwins' later and bring my headdress. I can't possibly wear it to the stuffy dinner but I'm damned if I'll go to the Zambesi without it.'

'I could put it in a bag,' said Laura helpfully.

'And look like a char? Really, you're too much.'

She got up and went through to her sister's room to regale her with the exchange, not bothering to lower her voice. Laura heard her say, 'I honestly don't know why we bother educating the masses. They're genetically incapable of logical thought. Can you imagine the picture I'd make, staggering into the Baldwins' hall with a great suitcase in my hand? They'd think I'd come for the weekend!' Both girls shrieked with laughter.

Laura felt a surge of hatred. Her arm throbbed where Evelyn had pinched her. What's more, she would have to spend much of her evening standing around outside some house or other, clutching the headdress, waiting until Evelyn's half-witted escort decided to take her dancing.

She went through to Gloria's room and said, 'If I take your headdress to the Zambesi, Miss Evelyn, I can leave it with the cloakroom girl.'

'But suppose we don't go to the Zambesi?'

Gloria said, 'Come off it, Evelyn. We're bound to, it's the only place just now. And Laura's been very good lately. She's worked very, very hard. Yes, Laura, take the headdress to the Zambesi at around nine. That's when it opens. Do my hair now, will you, there's a good girl?'

Despite herself, Laura warmed to Gloria, although she knew

she was being manipulated. The mantle of tormentor moved from one sister to the other with the regularity of a metronome and Laura was by turns victim and ally. Was this honestly better than the Rue de Claret? she asked herself. She was beginning to wonder.

When at last they were gone, Laura went to her room and changed. It was a cold evening, with a blustery wind sending clouds scudding across the darkening sky. She put on her dark coat, still slightly stained, and a new hat. It was the one thing she had bought since arriving in England, a small, close-fitting design in dark red with a brim that turned up at one side. She liked the curve it made against her cheek. To disguise the worst marks on her coat she swung a patterned scarf across her shoulders, fastening it with a shiny clip. She slipped the headdress, which was no more than a loop of dangling beads, into her bag.

Jane and Susan were admiring. 'My, don't you look fancy? I'll say this for you, Laura, you've had an effect on them girls. Since you came they've been looking a lot better than usual. Style! That's what you've got.'

Laura grinned. 'They couldn't have looked much worse. But I wish they wouldn't wear so many beads.'

'It's the fashion, lovey,' said Jane, adopting an attitude. 'You know our ladies, if it's fashion we must obey!'

'Oh, so we must!' agreed Susan, waving her arms in a parody of Evelyn. They all collapsed in giggles.

Laura pulled herself together. 'Do you know which bus I have to take?'

'Number nine,' said Susan, pulling off her nasty uniform cap. 'And just you watch who you talk to! You're new to London, but a girl's got to watch herself. You could be murdered. Worse!'

'Worse?' Laura looked blank, but Susan merely folded her lips and nodded meaningfully.

To Laura's disappointment, nothing happened. No one spoke to her but the conductor, who said, 'Leicester Square? Half an hour, love, I'll give you the nod.'

She sat holding tight to the rail in front of her, the bus caught up in the traffic like a fly in honey. As they edged through the streets lights came on in the houses, and people drew curtains against the night. But nearer town, the night was just beginning. Taxis carried women in furs and diamonds to the theatre or the ballet; men in evening dress saw friends across the street and lifted elegant canes in salute; a blind beggar saw a policeman coming and shuffled off down the road. Laura laughed delightedly. Life, at last. She felt a pang, sharp as a splinter, for the life of Paris.

Alighting in Leicester Square, she stood at first bewildered in the crowd. To think that as she sat at home every evening, listening to the clock, people here thronged and bustled and argued. To think that young and pretty as she was, younger and prettier by far than the Monk sisters, she had nothing and they had all this.

Gradually she began to make sense of the throng; people late for the theatre, early for the ballet; men fresh from dinner at their clubs, or on their way to them; East Enders, going to the music hall or the cinema, already a little drunk; and all around, on the corners, in the alleys, girls. Laura could spot them instantly. One had a poodle, like some of the better class street walkers in Paris, but most simply stood and waited. Now and then a man would catch a girl's eye, and she would lead him away into a sidestreet to haggle. Laura looked instinctively for the police. There they were, two uniformed bobbies, just watching.

She felt suddenly as guilty and furtive as if she too were 'on the game'. That misleading, almost cheerful expression the English had. She gave herself a slight shake. That wasn't any part of her now. She was simply a lady's maid on an errand. Taking her courage in both hands she approached the two policemen.

'Excuse me. I'm looking for the Zambesi Club.'

They looked down at her from beneath their improbable helmets. 'Not the sort of place I'd expect a young lady to be going on a Saturday night,' said one, disapprovingly.

'I'm not! I mean – it's an errand. My employer's going on there from a dinner later tonight and she wants to wear a special headdress. I'm to leave it for her.'

'One of them flappers, is she?' The other bobby, younger, looked intrigued.

'Never you mind what she is,' said his partner. 'Now, young

126

lady, the Zambesi's first on the left down there. You hand over
your parcel and get straight off home. None of this smoking and
drinking girls get up to nowadays. Mark my words, if you want
to keep the bloom on those pretty cheeks, get yourself off for an
early night.'

She nodded. 'Yes, sir. Thank you. I will.'

They must think her no more than a schoolgirl. She hurried
off down the street, slightly ruffled. She had imagined herself as
an effortless part of the sophisticated night, not an obvious
misfit. She caught sight of her reflection in a darkened shop
window. Perhaps the shoes were the problem – she must wear
higher heels. And she must reject any hint of the servant that
might infect her. It was all too easy to adopt the manner.

The word 'Zambesi' was inscribed in a huge illuminated swirl
ahead of her. As she drew nearer she saw that pillars either side
of the door were painted to look like trees, each with a snake
dangling from the branches. Inside the doorway a monkey sat
on a perch, wearing a fez, chattering angrily at a group of people
trying to get in. 'Honestly, Andrew, I thought you were a
member?'

'I am, darling. They're just being cretinous. Look here, I
know the manager.'

Laura hovered, unable to attract the doorman's attention.
The monkey began to bounce up and down, straining at its
leash, shrieking. Suddenly the leash parted and in a flash the
monkey was free, off the perch and fleeing. A woman screamed,
the doorman cursed and the monkey, staring desperately at a sea
of legs, flung itself at Laura's ankles. It clung there, shuddering
and whimpering. She reached down and gathered it like a baby
to her breast.

A man in evening dress burst from the club, saw the monkey
and said, 'For God's sake! Be careful, will you! It's known to
bite.'

'Of course it bites,' said Laura calmly. 'You shouldn't treat it
so. The noise and the lights disturb it.'

'Well, that's what you have to put up with when you're
famous. Half London knows Jacko.'

Laura said, 'I think he's got a cold. How can you keep him on
that perch in the open? He's half frozen, poor thing.'

'We give him a coat when it rains.'

She looked up at the man before her. Tall, blond, with blue, almost lidless eyes set deep into his head. He was wearing the Zambesi tie, a silk bow entwined with snakes. As Laura looked at him, an ironic stare from beneath the brim of her hat, he drew in his breath. She felt a slight disorientation. Did he know her?

'Won't you bring Jacko inside?' he suggested diffidently.

The would-be party-goers set up a chorus of complaint. 'I say, if you have to catch the bloody monkey to get in, then give it here!'

'Leave him alone,' said Laura firmly. Jacko was clinging to her and mewing, as if begging to be saved.

'Let them in, John,' said the blond man. 'I'll be responsible.'

'Well, about time too!' declared the bogus member, ungratefully.

The famous Zambesi club was a huge room with tables surrounding a stage and dance floor. A stuffed baby elephant loomed against walls covered with mirrors and painted greenery, and the jazz band wore feathers in their hair. As yet there were few customers, but a singer was crooning mournfully.

'You'd better come into the office,' said Laura's escort, leading the way through a screen of bamboo.

He took her into a quiet, bare room with a cocktail cabinet, a desk and a safe. The man said, 'Do sit down. Can I offer you a drink or a cigarette? Turkish or Virginia?'

'No, thank you. The policeman down the road said it would spoil my bloom.'

'And why were you talking to a policeman?' He was lighting a cigarette himself.

'To ask the way, of course.'

The monkey, reviving in warmth and peace, removed his head from the crook of her arm and looked around. 'Here, Jacko,' said the man, and offered some apple from a bowl. The monkey took it and gobbled, climbing down from Laura's lap to take up station by the bowl.

'If you must keep him here then at least let him be warm,' said Laura.

The man looked at her through wreathing tobacco smoke. 'Actually, I think his days here are numbered. His temper's getting foul. I'll take him home with me when next I go.'

'Do you live in the country? He oughtn't to be cooped up in

town. He oughtn't to be here at all, in the cold.'

'You keep talking about cold. Are you cold?'

'Of course not. It's warm in here. But the monkey—'

'Why don't you take off your coat?'

He came towards her and made as if to unfasten her scarf.

'What are you doing?' She pushed him away and got up.

'What on earth's the matter?' He extinguished his cigarette half-smoked. 'At least take off your hat,' he said.

'No, thank you.'

'Well, I think you should.'

He made a lunge and grabbed it, wrenching it from her head. Her hair fell about her shoulders in a dark, flowing mass and the man said, 'I knew it! It is you. Just as I remember.'

Laura ran a tongue across dry lips. 'Please return my hat,' she said slowly. 'I don't know you at all.'

'I don't expect you to. I was one amongst millions.'

'Millions of what? Who are you? Are you mad?' She reached for her hat but he held it away from her, smiling oddly. Laura was suddenly afraid.

'I was cheated,' he said softly. 'Cheated and made a fool of. How you must all have laughed.'

'I'm not laughing now.'

'So you admit it, do you? How can you not, you look French as hell. Sound it too, a bit. Down on your luck though. A coat in that state would never do for the Rue de Claret. And let me tell you, sweetheart, you were a lousy whore!'

Laura laughed. She couldn't help herself. Suddenly the memory of this boy came back in all its vivid detail, her first client, the very first, who had made her ill. Madame had personally supervised his eviction, minus shoes, clothes and money. The shoes and clothes had followed him through the door. Not the money, of course.

She stopped laughing and looked into his furious face. 'Are you still so cross about it?' she asked simply.

He blinked. 'Well – yes. Why shouldn't I be?'

She assumed the air of worldly wisdom with which she used to overcome difficult customers. 'You realise it was all your own fault? You asked for a young girl, but you didn't know what to do. You were so inexperienced! So English. Any of the other girls would have suited you better, and taught you a very great

129

deal, but you were arrogant. And you still are.'

He went a deep red. 'I'm damned if I'll have a prostitute tell me what I am or I'm not!'

Laura went to him and snatched back her hat. 'And I'm damned if you'll call me names! I don't do that work any more. I came to England for a fresh start. To be finished with men like you, who know nothing but think they know it all. Let me tell you, I don't envy the girl you marry. You're no good in bed or out of it.'

He lunged and grabbed her by the upper arms. 'Don't you dare say that to me!'

'Why not?' She was angry and past caring. 'I bet you still use a girl like a mattress.' She pulled herself free and began to put on her hat. 'The monkey says so much about you. Such selfishness. You can't see what anyone else needs.'

She straightened her hat in the mirror over the safe. She could see his face behind her, a mixture of rage and puzzlement. Finally he said, 'But no one goes to a prostitute to give the girl a good time!'

Laura lifted a contemptuous shoulder. 'No one of your sort, certainly. For you, it's all so brutal and basic. Just a little, trivial pleasure.' She turned and met his bewildered eye. 'What a pity men like you never know what they're missing.'

The door opened. An older man came in, looking annoyed. 'Gabriel! The club's full of gatecrashers, why are you hiding in here?' He took belated note of Laura's presence. 'Excuse me, Madam. Are you a friend of Gabriel's?'

'Not in the least,' said Laura. 'I was troubled by your monkey. The creature's becoming vicious from cold and bad treatment. You're lucky I wasn't savaged. Please ensure that someone of a responsible and civilised nature has control of the animal and treats it as a living creature and not – not as a toy!'

She swept out, leaving both men open-mouthed.

Only on the bus home did she remember that the headdress remained in her bag.

Chapter Two

Laura lay sleepless in bed. The house was quiet at last. The Misses Monk had returned home for once united in fury against their maid, who it seemed had exposed them to total humiliation. They had first accused the cloakroom girl of stealing the headdress, and then the manager of colluding in the theft. They had finally been convinced of the non-appearance of the vital piece only to discover that Evelyn's escort was so disgusted by her behaviour that he wanted to take her home that very instant. He was, as Laura knew, a favoured bedroom companion, but that night: 'He wouldn't even let me have a dance!' as Evelyn hysterically described it.

They were equally united in Laura's dismissal. 'Without a reference!' as Gloria declared dramatically.

Jane and Susan crept from their beds to comfort her. 'They'll take it back in the morning. Just say sorry and offer to have a day's wages stopped.'

Laura shook her head. 'I don't want to stay. I'll go back to the agency and ask for something else.'

Susan snorted. 'Without a reference? You'll be lucky. Swallow your pride and have done with it.'

Laura knew she should. When you were a servant there was no room for anything that prejudiced employment. You were at the beck and call of others, and if that meant pretending humility, apology, simulating regret – she turned over and placed her hot cheek against the equally hot pillow. Everyone was always telling her to be ashamed of herself. She was never going to be ashamed of herself again!

At breakfast, when she would provide neither explanation nor apology for her aberrant behaviour, she was given a week's notice. 'Just don't go telling everyone how beastly we've been to you,' said Evelyn. 'I know what you girls are like. Never a good word to say about anyone. We were so pleased with you, Laura! I can't understand why you should turn on us like this, I really can't.' She sniffled into a handkerchief and Laura found herself on the verge of blurting out an apology, an explanation, anything. They wouldn't believe her, though, whatever she said. They wouldn't understand.

In a free hour later that day she went to the agency, but it was as Susan had said. Without a reference, with only a garbled tale of what had happened, she hadn't a hope. 'I'm sorry,' said the woman, very stiff and unyielding. 'Our staff have privileged access to wealthy homes. Any taint – any suspicion—'

'I assure you I didn't steal anything!' said Laura fervently.

'Indeed. I'm sorry.' She pointedly closed her appointments ledger.

Dejected and tired by her late night, she went again to the big department stores. At one they looked up her application and said, 'Oh yes, Miss Perdoux. In fact we wrote inviting you for interview. You never replied.'

'You – wrote?'

'Yes. I'm sorry, we can't give you a second chance. Good day.'

She reeled into the street, seeing again Gloria's morning routine of sorting the post. They had taken her letter. With all their experience of staff they must be adept at foiling ploys to escape. Apologise? To them? She would rather die.

She trudged wearily back to Grace Square. The afternoon was warmer than of late; the air smelled of spring. Even the beaten-down evergreens in the central iron compound seemed fresher and less grimy. She thought of the man at the club the night before and smiled to herself. He had been so terribly annoyed!

Someone swung easily over the shrubbery railings, long coat flying. Laura choked back a cry. It was him. The man. She pulled herself together. 'What are you doing in there?' she asked.

His hat had fallen off and he picked it up, dusting it with his hand. 'Waiting for you.'

'But you don't – you couldn't—'

'We had a hell of a night after you left. These two women came screaming in like something out of Homer. Harpies or

132

something. You know, I expected at any moment to have my eyes pecked out. I'm surprised they didn't peck yours, actually.'

'You can see why no one wants to marry them,' said Laura. He made a face. 'Someone will. For the money.'

'It's amazing what you'll do for money.'

The hat turned in his hands. He had matured rather well, she thought, developing from a boy too tall and too thin into a well-muscled man. But his face was hard and somewhat expressionless, a series of flat planes connected by unyielding bone. She knew the type. If he turned up now in the Rue de Claret the girls would say to each other, 'Watch this one. He's trouble.'

She moved away towards the house, saying, 'I'm sorry but you can't come in. We're not allowed visitors.'

'I thought perhaps I might take you out to tea?'

She raised an eyebrow. 'Are you in the habit of buying maids tea?'

'No. But you're not in the habit of being a maid. We both know that.'

She snapped, 'My life's changed. You don't understand.'

'I'd still like to talk.'

What had she to lose but a week's meagre wage? She was late already and would only go in to more recriminations. All her plans seemed to have failed and she had lost her faith in planning. She would let life take her for a while, a leaf on the stream.

He walked very quickly and she found it hard to keep up, but then he was very tall. Her head barely reached his chin. She caught his arm and said, 'Will you slow down, please? I almost have to run.'

He said nothing, but slowed his pace. When they reached a teashop and found a table he took off his coat and sat down. He said, 'Nothing I do pleases you, does it? Not even the way I walk.'

Laura blinked. 'But you don't want to please me. That's obvious.'

He said, 'That's where you're wrong.'

The waitress came and he ordered for them both. Laura said, 'I wonder if I could be a waitress? Everyone wants references though.'

'You'd be a worse waitress than you are a maid.'

'I'm a very good maid. It's my employers.'

'What? They don't suit you either? Dear me.'

'You said just now they were harpies.'

'Yes. So I did.'

He sat back and looked at her. He said, 'You're better than I remember. Prettier. And you don't look so scared.'

She laughed. 'This time you're only buying me tea.'

'So I am. I've thought since – you really hadn't done it before, had you?'

She shook her head. 'We won't talk about it. I'm sorry I was so rude last night, it wasn't fair. Two beginners together—'

'We should try it again some time.'

She met his hard blue stare. A surge of anger began, sending twin flags of colour into her cheeks. Just then the tea arrived, and she sat staring at him, quite silent, while the waitress arranged plates and cups and pots. When she was gone Laura hissed, 'How dare you say that to me? Don't you know that's finished? Done with? I will not – *will* not – be treated like that. No more! Ever!'

He said mildly, 'No need to excite yourself. It was just a thought.'

'I won't go back to it. Not even if I starve.'

'Better eat your cakes then, and put off starvation.'

Saying nothing, he let her rage subside. In its wake she felt foolish, almost tearful. It wasn't as if he knew that she'd given all that up. She was being unreasonable. This was the only person to show any real interest in her since she arrived in the country and she was being difficult and French. 'I'm sorry,' she said at last. 'It's been a bad day.'

'Losing your job and all that.'

She nodded. 'They won't give me a reference and I can't get another place. I'm frightened I'll be forced – but I won't, you see.'

He said, 'Actually, I could offer you something. And before you bite my head off, it isn't that sort of job. Not if you don't want it to be.'

She gave him a very French look. He was as he appeared, hard and tricky. Well, she had learned her lessons in a hard school and wasn't about to be deceived. She said, 'Tell me.'

'It's in the club – the Zambesi. I'm the manager. The owner's Peter Kennedy, you saw him last night, bit of a soak but otherwise all right. Anyway, I've persuaded him we need a hostess. Someone to look glamorous and lead people to their tables. And talk to men on their own. We get quite a few of those, older men, never made a go of things after the war. We need someone intelligent, with a bit of sophistication about them, of course—'

'Last night someone took me for a schoolgirl,' said Laura bluntly. 'Now you're telling me I have sophistication and glamour. It all sounds a little—'

'Paradoxical?' He grinned. He had a gap in his teeth, just at the edge of his smile. 'You are an odd combination, you know. Like a Sybil, very young and very old, innocent as the day and at the same time steeped in every wickedness.'

'You must do a lot of Greek in British schools,' said Laura prosaically. 'Does it always give young men wild ideas about women?'

'I've always had wild ideas about them. Come on, take this job. We'll supply a room at the club and some evening dresses. All you have to do is glide around being charming and interesting. That's all.'

She poured them both another cup of tea. Her heart was beating a little too quickly. Was this really an offer or merely a sly attempt at seduction? He would certainly try and seduce her, but that was nothing. If this job gave her a breathing space in which to gather her wits then she was in no position to refuse. She thought of Madame Bonacieux and what she would say to such a proposition. If Laura had learned anything from her it was to set out one's terms without flinching. 'I will of course require good quality clothes,' she said demurely. 'There's never any point in skimping, it always shows.'

A slow, wide grin spread across his face.

Gabriel Cooper had been manager of the Zambesi for a scant three months. The entire life of the club had only been three months longer, but the owner had soon found that everything palled after a while. He preferred to relax in the evening, he realised, and hired the first personable intelligent chap he could to do all the work. Sadly, Gabriel was no more inclined to engage in boring routine than his master, so first a doorman had appeared, and then a floor manager, and now Laura.

They gave her a room above the club. It was dingy and full of junk furniture, but compared to the box room at the Monks' it was a palace. How she longed for somewhere of her own. She wanted cleanliness and beauty, to wake up in the morning and look upon her own special things. She began to move broken chairs and piles of old music, enlisting the help of Carol, a girl from the kitchen, who seemed to have little to do.

'Couldn't run a knees up in a brewery, this lot,' she confided to Laura. 'Kitchens are filthy. Chef's always sloshed so the food's terrible. Owner's never sober either if you ask me, and as for the Archangel Gabriel – he never turns up until eight, so what can you expect? Last night half the band went missing. He had to rush round to one of the theatres and bribe the pit orchestra to come here in the interval.'

'How did they manage for the rest of the performance?' asked Laura in fascination.

Carol giggled. 'It were one of them Russian things. Not a lot of music second half, and they left them the pianist.'

Because she didn't yet have her dresses, Laura was spared work the first night. But she came down anyway, in a plain black frock enlivened by a massive silver brooch on one shoulder, and wandered around watching what went on. Few people arrived before eight, but those that did often wanted to eat. As Carol said, though, the food was indifferent and service slow. Drinks, too, took forever to reach a table. Nonetheless the band was good, presumably in full force tonight, and as more and more people arrived the atmosphere grew electric. Couples dipped and swayed on a dance floor that was soon so crowded that no one could do more than shuffle. The lights grew dimmer, and soon the Zambesi trademark of a low, insistent drumming pervaded every tune. Despite standards that would never have been tolerated in the Rue de Claret, it was a wonderful club.

Towards two, Gabriel Cooper intercepted her on one of her slow circuits of the room. 'What on earth are you doing?' he asked blearily. 'You should be tucked up warm and cosy in your chaste little bed.'

'It's as noisy up there as it is down here,' said Laura. 'Besides, I'm learning.'

He shrugged. 'Nothing to learn. Food, drink, music, and take the money.'

She eyed him thoughtfully. 'Let's talk in the morning.'

'Morning? I don't start my day 'til lunch.'

'Let's say eleven. Here, in the club. Really, we must talk.'

She didn't get to bed until four, when the last few revellers had been thrust into the street still dancing to the remembered beat of the drums. The sudden quiet seemed to press against her temples like soothing pads. To endure such noise, all night, every night – it was better than the Rue de Claret, she told herself. It was one of those things you got used to.

At eleven the next morning she was up, dressed and downstairs in the wreckage of the club. Two cleaners moved desultorily amongst the tables, emptying ashtrays into a bin. Broken glass crunched underfoot, and in the corner a man was dismantling a cracked mirror. The monkey, Jacko, she found curled up miserably in a corner of the manager's office. She went to the kitchen and made him a meal of left-over fruits, of which there were a surprising number. The monkey sat up and ate, chattering to her between mouthfuls.

She sat with him, eyeing the shambles all around. Madame would have tolerated none of this. Wasted food, half-finished bottles, overflowing bins. The staff moved hopelessly, as if the magnitude of the task before them was too much for them even to begin. Laura felt Madame's disapproval as if it were her own, imagined her wrath at the waste and the disorder. This was what happened when you ceased to check deliveries, she thought to herself. Or perhaps they had never begun.

Gabriel appeared at half-past twelve. Laura was annoyed, and showed it. 'We had an appointment,' she said coldly.

'We had an arrangement. Your servant days are still with us, I see. You really will have to learn to loosen up.' He flicked open the office cigarette box, lit and inhaled luxuriantly.

Irritating her could well become his hobby, she thought. He mustn't know how easy it was. She sat down in Gabriel's own chair and trailed a casual hand across the desk. 'Does this place make any money?'

'What? Yes, pots.'

'I don't believe you.'

He was silent for a moment. Then he said, 'Well, obviously

there are start-up costs, one-offs, that sort of thing—'

'What you mean is, for a successful club it's doing terribly badly.'

'Do you have to be quite so dull?'

She leaned forward and met his eyes. 'You're not taking this seriously, are you? It's just a game, a way of passing the time. I've heard what London's like. A new club every month, none of them last. But this one could! If you tried. If you cleaned up, and got good waiters, and stopped people bringing in their own drink. Did you know the bar staff put the price of every third order into a separate box? They split it amongst themselves every night. And the kitchen's full of rotting food and no one feeds the monkey. It's a mess.'

Gabriel said nothing until he had smoked his cigarette. He extinguished it carefully, studying the pattern it made in the ash tray as if it might help. 'You'll do all right out of it for a while, at least,' he remarked. 'I've ordered the dresses, you'll have those. And you'll get tips. When the whole thing goes down you'll be floating amidst the wreckage.'

She rapped a hand on the table. 'It need not go down! Oh, Gabriel, are you really so lazy?'

'Do you really think I want to spend my life chasing waiters and cleaning women?'

'That's your job. It's what you're paid for.'

He laughed in her face. 'What a very bourgeois thing to say! Oh, bully them yourself if it bothers you. Tell them – tell them it's on orders from me.'

The interview left her light-headed. Did he really not care? It seemed so. He could watch dirt and mismanagement and downright thieving taking place under his nose and see no necessity for action. Well, she was differently made. All those years with Madame Bonacieux had taught her how an establishment should be run, with vigilance, and pride. This was like a party in a riverboat, making merry when you knew that round the next bend was a thousand-foot fall.

She had said she could put it all right. Well, now she must. But it was easier to see what should be done than to do it. Madame's gimlet eye was a weapon in itself, but she didn't have that power. How was she to change things? She had never ordered more than a cup of café au lait.

138

She checked her appearance in the mirror. She was wearing a pink sweater, and looked young and girlish. Perhaps if she wore black – and earrings. When she had changed she looked no older, only a sombre version of herself. But she had authority. Gabriel had given it to her. If they refused to do as she said, he must simply back her up.

She returned downstairs, and stood for a moment watching a woman push a mop ineffectually across the tiled entrance floor, leaving a tidemark of scum. Only the thought of Madame's roar of protest stiffened her. She clapped her hands. The woman stopped her mopping and five or six others emerged from behind potted palms and plaster trees. They really were the most slatternly crew. They must have been hired while Gabriel was blind drunk.

'I am Miss Perdoux,' she began. 'The club hostess. Mr Cooper has asked me to supervise a really good clean, so we'll have the tables piled up over there, please. One of you can wash them. The others can clean the carpet.'

'*Wash* the tables, Miss?'

She drew herself up with what she hoped was Madame's hauteur. 'Certainly. They're unpleasant. As for the cloak-rooms, they must be scrubbed with bleach. Oh, and someone can get a ladder and shake the cobwebs off the snakes and greenery.'

Uncomprehending faces looked back at her. For a moment her resolve wavered. But they must at least know how to clean! And if they didn't . . . well, she had watched it often enough. What was a little scrubbing? Somewhat doubtfully she said, 'Shall we go and find buckets? Perhaps I can show you what I mean.'

They followed her like lambs. But in the kitchen revulsion overcame her once again. 'This is so horrible!' she burst out, and one of the women said, 'Ain't it just? About time someone took it in hand. Kill someone, they will.'

Laura smiled thankfully. 'I'm glad you agree. We can come in here after we've seen to the tables. Are there buckets, do you know?'

'Got some big saucepans,' offered someone. So they fetched down the giant cauldrons that the chef never used and filled them with suds.

There was something very satisfying about cleaning, Laura discovered. She and her little band worked side by side, until she was sure that they were capable of reaching her standard. Then she turned to polishing the mirrors and the bar, removing weeks of grime. It was an almost sensual pleasure to see everything sparkle. She sat back on her heels and saw a bundle of paper nestling beneath the bar. When she investigated it turned out to be five-pound notes.

She was aghast at such profligacy. The bar staff were so blasé they didn't even bother to collect all their loot. She took the money into the office and found Gabriel asleep, so she extracted the keys to the safe from his pocket and deposited her find. She felt zealous and full of energy. She revelled in being in charge!

Later that afternoon her dresses arrived. She went up to her room to try them on, but found she couldn't see properly in the dim little mirror. She went downstairs and stood on the clean carpet, looking at her reflection on each of the four walls. Her favourite frock was in grey silk, which was barely grey at all. It matched her colourless eyes. The fabric clung and shimmered, and the dress was cut away at the back to reveal her spine. Bows were at the point of each shoulder and at her waist. She turned and turned again, but from each and every angle the dress was superb.

Gabriel was watching. She said, 'You have a good eye, Mr Cooper. The blue you ordered's too big, though. I'll get it altered.'

'What a lot of things you alter, Miss Perdoux.'

She flushed and stole another look at herself in the glass. A high colour suited her. Did she dare to use make-up? In the brothel she had of course, but here? Yes. Why not. In the evening.

She moved to go back upstairs. Gabriel was in the way. As she passed him he rolled against her, sliding her into the passage and pinning her against the wall. He whispered, 'I don't think you're grateful enough, you know.'

Laura looked up at him. She had expected this, but not so soon. She said, 'Oh, I'm grateful enough. You haven't seen half what I can do, though. Just you wait.'

His hand moved softly up to her rib cage. Her heart thudded uncomfortably against the pressure and she was angry at showing nerves. A man like this wasn't difficult.

He murmured, 'Why don't I come up to your room and stop waiting? There's a lot about me that you might like to discover.'

She leaned back a little to look into his eyes. 'If only I could,' she said lightly. 'But we open in an hour. And discoveries take so much longer than that.' She put her fingers to her lips, kissed them, and patted his cheek. Then she slipped out from under the weight of his body and ran quickly upstairs. Really! The man had all the sophistication of an ape.

She wore the grey dress that night, and red lipstick. Her eyes were ringed in black and in the gloom of the club she looked matchless, her dress of some shimmering steel. She felt in need of armour. The bar staff were mutinous, and she made no attempt to placate them. If they wished they could leave, she told them, but from this night on there would be no more thieving. There was no source of extra cash but tips for good service, so they'd better start serving well. 'And if you see a customer drinking from his own bottle, please tell me,' she added. 'I'll have a word. Bringing your own drink into the Zambesi is forbidden.'

The early hours of the evening were always quiet. The waiters stood about in groups and plotted against her. Laura took up station inside the door, with the monkey on its perch just beside her. When each new customer entered and stopped to talk to the monkey, she gathered them up and led them to a seat. Good seats by the dance floor for the young, the beautiful and the rich, the hinterland for the rest. Parties of men, or men on their own, were seated by the bar, and from time to time Laura drifted across and engaged them in conversation.

'Can I get you another drink, sir? My name's Laura. I'm the hostess. Have you been to the Zambesi before?'

They always responded. They might order champagne and pour her a glass, or try to impress by ordering a cocktail they couldn't really afford. She felt again the sense of power that had buoyed her up in the Rue de Claret. She knew all there was to know about men. Dressed like this, she was irresistible. She could make them do anything she liked.

Around midnight one of the waiters came and said to her, 'Man at the edge of the dance floor. He's got a hip flask. Watch.'

A short, chubby little man was topping up his glass at minute intervals. Laura wondered how he had come to be in a good seat at all, but she hadn't seated everybody. Gabriel had presumably taken it into his head to indulge this unprepossessing soul. She went quickly across to him, placed a hand on his shoulder and murmured, 'I'm so sorry, sir. You're not allowed to bring your own alcohol into the club. It's a house rule.'

Before her eyes the man turned a deep, turkey red. 'What's that? Since when? Are you telling me, Miss, how to behave in my own brother's damned club?'

Laura drew in her breath. A trap, into which she had neatly fallen. Oh well, she must brazen it out. 'I didn't realise you were Mr Kennedy's brother, sir. I'm sure he'd make an exception in your case, but – well, we are trying to encourage people to use the bar. I wonder if you'd be kind enough to be discreet?' She gave him her most winsome smile.

He said, 'I still say it's a bloody cheek.'

Trained to spot the least change in a man's demeanour, Laura saw that he was close to being mollified. Seizing her chance, she allowed herself a flirtatious giggle. 'Yes, isn't it, sir? I wouldn't have said anything if I'd known who you were.'

'Wouldn't you? Pretty girl like you could say anything to anyone, I'd have thought. Would you care to dance?'

It was going to be all right. Her mouth was dry with the dregs of panic. But to her relief, and the waiter's chagrin, she was soon in close embrace with the elder Kennedy. He was saying, 'How did my brother ever get the idea of hiring you, then? Not too bright as a rule, our Peter, and never good with the girls.'

'Mr Cooper hired me,' replied Laura, uncomfortably aware that her partner was stroking her bottom. He was pressing into her with obvious intent. Her thoughts raced ahead.

'Sleep here, do you? Got your own place?'

'No,' she lied at once. 'I went to school with Mr Cooper's sister. We have a flat near here – in the house of some friends whose daughter came out ahead of us. It's a super place. So central.'

It was the sort of thing the Monk girls said. But it was as if a switch had been thrown. She wasn't 'that sort' after all. She wasn't 'one of those'. The crushing embrace was no more. Space appeared between them and the man said in avuncular tones, 'Smashing to see the way you girls get out and about nowadays, don't you know? Your mother not object to this place, then?'

'She knows Mr Cooper will take care of me,' said Laura demurely.

Within three months, Laura was queen and in heaven. The staff greeted her with respectful murmurs of 'Good evening, Miss Perdoux.' Out on the floor men called, 'Laura my angel, come and amuse us and drink our champagne.'

The kitchen was clean, although the food remained variable, depending on the sobriety of the chef; and profits had soared. Even Jacko the monkey was better tempered and better dressed, in green and gold fez and jacket, the colours of the club. And while she worked and worried and lost sleep, doing it all for a few evening dresses, occasional tips and a meagre wage, Gabriel Cooper did nothing.

It annoyed her, and he knew it. In fact, far from helping he seemed determined to disrupt the smooth running of the club. When they were full and stretched to the limit he had a habit of ordering cocktails, supervising their creation amidst a great press of waiters and impatient guests. Flying to and from the kitchen, talking to regulars as if she had all the time in the world, from the corner of her eye Laura would see him sprawled at the bar, speaking only to hinder things, like a child putting a stick in the spokes of a wheel.

It seemed she had underestimated him. He could be devious. There was no question of approaching him about it, so she began a silent battle. She trained waiters as cocktail barmen, promoted kitchen staff to wait at table, encouraged cloakroom girls to emerge from their fastness to sit with the customers and talk. The moment Gabriel entered the club she swung reinforcements into the fray. So he started to bring friends in, a dozen at a time, all free.

The strain began to tell. She rarely slept before dawn, falling exhausted into bed, only to rise mid-morning, when the clatter of the street outside prevented further rest. The moment she appeared downstairs she was in demand, in the kitchen, in the cellar, discovering almost too late that Gabriel had given the band a night off. Hanging desperately on the telephone, pleading with the operator to try a number just once more, she knew that she hated Gabriel. And he clearly hated her.

143

She didn't know why he had changed. After all, she'd made it plain from the start that she'd refuse him. But he'd thought to persuade her, using his charm and evident good looks. He was attractive to women, no doubt of that, she watched him in the evening, girls hanging on the curve of his lazy smile. And she was quite unimpressed. Gabriel wanted women not for themselves but for his own, masculine pride. She felt almost contemptuous of him, not realising that it showed. Say what he might, cajole as he might, she was never going to fall for his charm.

One Saturday in June, when the club was filled to capacity and solid with heat, he brought twenty friends. As they filed past her, already drunk, already noisy, disrupting the smooth rhythm of a successful evening, Gabriel called out, 'My friends would like to try my cocktail, Harry. Get on with it, man, don't hang about.'

It was too much. The band was playing 'The Sheikh of Araby', in long, sliding cadences. A girl on the dance floor was attracting all eyes in a wonderful tango. Laura, her cheeks hot with colour, moved towards Gabriel. She was wearing a white dress, halter-necked, the least favourite of all that he had bought. How could he do this to her?

'Take these people away,' she said in a low, throbbing voice. 'Get out of here and take them with you.'

'Goodness me, Miss Perdoux!' Gabriel pretended to reel back in amazement. 'Didn't anyone tell you I'm the manager of this club?'

'You do nothing! All you want is to hinder me, trouble me, make my life hell!'

His cocktail arrived on a tray. Laura hit at it, sending the drink showering over them both. Gabriel ran his fingers across his cheek and then licked them. 'A little too much brandy, I think, Harry.' There was a burst of laughter.

There was no defeating him. She had been stupid to try. She turned to go, but he caught her arm. 'Don't look so upset, Laura,' said Gabriel loudly. 'You must have seen worse than this in the Rue de Claret.' She froze, waiting for the words that would ruin her. His face came towards her. 'Finishing school, wasn't it? My, my, what things you girls learn. Come along, my dear, you must change your dress.'

She looked down at her stained skirt. She had made a scene and ruined her dress for nothing. Everyone was staring. Why did Gabriel torture her so? He walked her to the bamboo curtain and pushed her through.

Once out of sight of the club, Laura pulled away and put her face to the wall. She hammered gently with her fist. 'Why do you do this? Why?'

He stood behind her, his thighs against her own. 'You deserve it.' He put his arms around her from behind, cupping each of her breasts. She was shaking and incoherent, but the touch of his hands seemed to calm her. The noise of the club seemed a long way away, and there was nothing but their own harsh breathing. He began to kiss her shoulders, pulling her hair aside. She was damp with sweat. He licked her neck, lasciviously, and she groaned.

The bamboo curtain rattled. At once Gabriel pushed her ahead of him to the stairs. Her dress caught on a nail, and he ripped it, and somehow the noise sobered her. Madame always said that desire was the ruin of a girl. 'When you're eager, they use you. When a man knows you want him, he loses all respect. Then he loses interest. Then he starts selling you to his friends. Desirable men are all the same.'

She fell through the door of her bedroom and turned to face him. 'I won't do it. I won't let you.'

He turned away from her. He went and sat on the bed. After a moment Laura went and sat next to him. She took his hand. 'Why are you still so angry with me?'

He looked at her out of clear blue eyes. 'You are the author of my worst ever humiliation. Did you know that? Of course you did. I thought I'd forgotten, but no one forgets things like that. Not if they live to be a hundred. I got you a job, I helped you – it isn't so much to ask, is it? I want to obliterate the past. To show you how different I can be. And you've had hundreds of men, what's one more?'

'I don't owe you anything,' said Laura tightly. 'I work hard. I'm not obliged to you.'

He let out his breath angrily. 'Selfish little bitch, aren't you? What do you care about the damned club? Kennedy's rich as hell, this is a plaything for him. And everyone's laughing at you. All those lies. You were this, you were that, you went to the best, oh, the very best schools – no one believes you, Laura. They know you were the Monk sisters' maid.'

She blushed a dark red. 'Do they? I didn't realise.'

She sat round-shouldered on the bed. He thought how rare it was for him to see her anything but composed. He said, 'I'm sorry. That was cruel.'

'I suppose you think I deserve it.' She glanced at him. She hadn't expected an apology. She said, 'I must seem very silly to you. Trying to change my life. Rubbing at a stain that won't come out. But I do so want to be different.'

He sensed a softening, and trailed a finger up her arm. He slid his hand under her hair and touched her neck. She had liked it before. He whispered, 'You're perfect as you are. As you were. If there's any kindness in you, let's pretend we're back in the Rue de Claret and do everything again.'

The room seemed stiflingly close. The music seemed to beat up through the floor like pulsing arrows. Madame didn't know everything, and besides, to give in was to defeat him. He didn't know the risk he ran.

But she was done with all that. Once she started again she would never stop. First Gabriel, then the men downstairs, then anyone. You began by being choosy and ended taking the cash. Before he could move she flung off the bed and went to the cupboard, taking out her blue dress. She had worn it the night before, but what matter? Each night was different.

Gabriel was watching her from the bed. He said, 'God, but you're a bitch. It wouldn't matter a damn.'

'It would to me.' She slipped casually out of the white dress and stood naked but for stockings and wide-legged French drawers.

He said angrily, 'To be brutally honest, you don't even have much of a figure.'

Her eyes flicked towards him. 'You don't like the merchandise? How fortunate it's not for sale.'

'Once! That's all I'm asking for!'

She slipped her arms into the dress and stood with her back to him, waiting for him to fasten it. Instead he put his hands inside and cupped her naked breasts. 'Please. Please,' he whispered.

She caught her breath. Then, calmly, she said, 'Fasten my dress, please. If you want a woman you can go to the square and pay. Or try someone downstairs. I'm told one or two society girls do it for nothing.'

His mouth was against her spine. 'All I'm asking for is a little kindness in return for a very big favour.'

'Gabriel, the answer's no.'

His face in the mirror was utterly grim. She knew she was afraid of him. He was an enemy it was unwise to make. But he fastened her buttons, suddenly brisk. She walked away, to her dressing table, to put on some lipstick.

She said, 'Does everyone know I was a maid?'

He said, 'Actually, no. And those that do don't believe it. They think the Monk sisters are finally going crazy.'

Laura said, 'Oh,' and took a deep breath. She relaxed visibly. 'That's all right then.'

He appeared in her mirror. He looked hot and unhappy; she felt a sudden weakening. But he would never know. They were always wary of young, virile men at the Rue de Claret. They expected so much.

He took two strands of dark hair and held them up on her head. 'Everyone thinks you're my mistress,' he remarked.

She spun round to face him. 'They don't! They couldn't! I've done nothing, I've always been respectable!'

He laughed at her. 'But look at you! What else could you be? So much perfume that even your hair smells good. You walk across the floor as if your knees are tied together. You pluck your eyebrows to look as if you've had the most terrible shock, then put on the paint like a mask. And you wear nothing under your dress. The motion of your unfettered bosom has the men of London drooling.'

She put the lid back on her lipstick with a snap. 'You're simply trying to upset me.'

'I'm telling you the truth. You work in a club, what did you expect?'

'You said I looked innocent! It was what you said, I remember – you didn't mean it. You took me on because I look what I am! You lied, you always lie. Oh God, I'm so tired of this. Why does everyone always know?'

She began to plaster cold cream on to her face, wiping off the lipstick, the powder, even the eyebrows. Gabriel, stunned by the effect of words spoken only for revenge, said slowly, 'They don't know. That wasn't what I meant at all.'

She paused, in the very act of ripping off her dress to put on a corset, a basque, anything. 'Then what do you mean?'

Some of the fog of drink was clearing from his brain. He'd been stupid, was in danger of losing the club's best asset. Since Laura arrived the takings had doubled, and no one minded the manager dipping his hand into the till. If he played this wrong she'd leave.

He said, 'People talk. They wonder about us. It's just—'

'I'm on the outside,' Laura finished bitterly. 'And always will be.'

'Don't know why that worries you,' said Gabriel. 'I'm on the inside and I've spent years trying to get out.'

There was a knock on the door. Laura froze. With Gabriel here, everyone's suspicions would be confirmed. She hardly cared any more. She called out, 'Yes?'

One of the waiters came in. 'Excuse me, Miss Perdoux. The monkey's gone mad.'

Chapter Three

Laura sat amidst empty tables. It was very late, or very early, depending on your point of view. Milk carts were clattering by in the street outside. She glanced at her watch – it was almost six. It seemed hardly worth going to bed.

The door opened and Gabriel came in. He shrugged. 'They want him put down. Talking about rabies, of all things. You were right, I should have taken him out of the club. What do you bet someone will sue?'

'I wonder what Mr Kennedy will say.'

'Don't suppose he'll mind. He was bored with the place.'

'You don't mean he'll want to close? We were making money!'

'He's got buckets of that anyway.'

He went to the bar and fetched a bottle of champagne, pouring each of them a glass. 'Cheers. Here's to today.'

She pushed her glass away, but he caught her hand. 'To uncertainty.'

She lifted her glass and said, 'To everything always going on.'

It was hard to be as casual as Gabriel. His dark mood of the evening before had vanished like mist. The club had been getting him down, she thought miserably. He had struck out at her simply as a diversion. In the light of day he didn't want her, at least no more than any other girl. But she had been nagging him, talking about duty and responsibility, irritating him as much as he did her. She looked into his young face, wondering if she looked as fresh and unscarred. She doubted it.

But the champagne revived her. When the cleaners arrived she at once set them to work to remove the blood from the carpet. It wasn't easy. She resolved to put a table over the stain.

The police arrived just after nine. Laura knew them, they toured the club quite often, checking on membership and the arcane drinking laws. But officialdom always made her nervous. She took them to the office, knocked and opened the door. Gabriel was slumped at the desk. The empty champagne bottle was beside him.

'Oh dear,' said the policeman heavily.

'Mr Cooper's very – tired,' said Laura in a flat voice. 'No one had any sleep last night. Perhaps I can give you the owner's address? Mr Kennedy—'

'If you would, Miss. And I suggest you give up any thoughts of opening for some time to come.'

She put her hands together, struggling to remain composed. This was her livelihood. If this failed, she didn't know what she would do.

'It was only a monkey! Nobody was killed!'

'So far, Miss. But rabies is suspected. And between you and me, magistrates don't like clubs that keep going too long. You've had a good run, after all.'

She saw them to the door, automatically polite. Then she went back into the office and sat on the desk next to Gabriel's sleeping head. He yawned and sat up. 'They've closed us down,' she said dismally.

He stretched, extending his arms above his head. 'About time too,' he said. 'Nothing worse than a nightclub you can't leave, if you ask me. Don't look so worried, Laura! You can get a job anywhere.'

She looked at him sardonically. 'What will you do?'

'Go back home and continue annoying my family.' He leaned back in his chair, clear-eyed, refreshed. He had an amazingly resilient constitution.

Everyone had a family except her. Everyone had someone to go back to when things went wrong. She felt very lonely suddenly. All she had was Sophie, dear Sophie, in her expensive institution, costing more than Laura could afford. She felt tears behind her eyes. She mustn't think of Sophie until things were going well. Depression loomed, a great black slug, waiting to devour her. If she wasn't so tired, perhaps – but she knew she couldn't sleep. She yawned, but knew she was beyond rest. Besides, there was no time for sleep. No casual optimism for her, no leisurely consideration of what she might do next. She had to look for a job.

Mindful of Gabriel's comments the night before, she dressed carefully, striving for an English respectability. Clearly it was time to stop plucking her eyebrows; she must let them grow naturally, a style which she privately considered very sloppy and little girl. Her hair – she put it up at the sides, a style which she had often thought distinctly juvenile. If it was English, so it must be, she decided, abandoning rouge for powder and discreet lipstick. She looked like a schoolteacher, she decided dismally.

Gabriel saw her as she came downstairs. 'My God. You look as exciting as wet flannel.'

'I look respectable.'

'What on earth for? Respectable people are crashing bores.'

'You know nothing about it,' she retorted. 'The only person you ever met who wasn't respectable is me! And I need a good job.' She made for the door, but he came after her and got in her way.

'If you want a job in a nightclub, you won't get it looking like that. Boring Miss Perdoux won't do anything for the temperature. Not like enigmatic Laura, so charming, so mysterious, who might or might not be the most wicked girl you ever met.'

She eyed him dispassionately. 'You English make so much fuss about sex.'

But she went back upstairs just the same. She took down her hair and put on more make-up, pencilling in her brows in a soft, almost natural line. To her surprise, when she went downstairs Gabriel was waiting for her. He said, 'At least now you look like a pretty vicar's wife. Come on, I'll take you to the Palm Tree. I know the bloke there.'

'You don't have to bother. Really.'

He glanced at her, looking very young, as he often did when he let his better nature show. 'He wouldn't see you without an introduction. Besides, I'll feel better when you're settled.'

She was touched. It wasn't like Gabriel to be unselfish. He hailed a taxi, and she was transported in memory back to the days of Henri. How pleasant it had been to have someone take care of her.

The Palm Tree was on the fringes of Soho. It was smaller than the Zambesi, its door manned by a one-armed war veteran who had once worked for the Taggart-Joneses, a good family quietly sliding off its perch. A younger son, Timothy, was in amateurish charge of the club.

'How's things in the jungle?' he enquired exuberantly, despite the early hour shaking cocktails and pouring them into smudged glasses.

'Closed down,' said Gabriel. 'That's why Laura's here. Need a hostess, do you? She's brilliant. Runs the place singlehanded. The customers love her.'

'Yes.' Taggart-Jones cast her a nervous glance. 'I'm sure they do.'

They went to a table under a ragged paper palm, and sipped their drinks. Laura felt her depression advancing once again. The place was shabby and dull, with none of the glamour of the Zambesi. It seemed a very ordinary sort of club. She imagined herself in evening dress, trying to add some sparkle, and felt heavily despondent. There must be other clubs, she thought. If the job was offered she would refuse.

Gabriel was nudging again at the reason for their visit. 'How about it, Tim? She'd do wonders for the place, you've no idea.'

'I'm sure you're right.' Taggart-Jones looked uncomfortable. In a low voice he said, 'Quite frankly, Gabriel, I daren't. The people who come here know my parents. They'd find out in a week.'

'Find out what?' asked Laura in icy tones. 'What's so terrible about employing me? What do you think I am?'

Colour flooded the young man's face. He stammered, 'I didn't mean – obviously in this sort of place—'

Laura rose to her feet. 'This sort of place?' she repeated bitterly. 'This unpleasant sort of place. I wouldn't work here under any circumstances. It's run by a man with a very dirty mind.'

Gabriel put his hand on her arm, trying to soothe her. 'It's a misunderstanding, nothing more. He just assumed you were something different.'

'A prostitute,' said Laura furiously. 'He thinks I have sex with the customers for the price of a drink! Does he think I'll go upstairs with him, in return for this disgusting cocktail?'

Taggart-Jones was almost gibbering with embarrassment. 'You stupid man,' she said forcefully. Stalking to the door, she passed the war veteran, who gave her a very old-fashioned look. She wished she could spit on him. Behind her she could hear Gabriel apologising. How dare he?

He caught up with her at the end of the road. Her look should have turned him to stone. 'It wasn't my fault,' he said innocently.

She spun on her heel to face him. 'You didn't have to take me there! You knew what he thought.' She rubbed at her eyebrows, pushed at her hair. 'You dressed me up to help him make up his mind!'

'Now you're being silly. You look fine.'

'I look like a prostitute! I must do. Everyone must know!' She was crying tears of anger and shame. Gabriel put his arm around her shoulders, let her sniff and snivel into his jacket. He found her his handkerchief and she blew her nose.

'You're being very kind to me,' she murmured. 'I'm sorry to be such a fool.'

'That's all right.' He waited a moment. Then he said, 'Why don't we go somewhere? Somewhere quiet?'

She stepped away from him, almost reeling. How could he? After everything? She backed away into the traffic and a taxi hooted. She turned and ran helter-skelter away. Gabriel called, 'Laura! Laura!' But she was waving at a taxi and it stopped. He ran across the road, narrowly missed by a bus, but he was too late. He saw her face in the window staring back at him as she drove away and he felt suddenly helpless and bewildered. Why not, for God's sake? Whatever she wanted others to believe, he knew she was that sort of girl.

The summer's day faded into a warm summer night. Laura thought how strange it was to see the Zambesi in darkness. As she walked to the door a bird fluttered up from the extinguished sign, already broken, with two of the bulbs smashed. Who had done that?

The door was locked. She knocked but there was no answer, and she wondered if the place was quite deserted. What would she do if she couldn't get in? But after a while someone came. It was Gabriel.

He stood aside to let her pass. He looked a little bleary, as if he had been asleep. 'Any luck?' he asked.

Laura sighed. Sooner or later he would have to know. She shook her head, threw down her gloves and went into the kitchen. Without a word she cooked them both an omelette aux fines herbes. Equally silent, Gabriel opened some wine. They ate sitting either side of a table in the totally deserted club.

When she was finished Laura sat back and sipped her wine. She was the oddest girl, he thought, furious this morning and now this.

He lit a cigarette. 'What are you going to do? Go back to France?'

'There's nothing in France. I'd be all right here, but I've no references, you see. If there was some family to recommend me – perhaps I could learn to use a typewriter?'

'You don't really want to do that, do you?'

She shrugged. 'If I must.'

He watched her through wreathing smoke. He had never seen her look so tired and dispirited. He felt an unaccustomed gentleness towards her. 'Kennedy's closing this place up,' he said abruptly. 'You'll have to move out.'

She nodded. 'I'll find a room somewhere. Should I move out of London, do you think? Would it be easier?'

'I don't know. Perhaps.'

He thought how little she complained. Laura seemed to accept all that life threw at her as no more than she expected. Almost as if it were her due. Her brief flashes of rage subsided into dull resignation. He was conscious of wanting to apologise. For something. He said, 'I'm sorry about the monkey. You warned me. It was my fault.'

She sighed. 'Poor Jacko. He doesn't deserve to die.'

'They might send him to a zoo.'

'Do you think so? He might not fit in. You know how he likes cocktails.'

They laughed, as people do when everything seems lost. He reached out and took her hand, and they sat peacefully and in accord. The quarrel of this morning seemed a very long time ago.

He said, 'I've an idea.'

Laura withdrew her hand. 'Not that again, Gab.'

'No, no! You can come home with me. To my family in

154

Yorkshire. Then, when you go for a job, you can forget about here altogether. Say you came from France to stay with the Coopers and now find you need a job. My mother can write the reference. I'll make sure she does.'

She felt a surge of relief, and slight dizziness. Tired as she was, the wine was going to her head. The British lived in boxes, she thought, boxes with tight lids. She had prised at the lids until her fingernails snapped, only to have Gabriel lift his just enough to let her scurry through. He wouldn't have done it if she'd slept with him, she thought wryly. Everything would be on quite a different footing. Now, awkwardly, she would be in his debt.

'Of course, if you don't want to come—' said Gabriel.

'I do! Oh, I do. But what will you tell your mother?'

He thought. 'You're the sister of a friend of mine at school. Half-sister, perhaps. Brought up in France. You were staying with him in London, but he's had to leave town and asked me if I could take you home.'

'Why can't I stay with my parents?'

'You're an orphan,' said Gabriel grandly. 'Both parents killed when the *R101* crashed.'

'Why were they on that?' asked Laura, giggling. 'Was my father an airship designer?'

'I don't know. It could be your mother. The French touch.'

'My mother was English. Really.'

'And your father?'

A shrug. She blinked at him sleepily, the club's cold air unpleasant against her face. There was nothing to stay for. They would go to Yorkshire in the morning.

The train puffed slowly into the station. It was the express and wasn't scheduled to stop, so people leaned from the windows trying to see what was going on. The platform was thronged with people, thronged with men. They wore long coats and flat caps, and all along the edge of the platform were pieces of painted wood on which were written 'Ban the Means Test' and 'Yorkshire Needs Work'.

Laura got up and went to the window, but Gabriel said, 'Don't get too close. They might throw things.'

'Why? We're not to blame. Oh, Gabriel, they look so poor!'

Another passenger flicked open his newspaper. 'Damned ruffians, if you ask me. They've got more than you know, young lady, it's all a sham.'

She went again to the window. In the flickering lights of the station the faces were gaunt and thin. As the train moved slowly on, pair after pair of eyes met hers and passed by. She had never seen such dumb misery. Such shame.

She said, 'Ought we to give them something?'

Gabriel shook his head. 'They don't want charity, they want work. They're miners or steelmen, I suppose. Poor devils.'

The train slid away up the line, gathering speed as the last carriages broke free of the iron stares of desperate men. Laura sat down again, deeply unsettled. She said, 'People are in trouble everywhere, but so many! Is there nothing they can do?'

'Perhaps they'll move away,' said Gabriel.

'To London? There's no work there.'

'No. Birmingham, perhaps. To the car factories.'

She nodded. To think of those men standing dumbly before train after train seemed to touch some well of pain deep inside her. She knew how it felt to have no way out. She could bear it better for herself than for others.

They drew into Leeds just before ten. Gabriel said he had sent a telegram but there was no car to meet them. 'We'll get a room at an hotel and take a taxi in the morning,' he said airily.

Laura stood her ground in the station forecourt. 'Why not tonight? We don't need to go to an hotel.'

'They won't be expecting us.'

'You said you'd sent a telegram! You didn't, of course. Gabriel! Gabriel, how could you? You've brought me all this way, for nothing!'

She was gasping for breath, as she did sometimes when panic overtook her. What did Gabriel mean by it? Was it all just one of his tricks? What would she do now, in a place she didn't know?

'Look,' he said soothingly, alarmed by her manner. 'No need to get hysterical over nothing. I will send a wire.'

'Your mother might not want me. She might not let me in the house.'

'My dear girl, she'll be so pleased to see me she wouldn't care if I'd brought a camel to stay. Let's just go to an hotel. Separate rooms, I promise.'

She shook her head. 'I couldn't sleep. Couldn't we go now, Gabriel, please? And get it over with?'

He sighed heavily. It was nearly thirty miles, they wouldn't be there before midnight. He had imagined a quiet meal in a small hotel he knew, connecting rooms, a whisky nightcap; warmth and relaxation, nothing sleazy or rushed. He'd played it wrong up to now, been too pushy. But now she was properly in his debt. She had to give in! Yet somehow here he was, being persuaded to take her home. She looked so small and anxious, he thought angrily. Just like that night.

The station was emptying now the London train was gone. A chill breeze stirred the hair on Laura's neck. He resisted a foolish urge to put his arm around her in comfort; he would surely be misunderstood. He turned his gaze towards the taxi rank. One single dusty vehicle remained. There was no excuse then. He must take her to Gunthwaite Hall.

Chapter Four

Laura woke slowly, sunlight brilliant against her face. She blinked and sat up, for a moment bewildered by the strange room. It was low-ceilinged, with rosebud wallpaper, an old-fashioned washstand with bowl and ewer, and a huge worm-eaten oak wardrobe. She got out of bed and knelt at the low window. In the distance a wood spread heavy branches across the horizon, and pigeons rose calling into the air; a little nearer and she saw fields full of dark red cows, and nearer still there was an orchard with sheep bleating and nibbling between apple, plum and pear trees. She felt quite amazed. She had never imagined Gabriel amidst this.

A dog was barking somewhere close by. She opened the window, not without a struggle, and breathed deep of the soft morning air. The smell of a farm – she had only to fill her lungs with that rich mixture of dung and flowers and hay and cattle to be transported at once to her childhood. She felt tearful suddenly.

She got up and began to wash, shuddering as cold water met warm skin. Presumably they had a bathroom here, but she couldn't be sure. Arriving so late last night, everything had been muddled and she had wanted simply to be no trouble. Now she saw that the house was ancient, walls, ceilings, floors all at angles to each other. Her door was a series of boards massively nailed and fastened with a stiff stable latch, and last night, doubtfully welcomed by Gabriel's mother in a dressing gown, Laura had climbed a staircase so wide and so uneven that she expected at any moment to slip to her doom.

There was no electricity, or even gas, simply candles and oil lamps, and no telephone of course. The house was lived in now as it must always have been, a defence against the elements, as dark and enclosing as a cave. It was so like the farm, she thought again, eyeing the chamber pot beneath her bed. Clearly that was meant to be used.

No one had offered any food last night, and she was hungry enough to feel sick. She thought of the welcome she had received. There had hardly been one, in fact. Mrs Cooper was a tall, thin woman with a mass of grey hair, who had fallen on her son with cries of: 'Gabriel! Gabriel!' He had fended her off with an ironic, embarrassed, 'Hello, Mother.' Laura felt uncomfortable watching them. She didn't know about mother love, it was nothing but a long-ago memory.

She dressed in a tweed suit. It was unsuitable town clothing, but she had nothing else and felt she must go down. Was it early or late? She had no watch and no way of knowing, but just then a clock in the hall struck the hour. It was only six.

There was no one about. She stood on the landing, full of hesitation. How did a guest behave in an English house? Was she to go down to the kitchen or did she hunt for a room where she might sit? Was it correct to help domestically, or would that reveal the bourgeois in their midst? Perhaps she should wait in her bedroom until someone came – but she couldn't sit there. The morning was waiting, and the sun was up.

She ran lightly down the uneven stairs, noting that they were every bit as wormy as her wardrobe. There was no one in the hall and she looked round at a sea of closed oak doors. There was nothing for it, she would have to go out. After all, a morning walk might be the English thing to do.

She wrestled her way out of the front door and into the sunshine. A hen, seeing her emerge, clucked stiffly from the base of the huge creeper that clung to the house wall. Peering into the dense mass, Laura saw an egg and took it, still warm. When she was small and very hungry, and if she was sure Madame didn't know, she would take an egg like this and eat it raw. She closed her eyes for a second, and then opened them again, half expecting to see Jean in the tumbledown cow shed. But the orchard stretched before her. Ewes were calling to their lambs.

She walked briskly away from the house. Two flint pillars guarded the entrance to Gunthwaite Hall, and the drive divided, a branch to the house and the other to the buildings. One huge barn dominated everything. It was stone below and timber and plaster above, mellowed to a rich creamy brown. Dogs were chained either side of a giant arched door, but when Laura approached they squatted and wagged their tails. Then she saw why they were there. The barn was full of sheep.

She stood cautiously near the door, wondering if she dare go forward and look. Someone might be inside. Belying appearances, the dogs might bite. Then a voice behind her said, 'Hello. Didn't you come with Gabriel last night? How do you do? My name's Michael, Gabriel's brother.'

She turned, a little flustered. Her first thought was that he was like Gabriel, only dark. At once she revised her opinion – he was much older. His eyes were brown and peaceful and his shoulders thick with adult muscle that Gabriel still lacked. He wore cord trousers and an open-necked shirt, and his hands had the permanently grimed appearance of the farmer. Unsure of herself or him, Laura said stiffly, 'How do you do?'

'Well,' said Michael, leaning on a shepherd's crook. 'What are we to call you?'

Since she was already blushing, the colour merely deepened. 'Oh. Sorry. I should have said. I'm Laura. Laura Perdoux.'

'A friend of Gabriel's?'

She gulped. 'Yes. He – he's a friend of my brother. He asked Gabriel to look after me and he kindly – very kindly—'

'No one would ever ask Gab to look after their sister!' said Michael in amazement.

Laura rushed in, 'He only offered to bring me here. Really, I can look after myself.'

Michael came towards her and took her hand. 'My dear, I doubt that very much. You're far too young and pretty. I don't suppose anyone else is up, so come and sit on some straw and watch the sheep. I'll take you into breakfast soon and introduce you to everyone. You won't see Gabriel for hours.'

He was trimming feet. Laura sat mesmerized by the rhythm of it all, catching, turning, this foot, that foot, tar brush and gone. The ewes bounded back into the flock, shaking their heads and bleating. Laura was fascinated by their flat, almost glassy eyes. They hadn't kept sheep in France. After a while, Michael paused and stretched his back.

Laura said, 'Are you Gabriel's only brother?'

He glanced at her. 'Yes. There's a sister in between, though.

Rosalind, she's married. I'm sorry, I thought you knew. Hasn't he told you anything about us?'

'Nothing at all, I'm afraid. I didn't even know he lived on a farm.'

'As far as Gab's concerned, he doesn't. It's merely a backdrop to his life, a picturesque pastoral scene. I wish we could all be quite so casual about it.'

He spoke with a touch of bitterness. Laura said, 'Has your family been here long?'

'About two hundred years, give or take. The farm's much older of course, this was a tithe barn in Norman times. The house was a fortified settlement, about as high as you can go and still have a decent farm. The Coopers bought it from some aristocratic lot down on their luck. Don't let Mother give you the wrong idea about us. We were all sent away to school, but we're still just honest farmers, no more than that.'

She said shyly, 'Is your father still alive? I'm sorry, I wish Gabriel had told me something about you all. I feel so rude asking questions.'

'There's no need. And, yes, Father's alive.'

He stopped talking and turned back to catch a ewe. There was something the matter with Father, she thought astutely. Suddenly three sheep made a sudden dash past the dog, eluded him and raced off down the track. 'Blast! Always the same three. I'll have to take the bike and the dog and go after them. They'll get into the village again. They're old pet lambs.'

'Why don't I go?'

He looked doubtful. 'It's a very long way, right down the hill. A devil of a pull coming back.'

'I don't mind. Please. I'd like something to do.'

The sheep in the barn were milling about, with a clear loss of patience. He couldn't leave them to chase the miscreants. He said, 'If you're sure you don't mind – the bike is under the eaves. Take the black dog, Glen, he knows what he's doing. They'll make for the churchyard, they always do.'

She scrambled down and unfastened the dog. It set off at a run and she hurried to look for the bike. It was an old ladies' model, creaking and uncomfortable, and her shoes slipped off the pedals. She had never once possessed good country shoes, she thought, bouncing uncomfortably over the ruts. She wondered if she might be able to afford some, and rattled down the hill doing sums in her head. If she didn't have to pay for Sophie she'd have done quite well out of the Zambesi. How would she pay for Sophie now? The wind was blowing her hair back from her head and her eyes were watering. In the distance she could see the black rump of the dog.

The village was still wrapped in sleep. As she whizzed round the corner she spied the runaways dining on roses and rockery flowers in a cottage garden, but the moment they saw her they scampered off and vaulted the churchyard wall. But the dog was before them. He raced through the gravestones and met the sheep head-on, snapping in revenge for his previous humiliation. The sheep turned and bounded back the way they had come. Laura put down her bike and flailed her arms saying 'Whoosh, whoosh!' as she used to do with cows. Off went the sheep, cantering back to Gunthwaite, but just as Laura was about to follow, a window in the cottage opened and a furious head looked out.

'I seen 'em! I knows them yows! Them's my prize blooms they's 'ad and t'show's next week!'

It was beyond Laura. She couldn't understand a word. She mumbled an apology and hurried off.

The steep hill she had flown down was a mountain she had to climb on the return leg. She glanced at her watch and saw that it was almost eight. The bike was heavy and her suit too warm; she kept stopping against the hedge to catch her breath. How far was Gunthwaite from the village? Two miles? Three? Gabriel's brother shouldn't have accepted her offer so quickly.

She stopped in a gateway and took stock. Below her the valley was brilliant in the morning sun, a patchwork of fields and copses. The village, with its church, nestled in the lee of the hill. Turning the other way, Gunthwaite was still beyond the shoulder of the hill, but to her right, lower down, there was a very large house. She could see gardens and a stable block, complete with clock tower. She began walking again pushing the bike uphill. At last the dark walls of Gunthwaite came into view, a stronghold still.

As she pedalled in she saw that the somnolent early morning had turned to bustle. Two men were moving a herd of cows through the yard and the sheep were pouring in a woolly mass back to their pasture. Laura looked for Michael, but he was nowhere to be seen. Perhaps he was in the house. She went to the open front door, doing her best to wipe mud and sheep muck off her shoes. A woman in an apron was passing through the hall. 'Best do that at t'back door, love,' she said. 'Front door's for vicar, that's all.'

Laura hurried round the house and found a porch full of boots and mackintoshes. There was a mudscraper too. She attended to her shoes and then crept shyly into a huge, open kitchen. An old man, the only occupant, said, 'Rosalind, dear.'

'Er – my name's Laura. Laura Perdoux.'

'Don't be silly, dear. What's that in your pocket?'

She glanced down. 'It's an egg.'

'You shouldn't keep eggs in your pocket, you know. Silly girl. Give it here.'

She handed over her prize. The old fellow took it and put it on the table. He had eyes as blue as Gabriel's, but ringed with the white of age. He might once have been tall too, but the years had bent him. He said conspiratorially, as if to a very young child, 'Let's surprise Mother, shall we? We'll give her the egg.'

Carefully, as if it was precious, the old man wrapped the egg in a teacloth. Just at that moment the door opened and Gabriel's mother bustled in. She said, 'Ah, Miss Perdoux. You've met my husband, I see.'

Laura said, 'I was trying to introduce myself.'

'I shouldn't bother, he won't know you. Gets us all muddled up. Still, he'll be happy now Gabriel's here.' She saw the teacloth on the table, and swept it up. The egg crashed to the floor.

'Norma!' complained the old man. 'You've broken Rosalind's egg!'

'I'm sorry, I meant to tell you—' began Laura.

Mrs Cooper sighed heavily. 'Never mind.'

Laura knew she was off on completely the wrong foot. Arriving late and unannounced, going off on her own this morning, and now the cause of a mess on the kitchen floor. She should have listened to Gabriel and stayed last night in town. Why had she believed she would be welcome here, when she knew he couldn't be trusted?

Trying to improve Mrs Cooper's opinion of her, she said,

'Can I help with the breakfast? I chased some sheep for Michael just now.'

'Yes. I thought I detected a lingering aroma. Everything's done, you might as well go through. Second on the left.'

Laura's cheeks flamed. The woman had been deliberately rude. It was because of Gabriel, of course; she didn't want another woman on the scene. Why hadn't Gabriel realised how it would be?

She went through the hall into the dining room. The woman she had seen earlier was there, folding napkins. When she saw Laura she said, 'Hello, dear. Find Mrs Cooper, did you?'

Laura nodded. Something in her face must have given her away, because the woman said, 'Don't mind her, she's always been blunt. Worse with young Gabriel around. Dotes on him. My name's Dinah. I'm the help.'

'I'm Laura. It was awful of Gabriel to bring me without telling anyone. I didn't know. He said it would be all right.'

'That's Gabriel for you.'

After a moment, Laura said, 'Is Mr Cooper quite well? He seemed very odd.'

Dinah grimaced. 'Senile. Started ten years since, and getting worse. Wanders off sometimes now, and if she didn't dress him no one would. Has to feed him too, sometimes. Thing is, she doesn't like strangers seeing him. Embarrasses her. If Gabriel had asked to bring you she'd most like have said no. She don't have visitors. Not any more. You've caused a right fuss.'

Laura looked around the room. Tarnished silver dishes stood over bowls of hot water on the sideboard, and a hastily arranged bunch of flowers was stuffed into a vase. The top of the table bore traces of beeswax still, while the legs were thick with dust. She felt consumed by guilt.

Dinah patted a chair. 'Sit yourself down and have a cup of tea. Don't upset yourself. It does her good to have a bit of company. Turning in on herself, she is. Not getting out. And everything falling to Michael. Now if he kicked up his heels she'd have cause to worry.' She nodded decisively, and handed Laura a steaming cup of milky tea. She preferred her tea black, but said nothing. In England it was best to conform.

Dinah was settling her broad hips against the heat of the sideboard, ready for a prolonged gossip, when the door opened and Michael came in. He was scrubbed and changed in a neat shirt, tie and sports jacket. Laura stood up hastily. 'You've changed. So must I. Your mother said I smelled of sheep.'

'Did she really?' Michael grimaced. 'She must be ratty this morning. Actually you smell fantastic. Some special scent, is it?'

'French,' said Laura, giving him a shy smile. 'Gabriel says I wear too much, but I was brought up in France and we all do.'

'Gabriel talks a lot of rubbish,' said Michael. 'Now, since no one else is making an appearance, why don't we eat? Thank you, Dinah.' He nodded pointedly and Dinah made a reluctant exit.

The breakfast was unexpectedly delicious. Michael said they killed and cured their own pigs, and the bacon was crisp as dry leaves. Fresh eggs had been scrambled to fluff, and there was black pudding and mushrooms, golden butter and crusty homemade bread. Laura thought of all the unwholesome meals she had consumed since she first came to Britain. It was a relief to find that good food still existed. She ate in silent concentration.

After ten minutes, Michael said, 'Can I offer you some more?'

Laura looked up and blushed. 'I don't think I could. But it's so delicious, I haven't eaten anything so good since—'

'Since you left France,' supplied Michael. 'The French take food rather more seriously than we do, I believe. But I've only been there once, about three years ago, with Gabriel. Paris. We had a bit of a mixed time.'

Laura opened her eyes wide. 'Did you? I am sorry.'

'Don't be. I'm not very good at towns. When it comes down to it I'm something of a bumpkin, I'm afraid.'

She laughed obediently. Just then the door opened and Mr and Mrs Cooper came in. 'Mother.' Michael stood up and held her chair, but she said, 'Don't be silly, Michael. I've to see to your father.'

Mr Cooper said, 'Hello, Rosalind!' and evaded his wife's grasp to get to Laura. 'Don't you look well? Such a pretty colour in your cheeks.'

He sat down in the place next to Laura and Mrs Cooper said in exasperation, 'Come over here, John! I can't see to you there.'

But he sat where he was, looking mutinous. Laura said, 'Why don't I see to him? Would you like some egg and bacon, Mr Cooper?' She got up and went to the sideboard.

'Sit down, Miss Perdoux!' said Mrs Cooper urgently. 'Have a proper breakfast, do!'

'Laura's finished, Mother,' said Michael.

She snapped, 'She's got a tongue of her own, hasn't she?'

There was a clatter in the hall and Gabriel came in. He was wearing pale cricket trousers and a sweater. He said, 'Morning all. What are you doing, Laura? Is Mother making you do penance for arriving in the middle of the night? I told you we should have stayed in Leeds.'

Mrs Cooper looked shocked. 'Take a young lady to an hotel? What would her mother say?'

'My mother's dead,' said Laura in embarrassment. 'Both my parents are.'

'Which is why her brother entrusted me with her care,' declared Gabriel. 'I had to bring her here, Mother. It was only right.'

Laura was aware of Michael's sardonic eyes on his brother. 'He can't know you very well, Gab,' he remarked.

It was innocuous enough, but Gabriel flared. 'What on earth do you mean? Are you saying I can't look after her?'

'How should I know? Last I heard you were running some dive full of heiresses and ladies of the night.'

'Michael, please!' said Mrs Cooper. 'I'm sure it was respectable. Please don't use such language in front of Miss Perdoux.'

'Do call me Laura,' she said breathlessly.

'And watch what you say, Mike,' said Gabriel, piling bacon on to his plate. 'I take my responsibilities very seriously. Can't have Laura's shell-like ears corrupted.'

The breakfast was over at last. Laura hung about the hall, trying to intercept Gabriel and find out how she could leave. She was an unwelcome guest, knew she should never have come. Sure enough, after a few minutes Gabriel appeared. 'Are you coming then?' he demanded. 'I've got the car. We can go into Bainfield.'

She didn't know where Bainfield was. But at least in the car they could talk. She ran upstairs to brush her hair.

The Coopers ran a large and old-fashioned car with worn leather seats and headlamps as big as half barrels. Gabriel drove fast, and Laura had to beg him to slow down. He took no notice.

'What's the point of a car if you don't enjoy it?'

'Gabriel, please!'

They rounded a bend and plunged straight into a herd of cows. Laura shrieked, the cows bolted, and everything slid off the back seat.

'Damn!' said Gabriel. 'I should have known. There isn't a decent clear road for miles.'

All thought of conversation was driven from Laura's mind. She clung to the dashboard with tense fingers and Gabriel said, 'Honestly! You're not going to die!'

'How far is Bainfield?' she asked tensely.

'Ten miles or so. It's market day. Laura, will you please relax!' But she sat with gritted teeth for the rest of the journey.

The little town was bustling with people and Gabriel was at last forced to slow down. Laura sat up a little, feeling a familiar charge of energy. A purposeful town never failed to remind her of her first days in Paris. Remembered fear and excitement seemed to crystallise into a new sense of herself and life's possibilities.

They parked in the market square, beside a stall selling vegetables and another selling jam. Gabriel opened the boot and cursed. In the skirmish with the cows, the acid battery they used for Gunthwaite's wireless had fallen over. Acid had leaked on to the carpet and burned several holes. 'Michael will have a field day,' said Gabriel crossly. 'He's always pleased when I do anything wrong.'

'Shall I try and mop it up?' asked Laura, but Gabriel shook his head.

'Not worth it. Look, I'll drive to the garage and have them do it. Get the battery charged at the same time. You can look after yourself, can't you? I'll meet you back here in an hour.'

She was alone. She fingered the letter in her bag. It was to Madame Bonacieux, enclosing the usual monthly postal order, and giving Laura's new address. She wasn't sure if she should send it now. She wandered down the street, ostensibly looking for the post office but in reality looking at clothes. Skirts were longer here, and hats less close-fitting. Stout Yorkshire housewives marched past, their baskets full, their feet in sturdy leather. Laura stopped outside the post office and debated with herself. Whether she stayed at Gunthwaite or not she needed

167

new shoes. If she sent only half the money this month, surely Madame would make the shortfall up? Suppose she didn't send anything at all? No one would notice for a while. They would think the post was at fault.

Her feet were hurting again. She had to have those shoes! Her mind made up, she ripped open the envelope, took out the postal order and strode into the post office to cash it. But once the clerk gave her the money she felt wretched. Sophie had never stinted, ever. She stood before the window, cash in hand.

'Have you finished, Miss? Was there something else?'

'Yes. I'll have an order for half as much, please.'

'Well. If you'd make up your mind.'

She stuffed the order into the envelope, borrowed some tape to seal it shut and posted it before she could change her mind. The deed was done. All she needed now was some cheap shoes.

She bought a pair of brogues, heavy, serviceable footwear that made her feel at once much older than seventeen. She might be older, she thought. No one really knew how old she was. She counted the money remaining in her purse and thought of her little hoard in the corner of her suitcase. Not much. Not enough. And Mrs Cooper didn't like her, she'd never give her the reference Gabriel had so glibly promised. What was she to do?

She was near the cattle market. She could hear cows lowing, and knots of farmers stood on street corners talking. There were pubs too. The Spread Eagle, The Commercial, The Rose and Crown, all thronged with men, and Laura thought longingly of a glass of wine. If she was still what she used to be she would go in and order what she pleased, but now, Miss Respectable, she could not. Her blouse was sticking to her beneath the tweed jacket. Might she not even try for a lemonade?

Just as she was plucking up courage to enter The Commercial, the doors burst open. Two men were flung to the pavement at her feet. She recoiled, resolving to go elsewhere, until a familiar pair of pale trousers caught her attention. 'Gabriel?' she said waveringly. 'Gabriel, not you?'

He got to his feet. One eye was closing and the trousers were stained with blood and beer. The other man staggered up, his nose pouring blood. 'Bloody Commie,' he muttered.

'Fascist,' retorted Gabriel.

Laura thought for a moment they would fight again, but neither had the stomach for it. As she and Gabriel began to walk away Laura found herself shaking. Partly it was surprise. The bustling streets of Bainfield seemed far less suited to conflict than the mirrored and ambiguous halls of the Rue de Claret.

They went quickly back to the car. 'What was it about?' asked Laura. 'You said you were going to the garage.'

'I did. Fancied a pint on the way back. He was sounding off about Jews, the usual stupid stuff, and I took him up on it.'

'What did you say?'

He squinted out of his one good eye. 'I just pointed out that you couldn't blame Jews for unemployment in Bainfield. Apart from the watchmender, there aren't any. But he's one of those idiots that likes to have someone to kick. I said we'd have more jobs if we didn't import food grown by slave labour abroad, and he called me a Jew and I laughed.'

'You asked for it, then,' said Laura grimly. They had reached the car and stood looking at each other across the dusty bonnet.

'You can't let people talk rubbish like that. It gets to be believed.'

'People always talk rubbish. It doesn't change a thing.'

He was silent on the drive home. They should be discussing her future, but she knew that in his present mood he'd be difficult. Her heart sank as she thought of Mrs Cooper's face when she saw Gabriel. Perhaps she'd blame Laura and lay that at her door as well.

As the car drew up she saw Michael coming out of the barn. 'Damn,' said Gabriel. 'Here comes the lecture. He never misses a chance.'

'Perhaps it's because your father's ill?'

'Nonsense! He enjoys it. That's why he's so pleased to see me home. Someone to criticise at last.'

'Hello, you two,' called Michael, wiping his hands on a cloth. 'Get the battery, did you? Good God. Gabriel! Your face!'

'An argument with a door,' said Gabriel sardonically. He looked like a sulky schoolboy, all scowls and untruths.

Michael sighed. 'Some door. Don't you think Mother has enough to put up with? Get inside and bathe it, man! What are you thinking of, fighting, with Laura in your charge! She must have been terrified.'

'I didn't see it,' said Laura quickly. 'Only the end. He broke the other man's nose.'

'No doubt some undernourished labourer who's never had a boxing lesson in his life! My God, Gabriel, will you never grow up? The Coopers of Gunthwaite don't brawl.'

'They don't stand by and let idiots talk persecution either,' flared Gabriel. 'Do you have to be so bloody sure of yourself?'

'Don't swear in front of Laura, please.'

Gabriel snorted. 'I doubt if that shocks her. Believe you me, she's tougher than she looks.'

Laura felt her cheeks grow hot. Muttering about a cloth for Gabriel's face, she pushed past them both and went into the house. Michael said, 'Satisfied? The poor girl's speechless with embarrassment. Why on earth did you bring her? You knew what Mother would be like.'

'She hadn't anywhere else to go.'

Michael stared at him grimly. Then he said, 'I don't know what you're up to, Gabriel, but I won't have you messing about with that young girl. She's too sweet to have a rotter like you taking advantage.'

'A rotter! I'm nothing of the kind. Good God, Mike, it isn't my fault you try to be a saint. Anyone who drinks more than a pint of beer is a rotter to you.'

'What would you like to be called? A waster? A parasite? No profession, no ambition, nothing but the desire to have fun and chase girls, all at my expense.'

'This farm is still Father's,' said Gabriel in a low, angry voice.

'And I'm the one who runs it! If you want to spend farm money, Gabriel, I suggest you give some thought to earning it.'

He strode away across the yard. Laura, who had been standing for moments behind the door, cloth in hand, came cautiously outside. 'I thought you could clean up,' she said diffidently.

'That bloody man! He's got no sodding right to tell me what to do!' Gabriel visibly fumed.

Laura said, 'If you sit on the wall, I can do your face.'

He sat somewhat grudgingly, and she dabbed at his abrasions. They weren't serious and would soon scab over. For the moment, though, they looked alarming. 'Your mother's glad to have you home,' she ventured.

'That's half the trouble. Mother prefers me to Michael and he's jealous.'

'Why does she prefer you? He seems very nice.'

'Oh, Michael's nice. Much nicer than me, if that's what you're thinking. It doesn't matter what he's like, Mother had a terrible time having him and almost died. Holds it against him in some way.'

'But that's awful! It's not his fault!'

Gabriel got up, brushing at his stained trousers. 'Mother's not too interested in whose fault things are. And look how it's turned out. Michael's as true a metal as I am base. Rosalind, of course, being a girl, hardly counts.'

He grinned widely, but his eyes were cold. Suddenly he took hold of Laura's shoulders, pulled her towards him and kissed her. He tasted of blood. She said quickly, 'Don't do that. Not here.'

'I suppose you think Mike might see? He might think you're not as sweet as you seem. But I shall do as I please. After all, if I was your first, you must have had hundreds of men since.'

Still gripping her shoulder, his free hand reached up under her skirt. She felt a shock go through her, a pulse of blood to every nerve in her body. His fingers drifted into the wide leg of her drawers. At the last moment, as he reached moisture, she jerked away.

He chuckled. She thought him the cruellest man she had ever known. Without a threshold of modesty, she was undefended against him, her body gave in before her mind could rally. Perhaps in time she would become like other women. For them, a sense of outrage seemed as much an habitual accompaniment as a purse. If someone had seen she would die of shame, she thought, and ran up to her room. She stayed there, in solitude, until dinner.

The atmosphere at table was grim. Gabriel and his mother had quarrelled and now wouldn't speak. Mr Cooper wouldn't eat when his wife tried to persuade him, demanding, 'Rosalind! Rosalind!' So Laura passed the meal in alternately feeding herself and him. Sadly, the food did not reach the standard of breakfast, although the vegetables were fresh and well cooked. But the pie was dull and too salty.

Michael said, 'Are you not very hungry, Laura?'

She smiled at him. 'Not really. And it's been quite a day.'

'Yes.' He looked at his brother. 'All right, Gab, let's hear what you have to say for yourself. We're not interested in the fight, but it's all part of the same thing. What do you mean to do?'

The bruise over Gabriel's eye was turning blue. He looked piratical, thought Laura, a look that suited him more than his usual unblemished charm. Gabriel was an opportunist rogue, whose principles, such as they were, seemed more occasional than constant. He said, 'When I wish to tell you my plans, Michael, I shall do so. Not before.'

Mrs Cooper said, 'Gabriel! Gabriel, please. Michael thinks you should try for the army.'

'No doubt he thinks I need the discipline,' said Gabriel thinly.

'Yes,' said Michael frankly. 'I don't think it's a bad idea. There's been a Cooper in the King's Own Yorkshire for generations.'

'Why don't you join then? Or Rosalind? Or one of the sheep? Much as it grieves me to disappoint you, Michael, I'll not join the army to suit your sense of tradition.'

'But you must do something!' wailed Mrs Cooper. 'It's been one idea after another, ever since you left school, and all of it costing money. Michael's foolish about the army, of course, you mustn't do it if you don't want, but isn't there something you'd like to do?'

Michael said, 'Whatever it is, he'll be sure it won't please me.'

An uncomfortable silence fell. Mr Cooper said, 'Where's the fruit tart? I must have my fruit tart.'

'Will you shut up, John!' said Mrs Cooper through clenched teeth. Laura got up and went to fetch the old man what he wanted. It must be awful for him, she thought, at the mercy of Mrs Cooper's scarcely concealed rage.

Michael said, with forced jollity, 'And what about you, Laura? Do you have any plans?'

'There's always the army,' said Gabriel. 'She's not a Cooper, of course, but she's the best we can do.'

'Don't be silly, Gabriel,' said Laura quietly. She sat down again, shaking sugar liberally on the old man's sour pie.

He smacked his gums and Mrs Cooper said, 'Please don't

pamper him, Miss Perdoux. He's lazy, that's all.'

They were still waiting for her reply. At last she said, 'Actually, I need a job. But I can't give English references. I don't know anyone.'

'What sort of job?' asked Michael, perplexed. 'Teaching, something like that?'

'I thought – in a shop.'

Mrs Cooper made a derisive noise. 'I can see you're from France. My dear, girls of your station do not work in shops. Unless in Harrods. Doesn't your family have money?'

'No.' She looked wildly at Gabriel, who raised an eyebrow, no more. 'My brother's got plans,' she declared. 'Travelling – investments—'

'What sort of investments?' Mrs Cooper looked down her long straight nose.

'I really don't know.'

Mr Cooper was gobbling the last of his fruit tart. Michael said, 'I'm sure Laura will manage wonderfully, Mother. If she thinks of something she'd like to do we can give her a reference and get her started. Mark my words, it won't be long before some young blade has noticed what he's missing and taken her off to keep house.'

'Surprised you can't find one for her,' snapped Gabriel. 'You're really very good at running other people's lives, never having had to make a single decision about your own.'

Michael said, 'If I thought you wanted the farm for any other reason than that it's mine, I might take you more seriously. It's time you did some thinking, Gabriel. We'll talk again.'

It was a relief to escape the table. Michael hovered, ready to suggest entertainment for their guest, but Gabriel took her hand and said, 'Come on, Laura. Let's walk.'

It was the last thing she wanted, she was longing for rest and sleep. But Gabriel was in a mood and she couldn't face a row. She put on her stiff new shoes and felt them rubbing blisters as they walked through the wood.

'He's such a bastard!' burst out Gabriel. 'Thinks he can tell me just what to do.'

'What would you do if he didn't tell you?'

'God knows. Fly, perhaps. I always wanted to.'

'But why not?'

'Because Mother wouldn't hear of it. I wanted to apply straight from school, but she wouldn't sign the forms.'

'Now you're older you can do as you please.'

The light was fading beneath the trees, and a fox slipped by in the distant shadows. Gabriel stopped by an elder bush and pulled her to him. She felt him hard against her, an angry young boy. But then anger and desire are very close.

'I need you,' he whispered. 'Please, tonight I need you more than ever.'

'You're angry at your brother. You don't need me.'

'Of course I do. You're so good for me. Laura, please!' His mouth was on hers, wide-lipped, searching. Her breasts felt hot and expectant. Why did her body always let her down? But she thought of Michael's face at the dinner table. If she gave in to Gabriel now Michael would be sure to know. There'd be no new and pure beginning. She pulled away, so suddenly that Gabriel was left gasping, and ran clumsily back through the wood.

Chapter Five

The next morning Gabriel wasn't at breakfast. The car had gone too, and Michael fumed and fussed in case Gabriel had run off with it.

'I wouldn't put anything past him, Mother,' he declared.

'He's gone for a drive,' she replied loyally. 'You were too hard on him yesterday. It's difficult for a young man, making his way in the world. You're too grudging, but then you always are. You should count yourself lucky, having the farm.'

Laura watched Michael's face as he bent over his bacon and egg. He was weary beyond measure with his mother forever taking Gabriel's part.

When the meal was finished Laura went out in the yard. She had discarded the jacket of her suit and wore only the skirt with a simple navy jumper. She felt better this morning, rested and less fraught. They all knew she had no money, and they hadn't thrown her out. Hadn't Michael mentioned teaching? She had little enough general education, but surely she could teach French?

She saw Michael taking the bull back down the track. It was a large, quiet, reddish beast, and next to him Michael looked wide-shouldered and competent. She walked briskly to catch them up, saying, 'Can I come? I could open the gate.'

He smiled, he needed no help. But he said, 'Do come. I should like the company. This is Hercules, he won a prize last year.'

'He's very handsome.'

They walked together, and the bull sighed now and then, great gusty breaths. Michael said, 'I wonder if I might ask, Laura? Are you Gabriel's girl?'

She blushed scarlet. 'Did he say I was? I'm not and never was. He's a friend, nothing more.'

'Gabriel didn't say anything. I wondered, that's all. Do you really have a brother?'

He stopped and turned to her. The bull, thwarted in his visit to the cows, let out a long, mournful bellow. Laura twisted her hands together, wondering why she hadn't seen that Michael was clever enough to recognise lies. His mother was too self-absorbed, but not Michael.

'I haven't any family,' she said at last. 'I couldn't get work in France so I came to England and worked as a maid. But it was horrible and the pay was bad, so Gabriel offered me a job. In his club. I just – showed people to their tables and things.' She took a deep breath, watching to see if his face changed. 'It isn't respectable, is it?' she went on. 'In England nice girls don't work in clubs. I didn't know. I can't get a job and I don't know anyone and Gabriel said he'd get me a reference. I'm sorry.'

She began to cry, unhappy tears dripping soundlessly on to her hands. Michael said, 'There's no need for that. I don't mind and I won't tell Mother. But I prefer to know where we stand.'

'I'm not Gabriel's! I don't want you to think that. It was stupid of me to trust him; he said it would be all right.'

'Gabriel always says things will be all right.' Michael sighed. 'Dry your eyes, Laura. If we all got upset over one of Gabriel's little tricks, we'd never stop crying.'

'I'll go,' she said, blowing her nose. 'I'll find something to do.'

'But we need help here. Why not stay for a while? We know people. Something might turn up. And stop crying! Please. For me.'

She smiled tremulously up at him. He was a kind man, gentle with animals and people. It was hard to believe he was Gabriel's brother.

Gabriel returned with the car at noon. He was clutching a sheaf of papers, and rushed into the house calling, 'Mother! Laura! Come and look at this.'

They gathered in the kitchen, where Laura was peeling carrots, and Gabriel spread his booty amongst the peelings. 'Look! I'm going to join the RAF.'

There was a picture of a smiling man in front of a small grey aircraft. Mrs Cooper picked it up and looked closely. 'No,' she said in a trembling voice. 'We talked before. It's out of the question.'

'But why? They need people and it's what I want to do. A lot of people fail the eyesight test, but I've got excellent vision. I've got a very good chance because I wanted to join before. They think it shows tenacity. I'll be interviewed as soon as they have the forms.'

His mother said, 'You could be killed. It's dangerous!'

'The army's dangerous, Mother, and you didn't mind that.'

'This is worse! You know it is. I won't permit it.' She glared at him with frightened, tearful eyes.

After a moment he said, 'I'm sorry, Mother. I don't need your permission any more. I'm of age.'

There was a clatter outside. They could hear Michael taking off his boots. Mrs Cooper called, 'Michael! Michael, come here and stop Gabriel being so foolish.'

When he came in, quiet, slow, they all looked at him expectantly. Gabriel said, 'It's a fuss about nothing. I'm applying to join the RAF.'

Mrs Cooper burst out, 'Tell him he can't! He'll be killed, he hasn't the right, he shouldn't upset me so! We'll stop his allowance, won't we, and never let him home?'

'Calm down, Mother,' said Michael. 'To be honest, I think it's an excellent idea. I wouldn't have stopped him before if you hadn't been so upset.'

'Oh, blame me,' she replied in ringing tones. 'Blame me, when all I want is to keep my son safe. It isn't so much to ask.'

Laura had been looking through the pamphlet Gabriel had tossed down. 'I think it's quite hard to be accepted,' she said diffidently. 'For flying, that is. He could be ground staff, anything.'

'They said I was definite for air crew,' retorted Gabriel, and Laura hid a smile.

'Laura's right,' said Michael. 'Why argue over something that might not occur?'

'And if it does?' demanded Mrs Cooper. 'If it does, what then?'

'I'll have some more facts,' said Gabriel. 'Honestly, Mother, I won't do it if it's too dangerous. I don't want to kill myself.'

His mother put her knuckles to her mouth. 'Young men don't realise,' she whispered. 'They didn't in the war. They never thought it might be them.'

Laura knew she was intruding. She said, 'I'll make a cup of tea,' and bustled about with the kettle. Michael began tidying the papers and Gabriel, awkward and unwilling, put an arm around his mother's shoulders. 'Oh, Gabriel,' she said, in a forlorn voice, and wept into his shirt.

The household settled down once the application had been made. There was nothing to do until they received a reply, and until then everyone relaxed into unlooked for harmony. Laura seemed to be accepted, if not without question then certainly without remark. Gradually, little by little, she carved herself a place in the pattern of the days. She rose early, soon after six, and went out to help Michael with the stock. When she returned Dinah would be serving breakfast – in the kitchen after that first, stressful venture into the dining room – and Laura would see to Mr Cooper. His wife meanwhile, able to eat peacefully for the first time in years, responded with sharp remarks and criticism. Laura tolerated it. The strain of caring for a mad old man was bound to tell.

After breakfast she helped in the house, and on market day went with Michael or Gabriel to town. Entrusted with food shopping, she enjoyed market days, although the stallholders were frosty. They couldn't get used to her French habit of picking and poking at food, while she for her part wouldn't buy on trust. She had seen the gristly meat foisted off on young women, and she'd have none of it. She approached shopkeepers with what she considered to be well-founded suspicion, and couldn't understand why they didn't think it just.

On one such expedition Gabriel said in exasperation, 'Does it matter if we don't have quite the best? At least we'd be spared all this glowering.'

'For somebody who fights in pubs over nothing very important, I think that's a bit rich.' Laura put her nose in the air, although she too wished she need not bolster her courage to quite such a degree just to buy beef. She thought how welcome a drink would be, and said to Gabriel, 'Can we go to a pub? I'd like some wine.'

'A pub? In Bainfield? I should think not. You're a lady now, everyone knows you're from Gunthwaite.'

'Even ladies have to drink!'

Gabriel laughed. 'Not wine, my dear. Perhaps sherry in the privacy of home.'

'Sherry then. Go into the pub, Gabriel, and buy me a sherry. I'll drink it outside.'

'And let everyone see you? If you fainted, possibly. It's like – it's like decent women in the Rue de Claret. Not done.'

The phrase flicked her on the raw. Who made these rules, who insisted upon them? It wasn't all men, there were women enough to point the finger. Women like Mrs Cooper, soured by work and worry, who seemed pleased if others were denied pleasure. Laura felt a small urge to rebellion; things weren't right merely because they were English, after all. Or French for that matter. Was it so important that she buy the best beef?

It was all confusing and difficult, and she very much wanted a glass of wine. She stopped outside the pub, tilted her head and said to Gabriel, 'Dare you! I want a drink.' He hesitated for a brief half second. She added, 'Coward.'

He said, 'Oh, very well! Don't say I didn't warn you.'

The place was crowded with farmers and auctioneers. The bar was high, like the stern of a ship, which in fact it once had been, brought from Hull by cart some fifty years before, but there all nautical resemblance ended; the faded prints on the wall above the fire depicted hunting.

When Laura entered there was an immediate lull in conversation. A group of men by the window failed to notice her, until their guffaws fell into silence. They looked round and took in the apparition. Laura smiled at them shyly. They stared in horror.

'A glass of sherry and a half of bitter, please, landlord,' said Gabriel loudly.

Laura glanced at him. His voice was full of obvious bravado. Was this really so terrible a crime?

For a moment it seemed as if they might not be served. But the landlord pulled the beer without a word, and then administered a silent sherry. Laura sipped and it was sticky sweet. All she had wanted was a glass of good wine.

'Can we sit down somewhere, Gabriel?' Everyone except the oldest men was standing.

'If you like – yes.'

She went to a corner and slid on to a bench polished by years of use. A man nearby said loudly, 'Comes to sommat when a man can't keep his bit of stuff in hand.'

Gabriel paused in the act of sitting down. 'Excuse me,' he said stiffly. 'Miss Perdoux is a lady. She's French.'

'And what bloody difference does that make?'

'It means – it means that she doesn't understand why she can't take a restorative drink in comfort and civility. And I must confess I don't understand it either. And if you've any further comments to make, I suggest you make them to me outside.'

His colour was very high. The belligerent man was drunk and wouldn't back down. Laura thought of the trouble over Gabriel's last fight, and wished suddenly that she'd never started this. If men wanted to keep their beer-smelling pubs to themselves, why should it matter to her?

She got up and said, 'Please, Gabriel, it's not worth it. I didn't realise there'd be a fuss.'

'This man insulted you. He should apologise.'

'You're making trouble. There's no need.'

She turned on her heel and pushed her way between the tweed-clad backs to the door. Gabriel followed, and as they left a voice said lugubriously, 'The beer must be off.' There was a roar of appreciative laughter.

Laura said, 'I didn't realise there'd be a fight.'

Gabriel whistled through his teeth. 'Neither did I. They took it terribly badly, didn't they?'

Laura nodded. She felt as she had when she and Marie had been asked to leave the café; angry, ashamed and tearful. She said to Gabriel, 'Let's go back to the car.'

'We haven't finished the shopping.'

She closed her eyes for a moment to compose herself. They couldn't go back yet. Mrs Cooper had ordered flour and nails and Mr Cooper's tonic from the chemist, said to 'feed the brain the food it likes – recommended for invalids and scholars'.

They visited the chemist last and it was clear that already the tale had spread. The girl behind the counter turned pink and said, 'I don't know how you dared, Miss! My mum'd half kill me.'

Laura dropped her eyes. 'I didn't know it was quite so daring.'

'Don't know as it was. Not as if you danced the can-can. Lot of old fuddy-duddies in Bainfield, if you ask me.'

'Hilda!' roared the chemist from behind the scenes.

The girl thrust Laura her change – plus a packet of pins for the last farthing – and fled.

Michael was waiting for them when they got home. Laura could tell by his face that he knew, although it was a mystery to her how news could arrow its way back here before them. His calm brown eyes were like pebbles in stone. He said to Gabriel, 'How dare you? In Bainfield of all places? You ought to be thrashed.'

Gabriel said defiantly, 'She wanted a drink, that's all. A sherry.'

'And you allowed her to expose herself to ridicule! To expose us! As if Mother hasn't worries enough.'

'Don't bring Mother into it,' said Gabriel, and Laura added, 'It was my idea. I didn't know it would matter.'

'Gabriel knew. In a place like this no lady worth the name would ever enter a public house, let alone order alcohol. We've been invited to dinner at Fairlands on Friday, and I wanted to ask if you could come, but now you could be ostracised. They'll think you're fast.'

'Fast?' Laura boggled.

'They have a daughter. They wouldn't like her to mix with someone who goes beyond the line.'

The colour flooded Laura's face. She turned and ran up the stairs to her room, while downstairs Gabriel said viciously, 'You're a pompous ass, you know that?'

Michael said, 'I'll thank you not to smear Laura's good name.'

The brothers glared at one another in mutual dislike.

But Michael had underestimated the times. When Friday came Laura and Michael went to dinner at the Fitzalan-Howards', to be greeted by Dora, the pretty daughter, saying, 'Did you really ask for a drink in a pub? I wish I'd been brave enough. Even Mother said it was about time someone shook them up a bit.'

'I didn't realise it would shake them up so much,' said Laura ruefully. 'Gabriel nearly had to fight someone.'

'I should think Gabriel's good at that sort of thing,' gasped Dora, blushing. 'I wish he'd come tonight, we so love to see him. Is he really going to join the RAF?'

'We don't know yet. We had a letter today, though. He's got an interview on Monday.'

The girl looked suddenly despondent. 'Oh. Really? It's always awfully dull when Gabriel goes away.'

It was a small country dinner party. Laura was wearing her plain black dress, her only jewellery the small gold ring Henri had given her. She had thought her clothes understated but now she seemed to bear unmistakable town gloss. The Fitzalan-Howard daughter stared in open admiration, and talked constantly of Gabriel. 'Why didn't he come?' murmured Laura to Michael.

He gave a slight grimace. 'He wasn't asked. Dora loves him, of course, but no Fitzalan-Howard ought to fall for a wayward and impoverished younger son.'

Laura made a face. It must be very hard for Gabriel, knowing that Michael had a house and a farm and a life, while he had nothing. People managed these things so oddly, she thought, holding on to the land as if it were all that mattered, and the sufferings of its sons meant nothing at all. Michael was respected and invited to parties, while Gabriel was left out in the cold.

There was a general murmuring at table. It was clear that a schoolgirl had been expected and Laura's sophistication put everyone in a quandary. Mrs Fitzalan-Howard, imagining her young guest at a loss, had seated her next to Michael when really she would have liked Dora to sit there. Mr Fitzalan-Howard was heard to comment pettishly, 'I'm sure I ought to merit an interesting foreigner, my dear,' but no one took any notice. After all, someone had to sit next to Mrs Fitch, the huntmaster's leathery wife.

'Do you ride, Miss Perdoux?' she demanded, halfway through the soup.

Laura lifted her head. Against the black of dress and hair her skin looked like porcelain. 'I haven't ridden in England,' she said, looking for all the world as if she had never set foot beyond an elegant salon.

'I thought not,' said Mrs Fitch, turning up her nose.

But Laura added, 'If the chance came, I'd love to of course. I rode as a child.'

Michael said, 'The horses are all turned out for the summer. When autumn comes I'll take you hunting.'

Laura said, 'Autumn? I won't still be here.'

'You never know,' said Michael.

When the main course arrived, overcooked lamb with glutinous mint sauce, conversation became less general. Michael said softly to Laura, 'Don't you wish Gunthwaite was like this?'

She looked down the table, at the pale walls, the electric lights, the elegance of a large, graceful home. 'It wouldn't suit Gunthwaite,' she said. 'This is a mansion, Gunthwaite's a farm. That's its charm.'

'I used to think so. Lately, farming hasn't been very charming, though.'

He looked a little bleak. Not for the first time, Laura wondered about the farm. Michael had three men working for him, but discussions in the kitchen often centred on someone going. Bill Mayes was the foreman and had to stay, but another was too old to find anything else and the third was invaluable with stock. It all came down to money, of course. The farm, like everything, was doing badly.

'You shouldn't stay on the farm if you don't love it,' she said.

He glanced at her. 'Do you know, if I hated each day I don't think I could leave. What would I do in the spring, wondering if the blossom was out? How could I sleep without lambing ewes to worry over? Once Gunthwaite has you, she doesn't let you go.'

'Do you feel that?' She shot him a laughing glance. 'I thought it was only me. The house gathers you up, don't you think? You give love, and in return she keeps you safe.'

Unexpectedly, his hand reached for hers beneath the cloth. 'I knew you understood.'

She sat absorbing this unexpected development. But Michael went on talking as if nothing had happened until quite out of the blue he said, 'What was your life in France?'

She thought of all the things she might say. She had a dozen prepared answers, none of which seemed right. She turned her hand within his, pressing her nails into his skin, gentle, telling indentations. 'I wasn't happy,' she said softly.

183

'So I imagined. You don't leave happiness. But you write to France still, so someone's there.'

She smiled, a little stiffly. Michael always noticed things. 'I send money to my Aunt Sophie. She brought me up. She's in a nursing home and doesn't need me any more.'

'But you need someone, Laura. You're so young and beautiful.'

'There's always Gabriel!' she said flippantly.

'For your own sake, I'd much rather you trusted me.'

His eyes were boring into hers, not caring who saw. She was embarrassed and a little alarmed, drawing her hand away in case he thought she meant more than she did. Michael sat very still, the food on his plate hardly touched, while Laura turned her shoulder to him and began talking about hunting to Mr Fitch. Michael's presence was like heat on her back. He had been so very kind.

Mr Fitch said, 'Michael's a bruiser to hounds, of course, damned sight better than Gabriel. Takes such chances, that boy. Doesn't do himself or his horses justice. It's his mother's fault. Odd woman, urging him on with one hand and holding him back with the other. Never had any time for Michael, or Rosalind for that matter. I'll say this for my old girl, she liked her brats equally, even if she did mount them on thoroughbreds at two.'

Perhaps it was better not to love your children, thought Laura ruefully. Gabriel's nervy, high-strung nature contrasted so oddly with Michael's solid worth.

Over pudding she turned to him again and said abruptly, 'You must tell me if there's anything I can do that will make things easier for you. You've been so kind to me.'

'By letting you stay? It isn't kindness. You do so much for us all. If you left I should miss you a very great deal.'

She turned her head from him a little. 'You mustn't talk as if I could stay for ever. I can't and it isn't fair.'

'Don't you want to stay for ever?'

She gasped. 'You know that isn't fair! I want to be settled and secure, of course I want that. But I don't ask you to do it for me. I wouldn't accept it if you did. You've been too kind.'

He blinked at that. And Mr Fitch addressed her, and she turned away and chatted to him until she rose from the table with the ladies, and talked in the drawing room about Paris until it was time to go home.

The car was dark and quiet after the house. Michael and Laura drove in silence for some minutes. It was a moonlit night, the sky almost cloudless. A stand of trees came hard by the road, and without warning Michael pulled in and switched off the car.

'What are you doing?' asked Laura softly.

'I – I don't know.' He was looking at her almost with desperation. He said, 'You're so very beautiful.'

All at once her heart went out to him. He worked so hard and so responsibly, and his mother and Gabriel hadn't a good word to say. She reached to touch his shoulder, a gesture of sympathy. In a rush that blotted the light his head came down on hers.

It was a clumsy, inadequate kiss. Laura leaned back and let her lips fall open, and his great head pressed its weight against her neck until all at once he pulled back, saying, 'Sorry. Sorry!'

Laura held on to his wrist. She leaned against the seat, gently rubbing his flesh. 'You can do it again, if you want,' she murmured. He looked at her, challenging and bewildered. She reached out, took his face in her hands and pressed her lips against his in tiny, birdlike kisses. His mouth opened, as she knew it must, and hers opened too. With a groan, of failure and delight, Michael's tongue came into her, probing, stretching, seeking. His hands were in her hair, kneading and writhing in mimicry of his tongue. She turned her head and let his mouth travel down her neck to the soft skin of her throat. Then, with a cry of pain, he pushed her away.

After a moment he said thickly, 'I really am sorry. You don't know how attractive you are, I think. Your innocence and kindness betray you.'

She felt an odd sort of triumph, and an urge almost to laugh. That she, a dirty, tongue-tied farmbrat, could be held in esteem by a man like Michael seemed ridiculous. He thought her innocent – she had known everything before she was six. He thought her beautiful – and that was deceit too. She had learned to dress well, that was all. And if he thought her kind, it was simply that he didn't know what prompted her. She cared for Mr Cooper only partly because she was sorry for him, more to win the good opinion of his wife. He didn't know her and he never would.

She said, 'You've been so good to me, Michael. It was kind of Gabriel to bring me here, but you know him – he doesn't think. You've made me so welcome.'

He chuckled ruefully. 'And then I abuse your youth and your innocence in a car? I'm not usually like this, I do assure you, it's just – from the first you had an effect on me. When I saw you with the sheep. Quite honestly, I'm ashamed of myself.'

'Why? Isn't it normal for men to want women?'

He said nothing. Then, laughing, he managed, 'I'm sorry, my dear, but you've shocked me somewhat. You're so French, so – original. Yes, it is natural for people to be attracted, but we're not animals. We don't mate as the mood takes us, we don't do what we feel. If we did, I've no doubt we'd all be very unhappy.'

Laura leaned back in her seat and looked out at the night sky. The stars were pale against the moonlight. The Milky Way was no more than a mist across the heavens. 'You're so different from Gabriel,' she said.

'He's very young. And to my mind over-indulged. He never learned what it was to do what he didn't like. Or to deny himself, for that matter.'

Laura looked at him. 'You deny yourself too much. You could kiss me again.'

His lips were softer this time. There was more confidence and less desperation. Laura thought how much Gabriel would envy his brother, and almost laughed. A chuckle broke from her mouth to Michael's, and he whispered, 'Do I amuse you so?'

'I was just thinking how much Gabriel would like to be doing this. He'll never understand why it's you and not him.'

'I don't think I understand, for that matter.'

She extended her tongue and traced its tip around his mouth. 'And that's the reason, my dear.'

The lamp was burning in the kitchen when they returned, although no one was up. In the yellow light Laura knew that she and Michael felt the same odd mixture of closeness and embarrassment. They had turned to one another and admitted a need, in one way showing too much and in another not enough. If there was no going back, where did this path lead? Neither knew what the other might expect.

Laura poured herself a glass of water, and lit a candle to take her up to bed. Michael said, 'You wish it had never happened, I suppose?'

She smiled and shook her head. 'No. But you might wish it in the morning. You won't think things, will you?'

'What sort of things?'

He looked puzzled and bemused. Her heart went out to him in a rush of warmth, and she said, 'Oh Michael, won't you kiss me goodnight?'

He came over suddenly, and the water spilled and the candle went out. When, finally, Laura went up the stairs to bed, she floated on clouds.

At breakfast she found it hard to look at him. Fortunately old Mr Cooper was at his most bewildered, and Laura busied herself settling him. His wife said, 'You were very late last night. What time did you come in?'

'Not long after twelve,' said Michael briskly.

'About two hours after it!' said Gabriel. 'Don't tell me you were canoodling with Laura in the car?'

Michael said nothing, but Laura intervened with a cool, 'Don't be silly, Gabriel. We could hardly get away, that's all. Everyone wanted to know about you.'

'What about me?'

She laughed at him. 'Wouldn't you like to know?'

'What about Gabriel?' asked Mrs Cooper snappily. 'If they wanted to know, they could invite him to dine. I don't understand the Fitzalan-Howards. Hot and cold, hot and cold.'

'Dora's in love with him,' said Laura.

Michael said, 'Laura!' in a shocked voice, but Gabriel chuckled.

'Ah, the divine Dora. If only she didn't blush. I think I prefer the iron-clad charms of Mrs Fitch – or even of her horse.'

'Gabriel,' said Michael warningly. 'You're going too far.'

Mrs Cooper said, 'Really, Michael, you can be so stuffy sometimes.'

Mr Cooper said, 'Are there muffins? When are we having tea?'

The men were shearing sheep all Saturday, and even Gabriel

was prevailed upon to help. Laura fetched and carried, tiptoeing through the grease. She found the scene strangely alluring. The men were stripped to the waist, sweat running on chests and shoulders. Gabriel was a soft smooth brown, while Michael's tan ended at elbow and throat, leaving his body pale as milk. Bill Mayes, the foreman, had a belly that bulged over his belt, and muscles gone slack from idleness. Alan, the stockman, not yet thirty, straightened up whenever Laura walked past, and smiled at her. At the first break Michael sent him off into the catching pen and brought Dinah's son from outside, even though he was a recovered consumptive and not strong.

At lunchtime Laura brought cider from the house. Dinah had spent the morning making pies, but in the warmth of the day they had not cooled and dripped unset pork jelly. Michael said, 'I'm so sorry, Laura. Not very elegant fare, I'm afraid.'

'I don't think the girl who stormed one of Bainfield's more popular pubs is all that concerned with elegance,' said Gabriel, licking an oozing runnel from his fingers. 'Are you, Laura?'

She grinned at him. 'There's a time for elegance, and this isn't it. Shall I press your suit, Gab? For the interview?'

He turned away. 'I shouldn't bother. I'm not sure I'm going to go.'

There was a silence. Michael stood staring after him. Then he said, 'Gabriel! Gabriel, come back here and explain yourself!'

Gabriel looked back over a sea of unclipped sheep. 'I'd rather not, if you don't mind. In front of everyone.'

Michael gestured with his shears. 'Can't you ever follow anything through? I thought you wanted to fly! This isn't the end of it. Not by a long way.'

Gabriel turned his back.

But it was Laura who talked to him. When the men had gone home Michael stayed on folding fleeces. Gabriel, reeking of sheep and sweat, went to the pump and Laura followed. She stood watching him shower in icy water, mouth wide, eyes screwed shut, hair in a long blond streak. She picked up the towel and waited until he was done. When he saw her, he grunted. 'Dry my back, would you? I wouldn't normally ask, of course, but I'm sure you've done it before.'

She rubbed without comment. Then, when he took the towel and used it to scrub chest and arms, she said, 'Why won't you go to the interview? Is it because of Michael? Or me?'

He looked at her grimly. 'How perceptive of you. As it happens I'm not all that keen to leave you here with Michael sniffing at your skirts.'

'He's doing no such thing! He – he likes me.'

'Don't fool yourself. All he wants is to cut me out.'

Laura felt cold suddenly, as if she was the one under the pump. 'There can't be anything with you. I told you that. Whether you go away or not, it wouldn't matter and nothing will change.'

Gabriel stared at her. Some part of the day seemed to have charged him with heat, his eyes blazed in his head like fires. She felt the desire, fierce and unexpected, to put her hands on his chest and feel his warmth. Why, oh why, did he attract her so?

'Do you want me to tell him all about you?' he said softly. 'What will he think of you then?'

'I don't want – it isn't fair—'

'If you don't want that, then keep away from him! I won't have it, Laura. I swear that I won't. Not my own brother!'

Laura ducked her head. 'You think I'm not good enough? Why am I not good enough, if you are? We're both the same. What I did you did too.'

'Come off it! You sold your body.'

'Yes. But I sold it to you.'

A light breeze flirted in the grass and skipped into the courtyard. Gabriel's face was losing its rage. He was capable of the wildest swings of mood. He said, 'He won't marry you. You realise that?'

Bewildered she said, 'I don't know. I hadn't thought—'

'Come off it! Of course you had. What a prize that would be. Michael and Gunthwaite in one fell swoop! But this farm needs money and he's got to marry it. Dora Fitzalan-Howard is the preferred candidate. You may have noticed her parents looking keen. Added to which, if it got that far I'd have to tell him about you. And I know how much you'd hate it.'

Laura felt as if a hand was closing around her skull. 'If he asked – I won't let him ask. There won't be anything between me and Michael, so you can go to your interview, Gabriel. You can relax in the knowledge that nothing will be happening behind your back.'

She turned away, but he took two strides and was behind her. She felt his body against hers, his hands on her upper arms pulling her against him. 'Don't you have any gratitude?' he whispered. 'What would it matter? I'll give you money, if you want. Anything. Please, Laura.' The smell of sheep still hung about them both. She felt animal herself, the sweat trickling between her breasts. She reached back and touched him, feeling a slow shudder run through his body. It was as if they were shrouded in the long, tired afternoon.

'Laura? Gabriel?' Michael's voice. She pulled away, seeing Gabriel's hard, hawkish look. She hated him to look like that.

'Michael? I brought Gabriel a towel. Did you want him?'

Michael was pulling on his shirt. He looked rumpled and weary. 'About the interview—'

Gabriel forced a laugh. 'Oh, that. Of course I'm going. Time you learned to take a joke, old man.' He walked abruptly away.

It was raining on Monday. Gabriel wore a soft hat and a mackintosh, but Michael wore his pork-pie trilby and carried an umbrella. Laura laughed at him. 'You look like a farmer! A real one, who can't say "horse".'

Michael looked puzzled. 'Who can't say it? Everyone can!'

'Not round here they can't. They say "oss". "My 'oss 'ates 'ay." And I don't know if that means he can't bear the stuff or if he eats it every day for breakfast.'

Both men laughed, and Mrs Cooper, emerging from the study, said, 'You're dawdling, Michael. You'll make him late and then what? I shouldn't be surprised if you'd rather he didn't join at all and stayed here helping you.'

Michael said, 'I was just going, Mother,' and put up his umbrella to make the dash to the car.

Laura stood at the kitchen window, watching them leave in a slow swish of rubber.

The rain fell continuously, shrouding the road in a watery haze. The wipers struggled but they drove on, despite the poor visibility. They dared not be late. Towards Wakefield in thunder and lightning, the rain hammering as if powered by Thor himself, a stationary car loomed suddenly out of the gloom. Michael swerved to a halt and Gabriel swore vilely. 'You ought to let me drive. Why on earth's the fool stopped there?'

He peered through the window. A man in a mackintosh was struggling to change a wheel. Even from here Gabriel could see that his wheelbrace wasn't up to the job. 'He'll never do it with that thing.'

Michael said, 'We haven't got time to help. And in this weather—'

At that moment the stranded driver looked towards them, rain running in a river from the brim of his hat, his expression a mixture of hope and resignation. Gabriel cursed. 'We ought to do something. Have we got a decent brace?'

'Yes. And a better jack. All right, Gab, if you don't mind turning up like a drowned rat. I suppose it's the decent thing.'

As they got out the stranger said, 'I hope you don't mind all this rain?'

'You've got a duff wheelbrace,' said Gabriel, pulling their own from the boot. 'And you shouldn't have jacked it without loosening the nuts first. It's easier.'

'I was trying to hurry,' said the stranger. 'It's my sister's car and the tools are lousy.'

'We'll soon have you right,' said Michael. He lowered the inadequate jack while Gabriel fitted the wheelbrace. It was a long-established routine; they were used to flats, taking their old car over flint track and country lane. But the worn brace had chewed the nuts and they were hard to turn. Gabriel wrestled with them, rain pouring down his neck, the scene lit at intervals by white sheets of lightning. At last the wheel was off.

'Go and sit in the car, Gab,' said Michael. 'You'll look a sight. I can manage from now on.'

'No. I can't get any wetter. Got the wheel?'

In their haste to be finished a nut fell in a puddle. A bus swished by, dousing them in water. The last remaining creases in Gabriel's trousers dropped away. When they were done the stranger said, 'Thanks. Thanks very much. I couldn't have managed on my own. Are you going far?'

'Only to Leeds,' said Gabriel. 'Interview.'

'Really? You shouldn't have stopped.'

'Perhaps you'll do the same for me one day. And you should get your sister some decent tools,' advised Gabriel, already running towards the car.

'I will. Take my advice and scrub up at The Queen's. And thanks again.'

Michael had already started the engine. He took off his sodden hat and tossed it on to the back seat. 'Look at us both. Look at you.'

Gabriel said, 'It doesn't matter. I doubt they'll take me whatever I look like.'

'I thought you were a sure thing. You said—'

'I know what I said. But let's face it, Mike, I'm not the type. No university, expelled from school, that sort of thing.'

Michael slapped a hand on his brother's wet knee. 'Don't throw in the towel yet, Gab! They might be looking for greasy drowned rats. You can't tell with these things. Tell you what, why don't we stop at The Queen's? We should have time.'

As they drove into town the rain was easing. Michael drove slowly, in case they got lost, and people scurried across the road in front of him. The hotel was near the station, very large and very smart, so much so that they were stared at in disapproval by the commissionaire. The foyer was wrapped in expensive silence.

'My God,' said Michael softly. They left wet footprints across the carpets on their way to the cloakroom, and at last found warm towels and soap. After Gunthwaite it seemed the most sinful luxury.

But even the facilities at The Queen's could do little to eradicate grease from Gabriel's cuff, or restore the creases in his trousers.

They went back to the bar. Michael was drinking whisky, but Gabriel declined. He didn't want to smell like a distillery. His confidence had collapsed completely and he said, 'Laura was right. I'll never get in.'

'She's right about a lot of things.'

'Oh, for Christ's sake, Mike!' flared Gabriel. 'You ought to watch yourself, it's no use falling for the girl. She's a lot tougher than she looks.'

'I should think she'd need to be. I know she worked in your club.'

Gabriel drew in his breath. 'Tell you that, did she?'

'I know she hasn't a brother. Just an aunt in a nursing home in

France.' He met his brother's wide blue eyes. 'I know all about her, you see.'

Gabriel got out a cigarette and tried to light it. The packet was damp. He threw it in the ashtray and said, 'There's more to Laura than that, you know. I met her when she was desperate for a job, fresh from France and all she could get was maiding. She was damned good, ran the kitchens, straightened up the bar, that sort of thing. And softened up the customers, of course. I bought her some very sleek dresses, everything showing that could. I tell you, Mike, you're not the only man to fall for what looks like youth and innocence. It's glued on top of a very old soul.'

Michael turned his whisky glass in his hand. 'Is this true? Or another of your tales?'

'Quite true,' said Gabriel. 'You should see her dance. Bends like a willow. God knows what she was in France.'

'She's lived on a farm,' said Michael. 'That's obvious.'

'See her in town, and you'd think she'd never seen grass. I'm telling you this for your own good, Mike. Laura's never what she seems.'

He should have said this before, he thought. Before Michael had time to form his own opinion. The tension of the moment, the strain of the day, seemed to make honesty – or something like it – almost possible.

It was time for the interview. Gabriel shot his cuffs and left, giving his brother a grim smile. 'Good luck,' said Michael.

'I bet you really mean that,' replied his brother. 'Anything to get me out of the way.'

When he had gone, Michael sat on in the bar. He ordered another whisky, and let his mind experience the rare luxury of peace. No work to do, no voices at his elbow, just minutes of space in which to think. Gabriel had brought Laura home intending to sleep with her, no doubt. If she was the sort of girl he wanted his brother to believe she was, he'd surely have succeeded. Instead, she gave her kisses to his older, duller brother, and lit a fire in the dark, peaty depths of his soul.

Michael had never known a woman. At haytime one year when he was about eighteen, a girl from the village had stayed in the fields at dusk and told him to put his hand up her skirt. He had touched hair and heat and tight wet thighs, and then she pulled down her bodice to let breasts like udders hang free. But it got no further. When she pulled at his clothes and touched him his body disgraced itself. She had flounced off home in a huff, and he was thankful. In the calm of the evening he knew she only wanted him to put her in the family way, and make Gunthwaite pay.

Since then there had been nothing. It was beneath him to seduce girls from the village, and out of the question to suggest it to someone like Dora Fitzalan-Howard. Gabriel had no such scruples, of course, and Michael well knew of his afternoons with Alicia Allenby, his mother's last friend. But for Michael there was no one. The Fitches invited him to dine and introduced him to horsy girls, but usually Gabriel was there to entrance them, and besides, he found strange women difficult. The more they excited him, the less he could talk. Until Laura.

She was the easiest of people to get along with, he thought fondly. She seemed to know what he wanted to say and helped him to say it. When she seemed shy and uncertain his heart went out to her, although he knew that in an instant she could change to a hard diamond sparkle. Yet she had nothing and no one, she was utterly alone, forced to earn her living as best she could. Michael loved her courage, loved her innocence, rejoiced in her rejection of Gabriel. Sitting there, in damp clothes in a dark bar, he acknowledged that love.

Gabriel breezed in an hour later. 'Mike! You must be tight as a newt. Let's have lunch and some claret, we've got to celebrate.'

Michael sat up. 'I take it they liked you?'

Gabriel rubbed his hands together. 'Not at first, no. "What was it about your character, Mr Cooper, that made three of our finest schools find you too much for them?" That sort of thing. But one of the men on the board was the chap with the flat this morning! Came out strongly for me, said they needed adventurous young men with a mechanical turn of mind. So I'm in!'

'My God!' Michael gripped his brother's arms. 'My God, what a stroke of luck!'

'Fate if you ask me. Aren't you glad I'm getting out from under your feet? I'm starving, do let's eat. They're going to write and tell me what course I'm on. Pilot Officer Cooper, that's me!'

He was so young and so exuberant. Michael felt a pang of envy. He was condemned to the farm, to work and worry and responsibility, while Gabriel, with all his gifts, could court adventure. But then he thought of Laura, and the envy fell away. Yes, it was a day to celebrate. They were both within reach of their dreams.

Chapter Six

Laura was in the garden. Dinah and Mrs Cooper were discussing Gabriel's packing, and Laura was deputed to supervise Mr Cooper in the sunshine outside. She took a basket and busied herself tidying the few clumps of herbs in the border, a tangle of sage, a riot of mint and a few spikes of chives. There should be more, she thought, with one eye on Mr Cooper's wanderings and the other on her work. There was no excuse for the absence of tarragon or fennel, parsley or thyme.

Mr Cooper settled on the garden bench. Laura relaxed, and thought of Gabriel. He was making her uneasy. Just then, he stepped on to the lawn.

She said, 'I thought you were busy with the car.'

'That can wait. I wanted to talk to you.'

'Oh. What about?' She shifted uneasily, digging her trowel deep into the soil.

'About what you intend to do.'

She looked up at him. He was against the sun, his face shadowed, his hair surrounded by a halo of light.

'I didn't mean you to stay for ever,' he said.

She got up. 'I know what you meant. I'm sorry.'

'Are you? I doubt it. But I've got other things to do now. Only you can't stay.'

She turned the trowel in her hands. If she went into Bainfield she might get work – but not after the incident in the pub. Perhaps in Leeds? But she quailed at the thought of asking Mrs Cooper for a reference. The woman didn't like her. She hardly liked anyone.

'Has your mother told you to make me leave?'

'Not yet, no. You've been so cunning, helping with Father, wrapping Michael round your thumb. You're very good at getting what you want, it seems to me.'

Laura said, 'Better than you, you mean? I should be. I take care to consider other people.'

'Well, you don't consider me! And I've done more for you than anyone. Laura, you've taken me for a fool!'

It was petulant, and sounded silly. She let a smile cross her face, and when he saw it his hand snapped out and struck her. Hard enough to hurt but not to mark. A bully's slap.

Shock brought tears to her eyes. Old Mr Cooper got up from his bench and said, 'Whatever's this? Striking a lady? I won't have it, I say.'

Laura turned to him. 'He didn't. It was a bee. Sit down and rest.'

'A bee? We don't have bees. You don't strike bees.'

'Sit down, sir, do. In a moment we'll go in for tea.'

He calmed and sat down once again. Gabriel muttered, 'Don't expect an apology. I don't apologise to you.'

'Or to anyone, I suppose?' said Laura. 'Go away, Gabriel. You're nothing but a child.'

He was behind her, his hands on her waist, his face in her hair. 'I'm sorry. God, I'm sorry! You make me mad. Why won't you let me touch you? It isn't much!'

'I'm different now. You wouldn't ask Dora Fitzalan-Howard, so why ask me?'

'I want no one but you. God, but you're exciting!'

His hands moved down to the hollows of her hips. Laura took in her breath. As the interview board had said, he had mechanic's hands. He could make any machine run sweetly, she thought. Hamfisted men could never make good lovers, nor eager ones, nor stupid ones, nor men in a hurry. She felt a softening, deep inside, as if heart and lungs and veins and arteries were dissolving into a viscous, golden pool.

Mr Cooper got up from his seat. 'I've had enough of you, young man,' he said belligerently. 'Leave Rosalind alone. Be off with you. Get away! More of this and I'll have you taken in charge.'

'Yes,' said Laura slowly. 'Be off with you.'

'Come to the barn this evening,' whispered Gabriel. 'At nine.'

'I can't. Everyone would suspect.'

'Say you're going to bed. If you come, I won't make you leave Gunthwaite.'

'You can't anyway.'

'Can't I? The truth is such a very dangerous weapon.'

His hands moved to her back, slid down to caress, pushing her summer dress into the cleft of her bottom. Involuntarily her legs parted an inch, and his hand was there. She gasped. She felt like a virgin once again, and yet it was all so well remembered. If Henri were here, would she deny him too? Henri would never permit the act of love to be used as blackmail. She stepped out of Gabriel's embrace.

But the evening seemed terribly long. When dinner was over, an everyday meal of overcooked shepherd's pie and stringy runner beans, Michael and Gabriel went to walk outside. Laura stood at the window watching, wondering if they were talking about her. Once, Michael glanced towards the house.

Gabriel was saying, 'You're going to have to be firm with Laura, you know. Given half a chance she'll stay here for ever. It's a terrible imposition for Mother, don't you think? I expected two weeks at the most.'

'Mother seems to find her a great help,' said Michael.

'Yes, she's good at making herself useful. Bit of a schemer, if you ask me. Honestly, Mike, I'm a bit anxious about leaving you alone with her. You know nothing about women.'

Michael laughed. He could see exactly where Gabriel was headed. He put his hand on his brother's shoulder. 'Don't worry, old chap. I'll see to things. I won't let all this drift on. You just get yourself settled at this aerodrome and let me worry about Laura. She's doing no harm, you know.'

'But we know nothing about her! She could be anyone. A thief.'

'You said she was absolutely honest at the club. I remember distinctly.'

'Did I say that? We discovered nothing, I grant you. But really, old chap—'

'Leave it.' Michael's hand tightened its grip. He wasn't laughing now. 'I'm not a fool, so don't treat me as one. Laura's future needs to be decided. Point taken.'

There was no more to be said. Gabriel walked restlessly to and fro on the gravel paths, the dusk gathering in the shadows of the walls and the depths of the hedges. Night-scented flowers were opening their blooms, and the honeysuckle wafted a last breath

198

into the cooling evening air. He was suddenly assailed by the beauty of this place. If things were different – if it was not Michael's – he knew he might love it.

It was almost nine. Gabriel said, 'I think I'll turn in early. Big day tomorrow.'

Michael was surprised. It wasn't like Gabriel ever to plan ahead; he had expected him to stay up drinking until dawn. But he said, 'All right, old chap. I'll call you at six. You go in. I'll walk down to Long Meadow, there's a heifer due to calve.'

It was quite dark when he returned. The cow was peaceful and wouldn't calve that night, but he had stood in the gloom while the nightingales sang. He felt a little melancholy. Gabriel was at last growing up. Now that he was settling to something, he would be the son his mother would speak of with pride. To his surprise, as he turned the corner by the barn, he saw Laura. She stopped at once. 'Michael! Hello. I thought – I'm just going in.'

'Lovely evening, isn't it? I was looking at a cow. You should have come, the nightingales were singing.'

Laura hesitated. In the darkness her eyes shone like glass. 'I wish I'd known. Will you take me another night?'

He took her hands, and they were warm and dry. 'Of course. On a special night. We'll listen together.'

Gabriel fastened the buttons of his tunic, watching himself in the glass. He looked every inch a flyer, he thought. He even had the required casual flick of his cigarette. He posed for a moment, thinking how much easier it would be if all one had to do was look the part. Sadly, it wasn't enough.

There were approximately three types of student on the course; those to whom flying came as naturally as breathing, those who were acquiring the skill by dint of ceaseless practice, and those who could practise 'til they were blue in the face and still couldn't land without a full-scale fire alert and an apoplectic instructor. Gabriel, to his amazed humiliation, was one of the last.

He knew full well that but for his empathy with engines he'd be off the course by now. They talked about him in the mess, falling silent when he came in. 'Like a bloody vicar in a bathtub,' Squadron Leader Jenkins had drawled, secure in the knowledge that he himself might have been born knowing how to land a Moth. Gabriel burned with rage and shame. For the first time in his life he was exerting himself at something he wanted to do, only to fail. What would they say at home?

He went into the mess and ate bacon and egg, forcing it down. He wasn't hungry, but if that showed it would look bad. They'd think he cared. The food sat unpleasantly at the bottom of his chest, and he began to feel sick. It added a new anxiety. To crash was one thing, but throwing up would make him a laughing stock. He thought about a brandy, but the thought made him greener still.

'All right, Cooper?' Jenkins, forcing a smile. 'Get your togs on, won't you? Bit of a breeze but nothing untoward. Give her a punt around, show us what you can do.'

'Yes, sir.' Pointless bloody exercise. They were finished with him, he knew that already. This flight was a mere formality.

The faces of the rest of his course swam at the corners of his vision. Everyone would be watching. There was no greater amusement on the airfield than watching someone balls it up, and this time there was the added piquancy of the final fling. He went for his helmet and flying jacket, knowing that he looked like Biggles himself. He felt utterly hollow.

His mechanic greeted him with sympathy. 'Do your best, sir. Remember, she don't like sharp turns. Planes is like women, they like everything soft and slow.'

He thought at once of Laura. She could have told him he'd be useless at this. Michael would be better. Where was the justice when his brother couldn't tell a piston from a crankshaft, yet drove with smoothness and rhythm, learning in a tenth of the time it had taken Gabriel? Did he make love like that too? Was he even now making love to Laura?

He was distracted, and sat on his map. The mechanic fished it out and smoothed it for him. 'Keep an eye on the field, that's the best plan, sir. For God's sake, don't get lost. No need to go far, just three times round and a bump each time. Nothing to it.'

It was nice of the bloke to be concerned. He'd give him a decent tip when he left, and he'd buy a few rounds. He wasn't sneaking away like a criminal. What then, though? Laura was right, he should have taken the club more seriously. He had thought it a stopgap kind of thing.

The propeller swung and the engine started with a roar. They were flagging him away, and he tried to concentrate on all that he knew. It was little enough, God knows, just a matter of hands and feet working together and in unison. He lifted his hand to the mechanic in a perfect insouciant wave, gunned the engine and sent the plane buzzing across the grass. What speed was he doing? To hell with that – if he crashed the thing and died, did it matter?

He drew back on the stick. The plane rose like a dragonfly from the surface of a pool. Gabriel allowed himself a grin. That would have impressed them. But of course, it was landings he couldn't hack. It was always pretty well all right in the air, although he'd once done something – neither he nor the instructor knew what – and caused a spin. A little too eager with the rudder, perhaps. He tried a gentle turn or two, left and right. Up here the sky was a perfect blue, shading to white near the sun. Was it time to land? He looked down. The airfield was nowhere to be seen.

A chuckle broke from him. Damn it all! Lost, as well as everything. He swung the plane to the right, reaching for the map and searching for somewhere, anywhere, for something he recognised. Was the tank full? Like hell it was! A few gallons, just to see him through the test. They didn't want him crashing in an inferno. So soon he'd be falling out of the sky. Marvellous.

A train passed beneath him, smoke drawing a long fluffy line across the ground. The railway. Thank God. He turned the map a couple of times, lining it up. Top left then, for the airfield. He turned the plane – no spin, no nothing, a good turn – and a moment later the ground unrolled like a sheet of drawing paper, with the airfield at its edge. Even from here he could see the line of concerned figures gazing up at the sky. He chuckled again, putting the trees on one side and the huts on the other. All he had to do now was find the ground. The time he'd dropped the last six feet like a stone had not gone unremarked.

The wind gusted across the field, sending the little plane up and away. Damn! He'd forgotten the wind! If he'd looked at the sock he'd have seen how stiff it was. He'd overshoot, they'd laugh themselves witless. Like hell they would! He put the stick down, left rudder, hard, correct, straighten, pray for no gusts.

There was a bump as he touched grass. He let the plane run for a few yards, opened the throttle and took off again. One down. Two to go.

On the next pass the line of figures had thickened to a huddle. Load of bloody optimists, he thought, and came in fast. Let them see a crash then. He'd bend this bloody plane into a bloody coathanger. Straight and level, watching for wind, thwarting it. Touch, throttle, go. He looked down to see the roofs of the huts passing below his wheels. Brilliant. Two down.

This time he made his circuit wide and high. The wind in the struts made a noise like singing in a cathedral, heard from a long way away. Perhaps he would leave tonight after all, make for London, see if Peter Kennedy wanted to have another go at the Zambesi. He felt a spark of anger. There'd be war soon, no doubt of it. Was he to spend his time in a nightclub?

The airfield was a green square on a patchwork quilt. All at once he wanted it over, finished, he wanted to rush at his fate. He put the plane into a dive, heard the rising screech of the wind. The engine stalled if the fuel supply was challenged, he thought. He pulled back and levelled out, thinking they ought to find ways to keep fuel coming whatever the angle of flight. Trees, huts, a positive congregation of people waiting to see the crash. The grass of the field was striking the wheels like rattling stones. Half an inch and he was down. Finished. Flying career done.

When he went into the mess Squadron Leader Jenkins was there with two glasses of whisky. He gestured to Gabriel to sit down. 'Have a scotch, Cooper. Jolly good show. You took a long time to show what you could do, but it seems you have. You've passed.'

Gabriel kept his face very still. Not one flicker of pleasure or relief would he show. He sat down and took the drink. 'Cheers.'

Laura looked through the letters on the hall stand. The vase of roses she had picked only yesterday had already showered them with petals. The deepest pink, like a sunset; like a cow's tongue. She grinned to herself and Michael, passing through, said, 'What are you laughing at?'

'I was thinking that the rose petals look like cows' tongues. Isn't that dreadful?'

'Commendable, I should say. You'll be a farmer before you're done. Anything for me?'

'Bills, only.'

'Isn't that Gabriel's writing?'

She glanced at the scrawled envelope in her hand. 'Yes. But it's for me.'

He was surprised, but said nothing. There was another for her too, in Madame Bonacieux's italics. Madame wrote like a very small woman, Laura always thought. She went into the dining room, where the air held the stillness of disuse, and opened the letter from Madame:

I am sorry to report that your dear friend Sophie is once again unwell. Her chest is weak, as you know. The nuns insist on their money (that's what the world is coming to nowadays) and as always I don't refuse. It is my belief that we are here to help each other and I do my best. Business is poor, I'm afraid, and I cannot afford all the expense, but I have told the nuns that all will be paid the moment I hear from you.

Yours in expectation,
Hildegarde Bonacieux

Laura drummed her fingers on the dusty table. She didn't know what to think. According to Madame, Sophie had been in hospital over a year now, with the bills increasing all the time. It seemed a little fishy, to say the least. And yet – suppose it was true? Suppose Laura didn't send the money, and the nuns threw Sophie back on the streets? What would there be for her but pain and misery and a shameful death? Laura shivered, as if she too felt the clammy cold of an upstairs room in a rat-infested house. Anything but that.

She made some swift calculations. She hoarded her money so carefully against the day when she would have to leave Gunthwaite and start again, but it was dwindling nonetheless. There were stockings to buy, and soap, pins, make-up, a small birthday present for Dinah and some handkerchiefs for old Mr Cooper who seemed to have nothing but rags. Now Madame Bonacieux again. This would almost exhaust her little store. What would she do when the next letter came? What would happen then?

She would send the money, of course. Perhaps Sophie was ill again because she hadn't paid enough before? But she was being too trusting; didn't she of all people know what Madame was like? This time she would ask for a receipt of some kind, from the hospital. She sat absently down in a chair and opened her other letter.

Dear Laura,
I thought I should let you know that I've passed the basic flying course. I wonder if you'd tell the family for me? It was more or less a formality (rumour has it they passed a three-legged dog last year), but it's nice to have it behind me. The thing is, they're sending us to East Anglia for a bit, a few months at least. More training and so on. Would you break it gently to Mother for me? I don't want her getting in a state about no leave.

Everyone's very tense and in a bit of a hurry round here, because of Hitler of course. The news is dire. One of the chaps here has relatives in Munich. He thinks they may have been killed. Jews, of course. The whole thing's a farce.

What are your plans, may I ask? Unless I hear in the next few days I shall have to write to Michael. I've given you every chance, Laura. Now it's up to you. Yours with patience running out,

G.

She folded the pages very quickly and stuffed them back into the envelope. How like Gabriel to ask her to do something for him and then to threaten her. If it wasn't for him she'd be happy, she thought. He was like the bad fairy at a christening, holding the promise of disaster above her head. What would she do if he told Michael? Perhaps he wouldn't. He'd tell his mother, and have done.

The thought was terrible. She imagined Mrs Cooper telling Dinah, or Mrs Fitzalan-Howard, and the word travelling as far as Bainfield where they'd say, 'You could tell, really. I mean, what sort of woman goes into a pub?'

She went out of the room and found Michael lurking in the hall, waiting for her. 'Any news? Sorry to pry, but Gabriel's the world's worst letter writer. I thought perhaps something had happened. He might want you to tell us.'

'You know him very well.'

Michael grimaced. 'I hope so. Come on, what is it?'

She relayed the news about the flying. Then she added, 'He wrote to me because – well, he wants to know when I'm going to leave. And really, I must. You've been so kind.'

'No, we haven't. You've earned your keep, you know. Mother doesn't say, but you've been invaluable. An extra pair of hands.'

She smiled dutifully. She'd been foolish to stay so long, perhaps. But Gunthwaite was insidious, wrapping you in its age and calm. The routines of farm and house and garden seemed to be timeless and everlasting. Soon it would be harvest, and the barns would overflow with corn and potatoes and apples. She had to be gone by then. The longer she waited, the more bitter it would be to go.

'Do you want to leave?' asked Michael suddenly, as she opened the kitchen door.

She glanced up at him. 'You know I don't.'

'And I don't think that I can bear it if you do.'

She put her hand against his chest. 'Michael—'

He said throatily, 'You know how I feel about you. Surely?'

They stood quite still. In the kitchen Dinah and Mrs Cooper were talking in a barbed way about pastry. 'Hot hands never make a good crust,' said Dinah, with the smug voice of success. Laura's mind divided its thoughts. What was the pastry disaster? What did Michael mean?

'I suppose you'd rather have Gabriel?' he whispered thickly.

'Gabriel? What?'

'More your type. Lively and adventurous. I know how dull I must seem to you. I can only offer you dullness. That's the trouble, isn't it? I must always be here and always be dull.'

She stepped away from the door, letting it close with a soft sigh. 'I don't mind about dullness. What do you mean?'

'He's asked you to wait, hasn't he? I'm sorry to embarrass you like this. You needn't leave Gunthwaite, you know, despite everything.'

She took a long breath. Michael's face was drawn down with misery.

She put her hand up to his mouth and traced the sad, dipping lines. 'Gabriel hates me,' she said. 'He thinks I'm tricking you. Because of my past.'

'Because you worked in his filthy club? I don't care about that. Laura – Laura – I don't want to ask what I know you'll refuse. You'll feel you have to go.'

The tumult in her head became suddenly very still. Was this how it happened? The rescue? If time would but continue for a moment more, she would have safety in her hands. She said, 'Ask me anyway. Please.'

'Will you marry me?'

She closed her eyes. She couldn't bear him to see her relief. Let him not know what this meant to her, let him never know. Nothing she could ever do would repay him. She opened her eyes. 'Yes,' she whispered. 'Darling Michael. Yes.'

Chapter Seven

The big, stone, foursquare house was as cold as charity. In the dining room a coal fire burned, but it was possible, in the evening, to see steam above your soup bowl and not know if it was the soup or your breath. Gabriel thought longingly of the kitchen at Gunthwaite, warmed by its range. Here, amidst the dykes and fens of Norfolk, warmth was a distant memory.

He shared his room with a yawning, drawling public schoolboy who had joined the RAF despite his army ancestry and was in danger of disinheritance. Since he was due to become lord of several thousands of Scottish acres, Gabriel was surprised to say the least, but as Philip said, 'My God, Gab, I'd have to live in a house even colder than this! No thanks, old man.'

They got on famously. They pooled funds to buy a motorbike and sidecar, and racketed the lanes terrorising horses and children. They found an inn on a lonely road, surrounded by birds and flooded acres, and spent the evenings by a fire, drinking whisky and talking to the locals. The flyers were thought to be strange, to say the least. They became consciously dashing.

Their presence in so remote a place was something of a mystery at first. But soon it was apparent that development was afoot. In belated response to German re-armament, Britain was researching a new plane. Gabriel, Philip and their colleagues were cannon-fodder in the cause of progress. Young and inexperienced, they were unimportant enough to see if it would fly.

For the first month, Gabriel was in imminent danger of being grounded. He seemed a hopeless case, unable to adapt to even the smallest modification in the aircraft he usually flew. His saving grace, and in the beginning it was little enough, was his ability to produce lucid criticism.

'At least he can tell you why he can't fly the bloody thing,' said Jenkins to his adjutant. 'On the rare occasions he links hand to brain, he's good. The rest of the time he's bloody dire.'

He went to the window and watched Philip Lansbury make a textbook landing. Good flyers weren't rare, that was the thing. Good mechanics were like hens' teeth. If he wanted to keep Cooper's mechanical insight, the boy just had to learn to fly. So he was tolerated. He improved, but slightly. If he was to stay he would have to improve a great deal more.

All in all it was an intense few weeks and it was some time before Gabriel noticed the lack of letters. But then, he wrote so few himself that he could easily understand others following suit, although his mother usually wrote once a fortnight, at least. He thought of Laura. He'd written to her, but she hadn't replied.

He went to the telephone in the icy hall. It stood on a desk, in full sight and hearing of anyone passing through. He picked it up and swung the handle for the operator, who as usual was busy elsewhere. He snapped at her when at last she answered, which made her less than helpful. He apologised, explaining that his call home was urgent. Could she place it for him? Please? Now? 'Well, Mr Cooper,' she said, clicking her knitting needles audibly. 'We'll see what we can do.'

It was Michael who answered the telephone. The operator intoned, 'I have a trunk call for you, from Mr Gabriel Cooper, in Norfolk.'

'At last,' said Michael, and then, 'Gabriel? Gabriel? Are you all right?'

Gabriel said, 'Yes, I think so. Has everyone given up writing letters in Gunthwaite? I've heard nothing for weeks.'

'You damn' fool, we haven't got your address,' said Michael. 'We've been trying to get in touch for ages. Didn't they forward anything?'

'No. Not a word. Send it to the King's Lynn Post Office, that should reach me. Look, could Dinah put up some bacon and stuff and post it? Everything's a bit spartan here, freezing cold and not enough to eat.'

'Sounds like boarding school again,' said Michael. 'How's the flying?'

'Brilliant,' lied Gabriel. 'Just the ticket. How's Laura?'

There was a silence. Nothing could be heard but the clicking of the operator's needles as she listened in. At last Michael said, 'Actually Laura and I have decided to get married.'

Gabriel felt the blood drain from his cheeks. When he spoke his lips felt stiff and inflexible. 'You utter, bloody fool!' he burst out. 'She's trapped you. The little French bitch just waggled her arse in your face and that was it!'

'Really!' broke in the operator. 'This is a public line.'

'And a private call, so please mind your own business,' snapped Gabriel. 'Michael, you've no idea what she's like.'

Michael said steadily, 'I know all that I need. I'm sorry, Gabriel, I knew you'd take it badly. I hoped my letter would explain. Remember, this is still your home and you're always welcome in it. But I won't hear a word against Laura. She's made me very happy.'

'I bet she has!' yelled Gabriel. 'Do you think she'd look at you twice if it wasn't for Gunthwaite? Do you think she'd care? You've put yourself in the hands of the hardest, most corrupt, most conniving—'

The telephone went dead. Michael had hung up.

When Gabriel turned round he saw Squadron Leader Jenkins watching him.

'Sorry, Cooper,' he said. 'We could hear you shouting in the dining room. Trouble at home?'

Gabriel nodded. 'My brother's engaged to marry a French whore. Would you believe it? A whore!'

Jenkins looked perturbed, but not about Gabriel's news. He thought the strain of flying might have sent the lad off his head. 'Come and have a scotch,' he said encouragingly.

Gabriel said, 'You don't believe me and neither will he. If you saw her you'd believe it still less. She's after the money, that's all. Desperate for it. He's a good bloke, Michael, but he knows nothing about women. She'll rob him and cheat him. It's all she knows.'

Jenkins took out his cigarette case and offered it. Gabriel took one blindly. 'I take it you liked her yourself?'

'What? Me?' Gabriel grimaced. 'I might like her, but she's

not the sort a man marries. Not if your name's Cooper anyway. She's deceived him, you see, everything about her's false. Once she's got him she'll show her true colours.'

Jenkins clicked his lighter, first for Gabriel and then for himself. He said, 'How about some leave at the end of the month? We can only spare you for a couple of days, but it might help.'

'Thank you, sir.' Gabriel smiled wanly. 'You never know.'

Laura looked up as Michael came into the kitchen. He saw her strained expression and smiled encouragingly. 'As you might expect,' he said, 'Gabriel's less than pleased.'

'I said as much.' Mrs Cooper was sorting apples for winter store. She rubbed one briskly on her skirt. 'You can refuse to listen to me, but Gabriel won't stand for that. I've told you before, Michael, you're letting everyone down!'

'I'm sorry,' he said to Laura. 'I have asked her not to say these things.'

Mrs Cooper flared, 'You know we need money! You were supposed to marry Dora Fitzalan-Howard!'

'Who wouldn't have me in a thousand years. She's a child, Mother, and she wants Gabriel. Doesn't he deserve her more than me?'

It was a subtle stroke. Mrs Cooper bridled and turned away.

Laura said, 'It would be so nice if they did marry, wouldn't it? Gabriel would have something at last.'

Beginning to mollify, Mrs Cooper said, 'I'm glad you see it. These trusts are so unfair. Gabriel doesn't get a thing!'

Michael put his arm around Laura's shoulders. 'He can have Dora and her fortune. I'll have my girl any day.' He pressed a light kiss to her forehead.

Mr Cooper said, 'You young men nowadays! Poor Rosalind. All these young men.'

'There's only one, Mr Cooper,' said Laura hastily.

'Nonsense! So many. All the time. One of them even struck her.'

'What?' Michael turned perplexed eyes from one to the other.

Laura shook her head pityingly, and felt ashamed. Poor old man. He was lost enough without casting doubt on his few stabs at coherence.

For the next few days she awaited the post with trepidation. Each morning at ten the postman came creaking along on his bicycle, taking an age up the potholed drive. Suppose Michael came out of the barn and saw him? She hovered in the orchard, pretending to look for windfalls, her nerves like frayed string. She was so close to happiness. Surely it wouldn't end now?

The day the letter came she knew it even before Tom Gill got off his bike. The knowledge was there, in her breast, as if she had swallowed a stone. The familiar hand.

'One for Mr Michael,' said Tom, handing it over. 'Nowt for you today, Miss. Waiting for those letters from over yonder, I expect?'

'From where?' Laura clutched Michael's letter bemusedly.

'From France! Them letters you get. Brings it all back, it do. The war, like. Frenchie stamps all the time.'

He was hoping for a cup of tea, but Laura didn't offer. Her mind was in a turmoil, thoughts speeding by so fast she couldn't catch them. She retreated, back into the orchard, amongst the smell of ripe fruit. The ground was thick with leaves and rotting plums. She went on until she was hidden in the trees, and looked again at the letter. Should she open it? Dare she? Michael might know.

She tried to concentrate and think logically. People hated to look foolish. At school, when Anabel rejected her, it had been that. Only that? It must have been! When this all came out Michael was going to look a fool. He'd say she'd betrayed him, he'd throw her out. He wouldn't see there was nothing she could do. If only she could talk to someone. If only there was one person in all the world who could be trusted.

But the letter, the letter! She couldn't concentrate. Could she open it and Michael not know? She tugged gently at the flap, but it did not rise. Perhaps she could steam it over a kettle, but not in front of Dinah or Mrs Cooper, one of whom was always in the kitchen. She felt an hysterical urge to scream. To hand Michael this letter would be the same as shooting herself. And she didn't want to die. She was crying in short, harsh breaths. Why didn't Gabriel die, why didn't he crash in a plane and burn to nothing? That time with him was so short and she remembered it so little. A boy, jerking inside her, grunting like a pig. An image came back to her, and she put her hand up to her eyes. She could see him still, struggling with the *préservatif*. Why did she think of that now?

So much had happened since. So many men. A room in Montmartre, and a disqualified doctor scraping her out. Gabriel knew so little about her, and yet it was enough. Once Michael knew she'd be done for. She looked at the letter. How foolish of her to believe she could marry Michael before Gabriel told. She had been deceiving herself for weeks, her happiness thinner than the skin on a rotten apple. She trod on one and watched its brown insides erupt on to the grass. She knew that what must happen was more than she could bear. She went out of the orchard, into the barn and gave Michael the letter.

He said nothing all day. Laura was in a state of suspended misery. Had he read the letter? How much did it say? After lunch she went into Michael's study, a chilly room stacked with papers and books, to see if the letter was there. She couldn't find it. He had it with him still.

Finally, at eight that night, when Dinah had gone home and Mrs Cooper was at last taking her husband up to bed, they were alone. Laura took the tongs and put more coal on the range fire, and took a pan and refilled the side boiler. She saw that her hands were quite steady. Did none of her anguish show?

Michael said, 'I didn't think he'd take it quite so hard.'

Laura tried to speak, but her voice failed at the first attempt. She tried again. 'What does he say?'

'Nothing interesting. A lot of stuff about your character, things he can't possibly know. I wonder about this flying stuff, actually. He's a clever sort of chap, but it could be too much for him. After all, we've got Father.'

'Are you saying he's mad?'

'I assure you, darling, it doesn't sound sane. And there is a family problem.'

She gestured furiously. 'Your father's old. It's age, nothing else. Gabriel's quite ordinary, he – he has a lot of prejudices. Like the Germans with the Jews.'

'But you're not Jewish! You're French. And more English than French, it seems to me. Is it jealousy, do you think? Just that?'

Laura struggled to speak. 'It must be,' she whispered. 'I thought it was just that I was – you know – one of those nightclub women. He thought I was a woman you could buy. And when he found I wasn't for sale, he invited me here. And then I was even more out of his reach.'

Michael was standing behind her chair. 'My darling,' he whispered. 'My dear one. Don't think about unpleasant things. Gabriel's one of those men who seem to need a woman, who can't survive without that outlet. He's always been that way. And he can't resign himself to knowing that he won't ever have you. Knowing that I will.'

He knelt behind her chair, and pressed his face into her neck. She sat very still. Michael believed nothing that Gabriel had said. He believed what he wanted to be true. That she was a virgin, from first to last.

'Will you write to Gabriel?' she asked.

He mouthed her skin. 'Yes. Yes, I will. And we'll be married as soon as we can, while he's away. It's kinder. Better. When he comes back and finds it all done, he'll come to terms.'

Relief, and a sense of God's benison, flooded through her like a tide.

Suddenly every day was a delight. Michael insisted that she go shopping and buy clothes, although she couldn't imagine what she would need. They were to be married in Gunthwaite village church. Michael drove Laura and his mother to Leeds and told them he would meet them in a tea shop at four, when he would expect everything to be done.

The two women, left alone, eyed each other warily. 'I don't know where all this money's supposed to come from,' said Mrs Cooper testily.

'I don't need much,' said Laura. But the humility in her own voice flicked her into irritation. If Mrs Cooper had her way Laura would be married in rags. She owed it to Michael to look pretty for him – more than that, to look beautiful. He was giving her a home, security, love – everything she had ever wanted. She caught sight of herself in a shop window; a neat, ordinary girl in a coat that had seen very much better days. Michael deserved better than that on his arm.

She said, 'Of course, Michael's wife is bound to need things I haven't even thought of. Afternoon dresses, for paying calls. Tailored things for town. And a wedding dress, of course.

Something I can use later when we entertain.'

Mrs Cooper said, 'I wasn't aware that you were going to entertain. I'm still mistress of Gunthwaite, I believe.'

Laura bit her lip. Mrs Cooper was the fly in her ointment, and no mistake. 'But of course you're still the mistress,' she said hastily. 'It's just – well, Michael says there are ever so many people who used to invite the family, but don't any more because – well, because they weren't invited back. Obviously, with Mr Cooper, it's difficult. But I shall have the time.'

Mrs Cooper looked at her balefully. 'Don't say "ever so many" please. It's vulgar.'

Laura's heart sank. She had started this day with such enthusiasm, and it was dying on the altar of Mrs Cooper's illwill. She wouldn't let it. To give in now would mean a lifetime of condescension. She looked up and down the street, and saw the bustle outside a large department store. 'Come along,' she said to Mrs Cooper, as if she was training a dog. 'We shall go along here. It looks ever so exciting.'

They went first to Modish Gowns. Mrs Cooper sat on a red plush sofa, face set in grimly handsome lines. 'Would you like some tea?' asked an assistant nervously.

'Tea? I'm surprised you still serve it. This place is quite tawdry nowadays.'

Laura gritted her teeth. The assistant turned startled eyes to her. She said, 'Thank you, tea would be nice. I mean, lovely.' 'Nice' was another word Mrs Cooper didn't like. She was regretting her jibe with the 'ever so' already. Mrs Cooper would gang up with Gabriel to say she was vulgar.

She remembered the aristocratic ladies in the café in Paris, looking down their long noses at her and Marie. She summoned up a vision of their high-chinned, straight-backed haughtiness, and took several abrupt steps to and fro. The modiste, who had not before noticed the young lady, turned like a marionette and trotted over. 'Can I help you? Was it something special?'

'The place looks utterly vile,' said Mrs Cooper, as if the modiste wasn't there.

Laura said tightly, 'I'm getting married. I need a wedding dress, a suit, several dresses, night things and underwear. I prefer my underwear to be French.'

'French?' The request was obviously impressive.

Laura nodded. 'Is that not possible? French. Silk. I suppose I could write to a friend and ask her to send some, but I'm sure French underwear can be bought here.'

'In London, perhaps, Miss—'

Laura sighed. 'Very well. Let's see some dresses.'

She chose a wedding dress in royal blue. The shoulders were wide and padded, which disguised her less than perfect waist. The skirt was a little dowdy, cutting off at the widest part of Laura's calves, but she saw at once that it could be looped with ribbons. That would be dashing. She commanded the alteration.

'A hat, Miss. Blue velvet, with a feather?'

Laura tried it on. The feather stuck straight up and was out of keeping. 'Retrim it, please,' she commanded. 'Blue maribou curving down to the shoulder should make it presentable.'

'I don't know if our millinery department—'

Laura fixed the woman with a glittering smile. 'Of course they can. A good milliner would do that in minutes.'

By now they had a bevy of girls surrounding them. The modiste was on her mettle, calling for suits and dresses from all corners of her department. Laura was implacable in her criticism. No French aristocrat with a thousand years of breeding behind her had a more steely smile, toss of the head, grim regard for a price ticket. The modiste altered and discounted like a woman possessed, and offered her English underwear humbly.

But there Laura drew the line. The girls in the Rue de Claret had been carefully dressed. Madame Bonacieux selected knickers, corsets, brassieres and slips with the eye of a connoisseur. A woman looked good wearing them alone, unlike the English versions, great bolsters of elastic and bone. Laura didn't want Michael's first view of her skin to be marred by weals and creases. She wanted to look dainty, fresh, her breasts lifting a little, her legs almost endless, her waist nothing at all. Her underwear would come from France.

When at last they emerged from the store, Laura longed for a glass of good wine. She felt celebratory, as if a battle had been won. Who would have thought that two unpleasant women being cruel to the whores in a French café could one day be of use?

Mrs Cooper said, 'You were very dictatorial, Laura. I was surprised. It doesn't do to upset these people. Gabriel said you were difficult in shops.'

Laura was annoyed. Didn't she realise how hard it had been to insist on what she wanted? Not even Gabriel understood. People in England viewed life as an obstacle course in which you could do nothing but clamber over what was in your path. It never dawned on them to insist that the rocks be moved. She almost felt that an Englishman could pass through life and leave it totally undisturbed, like a pond with a slow-swimming fish.

They went for lunch to a restaurant in Briggate. Laura ordered a glass of red wine, which wasn't exceptional; other women were sipping wine. But Mrs Cooper raised her eyebrows. 'I hope you're not going to be one of those women who drinks,' she remarked.

'Probably,' said Laura, and stirred the depths of her mock turtle soup. How old was Mrs Cooper? Sixty? She might live twenty more years. The thought was dispiriting.

When they arrived at the teashop where they were to meet Michael, he was already there. Laura felt her heart lift. Dear Michael, with his kind, open, above all welcoming face. 'Where are your parcels? What did you get?'

'Everything's being sent,' explained Laura. 'Really, I've bought so much! A lovely wedding dress, which I won't tell you about, and a hat, and shoes—'

'We'll have to sell some cattle,' said Mrs Cooper lugubriously. 'There's nothing else.'

'I doubt it will come to that, Mother,' said Michael, and waved to the waitress. They all had tea.

Three days before the wedding, Laura tried her dress on in her room. It was cold there, and the low ceiling made it dark. She squinted at herself in the glass, suddenly wondering what Gabriel would think, if he should see her in it. Perhaps it was too frilly? Could you be too frilly for a wedding? She thought of oozing up the aisle in slinky sophistication, and shuddered. Michael thought her a girl, and that was what she must be. No matter that she was older than time itself.

She went to the big, wormy wardrobe and drew out the box

sent by Madame Bonacieux. Silk underwear, running through her fingers like water. Its pale peach colour was almost like flesh. What would Michael say? Would he prefer lace and frills? Whatever Michael wanted she would be, she thought desperately. If only he didn't want children.

A headache began. She wanted to think about anything but this. She was deceiving him so. She wasn't as she seemed, she wasn't whole, she had secret, hidden damage. But she didn't feel damaged, she reasoned. The doctor had himself said he didn't usually discover what happened to girls like her. It wasn't as if there was anyone else Michael wanted to marry, or who would marry him. What future for him then, if Laura allowed scruples to get in the way? He wouldn't be happy. There would be just a lifetime with his parents in an ancient house, spiritually alone. Laura closed her eyes, praying to the God Who had saved her, rescued her, offered her this chance, that Michael would find her enough.

There was a commotion downstairs. Laura slipped out of her dress and put on her everyday clothes of tweed skirt and warm jumper. She tied her hair up in a ribbon of vibrant red.

She went to the top of the stairs to listen. A voice, unmistakably Gabriel's, was saying, 'It's all right, Mother. I'll put a stop to it. I won't let her marry him.'

She crept step by step down the stairs. The kitchen door was closed, but she could hear the murmur of voices. At last, unable to bear it, she leaned silently against the wood.

'You like her, Mother,' Michael was saying. 'She's invaluable. Before Laura came you never had a free moment, you said so yourself.'

Mrs Cooper said, 'But she isn't what she seems. I don't know why, but sometimes she's one thing and sometimes another. Vulgar. Or a lady. Or very young, and the next moment ordering waiters and people about with the confidence of a matron of fifty.'

'What did I tell you?' said Gabriel triumphantly. 'Everyone can see it except you, Mike. She's a fraud. God knows what she's really like, but believe me, I can guess.'

Laura pushed the door open. She stood there, framed in darkness from the hall. She was very stiff and very erect. 'I've never been anything but honest with you, Gabriel.' Her voice was a whisper, she couldn't manage more. 'You know nothing about me, how can you say you do? I worked in your club and you were the one who took money and did nothing.'

His eyes met hers. He was pale, his blond hair falling into his eyes. He wore a flying jacket in leather and sheepskin, seeming too big for the familiar jumble of the farm kitchen. Laura found she was shaking. Gabriel seemed a powerful and alien physical presence.

Michael said, 'It's all right, darling. He's spoiled, that's all. He never could bear it if I had the best chocolate in the box.'

'Best! You must be joking! She's a slut, that's what she is. A French slut. She'll rob you and break your heart.'

'If anyone breaks his heart, it will be you,' said Laura. Her voice was stronger now. Strong and clear. 'Shall I tell them how often you've tried to seduce me? The things you've offered, the things you've said?'

Gabriel approached her. 'I don't deny it. Why not? Once a whore always a whore, that's what I say.'

Laura drew back her hand and slapped him.

Michael came and took her in his arms. She put her face to his chest, although she was never further from tears. She wanted to kill Gabriel. She wanted to stab him in the heart, to bury the blade to the hilt again and again. Michael said, white-faced, 'Take that back, Gabriel. Take it back or you'll never be welcome in this house again.'

'It's my house,' broke in his mother, harshly. 'My son will always be welcome.'

Michael said, 'I warn you, if he insults Laura one of us will go. I'll leave the farm, take Laura and go away. Gabriel can spend his life calving cows and dipping sheep. Is that what you really want, brother mine?'

Gabriel said, 'If you'd but realise, I'm telling you for your own good!'

'You're telling me nothing. Nothing! All you do is spew up the vile product of your vicious imagination. I never thought I could hate you, Gabriel, but I'm close to it now. You revolt me!'

He drew Laura out of the room. 'I'm sorry,' he said. 'That was terrible for you. Let's go into the morning room.'

Like so much of the house it was a large, cold, empty room they seldom used. The chairs felt stiff and new, although years of sunshine had faded the covers. 'You didn't believe what he said?' she asked helplessly.

'Of course not! Darling, of course not. But – but you do realise that as long as you tell us nothing about your life before, Gabriel can say what he likes?'

She nodded. Michael took her hand. 'Nothing's so awful I can't try and understand.'

She took in her breath. Hundreds of men were impossible to understand. How could he sleep with her, knowing about that? His innocence betrayed him. He could imagine nothing as bad as the truth.

She said, 'You'd pity me. I don't want your sympathy.'

'What for? Were you illegitimate, perhaps?'

She shrugged. 'I don't know. My mother died when I was a baby. I was left on a farm – they were unkind. The priest took pity on me, and Sophie came. She isn't a real aunt. I lived with her. She took to drink in the end. I came here to – to start again.'

'You had no one to love you?' said Michael softly.

She looked at him. 'Neither did you. You weren't loved in this house.'

He was silent. She felt a great heaviness inside her. Why need she tell him anything, why need she lie? But he said, 'Why does Gabriel say what he does? What makes him?'

She shook her head blindly. 'He wants to despise me. Then he need not care.'

'So he does care?'

'He doesn't love me! He can't. He only loves himself.'

Michael held her very close. He said, 'Don't let it spoil things, Laura. We can be strong enough, together. We may not understand Gabriel but we don't need to let him harm us. If we love enough, no one can.'

Chapter Eight

Laura rose very early the next day and padded through the silent house. The range had been banked for the night and the coal made gentle clicks and sighs as it collapsed on its bed of ash. She pushed a poker in and gave it a blast with the bellows before putting the kettle on to boil. Flames leaped up obediently.

But tranquillity eluded her. All her peace had departed. Her very insides seemed to tremble, when only a few hours ago she had thought herself safe. She felt suddenly angry, because it was the same fear, the only fear, a predator that pursued her through the days and years, across seas and boundaries, a wolf that no walls could exclude. When it hungered, it lived on her flesh.

She linked her fingers together and tightened her grip until her nails were cutting the backs of her hands. Pain was the only release. As long as it lasted she could defeat the inner gnawing.

'Stop it, Laura. That looks horrible.'

She looked up, startled. Gabriel.

He was dressed in worn twill trousers and a sweater. He hadn't shaved and his chin was covered in thick, golden down. She began to feel calmer. Her enemy was here.

She said, 'I'm making some coffee. Would you like a cup?'

'Yes, please. I remember your coffee, it's always good.'

'Always remembering! Haven't you learned, Gabriel, that the art of living is to be able to forget?'

'That isn't living. It's just getting through.'

He sat in the chair opposite. It was a rocker, and he began to move backwards and forwards, backwards and forwards, squeak – squeak – squeak. 'Dammit, Gabriel, will you stop?' She leaned forward and banged her clenched fist on his knees, holding the chair on its forward swing. He moved towards her, took her face between his hands, and kissed her.

220

The kettle began to boil. Bemused, hardly knowing what she was about, Laura got up and took it off the fire. She made coffee in a big, blue and white jug and stood waiting for it to brew.

Gabriel said, 'I know I've hurt you. I'm sorry. Michael's my brother, I can't let him fall for this.'

Laura kept her eyes on the jug. Coffee grounds were gathered on the surface, and were sinking, one by one. She had to explain, to justify herself. To make one last throw. 'If I marry Michael – when – I shall be a good wife to him. Kind. Loyal. Faithful. I shan't mind about his mother, or his father come to that. I'll help with the farm and the cooking. I'll – I'll be careful with money. I'll pay calls and go to church. I'll do everything – everything!' She turned a ravaged face to him. 'So why won't you let me? Why do you want to take everything away from me, as if I was cruel, or evil, or a thief! I was a child when you knew me. A child! I did what others said.'

Gabriel looked away from her. He had intended this last night, an attack so acid that it burned away the pretence. But when that was gone, what was left? At bottom, underneath, was raw pain. Perhaps there was no real Laura Perdoux. Perhaps she was only the layers of learned mannerisms, styles of dress or behaviour. She was just a naked, helpless soul, grabbing this and that to clothe it, and let it survive.

He had never been good at torture. At school when they were persecuting some wreck of a child, he'd faked a nosebleed so matron came and saw what was going on. It wasn't kindness. It was his own weak stomach. He had too much empathy to endure the suffering of others.

He said quickly, 'Look, I'm going to sit down with Michael today and tell him everything. He'll remember the time in Paris. He'll know it's true. So why don't you just pack and go? I'll give you some money and you can start again somewhere else.'

Laura put her hands to the sides of her head. She wanted to still her thoughts, hang on to them, because otherwise she would be mad. 'Why? Gabriel, why? There's no rich heiress who'll marry him instead of me. I'll be a good wife, the best. Gabriel, please—' She clasped her hands to her breast in the age-old gesture of pleading. He had never before believed that people did that. But he had never before seen such desperation.

He turned away, reaching for a cigarette that wasn't there.

'For God's sake, Laura! Can't you see? It isn't only him. If you stay here – if you marry Mike – I won't ever be free of you.'

'But why should that matter? We weren't important.'

He gaped at her. Did she still not realise? 'You – you don't understand. Maybe to you it was nothing. Just a stupid boy who didn't know what he was about. But not to me!'

'It wasn't nothing,' whispered Laura. 'It hurt me. I took a long time to forget.'

'And I can't, Laura! It's been years and I'm still no good! You understand, don't you, what I'm saying? When I'm with a woman, it's no damned good!'

She stared at him with dawning comprehension. 'You mean you can't do it? You can't make love?' They'd had men like that at the brothel, lots of them. They had to be tied up, or beaten, or fed with bottles, anything that strange people could desire, just to make sex possible. Was Gabriel, golden-haired, handsome Gabriel, really one of those? He was looking at her with grim embarrassment. 'I can just about do it, I suppose. It's all a rush and a scramble. I keep thinking – keep remembering. When it's over, I can see they felt the whole thing was a bit of a sham. They don't exactly get up to be sick in the hall, but it's as good as. As bad as. You don't get over a thing like that. I don't get over it. I haven't.'

Laura drew in her breath. The turmoil in her head began to steady. Men were so foolish about these things, so unreasonable. It was nothing, an incident, no more. He'd been just a boy! She'd learned in time to overcome it, even to expunge thoughts of Jean, and what had it taken? Henri, said a small, clear voice in her head. Henri's kindness, gentleness and understanding.

She fingered the ring on her little finger. She said, 'And this is why you keep asking me? You think that if I made you ill then I can make you well again?'

'Yes. Actually it isn't so stupid as it sounds. You know the worst of me, no one more. I can't – I can't fail with you. Or if I did, it wouldn't be so bad.'

'Men don't fail with me. I've never had one yet.'

He said, 'It really is all your fault. The summer before I met you I started with a friend of my mother's. She never even undressed. We just went to the old summerhouse and lay on the bench. I could do it three times a day!'

222

Laura felt herself smile. 'I'm sure you could. But how unpleasant, Gabriel! Like an animal.'

'When I came to you, that was all I knew.'

All her anger towards him seemed to crumble to dust. She tried to cling to it, restore it again, because she was safe against Gabriel when she hated him. How like him, to breach her defences with his own failure.

He went to the window, fumbling again for the cigarette he couldn't find. 'Shall I tell you something else? I know this sounds stupid and it is, but I can't help that. Because of you I can't fly. I'm no bloody good, Laura, that's all there is to say. Nearly failed training, and now they only keep me on because I can tell one end of an engine from another. It's the same as this business, you know, it's all the same thing. A matter of belief.'

'Why can't you believe you can fly?'

'I don't know! Sometimes it works, but most of the time I remember nothing but mistakes. I'm not frightened, it's not that. I don't care if it kills me. I just want – I need to get it right!'

'I wished you dead,' said Laura dispassionately.

He looked up at her. 'Don't you think I've wished that about you?'

The coffee was done. She fetched a strainer and poured it into two large mugs. Then she cut some bread and they each sat dipping and chewing, like a couple of toothless peasants.

Laura said suddenly, 'What will you say to Michael?'

Gabriel shrugged. 'Nothing. What's the use? He wouldn't believe me. And if he did, I don't think he'd give you up. He's a stubborn chap.'

'I wouldn't marry him if he knew,' said Laura. 'It would come between us, like it or not. So it's up to you. Tell him if you want.'

He shook his head, wearily. 'I don't want. You're safe, Laura. Go on and live your little life, mopping up after Father, putting up with Mother's gibes, not going in pubs in Bainfield. After all that you've seen? I tell you, it won't be enough.'

Laura closed her eyes to the heat of the fire. 'It will be for me.'

They were silent together. She thought of all he had said. She didn't believe what men told her, most of the time. Not about sex. But this she did. It matched with Gabriel's insistence, his pursuit of her when there were others far more willing. The ghost of before was with him still.

She said, 'We couldn't do it here, at Gunthwaite. And after I'm married I won't. If you can think of somewhere – how long before you go back?'

He stared at her. 'Two days. But I don't believe you.'

A small, deprecating smile. 'That's up to you. I know what it's like for you. When you can't reach out to people you're shut off from life. There must be somewhere we could go.'

'What would you say to Michael?'

She shrugged languidly, suddenly sexual, suddenly aware. 'Bainfield. Shopping. To establish a truce. He won't mind.'

Gabriel had a friend with a shooting box high on the moors. It wasn't much of a place, an old keeper's cottage in a fold of the ground, surrounded for miles by curlews and grouse. The roof was sound but that was all. Used for perhaps two spartan weeks a year, it was damp and mildewed, inside and out.

The car was conspicuous on the high moorland road. At every hamlet faces appeared at the windows. Gabriel told Laura to crouch down.

'They'll think I'm a land agent, or someone to rent the shooting.'

'Suppose we can't get in?'

'There's a key under the eaves.'

It was starting to rain as they arrived. A hawk detached itself from the clouds and flapped slowly away. In the water butt frogs began croaking and Laura felt the urge to laugh. The whole thing seemed farcical. She and Gabriel could have made love in comfort so often in the past, and now they came to this.

Gabriel pushed open the rickety door and led the way inside. His friend had left the place ready for the next visit, with a stack of wood in the hearth. There was a table and chairs on the flagged floor, a wooden settle covered in mildewed cushions, and damp beds in the rooms above. 'Oh, Gabriel,' said Laura, chuckling. 'We can't even lie down!'

'It's the best I can do, dammit!' He was already on edge. Laura went to him and put her arms around his neck, turning her face up for a kiss. He said, 'I'm not ready. We can't.'

'Ready for what? It's just a kiss.'

She drew his head down, feeling his mouth hard and closed against her. She whispered to him, brushing his lips, until suddenly his mouth was wide and hungry. To every rough invasion she returned gentleness. Gradually, inexorably, he began to respond. Each kiss was a long, liquid sigh.

'Now.' She eased herself away. 'We must light the fire and spread blankets on the floor in front of it.'

'Do we need to bother with the fire?'

She blinked. 'Certainly. We shall be here for hours.' Seeing the horror in his face, she smiled. 'It's all right, Gabriel. It's easy. Let me decide what happens.'

The fire was soon crackling merrily. They took blankets from the car and laid them on top of blankets from the house, creating a mattress as soft as it was warm. Laura began to move in a consciously sensual way, sliding from her coat, easing her skirt over luscious stockinged thighs. Gabriel watched like a trapped animal, the muscles of his jaw rigid with strain. Slowly, inexorably, she unfastened her blouse.

She stood before him in high heels and stockings, her breasts covered by the merest film of silk. Her crotch was naked. Black body hair curled tantalisingly.

Gabriel said, 'This is all a mistake. You don't want this, you don't want me—'

'Yes, I do.' She put her hands behind her neck and lifted her curtain of hair. 'It won't be the same with Michael. For him I must be innocent. But not for you. I can be wickedness itself.'

She stood with feet apart, arms raised, hips tilted. A pose of conscious provocation. It was a side of her he had only ever glimpsed, and here she was, abandoned, tempting him. He found himself wishing he had never started this. Wasn't one humiliation enough for anyone?

She came towards him and pulled at his tie. 'Come on, Gabriel. It isn't fair to excite me and not go on.'

'I keep thinking of Michael.' He did, he did, but only to stop thinking of her!

She put her hand across his mouth. 'Don't. This has nothing to do with him. Now, I just want you.'

He didn't believe her. But her hips pressed against his, the rough tweed of his trousers rubbing against her soft flesh. The thought was unbearably arousing. Somehow his hands were on

225

her, passing again and again from shoulder to thigh. She was moaning, head back, eyes closed, throat a long column of white. He couldn't wait and she was saying, 'Gabriel, please – please.'

He pushed her down on the bed. She barely opened her eyes, but simply lay spreadeagled for him, a willing vessel. He dragged at his clothes, freed himself and went into her.

When he came to himself he rolled away, filled with the usual dismay. He'd been too quick, too rough. She hadn't been satisfied. But he felt her hand against his cheek and when he looked she was smiling at him. 'That was wonderful,' she said. 'I'm sorry I rushed you, but it's been so long. I'd forgotten how good it can be.'

'Don't give me that.' He rolled away, searching for the cigarettes in his discarded jacket. He glanced over his shoulder and saw her watching him, propped on an elbow.

'I enjoyed it,' she said simply. 'You excited me. Now you can take your clothes off and we'll do it again.'

'I can't. You don't understand—'

'No, Gabriel. You don't.' She reached across, took him by the shoulder and pushed him down on the bed. She knelt astride him, slowly and carefully unbuttoning his shirt. Then she spread it open and ran her hands across his naked chest, pausing at his nipples to touch them lightly with her fingers. 'You'll be amazed what you can do. Relax, Gabriel. Let me amaze you.'

He lay while she stripped him naked, touching each and every part of him. His body felt separate from his mind, responding despite itself. As his excitement mounted she made him lie face down and pressed against his back, letting him feel her body. His thoughts began to spin, he lost hold of them and they were gone. There was nothing but feeling, nothing but instinctive, natural response. Clumsiness was gone, awkwardness didn't exist; whether at her desire or his he was on his back, reaching up for her as she bestrode him. They met like two halves of a whole.

When it was over, Laura said, 'How do you feel now?'

'Wonderful.' He let out a deep, contented sigh. 'Are you always so good?'

'Always.' She laughed at him. 'It wasn't me. It was you, doing what you felt. You were thinking too much before.'

'You did really enjoy it too?'

She leaned across and brushed his lips with a kiss. 'You know I did. But today wasn't important for me. You were learning about pleasure.'

When they were dressing, he said, 'Will you teach all this to Michael?' He tried to imagine firm, straitlaced Michael letting his wife ride him like a horse.

She shook her head. 'Of course not. He won't need it, after all. We'll be married.'

Gabriel stood watching as she put on her stockings. The allure of before was gone, she was ordinary now, checking her seams quite straightforwardly. The change in her seemed touching in the extreme. He thought of her breasts hanging above him, and felt a rush of saliva into his mouth. At that moment she slipped matter-of-factly into her blouse and skirt, and said, 'Is there a fireguard? We don't want to burn the place down.'

Gabriel found it hard to meet her eyes. She'd think he was insatiable. 'I think there's one in the outhouse. I'll go and look.'

Michael was waiting anxiously when they returned. Laura went to him and kissed his cheek. 'We didn't go to Bainfield. We talked. I think it's going to be all right.'

Michael looked at his brother and Gabriel blushed. 'Sorry, Mike old chap. Laura says – well, she's convinced me. I know she loves you. She'll do her damnedest to make you happy.'

Michael went to his brother, took his hand and shook it. 'Thank God for that. Honestly, Gabriel, sometimes—'

'I know, I know. Put it down as jealousy. She's a lovely girl.'

When Gabriel went upstairs before dinner a row of hot water cans stood outside the bathroom door. Someone was splashing and humming inside. He knew it was Laura. He wondered if she was trying to wash away the taint of the afternoon, and a sudden sick tide rose up in him. It was all a sham; she hated him, she hated what they'd done. He waited in his room, the door open a crack, until she came out. She was wearing her old woollen robe. He rushed out of his bedroom to confront her, and she stopped and smiled at him. 'Hello, Gabriel.' She reached out and took his hand, as if she liked him, as if she was happy. He felt a terrible urge to cry.

227

Chapter Nine

The church bell was ringing, the unmusical jangle that passed for Gunthwaite's celebration. It was heard only faintly at the farm, distance working magically to render the sound sweet. Laura sat in her cold room for the last time, listening to the bell and staring at the dress hanging on the wardrobe door. She should be ready by now. The wagon was already outside, scrubbed and decorated with an old coach seat, its two great horses stamping and blowing, let off for the day from the plough. One of the men had dressed them as they used to do, manes plaited with ribbon, tails bound up with lucky twists of corn.

Dinah knocked perfunctorily and came in. 'Really, Miss! I never knew a girl take so long. Into this dress, right away now.'

Laura looked up at her. 'I don't think I can.'

Dinah sat down on the bed with a thump. 'Don't tell me you're going to let Mr Michael down? Not after everything.'

'Oh, I want to get married! But I didn't think so many people would come. All Coopers. No one for me.'

'Yes.' Dinah nodded. 'Everyone's talking about that. I said it's due to your being French, but that's not the end of the world now, is it? Wasn't anyone willing to come?'

Laura sighed. Of course people talked, she'd known they would. 'I haven't anyone. My parents are dead, and the woman I lived with's ill. But it's going to seem as if Michael's marrying a nobody. I don't want to walk in and see all that space.'

'I'll sit on your side,' said Dinah, patting her hand. 'And how about I send a message to the village? Anyone wants to see the service can sit on the bride's side. You'll get the postman, and Mrs Thwaite, and the Hinchcliffe mob at least. Fill the place up a bit.'

228

Laura beamed. 'Would you, Dinah? Oh, please!'

She finished dressing while Dinah sent her message. She had sat still too long, she was quite chilled through, and the church would be icy. But her heart was thundering, sending the blood racing through her veins; she felt shaky and excited at one and the same time. Would she faint in church? She almost thought she might.

The dress was loose on her. She'd lost weight. Her waist and legs were the same, but her breasts and arms were thinner. It was the food. When she was married she'd never let good beef be cooked to leather, or serve cabbage boiled to rags. But it wasn't only the food. Since Gabriel, she'd found it hard to sleep, and when she did she dreamed. Perhaps it was guilt, although as far as she knew she felt none. You couldn't feel guilt over something you had done guiltlessly so many times before. She opened her handkerchief drawer and stuffed squares of lace into the cups of her brassiere. That was better.

She finished her make-up, applying lipstick and rouge. Her eyebrows annoyed her, as fluffy and unkempt as an Englishman could wish, and to her eyes still unsophisticated. But wasn't that what she was about? Michael was marrying a virgin bride. She looked askance at her black eyelashes. Too much? Too late. She would have to go.

Old Mr Cooper was to travel with her in the wagon, and blunder with her up the aisle. He was totally confused, poor lamb. She was his Rosalind, and yet the real Rosalind had arrived last night. She was neat, well dressed and charming, seeming not to care that her father had replaced her with another daughter, just as well liked. Married to Howard Dalton, a diplomat some years her senior, she had travelled from The Hague for the wedding, leaving husband and two boys behind. Laura was a little afraid of her. Fortunately when old Mr Cooper saw them both together he became agitated, so they hadn't had an opportunity to talk. Now, with his real daughter at the church, he could turn confidently to Laura once again.

'Rosalind dear, you'll catch your death,' he said when he saw her. 'Go in for your coat, at once.'

The wagon driver chuckled. 'Look a bit daft in that, guvnor. Is a bit nippy though, Miss, want a rug or sommat?'

She shook her head. The wind was blowing, threatening her

229

carefully assembled hair, and it looked like rain. She just wanted to get there, and have it done.

A small crowd was gathered outside the church. When they saw the wagon they set up a ragged cheer, but it was mostly for the horses.

'By, that's not a sight you see right often.'

'Reminds me of when I were a kid. Right pretty sight, that. Remember old Blackberry? Eighteen hands before shoes. Won everything for miles, and just as well. Too tall for a plough horse, like.'

Laura felt better. No need to worry that she would be noticed when the horses were around. But as she alighted, the wind catching the ribbons in her skirt, there was a moment of hush. A woman's voice, carrying clearly, said, 'She's got sommat, and no mistake. Must be the French in her. Eh, she do look grand.'

She looked grand! The words strengthened her; she no longer felt the bitter cold, no longer worried about old Mr Cooper getting confused and demanding to be taken home. Gunthwaite's judgment might not count for much, and in Parisian terms would be laughable, but it was Gunthwaite she wanted to impress. And Gunthwaite thought she looked grand.

There was a pause at the church door as all those who had waited to see the bride arrive scuttled past her to get a seat inside. The rain was beginning, blown on the wind and thickened with sleet, the hills like huge old women cloaked with clouds. The wagon driver put rugs on the horses and covered the bench with a cloth. 'Need your brolly when you come out wed,' he remarked to Laura. 'Don't take too long on it, Vicar. Horses'll take a chill.'

'I think we're nearly ready,' said the vicar, craning his neck to catch the organist's eye. When nothing happened he stepped into the church and raised a discreet finger. Finally he windmilled his arms, and at last the music began. As for every Gunthwaite wedding, it was 'Here Comes The Bride'.

Old Mr Cooper straightened his back. What did he think was going on? No matter. Following the vicar's ponderous tread, they began processing between rows of decorous Cooper faces and goggling village ones. But all Laura could see was Michael, his strained expression dissolving into smiles as she came in. Had he doubted her? If she had ever led him to doubt then she hated herself for it. He had reached down into the abyss and pulled her out.

The vicar began, weighing his words, enjoying the sonorous echo in the little church. Laura let it wash over her. She had never attended a wedding before this, her own. The vicar began to speak, talking of the reasons for Christian marriage.

Laura thought, It's a wall, a strong high wall, protecting those within from lust and loneliness. She would be safe there, warm and happy, earning her great blessings with loyalty and hard work. Michael would never regret doing this, she promised. He would want for nothing that was in her power to give.

The vicar said, 'First, it was ordained for the procreation of children.'

She felt her heart turn over. She hadn't known that was so! She didn't believe it could be right. Was there no marriage without children, was that what it meant? All at once the chill air of the church raised goosepimples on her arms and she began to tremble almost beyond control. Now she listened hard to what the vicar was saying, about sin and continency, comfort and help. Pausing, surveying the throng, the vicar asked if anyone knew of a reason why Laura and Michael should not marry. Words beat at her throat, forced themselves almost to her teeth, were trapped behind that close-clenched wall and silenced. 'I can't bear him children!' she wanted to shout. 'I'm a whore, a corrupt and evil thing!'

No sound broke the hush. The service went on. She heard nothing, was conscious only when Michael took her hand. She looked up at him, sure that he must look inside her and see the truth. But he was gazing down at her with eyes full of warmth, as comforting and reassuring as a fire on a winter's day. Her trembling hands stilled. Michael needed her, poor thing that she was, and she knew she could make him happy. There would not be a day, not an hour, not a moment when she didn't strive with all her might towards that end. If Michael loved her she lacked nothing. Suddenly, wonderfully, she felt on the brink of complete happiness.

The rain was coming down in earnest as they left. 'Hard winter coming,' said the wagon driver, putting up the brolly. 'Here, Miss, want old Major's rug do you? Keep the chill out, any rate.'

231

Laura looked at the horse blanket and laughed. Michael said, 'Wait until we're out of the village. You need it, you look frozen.'

'I'm warm inside,' she said. And she was. It was as if a brazier burned in her heart, lit by the warmth of his eyes. Because of him she was safe at last. She was somebody. All her life she had lived on the edges of other people's security, with nothing of her own. But this was her chance. Now she could begin to live as they did. She had been no one, without even a name.

'Laura Cooper,' she said softly. 'Mrs Laura Cooper.'

'Mrs Michael Cooper,' said Michael, taking her hand and turning the slim gold ring. 'That's what will be on your visiting cards.'

Visiting cards! What a symbol of respectability. Let Gabriel mock the littleness of this place, let him say what he pleased. Little pond maybe, but she would happily swim to and fro in it for ever.

They were nearing the end of the village, a straggle of cottages drenched by winter rain. The great backs of the hills stretched away against the sky, as solid and dependable as any Yorkshireman. No wonder Michael was as he was, living by these hills. She took a long breath of air. Some might think it a dull, cold, empty Yorkshire scene. But for Mrs Michael Cooper, seeing the world for what felt like the very first time, it was blessed. She would never ask for more.

The wedding breakfast had taken Dinah, Laura and Mrs Cooper the best part of a week to prepare. Ham, roast goose, a saddle of mutton and a sirloin of beef all stood ready for carving. Against everyone's advice, Laura had insisted upon some French touches; a ratatouille, a good *demi-glâcé* sauce made with wine, and instead of the usual apple pie, *Tarte Tatin*. But her most successful innovation was *crème brûlée*. The Cooper clan were mostly farmers who believed in substantial fare, and at first they viewed the strange concoction with suspicion; but once Uncle Percy pronounced it, 'Not half bad. I'll have another, thank you, Dinah my girl,' it was open season. Topped with brandied raspberries bottled in summer, and washed down with homemade cider, it reduced several of the guests to hunting armchairs and sofas in secluded corners in which to fall peacefully asleep.

The hours passed in a whirl. The years in the Rue de Claret had taught Laura all about parties, and she moved ceaselessly from room to room, making sure everyone was happy. Some of the down to earth relations took control in the kitchen and dealt with the tide of washing up, while the more elevated Coopers sat in the parlour and made barbed conversation. Rosalind, elegant in pleated navy silk, sat in a window seat, talking to the Fitzalan-Howards.

'What will they think of us?' hissed Mrs Cooper distractedly. 'It sounds so common. All this talk about sheep.'

'The Fitzalan-Howards are farmers too,' said Laura bemusedly.

'Farmers! That's how much you know. Gentlemen farmers, rather. At least if you'd had some decent relations we might have made some show, but now it's just Cooper everything, and all of it bad. Thank God for Rosalind, that's what I say.'

But Rosalind slipped from her perch and came towards Laura. 'Going well, isn't it?' she said easily. 'Are you dying to get away?'

Laura coloured. 'Not really. But it has been a long day.'

'And now you've got to drive miles and miles in the dark and the rain. I remember when Howard and I married, I thought I should die of weariness. Have you eaten something? You really should. I know you must have done the food, it's so wonderfully French.'

'Thank you.' Was this all she could do, make feeble replies to Rosalind's kindness? An image of Zelma rose before her, talking to the headmistress of Laura's school. Just the right blend of politeness and equality. Unconsciously Laura adopted the manner. 'How do you find The Hague? Have you been there long? It must be such fun.'

Rosalind looked surprised. Then she chuckled. 'Dear me, Laura. I don't know at all what to make of you. I think Michael's done very well for himself, my dear, and I shall tell him so.'

As Rosalind drifted away, Laura felt a stab of irritation. The wrong style, the wrong moment. She didn't often make such mistakes.

Michael caught her eye across the room. It was time to

change. They were to spend the night in The Queen's in Leeds, although it would be ruinously expensive. Michael had insisted. Some of the relatives raised their eyebrows. The Gunthwaite Coopers were putting on airs these days and no mistake. But then, Norma always was a rum customer, would never get over her daughter marrying so well, and herself with only a vague connection with Lord something or other who didn't know her from Adam. Polite she might be, but they could sense her distaste for them. 'That young lass'll have her work cut out,' muttered a Cooper aunt. 'Who'd have Norma for a mother-in-law? Cold as charity, that one.'

Laura's smile became fixed. Exhaustion was taking over. She wanted nothing so much as to lie in her bed in the little room under the roof, listen to the wind playing hide and seek under the ancient tiles, and go to sleep. But she would never sleep in that room again. She was Michael's wife.

She went upstairs, pushing the door of Michael's room with the caution of an intruder. Her going-away clothes were laid out in readiness, hat, gloves, everything. All they needed was a bride to bring them to life. She sat on the bed for a moment, letting herself slump against the pillows. The place smelled of Michael, soap and leather and horse. She thought of sleeping here and felt vaguely repelled. Marriage was so communal, such an invasion of one's own private space. Where now would she find room for herself?

There was a knock on the door. It was Dinah, with a glass of brandy.

'Thought you looked knocked up. Drink it down and let me do your buttons. Weather's closing and Mr Michael's itching to be off.' The room was growing dark. Soon the lamps would be lit but only the Fitzalan-Howards and other notables would bother to go home. A fiddler would come from the village, and someone would play the piano, and people would sing. The drunkest would stay until the morning, invited or not.

When she was dressed in her smart grey suit with a pink blouse and pink-trimmed hat, Dinah said, 'That's grand. Just what you ought. Take a tip from me, now you're wed don't let the old girl spoil things. She will, you know. If she can. You stand up to her. Start as you mean to go on.'

Laura looked at Dinah's warm, cheerful face and on impulse

bent and kissed her. 'Be off with you,' said Dinah, and gave her a rough pat.

As she came down the stairs it seemed the hall was full of people looking up. Michael came and took her hand, leading her down to them.

'Well, everyone,' he said. 'Time we were off.'

One of the old men came and prodded Laura with his stick, as if she was a cow. 'You've got a sturdy one,' he pronounced, to roars of laughter. 'Bit light in t'bag, but good calving hips. No need for t'ropes if bull's not too strong.' All the men bellowed, like bulls themselves, excited by a cow.

Michael turned a dark angry red. Laura whispered to him, 'Don't mind them, they don't mean any harm.'

'I won't have it! They're insulting you.' He went on loudly, 'We'll have no more vulgarity, if you please. My wife isn't used to our country humour. Keep it until we've gone.'

'Bloody spoilsport,' someone remarked. 'Thinks he's lord of the manor.'

'Take your hat off before you shove it up!' yelled an anonymous voice. 'The mark of a gentleman, that is!'

Lips folded in anger, Michael pushed his way through to the door. The car was waiting, with Mrs Cooper standing by.

'You can't leave me with them,' she said as Michael came up to her. 'I won't have it. You should have waited until Gabriel could come, he'd have known what to do. You've filled my house with greedy, dirty-minded peasants who haven't the manners to go home. You'll have to stay and deal with them.'

Michael said, 'Of course we can't stay. Rosalind's here, after all. If there's any trouble get Bill Mayes to help.'

'I need my son, not a hired man! How can you? How dare you? I shan't forget.'

Michael folded his lips and helped Laura into the car. Mrs Cooper stood gripping the open window, her face inches from Laura's but her eyes on Michael, as if the girl wasn't there. It was unnerving. As Michael slid behind the wheel and prepared to drive away, Mrs Cooper said, 'I don't know how you can do this to me. I'm still mistress here. You're still my son!'

'Goodbye, Mother,' said Michael grimly. As he let in the clutch and the car moved off, a shower of rice rattled against the paintwork and settled in Mrs Cooper's hair. 'Goodbye! Good luck!' Women and girls crowded in on them, rice poured through the open window on to Laura's lap. Someone pushed some pennies into her hand. 'For the village children. They'll be waiting. Forget our Norma, have a right good time.'

'Thank you. Thank you. Goodbye!' Laura turned in her seat to wave.

The dark was gathering around the old house, the sky so heavy it seemed to lean on the sagging tiles. One of the farm dogs was barking hysterically, and two crows rose from the elms and blew raggedly away on a rising wind.

At the outskirts of the village the children were waiting in the rain. Laura flung them their pennies and they raced for them, shouting good luck. Now she could close the window. Michael turned the heater full on, and reached for her hand. The lights of the car were a narrow tunnel in the night. Rain began to fall in earnest.

'I'm sorry about Mother,' said Michael. 'Family do's always get her upset.'

'Did she really mean us to stay behind?'

He nodded. 'Probably. Don't worry, darling. I don't allow Mother to tell me what I should do. And neither should you.'

They drove on in silence. After the bustle of the day it was welcome. The windscreen wipers swished to and fro, and once they caught a hare in the lights, bounding away huge-eyed into the wet night. Laura began to feel a little strange, as if she wasn't in the car at all, as if everything was a dream. Her head felt heavy and hot, but her hands were cold. Michael said, 'We'll be there in half an hour. We'll have a hot toddy and dinner in our room.'

She smiled at him. 'That sounds like heaven. What a day!'

The Queen's Hotel was very grand. Michael seemed to know it, but Laura was much impressed. The street outside was paved with rubber tiles, to prevent the guests being disturbed by traffic noise. The doorman brought an umbrella and sheltered Laura's path into the foyer, while porters unloaded their bags and took charge of the car. To her embarrassment, as she stood blinking in the lights, showers of rice fell from her clothes and hair. Michael was tipping the doorman and the porter, somewhat uncomfortably. He wasn't used to this after all, and she found it rather endearing. He was so precise, so determined to do the right thing. Her thoughts turned to bed. What did he know, what would he be like? For no reason that she could understand, her stomach knotted.

After Gunthwaite and its oil lamps, The Queen's seemed painfully bright. She went to the mirror in their room and her face was pale and tired, with too much make-up. She said to Michael, 'I look terrible. I'm sorry, I didn't realise. I'm a mess.'

'You look beautiful.'

They stood apart from each other, tense and silent. A knock came on the door. It was the toddy Michael had ordered. Laura took hers and sat in an armchair, sipping. It was strong and potent. Every mouthful seemed to pass directly into her veins. She watched Michael pacing restlessly to and fro, his face set. 'I wonder if you'd mind if I went into the bathroom?' he said suddenly.

Laura said, 'Of course. Not at all.'

'Thank you.'

As soon as the door was closed she heard him turn the taps, to shield her from unpleasant noises. The day's unreality seemed to coalesce into apprehension. They didn't know each other well enough to admit their need even to use the bathroom. And this was no whore's game, a few hours in which to pretend. It was for ever.

When Michael emerged Laura took his place, saying she needed a wash. His embarrassment was infectious. She imagined leaving the door open, talking as she passed water. She'd done that with men often enough. The thought shrivelled her. He'd think her depraved. So she too turned on the taps. When she came out she said, 'It's very convenient. A bathroom like this. We could have one at Gunthwaite one day.'

He laughed uncomfortably. 'A bit too intimate, if you ask me. All this sort of stuff seems a bit – well – shocking.'

'Yes.' Why pretend to agree? She wasn't shocked at all. But if Michael wanted a shocked wife, then that's what she would be.

Dinner arrived. She wasn't hungry, and neither it seemed was Michael, but the ritual of the grisly evening must be played out. She could almost wish they had stayed at Gunthwaite amid the bawdy revellers. All the ease with which she and Michael normally conversed was quite gone.

She drank wine, too quickly. Michael drank almost nothing. Waiters came and took away the remains of the meal, and Laura went into the bathroom to get ready for the night. She washed and dabbed perfume in her hair, then drew out her French nightgown, pale sheer silk. It clung to every contour of her body, breast, belly, pubic mound. Michael would hate to see her wearing this. He would think her a . . . She shied away from the word.

When she opened the bathroom door she stood behind it and said, 'I wonder if you'd mind not looking? I want to get straight into bed.'

'What? Oh. Yes, of course. I'm sorry this is all so—'

'It isn't your fault.' She ran quickly across the room. 'There. You can look now.'

'Thanks.'

Now it was his turn. He came out in fully buttoned pyjamas, still showing the marks of Dinah's iron. Laura felt the beginnings of panic. How could they enjoy each other when he was trussed up like this? How could she excite him when he could not look at her body?

He cleared his throat several times, put his watch on the bedside table, blew his nose, and got into bed. Then he reached across and put out the light. It was pitch dark, sooty dark, the alien sheets felt like pages of a book.

'I – don't know how you want to go on with this,' said Michael nervously.

She said, 'I wish you'd kiss me. Like before.'

He was inept and unsure. His lips were stiff, and Laura reached up behind his head and pulled him down to her. She opened her mouth for him, received his tongue, and as he drew back from her nibbled his lips with tiny kisses. This was the beginning, known and trusted, they could move from this to greater, more difficult things.

Suddenly he was heaving himself on top of her. He said, 'I'm sorry. Believe me, I won't take long.'

He was pushing her nightgown up around her waist, although his pyjamas remained resolutely intact. But she could feel him nudging her. He had poked himself out of a hole, and was struggling to find the place. She was amazed, almost amused; she had never imagined him like this!

She dared not help him. She wasn't supposed to know what to do. He was very hard, his inaccurate thrusts were hurting her.

238

She lifted herself fractionally, and his penis slid backwards and in. She let out a cry of simulated pain.

'My darling – so sorry – rather die than hurt you—'

He was pounding at her, quite inexperienced. He was like Gabriel, she thought suddenly. Her first time in the Rue de Claret. Claustrophobia was suddenly overwhelming. This big man with his thick pyjamas seemed ready to smother her. She moved her head from side to side, fighting for air, eyes wide open as he gripped the brass bedhead to steady himself for his thrusts. She'd never pass water after this. She'd have to put ice up herself, as Madame used to tell the girls, to try to bring down the swelling. Mon Dieu, this one was like a horse!

The thrusts kept coming, faster, harder. Suddenly he paused, let out a strangled cry and collapsed. She could feel him twitching inside her. Thank God. If she'd really been a virgin he'd have split her in two.

He slept almost at once. She crept from the bed and went to bathe herself, touching swollen flesh. When could she teach him how it ought to be done? Not yet, needless to say.

Back in the bed, every inch of skin aware of Michael's presence, she realised that most of her hurt. Her throat was sore, her head ached, her limbs felt like lead. Michael had bruised the one part of her that didn't feel ill. She touched her face and it was hot. Perhaps she'd die, and Michael would always blame himself. She felt sad suddenly. Tears oozed from the corners of her eyes and soaked her pillow. So this was marriage, ill and sore and lonely in a strange and uncomfortable bed.

Towards dawn she was woken by Michael's penis coming into her. She noticed it far less than the sense of suffocation as her cold-thickened head was buried in Michael's pyjamas. She pushed him away, fighting for air, and heard his muffled apologies. 'Sorry – had to – won't take long—' Thankfully he wasn't so rough. She felt ill, she felt desperate, she wanted simply for him to be done. But he wanted her again before morning. When he rolled away for the third time she snarled, 'And that's all! Don't you dare touch me again!'

They lay silent in the dark without sleeping. Laura felt horribly ashamed.

They were stiff and embarrassed in the morning. It was intended that they move on to Whitby, for two nights in a guest house, so they talked in stilted tones about packing and paying the bill. Michael looked terrible, thought Laura, positively haggard. As he tucked in to salty bacon and brown-edged eggs, pretending enthusiasm he obviously did not feel, she couldn't bear it. She reached out and touched his hand. 'I'm sorry! I didn't mean – I wasn't used – I've got a cold, that's all.'

He put down his knife and fork. 'I don't know why you should apologise. Don't know what got into me. Of all the crass things—'

'It wasn't! You weren't!' She became aware of the waiters, covertly watching them. The honeymoon couple. She said, 'Can't we just leave everything and get out of here?'

The day was blustery and cold. Laura sat sneezing in the car, feeling lightheaded. Her eyes were streaming, her nose red, and from time to time she coughed like a bronchitic old man. They had intended to visit York but Laura was in no state for sightseeing. Michael drove straight to Whitby, and Laura was ensconced in bed by three in the afternoon, complete with hot water bottles and hot drinks. Yet still she looked woebegone.

'I'm letting you down,' she said miserably. 'I wanted to be perfect and last night – and this—'

Michael said, 'It's all right. I promise I'm not upset.'

'Aren't you? Really?'

'No. Not at all.'

But she knew he was. He had hoped for so much from her and she had given so little. Couldn't she have tried for a little understanding? He had been inexperienced last night, either virgin or as near as made no difference. There had been many men like that. But always before she had been in control, able to urge and instruct, calm and regulate. She hadn't before been a wife.

Michael said, 'If you're all right I'll take a walk through the village. No point sitting around here all day watching you sneeze.'

'No. Of course not.' She smiled at him anxiously. He smiled back. But they both could have cried.

Chapter Ten

Gabriel marched briskly across the airfield. He would have preferred to march briskly in exactly the opposite direction, but needs must. Aerobatics today, and there was no escape.

It was one of a series of tests to be performed on the new plane. Lately he had managed to avoid any sort of serious confrontation with the inadequacies of his flying skills, and life had relaxed into pleasurable routine. But today, the pilot least likely to succeed in aerobatics had to show what he could do.

He picked up his gear and went out to the plane. A small crowd of ghouls was gathered outside the mess, like spectators at the guillotine, he thought uncharitably. He was expected to climb steeply, loop the loop, come out straight and level, fly past the airfield, repeat the procedure and land. And crash, he thought to himself. The squadron was waiting to see him burn to death in a pile of twisted metal.

His mechanic was being kind to him again. 'You can do this one, sir,' he said encouragingly. 'Don't think about them lot watching. Just you get on with the job.'

Gabriel gave a sick grin. If only it was over. If only it was spring. If only he'd never started this flying lark, he could be sitting now before a roaring fire drinking scotch.

He felt better in the air. The plane was handling well, better than usual if anything. He adjusted the trim, then adjusted it back. There'd been nothing wrong in the first place. He checked his height – good, almost there. Anyone would think he wanted to do this thing. A nice shallow climb – damn! He was supposed to climb steeply. He turned the nose of the plane down and dived.

The engine cut. He levelled out and the thing sparked into life again, a reassuring roar. The great flat expanse of fen seemed to swing into place beneath him, a fugitive sun glinting on water in the dykes. What a godforsaken place, he thought distractedly. Who would live here if they had the choice? He'd do the steep climb and then try the dive again.

It was very cold in the cockpit. In fact, flying was generally quite unpleasant, if you analysed it bit by bit. Why had the engine stalled? Was it him? Something else? Probably the carburettor.

His climb was uneventful, the dive was not. Again the engine died. He levelled out and climbed again, noting engine revolutions and angles of descent on a pad. This time he'd loop the loop and see what happened.

At the top of the loop he knew he was in trouble. As the engine cut in the dive, at the exact point at which he was losing the sense of earth and sky, something jammed. He couldn't level. Nose to earth, the little plane was hurtling to its silent, engineless doom.

As he fought for control, odd thoughts distracted him. His mother's last letter: 'Laura seems to imagine that she is in charge in this house. I've spoken to Michael, of course.' Michael, at school, hitting the boy who was bullying his little brother. And Laura herself, astride him, her hair hiding her naked breasts, her face merging into the girl in the pub who said he was, 'Better than anyone. Never known a man do it like you.' Now he was to die, and everything would be over. He'd never know how it might have gone on.

He kicked the rudder, left, right. The plane slipped into a nose first spin. Gabriel was at once disorientated, he never could cope with this. But suddenly his tugging on the stick had its reward – the plane lurched drunkenly to an approximate level flight. The engine fired. Gabriel was conscious of tears running down his cheeks. He was spared. He was going to live!

He turned to land with no more ado. Enough of this idiocy; he was engaged in a senseless pursuit of the unattainable. This sort of thing was dangerous! Let everyone go by land or sea, let man abandon the air to those it suited better. He corrected automatically for a crosswind, prepared to touch – and the flap stuck, the engine cut and his aeroplane cartwheeled slowly into the turf, the propeller ploughing a ragged furrow until it shattered. Fuel gushed from the tank, a lethal river not yet in flame. The soft creaking of metal under stress mingled with the sighing of the wind. Everything was still. Amazed, disbelieving, Gabriel hung by his seat straps and felt blood running into his eyes.

The hours were hazy and filled with pain. Every now and then a nurse came and gave him an injection, which blurred the edges sufficiently for someone to come and dress his wounds. It still hurt like the devil, though. Sadists, all of them.

He wondered where everyone was. Mother. Michael. Time seemed to stretch towards infinity, a neverending ribbon of darkness. Just the nurses, the injections, the pain. But then, without warning, Michael came.

'Hello, Gabriel old chap.'

He turned his head. The pain was terrible, and he gasped. Damn. He must stop whimpering like a baby. 'Thought you'd given me up,' he managed.

'Not likely. They wouldn't let us in before because of your head. Apparently you need quiet and a darkened room.'

'Wondered why it was never bloody morning.'

In the half-light Michael seemed very big, almost as if Gabriel was a child again and Michael his tall protector. But he was just as tall as Michael. 'Is Mother here?'

Michael nodded. 'I said I'd see you first. To be honest, you're not as smashed up as they led me to believe.'

Gabriel grimaced. 'No thanks to them. Sent me up in a dicky plane with a blocked fuel line and jammed flaps. I think they're trying to tell me something. Did they explain what the damage is?'

'The plane's done for. As for you, concussion and compound fractures of your right arm and collarbone.'

Gabriel looked at him. His eyes were bloodshot, the blue faded with pain. 'Is it going to be all right?'

'Yes.' Michael took his good hand and held it firmly. 'You needn't worry. I know it hurts, but provided there's no infection you should be fine.'

Gabriel said nothing. Outside, in the winter afternoon, a bird was singing.

'So how are you and Laura getting on?' asked Gabriel suddenly. 'Mother behaving herself?'

'I think so. More or less.'

'I knew she'd be bloody. Going to show her in, are you?'

'If you want. I'll come again tomorrow, but after that I've got to get back.'

'Ah, the attractions of the marital bed. Best get Mother in to tell me her side of the story.'

Alone in the corridor once again, Michael listened to his mother's voice rising and falling unintelligibly on the other side of the door. If he had known she couldn't overhear he might have told Gabriel the truth. His mother was being impossible.

It was as if she had been waiting for Michael's bride all her life. At last she had a victim, someone upon whom she could heap all the years of bitterness. She seemed to blame someone – anyone – for marriage to a man who in his youth had seemed more than he was, and in age was less than he had ever been. She seemed to embrace hardship. Things were going downhill and they had never been rich, though at the very worst they would still have Gunthwaite and a decent life. But his mother yearned to be deprived of things, to blame others for her deprivation, to deprive in her turn. Her constant refrain was: 'Laura – you're so extravagant. Don't use so much butter.' Or wine, or cheese, or bread, or beef. It was nonsensical, since excluding the wine – and they brewed their own cider – they could take almost everything from their own land if they wished.

But that was an irritant, roughening the skin and no more. Less easily ignored was her desire to shackle Laura with her own responsibility. The old man. No longer did Laura volunteer to take care of him. It was: 'Laura – go and see to him. I need a rest.' Or in the evening: 'Laura, he's calling. He never settles for me.' Unless Laura was prepared to do battle, she had been appointed a slave.

From the other side of the door came his mother's harsh laughter. A strange sound, seldom heard. She was always at her best with Gabriel. He was the child permitted to be wild and irresponsible, as she had never been. She had married young, to a much older man. Was that the cause of it all?

He felt heavy and depressed. Would they send Gabriel home to convalesce? One more person between him and Laura, eating into their rare moments alone. Always his mother in the room, or Dinah, or his father to care for, or one of the men knocking on the window needing a hand. 'It's the heifer, guvnor. Calved in the ditch. I said we should keep her in.' Just now the farm was a turmoil of endless problems.

Even their room wasn't the haven it should have been. Going to bed at the same time seemed tantamount to a declaration of lust, so they went up separately, and sometimes Laura was asleep. Often. The days tired her, of course, up at six and barely a break before night, the incessant demands – his incessant demands.

If only he could want her less! Thoughts haunted him when he watched her raise the hair from her neck with her wrist while she was making bread, or saw her lift her skirt to climb on a chair to reach into a cupboard, or bend to fasten his father's shoe. He thought of her naked and willing, imagined himself behaving unspeakably, lived for the moment he climbed into bed and on to her – when it was all somehow wrong. He was ashamed of himself. She embarrassed him.

The door opened and his mother came out. She began to put on her gloves. 'What a poky little room they've put him in. They must think he's a nobody. I shall complain.'

'He's ill, he doesn't need anything bigger.'

'Well, you would think like that. Look at the place you've found for us to stay.'

'Gabriel's officer recommended it.'

'That jumped up little pipsqueak? No wonder. I wish you'd think for yourself sometimes, Michael.'

She aroused such anger in him! Unexpressed, it turned to lead in his stomach. Perhaps it was all his fault. He had failed his mother and was failing Laura too. What a time she was having.

The hunters, in from the meadow for at least a month, were stamping restlessly in their boxes. As if he had been waiting for Michael's absence, on the very first morning Bill Mayes, the foreman, came to Laura and said, 'What you going to do about them hosses, Missus? Eating their great heads off, night and day. Ain't right.'

'What did my husband say to you, Bill?'

'Nothing. Them hosses should be hunting, that they should.'

Laura dried her hands on a tea towel and went out to look. Behind the ploughhorse stalls were three large loose boxes. In each, gazing at her with liquid eyes, was a muscled, shining, restive horse. For weeks now the men had been leading them out and back, out and back, a purposeless, and so far unquestioned, routine. Bill Mayes was right. What were the horses doing if they didn't hunt?

'Pack was out four days last week,' said Bill. 'And these not with 'em.'

'What did Michael say? Why doesn't he want to go?'

The man viewed her with an unfriendly eye. 'Suppose he thinks a married man should keep at home. But them hosses needs hunting, that's what I say, Master wed or not.'

Laura went slowly back to the house. She needed no more proof that Michael was unhappy. He'd once told her that his greatest pleasure was hunting. Why would he give that up unless he was bowed down with care?

It was her fault of course. She had tried to change things and his mother had taken offence. She hadn't imagined that anyone would mind her cooking custards and soups and pâtés in place of the lumpen food that usually emerged at Dinah's hands, but it was soon made plain that her efforts weren't welcome. 'We don't like extravagance for everyday,' Mrs Cooper had told her pointedly. Only it wasn't extravagant to cook food well, it was wasteful to do otherwise.

She had compounded everything by taking Mr Cooper to Bainfield on market day. Since Laura appeared to be in sole charge of him she didn't think anyone would mind, but on her return Mrs Cooper had raged. 'I will not have our embarrassments paraded in public! You're the most insensitive girl I ever met. My husband's not to go out, and I'll thank you to remember it.'

'Yes. I'm sorry. Of course, Mother.' The hated, unnatural title.

If only she could talk to Michael. If only she could hold him in the dark and tell him how sorry she was, how she'd do better, how she'd do anything he wished! The look in his eyes always stopped her. It was almost a look of reverence, she thought despairingly. He didn't want a whore's dirty promises. She

246

couldn't tease him with her tricks. He wanted a respectable wife.

Evening brought a telegram. Gabriel was better; Michael and his mother would return the next day. Laura's heart sank a little. After the first shock, thinking that Gabriel might be dying, she had relaxed into life alone.

In the evenings, with Mr Cooper in bed and Dinah gone and no one but the sheepdog by the range for company, she found an odd mood of contentment. She would darn or knit, the radio playing gently in the background, bread rising quietly by the hearth. She imagined herself in charge of all this. Responsible for land, people, livestock, even the twice daily milking in the byre. Everything was hers, and nothing seemed beyond her. She was no longer Lori, the insignificant, despised hanger-on, she had suddenly, inexplicably, become Madame.

But the next day, only Michael returned. His mother was staying for a few days. 'She's found a grim sort of boarding house, and insists on staying. Poor Gabriel.'

'Yes.' Laura averted her eyes in case he should see the joy in them. She was gone and they could be together.

'Bill Mayes was saying about the hunters.'

Michael looked up from the post, all bills of course. 'He's got no business to be bothering you. I suppose I should have decided something. I'll put them up for sale.'

'Why? You love hunting. You know you do.'

'I can't go hunting and leave you here!'

She wanted to speak but her throat closed. There was no one kinder than Michael. He knew what she suffered and wanted to share the pain.

'It doesn't help to deprive yourself,' she managed. 'I want you to go. Who knows? One day I might go too.'

He looked doubtful. 'This is hard country. We'd need a sidesaddle horse.'

Laura said, 'Couldn't I ride astride? I've seen Dora Fitzalan-Howard do it a dozen times.'

Michael said, 'I dare say. It's all right for girls, I suppose. Not for married women.'

She said nothing. Clearly the sidesaddle was expected. She went to the range and inspected the pot roast she had prepared for dinner, brimming with onions and tiny turnips. She had cooked the potatoes earlier and would sautée them just before the meal. No Mother to turn up her nose.

'Did you miss me?' asked Michael suddenly.

She blinked. In truth, she had not. But that did not mean she wasn't pleased to have him home. 'I missed you every minute,' she declared, because that was how she should have felt. 'And I'm cooking a wonderful meal. Go and ride your horses until it's done.'

He came and stood in front of her, putting his hands on her shoulders. She wanted to reach up and kiss him, but knew he'd think her forward. And he stood looking down at her, longing to take her to bed, unable to tell her so and obliged instead to ride horses.

But that night was one of their better times. The exercise had exhilarated Michael, lifting some of his incipient depression, and they had drunk wine at dinner, in a little celebration of their own. When Michael began his silent, urgent thumping, Laura heard herself say, 'Not so hard, darling. I'm a woman, not a rock.'

He said grimly, 'It hurts you. I'm sorry. I won't be long.'

'I'd rather you were longer. And less hard.'

She slid her hands up inside his pyjama jacket, touching the pale flesh of his body. He quivered, like a strung violin, and she longed for him to touch her in return. It was as if she was sacred, and he had rights over one part of her alone. He simply didn't know what he was missing.

When it was over she said, 'I don't dislike it, Michael. Truly.'

He lay away from her, panting. Finally he said, 'I try not to need you so much. It makes me ashamed.'

She put out her hand to him. 'But – but I don't mind. I'm your wife, it's right that we should be together. It's proof of our love.'

'Or my unbridled desires!' He rolled towards her in the dark, his body urgent again, taking her by surprise. She opened her legs, arching herself up. It was no good. She had no hope of satisfaction. Suddenly he groaned and gripped her breast and she cried out in pain. His eyes were shut. In his haste to be done he used her like a machine, as if she wasn't living flesh at all. It was all such a painful, desperate rush.

When she looked in the morning her breast bore clear marks of his fingers. Yet this was the man who could strip out the inflamed udder of a cow so gently that the beast sighed in relief. She pressed a cloth to her nipple and closed her eyes. She wanted to be that cow. She wanted to discover her husband's tenderness.

Michael spent much of the day talking to Bill Mayes. In the afternoon a car came to the farm, and a gaggle of men went to the stables. Soon a groom rode away on one of the horses, to be replaced before nightfall by a neat little mare. Michael took Laura out to the barn to see. 'Her name's Sweetbriar. She's yours.'

And she had longed for tenderness! She put her arms around Michael's neck and hugged him. She hadn't cared about a horse, hadn't wanted one, but this proof of his love was sweeter than the little mare's name.

Her lessons began the next day. She rode in her breeches, with a heavy serge apron round her waist. 'There's an old habit of Mother's you can use when you hunt,' said Michael encouragingly. Laura schooled her face into a total absence of expression and allowed Bill Mayes to toss her on to the horse.

The mare danced a little and Laura felt a rush of apprehension. It was years since she last rode, and then only a child's pony in the park.

'Sits well, Master,' said Bill Mayes, chewing on his pipe. 'Take her down the field, Missus, and see how she does.'

All the men came out to watch. It was a trial of the new wife as much as the new horse. Would she prove herself a coward, no match for the Coopers of whatever sex? Or would she wring a triumph out of this uncomfortable situation?

The horse trotted and she bumped in the saddle. Everyone here posted to the trot, she knew, but in France it was seldom done. They would think she couldn't ride. At once she pressed her heel to the mare and set her into a canter, catching her lip at the first leap forward. '*Zut!* Slow down, you brute. Oh God!'

But the mare was a rocking horse, cradling her like an infant. Gradually Laura gathered herself, feeling the reins, settling herself more securely. It would have been hard to fall off. The sidesaddle pommels came up between her legs, fastening her down, two solid chunks of leather to which she could cling if need be. She thought of the old plough horse she had ridden as a child, inelegant grubby scrambling. Now see what she could do!

It was exhilarating. She turned the mare back to the farm and cantered up the field. Michael must teach her to post to the trot. Then they would put on fine clothes – let them not be her mother-in-law's – and off they would go. They might meet the Fitzalan-Howards. There might be others who would ask her to call. Dear Sweetbriar. Dear Michael. Laura's hopes soared.

The day came sooner than she expected. There was a meet near at hand and they need only hunt for half a day before returning home. The horses weren't fit enough for more. Laura's excitement knew no bounds, and even the necessity for wearing Mrs Cooper's habit could not depress her. It was in dull dark green, severely cut, with nothing to recommend it. Laura took it in hand, putting tucks in the waist and widening the shoulders with twists of ribbon. Looking askance at the obligatory bowler hat, she added ribbon to that too.

'Remember,' said Michael as he tied her stock, 'you're not to jump anything. It's your first time and you've got to take care.'

She looked up at him. 'I promise. Will you jump?'

'I'm afraid so. It's rather expected. Try not to get lost.'

She felt somewhat daunted. She had expected that Michael would be there to take care of her. But once she was mounted on Sweetbriar she felt better. What could harm her on this damp winter morning, the horses' feet brushing through piles of rotting leaves and filling the air with the smell of moss and earth? Birds watched them beadily from the skeleton branches of the trees and suddenly, to her surprise, something welled up inside. What was it? A warm uprising of unspecified emotion, a sense that she and the world were for once in accord. Realisation dawned slowly. She was happy.

Michael turned in the saddle to look at her. 'All right?' he called. She nodded, speechless. What could be better than to be Mrs Michael Cooper, on this day, in this place, at this moment in time? The trees gave way to a little cluster of houses and beyond, in the open fields, the village.

Hounds were gathered on the green, sterns waving like the masts of little yachts. As Laura rode up, somewhat shyly, she saw that only one other woman rode sidesaddle, in a habit of gaunt black with a veil. The ribbons on her own hat now seemed frivolous. Her mare began to sidle this way and that. Her happiness gave way to normality.

'How are you? You do look pretty.' It was Dora Fitzalan-Howard. 'Have you heard from Gabriel? Will he be coming home to convalesce?'

'I don't know. We're waiting to hear.'

'Do send him my love.'

Mrs Fitch the huntmaster's wife rode up, on a raking chestnut with a wild eye. 'At last, our shy new bride. Thought Norma'd got you chained in the cellar. Aren't you calling? Tuesdays I receive, unless we're hunting of course. But we don't hunt Tuesdays as a rule. I'll expect you.'

'Thank you. Of course. Delighted . . .'

Her mare danced away, bringing the inanities to an end. She barged into a man on a black, who touched his hat to her. 'If you'll forgive me, she might do better with a longer rein. Mrs Cooper, isn't it? I believe you come from Paris, I know it well.'

Her smile froze on her lips. She looked at him desperately, trying to see if there was something she might recognise. But in all the nights and all the men you didn't remember. They were just men.

He didn't seem to know her. Of course he did not. 'Are you all right?' he asked sympathetically. 'Is the mare too much for you?'

She blushed. 'I don't know. She may be. I'm out of practice, I'll have to see.'

'Might I suggest you stay at the back? Lot of bruising riders here today. You don't want to frighten yourself.' She wondered if she looked as if she frightened easily. They might all be laughing at her dress and her riding. She looked around but could see no one that she knew, not even Michael. Someone offered her a glass and she took it and drank. Cognac. Good.

Hounds were moving away. The air was filled with barking and the clatter of shoes on stony roads. A horse began bucking but its rider quelled it at once. She was an amateur amidst experts, quite clearly. She would take good advice and hover discreetly at the back.

They rode through a gate and across a field. Then they stood and waited. Michael came over to her, looking his best, eyes bright, sitting his horse as if born in the saddle. Laura's leg was aching where it was bent over the pommel, and they had hardly begun.

'Enjoying yourself?' he asked. 'Everyone says how lovely you look.'

'Do they?' She hung on to the fidgeting mare. 'Why don't we begin?'

'We're waiting for hounds to find. Ah!' The horn began blowing. 'We're off.'

The field waited, horses plunging, while hounds raced away, flowing over a wall like a magic carpet. Sweetbriar chewed on her bit, and a woman said, 'Don't hold to her mouth. She won't settle.'

But then they were gone.

Nothing Laura could do would check the horse. She raced across the ground, up with the leaders, holding to her mouth in earnest with no result. The wall loomed, Laura screamed, the horse leaped and they were over. She looked for Michael but he wasn't there. She was on her own.

Another field, another wall. Again she couldn't stop. But the first wild rush was abating, the horses were settling to a steady hand gallop. Laura pulled on the reins and felt Sweetbriar check. Two jumps! She felt elated. So much for staying at the back.

Now she could take Sweetbriar through a gate, but then, breath returned, the mare took charge again. A ditch. Laura clung to her pommels and let the mare do her best, a slither and a lurch and they were across. Into a wood now, the noise from the hounds coming back to her like the bells of Gunthwaite church. Were they near Gunthwaite? She didn't know. Thorns across her face, she tasted blood, and saw a riderless horse, not Michael's thank God. At the end, another wall. Huge. Unforgiving. The fallen rider lay groaning, one or two by his side, but the others were tackling the wall. Sweetbriar looked, considered, and turned away. Laura felt abashed.

She found her way to a gate and trotted through, reverting to the bounce bounce bounce of her childhood. Everyone was gone, there was nothing to prove. It was very quiet on the edge of this wood. A fox slipped from the trees and loped across a field, vanishing like smoke in the grass. Someone was riding towards her. Michael.

'I was looking for you. I thought you might be in trouble.'

She shook her head. 'The wall was too much. Sweetbriar refused.'

'She'd have jumped if you'd insisted.'

'You told me not to jump at all! But you didn't tell the mare.'

'No. Darling, I'm so proud of you.'

He reached out and took her hand. His eyes sparkled in the cold air, and he never looked so well as on a horse. Laura felt a stirring deep in her belly. Their knees touched. Michael said thickly, 'I wonder if we ought to go home.'

She nodded. 'Yes. I'm tired, I'd like to lie down. With you.'

He was breathing as harshly as the horse. Suddenly he leaned across and kissed her. She tasted spirits. He wasn't sober, that was it. Why didn't he take her against a tree, now, when he was hard and she was willing, when the blood was hot in their veins?

His hand brushed the front of her habit. She looked at him. She drew in her breath. Slowly, carefully, she unfastened her buttons. One, two, three. His hand reached into the opening, feeling for her satin-covered nipple. It was like a button itself, hard and knobby. He rolled it against his palm. She leaned from her saddle towards him, sinking against his iron thigh.

The horses squealed and parted. Laura slumped across the mare's neck, her groin hot with desire, her breasts aching for satisfaction. Why didn't they do it now? 'We must go home, go quickly home,' said Michael.

She imagined it. Running to the bedroom, throwing off clothes, clutching at each other. Michael naked at last, embraced by damp thighs, welcomed into a woman who wanted him. They must ride fast. Away down the track then, a gate at the end, stopping for a kiss. His hands at her breasts again, his newest toy. His breeches were distended against the saddle. She reached out and touched him there.

'Good God, Laura! What are you—' He pulled away, scarlet with embarrassment.

'I'm sorry. I thought—'

'What a filthy thing to do.'

'But I thought – we're going to make love—'

'That's not something you do.'

She took in her breath. 'But if it pleases you—'

'I'm not perverted, for God's sake! I don't touch it myself

253

more than I must. I'm not having my wife soil her hands just to – I wouldn't expect anything of the kind.'

She turned away and fastened her tunic. Everything was spoiled, the mood was gone. They rode back in silence, and Laura remembered her earlier happiness. Where was it now? She felt simple, consuming shame.

Chapter Eleven

Gabriel was lying on the sofa in the morning room. Usually cold as the grave, there was today a fire blazing merrily in the grate, some winter roses in the window and a scatter of books and papers on the floor. Mrs Cooper came bustling into the room and began tidying. Gabriel said, 'Don't bother, Mother. Then you can blame Laura later.'

She gave him a measured look. 'I don't know what you mean. The girl's impossible. No doubt she imagined a life of pleasant idleness once she'd landed her catch, but she's got to learn.'

'You don't give her a minute's peace.'

She smiled, her gaunt face suddenly alive. 'Don't I? Michael's besotted with the creature, of course. But at least I saved you.'

Gabriel levered himself up on his good arm. 'Saved me from what?'

His mother raised her eyebrows, as if the answer was obvious. 'Marrying her, of course.'

She passed behind his head, trailing chill fingers across his forehead. He felt weighed down by her, as if he had to carry her through life. From the moment of his birth he had been and must remain the focus of his mother's gloomy soul.

There was a knock on the door. It was Laura, with a tea tray. She struggled with the door and then with a small table on which to rest the tray, but Mrs Cooper lifted not a finger to help her. 'Don't leave the tea things for hours,' she said. 'Come back and fetch them when Gabriel's done.'

'Yes, Mother.' The obedient, servant-like response.

Gabriel said, 'You look exhausted, Laura. I can bring the things out.'

She flashed him the briefest smile. 'You'll only drop them. You're not in any condition.'

'I bet I look better than you.'

Mrs Cooper left the room, driven out by Gabriel's defection to Laura's cause. As the door closed, Laura said, 'You shouldn't annoy her. She'll take it out on me later.'

'You should chuck the tea at her. She's bullying you and getting worse.'

Laura sighed and sat on the edge of the sofa, next to Gabriel's feet. 'I know. She's enjoying herself. But if I stand up to her, all she does is go and bully Michael and worry him about money and the farm. And if I don't look after your father and she has to do it, she's unkind to him.'

'Unkind?' Gabriel looked askance.

'She slaps his hands and calls him an old fool.'

'She's always done that.'

'Has she?' Laura gazed moodily into the fire. 'I can't bear to see it, that's all.'

Her profile was turned to him. Large eyes, long nose, a mouth with the top lip too narrow and the bottom too full. Not a pretty face in the accepted sense. Yet somehow it held the eye. An interesting face. He felt again surprise that she could have slept with him with such abandon, but treat him now as if she was just his brother's wife. Perhaps in her mind the event was no more than the exercise of professional skill, as if she were an expert bellringer, brought out of retirement to ring one exalted peal.

Gabriel said, 'You'll have to do something. You can't go on like this.'

She smiled and glanced at him. 'She's no worse than a lot of people. I've begun calling, did you know that? I get all dressed up and Bill Mayes drives me in the car. He hates it, but Michael makes him. I take tea with ladies, and they're all on best behaviour and terribly dull, except Mrs Fitch, who talks about horses and childbirth. She wants me to stop riding sidesaddle. She says it causes accidents out hunting.'

'It does,' said Gabriel. 'If the horse turns over, you turn too. There was a woman killed once, when I was about fourteen. I saw the fuss by the ditch, but I didn't know she'd died until afterwards.'

'Killed?' Laura blinked at him. 'Michael wouldn't let me do anything dangerous. And Sweetbriar's so good.'

Gabriel leaned wearily back. 'Is she? I wouldn't know.'

Laura poured his tea and helped him to drink. He was easily tired just now. It was foolish of his mother to bring him home at all, to the boredom of the sofa interspersed with the painful attentions of Dr Hendon every day. His arm was a mass of half-healed cuts and tender flesh, within which the smashed bones struggled to knit. He nibbled at some bread and butter, but nothing more. 'I must get on,' said Laura, dragging herself to her feet and gathering the cup and plate back on to the tray.

'Don't go,' said Gabriel, reaching out with his good hand to restrain her. 'Why not stay and talk?'

Laura turned away. She felt faint suddenly, for no good reason. Perhaps it was sitting like this, taking her back to the Zambesi, as if she wasn't married, as if Gunthwaite wasn't known, no Michael, no future, just – emptiness. A curtain of black seemed to be rising from the floor. She reached out to steady herself and something crashed. She had dropped the tray.

'Mother! Michael!' Gabriel roared for help, and his mother rushed into the room.

'You foolish girl!' snapped Mrs Cooper.

Could she really spend a lifetime with this woman? The curtain rose and oblivion beckoned. Laura folded like a puppet losing its strings.

She woke in the bedroom. Dr Hendon, old and rather vague, was sitting on the bed holding her hand. 'Now, my dear,' he said, peaceably. 'If you're well enough, I think we should talk. Your husband says you've been looking peaky lately. How are your monthlies?'

'My – monthlies?'

'Your menstrual cycle. Have you been menstruating?' He was used to the hesitation. Women were always coy about the subject, and this was a new bride. She shifted uncomfortably in the bed. And he'd always thought the French were more open about these things. But women were women, it seemed.

'I – I haven't. Not since my marriage.'

'I see. Well, we won't jump to any conclusions just yet. It's not unusual for a big change like that to make a girl somewhat irregular. Let's have a look at your tummy.'

She lay quite still while he pressed the smooth expanse of skin below her waist. She felt almost detached from the process, as if he was examining a body which belonged to her but which she didn't at present occupy. Then he asked to look at her breasts, and she unfastened her blouse quite dispassionately. Against the white of her skin her nipples looked raspberry red.

'No doubt about that,' said the doctor with satisfaction. 'Your husband's going to be pleased with himself. You're going to have a baby, my dear, and I want to be the first to congratulate you.'

She stared at him. 'There must be some mistake,' she said in a small, bemused voice.

'None at all, Mrs Cooper. In just over six months I expect to deliver you of a son or daughter. Now, lots of rest and good food. You'll find everyone a great deal kinder, I dare say, now you're with child.'

'Will I?' She eased herself up in the bed. 'I didn't expect—'

'To be expecting? That's what comes of cold Yorkshire nights in a nice warm bed. Cuddles have consequences, that's the fact of it.' He was beaming at her, clearly delighted with himself. Anyone would think he had achieved the result.

She lay quite still when he had gone, putting her hand on her stomach. There was a small, hard ball beneath her exploring palm. She remembered the last time, all the anger, all the fear. It was always like that in the Rue de Claret. Sometimes a *préservatif* split, sometimes a girl took a chance for a bit of extra cash, or the man pulled a fast one and she realised too late. A few girls, touched by the idea of motherhood, let the thing go on. But there was no pleasure in it. Just pain and worry and poverty, and afterwards working twice as hard to keep the kid. Not many kept them long. It was hard to work with a baby behind a curtain, and in the end the offer of money and a better life got it carted off to some woman who couldn't have any of her own. Whores' children were worth quite a bit, if the mother was pretty.

The door opened and her eyes widened in alarm. But it was Michael, flushed with excitement. 'Is it true? Really?'

'He says so. I – I think so.'

'Darling. Darling, darling, I don't think I've ever been so happy.' He stood looking down at her. She felt quite detached

258

from him; she believed neither in his happiness nor her own.

'What shall we do?' she asked, and he said, 'Do? Take care of you, that's all. Mother's got to learn that she can't go on treating you as she does, not now. And I won't – I shan't trouble you at night.'

She reached for his hand and held it. 'You needn't say that. If you're gentle it should be fine.'

'Don't worry about that now. You're what matters. You and our child.'

He embraced her and they clung together. Quite unexpectedly she felt a surge of feeling towards him, a longing to hold him and cradle him to her breast. He reminded her, in his need, of Gabriel. This could be Gabriel's child, she found herself thinking. It could so easily be his. She had taken a chance, expecting nothing, and fate had seized on her inattention to play a practical joke.

Thoughts ran fleetingly through her head, not stopping to be considered. No bleeding since Gabriel. But none since Michael either. Faint and ill on her wedding day, but only through cold! Michael moved his lips against her hair, whispering endearments, and she murmured back, 'I love you. I'm glad you're happy. He didn't say when it would be.'

She could go to Leeds and get rid of it, no doubt. Once again endure the fear and pain, destroying not only this child but possibly all the others she might have. Marriage concerned children, she told herself. Gabriel's child, Michael's child, who would ever know? Not Gabriel, certainly. She'd never tell him.

Michael pulled away from her and looked deep into her eyes. What did he see there? Surely that she loved him. She would give him a child, Gunthwaite's child, the heir, however it was conceived. A child belonged to the people who loved it, and who could doubt Michael's love? A great surge of happiness was beginning inside her. This was what she was born for, the reason for her existence. Her scarred and battered body had taken Gunthwaite's seed, planted it and enabled it to grow. She harboured Gunthwaite's future, and that future would be glorious. No child would ever be so cherished.

Despite the momentous news, everything went on much as

before. For a few days Laura avoided Gabriel altogether, and Mrs Cooper grumbled that she had to work herself to death now Laura was shirking. Fortunately Michael took his wife's part, and sometimes in the middle of the day she could do as she pleased. Usually she went riding, which was generally considered to be good for the mother-to-be, provided she did not hunt. Riding past the kitchen window on her way down to the fields, she would see her mother-in-law watching her. It never failed to send a chill down her spine.

A little over a week after the announcement, Laura came upon an unfinished letter left lying on the library desk. It was from Mrs Cooper to Rosalind. She wrestled with herself for a few brief moments, but the temptation was strong. Didn't she deserve to know what they thought of her? She picked up the letter, leaned on the library door and read: 'You'll never believe what has happened! Michael's put his wife in the family way. A honeymoon baby, or so she'd have us believe. Gabriel won't hear of me talking to Michael, but really, the vulgarity of the girl! How are we to know she's not foisting some ill-conceived brat on the family? As you know, I've always suspected her. Whatever she may or may not be, she isn't a lady.'

Laura's heart was beating high in her throat, as if it would come up and choke her. This letter was meant for her to read. Mrs Cooper hated her, more now than before, and Laura didn't understand. This was her grandchild, and she would deny Laura before she would accept it. How strange that hatred could bring someone so much nearer the truth than love.

She said nothing, but the fire of her rage was intolerable. She found it hard to sleep, and lay in bed thinking of ways to be revenged.

'But it's true,' a small voice reasoned at the edges of her mind. 'Because she hates you she sees the truth.'

She got up, although it was cold, and went to the window. The courtyard was bright with moonlight, and a cat was padding noiselessly towards the barn. 'I know the truth,' whispered Laura to herself. 'I won't think of this again.'

But, returning to bed, she thought of murder. She imagined the house in flames with Mrs Cooper at a window and she with a ladder. She wouldn't put it up. Her mother-in-law's face would be a study in bitter amazement.

She tossed and turned uncomfortably, until Michael stirred and said, 'What is it? Can't you sleep?'

'No. I keep thinking. Why does your mother like Gabriel so much?'

'Because of his looks, perhaps. She used to say he resembled her father.'

'All the same. He's very spoiled.'

'Is he?' Michael lay on his back, gazing up into the dark. Gabriel wasn't spoiled in the usual sense, someone used to having his own way. If anything his mother's devotion erected a wall between him and his family. In her judgment he could do no wrong, he knew he would be forgiven any failure and lionised for any small success. So he struggled for some real measure of himself. All his life he had pushed at invisible barriers, trying this or that to see what would become of him.

'I wish he'd go,' said Laura. 'I wish they all would.'

'He'll go soon. He's nearly well.'

'But your mother won't.'

'No.'

Michael reached out and took her hand. She knew it was all he dared permit himself. 'I feel so lucky,' he murmured. 'You, and the baby. Mother's bound to improve, you know. Once you get to know her better, you won't find her so difficult.'

'She wrote a letter to Rosalind and left it for me to see. It said – she made it seem as if this baby wasn't yours. As if I had tricked you into fathering another man's child. Why would she say such a thing?' She turned her face to him in the dark. Her chest felt tight with misery.

Michael was very silent. When at last he spoke he said, 'I suppose I should have told you. I know I should. But I was frightened you wouldn't marry me. When I was seventeen I caught mumps very badly. My whole body was affected. It was thought I might die. When I recovered, the doctor gave it as his considered opinion that I would never father a child.'

'Dr Hendon? It was Dr Hendon?'

'Yes. Why?'

'He doesn't know anything!'

'Well – no. So it seems.'

Laura fell back against the pillows. She had the urge to

hysterical laughter. Michael had deceived her exactly as she had deceived him, and they had both been confounded.

'How dare she think that of me?' she said at last. 'Of course the doctor made a mistake!'

Michael chuckled. 'Of course he did. But it's not all to do with you. She doesn't want me to have a child. That way Gunthwaite goes to Gabriel's family.'

'Gabriel doesn't have a family, he isn't even married! And you're as much her son as he is! Why don't you loathe her, Michael? She's so unkind!'

He sighed. Sometimes Laura seemed so innocent. She thought she could change things that were simply part of life. Love couldn't be commanded, it wasn't possible to extract it by argument or force. He had always known that his mother's love was denied him. In fact, until Laura, he had believed he would never be loved at all. 'It doesn't matter,' he said. 'Not now.'

She lay back against the pillows. 'You could have told me. I'd still have married you.'

He buried his face in her hair.

They fell asleep soon after. But Laura kept waking, aware of Michael's body lying close. She felt a restless, nameless longing for comfort, excitement, release. If their loving had been easy perhaps she wouldn't now feel its absence quite so much. They didn't yet understand each other, that was the trouble. She thought how much more difficult it was to make love as a wife than as a whore, conforming to some ill-defined code of practice. At least as a whore she had only been concerned with pleasure.

Why did she still feel like this? She had expected pregnancy to bring that to an end, but apparently it was not to be. Her mind drifted, taking her pleasantly to that limbo in which thought and feeling combine to liberate the spirit. She thought of a man, a nameless man, faceless – she thought of Gabriel. She had taught him all about love.

She turned over, letting her hand drift across her breasts, imagining it to be Gabriel's hand. Why him, out of all of them? Why not Michael? Her pillow was hot and uncomfortable. She fought for sleep.

The next day, Michael was due to take his mother to Bainfield. But at lunchtime a heifer began to calve, and it was clear she wouldn't be done for several hours. He told his mother Bill Mayes would have to take her, and true to form she was unreasonable.

'Who's going to look after me? Bill Mayes is no use. I insist that you come.'

Laura finished spooning food into old Mr Cooper's mouth. 'I'll go with you,' she said.

'You will be too busy at home,' said Mrs Cooper.

'But I will come, if you don't mind. I need to shop.'

Mrs Cooper looked at the girl. They measured each other. Michael said, 'There, Mother. The perfect solution.'

'Indeed.'

Bill Mayes was a ponderous driver. The two women sat behind him, exchanging stilted conversation. Mrs Cooper began a long monologue about some friends of hers who had lately left the district, connections of some much grander family. She began to reminisce about her glorious youth, when she had danced until dawn and always travelled first class. It was all fancy, Laura knew. There had been no grand balls and first-class tickets. In the words of the Cooper relations, Norma was putting on airs.

'They don't have balls in France, I imagine?' said Mrs Cooper disdainfully.

'Not as many as you seem to have. But I never went.'

'I doubt you did. Gabriel was right, wasn't he? It's obvious you've married above yourself.'

Laura's temper surged. She choked it back, constrained by the back of Bill Mayes' head. 'I know you're not pleased about the baby,' she said tightly.

'My dear, if I might remind you? *Pas devant.*'

'Did you want to talk in French? Of course. If you wish.'

'I don't speak French, as well you know.'

Laura bared her teeth in a smile. 'How odd. The English culture.'

Conversation died. Bill Mayes, aware of the tension, began to put his foot down. The miles clicked by.

Once in Bainfield, they went their separate ways. Laura bought wool to begin knitting a layette, and material and a pattern for a maternity dress. In the draper's, as she was paying, Mrs Fitzalan-Howard came in. She extended her hands affectionately 'Laura! My dear, I've heard your news. I couldn't be more pleased.'

'You're very kind.'

'And how's Norma taking it?'

Laura hesitated, and the older woman laughed. 'I can guess. We all wondered what would happen when you produced the heir. Come and have tea, and tell me everything.'

In the tea shop, eating muffins and slab cake, the petty squabbles of Gunthwaite seemed rather ridiculous. 'Dora's longing to come and visit Gabriel,' said Mrs Fitzalan-Howard. 'Is he well enough? You know what these girls are like.'

'The doctor says he can get up tomorrow. Why don't you and Dora come to tea next week?'

Mrs Fitzalan-Howard made a face. 'Won't Mother mind?'

Laura chuckled. 'Yes!'

The meeting cheered her enormously. Gunthwaite was so isolated, so enclosed, that at times you could forget other lives, other worlds. She read the newspaper on the way home, putting flesh on the bare bones of the wireless news. Mrs Cooper said, 'All this silly talk about war.'

'Is it silly? I can't decide.'

'I wouldn't think you could. The French don't understand our position. Europe doesn't concern us, we have the Empire.'

'But still. The fascists, this man Hitler—'

'If he wants to do something about those encroaching Jews, then good luck to him. Someone has to stand up to them.'

'You know as much about Jews as you do about me,' said Laura thinly. 'But you're always ready to spread gossip.'

'What on earth do you mean?'

Laura looked her full in the eye. 'Do give Rosalind my love when next you write.'

She returned to her newspaper. Mrs Cooper sat rigid and fuming at her side.

Her little victory, and the promise of next week's entertaining, buoyed Laura up. When at last they reached home the kitchen seemed warm and welcoming, and Dinah had made tea. 'I'll take Gabriel's through,' said Laura impulsively. 'Dora's coming to see him.'

'He won't like that,' said Dinah. 'Pour him a whisky and you drink the tea.'

Laura laughed. She was feeling happy and confident for once. When she went into the morning room Gabriel looked up grimly, as if he was expecting his mother. Seeing that it was Laura, he said, 'Hello, stranger! Long time no see.'

'I've been resting. Everyone thought it was best.'

'Yes. Mother said. Congratulations.'

'Thank you.'

There was a silence. She put down the tray, gesturing vaguely. 'Do you want this? Or shall I pour you a whisky? Dinah said you might like one. Dora's coming to see you.'

'Is she? Oh, God.'

She poured the whisky. He could drink it whether he wanted it or not. She said, 'Did you know your mother wrote to Rosalind? She said the baby wasn't Michael's. I don't know how she dared.'

'No.' Gabriel avoided her eye.

Laura said breathlessly, 'Anyone can see she's just jealous.'

'Yes.' Gabriel took a gulp of his drink. 'You are sure, are you?' he said suddenly. 'I don't mean to suggest anything, of course but – you are sure?'

'I don't know what you mean,' she said coldly.

He looked her full in the face. 'We didn't use anything.'

'We didn't have to. It was the wrong time. I knew it was safe.'

'You're sure? You couldn't be mistaken?'

'Really, Gabriel! A girl like me? We don't make mistakes.'

He grinned, suddenly boyish with relief. 'No. I don't suppose you do.'

She took his glass from his fingers and sipped it herself. Delicious heady spirit. 'The snowdrops are out in the wood and two of the ewes have lambed. Michael thinks the tup must have got to them early. And everyone in Bainfield's talking about war. I've got the paper if you'd like it.'

'Please. My God, imagine war, and me laid up.'

'Not for much longer. You're getting up tomorrow.'

'I had a letter from Philip. The squadron's moved on, they're on Hurricanes. And I'm still here!'

'But they'll let you catch up, won't they?'

'There's to be an enquiry. If I'm found to be responsible, then no.'

She gave him back his drink. Poor Gabriel. At that moment

she could feel detached sympathy for him. So much to hope for, so little he could do. She was busy with her life, with everything going on, while he stood aside, watching his future recede into the mist. He might never fly again.

Chapter Twelve

To everyone's amazement, one night at dinner Mrs Cooper suddenly announced her intention of visiting her old friend, Alicia Allenby. Gabriel choked on his soup. When he could speak he said, 'Do give her my love, Mother.'

'Of course. She always asks after you.'

'You can tell her our news,' said Michael, covering Laura's hand with his own.

'Yes,' said his mother in a voice like vinegar.

They sent her in the car, surrounded by rugs and furs, like a Russian. In an excess of gratitude to see her gone, Laura made patties and dainty sandwiches, and packed them with a half bottle of elderflower wine. Her mother-in-law accepted the offerings stonily. 'I trust you'll take care of Gabriel,' she said, and closed the window of the car. Laura stood waving as she drove away.

The house felt lighter without her, thought Laura, wandering from room to room safe in the knowledge that Mrs Cooper wasn't there. She could fill her lungs with honest air, sing, shout, scrub the step or leave it filthy, just as she wished. There was little enough time for scrubbing though, Mrs Cooper or not. That night the first ewes began to lamb.

Laura had never experienced anything like it. Michael was out all night and half the day, returning only to sleep, and even Gabriel stood duty through the night, doing what he could with his half-healed arm. The stream of bedraggled infants never seemed to cease. Laura became used to stirring porridge with one hand and feeding lambs with the other, while Dinah cursed under her breath. 'Dratted things! Time was the shepherd saw to them out on the hill. Not in decent houses, upon my word!'

'Time was we could afford to lose a few,' said Michael prosaically, eating a well-earned breakfast.

'Where's t'shepherd?' demanded old Mr Cooper, who in age was forgetting his pretensions and betraying his origins. 'Or young Bill Mayes?'

'He's busy,' said Laura, expertly folding a napkin around the old man's neck. 'Don't worry about it.'

When Michael had again gone out into the yard the kitchen grew quiet. The old man was nodding off to sleep, and a row of apple boxes, each containing a lamb, stood before the fire.

'Peaceful without her,' said Dinah, folding her hair back into its bun. 'Why don't you get Mr Michael to move her into one of the cottages by the stream?'

Laura laughed. 'They're falling down!'

'They can be mended! I don't say she'd like Meadow Cottage, there's no road to it, but one of those by the stream would suit.'

Laura turned the thought over in her mind. The farm was littered with old dwellings, legacy of a time when they employed a dozen men. Cottages for shepherds, cottages for smiths, cottages for cowmen and labourers, they all stood empty. She said, 'She wouldn't go. She'd say I was pushing her out.'

Dinah snorted. 'Old folk always move out of the farm when the son takes over. Only right, with babies and that. She's just stubborn like she's always been. Stubbornness made her marry and stubbornness made her stick it. Better that than have everyone say she'd been jilted.'

'Jilted? Are you sure?'

'As sure as I stand here. Set her cap at the son of the big house, she did, went all out for him. Then he left her flat. Married a London girl. So all it took was young Cooper to cross her path, with his fine farm and his string of hunters, and she grabbed him with both hands. Next thing she's a farmer's wife, and it don't suit. Ruined him, she did. Foreign travel and extravagance. Then it were all his fault and she started to pinch. Never known a woman take to counting money like her.'

Laura licked her lips. She had to phrase this carefully. 'With this other fellow. Did she—?'

'What? Open her legs? Doubt it. Or she might have done and he didn't like what he found. Some women are like that. With others, men never get enough.' Dinah leaned against the dresser with all the confidence of a woman whose husband is long since dead.

Laura lifted one of the smallest lambs and began rubbing it with a towel. The creature bleated weakly, and tried unsuccessfully to stand. She resolved to choose her moment and talk to Michael.

But the next morning a note was delivered by Mrs Fitzalan-Howard's chauffeur, saying that she hoped it would be convenient if she and Dora called for tea that afternoon. It was a gentle reprimand; Laura should have written to confirm her tea-shop invitation, and she had forgotten.

She ran up to Gabriel's room, and burst in. He was shaving before the glass, the cast on his arm resting on the mantelshelf, his pyjama trousers looped precariously around naked hips.

'I'm sure we know each other well enough to forget to knock,' he remarked.

'Sorry. But it's urgent. Dora and her mother are coming to tea.'

Gabriel turned back to the mirror. 'Dora. Oh God. But her mother's charming, why the long face?'

'I forgot. We've nothing in. And your mother has the car.'

Gabriel dried his face awkwardly with one hand. Laura took the towel from him and completed the task more effectively. 'I wanted to serve something really good. Pâté, and a good soup, and—'

'My dear girl.' Gabriel caught her hand. 'Some sandwiches, any sort, a large cake, some small ones, some scones with jam and cream, and that's it.'

'But I like Mrs Fitzalan-Howard!'

'All the same. The English way. Believe me.'

She went dismally out into the long upstairs hall. She was sure Mrs Fitzalan-Howard would think her unwelcoming. She went back to the bedroom and put her head around the door again.

'Laura!'

'Sorry. You will be there, won't you? Not with the lambs?'

Gabriel sighed. The thought of Dora and her mother did not inspire him. 'All right,' he said at last. 'For you.'

'Thank you, Gabriel!' She ran into the room to press a kiss on his cheek. He put out his hand and held her. She stood very still, saying, 'Gabriel. Don't.'

His eyes were fixed on the swelling beneath her apron. She covered it with her hand, and he said, 'Can you feel it yet?'

'The baby? No. That must be later.'

'Four months, they say.'

'I wouldn't know.'

She pulled away from him and went to the door, but he was before her. He closed it in her face. 'Laura.'

'Yes?'

'You are sure?'

She looked him full in the face. Her eyes were so clear, he thought, there was nowhere deceit could hide. 'I told you,' she whispered. 'It's Michael's baby. Don't talk to me about this again.'

Already the first crop of lambs had lost their innocence and become bumptious, bullying their mothers unmercifully. They lambed early at Gunthwaite, considering how high they were, because the pasture was relatively sheltered, with huge banks of trees breaking the blast of wind and snow. In April though the woods harboured foxes with young to feed, which made them careless. As Mrs Fitzalan-Howard and her daughter drove into the yard a tall, red vixen flowed over the wall and away.

'Did you see that?' Mrs Fitzalan-Howard turned smiling to Laura. 'You'll have to ask the hunt to make you first on the list next season.'

Dora said, 'Are they taking the lambs?'

'I don't think so. Not yet.' Laura gestured to the front door, forced wide for the occasion. 'Won't you come in?'

The guests stood in the hall and admired the huge beams, crossing and recrossing in a tangle of dusty wood. 'It's really magnificent,' said Mrs Fitzalan-Howard. 'I haven't been here in years, I'd forgotten.'

'Yes.' Her daughter was more interested in other things. She said, 'Is Gabriel about?'

'He's joining us for tea,' said Laura.

They stood awkwardly together. She didn't know if she should take them through to the drawing room now, or perhaps show them something first? The lambs?

They went through to the kitchen. Old Mr Cooper looked up at them like a bemused crow, but the ladies said good day most kindly. Dora looked delightful, thought Laura, watching her bend over the most sickly lamb. She had dark blonde hair curling over her ears, and a small-featured face. She wore a neat wool dress that clung to a more than ample bosom. Laura looked down at her own skirt and sweater. She looked like a respectable matron, she thought. A good choice, for once.

Dinah was making faces. The guests should be taken to the drawing room. Laura looked desperately for Gabriel, and saw him coming across the yard. He looked disreputable, in cord trousers and shirt, the sleeve ripped to accommodate his cast. When he came in, he said, 'By Jove, you've arrived! You look super, Dora, quite grown up. And your mother barely out of the schoolroom, if appearances don't lie!'

'Really, Gabriel.' Mrs Fitzalan-Howard put her cheek up for him to peck. 'We're here to console your sickbed and I see you're hale and hearty.'

'All but for this.' He waved his cast and excused himself, promising to join them when he smelled less of sheep.

Dora was pink and breathless. In the drawing room, Mrs Fitzalan-Howard made stoical conversation about wallpaper and the weather, while Dora stared longingly at the door.

'Is Michael going to join us?' asked Mrs Fitzalan-Howard.

'No. He's with the sheep.'

'He's a very good farmer. Everyone says.'

'Yes.'

Would Gabriel never come? And then he was there at last, smart in collar and tie, smelling of soap and smiling. He sat next to Dora, making her giggle and blush, and Laura thankfully rang for tea.

Over the cake, featherlight and delicious, they talked of Laura's baby. 'I must tell you, Laura,' confided Mrs Fitzalan-Howard. 'I've asked the estate carpenter to make you a cradle. He does beautiful work, so detailed. A present for you. I hope you don't mind?'

Laura blushed and stammered. It was Gabriel, she thought desperately, robbing her of her poise. She could never behave properly in front of him. She pulled herself together, summoning all Marie's haughtiness, all Zelma's restrained style. 'You're far too kind. Michael and I will be delighted.'

Gabriel chuckled. He knew when she was acting, he could always see.

But of course he had to tease. 'Doesn't she look wonderful?'

he said cheerfully. 'No one knows when the baby's due though. When is it, Laura?'

Again, she was floundering. How could he? 'Dr Hendon said to expect it when it arrived,' she managed.

'Oh, good heavens! How like him,' said Mrs Fitzalan-Howard.

When they stood together, waving goodbye, Gabriel said, 'A success, I believe.'

Laura said, 'I was so worried. I couldn't talk.'

'Unlike Dora, who never stopped!'

'You make her nervous.'

'And who made you nervous? The Fitzalan-Howards are very kind.'

She looked away. 'It wasn't them. You were unfair, Gabriel. I wanted to do it right.'

'Oh, Laura.'

He was looking down at her with rough tenderness. She felt uncomfortable suddenly. He wasn't teasing now. Madame used to say that young men fell in love when the moon was full, with whatever crossed their path. She was too much in Gabriel's path.

In a fortnight there were no more ewes in the lambing pasture, Gabriel's cast had been removed and Mrs Cooper was home. Her visit had restored her. She was loud in praise of Alicia's staff, her cooking, her home. In comparison Gunthwaite was shabby and old fashioned. They should have new curtains for the drawing room, she'd order them at once. But of course she didn't want curtains. She wanted to discomfit Laura.

She resolved again to speak to Michael about the cottages. If only they could be alone! She'd hardly seen him in weeks, and now the lambs were done they were ploughing the last heavy fields, cramming a spring crop into ground already leaping into life. One afternoon, driven from the house by Mrs Cooper's presence, she walked up the hill to see if she could talk to him. Instead of Michael, Gabriel was there.

'Laura! What are you doing way up here?' He seemed young and golden, set against the brow of the hill. He had brought the seed corn and was coming down again.

'I was looking for Michael. I just wanted a walk.'

He gestured to the long meadow. She could just see the horses, moving quickly, instead of the slow plod of the plough. 'He's busy with the harrow. He won't thank you for stopping his work. I'll walk back with you.'

'No.' She pulled away. Her hair was blowing across her face.

Gabriel said, 'Don't be silly. The hill's steep, you shouldn't go on.'

'Then I'll stop for a while. I'll walk back when I'm ready.'

'Laura, have I upset you? Is it something I've done?'

She said nothing for a moment. The wind was fiercer now, as if it was in a chimney, whistling and roaring. Laura began to shiver. 'I don't like to have you near me any more,' she said distinctly.

'What?' He looked taken aback. 'It was when the Fitzalan-Howards came, wasn't it? Something I did that day upset you.'

'No. Yes. Gabriel, your arm's better. It's time for you to go.'

He stood looking out at the windblown fields, the cattle huddling against the slopes, crows fluttering like rags from hedge to hedge.

'It isn't all because of you,' he said.

'That you won't go?'

'Yes.' He swung to look at her 'Of course you want rid of me. And I know I should go. It's just – well. The enquiry. They may ground me.'

'Better to know, isn't it?'

'No! Believe me, no!' He looked away again, at the sky, the rushing clouds, the sun. 'I want to fly again. It's all I want to do. I'm no damn' good, perhaps that's why. Somehow, some way, I have to get it right!'

'I can't do anything about your flying,' said Laura decisively. 'It has nothing to do with me.'

'Yes, it does.' He was laughing down at her. 'My dear, I would give anything to have you proud of me.'

She lifted her shoulders in her dismissive, Gallic shrug. 'You don't care what I think. And if you do, it's only because you don't care enough for anyone else. One day you will.'

They stood together, so close and yet untouching. He wanted to kiss her, but could see from her face that he'd offend. She was right, he had to go, he thought, feeling his arm still ache from the effort of carrying the corn sack, almost wishing it would ache

273

more so he could stay. She turned to go up the hill and he turned down.

'Was there any evidence of flap failure, Squadron Leader Jenkins?'

'The plane burned, sir. But her flight did indicate something of the kind.'

'Something of the kind. Pilot error, perhaps?'

'I really couldn't say, sir.'

'No. I imagine not.'

The four heads at the table bent towards each other. Gabriel sat on his hard chair, wanting to shout, 'What about the engine failure? What about that?' He was doomed, he felt sure of it. The end of an inglorious career.

'Pilot Officer Cooper.' He stood up, rigidly to attention. 'At ease, Mr Cooper. On the recommendation of your Squadron Leader, and in view of the confirmed engine failure in the plane, we are prepared to permit your return to your squadron. You will be grounded for six months and undertake re-training. Thank you.'

Gabriel found his throat had closed. He swallowed audibly. 'Thank you,' he whispered.

As they left the building, Jenkins came up to him and said, 'Well done, old man. You got off lightly. So, it's back to Norfolk for six months.'

'I thought I was to rejoin, sir.'

'After the re-training, Cooper. Look on the bright side. You're not a natural at this game, so it's bound to stand you in good stead. Get some gunnery practice.'

'You think it's war, sir, do you?'

'I'm certain it is. See you in six months. Good luck.'

Alone on the pavement, Gabriel looked for a pub, but it was mid-afternoon and nothing was open. He bought a newspaper and scanned the columns. Mussolini, Hitler. And someone claimed to have invented a new type of bicycle, with more pedal for less push. He got up restlessly. There was nothing for it. He'd have to send a telegram home and head for Norfolk once more.

Chapter Thirteen

The summer was poor that year, with a lot of rain. The sheep in the river meadows suffered with their feet, and the cows poached the land to nothing by the gates, as if it was the middle of winter. Laura gave up going for rides after a near accident at the river, putting Sweetbriar across the ford. A log came hidden on the swollen stream, to crash into the mare's unsuspecting legs. She reared and plunged and Laura almost came to grief. The child inside her seemed to leap in fright, and afterwards, safely on the bank, Laura put her hand to her belly. She had only felt flutters before, nothing more. But there was a creature in there. An actual living child.

When Michael came in at the end of a long, tiring day, trying to snatch hay between rainstorms, knowing that the crop was poor, she foolishly told him what had happened. But she only succeeded in upsetting him, because the horse had almost thrown her. Thereafter she was banned from the saddle.

She didn't mind. Quite suddenly she was anxious that this acquaintance, this baby, should be well. She began to imagine terrible things. Why should she, who had lived as she had, be granted a perfect child? Dr Hendon, after fifty years of nervous mothers, had no time for her. 'We'll know soon enough if the baby's sick so there's no use fussing. You young mothers want everything cut and dried! Have patience, that's what I say. Soon enough all will be revealed.'

It was like waiting to open a present, hoping for something wonderful, fearful of something foul. The girls in the Rue de Claret used to play tricks on each other like that. Laura smiled as she thought of the time Sophie had given her a live frog, which had hopped along the corridor making everyone scream and customers run for their lives in case the police had come. She grinned to herself reflectively. Part of Madame's policy was to keep the police satisfied. Laura had seen to one of the captains herself.

The thought of Sophie made her pause. It was time to send money once again. Madame had written to say that Sophie was still unwell, in mind as well as body, and she attached a list of all the little comforts she had been obliged to purchase, for a not inconsiderable sum. Would there ever be an end to this? The shackles of responsibility grew no lighter, it seemed. But she thought of Sophie as she had first seen her, exotic and exciting. Someone kind in those hard and friendless days. And she thought of her in that mean upstairs room. If only a little of the money reached her it had to be worthwhile. So she rode the bicycle to the village and sent the postal order once again.

On the way back it started to rain once more. Laura began to hurry, pushing the bike, aware of a slight backache. She resolved to tell Dinah about it and ask for a cup of tea, but when she went into the kitchen only Mrs Cooper was there. Laura remembered it was Dinah's day off.

She said, 'Could I have some tea, do you think? I'm rather tired.'

'I'm sure it doesn't need biblical strength to put a kettle on,' said Mrs Cooper nastily. Laura said nothing, but went for the kettle herself. Her back was aching seriously now. If it wasn't for Mrs Cooper she'd go up to bed.

The backache came again, a strong pain radiating round towards her front. She gasped and Mrs Cooper said, 'Don't start that now! You've a month to go.'

'Should I lie down, do you think?' asked Laura, because after all her mother-in-law had borne three children. She must know.

Mrs Cooper looked at her with open dislike. 'When I had Michael I was too busy to fuss. Four days I struggled, the doctor thought he'd lose me. And he'd come in—' she gestured towards her husband, sitting vacantly by the fire '—he'd come in and cry. What use is crying?'

Laura leaned against the dresser, feeling the pain start again. 'I'm sure something's happening,' she managed. 'Could you go and call Michael, please? And send someone for the doctor?'

'I'll do no such thing. It's too early, and I won't go alarming people for no good cause.'

'But it is good cause—'

A cold, malevolent stare. 'Is it now? If this is a honeymoon baby, you've got weeks to wait. Of course, if it isn't, it might come now. Gabriel said Michael didn't know what he was getting into.'

Laura had had enough. She went cautiously out into the hall, aware that the pain was threatening once again. If Mrs Cooper wouldn't help she must help herself. If she had ever doubted the woman's hatred she knew better now. She would stand and watch while Laura suffered alone.

She tugged at the stiff front door, just as she had on her very first day at Gunthwaite. It gave and she crept into the yard, calling 'Michael? Michael?' in a voice high with anxiety. What would she do if he wasn't there? If no one was there? If she gave birth with no one but that witch for company?

But Michael came from the barn. When he saw her he hurried across. 'Darling, are you all right? You look frightened to death.'

'It's started. Your mother wouldn't call you or anything! She hates me, Michael, she wants me to die. She thinks the baby isn't yours, she thinks I'm a thief, she wants me to suffer for days!'

He put his arms around her and held her for a moment. 'There, there,' he soothed. 'There, there. You're in a state, aren't you? Come inside. I'll send for the doctor. Perhaps the baby wants to come a bit early, there's no need for any fuss.'

He was calm as only a farmer can be. Midwife to cows by the dozen and sheep by the hundred, he was used to birth in all its complexity. Laura was like a maiden heifer, in needless panic when the pains began. He walked her back into the house, resting a soothing hand on her belly. He felt it tense and harden, and held her close until the spasm had passed. 'There,' she said shakily. 'You believe me, don't you? It's begun.'

'Of course it has. Don't worry. Mother didn't understand, that's all.'

But Laura was beyond forgiveness. She longed for the woman to be gone, to be out of the house, out of her life, forever. When the pain came again she fought it, concentrating all her energies on focusing her dislike. This was all his mother's fault. Without her she could forget Gabriel's part in all this and give birth to Michael's baby. Michael's. She would have no other.

The door opened and she tensed. But it was Dinah, summoned by Michael to attend. 'Well, you've caught us on the hop,' she declared, taking off her hat. 'Best get ready. Babies that come early usually come quick.'

'Do they? Mrs Cooper said Michael took four days.'

Dinah sniffed. 'Believed her, did you? If he did she blames him for it. Great one for blame, she is. And bearing grudges. Sit up a bit, love, I want to put this towel under you. Never know, we might get finished before the doctor comes.'

But that was a hope soon dashed. The pains came with sickening regularity, one upon the other, building. But when Dr Hendon examined her, he made a face and said to Michael, 'Not much happening, I fear. We're in for a long haul.' He went to the bed and took Laura's hand. 'Now, you've got to be brave, for a few hours at least. Each time the pain comes, try to let it have its way. We'll be done by morning.'

She rolled her head on the pillow. 'But that's for ever.'

'When your baby's in your arms it will seem like nothing at all. I'll be downstairs if Dinah wants me. Do your best.'

The room was very quiet when he'd gone. Laura felt her heart contract a little, because she was trapped here with no escape. When the next pain came she fought it like a tiger, pushing it away, refusing to allow it to come. Dinah smacked her hand lightly. 'That's not the way. The pains are helping you, but you're not helping them. Next time, breathe all through. Lots of breaths.'

She tried, and it helped a little. But nothing helped a lot. After a while the doctor came back and patted her hand. How she hated him! But she hated Mrs Cooper more. If she could she would curse her, she decided. She would uncurl her enemy's fingers one by one from her grip on Michael's soul. Why did she want him? She had no love. She hadn't suffered as Laura suffered now, for love of him.

It was very late. She asked Dinah to draw the curtain back and saw that the moon was high in the sky. It leaned drunkenly, only the top edge shadowed, as if everything it looked upon that night was topsy-turvy. She felt dread, deep and inescapable. She was so alone here, so far from help. Dr Hendon was old, and didn't care. He didn't even like her, she thought. He wouldn't struggle to save her from death.

Tears pricked behind her eyes. She was a little girl again, crouched in her mother's high bed. She yearned for that time again, to be safe, safer than anything, in the circle of her mother's strong arms. But those arms had weakened and fallen away. They had let her tumble across time and space, into this pain.

Laura groaned and Dinah came to her at once. 'Want a drink, love?'

Laura shook her head. She wanted something – she didn't know what it might be. All of a sudden her body was wrapped in an alien sensation, contorting fists, face, everything. She let out a long, involuntary wail.

The doctor came, but refused to let Michael past the door. He stood in the hall, calling, 'What's happening? Is she all right?' Neither Dinah nor the doctor spoke. Laura screamed again, a shriek of intense pain that trailed away in exhaustion. And she screamed again and again, suddenly breaking into raw-throated French. *'Mon Dieu! Mon Dieu! Je suis morte!'*

The doctor was taking instruments from his bag. Laura saw the glint of steel, they were killing her, killing her baby!

'Hold her still!' shouted the doctor.

'Don't fret, lovey, he's getting the baby out,' gasped Dinah, throwing herself across Laura's straining thighs.

But Laura struggled, her hands gripping a towel tied to the bedhead, her body arched in a bow. It was as if her baby was being ripped out, dragged from her with violence and blood. All at once something gave. The pressure miraculously eased. The doctor grunted, without satisfaction. 'It's a girl. Quickly, Dinah, take her. I'll see to the mother.'

She felt weak with exhaustion and strain. The room was receding from her vision, as if she was sliding away down a long, narrow corridor. But she heard Michael's voice and roused herself. 'Let me have it, Dinah! I know what to do.'

The baby had made not a sound. It was dead, thought Laura hopelessly. All this and a dead baby. She would have cried but her strength was gone, and besides, the doctor was pummelling her. It was like a punishment for a thousand sins, to endure this as well as everything. The corridor beckoned once again. At least, she thought as she slid away, at least here was peace.

A baby cried. It was a weak, thready sound, but it cut through the fog in Laura's brain. She opened her eyes, aware that once again the doctor was pressing fists into her belly. He hated her, that must be it. He wanted her to die. 'Is she—?' She wanted to lift her hand but could not.

'Your daughter lives,' said the doctor, briefly raising his head. 'And so must you, my girl, to take care of her. Let's see some fight!'

But she couldn't fight anyone. She was helpless with exhaustion. Yet somehow a bubble began deep inside, expanding little by little. 'Can I see her?' she whispered. 'Michael?'

And he was there, the baby in his two strong arms. 'She looks a little battered, darling,' he said nervously.

'I did what had to be done,' snapped the doctor. 'It's only the forceps. Without them she wouldn't be here now.'

Laura struggled with the last vestiges of strength, gathering them together to find energy enough to raise her head. There was her baby. Her forehead was caked with blood. One eye was closed, lost in puffy flesh, and over it all was a tangle of wild dark hair.

'She looks like you,' said Michael softly.

'Me?' Laura glanced up at him. 'I don't know. So hurt – she looks like no one.'

She sank back against the pillows. Dinah was starting to straighten the bed, and the doctor to gather up his things. Soon all would be restored to normal – except she knew, without a moment's thought, that everything was changed. Nothing would be as it was only a day before. She was a mother now.

It seemed from the first that Michael and the baby were special to each other. He had saved her when she couldn't breathe, sucking out the fluid with a straw, swinging her by the legs like a stillborn lamb. Michael's skill had saved her, and she seemed to know. He could settle her when no one could.

Laura wondered if she was jealous. A mother should wish to be first with her child. But the sight of her husband, soft and tender, sure of himself with the baby as he had never been with her, moved her almost to tears. She didn't know if Michael was the father of her child, but she knew that she wished him to be.

They called her Mary, which from time to time Laura turned to Marie.

Once her eyes began to change they saw she might have Laura's colour, that see-through absence more blue than grey. Her hair stayed dark, so all in all she was like Laura. But for the scars of her birth. The marks on her forehead remained, turning purple whenever the baby cried or grew warm. Mrs Cooper said, 'She's blemished. I thought so. Marks like that never fade.'

Laura schooled herself not to care what the woman said. It wasn't as if her mother-in-law hated the baby, after all. She seemed in fact to appreciate her somewhat. She wasn't above rocking the cradle if she cried, or moving it out of the sun if it seemed the child might be disturbed. So she wasn't all cold. Laura replaced her nightmares of someone murdering her baby with ones of her being stolen away.

Her own vulnerability alarmed her. She felt as if she had allowed herself to come to this point without any clear thought of what it would mean. She was fastened now, tied down with silken cords. Never again would she decide to leave one life and start another, with no trace left behind. Never again could she imagine death and feel nothing but curiosity. How could you die with a baby to care for? Her head ached with the burden of so much care, a burden carried even in sleep. Her freedom had gone. For ever.

The summer bloomed late that year, a few weeks of sunshine when the apples were ripe. Laura took the baby out into the orchard and let her sleep shaded by sun-dappled leaves. Now and then Michael would come and look into the cradle, marvelling. They could spend hours staring down at the little girl, never tiring of watching her hands curl and her lips purse, as if she dreamed of sucking. When Laura fed her, Michael sat at her side, enthralled.

Visitors came. It seemed that they were finally accepted as a unit of their own, as if the baby signalled their establishment. People brought presents and asked about the christening. If they asked everyone, as they should, it was going to be a considerable event. One sultry afternoon, when the heat was making the baby fretful, Dora Fitzalan-Howard rode across. Laura took her into the orchard and they stood looking down as the baby mumbled and kicked.

'She looks terribly like you,' said Dora.

'Complete with black eye?' Laura lifted her baby, and stared into her still-battered face. 'Everyone says it will go in time. I don't care, though. She's beautiful to me.'

'My mother said you'd be besotted,' said Dora, throwing herself down on a wooden seat and unfastening her stock. 'She says everyone is except people like Michael's mother, who hate everyone, including themselves. Oh, isn't it hot!'

'Michael's mother? She loves Gabriel. Adores him. It's rather horrible, actually.'

Dora sat up. Mention of Gabriel always made her pay attention. 'Does Gabriel love her back?'

'Not really. At least, not that I can see. Perhaps he's the same as her, and doesn't love anyone.'

'Gabriel? Oh, no!'

Dora pulled at the net that covered her hair when she rode. The dark blonde curls tumbled about her shoulders. Laura watched her appreciatively. Why didn't Gabriel like her? She was pretty with the soft formlessness of youth, a slender, blossoming tree that would bear the sweetest fruit. It was a product of childbirth, she realised, this urge to make everyone around her realise the pleasures that lay in store. She thought of the night of Mary's birth and winced. Pleasure? She doubted that her body would please anyone again.

'When's Gabriel's leave?' asked Dora.

'What? Leave? I don't know. He doesn't say.'

'When he does come home, tell him Mummy and Daddy really want to ask him to dine. Because he's in the air force, you see, and might know something. Everyone wants to know.'

'Know what?'

'About the war, silly! Daddy says we're in a hopeless mess. The Germans are just going to flatten us. He says it's all going to be in the hands of the flyers and not the poor bloody infantry any more. He was a captain in France, you see.'

Laura looked at her squirming child. 'There won't be a war. There mustn't. Not with Mary—'

'Oh, Daddy's an old pessimist,' said Dora lightly. 'I don't care either way, really. At least it would be something, wouldn't it? Something happening!'

'They might take Michael,' said Laura fearfully.

'I shouldn't think so! He's a farmer. They always stay put.'

'Do they?' A spark of hope, then.

'Sure to. Miners and farmers always get off. Lucky devils, Daddy says.'

Laura sat for a long time after she had gone. War. The talk had gone on for so long she had ceased to listen. And life at home had absorbed her, so much more vital than an abstract piece of news. War. She thought of the bones of that long-dead horse; the bitter, wasted acres; Madame Girand, forged by struggle into iron. It should not happen here. It could not! Gunthwaite was her refuge from the storm, her place of safety. So far from everything, so steeped in beauty, it had to be secure.

Chapter Fourteen

War was declared in September. The women heard first, standing gathered in the kitchen around the wireless. Dinah was muttering under her breath, 'It can't be! No! Not my Timothy!' until Mrs Cooper slapped at her and said, 'Shut up, damn you!'

When the announcement was over Mrs Cooper sank into the rocker and cried. Laura didn't know what to do. She looked down on that narrow dark head, so heavily streaked with grey, and considered touching it in comfort. But the woman was her enemy, more than any German, ever. She wrestled with herself and said finally, 'Gabriel's only just finished training. He won't have to fly.'

Mrs Cooper turned her handkerchief in her hands. 'They might need everyone. We can't tell.'

'They don't need my Tim,' said Dinah firmly. 'No son of mine's getting himself turned into trench-mud. He'll stick to the farmwork, and like it.'

'They'll call him up,' said Mrs Cooper, the handkerchief now a rag. 'Like the last time, they'll have to go. They took all my brothers. Three of them. All gone.'

Both women looked at her. It was the first they had heard of it.

'They won't take my Tim,' said Dinah lamely. 'We should have learned our lesson the last time. We've no need to get involved in things that don't concern us. All this fuss about Poland. I don't know Poland! Nobody does.'

Mrs Cooper seemed to be getting a grip on herself. She took a deep breath. 'But next it will be France. And Belgium. Holland, Denmark, the whole of Scandinavia. They don't mean to stop.'

'Well then.' Dinah wriggled uncomfortably. 'I don't know France or Belgium, either. If it isn't us, we shouldn't care.'

'I know France,' said Laura softly. 'I know it very well.'

She went to the fire and stirred it, because suddenly the room seemed cold. Looking out of the window she saw Michael crossing the yard, his breeches stained with muck from the byre. He looked strong and tall and capable, striding over cobbles stained amber in the midday sun. She went to the door and called, 'Michael! It's war.'

He stopped dead in his tracks. After a moment he said, 'My God.' But still he stood there, as if all thought and action must be suspended to absorb this terrible news. What would it mean for them? What was to come? He took a bemused step towards his wife. 'They won't bomb here. Mary's safe.'

'And you. You won't have to go.'

'No. At least there's that.'

One by one the men gathered to hear the news. Far down in the valley Gunthwaite church began to toll its bell, as if they were already under attack, as if there were already men to bury. 'That Hitler's sure to back off,' said Bill Mayes with assurance. 'Now he knows we mean business.'

'He's had his chances,' said Michael. 'Like it or not, I think we're for it now.'

Dinah folded her apron and hurried off home, hours early but no one said. She was rushing home to Tim. Laura knew how she felt, she herself had an urge to gather her family close around her and keep tight hold. Danger threatened. She must hold to her most precious things and never let go.

There was a flurry of activity in the next few weeks. A number of men from the village volunteered, only to be sent home to await call-up. The offices were swamped, and could well do without eager young farmboys demanding jobs flying planes or sailing warships. And quite unexpectedly, Gabriel came home.

At first it was difficult to believe it was him. He had filled out, his shoulders almost as broad as Michael's, thickened by hard work. He was brown, too, his hair bleached in the sun.

'What on earth are you doing here?' demanded Michael, somewhat uncharitably Laura thought.

Gabriel grinned. 'The first hint of war and they send all the flyers home. Bit of a turn-up, don't you know?' He spoke like that a lot, all slang and catch phrases.

'Darling!' His mother came into the kitchen and flung her arms wide. He dodged her embrace and pecked her on the cheek. 'Hello, Mother. You're looking well. There's nothing doing in this damned war so they thought they'd let me have a couple of weeks off.'

She held tightly to his arm. 'They haven't forgotten your accident, have they? You're really not fit to fly.'

'Aren't I? That's probably why they've sent me home.'

'Not really?' Laura only half believed him.

'You never know.'

Gabriel met her eyes. He seemed to challenge her. She couldn't get rid of him that easily. He said, 'Can I see the baby? Or is she forbidden territory?'

'She's here.' Laura stood aside from the cradle and Gabriel came to look. She heard him catch his breath.

'She's lovely,' he said in a stiff, unnatural voice.

'Does her mark worry you? It was the forceps. Everyone promises it should fade in time.'

'We don't care if it doesn't,' said Michael, sliding an arm around Laura's waist. 'We love her as she is.'

Gabriel glanced at them both, and then looked back at the baby.

'She's still beautiful,' said Laura defiantly. 'Everyone agrees.'

They had a celebration dinner that night. Laura cooked pheasant in wine sauce, in marked contrast to Mrs Cooper's preferred style of dried-up roast with cabbage. But it wouldn't do to admire Laura's greater skill. She said, 'I'm sorry it's not your favourite, darling. But I'm so busy with your father, I have to let Laura cook.'

'Don't you like it?' Laura bridled.

Gabriel, catching Michael's amused eye, said, 'It makes a wonderful change.'

Both women subsided in an uneasy truce. When they left the table, each to put their respective charges to bed, Michael said, 'The baby's helped things. They're getting on a little better, I think.'

'Laura's standing up for herself, you mean. Mother really should move out.'

Michael grunted. 'You know she won't go. I suggested it,

even started doing up the cottages, but then she blew cold and said we were trying to turn her out.'

'Sounds like Mother.' Gabriel reached in his pocket and pulled out his cigarettes. 'While we're alone, old man, there's something I wanted to say. We're in a hell of a mess, you know. My advice is to stockpile everything you can. Grain, potatoes, fruit, everything. Hang on to it. When this thing gets going there'll be people going hungry, I promise you.'

'Is it going to get going?' Michael blinked in surprise. 'Nothing's happened yet. I thought it could be a false alarm.'

'Believe me, it isn't. The balloon's going to go up.'

He tapped his cigarette on the table, turned and lit it in one easy move. He exhaled with weary relish. 'God, I'm tired. We've been working non-stop for months. We're not going to have nearly enough planes, not enough spares, not enough anything. Not even enough pilots.'

'But they won't bomb us here,' said Michael quickly. 'Laura and the baby are safe?'

'Yes.' Gabriel gave him a wide stare. 'As safe as anyone can be. But you can't escape it. Not even here.'

Michael got up and poured two whiskies. He almost wished his brother hadn't come home. Then they could have gone on in their backwater, with only the occasional visit from officialdom checking on pigs or the blackout to disturb their rural peace.

He changed the subject. 'What are you going to do while you're home? Hunting's been stopped.'

'Has it? What on earth for?'

'God knows. Doing our bit. Dora Fitzalan-Howard keeps asking after you. Says her parents are anxious to encourage you after all. They want you to dine. Seems you've become respectable.'

'Hell!' Gabriel drew on his cigarette. 'I suppose I should be grateful. They made it pretty damned obvious I was the local pariah, so the least they can do is give me a good dinner to make up. I'll call on Dora and catch up.'

His mother bustled back into the room. 'Gabriel, darling! I've left Laura to finish, I had to talk to you. Tell me everything. All about your friends, everything. It's so exciting when you come home. Michael's the dullest person in the world.'

When Gabriel called at the Fitzalan-Howards he was welcomed with open arms. Everyone longed to hear about what was happening in the outside world, and an actual pilot was a gift from the gods. Gabriel sat in the drawing room enjoying being lionised for a while, reflecting that Dora was really very pretty nowadays. He felt restless and bored at home; things were different at Gunthwaite now the baby had come. Michael and Laura had no time for anything but her.

Mrs Fitzalan-Howard said, 'So you will dine next week, won't you? So many people are longing to see you again.'

'Michael did mention something. Thanks.'

'And you'll ride with me,' said Dora with emphasis. 'I won't let you say no. We don't know what to do with all these horses now we can't hunt. Daddy says if the war starts in earnest we might not be able to feed them. It's too silly.'

'They're an expensive luxury nowadays,' said her mother.

'I can't believe Daddy would have them shot!' Dora shuddered and turned back to Gabriel. 'So you will ride? Tomorrow? There isn't anything else to do.'

So Gabriel agreed. Michael's horses, like the Fitzalan-Howards, were under-exercised and over-fed, so the outings were hectic. Out of practice, Gabriel wrestled with his mount, watching Dora handle hers with consummate skill.

'I'm always being shown up on a horse,' he complained, as they racketed to a halt by a gate. 'After I broke my arm I couldn't even manage Laura's quiet little mare. Ultimate humiliation.'

Dora laughed, pulling off her scarf and tossing her hair. It was obvious coquetry. 'I don't think you could ever be humiliated! You always see the joke, even against yourself.'

'Do I?' Gabriel made a face. 'On one memorable occasion, I didn't. Not for years.'

'What occasion?'

He put a firm hand on her knee. 'Let's say it concerned someone not nearly as gorgeous as you. She wasn't a lady, either. In fact she wasn't a lot of things. Although I believe she became them, later.'

'Were you in love with her?' Dora prepared herself to be jealous.

'What? No! Darling Dora. I have never been in love.' He moved his horse closer, put his hand behind her head and brought her lips to his own. A brushing, promising kiss. Then he pulled away, rode his horse back ten feet, set him at the gate and galloped away. It took poor Dora, flustered beyond belief, three fields to catch him.

He kissed her every day after that. Soon they were tying their horses to a bush and embracing. There was something delicious about secret rendezvous, thought Gabriel. He liked the fact that from the very moment Dora's parents accepted him, he was giving them every reason to regret it.

Not that he disliked the Fitzalan-Howards. Far from it. It was simply that they had disapproved of him, and Gabriel responded as badly to criticism as he did to his mother's unjustified praise. Although he didn't kiss Dora simply to spite society. She was pretty, he was bored, and kissing was a delightful way to pass this time on the brink of war. He might die. They might all die! It was impossible to believe. Impossible, too, to deny the frisson of excitement that lent spice to an ordinary life.

By the time he went to dinner, he and Dora were almost intimate friends. She greeted him at the door with a hug that surprised her mother, and led him into the drawing room by his hand. It irritated him. She didn't understand the rules; he wasn't courting her, but in Dora's life, in her sheltered world, there was nothing else.

But the evening was pleasant in its way. They ate roast pheasant, as at every house where formal dinner was being served at that time of year, gamey and too well hung. Dora laughed at his jokes too loudly and too long, and he was aware of the parents watching him. When the ladies retired, Dora's father said, 'You're doing well, I hear, Gabriel. Flying again.'

'Yes, sir. I'm to rejoin my squadron after this leave. We're off to France.'

'Good God!' Mr Fitzalan-Howard sat up a little. 'Dora never said anything!'

'She doesn't know, sir. I didn't want everyone to worry.'

One of the other guests, a retired colonel, said, 'Making a bit too much of it, aren't you, young sir? Herr Hitler's been shown he's at the limit. I doubt he'll go further.'

'He always has in the past, sir.'

'But the Axis is against him now. We've shown him we'll stand and fight, and we're ready!'

Gabriel said nothing. But his very silence showed he did not agree. Mr Fitzalan-Howard said, 'Speak honestly, Gabriel. If the worst happens, can we hold them in the air?'

He opened his mouth for the platitude, and then stopped. There was no point in deceiving them any more. 'If I'm honest – we've got a prayer, but not much of one. We're not ready.'

'For God's sake! Do you want us to give up before we've begun?'

'No, sir. We have to fight. But it's going to be hard. Much harder than anyone understands.'

No one said anything for long minutes. Then Mr Fitzalan-Howard got up and went to the cupboard, taking out a single dusty bottle. 'Shall we treat ourselves? I think it's time. My father laid this down and I wasn't intending to drink it for another two years. But I'm dashed if I'm going to miss it because of some painter and decorator in Berlin.'

They sat so long over their port that eventually Dora came and demanded to know where they were. Her father, more than a little drunk, told her to sit down and drink a glass herself. One by one all the ladies drifted in, and it felt odd, and a little immoral. But it seemed to mark a significant moment. They were all beginning to see that this war would not fade away.

The strange mood was hard to shake off. Days later, when Dora and Gabriel rode, they found themselves talking of rationing and mass bombing. 'They're going to send the children out of the towns,' said Dora in amazement. 'We've been asked if we could take three. Three! Daddy said no, he's got his collections to think of. Imagine some East End brat among those.'

'He doesn't think a few fishing flies ought to be sacrificed to save the life of a child?' asked Gabriel sardonically. They were riding through leaves in the wood, to their trysting place.

'He might if anything was happening. But it isn't. I almost wish it would, actually. I hate waiting.'

Gabriel slid from his horse. 'So do I.'

Dora moved easily into his arms. After the first long kiss she murmured, 'Are you really going to France? I don't believe it. You just want us to think you're dashing.'

'Of course I'm going. So now what do you think?'

'Aren't you frightened?'

'No. Excited, more. I'm going to be back with my squadron and all my friends.'

'Do you have a lot of friends?'

'No, not really. One really good chum. Philip Lansbury.'

'Is he a better friend than me?' She moved against him, urging him on. He could feel her breasts sliding softly against his chest.

'I don't know about that,' he murmured. 'I'm not sure how good a friend you are.'

He didn't intend to go as far as he did. But Dora was so eager, so willing to go on. His tongue and hers, meeting, entwining, and those breasts, moving like living creatures. He had to touch them, and somehow her blouse came out of her breeches, and he was inside it. God! She wore nothing underneath. No wonder she felt so good. Her nipple was hard and tight. He rolled it against his palm like a berry. Dora cried out, a low gasp of amazement. Her head lolled against his shoulder, her mouth wet and slack. His erection was fierce, he found himself pushing involuntarily into her thighs.

She said, 'What do you want? What should I do?'

He put his hands on her bottom, pressing towards her centre. If she wanted him to stop, let it be now. But she looked up at him, teeth like cultured pearls. Suddenly, triumphantly, he thought, I can do it! Like a stag at last in his prime he could take what he wanted. It needn't be prostitutes, needn't be factory girls, needn't be women desperate for a man. It could be girls like Dora, well-respected, educated girls, longing to have him inside them.

He laid her on the ground and began kissing the skin beneath her breasts, unfastening her breeches and easing them down. Dora was lying with her eyes closed, whispering, 'Do it! Do it! I hope nobody can see.'

He pushed the breeches to her knees, and she was naked. Her pubic hair was darker than that on her head, a sombre bush. It reminded him of Laura.

He began to rub between Dora's legs, a gentle persuasive motion. She began to moan, clutching his wrist when he touched her most sensitive spot. 'Gabriel! Oh, Gabriel!'

He thought, she couldn't be a virgin. But whether she was or not, he didn't care. This was so delicious! He felt as powerful as God.

Suddenly it was impossible to stop. He was on top of her, struggling with his clothes, pushing himself between thighs held tight by the breeches round her knees. For a second he was obstructed, the place seemed closed to him, her body would not give. Her eyes opened wide and stared into his face, she let out a long, wailing cry – and he was home! Locked into her, they gyrated briefly, their hips shuddering with passion. The end was not as good as the beginning. In a moment he was spent. As Gabriel withdrew he saw that he was red with her blood.

Lying panting on the grass his body began to cool. The horses were stamping restlessly. He began to realise what he had done.

'Oh, Christ,' he said softly, reaching into his pocket for a cigarette.

'What?' Dora lay in the grass, her eyes clouded. 'I didn't know I could feel like that. Did you feel it too?'

'Oh, I felt it all right. Shit!'

Dora sat up. Her lovely, pale body was stained with grass and the marks of his hands. 'I don't understand. What's wrong?'

'Everything! What the hell are we going to do?'

She pushed her hair away from her face. 'Why should we do anything?'

He felt a sudden, sharp dislike. The girl was a fool. Very slowly and clearly, he said, 'Because you could be pregnant, Dora. That shouldn't have happened.'

'But we love each other. And no one gets pregnant the first time.'

He threw away his cigarette in disgust. 'Do you really believe that?'

'Isn't it true?'

'I assure you, you could easily be pregnant! Look, get dressed, we can't stay here.'

'What are you going to do? Are you just going to take me home?'

What did she expect? he thought. Immediate marriage? He bit back the words that had risen to his lips. She was a child still, barely out of school. She didn't understand. He said wearily, 'Look. We've got to try and stop this. We'll go and see Laura.'

'Laura. Why?' Dora looked amazed.

292

'Because she's the one person in the world who might be able to help.'

She was pegging washing in the yard as they rode up. The sheets were flapping madly and frightening the horses, and Dora tried to turn round, saying, 'I think I'll just go home.'

'No.' Gabriel's hand was hard on her wrist. 'No. Don't worry. She can keep a secret.'

She came across to them, her empty basket on her hip, her dark hair blowing across her face. She looked well and happy, thought Gabriel. She called, 'Why are you two looking so glum?'

Gabriel neatly looped the two pairs of reins over a rail. 'We've been a bit stupid, Laura. We want to know what to do.'

'Do?' Laura looked from him to Dora. The girl's face was suffused with colour and her hair was coming down. 'Have you had an accident?'

'In a way,' said Gabriel. 'The thing is – something happened that we didn't mean to happen. We only meant to kiss.'

'You haven't—'

'Just now. In the wood. We got rather carried away. We didn't – use anything. The thing is, what do we do now, Laura? I thought you might know.'

Dora turned her face away and started to sob. Laura took hold of Gabriel's arm and dragged him out of earshot. 'How dare you, Gabriel! What possessed you?'

'She was dying for it! I meant to go on until she told me to stop, but she never did.'

'She's a child. She loves you, of course she didn't say no. She didn't know what she was doing.'

'But what do I do now?'

Laura turned her face away. She fell cold towards him, icy cold. 'She's given you her virginity. For a girl like her, that's important. If she's pregnant, then so be it. You should marry her. You should marry her anyway.'

He let out his breath in an angry sigh. 'That isn't possible. I'm going to France, I can't get married. Will you just tell me how to stop her being pregnant.'

She looked at him, blank-faced. Behind it, her mind was racing. She had no control over these things, but that wasn't something he needed to know. Let him imagine that a woman of her experience held the keys to life loosely in her hand. Let him believe that everything was under her constant firm control. 'She could try a douche,' she said thinly. 'Salt water's best. If I was in France there's something she could take, but you don't have it here. That's all you should do.'

'What do you mean? What else is there?'

She glanced at him, almost with contempt. 'Abortion. She could be killed or her body wrecked. Is that what you want?'

He clenched his teeth and groaned. 'I didn't want any of it! If she hadn't been so willing I'd never have gone on. If you ask me it's pretty damned decent to concern myself at all.'

Laura reached out and slapped him across the cheek. The force of the blow ran up her arm like an electric shock. Gabriel stood transfixed and Dora, drying her eyes, said, 'Please don't! It was my fault as much as his.'

Laura felt quite shaky. Her own viciousness had taken her by surprise. It was just that she couldn't bear to watch Gabriel steadily rejecting the reality of what had happened for a truth which allowed him an escape.

She tried to pull herself together, saying to Dora, 'I'll explain something which you might do. There are things a man can use, you know, to prevent accidents. If you want to make love with people you must take care.'

'But it was Gabriel! I didn't know it was going to happen. I thought—'But there was no need for her to continue. She thought she had found love, believing that everything was simple when in reality nothing was. What she and Gabriel wanted were so very different.

'You may be lucky.' Laura patted her hand. 'Let's hope for the best.'

They rode away together, Gabriel acting the gentleman a little too late and taking Dora home. Laura felt a sense of gloom clouding her day. Poor Dora. What a brutal beginning.

Relations were strained with Gabriel for the rest of his leave. Laura took care never to be left alone with him, although he was ever-anxious to be alone with her. It became a silent battle, and eventually he won. He ran her to ground in the old stone wash-house, coaxing the fire under the boiler to light. As she straightened and headed for the door he leaned against it. 'Sorry. Not this time. I want to talk.'

'And I don't. There's nothing to say. You behaved atrociously and I despise you for it.' It was a relief to have said it at last.

'But I never meant it to happen! You must know what it's like, somehow passing the moment when there's no going back.'

'There's no such moment. There's only greed and stupidity.'

He shrugged. 'Then I'm greedy and stupid. I wish I wasn't, but there you are. And afterwards I tried to put it right.'

'You should marry her.'

'Even if I wanted to, her parents wouldn't have it.'

'They might. And Dora's a lovely girl.'

'While I'm greedy and stupid. She doesn't know me. She's like – well, she's almost a child. Charmingly innocent of course – but then I never did find innocence charming. And I hate being at odds with you. It's such a strain.'

So it was. There was only so much room in their lives for tension, it seemed. 'What will you do?' Laura asked in a different tone. 'If she's pregnant, I mean. You can't send her to some quack who'll tear her apart. Some stinking place where prostitutes go. The girls are scraped out, and some of them live and some of them die. They bleed, or get infected, and they die just the same. Then it's all the police, and everyone terrified, and the parents find out. Can you imagine?'

Gabriel said, 'But she won't be pregnant! I mean, it would be such bad luck.'

Laura turned her attention back to the recalcitrant fire. In her opinion, luck hardly came into it. It was the life force, strong and insistent, brushing aside human stratagems. Sometimes nothing would thwart it, and a child would come. Dora and Gabriel might not know it, but they had done what they were meant to do. The consequences were beyond their guessing.

'You could do a lot worse than Dora,' she coaxed. 'Good family and all that. No sons. You could end up living at Fairlands. More comfortable than Gunthwaite, at any rate.'

'Everywhere's more comfortable than Gunthwaite. When's Michael going to do something about electricity?'

'When we come into money,' said Laura, at last succeeding with the fire. She flapped dirty hands at Gabriel. 'When you come into money. Get hold of Fairlands and lend us some.'

They both laughed. It was such a relief to have talked together and to be normal again.

He left at the end of the week. On his last day Dora's parents invited him to tea. He would have refused, but Laura would have none of it. When Dora asked him, her voice light with hope, she stood behind the girl and fixed him with a stare of pure ice. When he returned, glum as could be, he said, 'It isn't any use, you know. Sooner or later she's got to realise it didn't mean anything. It's just cruel keeping her hanging on.'

Laura had the baby against her shoulder, trying to settle her. 'You never know. You might think differently in a few months. No need to burn your boats. She's such a sweet girl.'

He sighed. 'I know. Perhaps that's the trouble. I don't have a very sweet tooth.'

The baby grizzled and Laura patted her rhythmically. Gabriel was so perverse, he never wanted anything he could have. He cooled to Dora the moment her family warmed to him. She said, 'You'll have to write to her. If everything's all right, you could say you'd found someone else.'

Gabriel eyed her cynically. 'I do believe you'd be thrilled if I had to marry her. It would fit your warped sense of justice. Finally, a man gets what he deserves.'

'You make it sound as if I hate men. I don't at all.'

'You do a little, though,' said Gabriel. 'It adds to your spice.'

The door opened, letting in Michael plus a blast of cold air. The baby woke from her doze and began to wail in earnest, bringing Mrs Cooper downstairs to say, 'Let me have her. I knew she'd not settle.' Laura was angry at them all, except the baby. She turned a rude shoulder to her mother-in-law and went upstairs, to lay Mary in her cot.

The child cried for a minute or so, before sighing, nestling her head into the mattress and letting her eyelids sink. The crying had brought her forceps marks into sharp relief, a great thumbprint on her forehead and a smaller red blotch beneath one eye. It might be that one day, far in the future, someone like Gabriel would despise her because of those marks. Yet Dora, unblemished Dora without visible flaw, was set aside simply for being too loving.

Gabriel was right, there was a small part of her that hated men. She hated the power they had to dole out happiness or despair. Even Michael, who had given her everything, wasn't entirely immune, because although he was wonderfully kind, she depended on him. She would love Michael whatever happened, of that she was certain, but how much more would she love him if he didn't hold her happiness in his hand?

Just then he came into the room. He stood beside her at the cradle, his hand on the small of her back. 'Don't mind Mother,' he said softly.

Laura shook her head. She tried not to mind. Michael's brown weathered cheek was close to hers, she was struck anew by the strength and size of his body. She and her baby were fortunate indeed to have a man like this to take care of them. She turned towards him, letting her lips brush his dark skin. They hadn't touched since the baby was born and for so long before. He was so patient. So kind. Suddenly he held her close, his body against hers, hot and eager. 'Let's go to bed,' Laura whispered.

'We can't! It's Gabriel's last night.'

She let her breath whisper against his ear. 'I don't care. I want to be with you.'

In the tent of their bed Michael hung above her, eyes closed, his body labouring towards the end. Laura clenched her teeth. It was awful, unbearable. Every thrust seemed to rake against barely healed flesh.

Her fingers began to claw into his shoulders, and suddenly she thought of Jean. It was as if his face was above her, and not Michael's at all. She choked back a cry, put her fist to her mouth to hold back the bile that was rising there. With an agonised groan, Michael finished. He rolled to the side and lay panting.

Later, when he slept, she lay wakeful. You thought you had buried the past, but it was always there. It was like a fungus, waiting its chance to surge into mottled, repulsive life, unassailable. Why did it surface now? Just when she needed all her intelligence and energy. She turned restlessly on her side and tried to sleep.

Chapter Fifteen

About ten days after Gabriel left, a letter came from Rosalind. It was postmarked London, and immediately Laura was on the alert. She thought she would have to wait for Michael before she found out what was happening, but to her surprise Mrs Cooper laid the letter on the kitchen table and said, 'Now what are we going to do? Rosalind's come home.'

She would say no more until Michael came in at mid-morning. He read the letter in silence. 'Well,' he said at last. 'Now what?'

'Is she coming here?' Laura demanded. 'What about the children? Is her husband in London too?'

'Howard's been called back to some hush-hush job in Whitehall,' said Michael. 'He's quite a linguist and they need people like him. Rosalind too apparently, something to do with refugees.'

'What about the children, though?'

'She asks if she can bring them to stay.'

Nobody said anything. Laura looked at her mother-in-law, trying to gauge her reaction. Mrs Cooper said, 'I can't believe she can ask such a thing. She knows how much strain we're under.'

'She can't keep the children in London,' said Laura. 'It isn't safe.'

'Nothing's happened,' said Mrs Cooper.

Michael said, 'Let's not wait until it does, though. Of course they can come.'

'You're not the one who'll have to take care of them,' snapped his mother. But her tone was ambivalent. Laura realised with sudden clarity that Mrs Cooper wanted to be the one to approve the idea. She had merely been building tension.

Laura said mildly, 'I've got Mary to worry about. So it really is up to you, Mother.'

Mrs Cooper sniffed. 'Never let it be said that I refused my own grandchildren. Really, I don't know why Rosalind couldn't find somewhere in the country and look after the children herself. But she never was in the least domesticated. And it isn't as if we have help. She knows we have to do everything ourselves, here.'

Dinah, coming in from the yard with an armful of washing, banged it down on the table. But Mrs Cooper ran on. 'I suppose we'll have to take them, though. As long as Rosalind doesn't want them to stay indefinitely. They can have the attic room.'

But it was Laura who made the room ready. She made up the beds with patchwork quilts sewn by some long dead Cooper, and put a rug by each on the boarded floor. She found two chamberpots, and rummaged through the bookshelves for something children might like to read. She found several worn little volumes of Beatrix Potter, opened one at random and was at once lost to the world. It was all as she remembered.

After a while Michael came to find her. She stood up guiltily and he said, 'The baby's crying. We wondered where you were.'

'I was getting the children some books.' She smoothed her skirt, closing the door as she always did to her past. But something made her say, 'I had this book. When I was small. I remembered it.'

'Beatrix Potter?' Michael flicked through the pages. 'Never one of my favourites, I'm afraid.'

'My mother read it to me,' said Laura jerkily.

'I thought she died when you were very young?'

'She did. But I still remember.'

She brushed past him and went quickly out. Michael stood looking after her. When Laura was in this mood he felt helpless. If there was one subject on which he dared not question her it was the past. But he saw how much it troubled her. Now she would be quiet and withdrawn, busy with her thoughts, which she never shared with him. He folded his hand around the little book, the binding slack after many many readings. She had told him often enough that she couldn't remember her mother. He felt bewildered.

★ ★ ★

The day Rosalind arrived was one of tension and bustle. Mrs Cooper snapped at Dinah all the morning, and Laura whenever she could.

'Didn't they used to get on?' Laura asked Dinah when briefly they were alone.

'Not so's you'd notice,' said Dinah prosaically. 'Fought like Kilkenny cats. Rosalind was jealous of Gabriel, you see, and she had good reason. But mostly it's just girls and their mothers. You saw how they were at the wedding. You know how it is.'

But how could Laura know? She had no experience.

Rosalind arrived looking svelte, her hair in a pleat, wearing a suit in tailored grey. At her side were the two children, both boys.

'This is David, and this is Alan,' she said brightly. 'David is eight and Alan is six. Say hello, boys.'

They stuck out well-drilled hands. 'Good afternoon,' they said in unison.

They wore short grey trousers, identical pullovers and caps. But the clothes seemed to make them uncomfortable, and there were lines on their thighs where the short trousers rubbed. Mrs Cooper said, 'At least the boys are properly dressed, Rosalind. I thought you'd have them rigged up in something outlandish.'

'Of course not, Mother,' said Rosalind, with a high, false laugh. Laura realised she was very much on edge.

'I don't know why you're got up as if you were in town,' said Mrs Cooper.

'Ah, well.' Rosalind extended her long arms and fluttered her fingers. 'You know what it's like for a diplomat. All parties and cocktail frocks. But I've brought my woollens, I can assure you.'

'Really, Rosalind! This isn't exactly a cave.' Mrs Cooper automatically tidied Alan's mop of unruly hair.

'It's as dark as one,' said Rosalind. 'Michael dear, when are you going to put in electricity? This stygian gloom is ridiculous.'

'The expense would be farcical,' he said.

'We had to have oil lamps when we lived in India,' remarked David.

Mrs Cooper's nose wrinkled. Clearly she didn't like talkative children.

'We had snakes and scorpions,' added Alan. 'My *amah* used to kill them with a stick.'

Rosalind giggled. 'You don't really remember that, do you? She killed one once with a stick. You make it sound as if we were overrun, darling. And, yes, we had oil lamps, just like here. But that was a long time ago.'

How well travelled she seemed! At home in India, London, The Hague. Laura could see her at grand diplomatic functions, moving from group to group, always poised, always elegant.

They had tea, with Laura's cakes and Dinah's scones, and Mrs Cooper decried one for being too fancy and the other for being too plain. Laura took no notice. In the hectic rush of the wedding she had failed to notice how Rosalind and her mother sparred. She watched in fascination.

Later, Laura took some towels up to Rosalind's room. Rosalind followed, closing the door and saying, 'Phew! Peace at last. I don't know how you stand her, Laura. She can't open her mouth without finding fault.'

Laura said cautiously, 'Perhaps she's got worse as she's grown older? And your father's obviously a trial.'

'She found him a trial even when he was well. She made him miserable, you know. Made him take us all to Biarritz when he would much rather have stayed on the farm. She forgets it all now, of course, but it was her fault we lost the money. She wanted to live as if she was rich.'

'Michael says farming's worse now than it's ever been,' said Laura. 'That's part of it, surely.'

Rosalind sank on to the bed. 'I suppose so. Michael should take his chances when he sees them. The war's bound to put prices up, he could make a killing.'

Mary was crying. Laura went to fetch her, and Rosalind followed. She said, 'Mother's quite fond of her, isn't she? I'm surprised.'

'I know what she wrote.'

Rosalind took in her breath. 'I suppose you do,' she said finally. 'I didn't believe any of it, of course. It's just Mother's spite.'

'It was all foolish. If people say awful things about me, I hope you won't believe them?'

'No. No, of course I won't. Laura, you must realise if I didn't like you and trust you, I'd never be letting you take care of my boys!'

The praise was sweet, even if Laura suspected it came from a mouth that usually said what people wanted to hear. 'Do your boys always wear those clothes?' she asked.

Rosalind chuckled. 'I knew you'd noticed. Of course they don't, I just thought it wouldn't hurt to get off on the right foot. I got them at Harrods yesterday, and the poor dears are being scratched to death.'

'Did you come back through France?'

'No. But there's nothing happening yet, you know. I gather everything's more or less as it was. Do you have family there still?'

'Friends. Do you think it's going to come to anything? Are we really going to have to fight?'

Rosalind's gaze was steady. 'Actually, yes. I do. Geoffrey was at Munich, he saw what Germany's like. We can't permit that sort of thing here. Whatever happens, bombs, everything, we have to make a stand.'

Laura felt bleak, as she often did when she thought about the war. She had no patriotic fervour, made no principled stand. She wanted life to go on as it was, for her family to flourish and the farm to prosper. Did anything matter so much that little boys must be deprived of their mothers, and mothers deprived of their husbands and sons? Wasn't anything better than bombs raining down on the innocent?

But she knew without asking that no one agreed with her. The English were a belligerent race. They had no French pragmatism at all.

She thought of Madame Girand, that impossible old hag, no doubt at this moment profiteering, and allowed herself a small, reflective chuckle.

Rosalind said, 'What on earth are you thinking? Mother says you're enigmatic, and for once I agree. I don't suppose even Michael knows what makes you tick.'

Laura coloured. 'Perhaps it's being French. I don't think the English understand the French mind all that well.'

They fell silent. They were, after all, so very different. Rosalind went to the window and stood looking out at the orchard, the woods, the shoulder of hill behind. Her two little boys were marching across a field, purposeful and dishevelled. Rosalind said, 'It's so lovely here. Every time I miss my boys I'll think of them like this.'

Her voice broke. Laura saw that there were tears running freely down her cheeks. 'I've got to go in the morning,' she whispered.

'So soon? Why?'

Rosalind turned and forced a smile. 'Because otherwise, Laura dear, I won't go at all. Enjoy my boys, won't you? Love them for me.'

Apart from the clothes they came in, the boys had very little that was suitable for life on a farm. Laura rummaged in the attic and found some old dungarees that must once have belonged to Michael and Gabriel. They were too large, but folded, tucked and pleated they made do. The weather broke, and each morning they woke to rain slashing against the windows, but just the same within days they had a den in the straw stack, a pet calf, and were tentatively enquiring about a pony.

They were interesting children. Alan was a stolid and practical little soul, while David was wildly imaginative, inventing reams of tales about his barely remembered time in India.

'Daddy had a chauffeur. He took him to hunt tigers most days. On Sundays we'd ride on an elephant.'

Laura listened with only half her attention. She was baking. 'What was the elephant's name?'

'Pindar. Alan couldn't ride him, he was too small and too afraid. Daddy said I could only because I was brave.'

Laura trimmed pastry on the edge of a pie, handing the trimmings to David to play with. He at once began rolling elephants' trunks. 'Pindar was the bravest and most dangerous elephant in all India. He once killed ten men. He knelt on them because they were throwing stones.'

'Good old Pindar,' said Laura.

She wasn't sure if she ought to encourage him. Mrs Cooper's view was that stories would soon turn into lies, but Laura thought not. It seemed to her that David was missing his mother, and the stories filled the gap.

They worked in silence for a moment. Then she said, 'Let's imagine Pindar had a baby brother. We could call him little Pindar. Alan could ride him.'

David looked at her doubtfully. Were other people allowed to add elements to his fantasy? He preferred unqualified belief. 'He'd still be too frightened.'

'Are you sure? Little Pindar could be known as the kindest, most gentle elephant in all India. As kind as big Pindar was brave. He liked to take little children on his back and give them rides, and when they got down he tickled them with his trunk and made them laugh.'

'So he wasn't just Alan's elephant?'

'Of course not. Alan couldn't have an elephant all his own, could he? Pindar wasn't anyone's own elephant, after all. Unless he was a king, perhaps.'

'Couldn't Daddy own Pindar?' asked David wistfully.

'I should think he'd cost rather too much to keep. And the best elephant in India would need jewels on his headdress and things. I should think you rode Pindar on Sundays because the king liked you.'

'The Maharajah,' said David decisively. 'He rewarded my father for saving his baby son's life.'

It was wonderfully satisfactory. David ate the rest of the pastry and ran out into the garden to play. Dinah, washing up at the sink, said lugubriously, 'He'd better not try that on at school. You should stop him, not join in.'

'I let him know I don't believe it, though.'

'All the same. It's best put a stop to. He's got little Alan foxed with it all. Doesn't know if there was gold and elephants or not. Poor little chap.'

Laura went out into the garden to see Mary asleep in her pram, and watched at a distance as David tied Alan to a tree.

'You're my prisoner,' he announced grandly. 'I'm the Maharajah and you're the thief. You tried to steal my elephant and I shall kill you soon.'

Alan looked suitably anxious, and Laura called, 'You're not to tie him up, David! He can be your elephant keeper, can't he?'

'No!' David prodded his brother with a stick.

'David! Let him go at once!'

The grandiose fantasy fell away. There was just a harassed woman trying to discipline two yelling little boys.

'Told you so,' said Dinah, with a smirk.

It was time the boys were occupied. After lunch Laura cycled down into the village to look at the school. It was a small building with a pointed roof, surrounded by an iron-railed playground. The lavatories were housed in a separate brick shed, and they smelled. Even Gunthwaite's earth closets, which did not have the benefit of a flush, weren't so unpleasant, thought Laura. Fresh from their cosmopolitan life, Alan and David would be shocked.

It was playtime. She stood by the railings, watching a tide of children flow out of the little school, filling the yard to capacity. It must be the evacuees, she realised. Children large and small, dressed in an assortment of home-made woollens and scuffed shoes, raucous, wild. It was intimidating.

When playtime ended she followed the crowd of children into the school. The headmaster's office had been commandeered for teaching space, and there wasn't an inch of room. The headmaster himself crouched behind a thin partition at the end of one classroom. Laura knew him quite well, he sometimes took a gun out on Gunthwaite land. 'Mrs Cooper,' he said expansively, trying to rise behind his desk. It was an impossible feat and she waved him down again. He sat, smiling and flapping, overwhelmed by circumstance.

'It's about my nephews,' she explained, perching on the edge of a rickety chair. 'I wish to enrol them in the school.' Next door and clearly heard there rose the sound of chanted tables. 'Once two is two, two twos are four . . .' The headmaster looked at her wearily before extracting a large register from his desk.

'Ages?'

'Six and eight.'

'I see.' Even at this distance Laura could see that the page for eight year olds was entirely full. It seemed that mothers were more easily persuaded that eight year olds should be sent away than any age younger.

The headmaster raised his hands in a gesture of helpless despair. 'As you can see – the six year old, perhaps? But we don't have the capacity for more. I simply don't know what I can do.'

'Surely you'll be moving to bigger premises?'

'The top class already assembles in the church hall. Is there any possibility – I don't wish to seem difficult or unwelcoming – but could you perhaps educate them at home? For the time being? Until something's sorted out.'

'But when's that likely to be?'

Through the wall came the shouted climax, 'Twelve twos are twenty-FOUR!' The headmaster sighed. 'I really don't know. Some of these evacuees are very difficult. Very difficult indeed. I can't honestly say that your nephews would benefit very much as things stand at present. Perhaps we could talk again in, say, six months?'

Laura emerged into the afternoon sun bemused. The table chanters were on fours, slogging on towards home time. From a side door two boys crept out, like snails at first, then haring across the playground towards freedom. Their outsize trousers and wrong-sized shoes declared them evacuees. They were the talk of the village. 'Little tykes,' people would say. 'More fleas than a dead dog, some on 'em. Not a stitch of clothing they could honestly call their own. Poor little beggars.'

She thought about reporting the truants, but did not. She couldn't blame their flight from those cramped, dull classrooms. She could make David chant tables, she supposed. No harm in starting little Alan, either. And she could teach them French!

Suddenly she was excited. The dining room would become a proper schoolroom, and they would work every day. There would be neat exercise books, full of creditable achievement; drawings of butterflies, maps of the world, spellings. David would no longer tie his brother to a tree.

She pushed her bicycle doggedly up the hill, stopping as she always did to gaze down on Fairlands. There was a figure by the hedge. At this distance it could be anyone. She waved, hoping it was Dora, wondering if she should call. She hadn't seen her since Gabriel left.

The figure did not wave back. She resumed her slow progress up the hill, not stopping again until she could mount and cycle the length of Gunthwaite's drive.

Mrs Cooper was in the kitchen. Laura took off her hat and said breathlessly, 'The school's full. David can't go. We've got to teach him at home.'

Mrs Cooper said, 'Be quiet! Listen.'

A voice on the radio said, 'First reports indicate heavy loss of life.'

'What is it? What's happening?'

'What do you imagine? It's begun.'

From calm to chaos took so little time. Suddenly the Germans were on the move, rolling up the opposition as easily as if it was a carpet left by the old householder ready for throwing out. A sense of disbelief, almost of shame, seemed to dog every news broadcast. Was there never to be a resistance? When were they going to stand?

They thought of Gabriel constantly. There was no news at all. One letter since he left and nothing more. In the village two families received telegrams. One son dead, another wounded. A frisson of fear seemed to shake everyone. This had happened before, they remembered it. The list of names in the church filled an entire, windowless wall. Dinah's son Timothy tried to volunteer and was sent home, to his mother's fierce relief. But that was short-lived. He was called up the next day. Then, when world events seemed so important, so all-concerning, Dora Fitzalan-Howard paid Laura a visit.

She came by bicycle, wearing a long woollen skirt. Laura took her into the drawing room. Sunlight was falling through the window, and they sat in its glow. It softened the colour of Dora's skirt to a warm peach, the colour her cheeks used to be. As soon as the door closed and they were alone, she said, 'I think I'm having a baby. I don't know what to do.'

From the first it had seemed inevitable. Laura licked dry lips. 'I take it you've missed?' she asked hoarsely.

Dora nodded. 'And other things. I feel so sick. I – my breasts hurt. Is Gabriel going to hate me? He hasn't written. Just a note when he left and then nothing. What am I going to do?'

What indeed? Oh, Gabriel, Gabriel, Laura wanted to cry, how did you imagine this would end? She said weakly, 'They're fighting. He won't have time to write.'

'Will he marry me? What if he's killed, what happens then? I'm sure he hates me. I can't bear my parents to know.'

Laura sighed. She remembered Madame's matter-of-fact practicality when this very thing had happened to her. That was out of the question for Dora. The girl was practically a virgin still, she knew nothing. Laura had been different. Her fate was something no innocent should endure.

'I'll write to Gabriel,' she said. 'He's got to be told.'

'Does he despise me? I'm sure he does. Men do despise women who let them, don't they? I didn't realise. I've been stupid and – and loose, and he won't want anything to do with me ever again!'

'Don't waste your sympathy,' snapped Laura. 'He knew what he was doing, and he knew what to use, he was just too selfish to care!'

'It was my fault. Really, it was.'

They stood looking hopelessly at each other. There was no use apportioning blame. What was done was done.

Dora said quietly, 'What if he doesn't want to know?'

'Then your parents must be told.'

In a desperate, hopeless voice, Dora said, 'I'd rather die.'

Laura felt her heart miss a beat. She remembered when she too thought of death. 'You don't have to be silly,' she said briskly. 'It's only difficult because Gabriel's had to go away. I'm sure he wants to marry you. Not yet perhaps, he won't like being rushed, but it's his own fault, after all. Once he knows it's bound to be all right. He isn't cruel.'

'Please don't tell him I cried,' said Dora, gathering her handbag. 'I don't want to trap him, you see. If he doesn't want me then that's that.'

'He does want you,' said Laura desperately. 'He thought you were too young. He thought you might find someone else.'

'I wish I could believe you.'

Laura seized her hand. 'Do. Please. If I'm wrong we'll know soon enough. But I don't think I am.'

That night she lay wakeful beside Michael. Suddenly, with that sensitivity which sometimes so surprised her, he put out his hand and said, 'Laura? Why can't you sleep?'

She thought of all the prevarications she had planned and saw there was no need for them. 'Gabriel's got Dora pregnant.'

After a moment Michael said, 'The poor girl.'

'It was just once. They were terribly unlucky.'

'It isn't a question of luck, Laura! He had no right to take advantage of her. Sometimes he disgusts me.'

'It wasn't all him. I've got to write.'

Michael rolled on to his back and stared blindly into the dark. 'He'll have to marry her. Her father will insist.'

'We don't want to tell him. And you won't, will you, darling? It's Dora's secret, not ours.'

'She should have had more sense. Was it her, do you think? Tempting him? She's been after him for years.'

'You can't say that. She's a nice girl.'

'Hardly. But it's like you to say so, darling. Dora might have a pedigree a mile long but you're ten times the lady she is. To my mind, she's something of a slut.'

'Michael! Really, that isn't fair.'

He rolled over and kissed her, his mouth hot and searching. Her senses flamed, but she was a lady, and Dora a slut. She couldn't respond. Suddenly he pushed her nightdress above her waist, covering her at once. She tensed as he entered, expecting pain, but now there was only discomfort. Flesh healed, scars faded, there was no knowing what had happened before. Her desire seemed to turn back on her. She felt dry and resisting. She couldn't let go of the day's events and think of pleasure. When he finished, lying blowing on her like some giant sea-mammal, he murmured, 'We're so lucky, you know.'

She put her fingers gently in his hair.

Chapter Sixteen

The airfield was the third in six days. No more than a cluster of tents around a field, it provided nothing except a fuel bowser and a mess tent. Damaged planes, if they could make it, were sent post haste across the Channel. Anything that couldn't be repaired was torched.

Gabriel lay on the grass beneath the wing of his plane. The earth beneath him felt warm and more alive than the body it supported. He ached from the hours crammed in the cockpit, and his legs shook with a continuous tremor. It was the unreleased tension, confined in a box being shot at, his whole self longing to take flight. If he had the energy he'd go for a run, he thought. But they'd be scrambled again soon. Had he hit that last Me? Philip might have seen. He'd ask him if they made it to tonight.

The grass smelled wonderful; he could get drunk on that smell, driving out the stench of ethylene glycol and aviation fuel. It soothed his senses, slowing down the endless snatches of conflict that repeated and repeated in his head. How long were those dog fights? Two, three minutes? A lifetime of climbing, diving, turns and spirals, his thumb on the button, his thoughts like huge balloons. He had discovered lately that he was a good shot, better than most. Perhaps the best. It was the extra six months training, he supposed. And he was always good with a shotgun. It was harder in a plane, of course: your speed, his speed, the speed of the bullets, shells, whatever. But the end result was worth it. The other man dead, and not you.

A telephone buzzed in a tent. Gabriel lay quite still, savouring the last moments of rest. Jenkins came out of the tent. 'All right,' he called. 'We're off.'

'Off where?' Philip Lansbury levered himself into a sitting position.

'Another field. We're moving back.'

'Bloody hell! Much further back and we'll need seaplanes.'

'Point taken. Actually this is only a refuelling stop, then it's a hop to dear old Blighty. We'll go in formation. If you see bandits, squawk and then leg it. These planes are needed at home.'

'They're needed here,' said Gabriel incredulously. 'We can't let the Luftwaffe have it all their own way.'

'Sorry, old boy. Not much choice. We're pretty well rolled up.'

No one said any more. After all, they should have realised it had come to this. Day after day they flew across long, weary lines of refugees, clogging the roads, impeding the troops. Day after day they saw the front lines pull back and back again. Day after day they fled skies filled with enemy planes. They engaged stragglers and lone Stukas, or the odd bunch of sightseers out for a spin. But the massed formations of enemy fighters were beyond them.

They were all putting out their cigarettes. Already the tents were coming down, and the fuel bowser was dragged clear, ready to be set on fire. An old woman stood at the edge of the field, watching them.

Gabriel lifted his hand in salute. '*Au revoir, Madame.*'

Laura fingered the telegram in her handbag. 'Returned Norfolk safe and well stop Gabriel.' Beyond the window of the taxi stretched a vast expanse of open space, now and then punctuated by a low building or a plane. In the far distance vehicles were moving about, and a klaxon sounded.

The driver stopped. 'Main gate,' he said laconically.

'Thank you.' She counted out coins to pay him, aware of the men on the gate watching her suspiciously. As the taxi drove off one of them advanced on her.

'Can I help you, Madam? Sightseers aren't allowed.'

'I've come to see Pilot Officer Cooper.'

The man looked askance at Mary, as if they had a lot of women with babies asking for flying personnel. Laura gave him a cold stare, the sort Madame Bonacieux reserved for undesirables.

'He's my husband's brother. I'm here to discuss a problem on the farm.'

He responded as she had hoped. 'Certainly, Madam. Yes, Madam. If you'd like to come into the gatehouse, I'll see.' He went off to telephone.

She laid Mary on a seat and wandered around the bare room. From the window she could see three planes taking off, in a slanting line abreast, each nose level with its neighbour's wing. The smell of aviation fuel drifted towards her and she felt a thrill suddenly. Everything was busy and purposeful. She was glad to be away from Gunthwaite. The place had been making her timid.

A young, urbane man knocked on the door. 'Mrs Cooper? Mrs Laura Cooper? Hello, I'm Philip Lansbury, Gabriel's friend. He's having a bit of a dodge round at the moment. Would it be too much of a bore if I took you to the mess? He shouldn't be long.'

'He's having – what is he doing?'

'Flying. You may have seen him take off. Just an exercise, half an hour at the most.'

She picked up the baby and went with him. A petrol tanker drove past at speed, and a lorry full of young men in flying kit. 'Are you sure you shouldn't be doing something else?' she asked her escort. 'I don't have to be looked after if you've important things to do.'

'I can't imagine anything more important than looking after you,' he said, flashing a white-toothed smile. 'Gabriel told me you were French. Your English is spot on, I must say. And just remember, all this bustle is going towards keeping France safe. You've no need to worry.'

'Are you saying France isn't going to fall?'

He looked a little embarrassed. 'If it does, I'm sure it won't be for long.'

She snorted with laughter.

He took her to a warm room furnished with good leather. Mary woke, but seemed fascinated by her change in surroundings. Laura accepted a drink, gin and Italian vermouth, although only a few sips made her feel woozy. She was desperately out of practice. Philip said, 'If you'd like to see to the baby, you can always go to our room. Mine and Gabriel's.'

'Perhaps I'd better. If I don't she'll scream when we're trying to talk.'

'A farm problem, you said?'

She nodded. 'Everyone's going to war. We're terribly short-handed.'

'I didn't think Gabriel knew anything about the farm.'

She said nothing, but accepted the use of the room with smiling thanks. When she was alone she laid Mary on the bed and took off her nappy, letting the baby wriggle and kick for a minute or two. There was a photograph by Philip's bed of a girl with long curly hair, and another picture of a horse. Gabriel had no photographs at all. On an impulse which she made no attempt to curb, she opened the cupboard next to his bed and saw his leatherbound letter writing folder. Papers overflowed the seams. She took it out, opened it – and found herself staring at her own face. He had her photograph.

It was a large picture, some four inches square. She wore a pale spotted dress and her hair was loose on her shoulders. She wasn't smiling, although it looked as if at any moment she might, looking up through leaves and petals. The orchard, then. On Gabriel's last leave, she hadn't had that dress long. He had taken a secret picture, in the very midst of a hectic romance!

She changed the baby, fed her, and put everything carefully away. The picture might mean nothing, of course. He retained a soft spot for her, as well he might, until he developed a softer one. But why not Dora? All at once she wished she had let Michael come. Gabriel would speak honestly to her, and the last thing she wanted was honesty.

There was a knock on the door. She drew in her breath. 'Gabriel? Do come in.'

'Laura? I didn't believe it when Philip told me. I thought he was pulling my leg.'

He still wore his bulky flying jacket, with something hanging at the back, parachute straps or something. He looked dashing and capable, a real pilot, not Gabriel at all. His hair was damp with sweat. 'He said you were flying,' said Laura awkwardly.

'Yes. We all are. We've got heavier cannon since France, thank God. But has something happened at home?'

She shook her head. 'At least – I suppose it has.'

'Everyone's well, aren't they?'

'Yes – yes. You didn't get my letter?'

'No letters at all in France. Laura, what's happened?'

'Dora's pregnant.'

He stood quite silent, his face perfectly still. He didn't mind, she thought with relief. It wasn't even a surprise. But suddenly he took a pace and kicked out. A hole appeared in his bedside cabinet. Splinters fell rattling on to the floor. 'Fucking shit!' he said simply.

Laura said nothing. She wondered if the cabinet was government property and if Gabriel would get into trouble. She settled the baby more firmly on her knee, in case he lashed out again. But the violence had been expended. He said wearily, 'I'll swear you wanted this to happen. I'll swear you willed it.'

'It has nothing to do with me. Except that Dora came to me. She's terrified, Gabriel. She really needs you.'

'She doesn't need me! She doesn't even know me. She's just a girl with an itch that needed scratching. It could have been anyone!'

In a low voice, Laura said, 'She's known you forever. She knows you as well as anyone ever will. I think she even suspects that this is what you'll say. She says she'll kill herself.'

'She can get rid of it, can't she? It's not like you suddenly to develop scruples.'

Laura said, 'I won't hear of it! It isn't so bad. All you have to do is marry her and put everything right!'

He put his hand to his head and groaned. Then he began to talk to her, appealing to her, as if she could somehow let him out of this trap. As if her good opinion was all that mattered. 'I'm going to war, Laura! The real thing! I could be killed, she'd be a widow.'

'At least you'd leave an heir,' she remarked.

'Oh, very funny! It would inherit my four pairs of badly darned socks. Suppose I don't die, and I'm married to Dora? For God's sake, I don't want to marry her. I don't want to marry anyone.'

'But you liked Dora before all this. You liked her a lot. In the end you might find she's perfect for you.'

He looked at her balefully. 'And I might not. What are you

going to do when I come to you in two years' time, saying my marriage is driving me mad? Saying I'm going to kill myself? What then?'

She ran a gentle hand over Mary's dark cap of hair. She didn't believe Gabriel's histrionics. 'At least you'll have a baby. And the baby will have a proper start in life.'

Suddenly all the fight seemed to go out of him. He slumped on Philip's bed. He said, 'I don't think you care about Dora. You just want to see me locked up. It's your revenge for what I know about you.'

She met his stare for a long while. Then she said, 'You don't know much. Not even half.'

He rolled on to his stomach, obviously weary and worn out. 'No one can ever know everything. Even I have secrets, unbelievable though that may be. Just imagine. Dora will want to know everything. She won't be content, Laura. She won't be another Michael.'

'What on earth do you mean?'

'Michael's happy to live with his enigma. He's not stupid. He accepts what he knows he can't change. It's a very rare quality.'

'He's a very rare man,' said Laura softly. Gabriel made no reply. When she looked more closely she saw that he was asleep.

She took back a letter for Dora. Gabriel had written it under duress, subjecting it again and again to Laura's scrutiny. 'You make it sound as if you're writing to your aunt,' she complained. 'Be more affectionate.'

'I don't feel in the least affectionate.'

'Nonsense! You like Dora, you know you do. If you didn't you shouldn't have screwed – I mean, seduced her.'

Gabriel laughed. It wasn't often Laura made a slip. Her conversation was usually absolutely genteel, almost to the point of prissiness. The functions of the body were subjects she seemed to consider taboo, extending the ban even so far as spitting or a belch. If someone else mentioned them she cultivated temporary deafness until the conversation returned to more acceptable realms. Knowing what he knew, Gabriel found it endlessly amusing.

'You could say how much you've missed her,' encouraged Laura. 'You didn't write because you hoped she'd forget someone as unworthy as you.'

'You've been watching too many films,' said Gabriel.

'You know I never watch any.'

'What? I suppose you don't. Well, let's go tonight.'

'But there's Mary—'

'Philip can babysit. Come on, Laura! We'll run into town, have a meal and take in a film. Consider it my reward for marrying Dora. Look, I'll write a brilliant letter. "I can't believe that you really care for me, darling. But if you do, and will do me the honour of becoming my wife, I'll be the happiest man on earth." Will that do?'

'Yes. Wonderful.' Laura felt flustered.

'Well then. Let's tell Philip what's in store.'

Laura was staying at a small hotel in town. Bathing and dressing by electric light that evening, it felt like the height of luxury. She put on a lilac frock she had intended to wear the next day. It was fresh and smart, and she put up her hair in clips on either side of her head. It was the new fashion. When Gabriel and Philip arrived and she came downstairs they both looked at her with obvious admiration.

'I don't think the town's seen anything as pretty in years,' said Philip gallantly.

Laura looked at herself doubtfully. 'Is it too much, do you think? It's only a travelling dress. It's all I've got with me.'

Gabriel said, 'It isn't the dress. It's your professional way of dressing.'

She said nothing. She could tell a barb when she heard one. Gabriel was in an odd mood, half pleased to be in her company, half vengeful over Dora. She quickly took Philip upstairs and settled him in a chair, a screen between him and the cot, the radio playing softly. Mary was still awake, smiling and gurgling. Laura kissed the tip of her own finger, and touched it to the child's nose. 'Be good, darling. Mummy won't be long.'

They ate at The White Hart, a somewhat dire repast of poached salt fish, tough beef and bitter apple pie. Gabriel ate heartily, but Laura picked at hers. 'Not up to Gunthwaite standards, I'm afraid,' said Gabriel.

She smiled apologetically. 'Not really. We're very lucky, aren't we? Everyone else eats this sort of thing all the time.'

'How are Rosalind's boys? Eating like horses?'

She smiled and nodded. 'They're lovely. I have to teach them, did you know? The school hasn't room.'

Gabriel looked amazed. 'What does Michael say to that?'

'Nothing. At least, not much. Mother said a lot, of course, but that's just her way. I think she'll help, actually. Hearing them read, that sort of thing.'

Gabriel's face was rather set. 'Why do you do it, Laura? Do you realise how many people have shed their responsibilities on to you? The school, Rosalind, Mother – even Dora. Why didn't she tell me she was pregnant herself?'

'Why don't you ask her to marry you yourself?' countered Laura. 'You're as bad as anyone. If it is bad. I don't mind.'

Gabriel looked away. The room was full of people like themselves, men from the airfield with wives, girlfriends, sisters. Everyone was either in uniform or something sober. Laura's frock seemed almost unacceptably light-hearted in such company. He felt depressed suddenly. The ambivalence of his mood had crystallised. He did not want to marry Dora, he did not want to fight in this war, he did not want to die.

She was looking at him in that way she had, as if she knew what went on in his mind. He presumed it was an illusion, a trick. She knew him no better than anyone. He wondered if she looked at Michael like that – he often wondered about Laura and Michael together. He thought of the long, dark evenings in the kitchen, his father's mumbling, his mother's taunting, the children. Did they talk despite it all? What could they say?

Suddenly she put her hand over his. 'Don't worry so much, Gabriel. It's going to work out. I'm sure of it.'

'Is that supposed to reassure me?'

'Yes. You never worried about the club.'

'That wasn't serious. It was just one of those things.'

'Tell me honestly. France is lost, isn't it?'

He nodded, catching the waiter's eye and signalling for the bill. 'I don't think any of us will be in France much longer.' He got out his wallet, saying with forced gaiety, 'So it really doesn't matter a damn about Dora or anything else. Spare me your elaborate concern and let's get off and see this film.'

It was an American comedy. Laura was unused to the genre and couldn't understand much of what was going on. Halfway through Gabriel put his hand on her knee. Without fuss or hesitation she removed it. Before he could decide whether to try again, the air-raid warning sounded.

The lights went up. A girl in the back row was caught in a state of some indecency and Gabriel laughed. Nobody seemed to know what to do.

'Mary,' said Laura desperately. 'I've got to get to her.'

'If you would please leave in an orderly fashion,' intoned the theatre manager. But Laura was in a panic. She pushed and shoved like a woman possessed, bursting out into the dark street and starting to run.

'Wait!' Gabriel was hard on her heels. 'For God's sake, nothing's happening. We've never been bombed. It's probably a false alarm.'

'I don't care. I have to get to her.'

The klaxons were wailing like banshees in the night. Here and there people's eyes gleamed as they stood in the street looking up into the sky. There was nothing at all to see. But suddenly, in the distance, they heard the drone of engines.

'Christ!' said Gabriel. He caught Laura's hand. Together they raced down the street.

They found Philip standing in the open, holding the baby, looking for them. 'Come on, Gabriel! They're making for the airfield, we've got to get back.'

'Then they'll bomb you too,' said Laura. Now that she held her baby again she felt calmer. She could begin to think.

'We'll have to get the planes up,' explained Philip. 'There's a shelter down the street, you go there. Come on, Gabriel!'

He set off at a run for the car. Gabriel stood for a moment, looking down at Laura. Then he took her face in his hands, bent, and kissed her passionately. Crushed between them, the baby began to cry. 'Goodbye,' he said softly. The siren and the baby's wails made it difficult to talk.

'I'll give Dora your letter,' said Laura. 'Don't get killed, Gabriel.'

'Go and be happy,' he said.

He let her go. She stood in the street, watching him race away, the tails of his coat flapping. Without thought she soothed her crying child. The engines were louder now, and air raid wardens were using loud hailers to get people off the streets. Everybody wanted to look. She too stared upwards, into the sooty chimney of the sky.

'Get that child out of here!' yelled an elderly man with a moustache. 'Do you want to get it killed?'

She allowed herself to be pushed towards the shelter, but she felt more in danger there than in the street. She imagined herself crushed and without air, in a tangle of bodies. Dimly, through the concrete of the walls, she heard explosions. 'They're after the airfield,' someone said. 'Just shows how close they've got. What are our boys doing, that's what I'd like to know?'

The explosions went on, like distant thunder. It seemed that no one was doing anything. But then, a different sound intruded – the whump, whump of an anti-aircraft gun. The people in the shelter raised a cheer.

Within thirty minutes it was over. The consensus was that the raiders were at the limit of their range with little time to spare over the target. Nonetheless, an air of foreboding hung over the little town.

'It's started,' said one old man. 'This is it.'

'We'll hold 'em in France,' said another. 'Retreat and then stand, that's the plan.'

'Oh, aye. I remember the last time. Not so much a plan, more a bloody cock-up. You mark my words.'

Although the All Clear hadn't sounded, Laura slipped from the shelter and back to her room. What had happened to Gabriel and Philip? She fed and changed the baby, laid her down in the cot and tried to sleep herself. Just as she was drifting off, the All Clear howled its message and woke her up.

All of a sudden Gabriel and Dora were getting married. The moment Laura delivered the letter, Dora telephoned the airfield. It had been bombed, and communication was difficult, but for some unexplained reason in three weeks' time Gabriel could take a weekend off to get married.

Dora said, 'He saved up leave in France, perhaps. Oh, and then Daddy telephoned and spoke to him and said he was very pleased, and Mummy's absolutely thrilled. Oh, Laura, I can't tell you how grateful I am.'

Her eyes were dewy with unshed tears. Dora was the least complicated person in the world, thought Laura, and she didn't understand complexity in others. But she would learn, she told herself. Dora's faults were those of a girl sheltered since birth, learning none of life's lessons. This was her first hard experience. Soon she would be married with a husband in action. In a year or two Gabriel would find himself married to a woman, not a girl.

A wedding dress was found in the attics of Fairlands. Mrs Cooper, delighted with Gabriel's luck, sent over an antique brooch for the veil. She had given nothing to Laura. It was hard not to be hurt, especially when she stood in the Post Office queue and heard someone say, 'Should be worth watching, this one. The Fitzalan-Howards'll put on a show, not like that last do. Married a pauper, Mr Michael did.'

Silence fell as they realised who was there. Laura said nothing, passing to the counter and handing over her usual money order for France. The woman sucked her teeth and said apologetically, 'Don't know that this can go, Mrs Cooper. Everything's upside down over there, you see. Bombs and that.'

Laura felt a slight shock. This was her habit, her usual practice. So much had changed, nothing was as it should be. 'I send it to a relative,' she explained. 'She needs the money. What can I do?'

'Send it to Hitler and ask him to drop it in,' said a voice lugubriously. Everyone roared with laughter.

She went home with a feeling of lasting disquiet. It nagged at her like a bad tooth, something she couldn't shake off. Every day the news grew worse. In her mind she kept making accommodations, this will happen but not that, and if that must occur, at least this will remain the same. But, like the army, she was constantly retreating. Danger was advancing even to the walls of Gunthwaite itself. What had before seemed inconceivable now seemed almost likely. Daily more enemy planes were flying over the country, seemingly at will. How long before enemy soldiers were knocking at the doors?

Perhaps her mood was a presentiment, her senses tuning in to a collective fear and panic. The British Expeditionary Force was in full retreat, its soldiers strafed and bombed on the exposed beaches of Dunkirk. Routed, beaten, they abandoned their equipment and fled France, to the island that was all that still was free. And when Winston Churchill said in the House of

320

Commons: 'We will fight them on the beaches. We will fight them in the streets and in the hills,' the people of Britain fully expected that that was what they were going to have to do.

Chapter Seventeen

The fall of France seemed to crystallise everything into tiny knives of possibility. With life itself in danger, happiness must be gathered on the run, without fear or contemplation. The wedding of Gabriel and Dora fitted perfectly with this desperate mood. What more natural than for a girl to marry her man on the eve of battle?

Mrs Fitzalan-Howard stripped her hothouses of flowers, her attics of satins and lace, her stores of food and her cellars of drink. If anything was less than perfect it would almost be a defeat in itself. The Germans would not have their way, even so far as spoiling a young girl's wedding. The atmosphere at Fairlands grew feverish. Dora and her mother could be heard screaming at each other at all hours of the day and night. But then again, sometimes they would both dissolve in tears.

Gabriel came home on the Friday afternoon, went to see Dora, stayed for dinner, came back to Gunthwaite and got stinking drunk. Michael sat up with him, listening as he always listened when Gabriel grew maudlin. It was mostly about flying; gaining height, losing height, wireless problems. He had manufactured a thin fiction of never being in action, an observer merely, always after the fair. Michael hoped it was so. He hated to think that Gabriel, the youngest one, the wayward one, had triumphed in the ultimate test, while he, Michael, stayed safe and sound at home. Some part of him felt guilty. He, the eldest, should be the one to take up the challenge. It wasn't Gabriel's place.

After a while he fell silent. Michael thought he might leave him and go to bed, letting him fall asleep where he was. But suddenly Gabriel looked at him and said, quite soberly, 'You should have seen them in France, Mike. The people on the roads. Thousands of them, walking away. And the planes

322

coming, strafing them, just for the hell of it. I keep wondering where all those people are going to go.'

Michael felt uncomfortable. This wasn't the time for talk of that kind. Gabriel too often worried about things that couldn't concern him. As a child, sending cattle to slaughter, he'd worried how the bullocks would die. He worried about the tramps in winter, wondered where they would sleep. And that thing about the Jews. The trouble with Gabriel's concerns was that they made you think too, when it was easier – better – not to.

Michael said, 'You don't have to think of that now, you know. You're getting married tomorrow.'

Gabriel got up and went to pour himself another drink. 'What would you do if I made a run for it now? Stop me? Drag me back?'

'No. It's Dora who'd suffer.'

Gabriel took a large gulp of whisky. 'God forbid we should any of us upset Dora. Does it never occur to any of you that it might be quite cruel to marry her to someone who doesn't love her, doesn't want her, and consoles himself with the thought that at least it might mean he ends up living in a nice house?'

Michael sat and said nothing. Gabriel said, 'God! I hate your silences.'

'You'd hate my talking even more. If you'd let yourself, you'd admit this isn't so bad. You know it's best.'

Gabriel tossed the hair out of his eyes. He had changed, thought Michael. The laziness was gone from his eyes. At least war had achieved that. It was a side of Gabriel that had no counterpart in him, who was always on the go, always doing. When it came down to it Michael was happiest in with the sheep, instead of in the house, talking about what they might do next year, next week, sell this, buy that, whatever. He knew it was a weakness in him. Nowadays it wasn't enough to farm as you had always farmed. In a changing world, Michael was beginning to feel like an anachronism.

It was Gunthwaite, of course. Up here the nearest he came to conflict was the monthly interview with the assessor, checking on pigs and hens. Gabriel was lucky, though he might not see it. He wasn't on the sidelines, growing old. For a brief, untypical moment, Michael envied his brother. He might not have

Gunthwaite, he might not have Laura – but he did have opportunity. He had the chance to test himself in life.

When at last they went up to bed, Michael was the one who lay awake. Laura was sleeping beside him. He wanted her, he realised. He wrestled with himself for five minutes or so, but it was no good. His groin ached with need. Saying nothing, he swung himself on to her and reached between her legs.

She mumbled but did not wake. He probed for her opening, found it and rammed himself in. Good. Very good. Although still asleep, she put up her knee to help him, murmuring in French. He didn't understand enough to know what she was saying. He wondered how far he could go before she woke. He slid his hands up inside her nightdress and took careful hold of her milk-filled breasts.

The whisky made him a long time in coming. His fingers tensed, digging in as he thrust at her, and as he watched she opened her eyes. He said nothing, locked in her, shocked at himself, struggling to reach the end. It seemed as if it would go on for ever. Then, without speaking, she reached down and gripped him. He felt a thrill of awareness, as each time he thrust he passed through a collar of her fingers. They seemed to flutter, touching the point of him, shameful but unstoppable. Suddenly he was aware of a great rush of pleasure, and she held him, held him – until she let him go. He exploded into bliss, and slid away.

Laura sighed and snuggled back into her pillow. But Michael's panting kept her awake. All at once she was quite awake, her mind clear and appalled. Had she done that? To Michael? She went cold. But she had woken to find him hurting her, and taking so long. All she'd wanted was to go back to sleep.

Her groin throbbed unpleasantly. It reminded her. Big men, paying for all night, first time quick, third time slow as treacle. It was a trick she'd learned from the girls, a quick way of getting it done. But what would Michael think?

He'd been drinking. He might not remember. She turned over again and tried to get some more sleep.

The morning dawned with the haze that promises a wonderful day. The orchard was in full leaf, dipping and swaying in the breeze like ladies at a ball. Some of the hens had hatched broods and clucked about the yard, their babies like balls of cheeping fluff with matchstick legs. Everyone was excited; even the milk came in early, as if the cows were anxious to get done and get off. But Gabriel lay in bed.

At nine, Laura took him a cup of tea. She opened the curtains and he blinked blearily at the light. 'You can't be ill,' she said threateningly. 'Dinah's filling the bath and your mother's pressing your uniform. And I've brought you some aspirin.'

He groaned painfully. It was an act designed to arouse Laura's sympathies, for he never had much of a hangover. Gratifyingly she sat on the edge of the bed and took his hand. 'You know you're doing the right thing, don't you?'

There wasn't an easy answer to that. Eventually he sighed, 'I suppose so. I blame you entirely, you know. If it hadn't been for you I'd never have got her to sleep with me in the first place. I pressed all the right buttons and she couldn't resist.'

'It's nothing to do with buttons! She loves you. She really does, Gabriel, you're terribly lucky.'

He leaned back on his pillows and looked at her. The summer morning touched her pale skin with gold, and filled her eyes, those strange light eyes, with sunshine. Dora was prettier, in the conventional sense, neat and charming. But Laura had something else. Character, perhaps. When you looked at Laura you didn't know what she was, by any means, but you couldn't help but try and guess.

He lifted her hand and put it gently to his lips. She didn't pull away. But after a moment she got up, detached herself easily and said, 'Do get ready, Gabriel. Then we can all follow. It's going to be a wonderful day.'

When Gabriel walked into church at noon, he felt a certain surprise. There were so few men. If anything were to bring home the totality of this conflict it was that. There was almost no able-bodied man left in the village, the church was full of thin grey hairs. Of the Cooper clan, only Michael was under the age of forty.

'Where are all the relatives? I thought farmers didn't have to go,' said Gabriel in an undervoice.

'They don't,' replied his brother. 'They've all gone anyway. Everyone except me has someone to look after things. You can't blame them for wanting to show Hitler what's what.'

'Not you,' said Gabriel. 'Sensible man. Believe me, it's a

damn sight better to look after things at Gunthwaite than to be shot at by aggressive foreigners. I tell you, it's much over-rated.'

'So you were shot at?' said Michael. 'I thought as much.'

Gabriel grinned. 'Only when I couldn't run fast enough, I assure you. And don't tell the women.'

Laura hovered at the door, waiting for Dora. Mrs Cooper, flanked by Alan and David in their smartest clothes and obliged to carry Mary, said, 'They don't want you hanging around, you know. It isn't your place.' So, although Dora had asked her to wait, she felt uncomfortable about it. She wasn't anybody, and the Fitzalan-Howards were the nearest thing to gentry there was around here. But Dora had asked after all, and she had promised.

The organist was playing restful music. The church looked magnificent, a flower-decked hall, opening on to the sunny, scented churchyard. There seemed to be nothing in the air but peace and the expectation of happiness, it was impossible to believe in war. There had been wars before, she told herself. Gunthwaite had always survived. It would always survive. For ever.

A Rolls-Royce was purring down the street. It held the bridesmaids and Mrs Fitzalan-Howard. When she saw Laura she said, 'He is here, isn't he? Dora said to make sure, she's being so silly.'

'Of course he's here,' said Laura, with an insouciance she did not feel. 'Is it all right if I wait for her?'

Mrs Fitzalan-Howard squeezed her hand. 'I hoped you would, my dear. I'll go and sit down, she'll be better with you. We make each other nervous, you know.'

So it was all right after all. The car arrived with Dora, in a great froth of antique lace. But she looked pale and frightened. 'Don't worry,' called out Laura at once. 'Gabriel didn't get drunk or anything. He's here.'

Dora's face lit up. Her father said, 'I don't know why you women fuss so. Of course he's here, where else would he be?'

Dora and Laura exchanged glances. And then Laura felt uncertain, for the very first time. If Dora knew what Gabriel felt about this, why was she letting it go on?

The bridesmaids were ready, the bride's dress pulled

straight, the bouquet placed just so. Laura hurried to her place, her heart beating rapidly, and took the baby from Mrs Cooper. David and Alan were kicking each other surreptitiously under cover of a kneeler. She fixed them with a wide-eyed stare and they subsided. As the organ began to play the march, Michael caught her eye and smiled. Last night hadn't mattered, then. He didn't remember. Gradually her heart began to slow. Really, there was no need to worry. Gabriel looked like a handsome young flying ace, Dora his eager young bride. The ancient serenity of this place would cast its spell over all of them once again. Everything was perfect.

No one would have imagined that a wedding breakfast of such magnificence could be held in wartime. There was champagne and caviar, Scottish salmon, and trifle with good, thick cream. If there was any lack it was in the little foreign delicacies that might have been expected; truffles and chocolate and dates. And behind the scenes things were not quite as they seemed. The caviar had come from Russia in 1936 and they hadn't known what they would do if it had been off when they opened the tin this morning; the champagne was supplied by a relative whose house was being requisitioned by the army and who wanted to empty his cellar, and the salmon was poached from the Spey and transported by dubious means and a great deal of ice.

Gabriel and Dora looked wonderful. The slate blue of his jacket made the perfect foil for her ivory veil. 'Everyone should get married in uniform,' said Laura happily.

Michael said, 'He's drinking too much.'

'It is his wedding, darling!' She felt drunk herself, in actual fact. She leaned her head against Michael's shoulder. He felt unresponsive. Instead of softening to accommodate her, he seemed not to have noticed. She sat up, suddenly cold.

He said, 'It's all a farce, really, don't you think? Fiddling while Rome burns.'

'It isn't burning. We won't be alone for long. The Americans will come in.'

'It could be over before they make up their minds. Sometimes, Laura, I don't think you realise how serious it is! Gabriel was saying France is full of refugees, great rivers of them, trying to get away. The German tanks keep rolling on, with nothing to stop them, just a little bit of sea. And our artillery's smashed, half of it left at Dunkirk, we've lost hundreds of planes we haven't a hope of replacing – and here we sit. Celebrating.'

'It wouldn't help if we didn't,' said Laura.

'I don't mean that! I mean we should be doing something positive. *I* should be doing it.'

She blinked at him. 'You are. You're growing food. It's vital.'

'Laura, anyone could run the farm. Bill Mayes knows every bit as much as me.'

'He doesn't! He's a hired man, he's not in charge. He couldn't do all the planning, and the buying and selling—'

'He's been doing it for thirty years or more. He'd do it better than me, most likely. He's been at it longer.'

Laura was silent. She wished the baby would cry, so she could get up and go to her. This was all Gabriel's fault, coming home in his dashing uniform, telling tales of France and conflict. It was all exaggerated, of that she was sure, but it was bound to unsettle his brother. That might even have been his intention.

Down the table, David was using a fish bone as a catapult, flicking salad at his brother. She was too preoccupied to care until one piece took off, sailed over Alan's head and landed in an oblivious lady's hair. It nestled there, like a rare jewel, and Laura got up and leaned over the boys. They were giggling like fools.

'Just stop it, both of you!' she snapped with unaccustomed heat. 'If you don't, I'll make you get down with no pudding.'

They put their hands in their laps, but the suspended piece of salad kept catching their eye and sending them off in fits again.

Everything always went wrong, she thought helplessly. What would she do if Mary woke up and screamed, or if Dinah rushed in to tell them Mr Cooper had got lost, or if Gabriel stood up and walked out of this wedding breakfast and refused to be properly married? But even as she worried about them, she knew none of those things mattered. The only important thing was Michael. He wanted to go to war.

She went back to her place and lifted her champagne glass, emptying it in one long swallow. Someone came and refilled it, and she drank most of it again. Michael said, 'Save some for the toasts.'

She glanced at him. 'Why bother? As you say, it's all a bit meaningless. Gabriel could be killed next week.'

After a moment Michael said, 'We can wish him well, all the same.'

'You've changed your tune.'

She was being bad-tempered, and didn't care. Gabriel was right, everyone was weighing her down with responsibilities. Rosalind hadn't even bothered to come up for her brother's wedding, let alone to see her boys; she was content to let Laura bear the load. She felt aggrieved, knowing full well that Rosalind had a job in Howard's department and was busy. But then, everyone seemed to have concerns that were more important than Laura's. Only her life was flexible, it seemed. Only she could take on an endless series of tasks.

Her glass was empty again. She felt tearful and wished it were full. When it was filled once more she felt no better, though. How she wished she could go home.

When the toasts were done Dora came rustling across. 'I'm going to get changed now. Don't tell anyone but we're spending the night in Ripon, one of Daddy's friends is lending us his house. I'm so happy, Laura, and it's all thanks to you. Gabriel says he can't wait for us to be a threesome. Isn't he good?'

'Wonderful,' said Laura obediently. Perhaps Gabriel wanted to insulate himself from Dora with a brood of children. He was so defensive. So reluctant to let anyone really close. Suddenly she said to Dora, 'You don't want to crowd him, you know. Men like a bit of space. Michael's like that.'

'Michael!' Dora laughed indulgently and set Laura's nerves on edge. 'Dear old Michael. Aren't you lucky having him safe at home? I won't be able to rest for a minute, worrying about what Gabriel's getting up to.'

She was going to play the anxious bride for all she was worth, thought Laura uncharitably. She would boast at every opportunity about 'my husband the fighter pilot'. She looked into Dora's bright, innocent face and felt cruel. She excused herself, she had to look after the baby.

It was quiet in the upstairs room. Mary sucked peacefully at her breast, one hand waving delicately in the air, like a conductor trying to coax a perfect air from the violins. The door opened, but Laura didn't look up. It would be another woman looking for her coat.

But it was Gabriel. He stood watching for a moment. He said, 'I can't believe I married her. I did it. It's done.'

'Congratulations,' said Laura grimly. 'Don't you think you ought to go?'

'No. I like to look at you. I will never look at Dora and feel as I do now.'

Her throat was dry. She didn't want him to go on. But some perverse, untamed instinct made her say, 'How do you feel?'

'Restless. Lustful. Missing you, when you haven't even gone.'

A sudden frisson caused milk to begin oozing from her free breast. She bent her head over her child, gently detaching her from the nipple, turning her expertly and putting her to suckle where the milk flowed. There was something louche and unsettling about the situation. Gabriel groaned and Laura looked up and met his eyes. 'I don't want you here,' she said urgently.

'Where else should I be?'

She shook her head free of its wilder thoughts. 'Talking to Michael. He's going to join up.'

Her voice cracked. Gabriel said, 'Who? Mike? Of course he isn't.'

Bending her head over the baby, Laura wailed, 'It's your fault! Yours and mine. You make him feel he's being left behind here. And I – I upset him. Last night . . . He's tired of me. He wants to go.'

'That's just stupid, Laura. He's not in the least upset! If you want rid of me you'll have to do better than that.'

'I do want rid of you. I always have. I just want Michael to stay.'

She was shaking with dry sobs. He leaned against the door and took out a cigarette. When it was lit and he was puffing smoke, he said, 'That's telling me, isn't it? I never thought otherwise, you know.'

'Then stop this!'

'What? Wanting you? No can do.'

'You've got Dora now. You don't need to keep reminding me of – of what I was. You won't let me forget.'

330

'Pretend, you mean. Pretend to be respectable. Why bother, Laura? You're unique. Special. Been through hell and survived. You don't have to turn into a bourgeois bore.'

She looked at him. 'I won't sleep with you again. Whatever happens. I know you too well, Gabriel.'

The baby was finished. She laid her on the bed, carefully fastening her dress. She felt less vulnerable with her breasts covered. She wasn't shy, but Gabriel's stare had the ability to make her feel totally exposed. 'Aren't you going?' said Laura flatly.

There came a knock on the door. They looked at each other. 'Come in,' said Gabriel.

It was Michael. He looked from one to the other without curiosity. 'I was looking for you both. There's something I've decided and I thought you both should know.'

Laura took in her breath. 'I don't need telling. I'm not a fool. You want to join up.'

There was a silence. Husband and wife stared at one another. With an hysterical sob, Laura turned away.

Gabriel said, 'It's madness, Mike. We were just saying. You can't.'

Laura swung back to them. 'You see! Gabriel won't let you and neither will I.'

Michael said, 'I don't need anyone's permission, I'm afraid. I'm sorry. It's something I have to do.'

Laura put her hands to her head. She felt as if her brain was pulsating, would soon explode. Yet Michael was doing this to her, dear, kind Michael! She picked up the baby and tried to push her way out of the room. Michael put up his hands to bar her way. 'How can you?' she demanded. 'Leaving me, and Mary, and your parents and the boys. Everything, all the stock, all the farm. Not caring at all! Get out of my way!'

The jiggling unsettled the baby. She burped against her mother's shoulder and a trail of milk ran down Laura's dress. So now she looked a mess as well. She felt tears beginning to come. Tears of fright and despair.

Michael said, 'It's because of you and Mary and everyone I have to go. I can't expect others to fight for you. Not as I will.'

She turned and met his eyes. She was demanding, with the anger of desperation. 'You can't leave me! You shouldn't leave

331

me! I'll do anything you want, anything at all. You don't know how much you mean to me. You don't know how much I need you. Please, Michael. Please. Don't go.'

He held her shoulders, embracing her and the baby together. Gently, like a vicar bestowing a blessing, he kissed her forehead. She felt the walls of her security falling like so much paper, felt the cold wind of reality blowing across her naked soul. Everything had been an illusion, then. She had luxuriated in a fortress that wasn't there. He held her, but she felt nothing. She began to shiver uncontrollably, to choke on sobs. Now she knew that there was nothing in the world that she could trust. She was alone again. Without him.

BOOK THREE

Chapter One

A day had never seemed so long. The hours crawled past on leaden feet, although there was masses to do; David's lessons, Alan's drawing, Mary's bath, Mr Cooper to retrieve from one of his long wanders down the drive, from which he never thought to return; some men from Northumberland to entertain, down to look at some rams, and Bill Mayes out in the field and nowhere to be seen.

But still it was only four. Michael wouldn't be back much before six, later perhaps. He might have had a puncture. They might detain him for a medical check, or perhaps even now they were reasoning with him, explaining that he could do so much more if he stayed on the land. Just as she was deciding to believe that version of events the car turned into the yard. He was back.

She knew from his face what he was going to say. 'I'm to go next Monday. Officer training. They need Yorkshire officers. The southerners can't understand the men.'

She glanced at him. 'That's good, then. Having you. Don't you think you'd better tell your mother?'

'I will. But I wanted you to know first.'

Laura went to the fire and raked it vigorously. Mr Cooper, dozing in his chair, jerked awake and stood up, fumbling for his stick. Expertly Laura helped him to sit down again. 'Have I had my walk then?' he asked.

'Yes. You've had your walk today. You need a rest.'

'So I do. What a good girl you are, Rosalind.'

But what had goodness brought her? He was leaving. 'You'll be fine,' said Michael gently. 'Please don't cry.'

'I don't know how you can leave me with everything!'

'I've asked for a couple of land girls to come.'

She shook her head, helplessly. More mouths to feed, more

people to worry over. Michael, seeing that she was beyond persuasion, went out to the barn. She would come round, he told himself. All the women did, in time.

On the day he left she clung to him and sobbed. His mother said, 'Please spare us these foreign histrionics, Laura! He's going to Catterick, not Mars.'

'You will help her, won't you, Mother?' said Michael.

The woman snorted. 'She's been doing her best to take over the place since the day she arrived. I should imagine her dream's come true.'

Michael sighed. 'I really can't go if you're going to be unkind.'

'Then let her be unkind!' sobbed Laura. 'Let her be as cruel as she likes, I don't care. We can't manage with you gone.'

He took her hands and held them. 'Yes, you can. Leave everything to Bill, he knows. Don't let me remember you crying.'

She fought for control. Alan and David were watching, their young eyes sombre. She was frightening them. 'Is Uncle Michael going to get killed?' asked Alan suddenly.

Laura drew a shuddering breath. 'I hope not, Alan. He'd better be careful, hadn't he?'

'I will,' said Michael. His eyes were so dark, so warm. 'Don't worry. I will.'

She was better when he was gone. It was as if all her anguish had passed, leaving in its wake a solid, dull misery. Well, she could live with that. It was a fine morning, as so often that summer, and the sunshine revealed smoke-hung cobwebs in the corners of the beams. She would settle the boys to their lessons, listen to the wireless and clean. Dinah, watching her gather a ladder, brushes and cloths, said, 'I painted the scullery when Tim went. Tires you out, I suppose. Doing things.'

'No need to let things go,' said Laura curtly. 'You can do the windows. They're disgusting.'

'I'm doing the beds!'

'They can wait. Why don't we move things around while we're at it? I never have liked the dresser there.'

'Mrs Cooper won't like to have that moved.'

Laura's mouth set in a narrow line. 'Then it can definitely go.'

Dinah made a face. She was in a mood, and no mistake. If everyone took on like this when their men went off to war there'd be no need for anti-aircraft guns. The women could stand on the roofs and spit flame. Who'd have thought Mr Michael would inspire such devotion? Such a calm, gentle, unassuming sort of chap. But she loved him. By God, she did.

Lunch was a scratch meal taken out of doors, bread, cheese and pickles. David and Alan were delighted and chased each other in and out of the great arched doors of the barn. The knot in Laura's gut began to unwind a little. It wouldn't hurt to try conciliation. She said to Mrs Cooper, 'Dinah and I are changing the kitchen round. I hope that's all right.'

'Whatever for?'

'We have to move everything to clean, so it seems a shame to put it all back in the same place. It's good to have a change now and then.'

Mrs Cooper's harsh, handsome face remained set. 'You think you can take over, don't you? Have it all just as you would wish. But it isn't any use. Gunthwaite never changes, it will take all you have and ask for more. You could move a hundred kitchen cabinets and still not make a mark.'

Laura was taken aback. It was the story of Mrs Cooper's own failure, of course, the energy and ideals all come to nothing. But she didn't want to change Gunthwaite. She loved it. More than that, needed it. All she wanted to do was give it every care.

They worked less well in the afternoon, spurred on only by the desire to have the place tidy again. But the new arrangement was a definite improvement. Mr Cooper's chair could go close to the window, and the boys could get to their toy box without falling over the coal. Laura looked at the beams they had dusted that day. If they killed a pig and made ham they wouldn't be able to hang it in here any more. Perhaps there was an outhouse that would do, safe from the prying eyes of the assessor. When the next pig farrowed, the litter was going to be officially one short.

The sound of an engine cut across her thoughts. For a brief second her heart leaped with joy. It was Michael again, the whole foolish episode magically ended. But it wasn't Michael. It was a taxi from Bainfield, as old as the hills. And out of it, stepping with all the sinuousness of a lifetime selling themselves, came Sophie and Marie.

∗ ∗ ∗

Laura felt the world shift on its axis, the entire planet lurch in space. Sophie – Marie – here? They looked so old. Sophie's hair was dyed bright yellow, and she wore it in a girlish topknot above a ravaged face. Her lipstick was the brightest red, her eyebrows plucked to nothing, her cheeks stained liberally with rouge. As for Marie – her tight suit made the most of a still perfect figure, although her legs had thickened a little. She wore a hat with a veil, with a great knot of false hair at the nape of her neck. She looked out at the ancient stones of Gunthwaite like a gaudy town starling in a field. Laura felt an hysterical urge to laugh. She could see it now, when she never could in Paris. Everything about them screamed 'whore'.

'What on earth's arrived now?' said Dinah incredulously. 'Right couple of birds of paradise. Quick, they're paying off the taxi. Best stop him, they're in the wrong place.'

But Laura wasn't to be hurried. Moving deliberately, she took off her apron, wiped her hands and went out into the yard. At once Sophie and Marie screamed, gabbled in French, and advanced on her.

'My darling! My beautiful one! You look like a domestic, what's happened to you?'

'Sophie. Marie.' Laura kissed them both, in the French way, sliding easily back into it when it had taken so long to unlearn French manners. 'What are you doing here?'

'Need you ask?' Sophie waved a theatrical hand. 'The Bosch, my dear. Everywhere. Of course, Madame's making the best of it, German officers in every room, but it wasn't for us. We're not collaborators. So we left and went to Vichy, but we got a little involved in something.'

Marie said drily, 'We were passing guns for the Resistance. It's all a mess, you've no idea. But Sophie got drunk and talked, so we had to run before they caught us. Germans don't like Jews, gypsies, spies or ageing whores. They all go the same way.'

'Which way?'

Marie lifted her shoulder. 'Who knows? They put you on a cattle train to a concentration camp in Germany and you're never seen again. Even the children.'

She stood back to look better at the house. Laura knew how it

338

must seem to them, who hated the country. A tumbledown farm, a disaster. She said quickly, 'Won't you come inside? You can see my baby. Her name's Mary, she's four months old.'

'A tisane,' said Sophie, tripping across the yard in her cruel high heels, veined legs slithering. 'I could die for a tisane. We travelled in a wagon through France, you can't believe the suffering. And the food here! My dear, we could have starved.'

Dinah was standing open-mouthed in the kitchen. 'You don't see a sight like this more than once a Preston Guild,' she muttered.

Marie said, 'Is this the maid? A very ugly one, Laura.'

'It's just like the place you grew up in,' said Sophie distastefully. 'Ugly people and ugly things.'

It was a relief that Dinah had no French and the girls no English. Laura tried to explain them away. 'They're refugees from France.'

'Oh, aye?' said Dinah doubtfully. 'If Mrs Cooper sees 'em they'll be refugees from here and all.'

'Will you be staying long?' Laura asked Marie, as she cast herself wearily into Mr Cooper's favourite chair.

'My dear, you are all we have. We have nowhere else to go.' Laura stood with the kettle in her hand, absorbing the full enormity of her plight. She was in the midst of a terminal disaster.

She gave them beds in the room next to David and Alan. The boys saw them on the stairs and stood open-mouthed in amazement. Sophie bent and kissed little Alan. 'Little angel-face! I shall adore you. And your divinely serious brother. *Bonjour, Mon Capitan!*'

'Leave them alone, Sophie!' snapped Marie. She had lost none of her austere superiority. Sophie continued up the stairs, blowing kisses.

In the kitchen, Dinah said, 'Well! That explains a lot.'

'What on earth do you mean?' asked Laura, bristling defensively. 'I know they seem odd, but – well, you know how it is.'

'No wonder you didn't ask them to the wedding.' She was grinning broadly.

Laura grinned back. 'You can see why,' she admitted.

There was a familiar step in the hall. Dinah made a face. 'Now what?'

When Mrs Cooper came in Dinah was scraping carrots and Laura polishing an already polished brass. She said, 'At last I can use my own kitchen again. How very clinical everything seems.'

'I thought – it makes everything airy. For the summer. We'll change it back if you want.' All the fight about the kitchen was out of Laura now. She had something bigger to struggle over.

'My husband always likes his chair by the fire.'

'Not in summer, though. Now he can look out.'

The ritual skirmish over, Mrs Cooper sat down and waited for her usual cup of tea. In truth, she didn't care how the kitchen was arranged. Tomorrow she would go and see Dora at Fairlands and they would talk about Gabriel. That was something to look forward to. But Laura was standing in the middle of the floor, twisting a tea towel in her hands.

'Mother – I've got something to tell you. Some people have arrived.'

'People?'

'Yes. From France. They've come to stay.'

'Well, they can't. We don't have people to stay, my husband's not up to it. For tonight possibly, but no more than that.'

'I don't think they've anywhere else to go.'

There was a babble of French in the hall. Sophie and Marie swept in, loud, voluble, carrying Mary from her crib. 'Ah, Laura, this gorgeous little one! We couldn't leave her alone up there, all by herself.'

'She was asleep,' said Laura feebly.

'And now she's awake. *Bonjour, Madame*. Aren't you going to introduce us, Laura? Who is this odd-looking woman?'

Laura struggled with her introductions. 'Madame Cooper,' said Marie haughtily, and extended her fingertips.

'How do you do?' said Mrs Cooper, at maximum frost.

'You live with her?' said Sophie incredulously. 'Bet you wish you were back with Madame Bonacieux!'

Laura made a face at her. Perhaps Mrs Cooper understood French. But it seemed she did not. 'Is it some new order?' she asked in bewilderment. 'Do we have to take these people in? I shall have to complain.'

'You do that,' said Laura breathlessly. 'It's because I'm French, I suppose. They knew I could talk to them.'

'They don't look at all the sort of people I should wish to speak to. Are they actors of some sort?'

'I really don't know.'

Laura made tea and served cake, battered from all sides by disjointed conversation. The boys came in, and sat staring at the strangers.

'Are they mad?' asked David eventually.

'I'm not sure,' said Laura.

Would this crazy day never end? One by one the occupants of the house fell away. Mrs Cooper withdrew last, saying, 'You'll have to speak to someone, Laura. We can't keep these people, they eat enough for ten.'

'I will, Mother. Goodnight.'

Laura was left at the dinner table with her friends. 'Now,' said Marie, 'I'll go and fetch the cognac. We took the precaution of bringing a few bottles across. You look as if you need some, Laura.'

'Not as much as me,' said Sophie, kicking off her shoes and putting her feet on a chair. 'You should have told me you were in this hellhole, darling. I'd have rescued you.'

Laura said absently, 'I don't need rescuing. Did you get my letters, Sophie? Is that how you knew where to come?'

'Letters? Not since I left the hospital. Marie had the address. From Madame.'

'So when did you get out of hospital? I've been sending Madame money for your care for years.'

'Money? To Madame? I got out four weeks after you left! The old criminal! The bitch!'

Laura said resignedly, 'I admit, I used to wonder. How was she doing when you left?'

'She's got a lot of new girls,' said Marie, pouring three generous measures of spirits. 'Hundreds to choose from, all young and pretty. Stands to reason, everything upside down. So she threw me out. After all these years, just as if I was a worn-out horse. I hadn't planned anything, so I went round to see Sophie. She had a new place, she's given the other up, she takes in mending. But she'd just been chucked on the street too. Great German clean-up, or something. And it wasn't healthy, a Jewish neighbourhood – and my grandfather was a Jew.' She took a sip of her drink and leaned back expansively. 'Nothing to do but leave, you see. And then that trouble. I tell you, we got out of the house ten minutes before they came for us. Ten minutes! But they got a boy who came to warn us. A little kid, doing what he was told, no more than that. I ask you!'

Laura sipped her cognac. It was good, Marie still had refined tastes. 'What happened to him?'

She shrugged. 'No one knows. A train, I should think. You wouldn't believe what happens nowadays.'

Sophie sighed gustily, and began to cough. She wasn't so well, Laura realised. Beneath the determined sparkle and the paint, she was a tired old lady. Not so old, surely? thought Laura. It was the life, of course. 'What you going to do with us, then?' Sophie asked astutely. 'You're not so keen on us being here, are you? And Mother's giving us the evil eye.'

'Not at all,' said Laura, suddenly very English.

Marie laughed. 'I saw their faces! You fit in well, Laura, I'll give you that. You're about as sexy as a potato nowadays.'

'That's the English way. You should meet my husband. He's so nice. But he's gone to war.'

Marie waved a hand. 'Haven't they all? Ah, haven't they all?'

They sipped their drinks. Laura could feel the years slipping away, feel herself growing closer to these two than she could ever remember. They were all the same, united by experience, bred to the same sad life. Had she escaped? It was hard to recall.

Sophie yawned. 'How long can we stay, then? We won't let the cat out of the bag. Promise.'

Laura said, 'I don't know. We don't have visitors, with Mr Cooper in the state he's in. And we're supposed to be getting land girls. But they could sleep in one of the buildings, I suppose. If we could get you ration books, and tell Mrs Cooper you've been evacuated here and we haven't any choice – but it's all so complicated!'

She put a hand to her head. Marie chuckled. 'You've turned out well, you know that? I expected you to throw us out the moment we arrived. Respectable bourgeois that you've become. Little Lori Perdoux had her selfish streak, after all.'

'She never did,' purred Sophie, running an age-spotted hand

over Laura's bare arm. 'She was always good.'

'Not when she was the most expensive whore in Paris,' said Marie.

Laura started to giggle. To think of that now! What a conceited little bitch she had been.

She looked round the room, the oil lamps casting pools of yellow light on polished wood and leather. It seemed another life, another lifetime. She considered. If Michael was here, would she have been so welcoming? There were advantages, it seemed, in being left to make all the choices.

She lifted her near-empty glass. 'A toast,' she declared. 'To Madame Bonacieux. May she get all she deserves and give me all that she owes. The old battle-axe!'

'The old battle-axe!' cried Sophie and Marie.

They drained their glasses, chuckling.

'Some more,' said Sophie. 'We're alive, we should celebrate.'

'Not for me.' Laura got up, yawning. 'I've got work to do tomorrow.'

'Not much work for us around here,' said Marie. 'We'll have to look for some. I don't mind old men as much as I did.'

Laura opened her eyes at her. 'You wouldn't!'

Marie laughed. 'A joke, *chérie*. Go to bed.'

Laura left them finishing the bottle.

My Dearest Laura,

I'm sorry it's taken so long for me to write, but this is literally the first moment I've had to myself in days. We're kept moving from morning 'til night, running from weapons' training to map reading to communications, without a break. We fall into bed at night and haul out again at six the next morning for a kit inspection.

Some of the men, from banks and so on, are finding it very hard. I just wish we could have it over and get on with doing something. I feel almost as out of it here as I did at Gunthwaite, we hear nothing and see nothing of the war. The food is terrible, of course. I find myself lying awake at night dreaming of your cassoulet. And of you. Always.

How are Mary and the boys? I've had no letter from you. Perhaps you've written and it's been delayed? The army's like that, even the simplest things seem to go astray. Tell

Bill Mayes to make sure the ewes get on to roots a week before tupping, but to check their mouths first. Anything without good teeth had better be sold off, now I'm not there to keep an eye. Have you heard anything about the land girls? I'm sure they'll be a help.

I wait every day for a letter. I miss Gunthwaite, and you, more than I can say. Give my love to everyone.

Your faithful husband
Michael

Laura folded the letter carefully, and looked again at the scrawled sheets of her own abandoned communications. How could she tell him? What could she say that wouldn't have him worried to death? Out in the yard Sophie and Marie were teaching David and Alan to play *boule*, improvising with croquet balls and gabbling in French. Their fame was spreading. Every day there were several children and a couple of men taking peeks at them over the wall. She didn't know what the village was saying, but she could guess. When the vicar first encountered Sophie's waggling rear and wicked eye, he said, 'Ah, yes. The refugees. One wonders at their fleeing an invading army, doesn't one? Women like that usually run rather quickly in the other direction.'

Dinah, who thought the vicar an impossible snob, said tartly, 'Takes all sorts. Smuggling guns for the Resistance, they were. I'd like to see who'd do as much if the Germans walked in here. No use writing letters to *The Times* then.'

The vicar was a great *Times* correspondent. When he'd gone, rather sooner than he'd intended, Laura said, 'I thought you didn't like them, Dinah?'

She grinned. 'They're all right. Marie knows how to make pastry, I'll give her that. As for her sewing – it's the finest I've ever seen. And Sophie's a laugh.'

'She hasn't done much laughing, these last few years.'

'No? Doesn't surprise me. Must have been pretty, when she was young.'

Laura smiled. 'When I was little, I thought she was the most beautiful thing I'd ever seen. Everything shiny. She must have looked so vulgar, but I didn't know.'

'She's good with kids,' said Dinah. 'Kid herself at heart.'

344

Laura dragged her thoughts back to her unwritten letter. What to say about the sheep? Bill Mayes had been a day or two late in moving the hurdles in the turnip field, and the hungry sheep had broken into the wood. Six had died from eating yew and rhododendron, and a dozen more might yet give up the ghost. As for the cattle, they'd lost a calf, born dead, and the cow lucky to live. It might have happened if Michael had been there, but Laura doubted it. Bill Mayes didn't turn out for late night checks on the stock, he was too comfortable in bed. She knew what he'd say if she challenged him about it. 'Farmed here nigh on forty year, and I don't need no woman telling me my business.' But she knew negligence when she saw it. There was a row brewing.

She got to her feet. There was really no time to think about letters, she would write tonight, before bed. Now there was food to be cooked and children to be educated, as well as the room for the land girls to be sorted out in the barn. And she must talk to Bill Mayes.

Laura hurried into the yard. 'Sophie, would you please prepare dinner?' she called. 'We're having soup and I've killed a chicken, but it isn't very big so you'll have to stew it with potatoes. Put a little ham in if you think that would be good.'

Sophie made a face. 'I'm playing *boule*. I can't do it now.'

'The boys have to do their lessons,' said Laura implacably. Why was she always being implacable? 'Alan. David,' she called in English. 'I've set some things for you to do. Marie, could you supervise them, please?'

'I was going to lie down,' said Marie, carefully folding her false hair back into its bun. In the daylight the difference between that and her real hair was startling, but as she said, in wartime you couldn't get good dye.

'You can rest while David does his writing and Alan copies his letters. Please, Marie. I thought you might begin teaching the boys some French.'

Marie looked down her elegant nose. 'A good idea, Laura. Sometimes you're quite sensible. I can do something to give these boys a respectable accent, the English have no idea.'

So that was one problem out of the way. She ran indoors to check on Mary, and found Mrs Cooper in attendance. Although she needed her mother-in-law's help she resented it. What would happen to Mary, brought up under that baleful eye? She kissed the baby, evaded her reaching arms and said, 'Has anyone come about the land girls? They were supposed to be arriving this week.'

Mrs Cooper looked blank. 'But of course. This afternoon. I told you.'

'You didn't tell me anything! You mean they're coming today?'

'Laura, you're becoming quite stupid. I told you yesterday, at lunch.'

'You weren't at lunch yesterday. You went to see Dora.'

'Did I? Well, I must have told her.'

It was infuriating. She ran across to the barn, wondering if the land girls would object to climbing a ladder to go to bed. But the room itself was large and dry. Light came in through a skylight in the roof, and there was a paraffin heater. Laura wondered if it would set the place on fire, and then reflected that if all she had heard about land girls was true they would do that by smoking in bed. No one round about had a good word to say for them. Man-hungry minxes, the lot of them.

She slumped on one of the unmade beds. They were all man-hungry, that was the trouble. So many women, like a convent without prayers.

Weariness overcame her, and she lay back on the mattress, staring up at the rafters, wondering if she would see a mouse run. Her thoughts drifted, remembering a man, a nameless man, pulling her on to him. The feelings, deliciously remembered, made her tingle. Just once in a while it would be good. Now and then.

A noise in the yard caught her attention. Bill Mayes was bringing the sheep in, when she had specifically told him they were not to come in-bye. He didn't want to make a hurdle pen just for dagging and trimming feet. She climbed down the ladder and confronted him.

'Bill, I told you to put up hurdles. The land girls are coming. If the sheep go in the barn the place will stink.'

'That's not my affair.' The stocky, belligerent man stuck out his belly and swaggered past.

'Then what is?' snapped Laura. 'You've killed six sheep and a calf so far. I suppose that isn't your affair either.'

Guilt made him bridle. He turned on her with a pointing finger. 'Don't you go telling me what to do, Missus. I've been farming since before you was born . . .'

'I was born on a farm,' said Laura tightly. 'And I know poor stockmanship when I see it. Let's have it straight, Bill. My husband left me in charge here. I've let you have your head and it's not worked well. Now we do it my way.'

'I'm not taking orders from a woman. Nor one that harbours foreigners.' He looked at her darkly.

'They're French! The Germans drove them out. For God's sake, Bill, there's a war on, everything has to change. Look, I don't want to fight.' He turned away from her slightly, in a minor relaxation of hostility. She dropped her voice coaxingly. 'You're as good as anyone with crops, Bill, but you should follow me about stock. Really, I know what I'm doing. The horses, now. They should move to poorer pasture and let the cattle go in the meadow.'

'The government wants that meadow ploughed,' said Bill determinedly. 'Get a good yield from it, mark my words.'

'I'd rather leave it until they force us. Stock do well there, the grass is good.'

'Corn'd do better.'

They were relaxing, on safer ground. She talked a little longer, letting Bill air his preference for ploughed land. She felt a small thrill of triumph. He always seemed so against her, she had never expected him to back down. Perhaps he wasn't as tough as he appeared?

As the conversation drew to its end she said casually, 'So you'd better put the sheep in Long Meadow for now, Bill. You can trim them tomorrow when the land girls are here to move the hurdles.'

He avoided her eye. But he whistled the dogs and began to move the sheep away. Flushed with victory, Laura called out, 'You can have six eggs, if you like, Bill. Put them in your pocket.' An obvious bribe, and he responded with a sideways look. It was almost conspiratorial. What was that odd expression? You scratch my back and I'll scratch yours. Co-operation versus illicit eggs. A necessary trade.

The land girls arrived just as she was putting a vase of flowers in their room. She had found a couple of old hooked rugs and a

347

washbowl, as well as the usual chamber pots, but the place looked bare and rather spartan. The woman in charge of the girls said briskly, 'I doubt that this will be suitable in winter, Mrs Cooper.'

'There might be room in the house by then. And this is more spacious.'

The girls, not much more than eighteen, looked down-hearted. They were both a little plump, with round, innocent faces and soft hands.

'Have you done this sort of work before?' Laura asked.

They both shook their heads. 'My mother said it would do me good,' said one.

'My father said it would keep me out of trouble,' said the other. 'You don't get in trouble in the country, do you?'

Laura and the woman in charge avoided each other's gaze. 'We don't have bombs in the country, that's very true,' said the woman. 'Now, Mrs Cooper, are you going to help our girls settle in? They'll be collected on Friday evening. There's a dance in Bainfield. But if you could arrange transport at other times? They may want to go to the cinema, or to the shops.'

'Yes. Yes, of course.' So she was to provide a taxi service as well! She looked dubiously at her charges. As unformed as bread dough, both of them.

She led the way down the ladder and into the house. Her mother-in-law was in the kitchen. 'Not more people?' she said loudly, and took herself off. Her husband struggled out of his chair and quavered, 'Is it time? Is it time?'

'Not yet,' said Laura absently, and sat him down again.

'Time for what?' asked the woman in charge.

'Nobody knows.'

The land girls huddled together away from him. Just then, when the household was at its least inviting, Sophie and Marie appeared. 'My God!' said Marie, staring at the visitors. 'What are these three lesbians doing here?'

The woman in charge went purple. 'I beg your pardon?'

'You speak French,' said Laura in horror. 'She didn't mean – it wasn't—'

Marie insinuated herself between them. 'My apologies, Madame. One is so used to a lack of culture, one sometimes fails to realise that fine minds can exist in unlikely places. You know

348

France? You have travelled there? Perhaps you will join me in a cognac?'

Laura left them. She took the two girls and showed them the oil lamps and the privy. Their round, young faces became rounder and more anxious by the minute. 'I know it seems primitive,' apologised Laura. 'Perhaps after the war—'

'My dad said there'd be a privy,' said one, miserably. 'I didn't believe him.'

'I didn't think anywhere didn't have electric,' said the other.

Laura felt embarrassed for her home. Beautiful, tranquil Gunthwaite had fallen behind the modern world. But the modern world was upon it, upon them all. It was no use waiting for Michael to tell her what to do any more. Decisions had to be taken, changes had to be made. She had to take charge.

Chapter Two

Bill Mayes stood in the kitchen, thumbs looped into his belt. Well might he look smug, thought Laura angrily. She had been too quick to think her battle had been won. Bill Mayes had manoeuvred himself into a comfortable position, doing as he wished for the most part yet able to shunt responsibility on to Laura whenever he so chose. As now.

'I didn't say I definitely wouldn't plough the meadow,' she said uneasily. 'I said I'd wait until they forced us.'

'Well, this here inspector thinks you're being obstructive,' said Bill with satisfaction. 'Says you don't know there's a war on. The country needs grain, he says.'

'They need beef too. And that meadow floods every spring, we'd never get it sown. Did you tell him we'd plough Ten Acre instead?'

'Not my place to tell him anything,' said Bill, innocently.

She got up from the desk, and smoothed her skirt. 'I'm beginning to wonder myself what your place is, Bill.'

'And what do you mean by that, Missus?'

She gave him back his own oblique look. 'Whatever you like.'

In the dining room Marie was regaling David with a long story in French. If he understood one word in ten it would be a miracle, thought Laura. But there was a chorus in English of some sort, and at intervals both boys burst into tuneless song, bolstered by Sophie's surprisingly sweet soprano. 'The elephant said THANK YOU, the elephant said YES, the elephant said HOW DO YOU DO, I'd like to come in for a REST.'

Marie's invention, of course. Her rusty English was reviving at an amazing speed. Sophie spoke hardly a word, save, 'Want a good time, honey?' which she knew in ten languages at least.

Laura opened the door, and the boys turned bright faces to her.

350

'Boys,' said Marie, and they both chorused, '*Bonjour, Laura. Ça va?*'

'*Bien, merci,*' responded Laura, with a mock curtsey.

Alan said, 'Will you write and tell Mummy and Daddy we can speak French?'

David said, 'We can't speak it yet, silly. We just know some words. I mean, you can't just say hello and things, can you? We couldn't be spies.'

'Marie was a spy,' said Alan excitedly. 'The Germans caught her, but she didn't say anything. She was terribly brave.'

Marie waved a deprecating hand. 'Children – they exaggerate so.'

'Yes,' said Laura, with a dark look. Any minute now Marie would have invented herself as the architect of the entire French Resistance.

It was blowing hard outside, a summer storm. Leaves and twigs rattled against the dining-room windows. She slipped on a jacket and braced herself for the outside air, shuddering as the wind hit her. In the far field, the horses were harrowing one of the fields left fallow, with heads tucked in and ears flat, wandering away from the wind. Laura squinted. Who was driving them? It was Paula, one of the land girls, doing her struggling best. There was no need for reprimand, it was only the harrow, after all, breaking up the thistle roots to weaken them.

She went into the barn. Ruth, the other girl, was desultorily sorting potatoes. Laura sat down with her, and sorted a sack herself. 'I think it's going to rain,' she remarked. 'Paula will have to bring the horses in. Can she do it by herself?'

'She likes to try,' said Ruth. 'She won't let me help her, says I'm too nervous and they get upset. I didn't know there'd be horses. All the other girls drive tractors on their farms.'

'Yes. I know.'

Another implied criticism. But she was too sensitive, it was only natural for the girls to compare notes when they met up in town. Laura said, 'Do you wish you were somewhere else, then? If you wanted a transfer you've only to say. I know Gunthwaite doesn't have many modern things, and if it upsets you – I don't want you to be miserable, you know.'

351

'Oh.' Ruth coloured a little. 'We're not miserable. I mean, it were a bit of a shock, no toilet and that. And the barn, and everything so old. But Paula likes the horses more than anything, and I'm good with the sheep. Besides, it's pretty, isn't it? Not like town or even the park. I've never lived anywhere so nice.'

'Neither have I,' said Laura gently. 'I'm glad you see it, Ruth. Sometimes I think people only notice that we haven't electricity and don't see the rest.'

The rain began. In a while Paula brought the horses into the yard, stamping and blowing, anxious to get in from the weather. Her young face was red with effort and concentration, driving her team, stopping them charging the gate. 'Whoa, Banner. Whoa, Blossom. WHOA! Stand up, there.' She bustled round them, full of self-importance. Laura knew she would spend half the night brushing her charges and cleaning the gear.

The potatoes were finished. Ruth went to help Paula toss hay from the loft, and Laura went back to the house. It was good that the girls were happy here, not wishing to be off every night. But these other farms worried Laura. Almost everyone round-about had a tractor except them. Michael had held out against them, claiming that machines were bad for the land, because he loved his horses. In the spring he sometimes had four teams working, two from the farm and two brought in, and a man and boy to each. It was a fine sight.

But now they must plough Ten Acre. It was old pasture on heavy land, crippling work for a team. She considered a moment. Perhaps next market day she should go into Bainfield and see if she could hire a tractor. The auctioneer arranged contract work, she knew. Michael wouldn't like it, and Bill Mayes still less, but if they must plough then they must, and well. She wondered how much it would cost. Everything was expensive and in short supply. But if they grew barley on that field she might get a good price.

The figures turned and twisted in her head. Barley prices had been terrible of late, you couldn't grow it for what they paid. For years now the government had been happy to see the country flooded with foreign grain and foreign beef, while farms became derelict and the land went to nothing. Michael had held on through it all, keeping the land in good heart, keeping faith. Was she betraying him? If she used tractors to wring corn from virgin acres was she conspiring with an enemy and letting Gunthwaite go?

It was time the riding horses went at least. There was no point in feeding extra mouths when no one had the time or the energy to ride any more. Next time she saw Mrs Fitch she'd ask her to see them sold. And that was another thing she wouldn't tell Michael.

As she walked back to the house she saw Mrs Cooper talking agitatedly to someone. They turned as she approached and Laura saw that it was Mrs Betts, from the Post Office. She had battled up to Gunthwaite with a parcel and some tasty news. 'Thought you should know,' she said. 'Got it from Mrs Higgins' boy, he's in the navy, on weekend leave. Trouble in the Channel. German planes bombing convoys. The fighters have been after them.'

'Gabriel,' said Laura faintly.

Mrs Betts nodded. 'Didn't want you hearing when you were in the village, like. Best you're prepared.'

'I don't know what I shall do,' said Mrs Cooper, looking about her in a bewildered way.

'Gabriel will be fine,' said Laura staunchly. 'He got through France, after all.'

'He didn't fight in France! He told me so. I'll have to go and see Dora. Tell Mayes to get the car.'

Laura clenched her teeth. There she went again, using precious petrol on a social call. Remembering her manners she offered Mrs Betts a cup of tea, and sat in the kitchen with her while she drank it. The car roared off down the drive and Mrs Betts said understandingly, 'At least she'll be out of your way a while. Right bad do this is, left alone with all this lot to manage.'

'I'd rather be busy,' said Laura. 'Now Michael's away.'

Released from their lessons, Alan and David ran screeching past the window. 'We're getting another lot of them,' said Mrs Betts lugubriously. 'Message came today. Stands to reason, now it's hotting up. But where are they going to go, that's what I'd like to know? School's bursting as it is.'

Laura nodded, not really taking much in. She couldn't

pretend now that there would be no fighting. What would happen to Michael? Where would he go? She had built upon a rock, and it had crumbled beneath her feet.

Gabriel was sitting in a deckchair in brilliant sunshine, the squall that was flustering Gunthwaite that day nowhere to be seen. But it was a sham relaxation, more for effect than anything, since he couldn't bear to exhibit tension as obviously as everyone else. They all knew there was hell on in the Channel. They were standing by in permanent readiness to take to the air.

Someone strolled over to him. 'Nothing doing, so far. Don't know why they can't let us in on the act. Anything's better than waiting.'

'Yes.' Gabriel pulled out his cigarettes and they both lit up. He leaned his head back in the chair, staring up into a cloudless sky. A slight breeze was rustling the grass. He imagined the leaves in the orchard at Gunthwaite, and Laura's face. He ought to think of Dora. He must think of Dora. There was a small but brilliant twinkle in the cloudless blue.

'Bloody hell! Luftwaffe! Scramble, everyone!'

They all stared up where he had been staring. It was a plane certainly, but a German plane? Cooper had the best eyes in the place. Suddenly, the sound of engines was apparent. Someone came running out of the control tower. 'Get moving, you idle shower! Bandits.'

No time to think. In the midst of the rush to get airborne, bullets began to rain down. Planes raced down the strip, scuttling into the air without formation. One, driving unexpectedly into a hail of fire, exploded in flame.

They took off around him, momentarily blinded by smoke, clawing up into clear sky. The enemy had the advantage, diving on them out of the sun, covering the bombers that were even now approaching. Dark canisters began to drop like eggs towards the ground. Gabriel, head swivelling to sight the enemy, saw earth erupt in what seemed to be silent motion. A fly seemed to zip past his ear; instinctively he jammed the rudder bar down, twisting into a dive. His pursuer was hard on his tail, diving as fast, faster. He pulled back on the stick, heading into an abrupt climb. His enemy shot past and he dived again, now on the other's tail. His first shots were wild. He wanted simply to shoot, that was all. Then he began to aim, concentrating, seeing a flutter of fabric as some of his shells struck home.

He pulled away abruptly, sensing pursuit. Sure enough, in the sky above him an Me 109 was baring its teeth. The range was too great; Gabriel gave his machine full throttle and increased it. Anyone else around? Now what should he do? He had a desperate urge to turn his aircraft and run as far as possible from conflict.

Everything was very quiet. He realised that in his haste he hadn't connected the R/T. Abruptly he did so, and his headphones were filled with excited chatter. 'Yours went down, Gabriel. Hit the pilot, I guess. Christ! There's one on my tail!'

Gabriel craned his head and saw the deadly shape in the sky. He kicked the rudder and came round, anxiety about a spin somewhere on the periphery of his mind. No time for that now. Get above him, try to aim, tear through the sky in a murderous follow my leader. The Messerschmitt broke away, apparently undamaged. Gabriel checked his mirror, checked the sky, searched everywhere. Nothing. It was done.

Back on the ground they were all voluble. So much had happened in such a short time it was hard to remember that a plane had crashed and someone had died. Fire tenders were still hosing the blaze.

'Who was it?' asked Gabriel.

'One of the new blokes. I didn't know him.'

So they didn't have to mourn him too much. Instead they congratulated each other and went over everything again and again. Suddenly the tannoy blared. 'Scramble. Scramble.'

Gabriel ran for his plane. They had barely finished refuelling, was it some ghastly practical joke? He flung himself into the cockpit, plugging in in time to hear the R/T crackle with information, headings, enemy strength. This time they'd go up with wingmen and try to put some order into things. He felt calm, suddenly. It wasn't like France. At least here there was no chance this time that the airfield would get up and run away. He would think of Laura and the orchard, the things he must keep safe.

The sky seemed huge and empty. But then, in the distance he saw the telltale dark specks. So many of them, twenty, thirty? He pulled down his goggles, trading the sense of claustrophobia for the certainty of unburned eyes. Suddenly the formation in front of them began to scatter. They'd been seen. A thrill, almost a relish, for battle. Right then. On with the show.

Mrs Cooper sat holding Dora's reluctant hand. They were in the conservatory, with the doors open to the garden and a teatray on a table at the side. Dora wondered if she could extricate herself on the excuse of pouring more tea. But it seemed churlish when Gabriel's mother was confiding in her.

'Really, my dear, Laura's quite heartless. She doesn't understand how we feel. All she thinks about is Michael, who's safe as houses in a training camp and probably won't see action at all.'

'I suppose she misses him,' said Dora. 'After all, we miss Gabriel.'

Mrs Cooper sighed in dissatisfaction. She didn't want Laura's behaviour given a creditable gloss. 'And those women!' she went on. 'I'm sure we needn't have them. Laura says we must, but no one else has people like that inflicted on them. I mean to say, have you?'

'We've been asked to take evacuees,' said Dora, trying to disentangle her hand without Mrs Cooper noticing. 'I think we shall have to, this time. Someone came and looked at the house too, and upset Daddy dreadfully. They suggested they might use the west wing as a school.'

'My God!' Mrs Cooper reeled back as if shot. 'Have we really come to this?'

Dora looked at her unhappily. She very much feared that she was coming to loathe Mrs Cooper, with her dark gloom and her dramatic pronouncements. She hated too the way she seemed to think they were united in love for Gabriel. Dora didn't think Mrs Cooper appreciated that Gabriel was married. It meant that Dora was now the most important woman in his life, they didn't share the position.

She decided the moment had come. 'I think I should tell you, I'm expecting.'

'What?' Mrs Cooper stared at her in amazement 'Already?'

Dora nodded vigorously. 'A honeymoon baby.'

'We can't have two honeymoon babies in the family! People will talk.'

'Oh.' This seemed inadequate, so she added, 'I'm sorry. My mother's delighted.'

'You should tell the authorities. Then they won't take the house for a school.'

'They're only thinking about taking a part of it. Just for a day school. I don't think my baby will make much difference.'

This time she did pour tea. Why did Mrs Cooper visit her like this? She wanted her to fall in a heap and sob, when the news was really quite encouraging. British fighters were keeping the enemy at bay, with very few casualties. Dora was sure Gabriel would be all right. He was so alive, so exciting, it wasn't possible to think of him as gone. In all probability he'd be a hero and they'd all be terribly proud.

Mrs Fitzalan-Howard came in to join them. Dora cast her a look of pleading but her mother gave a little shake of her head. Dora would have to learn to cope with Mrs Cooper. Now she was a married woman there were responsibilities she could not shirk.

'Isn't it wonderful about Dora's baby?' she said companionably. 'We shall have such a lovely spring.'

'He could be killed. The child would be fatherless.'

Mrs Fitzalan-Howard said tartly, 'There's not a lot we can do about it now, is there?' and picked up a cup of stewed tea.

They were all three silent. Eventually, sighing, Mrs Cooper got to her feet and took her leave. When she was gone Mrs Fitzalan-Howard avoided her daughter's gaze. 'I thought we were being polite,' remarked Dora.

'She really is the most peculiar woman. I gather Laura wants to move her into a cottage, and really I can't blame her.'

'I can't bear her coming twice a week! I'm going to visit her. At least then I can leave when I like. And I can talk to Laura.'

Mrs Fitzalan-Howard picked a leaf off her wilting aspidistra. The hot summer was playing havoc with the conservatory plants. 'I don't know how much time Laura has to talk. Whenever I see her she looks harassed.'

Dora laughed. 'So do we all, after five minutes with That Woman!' Mother and daughter chuckled together.

Bainfield was different on market day. No longer were there gaggles of men on every corner, half-drunk and roaring with

357

laughter, or sober and intent. Now there were women hurrying about their business, and land girls by the dozen, seizing the chance to get out and about in a town. And there were uniforms, spotting the crowds like dark reminders of a world beyond.

Above all, it seemed to Laura, colour had gone. Clothes were drab, shops drabber, the fruit on the market stalls no longer lay heaped in glorious profusion. No oranges or bananas, not even the hothouse grapes that used to come from great houses roundabout. Perhaps the gardeners had gone, or the fruit itself was more precious now there was nothing else. All in all, it no longer reached Bainfield.

Laura walked quickly to the auctioneer's. To her surprise the senior partner, Mr Jones, was in the office. Presumably he considered the few sheep forward beneath him, and had delegated the task of selling them to the sallow youth who had avoided conscription because of bad lungs. Many a farmer with a son called up had given him a sour look and muttered, 'That one needs shooting, more than any of 'em.'

Jones rose as Laura entered. 'Mrs Cooper. How delightful. Sit down, won't you? Can I offer you a sherry?'

She was taken aback. She wasn't used to gentility in her frantic day. She sank into the worn leather captain's chair and accepted a drink. An elderly farmer, glancing through the window, remarked that it didn't take rams like Jones long to sniff out the untupped ewes. But Laura, comfortably relaxing, was enjoying Mr Jones' intelligent interest.

'You know what it's like at Gunthwaite, Mr Jones. We've done well, considering the times. My husband set his mind to being self-supporting, we almost never have to buy feed. And the surplus was profit. It got us through the depression in farming, the land's in good heart and we run good, healthy stock. But now everything's changed. We have to produce more; I can't run the farm as we used to. The Ministry want us to plough more land, and I'm wondering about tractors. We've never used them, you see. Michael felt they did harm to the land. And I'm not sure.'

Jones reached for the sherry bottle and topped them both up. 'I should come out and see, shouldn't I? Look at the fields and make an assessment. I must admit, in recent years Gunthwaite's fallen behind the times. I mean, looking at your pasture, I wonder why you don't run a dairy herd. You could use a machine with a good petrol engine, or electricity of course.'

'I don't think we could afford electric,' said Laura shyly. 'Perhaps after the war. But a tractor—'

'You're right to consider it. Now farms are short-handed, tractors make all the difference. The girls are willing, I'll give them that, but farming's hard for the weaker sex. I have to tell you, Mrs Cooper, it grieves me to see women like yourself – attractive women – wearing themselves to shreds with the work. Why, there's almost nothing of you.'

The sherry was going to her head. She got up, a little unsteadily. 'When can you come out and visit us, Mr Jones?'

He thought about his exhausted petrol ration. To hell with it, he'd buy on the black market and be damned. 'I think – tomorrow afternoon?'

'That's terribly kind.'

The day was hot once more. Harvest was approaching, and the corn stood tall and feathery in the fields. Laura took an ear, spread the grains in her palm and cracked one in her teeth. Soft yet awhile. When it was 'steely' and held against her teeth, then it was ripe.

She and the auctioneer stood at the edge of the field Paula had harrowed the week before. 'The thistles were bad,' explained Laura. 'We left it fallow, and cut them twice. Then we ploughed it, and harrowed in the seedlings. It should be clean for spring.'

'But a crop lost,' said Jones sorrowfully.

'For the sake of the land! Michael always says you can't do anything that's bad for the land. Cash cropping makes you pay in the end. Don't you agree?'

'There's a war on,' said Jones, smiling at her.

She grinned back. 'So there is.'

She was wearing a light summer skirt. As they walked up Ten Acre the breeze tangled it around her legs. The land girls wore trousers all the time, and shorts when the weather was warm. What would Michael think of that? thought Laura. If he saw her in shorts he'd be shocked.

Jones reached down and pulled a clump of grass. 'You don't see sward like this nowadays. Wonderful for cows.'

'We put them on here when the meadow's too wet, and then

the sheep follow. And in winter the in-foal mares come on, and the others on rest days. But we shall have to plough.'

'Let's sit down and think about it, shall we?'

The grass was warm and dry. Jones sat close, a tall man with thick greying hair. Laura wondered why he hadn't volunteered. Perhaps he had and was unfit? She looked down at the farm, a long way below, a cluster of stone in a stone-walled landscape. A flock of doves rose from Hanging Wood, swooping high before settling again. The crows were amongst them. If Michael was here he'd be out with his gun.

A hand crept on to her knee. She removed her gaze from the valley and looked at it. 'My dear Mrs Cooper,' said Jones. 'I can't tell you how much I admire you.'

The hand slid up to her thigh. Laura said idly, 'You can admire me all you like, Mr Jones, but if you don't remove your hand I shall be forced to do you some damage. We came to talk about tractors, did we not?'

'But if you knew how you've charmed me! The hours since yesterday have crept by. I couldn't wait to see you again. I've been on fire for you—' He strained towards her, ready to kiss. If they didn't repulse you it was always all right. Her calm, immobile profile was immeasurably exciting.

He pressed his face into her neck, mouthing the smooth skin. Her voice remained peaceful. 'Do you think we should plough this pasture by tractor?'

'Why do we have to talk about tractors now?'

'It's what I expected. Please, Mr Jones. Before we go on.'

'Then for God's sake, yes! You can always seed again later. You have the most beautiful shoulders – and your bosom. I could worship your bosom.'

Laura stood up in one liquid movement, drew back her foot and kicked the auctioneer sharply in the groin. His eyes bulged, he made a noise that resembled strangulation and rolled stiffly away. He lay on the sun-drenched grass, gagging and moaning. 'Don't bother calling at the house on your way back,' said Laura casually.

When he could sit up he watched her. She was walking to the house, her skirt blowing in the breeze, her carriage straight and proud. She looked every inch the gentlewoman she had just proved she wasn't. He felt aggrieved and misled. He had reached out to take a plum, and instead put his fingers in the mouth of a shark. Well, he'd discovered one thing. Mrs Michael Cooper was no lady.

Laura prepared carefully for her interview with the bank. She dressed in a dark suit with a small hat and gloves. She took with her all Michael's carefully written profit and loss statements for the past five years, and a wad of bank statements, just to prove they were orderly folk who respected these things. But sitting before the desk, under the unfriendly gaze of the elderly manager, she wished she had never thought to come.

She explained the need to buy a tractor in faltering words. 'But you could contract plough this acreage,' said the manager. 'I don't imagine your husband will be very pleased to hear that you've spent so much on a piece of machinery you could very well do without.'

'I thought of that first. I invited Mr Jones, the auctioneer, to look round. With the shortage of labour at present, he seemed to think we could justify buying a tractor ourselves.'

'Really? Jones said that?'

'I believe that's what I said.'

She bridled visibly, as she always did when challenged in a lie. The man subsided, looking again at her figures. It wasn't that Gunthwaite couldn't afford a tractor, or even justify its use, but this business of women coming in and demanding loans was somewhat rich. But it was wartime. No doubt things must change, although God willing they'd change back again as soon as all this unpleasantness was at an end.

'Very well, Mrs Cooper,' he said, sighing, 'You may have your tractor. Try and make sure you take a responsible man with you when you purchase. No use picking a pretty colour. A tractor is a working vehicle, you know.'

She didn't laugh until she was out on the street. It was part euphoria, part outrage. She imagined a tractor in delicate pink, and had to lean against a pillar box for support. Then she saw Dora across the road, and tried to sober up.

'Laura! What on earth's the matter?'

'I've just been advised against buying a pretty tractor. The bank manager thinks I might.'

'Buying what?'

She shook her head. 'It doesn't matter. Shall we have tea? I had no lunch, I'm starving.'

Dora nodded. 'Yes, please. I called on you earlier actually, but you were out. Mrs Cooper made me read through the deaths in the paper.'

'Did she? It's her new hobby. I think she imagines that if Gabriel's killed we won't tell her. Besides, they'd write to you. You're next of kin.'

'He won't be killed,' said Dora, with determination. 'You don't think he will either, do you? You're not in the least nervous.'

Laura considered. Truly, she wasn't nervous for Gabriel at all. 'Perhaps it's just that I can't imagine it,' she confessed. 'A world without Gabriel, I mean. He just is. And always will be. The same wild boy.'

They sat in the window of the teashop and ate plain scones with margarine. The school was definitely moving to Fairlands, and Laura envisaged sending the boys. 'But it would mean stopping their French.'

'Marie could teach at the school,' suggested Dora. 'Would she, do you think?'

Impossible. But in another life, without the teenage seduction that had started her on the road, Marie could have been a beautiful, cold teacher. A man was walking past on the pavement outside. It was Jones the auctioneer. He caught Laura's eye, blinked, and cut her dead.

Chapter Three

The tractor was small, grey, and seemed to wear an expression of round-eyed surprise. Everyone on the farm had come to admire the new arrival, and Laura stood to one side, proprietorial as a new mother. But she had felt more confident of handling Mary, tiny and vulnerable though she was, than this jumble of metal. She bolstered her courage with the salesman's repeated words: 'Ferguson tractors are by far the best. The equipment's attached by a unique eight-point system. You'll be amazed at the power delivered where you need it, in the soil.' Where else would power be delivered? she wondered. Was it something you could deliver? Like coal?

'Know how to drive it, do you?' asked Bill Mayes belligerently.

Laura hesitated. It had certainly been explained. But Bill was determined to upset her. 'Yes,' she declared. 'Of course. But you can too, can't you? It's just like a car.'

'That it ain't,' said Bill. He moved to lean against the wall, his opposition made plain.

She looked wildly at Ruth and Paula. They shook their heads. Bill and the men were openly smirking. The silly woman was learning her lesson after all. That's what came of meddling in things you didn't understand. She tried to remember what the salesman had said and done. It was simple. Quite simple. She merely had to begin.

She climbed on to the cold metal seat. Her skirt tangled on a lever and she dragged it free. She must start to wear trousers like the girls. She pulled out a knob, she remembered that part, and then you had to turn the key and press – to her horror and triumph, the engine roared into life.

Its vibrations set the little seat in juddering motion. But now

363

what should she do? There were levers and knobs everywhere, and she had no notion of how to make it move. Did she want it to move? She might trundle inexorably forward, crushing stone and flesh as she went. There was a brake, of course. She felt around on the floor for the pedal.

The engine was starting to belch smoke. Ruth climbed up on the step at her side and muttered, 'Push in the knob. You only use that when it's cold. Like a car.'

'I can't drive a car.'

But she did as she was told. The engine started to purr happily.

'I'm going to try and drive,' she confided to Ruth. 'Get off if you like.'

'It's all right. I want to know how to drive it too. Just to show them!'

Laura pulled a lever. Miraculously, the machine began to move. She clutched the wheel with white-knuckled hands. It wouldn't turn, she'd hit the trough – she turned too much and veered abruptly towards the house. Again she over-corrected, and again. In a series of swerves and bends the little tractor motored out of the yard.

'I'm doing it!' she shouted. 'It's working!'

A dozen cattle saw her, snorted, and raced away from the fence. 'Them cows'll slip them calves,' roared Bill Mayes. 'Mark my words, you'll ruin 'em!'

'Can you stop?' asked Ruth nervously. Laura tried. The machine stood panting obligingly, awaiting their pleasure.

They turned, not without difficulty, and drove back to the yard. 'It's easy,' declared Laura, springing down. 'You'll get the hang of it in no time, Bill. You'll be glad of it at harvest.'

He remained leaning against the wall. Then he pulled himself upright, turned and marched purposefully away.

The tractor remained in the yard, quite neglected. It was a symbol of the men's attitude towards an impertinent woman. After some days Laura decided to make a stand, and began driving it around the farm. Soon she was enjoying herself, and began eyeing the shiny new plough. But she was anxious; she couldn't run the farm without the men. There was no use making them hate her. What could she do?

Harvest was upon them. The reaper moved from farm to farm, followed by bands of workers gathering the sheaves. These would be stored in stacks until the thresher came, and the straw would be gathered and the grain secured. Bill was openly insolent. Laura had only to suggest they start with one field for him to determine on another. On one occasion the inspector came to discuss their crop, but the moment Laura approached, Bill turned on his heel and walked away. The others, following Bill's example, laughed openly.

The horses worked hard at harvest. The sheaves of corn had to be carted close to the house, and the wagons moved back and forth all day. In the early morning a light mist lay over the pasture, and the trees seemed to rise out of it like ships. The teams, fed at dawn to be ready, hauled the wagons down through misty meadows to the fields of uncut corn. No cutting would begin until the sun was up. People yawned and shivered a little, talking softly to each other. Boys came with sticks for the rabbits, and the earth smelled as it always did, rich and good. Then the reaper began to clatter, the day was started and all peace was gone.

Towards afternoon Blossom went lame. She was led back to the yard for a poultice to go on; she had probably stood on a thorn. Banner went with her, he couldn't pull by himself, which left only one wagon to cart sheaves. The stooks grew and kept on growing, as the reaper munched voraciously across golden acres. Laura went over to Bill.

'We'll have to use the tractor. We can't let it all pile up.'

He looked at her with cold dislike. 'I'll get another hoss from somewhere. We'll be right.'

'Please, Bill. It could take days to get another horse. Please try the tractor.'

But he didn't deem her worthy of a reply.

She walked back to the yard. Ruth was there, unloading the single wagon. She was wearing shorts and looked brown and happy. Suddenly Laura envied her, for her freedom, her simplicity, her youth. Had she ever been so free? It seemed as if she had always been encumbered by rules and responsibilities.

Ten minutes later Laura left the yard again, wearing a pair of shorts and driving the tractor. The wagon, unused to speed, bounced hectically along in her wake, and Bill Mayes, pushing the hat to the back of his head, said, 'That bloody woman! Who the hell do she think she is?'

'More than a match for you, Bill, that's for sure.' Men from the neighbouring farms chuckled. Old Bill was a fool to himself. Cling on as he might, the horses were done. Times changed. Even here, there was a war on. Throughout the day the tractor chugged, making two trips for every one of the horses. Laura drove 'til her back ached and her head throbbed. But she knew she was victorious.

It was evening, but there was no one at the house. Michael left his bag in the kitchen and walked into the yard, carpeted in straw and fallen grain. He felt a surge of gratitude to be home.

A bunch of dead rabbits swung in the shade of the barn eaves, but the only sound came from the stables. He went through and saw Blossom on three legs, with Banner her reluctant companion. That was a bad shoe, he'd stake money on it. He went back into the yard, and out to the fields, looking for everyone.

They were down by Hanging Wood. The horses stood in the shade of the elms at its edge, and old Mr Cooper sat with them, his aged panama hat almost white in the evening sun. Even at this distance Michael could see his mother, sitting by the pram, and the little boys running after rabbits in the stubble. Teams of men and girls were stacking the sheaves, slowly now, at the end of a long hard day. He couldn't see Laura. But then he spied a small, grey tractor leading a load down to the yard. Borrowed, no doubt, because of Blossom.

He watched it bump and jolt its way on to the track. Useful though it was he resented its presence, marring the gentleness of a Gunthwaite harvest. He had had enough of engines and machines. Lately his whole life seemed taken up with noise and the smell of petrol.

He noticed the driver. It was a land girl, black haired and full-breasted, her knees protruding from a pair of khaki shorts. He felt a start of admiration. These girls were rough but you couldn't help but admire them. Driving like a man. At that moment he recognised his wife.

His heart seemed to falter. The sight passed beyond belief. He started to run, then realised what a fool he would look,

366

arriving red-faced and gasping to berate her. So he waited, fuming, at the gate. The tractor slowed as it came towards him, but only to negotiate the gap. Laura's face was totally absorbed.

'Laura! Laura!' He had to shout above the engine. She looked up, saw him, and juddered the tractor to a halt. Her face was radiant.

'Darling! Oh, Michael, darling!'

Her arms were round his neck, his face was in her hair. She smelled of corn and places warm and dark and secret. His anger fused into hot desire, almost sinful pleasure. She was so beautiful.

He said, 'Let's go back to the house. It's been so long.'

'Yes. Come on the tractor.'

But it seemed to him all wrong, clinging on behind while his wife drove. When they got to the yard she turned to him in triumph. 'Did I drive well? I had to learn, no one else would. Oh, Michael, it's been so difficult without you.'

Her words disarmed him. Poor Laura. Poor sweet little Laura. He had gone away and left her to cope with difficult, unwomanly things. He took her in his arms again, found himself pressing hot kisses to her face. 'We'd best go in,' she whispered. 'They'll all come back soon.' They went silently up Gunthwaite's wormeaten stair.

The brown of her legs ended abruptly in white marks on her thighs. Her throat was stained in a deep vee between her breasts. As she stood naked before him, he felt a wild stir of emotion, loving her, desiring her – hating her brazen knowledge of her power. She had no timidity in this, he thought hectically. She smiled like a goddess, about to bestow gifts. His sex was hard, he couldn't wait. He took her by the shoulders and pushed her down on the bed.

He was still wearing trousers and a shirt. He knelt above her only long enough to release himself, coming at once to cover her. His hand came between her legs, and found the place. With one thrust he was in. Like a customer, she thought. It was Michael and not Michael; her lover, and yet nobody she knew. Just a man, needing a woman, invading her. She closed her eyes, not wanting to look at him, not wanting to know. In a moment he would be done.

When he had finished and lay panting at her side, she rolled off the bed. 'I'd better go back. Everyone will wonder where I am.'

He yawned, his mood lighter now. 'Tell them to stop. You've done enough today.'

She glanced down at him. 'I wanted to get this field finished before tonight. Then we can start on Gildersome in the morning.'

'We always do Gildersome last. It's cold land, stands a late crop.'

'But the summer's been so hot it's ready now.'

He felt a shaft of irritation. This was his farm. He was the farmer, not some visitor, giving unwanted advice. He got up and went to the cupboard to get out moleskin trousers and a rough shirt. Laura said, 'Why not your uniform? You look so grand, and everyone will see. It'll please your mother.'

'But not you.'

She blinked at him. 'Of course me!' What she felt wasn't important, she was his wife. Her welcome was without question. 'I don't care what you look like, Michael. It's just so good to have you back, I wish – I wish there was nothing to do and no one here but us.'

She held out her hand and he took it. They looked at each other, each deciding separately that they were being foolish. What did shorts matter, or tractors, or uniforms or fields, when they were together again?

The cold tea Laura had arranged turned into a celebration feast. To their credit, Sophie and Marie remained discreetly out of sight, merely passing Michael on the stair and nodding. When he asked who they were, Laura said vaguely, 'Oh, you know. Refugees. Everyone's got some.' And he didn't want to know more, happy just to be home again.

They opened a new cask of cider, and a jar of plums they were saving, to eat with dollops of yellow cream. Alan and David demanded to know everything. 'Did you drive a tank? Did you kill a German? Is the war over then, is that why you're home?'

Michael avoided Laura's eye. 'It's just a holiday. I've finished my training, that's all.'

Laura said, 'Do you know where you're being sent?'

'They'll post me a travel warrant in a few days. Soon enough to worry about it then.'

Mrs Cooper said distractedly, 'I wish Gabriel was in the army. He never has leave. And never writes, not even to Dora.'

'I imagine he's busy,' said Michael. 'There's been a hell of a lot of trouble in the air.'

'Do you think they'd tell us?' asked his mother wistfully. 'I mean, if he was missing, or something like that?'

'Dora would be the first to know,' said Laura.

It was a shadow at the end of a brilliant summer day. Another shadow, thought Laura. On the surface there was no reason for dismay, but they were all troubled. Even old Mr Cooper, seemingly long past caring, sat in his chair restlessly picking at his sleeve. It was as if he was beset by a nameless anxiety, when everyone else could name a dozen of theirs. Loving and being loved, losing, finding – what would happen to them all tomorrow?

In bed that night, Michael wanted her again. He took her like the soldier he had become, quickly, selfishly, wrapped up in his own silence. When it was done she said softly, 'You're going abroad, aren't you? That's why you've come home.'

The silence hung in the night, heavy and hot. At last Michael said, 'I didn't want you to worry.'

'Have they said where?'

'No. I think – the desert, perhaps.'

She tried to picture it in her head. Sand and heat, when Michael so loved his own green fields. No shade, no water. He might die in that alien place, all alone. She turned her face to his naked chest, her tears against his skin. He put his arms around her, holding her, soothing her. 'It's all right – it doesn't matter – of course I'll come home.' Suppose he did not? His heart lurched at the thought.

'It could be years,' sobbed Laura. 'I can't manage here alone.'

'But you can, darling. You must.'

Eventually he felt her slide into exhausted sleep. He lay at her side, feeling a great tenderness towards her, not unmixed with grief. She was changing, because of him. He had left behind a soft and lovely wife, and come back to a woman harder, more capable, less eager to please. If he was away for years, what would she be then? he wondered uneasily. What would his daughter be, growing up without a father?

Michael slid from the bed and went to the window. The

orchard was heavy with fruit, the weight of the plum trees held up by props. One of the farm cats was stalking in the moonlight, a silent wraith. He took a long, deep breath, trying to take in the essence of this place, to draw on in the months and years to come. He longed to encircle it, to hold the memory so safe and sure that danger and misery could not come here while he held on. The moon hung like a circle of silver on a blue velvet sky. A bat crossed its face, fluttering distinctively, and he thought of flying things. He thought of Gabriel.

He lay beside the woman, her bed smelling of cheap perfume and sweat. 'If you didn't want it, you needn't have come,' she said petulantly. He said nothing. At the start of the evening he might have wanted it, but now, with a scant four hours before tomorrow's show, his mind wasn't on his groin. Despite the whisky he'd drunk he felt cold sober. All he could think of was Davis, spiralling down in flames.

'I think I'll shoot off, if you don't mind,' he said, taking his arms from behind his head. 'Sorry and all that. Bit of a big day tomorrow.'

'All the more reason to make it a big night,' she retorted. But it wasn't any good, and she knew it. The flyboys were all on edge, not one of them behaved normally. She couldn't help but feel let down, though. All the girls said Gabriel Cooper was wonderful in bed.

Driving back to base, he too felt regretful. Sex was the best method he had yet found of relaxing and getting some sleep. If he could just get in the mood, then for a brief time he could forget the fear and the strain, drown it out in a rush of purely physical pleasure. He sometimes thought fear heightened all his senses, and that in particular. Sex was definitely better in war.

As soon as it was over though, he liked to to get up, get dressed and go straight back to base. Then he could fall into bed refreshed and relaxed, ready for the usual screaming panic of the day. Besides if he copped it after a good night, at least he wouldn't have missed anything. He'd have wrung as much as he could from an all too short existence.

When he got back to his room Philip was there. He was smoking, bright-eyed with tension. 'Worth it, was she?'

Gabriel shrugged. 'Don't know. Waited too long, couldn't

get in the mood. The chopper wouldn't rise.'

Philip lit another cigarette from the stub of the last. 'Your wife's been on. Worried about you. You don't write.'

Gabriel sat on the bed. 'No.'

'You could drop her the odd word, couldn't you? She's lonely. She misses you.'

'You know this is none of your business?'

'I couldn't not tell you. And she sounds so young and sweet. Worth ten thousand of the tarts.'

Gabriel closed his eyes for a moment. 'I know, I know. Of course I know. But I can't write. I – I just can't do it. I can't tell her the truth, so I try and write a lot of meaningless rubbish. But it *is* rubbish. It doesn't sound real. If I sent her that she'd be more hurt than anything.'

'But you write letters. I've seen you.'

'I don't write to Dora.'

Philip said nothing. He went to the cupboard and got out a whisky bottle, pouring himself a small nip. 'I'll write if you like. Say you've hurt your hand gardening.'

Gabriel chuckled. 'Growing petunias? Dashed dangerous stuff this gardening. All right. If you want. Bugger off now, will you? We ought to try and get some kip at least.'

Suddenly Philip said, 'Do you think he was dead? Davis, I mean.'

'Don't know. He didn't try and get out.'

'Could have been wounded, though. Trapped. Going down in flames, burning.'

'Keep your revolver handy,' suggested Gabriel. 'Then, if you get in a fix, you can shoot yourself and not fry.'

'Do you think he did?'

'Shoot himself? Davis? No. Didn't like guns. That was his trouble, he could fly but he couldn't shoot. Get to bed, Phil. You won't burn. It's only the good-looking blokes do that.'

Philip laughed, a little too shrill. He liked to talk to Gabriel. He had a certain honesty in the face of nightmare that Philip knew he didn't have himself.

Alone in the room, Gabriel finished the scotch. Then he got out his writing pad. He began to write 'Dearest Dora', but after he had sat for ten minutes he screwed up the page and began again:

371

Dear Laura,

We lost a man today. Charles Davis went down in flames, it shocked us all. He was a nice bloke, bit shy, probably a virgin still. Such a waste. We're all terrified of burning, it's the worst. They ship the survivors to some ghastly hospital where they try and glue skin back on, but mostly we'd rather be dead.

Philip tells me Dora telephoned. She wants me to write, but honestly I can't. She wants to hear of heroic deeds, when really we're all scared witless. It never stops, that's the trouble. No sooner are you down than you're up again trying to shoot some poor fellow before he shoots you. We daren't bale out too soon any more, either, because they'll shoot you down. We try and leave it until the very last moment, so you're even more likely to fry or drop like a stone.

You've no idea how odd it feels to have your flesh creep. When a bloke's on your tail and the shells start hammering, the very flesh on my bones starts moving and shrinking. And my mind has no control. You see, my body knows how much I want to live. That's the whole trouble, none of this would matter if I didn't so desperately hate the thought of dying.

I feel ashamed that I want to live so much. It isn't as if I want to do anything very great, I'm not a genius or anything. But I want to experience life again, know what it's like to wake on a summer's morning and have nothing special to do; take a horse on an autumn day and gallop through the woods; settle down in the kitchen with you for a long, lazy chat.

I can't write to Dora. I simply can't. If you get the opportunity, could you please explain?

Yours, always,
  Gabriel

He sealed it and stamped the envelope before he settled down to sleep. That way if he was killed in the morning show, someone would send her the letter. It seemed important somehow that she should know what was in his mind, more important even than deciding how to defeat a Focke Wulf that outpaced him at every turn. When all this was over he would go home again. He felt randy suddenly. Damn, he should have had that woman after all. But even as he thought it, he slept.

Sitting in the barn with the men, Michael felt strangely out of place. The chatter of a barracks was absent, this was the slow, thoughtful contemplation of countrymen born and bred. He found it irritating.

He got up and went through to see Blossom, standing patiently with a poulticed foot. They'd be poulticing for weeks yet, because as he thought, she'd been badly shod. A prick had gone septic.

'Worked too hard, she were,' said Bill Mayes, leaning in the doorway. 'Wanted to rest her, missen, but Missus wouldn't hear on it.'

'It was a bad shoe, nothing else,' said Michael curtly. 'She improved the moment we got the shoe off her and started some heat.'

'She don't know horses, that's the trouble.'

Michael glanced up at him. 'Neither do you.'

Bill fell into silence. Inwardly Michael cursed himself. There was nothing to be gained by blaming the hired men. It wasn't to be expected that he could leave the farm and have nothing go wrong; if so, what had he been doing all these years?

'I suppose you know what you're doing,' he said abruptly. 'You can see to this, can you? I shall be in the house.'

Muttering, but not enough to be heard, Bill said, 'Aye. With them Frenchies. Moved them in soon as you was gone, she did.'

In the yard, the land girls were carting boxes of plums; Laura planned to take them to market the next day. All the jobs put off while harvest was in full swing were begun the moment drizzle delayed them. He watched while Ruth loaded the wagon, then cautiously drove the tractor to the barn. Both girls looked at him shyly; an unknown quantity in their little world. He went over to them and said, 'Banner's standing idle, you should use him. He costs nothing.'

'Mr Mayes put him out in the field. And he's a devil to catch until he's hungry.'

There was nothing to be said. Michael stamped into the

house, as bad-tempered as he had ever been. When he slammed the door everyone in the kitchen froze. He looked at their anxious faces. Laura, the children, his poor bewildered father. Why had he come home to upset them? He should have stayed away.

Laura said, 'Did you want a cup of tea?'

'If you're making.' He went to sit down, uncomfortable in his own home. The little boys slipped out, off to see those Frenchwomen, he supposed. Even his little daughter cried when he picked her up. Laura put a cup and saucer in front of him and he stirred it desultorily. Even tea wasn't the same now sugar was on the ration. He said, 'The Frenchwomen. Whatever you told Mother, we didn't have to take them.'

Laura hesitated. Then she sat at the table beside him. 'No. Of course we didn't. I knew them in France, they had nowhere else to go.'

'Who are they then?'

'Sophie looked after me when I was small. Marie took me shopping when I was older.'

He looked at her in bewilderment. 'But what sort of women are they?'

She was silent. She knew how everything must seem to him, as if she had only waited until he was gone to do as she pleased. It was his last leave and they both wanted everything to be fine, but they couldn't achieve it by avoiding the things that troubled them. 'I didn't ask them to come,' she said gently. 'And I didn't mean to buy a tractor, but we have to plough and there wasn't any choice. I know Bill says things about me.'

Michael shook his head dismissively. 'I don't listen. He's causing trouble, I don't know what to do.'

'You can't do anything. He's good with the crops. I need him.'

'But the horses! They need someone with an eye. Blossom should never be this lame. And no hunters. I can't believe that you sent them off.'

Laura linked her fingers together. He wasn't talking seriously, she decided. He was anxious and unsettled, only now realising the task he had set her. If only he would see what she had achieved, and not just the things undone. 'Why don't you put Paula in charge of the horses?' she suggested. 'She loves them, you know. She can catch Banner when no one else can.'

'I didn't want to sell my horses! I don't want a girl in charge!'

'Then you should bloody well have stayed home, shouldn't you?'

She got up and stormed to the fire. Old Mr Cooper said quaveringly, 'Rosalind – my dear girl,' and she reached out a hand to him, holding his thin shoulder in the way that soothed him best.

Michael said, 'It needn't be like this. Things could go on, just as they used to.'

'No they can't! We've got to produce, the people need food! And don't you see, we can make some money at last? Prices are good again. If we got electricity, we could sell milk.'

'So that's what you want, is it? Everything modern and bright? You couldn't wait to have rid of me, so everything could be changed!'

She looked at him. Her heart dissolved into tenderness. 'I want everything the way it used to be,' she said gently. 'I don't want to change a thing. But wanting doesn't come into it any more, we have to do what we're told. If you were here, you'd do the same.'

He took a long breath. 'I thought I'd help by going. But now I don't know. One person doesn't seem to make much difference. And here everything needs me.'

Hadn't she told him so, a thousand times? Hadn't she begged him to think again? She turned away, her eyes hot with tears. The door opened and Mrs Cooper came in. 'I got the post in the village. One for each of you. Is that from Gabriel, Laura? It looks like his hand.'

'I don't know.' She took the letter, slipping it at once into the pocket of her apron. 'Michael? What's that?'

A brown, official envelope. 'My travel warrant. I'm to leave on Friday.'

'I thought you had longer.'

'Yes. So did I. They must want us out in a hurry.'

Mrs Cooper was spreading the newspaper on the table. They each came and stood to read it, the front page stamped with pictures of aircraft against a white sky. Bombers were making daylight raids on London. Fighter losses were heavy. Laura wondered if the figures were true, but if they were false, how much worse must things be? She closed her fingers on the letter in her pocket. Poor Rosalind. Poor Gabriel.

She turned to Michael and said, 'You were right to join up, you know. It might not seem it, but you were. We have to fight.'

Mrs Cooper said, 'It oughtn't to be happening. It all seems mad. I'll go and see Dora, she has to know about this. Gabriel's in danger!'

Laura took in her breath. 'Don't you think you might frighten her? I mean, she can see for herself what's happening.'

'I didn't suppose it would worry you,' said Mrs Cooper scathingly. 'After all, you have Michael at home.'

As always, it was manifestly unfair. But there was nothing to be done, nothing to be said. In the afternoon Bill Mayes roared off with Mrs Cooper in the car, using the petrol Laura had saved for market the next day.

'We've got tractor fuel,' said Ruth encouragingly. 'Take the stuff in that, couldn't we?'

Michael said, 'No. If it's fine, we'll be using the tractor for harvest. Paula can take Banner in the cart. Dress him up, attract some attention. Make a day of it.'

Everyone smiled. Sophie and Marie sauntered in from the orchard, baskets brimming with fallen plums. 'I shall use some of my cognac,' called Marie. 'The plums will be superb.' She went on her hip-swinging way. Sophie came up to Michael and nudged him with her elbow. 'What a piece of meat!' she said in French to Laura, and chuckled dirtily.

Michael looked helplessly at his wife. 'Who are those women?' he said again. She didn't reply.

Chapter Four

Michael was home only long enough to unsettle everything. Laura travelled with him into Bainfield on his last day, to see him off on the slow provincial train. They stood uncertainly together, wanting to say the right thing, hardly able to say anything at all.

'Don't worry,' said Michael earnestly.

She shook her head, in deprecation, not agreement. From this moment on, she couldn't think of him without anxiety. If she wasn't to worry, she wouldn't think of him at all. She searched for honesty and said, 'I wish you wouldn't go.'

'Laura!'

Now she had annoyed him. If only the train would go, and this could be over. Tears were brimming, and she couldn't hold them back. He said, 'Laura. Laura, don't.' And his voice was breaking too. Soon they would both be sobbing.

'I'm sorry about the hunters,' she managed.

'It doesn't matter. Really. You will be all right?'

'Yes. You will be careful? I mean – oh, Michael!'

She clung to him, sobbing openly now, making a scene in public. It was almost more than he could bear. 'The train's going. I've got to be off.'

'Michael! Michael!'

'I love you, darling. Goodbye.' He was on the train, wrestling with the window, his face tight with strain. The tears were pouring in little rivers down her cheeks. A woman standing next to her whispered, 'Smile for him, love. Don't let him remember you crying.'

So she pinned on a smile, a grimace, and held it in place until the train began to move, kept it fixed and staring until there was nothing but smoke, carrying Michael away. Then she put her face in her hands and stood shuddering until the woman next to her took her to the buffet and made her drink a disgusting cup of tea.

When she got home, Mrs Cooper said, 'There's been another raid. I'm so worried about Gabriel.'

Laura snapped, 'To hell with Gabriel! Can't you think about anyone except Gabriel for once?'

'Nobody is shooting at Michael, Laura! You really are the most irrational girl.'

Perhaps she was, perhaps she was. Laura went out into the orchard and wept beneath the trees. What was this terrible sense of foreboding if not irrational? She couldn't believe in it. It had nothing to do with Michael and everything to do with her. She was frightened only of what would happen while he was away. But what could that be? She looked up through the canopy of leaves into the still blue sky. Gunthwaite would always be here, holding, protecting its own. Her heart began to steady. Each breath shuddered a little less. She wasn't abandoned, after all. She was safe. At home. But still, lodged in her breast, was a leaden weight of despair.

Once again, time settled her. The old irritations overtook greater anxieties. Every day Mrs Cooper waved everyone into silence for the news. There was no greater crime than interrupting Alvar Liddell as he recounted the day's events. It was like a prayer meeting, thought Laura sourly, with the heavenly message always gloomy. Every day ships were sunk and airfields attacked, and Michael could be on one and Gabriel on the other. Sometimes, as the announcer recited losses, they couldn't breathe. Sometimes it felt as if the whole country was holding its collective breath, waiting for the moment when their rickety pack of cards would tumble into nothing about them. Men were drilling with broomsticks instead of guns. If the Germans came, and they must come, surely, there was so little to hold them back.

Mrs Cooper's visits to Dora became still more frequent, and in consequence there was never any petrol to go to Bainfield, even to have the wireless accumulator charged. 'You might once think!' raged Laura, as the set faded into unintelligibility. 'We need to go to Bainfield. Could you please not go to Fairlands? I'll take the accumulator to the garage and get some shopping at the same time. We need a lot.'

'I shall go to Bainfield,' said Mrs Cooper flatly. 'I shall visit Fairlands on the way.'

'But I thought I might like to go to Bainfield,' said Laura in exasperation.

'I'm sure you're indispensable, Laura dear. You always seem so. You'll do much better here.'

The spat may have ruffled them, but it also energised. Laura vented her exasperation on the men, galvanising them into a thorough cleaning of the foldyard, ready for winter. Mrs Cooper felt disposed to put on her good hat, smooth her gloves and set off purposefully on her outing.

She went first to Fairlands, only to find it in uproar. She stepped from the car in time to see the headmaster of Gunthwaite school, aided by two of his larger boys, remove a filing cabinet from the drive and stagger in through the door. All around were packing cases and boxes of books. A pile of desks rested haphazardly beneath the Virginia creeper while a trio of small girls amused themselves playing hopscotch on the terrace flags.

'Haven't you girls somewhere to go?' rapped Mrs Cooper.

They looked at her, wide-eyed and silent. They had the look of recent evacuees, a mixture of insecurity and barely concealed panic. At that moment the headmaster appeared again, dishevelled to the point of disarray, in Mrs Cooper's uncharitable opinion.

'What are these children doing here?' she demanded. 'Children are still sent to school to be educated, I believe.'

'These three have permission to play here, Mrs Cooper,' he said soothingly. Then, in an undervoice, he added, 'Sisters. Bombed out last week. They prefer to stay close to someone they know. They're lodging with one of these boys.'

She looked at them with renewed interest. She wasn't sure she believed half she read in the newspapers. But here were three victims, small, pale and defenceless. She adjusted her wrap a little more firmly around her shoulders. 'You know my son's a fighter pilot?' she said importantly. 'I can assure you, this won't last long. They're doing marvellously, you know.'

She spotted Dora's plumply pregnant body in the hall. The

girl was expanding quite visibly, it seemed. 'Dora? Dora! I came about the news, our wireless is out. Have you heard from Gabriel?'

Dora, who had been in the act of retreating upstairs to a hurriedly decided sickbed, said, 'I had a letter yesterday. From his friend. Gabriel's hand's still not better. There's no need to worry, he's just sitting around doing paperwork. He's furious, Philip says.'

They went through to the morning room. This too was in disorder, full of items rescued from the school rooms. A Chinese vase stood on the rug, and they sat either side of it. Suddenly Mrs Cooper said, 'I'm sorry to come like this, dear. It's – it's difficult at home. I worry so, and they don't understand. Gabriel's very dear to me. I like to talk to someone who loves him too.'

Dora didn't know what to say. At last she managed, 'Philip says he might have leave soon.'

Mrs Cooper drew in her breath. 'Take my advice, dear. Don't be like Laura. She and Michael did nothing but argue when he was home. He doesn't stand up to her, you know. You must let Gabriel be master still. Men don't like to feel we can manage without them, you know.'

'No.' Dora sat uneasily. She couldn't imagine her mother-in-law ever being careful of her own husband's feelings. Of anyone's feelings, for that matter. She sat on, feeling resentful, until at last her visitor took her leave.

It was hot, in the air. Gabriel felt the sweat beading under his helmet. Far below the patchwork of little England gleamed yellow and brown, the river a silver ribbon cast on a well-made bed. He glanced in his mirror, searching for the black dots that would make or break his day. The R/T crackled into life, they had him on radar, he was a couple of miles to the west. He adjusted his heading, and the formation followed suit. The tail ender was so new he'd barely unpacked. Gabriel hadn't asked his name, it wasn't worth it. New boys didn't last long up here.

He saw them. Bombers with fighter escort, bloody Focke Wulfs. Off to London probably, to plaster the docks. Again. He called out, 'Bandits. Let's go.' They turned like birds, swooping to their prey.

The enemy saw them too late. Gabriel began firing at maximum range, all the time thinking, deflection, deflection. Smoke began pouring from an engine. He left it and raked the sky for richer meat. Planes were everywhere, in aerial chaos. Forget the bombers. Someone else would crack those, once the fighters were done. Someone on the new boy's tail. He turned automatically, cannon hammering. The enemy plane began to spin, and in a moment a body fell away, parachute fluttering. The sight distracted him; he was suddenly aware that the new boy was gone. His plane tumbled towards the horizon, wreathed in flame.

Fury suffused him. Another! And tomorrow another still! All the fear and rage of weeks past bubbled up in an explosion of wrath. He kicked the rudder, turning inexorably towards that flutter of white silk. A face, terrified, helpless, turned to him. Damn him! Let him know what he'd done. Gabriel thumbed his guns.

In the bar that evening Philip said, 'They're talking, you know. Bit bloody unnecessary that.'

'He shot the new boy down.'

'Well, you knew he would. And the boy got out, you know. In hospital. Broke an ankle when he landed in a tree.'

Gabriel said nothing. He thought of the German face he had destroyed, turned to him in panic and hope. Such a young face. Murdered for a broken ankle. 'They do it to us,' he said defensively.

'But if we get down we go straight back into it,' said Philip. 'That bloke would only have been a prisoner.'

'That we'd have had to feed.'

'I'd rather feed them than shoot them. You're forgetting, Gabriel. We started this to fight brutality. Don't let's end up as bad.'

He had a woman that night, but it didn't help. When he got back to base he couldn't even remember her name. The day haunted him, he couldn't leave it behind, although it wasn't as if he hadn't killed before. He'd sent at least four planes spiralling out of the sky. But it was the first he had intended. And for a moment, for a few hot seconds, he had enjoyed the act.

At dawn the next day he was flying again. They met them over

the sea, took them head on, fought until his guns were empty
and landed damaged at an airfield not his own. He was trucked
back in time to pilot a new plane, delivered that day, and he had
a kill first time up. When he got back he found the airfield had
been shot up an hour before, there were craters everywhere. He
parked on a patch of clear grass and climbed out. There were
some shrapnel tears on the skin of the new plane, marring its
deadly beauty. He had heard it more than felt it, like demonic
wasps. He looked at the mess wearily, his brain too tired for
thought. The notion kept running through his head that he had
spoiled his nice new plane.

It was a mile back to the buildings, and not worth the effort
when they'd be up again in an hour. He slumped on the grass
beneath the wing but a second later a face appeared in the space
above his head.

'Get anything?'

'What?' His voice was coming from very far away.

'Your report. What did you get?'

'Oh. I can't remember. I think – one kill. Went into the
drink. Bugger off, will you? I've got to sleep.'

He cradled his head on his arms. A bee buzzed curiously
about him, inspecting the red puddle collecting beneath his
outstretched arm. But it had no use for blood. Gabriel was left
sleeping all alone.

Sophie and Marie were chopping toadstools. They had gathered
them in the morning and swore they were edible. Mrs Cooper
said that she for her part would not eat them, and neither would
the children. She hadn't lived this long to be wantonly
murdered by peculiar foreign food. Laura had established that
these people were genuine, she supposed. Were they in fact fifth
columnists, dedicated to destroy? Well, she wouldn't eat the
horrible things. Everyone else could decide for themselves, but
if they were struck down by food poisoning at the hands of a
foreign power, then on their own heads be it.

Ruth and Paula were thus left to set caution against curiosity,
while Dinah took off her apron with the relief of someone who
can go home to eat. 'Don't you try it,' she advised Laura. 'What
would happen to us all if you dropped dead?'

Laura smiled wearily. 'They might let Michael come home.'

'Not them! We'd be in a proper mess, we would. You eat the peas.'

When it came to it, no one ate the stuff. It tasted horrible. Marie declared it to be the fault of English margarine, while Sophie alarmed everyone by saying she couldn't quite recall, now that she thought of it, whether this was the deadly variety or the one that was good sautéed, but then it was many years since she had gathered them. In a spirit of enquiry they fed the remains to the hens, but none of them died. So the question went unresolved.

Just as Laura was going out to shut up the hens a car came puttering up the drive. She was surprised, they so rarely had visitors, and almost never at night. Then she recognised the Fairlands Lanchester, long and green, with sweeping running boards. Mr Fitzalan-Howard was driving and Dora was at his side.

'Dora! Has something happened?'

The girl's face was blotched with crying. She looked a mess tonight, her pregnant belly huge, her dress too small for it, her ankles swollen over far from sensible shoes. 'It's Gabriel. Gabriel!'

Mr Fitzalan-Howard said, 'She would come. I said there wasn't any point, but she insisted. He's been wounded.'

'He said he wasn't flying,' sobbed Dora. 'He said he'd hurt his hand and that's why he couldn't write. And all the time he was and it wasn't true.'

Laura took in the complexities at once. To Dora, Gabriel's faithlessness was just as bad as his wound. 'How badly is he hurt?'

'I believe it's loss of blood,' said Dora's father. 'I telephoned the aerodrome the moment the telegram arrived. Bit of a garbled tale, really. Seems he was sleeping beneath his aircraft and they were scrambled within minutes of touching down. Quite fortunate, because otherwise no one would have noticed. When he didn't get up they went to wake him and found him covered in blood, bleeding from an artery in his arm. Nothing serious in itself, but obviously – loss of blood and all that. Dora, there really isn't any need for this, you know. He's not going to die!'

'Why don't you go inside?' advised Laura. 'I'll come in as soon as I've shut up the hens.'

She took her time. In summer some of the younger birds hung around the henhouse in the evening instead of tucking up inside, and quite a few roosted away. Each day Alan and David were sent out to find nests and bring home the eggs, but now and then, to everyone's surprise, an absent hen returned with a clutch of chicks. Laura checked the usual places in the hedge but found no errant bird. She paused before fastening the henhouse door, listening to the silence of the coming night. She dreaded going in to Mrs Cooper's panic and Dora's grief.

As she neared the house, she saw Paula coming towards her in the gloom. 'Right state they're all in,' she said ruefully. 'I'd wait a bit if I were you. Marie's giving them cognac.'

'How many bottles does she have?' asked Laura in amazement. 'I hope it's hundreds.'

'Might be, knowing her.'

Paula pulled a packet of cigarettes from her pocket and lit up. It was a recently acquired habit, and she still had the stilted movements of a novice. 'You should try,' she told Laura. 'Settle your nerves.'

'Do you think they need settling?'

Paula grinned, her teeth flashing in the failing light. 'Course they do. Never get a minute to yourself, and everyone always complains.'

'Except you and Ruth,' said Laura gratefully.

'Well, stands to reason. Got the best billet of anyone, we have. Eggs when we want them, bacon, honey – and the horses. When the war's over I'll get a job with horses. Fun, they are. Better than the factory, any road.'

'You'll marry a soldier, and do what he wants,' said Laura. 'What's the boy you're going with? A fitter? He'll work in town.'

'They'll need fitters in the country now for all them tractors. I'll keep with the horses. You'll see.'

She went off to her room above the barn, and Laura walked back to the house. Paula's determination amused and depressed her. She had all the confidence of a youth undimmed by obstacles and failure. She assumed that the war would be won, that her boyfriend would survive, that there'd be money and opportunity to mould life to any shape you wished. How many Paulas were condemned to Europe's cattle trains? They could dream all they wanted but none of it would come true. Dreams were always false currency, thought Laura miserably. You could never exchange them for anything real.

When she entered the kitchen she found turmoil. Dora and Mrs Cooper were in tears while Marie was entertaining Dora's bemused parent to cognac and French conversation. David was prosaically completing a jigsaw at the kitchen table, the lamp was smoking and the baby was screeching unheeded. Laura went to pick her up. Marie was saying, 'Tell me, how does a man of culture like yourself find amusement in this eternity of green? Don't you yearn for a little – sophistication?'

'Go to bed, David,' said Laura automatically. Just as automatically he ignored her. Go to bed when a drama was underway? With any luck he could sit at his jigsaw and they'd forget him.

'I must go to him,' sobbed Mrs Cooper. 'Someone must take me tonight.'

'We haven't the petrol,' said Laura. 'And he's all right, isn't he? Are they sending him home?'

'That's really what we came to say,' broke in Mr Fitzalan-Howard.

Marie was purring, 'I do so admire a man who can retain his virility in the midst of rural suffocation.'

He tried to remove his arm from her clasp in a courteous manner, which was more than a little difficult. 'Gabriel's being sent home to recuperate,' he managed.

'Tomorrow,' wailed Dora tragically.

The baby was grizzling again. Laura sat with her against her shoulder, rhythmically patting her back. 'You'll find he's quite a good patient,' she said.

'I don't want him,' snapped Dora.

Laura sighed. 'Don't be silly. You can understand if you try, you know. There's something I should have told you. He – he wrote to me and asked me to tell you. But then you got that other letter and I thought you'd be happier thinking he wasn't flying. He's been in action constantly for weeks. He knew you'd be worried and he didn't want you to know, but he found he couldn't write lies. So he didn't write at all. I know it sounds cowardly, but I promise you, he's no coward. You don't know what it's been like. Dog-fights, danger. He's been under the most terrible strain.'

Everyone stared at her. David said, 'How many kills, Aunt Laura?'

Abstractedly she said, 'Four, I think. Go to bed, David.'

'How dare you?' demanded Mrs Cooper. 'How dare you keep such things from me?'

'Gabriel thought it would be best. And I didn't think it would help you to know.'

The older woman raised her hand as if to strike. 'We had a right to know! To hell with whether it helped us or not! You think you can take over everything, decide everything, as if we were children! I won't have it. This is really the last straw. Changing the farm, taking charge, behaving as if no one else has an opinion that matters, no matter how many years of experience they might have. Not even Michael can sway you any more. And now this.' Mrs Cooper stood up, looking as if she wanted to push Laura out altogether.

But she had a point, of course. It was not up to Laura to decide that this or that should not be told. Gabriel's wife and mother had their rights too.

Dora was looking at her accusingly. 'I don't know how you could,' she said.

Laura knew she must defend herself. 'I didn't ask him to write to me.'

Dora said, 'He asked you to tell me something. You just decided you wouldn't. I don't know who you think you are, Laura, but you've changed. You used to be kind and thoughtful, but you've become so hard. You do what you want and never mind who it upsets.'

Mrs Cooper turned and put her arms around her. 'Please, Dora. Don't distress yourself. Tomorrow Gabriel will be home and we can talk to him ourselves. He's stronger than Michael, he might be able to make her behave. She's so possessive, you see. She's always been the same – hanging on to Gabriel, hanging on to Michael. I know she resents me. She always has. But I'd hoped she'd have more charity where you're concerned.'

'You are so unfair,' said Laura in a low, throbbing voice. 'I was only trying to spare you! And if either of you had shown any sign of adult sense I'd have been only too happy to take advantage of it. Can you blame me for treating you like children? Look at you now, wailing and shrieking when he's lost some blood, for God's sake! He isn't dying, he's coming home!'

David said, 'I wish you'd all stop shouting. You're giving me a headache.'

Laura rounded on him. 'David, I told you to go to bed! Go! Now!'

Mrs Cooper said, 'Do you have to take it out on the children?'

Laura found she was trembling. Tears were very near the surface; in a moment she would disgrace herself and sob. She held her baby very close. At least Mary loved her, at least she wasn't always finding fault. What would they have her do? Behave as they did, weeping and wailing when there was work to be done? Where were they when decisions needed to be made? 'You see to it, Laura. It's more forms.' 'Laura! There's a man to see you.' 'Laura, the men have finished the wheat, they want to know what's next.'

She was biting her lip trying not to cry. Mr Fitzalan-Howard said awkwardly, 'I think we'd better go, Dora. You've all had a shock.'

Mrs Cooper said, 'And I shall go too. I think I must impose myself on you for a day or so. Then I'll be ready to greet Gabriel when he arrives. After that, Laura, you'll be pleased to hear that I shall take up residence in the cottage. You've wanted it long enough and just at present I shall be more than happy to live alone. I suggest you find the time to make the place habitable.'

Laura's breath deserted her. So, she was to be left with everything, Mr Cooper, the boys, the farm. It was all very well for Mrs Cooper to behave as if she'd been driven out, but in fact she was excusing herself from anything she did not wish to do. But she wouldn't ask questions. She wouldn't for a moment give the impression that she might be upset. She folded her lips and turned her head aside.

'Oh, là là!' said Sophie delightedly. 'How well I taught you. So *grande dame*!'

Laura sat immobile until she heard the car draw away. Then Marie said, 'Laura, the baby's crying.'

So she was. Round the edge of the door peeped the unrepentant David. Upstairs Alan slept the sleep of the just while old Mr Cooper sat dribbling by the fire. Crying was for babies and women with others to care for them. Laura could allow herself no such luxury. She was responsible for them all.

Gabriel sat slumped in the back of the car. The WAAF who had been designated to drive him had given up on conversation within five minutes, without one word of reply. He was a disappointment, she decided. This flying ace was certainly good-looking, but his nerves were obviously shot. His face was white, his eyes glassy, and he had a distant expression that hinted at horrors within.

But Gabriel was thinking no dire thoughts. He was feeling too ill. He remembered nothing of the blood or his rescue, although Philip said he had resembled a dying fish, losing all colour before their very eyes. The upshot had been a rush to hospital and a rapid blood transfusion. It had left him with a headache of mammoth proportions, his mouth tasting of metal and an arm like a dead weight of ice. In contrast to the casualties in neighbouring beds, though, his wound was trivial. Hence his departure to recover at home. And he had never felt this deadly in his life.

He began to slide down the seat, and jerked himself up again. It wasn't done to let people see a flyer in a state of collapse, it rattled their nerves. They were the invincible, laughing heroes of the hour, without visible human weakness. He looped his good arm through a strap in the side of the car, longing to lie down and rest.

The drive took for ever. All road signs had been dismantled and sometimes he lost his bearings and couldn't say which way to go. When at last they reached Bainfield his blood – someone's blood – quickened. Not long now. Soon he would be in his own cool bed, under the ancient beams. He would look up and know that he was threatened by nothing more than the dust of a million beetles, steadily gnawing their way through the rafters. Thank God for Gunthwaite.

Some of the elms were changing colour. Winter wouldn't be long now. Would he be flying again by then? There was no airfield that wasn't cold. His very flesh cringed at the thought of all the months that lay ahead, freezing to death on the ground, freezing for life in the air. He was cold now, shivering with the tremor of exhaustion.

'Is this it?' The WAAF, who in other circumstances he might have fancied, was pointing at Gunthwaite's long drive. Gabriel let out a groan of thankfulness. 'Well, is it?' she demanded petulantly.

'Yes,' he whispered.

The girl drove rapidly up to the house and stopped with an efficient but soul-wrenching jerk. 'Here you are, sir. What a lovely old house.'

'Yes. Thank you.'

'Want me to see you in?'

'No. Just put the suitcase down, would you?'

He waited until she had turned the car expertly on the cobbles and roared away. He wondered why no one was there to greet him. Didn't they know he was coming? Perhaps his mother was dead. Little else would keep her from him, he thought ruefully. And her absence, little though he missed her, brought tears to his eyes. In the end no one cared, he thought.

The door opened. Laura came out. She was wearing a pale skirt, white blouse and an expression of utter surprise. 'Gabriel! What on earth are you doing here?'

He swayed, steadying himself with a massive effort of will. 'Been wounded. Sent home. Didn't you know?'

'Yes. But you're supposed to be at Fairlands. With Dora.'

He felt a slow dawning of realisation. Dora. Of course. 'Even your mother's over there,' said Laura. 'They're going to be furious.'

He shook his head bemusedly, wearily. 'Don't care. Feel terrible.'

He knew he was swaying, knew that in a moment he would crash painfully to the ground. But then Laura was beside him. She was holding his good arm, how did she know?

'It's all right. You look awful, you should be in bed. Paula can ride over later on and tell them.'

'I don't want to see them,' whispered Gabriel. 'Not yet.'

'No. Just as you want. I'll get you a hot bottle and make you some tea. Poor Gabriel.'

Her hands on his body were light and cool. She undressed him like a child and he felt no embarrassment at all. She seemed as familiar to him as himself, a presence he had always known. 'You've lost weight,' she said, matter of factly easing his naked body between the sheets.

He whispered, 'So have you.'

She smiled at him. 'It must be the war. Dear Gabriel. If you knew all the fuss there's been about you.'

He reached up and touched her cheek. Then his hand subsided, inscribing a wavering line down her neck, across her breast, hesitating at her nipple. He spread his fingers, as if they weren't his own, and pressed the yielding flesh. 'I've never yet slept with a woman I didn't wish was you.'

'You're too ill to think of that,' said Laura. She was laughing down at him.

'Am I? I think of you all the time. You know I love you.'

Some of the laughter was fading from her face. She took his hand from her body and slipped it beneath the sheet. 'Sleep well, Gabriel.' She rose and left him.

Chapter Five

No one believed that Gabriel had come to Gunthwaite quite by chance. They saw it as another of Laura's plots. Dora recalled that when Laura first arrived she had been Gabriel's. Suddenly, belatedly, she was jealous.

She and Mrs Cooper drove over the next day. Laura met them with stilted politeness. 'I'm afraid he's still sleeping. He had a blood transfusion, which left him confused. He feels terrible.'

'She probably drugged him,' said Mrs Cooper, as if Laura couldn't hear. Ignoring her husband altogether, she ran up the stairs to her son.

Laura stormed into the kitchen. 'If I knew anything about drugs, I'd have poisoned her long ago,' she said viciously to Dinah.

Dinah grunted. 'I wouldn't have turned you in. Let it be. If that girl Dora thinks she's on to a good thing, siding with her against you, then she'll have to think again. Gabriel won't like it.'

Laura looked rueful. 'You know that won't make it any better! We were friends. It isn't my fault that Gabriel's here. I can't make him a good husband.'

'It's always the same when they're forced into it,' said Dinah. 'They don't take to it well.'

Laura was silent for a moment. 'Does everyone know?' she asked.

'Most people can guess. I mean, look at her. Size of a house. Must have been three month gone when she wed. Mark my words, she'll drop it any day.'

'Oh, no! I was relying on them having some time when he's better.'

Dinah made a face. 'Not the best idea you've ever had. He

likes his women gorgeous. Too much of her like a balloon and he'll start running and never come back!'

They laughed surreptitiously, not because it amused them but because it rang so true. Gabriel was never the sort to love a woman despite everything. When they ceased to attract him, he ceased to love.

Laura let her mind dwell for a moment on the act of love. She felt again the remembered pressure of Gabriel's hand. Her breasts contracted. He'd taken her by surprise, that was all, touching her at a time when she was defenceless and unprepared. Even the auctioneer might have stirred her, if he had touched her like that. It was what he had been hoping for, a woman so much in need that she would give what he asked without question. Why did women go on needing something that enslaved them so? Laura, of all people, should surely have had enough.

She thought of all the hundreds of times she had lain spreadeagled on a bed; the hundreds of men who had pierced her. Sometimes even a drunken sailor could excite her, and at others no amount of time or skill could bring her to orgasm. Why did it never work with Michael? He was ashamed of his sex, she thought sadly. He had no joy in it. And she could have no joy in hers.

There was a clatter on the stairs. Laura went out to see Mrs Cooper and Dora both in tears. 'He's all right, isn't he?' she asked.

'He said – he said he didn't want to see us,' said Dora brokenly. 'He said he felt too ill. But I'm his wife! I should be nursing him.'

'I don't think he needs nursing as such,' prevaricated Laura, who had spent half the morning carrying trays and bottles. 'He just wants rest. Why not come again tomorrow?'

'Yes. We'll do that,' said Mrs Cooper.

Dora shot her a surprised look. Surely, if Gabriel was at Gunthwaite so should his mother be?

But having slipped her feet under the Fairlands table, she wasn't about to remove them. Dora felt a gathering depression. Somehow she had acquired an appalling guest.

When they were gone Laura found old Mr Cooper in tears. He was standing in the yard, in his slippers, tears trickling down the creases of his face. 'What is it?' she asked gently. 'What's the matter?'

He sighed and the crystal tears ran faster. 'She doesn't want me. I see that now. She's left me and gone.'

She took hold of his hand. Confused and lost as he was, he could still experience abandonment. 'We want you,' she said. 'Dinah and me. And Sophie, and Marie, and the boys. Come inside. You can sit in your chair and have some tea.'

He allowed himself to be led away. The tears still ran, but in a moment he would forget why. Perhaps it was a blessing, thought Laura. At least his grief need not be suffered for more than a brief period of clarity. In the moment that he drank it, the pleasure of a hot cup of tea would fill his world.

Sophie came out of the house. She was wearing one of Mrs Cooper's tweed skirts. Laura felt familiar amazed wrath, at her nerve as well as her dishonesty. But Sophie at once disarmed her. 'I'll take him,' she said cosily. 'Come on, old chap. Now the dragon's gone, Sophie can look after you.'

'What? What did you say?'

Sophie burbled in French again. But his face cleared and relaxed, as if babyhood was once again his lot. Now even language was denied him.

'She doesn't know how to talk to me,' he said to Laura. 'Never mind. Never mind.'

'Are the boys with Marie?' called Laura, as Sophie and the old man tottered away.

'She's gone to Fairlands in the car,' called back Sophie. 'She wants to sleep with Dora's papa. His wife crosses her legs, you can tell.'

Laura stood frozen to the spot. Various courses of action presented themselves to her: sending Paula and the cart, jumping on Banner's giant back herself and galloping across – but why? What could she do? If Mr Fitzalan-Howard did or did not want to sleep with Marie there was nothing Laura could do about it. And did it matter if the whole world knew she was harbouring prostitutes at Gunthwaite? Michael was in a ship on an ocean infested with submarines, heading for a desert full of enemy tanks. He might never come home to discover it.

In the kitchen, Dinah was taking off her apron and fetching her coat. 'I've fed the baby,' she said. 'And them boys is off in

393

the fields. What happened to their lessons, that's what I'd like to know?'

'They've done a lot of French,' defended Laura, 'I'll start again tomorrow.'

'Send them to Fairlands on the cart,' advised Dinah. 'They're running wild here. It's not much of a school they've got there but they can catch up with learning when the war's done. Do them good to mix a bit with other kids. And you know that Paula – any chance to get out with Banner and the cart. She'd take them, night and morning.'

Laura wondered if she was allowed to use land girls for taking children to school. But it was a thought, nonetheless. In the winter there was little enough to do at Gunthwaite except feed stock and check on the sheep, so the discipline of a twice-daily outing might be welcome.

With Dinah gone, creaking off to the village on her bicycle, she looked around the kitchen. The fire was raked and burning well, the kettle hissed gentle steam, an apple pie stood beside vegetables and a roast, all waiting to be cooked. Out in the barn the men were getting ready to begin threshing when the machine came later in the week; Ruth and Paula were in with the sheep, dagging and trimming ready for tupping time. In short, everything was done. Quite unexpectedly Laura was like a balloon, adrift and floating in clear air. She felt light-headed and wild. She had forgotten what freedom was like. What was she to do?

She remembered Gabriel. Poor boy, he was so ill. With a feeling of justification she went and rummaged in the mêlée of Sophie and Marie's bedroom, discovering the cognac under the bed. Still a nest of bottles, one holding a scant inch of spirit. She would take it for Gabriel.

He was lying on his back, staring wide-eyed at the ceiling. His good hand was plucking restlessly at the sheet. 'You're supposed to be asleep,' said Laura, pushing the door with her bottom so she could enter with the tray.

He rolled his head to look at her. 'I was. The visitors woke me up. God, but you look delicious.'

She put the tray down and bent to peer at herself in the bedroom mirror. All she could see was a face with a paling suntan, eyes like clear windows and a cloud of dark hair.

Without make-up she looked dull, she thought. And her eyebrows were turning into a tangle. 'I look like a farmer's wife.' She sighed. 'Do you remember how I looked at the club? Those wonderful dresses.' She put a hand on her hip and crooked the other in a matching upward angle, undulating across the floor like a mannequin.

Gabriel laughed and sat up. He was naked still, his body lean and strong. His chest bore a tangle of golden hair that had never been there before.

'How's the arm?' asked Laura. She abandoned her pose and poured them both a drink.

'So-so. Is it shameful of me to say that Dora looked terrible?'

Laura sipped her drink. It was strong as raw mustard. 'Of course it is. Dinah and I said you'd think that, though. Only the best sort of men can see beauty in a pregnant woman, and you're not one of them.'

'She's like a bloody barrage balloon. What's beautiful in that?'

Laura sat on the bed and leaned back comfortably. 'She's carrying your child. If all you can see is swollen ankles and fat hands, then of course you don't see beauty.'

He looked at her for a long moment. 'If I wanted a child, it might be different. It isn't her body, really. I hate the way she looks at me. Like a kicked dog.'

'You kicked her. No one else. Even if she does blame me.'

She was lying like a queen on the bed. He reached out and took her hand, while her other held the glass. Just touching her skin brought him to hardness. Why? In ordinary circumstances, Dora was the more beautiful. Yet it was Laura he wanted to get inside.

He said, 'Do you miss Michael still?'

'Of course. All the time.'

'I mean – do you miss his body?'

She drew in her breath. It was hard to lie to Gabriel, hard to pretend. He always knew. She said, 'Sometimes. Michael isn't – he doesn't – it isn't always good. When he came home on leave he was like anyone, so quick, so hard. We both wanted too much. Because he was going away.'

'So you need a man.'

She turned her head to look at him. Why was she here?

Suddenly she didn't want to pretend. 'My body's hungry. Not my mind.'

Desire seemed to be thick in the air. They took it in with every breath, like fire. Laura felt blood engorging her, swelling the soft tissues between her legs, making them ache with the weight of her need.

She sat up with a jerk. What was she thinking? Why was she here? She was a slut indeed if she let this happen now. They were each married, each promised to someone who shouldn't be betrayed. She might want it, long for it, but she mustn't give in!

Gabriel said, 'It wouldn't matter. They'd never know.'

She met his eyes. 'We would.'

He said, 'I could be dead tomorrow,' and Laura laughed.

'Do you say that to all the girls? It must be like picking plums.'

He chuckled ruefully. 'It is. But very unsatisfying. Oh God, why does Dora have to be pregnant?'

'If she wasn't, you wouldn't have married her,' said Laura reasonably.

'You know what I mean! If we've got to be married, at least let us have some bloody fun.'

'You should go to Fairlands. You know you should.'

'Dammit, my mother's there. And I like it here. I like it very much.'

He ran his hand down Laura's arm once again. She felt the flame ignite and rush blazing through her limbs. Damn him! He must never know what he did to her. 'Do you have to be such a bastard?' she snapped.

She ran down the stairs, hearing him call after her. 'Laura! Laura! Come back here!' But she wouldn't sit with him again.

She went walking across the fields, on and on, until at last she felt calm again. The wind had cleansed her, cooling her blood and her appetites. At peace with herself again, she couldn't believe that she had been tempted. She thought of Michael, and felt soft with love.

In the evening, sitting across the fire from Sophie, she said, 'I'll go and see Dora tomorrow. Apologise. See if we can get Mother and Marie to come home.'

'That's a bloody bad idea,' said Sophie. 'We've never been so comfortable.'

'No. But I should anyway. Marie's playing games and Mother's not Dora's problem.'

'Put her in the cottage, like she said.'

Laura thought of all that had to be done. The cottage was sound but badly neglected. The chimneys were blocked with birds' nests and the range was useless, a mess of rusted metal. Perhaps it would be better to abandon it and put in a bottled gas cooker. Perhaps, while they were about it, they should provide a bathroom. Whatever they decided, it couldn't be done in a day.

'She doesn't mean to go,' she said despondently.

'All the more reason to call her bluff.'

They heard a noise on the stairs. It was Gabriel, in pyjamas and dressing gown, coming unsteadily down. When Sophie saw him she said, 'Oh, là là! What a beauty. Just what you need.'

Also in French, Gabriel said shakily, 'Just what I keep telling her. I didn't know we had a visitor, Laura.'

Laura got up. 'We don't. This is Sophie, someone I used to know. She and Marie are refugees. They're staying for a while. I thought Marie would be back by now, she went to Fairlands with your mother.'

'To sleep with Monsieur,' said Sophie, giving an awful leer.

'Shut up, Sophie!'

Laura felt herself blushing. She could see that Gabriel was vastly amused. She wanted him to go away, back to bed, anywhere, away from Sophie's dreadful little tricks. She couldn't make it plainer what she was. Why was Sophie here, dragging her back, dragging her down, keeping her forever mindful of the one thing she wanted to forget?

She turned away, her hand to her mouth. Gabriel said in English, 'It's all right. I do understand.'

'No you don't. No one does.'

'It's difficult, isn't it? Stepping out of one world into another.'

'Are you talking about flying?'

He shrugged. 'I suppose so. I can't go from that to this in a moment. I can't cope with them both. Life here doesn't actually seem very serious.'

'It is to us. It is to Dora.'

'What's the matter with him?' asked Sophie. 'You both look so damned glum. Got the shakes, has he? Just like last time. Half of them never got right.'

'I haven't got the shakes,' said Gabriel.

Laura said, 'She isn't used to people understanding.' She was conscious of wishing that Sophie wasn't there. But it was good that she was. She and Gabriel shouldn't be alone. 'When are you going back?'

'Supposed to be the end of the week.'

'You really should go to Fairlands. This isn't at all fair on any of us. People are bound to talk.'

'They must be talking already!' He looked at Sophie and grinned.

Laura closed her eyes for a second. 'It isn't funny, Gabriel.'

'Believe me, sweetheart, if I didn't laugh I'd cry.'

She looked at him, really looked at him, seeing through the illness and pain to the man beneath. His eyes were hard, unblinking, almost steely. He looked a little mad. 'Are we losing the war?' she asked quietly.

'I don't know. We're losing a lot of planes, I know that. I think I'll go back, you know. Tomorrow, perhaps the day after. If we older chaps drop out, they only send up young kids and they don't stand a chance. Easy meat, you see.'

'But what about you? You had such trouble learning to fly!'

Gabriel grinned, suddenly, frighteningly boyish. 'But I'm a hell of a good shot. I can drill them at maximum range. It's a thrill. A big thrill. Sometimes it's bloody marvellous!'

Bile rose in her throat. She turned away, pouring water from a jug and drinking it down. Gabriel's hand pressed her shoulder. 'I'm sorry,' he said. 'I really am. You see why I can't talk to Dora?'

'You should try. She might understand.'

'She'd think I was mad.'

'Aren't you?'

She turned to look at him. He shrugged a little, her own habit given back to her. 'I think it's best to be a little mad. Just now.'

The baby was crying. She went up to her, aware of Gabriel standing below. He made her uncomfortable. Tonight, in this house, she felt exposed to his needs and her own. They could so easily give each other comfort, she thought. Instead, she went into her room and pointedly closed the door.

Chapter Six

Mr Fitzalan-Howard was bemused. War was one thing but they hadn't lost yet and he was already invaded. First the cacophony of the school in the house five days a week, and worse, children roaming the estate, frightening the game. He hadn't seen a grouse in weeks. He pondered the problem, wondering how much was due to the absence of a decent gamekeeper. He might turn events to his advantage if he trained some of those East End boys to trap stoat. That sort of child was always keen to do violence, he decided.

The voices of women outside his study door brought him back to his train of thought. Somehow Dora had seen fit to introduce two of the strangest women imaginable into his house. God knows, they were used to Norma Cooper by now, they'd known her since the day she first came to Gunthwaite, but she wasn't a friend. Not in any sense. So why had Dora not dissuaded her from coming home with them? As for the Frenchwoman, he was in no way able to understand either what she was doing in England or why that charming girl Laura Cooper felt obliged to harbour her, war or no war. As to her presence at Fairlands, it utterly defeated him. Why?

A knock came on the door. He shuddered and ignored it, but it came again. It was too ridiculous to cower in here, unable to face a simple visitor. The knocking continued. At last, exasperated, he yelled, 'Come, damn you, if you must!'

It was that woman. French. All arched eyebrows and peculiar hair, her waist tightly laced, as used to be the fashion. She said, 'Forgive me. I know I trouble you. Is there a book I could read? Perhaps Maupassant or Molière? Or something philosophical.'

He turned to the bookshelves at his side. 'I believe we have some Molière. In French, although I confess not to have read it.'

'Why should you? I don't read your Dickens. Although I shall begin, now my English improves.'

'Very commendable.'

'I read for enjoyment, Monsieur, not to be commended. When I was in France and in daily fear of the camps, I always carried a book. To be ready, you see. An intellectual escape. And if you wish to retain your sanity you must begin reading. The school, and all us women! Your life's intolerable.'

He chuckled, despite himself. Really, she was at least amusing. He held the book, reluctant to give it to her. 'Why exactly are you here?' he asked bluntly.

She shrugged, that Gallic gesture so difficult for the English to understand. 'Does it matter? Of course, I inconvenience you. But then, you have never lived on an ancient farm. To have a light you must find a lamp, clean it, fill it, crack a glass on a terrifying flame, and at last succeed in dissipating some of the all-pervading gloom. To have a bath takes many hours. To have amusement means teaching French to little boys, and to have intellectual stimulation – my dear sir, the finest mind could not survive the drudgery. I became a sheep.'

'Baa,' said Mr Fitzalan-Howard.

'A fellow sheep! I knew it. Sir, I salute you.'

She came across to him, held his shoulders and kissed him on both cheeks. He felt himself blushing and fought it. She'd think him parochial in the extreme. He said, greatly daring, 'I don't suppose you'd care to join me in a sherry?'

'You're very kind.'

An hour later Mrs Fitzalan-Howard discovered them still in the study, drinking sherry and laughing together. She was surprised. Perhaps even a little perturbed. Everything was so odd nowadays, but at least one thing had always seemed constant. Reliable. She felt a strange and gnawing pain underneath her heart. What was it? Surely not – jealousy? There was nothing so foolish as jealousy of an overblown Frenchwoman with dyed hair and rouged cheeks and – an ability to make her husband laugh. She chewed her lip almost until it bled. Of course she was jealous. For the first time in all her married life her husband was giving her cause to doubt him. The sensation was nastier than she would have believed.

Throughout dinner, with Dora and Mrs Cooper talking

glumly about Gabriel, Mr Fitzalan-Howard and Marie continued their amusing conversation. He was witty, his wife realised miserably. It was years since she'd seen that side of him. In the humdrum routine of their daily lives she had failed to notice that she was married to a charming, educated man until this Frenchwoman, entirely true to type, arrived to try and steal him away.

She was too depressed to eat. Dora, equally gloomy, picked at the unpleasant, carrot-filled stew. Mrs Cooper said, 'You know, Laura feeds us nothing but foreign muck. I do prefer some good, plain food.'

Marie murmured in French to her host, 'How is it that this same person never rises from a Gunthwaite table until all the food is gone? We call her caterpillar, because she is constantly eating, without apparent enjoyment.'

He laughed more loudly than the joke deserved. Mrs Fitzalan-Howard felt as if her bones had turned to rubber. She drooped like a marionette with a broken string.

In the bedroom that night, she asked her husband, 'Why is the Frenchwoman here? She must have told you.'

He lifted his shoulders, in an unconscious imitation of Marie's shrug. Soon the whole village would be shrugging. 'Not really. I think she's a little worn down by Gunthwaite's lack of facilities.'

'She's not staying, is she?'

'I don't know. I should hate you to chase her away, my dear. She's the most amusing thing I've met in years. A truly cultured woman, charming, sophisticated – she looks like a French actress I saw once, in London.'

'She looks like a raddled old ewe,' said his wife, under her breath. She creamed her face vigorously, and wiped it off on cotton wool. Was she pretty? Dora was prettier, when she wasn't pregnant, that is.

But Dora's mother still had good skin and springing brown hair, with only a touch of grey. Better than that woman's improbable chestnut, at any rate. Perhaps she was a little fatter than she had been, but if keeping her husband meant starving herself – should she? Hunger wasn't such a demon when the alternative was a stew like tonight's.

401

She looked at her long, cotton nightdress. She had long ago abandoned seduction for practicality. Fairlands might not suffer as Gunthwaite did, battered by Pennine winds, but it was still a big house, hard to heat. She went into her dressing room, and opened a low drawer. Her silks gleamed in the lamplight, telling of holidays in Italy and hot, English summers, in those days not so long past when the world was at peace. She drew out a pale peach nightdress, its straps rolled and stitched to be thinner than string. Slipping it on, she looked at herself in the glass. Good heavens. She looked young.

When she emerged, her husband stood in the centre of the room, his striped pyjamas firmly buttoned, and said, 'Good God.'

'I wanted to pretend it wasn't wartime,' she said. 'I wanted to look pretty.'

'It is still winter, you know.'

'Yes.'

Goosepimples were rising in battalions on her arms. She scurried to the bed and jumped in, shuddering at the touch of cold sheets. If she had intended this she should at least have thought of hot water bottles. Geoffrey wasn't interested, that was plain. He wanted to flirt with Frenchwomen, not with her.

He said, 'Are you all right, old thing? You look a bit down in the mouth.'

'I'm perfectly well, thank you.' Her voice was muffled in the pillows.

He sat on the bed beside her. 'No, you're not. You're upset. Come on, dear, tell me.'

He was a darling, a dear. She loved him so much. 'That – that creature's going to seduce you. And you don't care!'

'Seduce me?' He felt a blush rising. 'I can't imagine – at least, I suppose – but I assure you, there isn't the slightest chance! Have you been worrying yourself about that? As if we haven't enough real problems. The school, and Dora – I don't know what to think.'

'Yes, you do. We both do. I never was sure about Gabriel Cooper. But at least he married her.'

'Did he?'

Her husband looked down at her tear-streaked face. Underneath all that womanly competence, organising this, that and even the blessed other, she was still the girl he once knew. 'There's a lot more to marriage than a ceremony. A lot of years, a lot of struggle – and a few silk nightdresses to boot.' He put his hand on the soft, unexposed flesh of her arm. Why had they let the sillinesses of life get in the way? There should always be time for this.

As they were making love she found her feet continually sliding into areas of chilly sheet. Hot water bottles, she thought abstractedly. They were going to do this much more often.

The screaming began at around four. 'Mother. Mother! MOTHER!!!'

Mrs Fitzalan-Howard shot out of bed and ran to her daughter's room. Dora was sitting bolt upright in bed, her eyes wide and her breath coming in gasps. 'It hurts,' she managed. 'Terribly!'

'Then you've started.' Her mother pushed the pillows more comfortably into her back. 'Relax, dear. We'll telephone Dr Hendon.'

'But it shouldn't be for months yet!' Dora struggled to maintain the fiction.

Her mother looked at her quizzically. 'Shouldn't it? I think this baby's about ready, don't you?'

Dora dropped her gaze. 'I didn't want you to know. To worry. I thought it had worked out awfully well.'

'So it has.' Her mother sat a moment, and took Dora's hand. 'Gabriel's ill, he's under terrible strain. When the baby's born, when you're better, things are bound to be different. It's the war, you know. Everything's out of gear. All we can do is wait.'

Dora nodded. Then her clasp on her mother's hand tightened, gripped, became a convulsion of fingers, body, everything. Her teeth clenched, reducing her wail of anguish to a high-pitched squeal.

'What is it? Is it really that bad? Geoffrey! Geoffrey, call the doctor urgently!'

They began to get organised. Nothing was ready, they had talked vaguely about having this baby in hospital. Mr Fitzalan-Howard belatedly telephoned the maternity home, only to find that it was one no longer and now took convalescents. But no one was particularly worried. Dora had herself been born at

Fairlands, and her father before her. If only the doctor would come!

They began to get ready. Between spasms Dora was fine, sliding off the bed so that waterproof sheets could be spread, changing her nightgown for a fresh one. But each time the pain came she was in agony. Her mother, knowing her daughter to be nothing of a coward, began to panic.

'Perhaps if you lie down – or turn on your side? Dora, don't wail like that, it isn't necessary.'

Mrs Cooper, standing in the doorway, said, 'It was the same for me when Michael was born. It's the way the baby lies.'

'But what do we do? She can't endure this for hours!'

'We give her this.' Sweeping in, her dressing gown trailing like a theatrical cape, Marie presented a small, crystal bottle. 'One drop, in water. No more. It's opium.'

Mrs Fitzalan-Howard went white. 'We can't – it's not good for her.'

'Not yet,' said Mrs Cooper. She brought a chair to the side of the bed and sat purposefully down. 'Too much is bad for the baby. She must wait until it's coming.'

'By then she could be dead!' Marie was not noted for her tact and Mrs Fitzalan-Howard let out a small scream.

'Cooper babies have killed their mothers before!' rapped Mrs Cooper, as if it were an honour to die in such a cause. She tapped Dora's wrist. 'Spread your hands. Breathe, don't scream. It does no good at all.'

Mrs Fitzalan-Howard slipped from the room. Her husband was in his study, trying to think of something to do. 'Telephone the doctor again, Geoffrey. Those women are like witches! Potions, spells – they'll be putting a knife under the bed next. I'll swear they're enjoying themselves.'

She stood beside him while he called. He was firm. 'Look, I must make myself clear. It's urgent. She's in great pain. We fear there may be something amiss.'

A muffled squawking at the other end.

'Do you mean to say that you took my message knowing full well the doctor would be away for another four hours? No matter, no matter, we're losing time. I must have someone here – all right, give me the name of him if you must, I suppose he'll have to do.'

His wife looked at him hopelessly. 'Another call. I knew it. We should have sent her to London.'

'She'd have been bombed. They've given me the name of some Pole in Bainfield. He's qualified in Poland, apparently. A refugee, volunteered to work here when he arrived, but no one quite fancied the idea. But at least he knows something!'

'They're going to dose her with opium!'

'I'll call him. Tell him to come at once.'

It was an hour before he arrived. The pains were coming more frequently, and between times Dora sobbed and clutched her mother's hand. 'I can't bear it. Is it supposed to be like this?'

'Cooper babies always come hard,' said Mrs Cooper lugubriously. 'You're never the same afterwards.'

Marie snorted. 'I've seen girls screaming for two days. And two months later they're back – dancing. Some women like to be ill, that's all.'

'And what would you know about it? How many have you had, may I ask?'

Marie stared back, implacably.

They were preparing for a complete row when the Polish doctor arrived, driving to the door in Bainfield's wheezing taxi. He clicked his heels to his dressing-gowned host, removed a top hat and declared, 'Goodness day. Colonel Wojtyla Zwmskorski, at your service.'

'You are a doctor?' Evening dress and an opera cloak lent a certain doubt to Mr Fitzalan-Howard's expectation.

A bow. 'For the last three years in the cavalry.'

'Then what on earth are you doing here? You can't know anything about childbirth!'

Zwmskorski removed his cloak with a flourish. 'Cavalry officers have wives, good sir. Besides, if a mare was in difficulties I was often called in to assist. I know babies. All babies!'

There was no help for it. They had no one else. He ran lightly up the stairs, discovering the room by the simple expedient of following the crowd. Maids with kettles, maids with teapots, and Mrs Fitzalan-Howard running from bedside to landing time and again to see if the doctor had yet arrived. When she saw Colonel Zwmskorski's unlikely but authoritative figure, she declared, 'Thank God!'

He took her hand and kissed it. 'Madame. Now, if you would all leave, please? I must examine this beautiful soon-to-be mother.'

'I have opium,' said Marie, waving her bottle. 'You will need it.'

He laughed. 'Perhaps for the patient. In Poland it is our custom to try and keep the physician awake. Ladies. Everyone. Excuse me.'

They all trooped from the room. Dora, who had been lying limply against the pillows, began to gasp with the onset of pain. The doctor, if such he was, put a cool hand on her belly. Try as she would to contain herself, she began squealing between clenched teeth.

'So bad?' he enquired. 'Yes. How fortunate that I am come.'

He emerged from the room drying his hands. 'The baby is – like this.' He gestured with his hands.

'Upside down,' said Mrs Fitzalan-Howard. 'A breech birth.'

'Indeed. It is also back and back with its mother. The spines are together. This is very hard. Much pain.'

'Opium,' said Marie comfortably.

'Your offer is accepted, Madame.' He bowed to her. As he rose he studied her carefully. 'Paris,' he said finally. 'Perhaps – four years ago? The Rue de Claret.'

Marie stood quite still. 'Perhaps. One meets so many – a soirée, I believe?'

'A delightful evening. We shall talk of it later. Recall old times. Now, I must return to my patient.'

Downstairs in the hall the taxi driver was complaining he hadn't been paid. 'He says he'll owe me, but I ask you! Owes everyone, he does, whole of Bainfield. I won't leave until I'm paid.'

Marie called down, 'You can wait, driver. You can take me to Gunthwaite Hall.'

'Oh, yes?' He looked bemusedly up at her in night attire, layer upon layer of old and somewhat dingy lace.

Mrs Cooper said, 'Going? Now? It's barely dawn.'

'She might die,' said Marie. 'Her husband should know. I see it as my duty.'

'I shall wait until the baby's born,' said Mrs Cooper, clearly intending to settle in for the duration.

Marie shrugged. 'As you please. By the way, that Pole – I do recall him. A man of bad character. He made me an improper suggestion. Don't believe anything he says.'

So she departed, a moth-eaten fur tossed over her lace, her clothes thrust willy-nilly into a bag. When the cab driver still complained that he hadn't yet seen a penny in payment, she thrust a note at him.

'*Vite! Vite!* Hurry, you ignorant man!' She hustled him out, bags and baggage everywhere, a blustery wind scattering leaves in the pool of light beyond the door. Suddenly all the noise and fluster was gone. For a moment, silence reigned, broken only by the piercing arrow of Dora's scream.

Hours passed. The day was grey and unfriendly. Colonel Zwmskorski was naked to the waist, as if at a foaling, and from time to time Dora looked up from her hazy stupor and was surprised. He looked like Gabriel, on their wedding night, or rather their wedding morning. His chest hair was beaded with moisture. Sometimes he came to her head, but mostly he was framed between her knees. Mrs Cooper held her on one side, and her mother on the other. When the pain came they held her legs in a position that ordinarily would mean death from embarrassment, while this strange man hunted for the baby. She had ceased to believe that there would ever be a baby. Probably she and the child would die.

The pain again. Even in her blurred state, she knew it was different. The doctor said breathlessly, 'Dora, please push, my darling. My angel, my desired one. Now, for me, push!'

He at least was kind to her. All she wanted was a little kindness. Something was slithering between her legs, like blood. 'Dora! No more.' He was crouching still. 'We must wait a little.'

It was very quiet. The only sound was of Dora's harsh breathing. Mrs Fitzalan-Howard stared in amazement at the tiny body protruding from her daughter. It was a boy, she could see that much, its chest compressed by the doctor's unyielding hands. How long could he last like that, the head still inside? Would the next pain never come?

Seconds ticked by. Mrs Cooper let out a sound, half moan, half laugh. The doctor looked wildly over his shoulder where scalpels lay gleaming like shark's teeth. In a moment would he cut her and be done?

The contraction came. 'Push now,' he said desperately, his voice grating. 'Dora, if you love me, push!'

Love? She didn't know about love, only pain. She pushed. The child, blue and still, was at last expelled into air. As they watched, quite hopeless, it sneezed, took a breath and began to live.

Later, when it was still day, Dora woke. Gabriel was sitting by the bed. She felt confused, as if she might not know him. He was a creature of her dream, something strange and unexpected. Was he really the doctor, had it been him all along?

He said, 'Hello, Dora. How are you feeling?'

'I – I don't know.' She tried to sit up and winced. She hurt, oh, how she hurt! She remembered Mrs Cooper saying she'd never be the same again. She started to cry.

Gabriel said, 'Why are you crying? The baby's wonderful. We have a son.'

'Do we?' She'd forgotten about the baby. It had died, hadn't it, somewhere in the night? She said, 'It hurt so much. I won't be a woman any more. Your mother said so.'

He laughed, quite loudly; it seemed out of place. He didn't want to be here, she thought. He'd come because someone had said he should. She turned her face away. 'You can go if you want. You don't have to stay.'

He took a breath that caught in his chest. 'I want to. I was ill before. Exhausted. You don't know what it's been like—'

'You could have told me. Me. Not Laura.'

'Yes.'

He looked down at her white, narrow face. She was pretty again, he realised. She looked bruised and weary. How could he feel sorry for himself and not for her? 'There never seems to be any time,' he said, knowing how inadequate it was, he was.

'Mother said that. She said we'd be fine once the war was over.'

'If I live that long.'

He shouldn't have said that. He wasn't supposed to admit that his chances were almost nil. Dora looked at him with what he imagined was reproach, but he didn't mind, suddenly. He felt calmer. If he was going to die, then so be it. No need to upset everyone and leave them with a bad taste. What had Laura said? 'You're going back tomorrow. Would it hurt to leave Dora happy? Think of the things she'll say to your son.'

He said now, 'If I do get killed – what will you tell him? The boy?'

'You won't be killed.'

'Yes! But if I was – what?'

She said nothing. She looked away. He felt that stabbing irritation that so often beset him with Dora. It wasn't that she was stupid, or uncaring – it wasn't a fault in her that she had lived all her life in tranquillity. She didn't know how to face death. But he hadn't time to wait until she learned. He persisted. 'For God's sake, Dora! What will you say?'

She was so tired. Her eyelids felt as if weighted with lead. He was asking her to think the unthinkable, when she would rather sink back into dreams of wreathing clouds of purple and pink. 'I'd tell him you shouted at me,' she murmured. 'When I wanted to go to sleep.'

He felt weak and amused. What was he thinking of? The poor girl was worn out. They knew so little of each other. They had married out of childhood acquaintance and adult folly. He reached out suddenly and touched her hair. 'If I come back – when – I'll try harder, Dora. We'll start properly. Have a holiday. Get to know each other again.'

She sighed, and her eyelids fluttered. She was asleep.

He went back to Gunthwaite as he had come, on the cart. One of the land girls drove, self-importantly delighted to be in charge of Banner. 'You drive very well,' said Gabriel as he alighted. The girl's face suffused with colour.

When he went into the kitchen Laura was kneading bread. He tried another compliment. 'You look so pretty doing that.'

She laughed and pushed at her hair with her wrist. 'Is this your new technique, Gabriel? Ingratiating?'

He grinned. Trust Laura. 'You didn't used to know words like that,' he remarked, pulling off a piece of uncooked dough and chewing it. It was, as ever, disgusting.

'I didn't used to know a lot of things. What's the baby like? How's Dora?'

'It's a boy. She's – not very well.'

409

'Were you kind to her? You promised!'

He nodded vaguely. 'I was. I tried to be. If I come back, I'm going to try and do better.'

She went on making her bread. The kitchen was so peaceful, he thought. In a moment the boys would come roaring in for their tea, and the baby would wake, and the Frenchwomen start arguing and discussing and disrupting. But Laura created her own silence and peace. It surrounded her like a small silver pool.

She turned her back to put the bread in the oven, putting up her hand to shield her face from the heat of the fire. When the door closed he came suddenly behind her and gripped her arms above the elbow. He held her close, crushed to him, knowing he must leave marks on her skin. 'Let go,' she said quietly. 'You have Dora, I have Michael. If you come back – when – you go to Dora's bed.'

'But I want you. I'll always want you.'

'And I don't care.'

He let her go. He felt like crying and thought, It's just the way things are. He was on a knife edge, flying so much. He felt weighed down with Dora and the baby. He couldn't rely on what he was feeling. When he came back he would feel different, he decided. And if he didn't come back – he turned and saw that Laura was standing at the sink, and she was crying.

'I want you to remember something,' he said. 'I want you to know that what I feel for you is different from anything I've ever felt before. I can't give a name to it. Perhaps it doesn't have a name. It's made up of desire and affection and gratitude and – well, some part of it is love. I don't want to die and not have you know it was in me. That I was capable of it and it was because of you. You put on so much of an act sometimes. Sometimes I don't know where you are underneath it all. But whatever – whoever you are, at least you made me feel more than I've ever felt.'

She watched the tears falling on the dishcloth in her hands. 'That's for your wife to hear. Not me.'

'I can't help that now. If I come back I'll try with her. That has to be good enough.'

In the morning, Gabriel came down dressed in his uniform. Bill Mayes brought the car round before eight. 'Go to Fairlands first,' instructed Laura. 'He can say goodbye to Dora. Mrs Cooper can go with you to the station, and then come back here. If she doesn't want to come, tell her she has to supervise renovating the cottage.'

'Soon you'll have everyone dancing to your tune,' said Gabriel.

She looked at him. 'It's probably for the best. Are you well?'

'As well as can be expected.'

She held out a small parcel. 'Something for the baby. Say it's from you.'

'Oh, God! All right. All right!' He took it, guilty, ashamed, angry. He couldn't feel what he was supposed to feel. None of this seemed to have anything to do with him.

Laura waited until the sound of the car had faded. He was going. He was gone. She felt empty and rather sad. It was best to be alone here, she thought, walled up in silence. People brought danger and challenge, they rocked her steadiness. People? Gabriel. She was better off alone.

Chapter Seven

Michael leaned against a lorry, feeling the heat come up from the engine and add to his misery. He had sweat rash under his arms and prickly heat in his groin; his tongue was stiff from the oily water, his throat raw from the cigarettes he smoked to keep the flies away; his head ached with the remembered throbbing of the engine and his eyes were raw from staring into the sun, searching for planes. Their sector had lost three lorries this week, and two men. The lorries were harder to replace.

But it was the flies that preoccupied him. They were on everything, clinging to food even as it went into the mouth. Michael was starting to make a study of them, noting several distinct types, each with its own particular habits, just like the planes. Stukas, fighters, bombers heavy and light – everything was replicated in the world of the fly. At least driving in the desert in the dark they could escape both the flies and the planes.

Some of the men were washing in an oildrum. It was a luxury, but one they could afford. They'd be in camp six hours after dark. Michael took his towel from the cab and went across, stripping to the waist and gritting his teeth against the chemical taste of the water. If only he had some clean clothes.

His mind began toying with the idea of nakedness. He imagined himself running through long, cool grass. He wasn't alone – Laura was with him, running through the orchard amidst the daisies. And she was naked too.

The prickly heat in his groin flared into wild itching. He cursed and splashed water down his trousers, while the men laughed. 'Dreaming of your old lady then, are you, sir? If she could see you now!'

'Best get packed up,' said Michael phlegmatically. 'Five minutes to sundown.'

They'd been stooging about all day waiting for darkness. Now they could make a brisk run for home. He felt a certain satisfaction because at least this convoy had avoided being bombed, despite sighting enemy planes on three occasions. They cowered behind sand dunes, surviving to steal away, unseen. Tonight they'd have a decent meal, in camp.

Two black dots appeared on the horizon. Flies, perhaps? It wouldn't be the first time he'd mistaken a fly on his nose for a plane high in the blue. He brushed his hand over his eyes and looked again. He took a deep breath, filling his lungs for the bellow. 'Here they come! Get in the trucks and scatter!'

Engines roared into life, setting up a drumming in the fuel barrels with which the lorries were loaded. Every man there was sitting on a bomb. Michael's driver, Ted, was hammering along with his foot to the floor, sending the lorry ducking and sliding across the sand. As long as they split up some of the convoy would survive, to unite again once the planes had gone.

An explosion roared out, sucking the very air from their lungs. One of the lorries had been struck without its engine ever starting.

'Tommy,' said Ted. 'Bet your life he wasn't in it.'

Could you blame a man for being a coward in these circumstances? No one else had baulked. Besides, Stephens was building a reputation as a shirker who'd let anyone down. Michael knew he had to deal with him.

Bullets were rattling on the sand. They were far enough now, should they get out and run? Just at present it was as dangerous out as in. Suddenly Ted jerked the wheel, sending the vehicle lurching to the left, reacting with that sixth sense which had kept him alive this long. Seconds later the sand shook as a bomb exploded. And then, with desert speed, while their stomachs still ached with the shock, darkness fell.

They limped into camp throughout the night. It was a good enough show, one lorry gone but no men. Michael was called to the CO's tent to give his report. The captain said, 'I'm pleased with you, Cooper. You keep your head and you know when to listen to the men. Just take hold a bit more, if you know what I mean. They respect you, but with a little more force they'll respect you a lot more. You can deal with this Stephens chap. A bloody backslider, ever since he joined.'

Outside the tent, the night was peaceful. The air was soft, cool, quelling even the mosquitoes that always swarmed where there was water. Michael felt very tired, but knew that until he had solved his problem he wouldn't sleep. If only, he thought, if only I was at home!

It was a nameless longing, one they all possessed. They didn't know what they wanted from home, only that home existed, and they must long for it. Leaves were all wrong, he decided. They gave you something but not enough. You were there only long enough to see the differences, and feel out of place.

He went to the men's long tent and said quietly, 'Stephens. I'll see you outside.'

Heads lifted. The little man rose, suspiciously. He reminded Michael of a badly bred terrier, small, thin and mean. A breeze had sprung up, moving his sparse strands of hair. Michael thought of the evacuees, full of lice and cynicism. This was what those children grew up to be.

He said, 'We lost a lorry because of you today. You funked it.'

'No I never! We didn't have a chance! Trying to get us killed, you were.'

'How far were you from the lorry when you heard the warning?'

'Didn't hear no warning. Had me head in the engine, working.'

Michael suppressed a grin. A more unlikely scenario he had yet to imagine. The engine of Stephens' lorry was more sandy than Hornsea beach. 'You'll be sorry the old girl's gone, then.'

He watched the little man in silence for a moment. There was a gleam of triumph in his sly eyes. Michael was thought to be a soft touch, he was expecting to get off lightly. The man's gaze slid back to the tent, to bed and a cup of tea. Suddenly Michael was annoyed.

'You're a bloody coward, Stephens, and this is your last chance. One more incident like today and I'll have you up for lack of moral fibre. For now, we'll see what a night of engine stripping will do for you. I'll inspect in the morning. And, just to keep you on your toes, from now on you drive for me.'

'I didn't do nothing, guv!'

'Call me sir! My God, if you had your way Jerry could land at Dover whenever he pleased. Whatever you did or didn't do, from now on you behave like a decent British soldier! Do as you're bloody told!'

Their faces were an inch apart. 'Yes, sir,' whispered Stephens.

Michael knew he had lost his temper and felt ashamed. It was the heat, that was all. 'We've got a lorry from the pound,' he said curtly. 'It's seized but I want it running by morning. No excuses.'

'Yes, sir.' Stephens was sidling warily into the night.

'Wait until I dismiss you!'

'Sir!'

'You are dismissed.'

Yelling like that in the open air, half the camp had heard. When Michael went into his tent someone lowered a book and said, 'You're not really going to drive with that idiot, are you? It's suicide.' Michael grunted. Perhaps it was. He was putting his life in the hands of a cowardly incompetent.

He sat on his bed and took off his boots, his toes relishing their freedom. He thought of tomorrow and flinched. Stephens for twelve solid hours! At Gunthwaite the days passed like golden drops of water, one upon the other, countless, nameless. A day here was just sand in the eye. He lay back, letting remembered peace wash over him, and fell quite asleep.

Laura was busy with the sheep. It wasn't that the land girls or Bill Mayes couldn't handle them, simply that she liked to assure herself that all was well. Ewes heavy in lamb needed care and gentleness, and she knew that while she was there no one would shout or chance an ill-directed kick. Pale, bony faces looked at her from every point of the hedge. Next year they would use a blackface tup, she thought. She had heard they were hardy and got early lambs. Nowadays her letters to Michael were full of talk about sheep and lambing, and very little else.

An old ewe with twins stamped as she passed by. Laura looked and saw one of the dogs following her, Michael's old bitch, Tam. That dog knew more about sheep than any of them, she thought, and called her up to ruffle her ears. The dog grinned and writhed in pleasure. Michael would think her soft if he saw her. To him sheep dogs were working dogs and that was that.

She stumbled on the ruts in the gateway, and slithered on frost in the yard. Sophie was slithering in the opposite direction. 'Lori! Lori!' The baby name always came back in times of stress. She came panting across, her bosom heaving like blancmange. 'A telegram. Marie says to open it, but I can't bear!'

Laura couldn't breathe. Try as she might she could not draw air into her lungs. Only when the pain became intense did her diaphragm heave and rescue her. She took the telegram in shaking hands.

'Did the man say anything?' The postman always knew what telegrams said. He always warned you if the news was bad.

'He talked. But I don't understand.'

They began to walk back towards the house. It was pointless to complain, Sophie would never learn more than a smattering of English. Besides, thought Laura, if she never opened the telegram, would it matter? If you didn't know someone was dead then you couldn't be sorry, could you? Years might pass in which their memory could gradually fade, until at last, when you discovered the truth, there would be no pain.

'Open it! At once! They're all waiting!'

Faces were crowded at the windows. In a while Mrs Cooper would come to the house for eggs or some baking, or to demand that Dinah help her in the cottage, and she too would want to know what the telegram said. It was Michael, it had to be. They'd send to Dora for Gabriel.

She felt very calm suddenly. The paper was growing warm in her hands. She opened it and read the brief message:

REGRET TO INFORM YOU LIEUTENANT MICHAEL COOPER MISSING BELIEVED KILLED STOP LETTER FOLLOWS STOP DEEPEST SYMPATHY MAJOR B GRAMPIAN STOP OFFICER IN COMMAND STOP

Her brain refused to work. She read the message again, and still it made no sense. Yet a storm was gathering in her breast, a conflux of emotion so strong and so terrible that her heart struggled for the next beat. It wasn't true. If she could move time backwards the telegram could be unread, the event undone. He wasn't dead! He couldn't be!

Her mouth was working soundlessly. At last she managed, 'Sometimes I dream. I don't believe my dreams. He's dead but I never see him die.'

Sophie said, '*Mon Dieu*. I knew it all along.'

Laura said, 'You don't understand. If I haven't seen it then it isn't so.'

Marie and Dinah were hurrying from the house. Dinah took the telegram in brisk fingers and said, 'Well then. No use standing here. I'll make us a cup of tea.'

'It isn't true,' said Laura, and smiled a little. 'He isn't dead. I didn't see it and it isn't true.'

Marie said, 'She's in shock. As a child she was hysterical. How could you see him die, Laura? It was thousands of miles away!'

She let them lead her to the house. It was better inside. Here were all the familiar, homely things; bread rising by the hearth, toys piled against the wall, brasses gleaming in the glow from the range. She went to the clock and fetched down Michael's last letter. He said so little about his life there, it was all about Gunthwaite, crops, cows, sheep. Where was he when he wrote this? What was he doing? She couldn't believe in a place, a time, a happening, when she knew nothing that surrounded it, nothing at all.

They sat her in a chair and gave her tea. She couldn't drink, it choked her. Mrs Cooper came in at the door, her face stark and white. 'It isn't true,' said Laura emphatically.

'Michael's dead,' said Mrs Cooper in amazed tones. 'Michael's dead!'

'It isn't true,' repeated Laura, and her mother-in-law laughed.

'Oh, it is, my dear. You never believe the first one. After that, you don't doubt a thing. But Michael – Michael.' She smoothed the telegram with long, vague fingers.

A car was drawing into the yard. It was the vicar. Laura got up stiffly, remembering the young priest all those years ago. She couldn't talk then and she wouldn't talk now. It wasn't true. There was nothing to say. She walked out of the room and up the stairs, closing her bedroom door with a determined thud. In the kitchen they all began talking, she could hear them quite clearly. She wasn't concerned. Michael's clothes still hung in the wardrobe. She opened the door and breathed deep of the smell of him. Her heart bled a little, a tiny drop squeezing out. It isn't true, she told herself. I cannot believe that Michael is dead.

Stephens said, 'Blimey, sir. Oughtn't to be going anywhere on a night like this.'

The stars were brilliant in a moonlit sky. Everywhere the dunes were outlined in shades of grey, their shadows no more than mist. Michael said, 'They're sending fighters out from Alex or somewhere.'

'Much good they'll do. Over us for ten bloody minutes and back home to bacon and egg. We're the ones that cop it. We're the stupid bastards.'

'Shut it, Stephens.'

But he never did. Night and day Stephens complained, like a cracked record. Food, water, flies, weather, bombers, fighters – he voiced every last irritation. They all felt them, of course they did, but they were best ignored.

He climbed in the cab and turned on his hooded torch to look at the map. According to the latest intelligence the Italians were somewhere to the west, with a section of German tanks stiffening the line. But hard experience had taught Michael not to believe everything he was told. He decided to take his men on a twenty-mile loop, sure then that they were in no danger of driving into an enemy position. They were to resupply mobile artillery, which in practice might mean a three-day chase across the sand. Somehow when he decided to defend his home, he hadn't expected this level of disorder.

The disgruntled Stephens at last got in the truck, and the convoy moved off. Michael shifted a little in his seat, trying to minimise the impact of its steel frame against his hip. It was really very bright tonight. His thoughts returned to considering the army and its rules. He supposed that from the outside it seemed to be running on oiled wheels, it was only from the inside that you realised the truth; all the organisation was retrospective. When a man was killed messily and unexpectedly, upsetting everything, routine ensured that he was disposed of tidily, replaced speedily, and recorded finally. No one remembered the confusion of the death, they were too busy

418

docketing and annotating, fitting the mishap into the rigid structure of King's Regulations. But out here, out of camp, driving in the moonlight with only a map reference to guide them, they were truly on their own.

After three hours or so, Michael signalled a halt. They climbed out of the lorries, half deafened by the engines, stretching and yawning. They would make a brew and move on. Michael took out his compass, checking their position against the stars. The night sky was brilliant with points of light, and all of them strange. He remembered spring lambings at Gunthwaite, looking up at the plough, the bear, Orion's belt, wondering if the hazy moon meant snow. Here, even the stars were different.

He felt the urge to relieve himself. 'Back in a mo,' he said to Stephens, and walked off towards a dune. At least out here he was spared the latrines of camp, a nightmare of flies, stench and futile carbolic. No wonder they all got dysentery. The sand was almost white here, millions of hard, sterile particles, you couldn't grow weeds in stuff like this. The farmer in him despaired of this landscape, despaired for its people. Hell to be born amidst this.

Before returning he looked up again at the sky. It intimidated him more than a little, so vast, so cold, so uncaring. Whatever his thoughts, whatever his actions, to those stars he was no more than another grain of sand.

He heard the drone of distant engines. Hairs rose on the back of his neck. Not here, not tonight, not when they were illuminated like actors on a bloody stage! Ours or theirs? He began to run back to the lorries, rounding the dune to see that he had come much further than he had intended; the convoy was at least two hundred yards away. The roar of the lorries drowned the sound of the approaching planes. Michael started to bawl at them, seeing them start to move. That bloody fool Stephens! That incompetent Stephens! He was the only one who knew that Michael was gone.

His breath was raw in his lungs. Stop shouting, they can't hear you. Run, damn you, run! The lorries were drawing away, obscured now in a cloud of moonlit dust. He could hear the planes again now, the engine note steady. Fighter escort. That's all it could be. And they'd run off and left him!

He stood in a patch of moonlight and began waving his arms. They might see him, you never knew. And what about Stephens? How long before it dawned on him that he had left his commanding officer in the sand? Would he come back? Pray God he came back. Or would he merely report that he had assumed Lieutenant Cooper had joined another truck? Michael could see him now, all injured innocence and glib explanation. Stephens cared for nothing but himself.

All sound was fading now. The night was quiet. Michael sat down in the sand and turned out his pockets, finding the compass, some biscuits, a handkerchief and a piece of string. Out here without water, he'd die after a few hours in the sun. How far back to camp? Fifty miles at least. And a great deal less from the enemy. He looked at his watch and saw it was almost midnight. He'd give them until three, he decided. If no one came back for him he'd take a compass reading and make for enemy lines. It was his only hope.

Dora lay on the bed, rocking the cradle with a lazy hand. The baby was almost asleep. She felt sleepy herself, as so often since the birth. The doctor, Zwmskorski, said it was to be expected. He came at least twice a week, which infuriated Dr Hendon, who for years had considered Fairlands the icing on his cake. But Dora was glad he hadn't attended her. Look what he'd done to Laura's little girl. Those terrible marks.

She propped herself on her elbow and looked down into the cradle. Piers Gabriel was asleep, his mouth working silently in memory of the nipple. At his feet rested a little teddy bear, sent by Gabriel from his station. 'I'm so sorry I was such a fool,' he had written. 'Put it down to innate stupidity, compounded by loss of blood. I shall try and get some leave soon, but I'm not too hopeful. Things are a bit hectic here just now.'

He was being brave, she could tell. And truthfully, she didn't want him home, for a little while at least. Life here was very pleasant, with the baby to amuse her, Zwmskorski to visit her, and a constant stream of cards and presents from everyone she knew. For the first time since the honeymoon, she was enjoying being married to Gabriel.

Her mother came into the room. 'We've had some news. Michael Cooper's been killed.'

'What?' Dora sat up, suddenly wide-eyed.

'Norma Cooper drove over. She wanted to telephone Rosalind and Gabriel, but she wouldn't stay. She looked absolutely white.'

'What about Laura?'

'I don't know. I thought I should go over. She might not want to see anyone. I can't decide.'

'Should I go, do you think? Perhaps I ought. It wasn't her fault about Gabriel, after all.'

'No. Poor Laura. I can't think what she's going to do!'

Dora tried to imagine what it must be like. Michael Cooper had always seemed to her a sombre sort of man. Unexciting, almost. But Laura adored him, that much was plain. She said, 'I will go. It could be Gabriel, after all.'

Her mother pressed her hand. 'I'll have the pony harnessed to the trap. We can't go jaunting in the car, we haven't the petrol. Damn this terrible war!'

Dora dressed in a pale blue jumper and skirt. The clothes were inappropriate, but she still wasn't slender enough for the rest of her things. She looked miserably at her thickened middle, and wished she could go to give comfort looking as she used to do. The Polish doctor assured her, implausibly, that it would soon go away.

She was more depressed by her appearance than her errand. Her mother pressed a note into her hand, a brief condolence. 'You won't upset her, will you, darling?'

'I can only try, Mother.' She picked up the reins and clicked the pony into his usual lackadaisical trot.

As she turned out of the drive, the doctor's car drew up beside her.

'My dear Mrs Dora! I have come to see you. An outing?'

'Of a kind. My husband's brother's been killed. I'm visiting Gunthwaite to call on his wife. His – widow.'

'And I shall visit too. A doctor is often needed at such a time. Come. I shall take the horse.'

He abandoned his car and jumped up beside Dora. She felt flustered. What would Laura say to see her arriving with a strange man? Zwmskorski took the whip and cracked it expertly in the air. 'Come, horse! Be off with you!'

Shocked into compliance, the horse rattled down the road.

An odd silence hung over Gunthwaite Hall. There was no one in the yard. Dora got down from the trap, leaving Zwmskorski to tie the pony to a rail. 'Is anyone around?'

After a moment a girl appeared in the arch of the barn. 'Oh. We didn't hear you. I'll get Paula to see to the pony.'

'He needs a rug,' said the Pole. 'And a drink.'

'Where is everyone?' asked Dora.

'She sent the men home. No one's doing anything. It's weird.'

Dora felt a chill run down her spine. Weird was the word. She went to the back door and knocked, and after a moment it opened. One of the Frenchwomen, the one with no English. The visitors went inside.

The old man was sitting by the fire mumbling to himself. Marie and the two boys sat at a table cluttered with unwashed plates and glasses, in the midst of a meal of some sort, although it was mid-afternoon. Of Laura there was no sign.

'*Bonjour, Mesdames,*' said Zwmskorski.

Marie glared. 'Why are you here? This is a house of sorrow.'

'We came to see the widow,' said Zwmskorski. He bared his teeth in a teasing, knowing smile.

'She'll see no one.'

Dora said, 'Is she upstairs? I'd better go and knock.'

Marie snorted. 'After all that you said to her, you're the last person who should be here.'

'All the same.'

She half expected Zwmskorski to accompany her, but instead he settled at the table. Now that she was here she felt diffident. What on earth was she going to say? But there was nothing for it. She climbed the stairs and knocked on Laura's door.

'Yes?'

Dora turned the handle and went in. Laura was sitting in the window. She was neatly dressed and her hair was combed. A pile of letters lay on the seat beside her, and she was dry-eyed and calm.

'Hello, Dora,' she said.

Dora twisted her wedding ring unhappily. 'Hello. I came – Mother sent a letter. We want to say how sorry we are.'

Laura said, 'Don't be. He isn't dead, you know.'

'But Mother said – wasn't there a telegram?'

'Yes. Missing believed killed. And I've been dreaming that

422

he's dead ever since he went away. I'm not dreaming it now so I don't think it's true.'

'Perhaps you wouldn't dream it – if it was over?'

The skin of Laura's face seemed to stretch into a mask. 'I don't believe that. I can't.'

Dora sat down beside her without being asked. Her legs felt too weak to support her. 'Are you still not well?' asked Laura.

'It isn't that. This is all so upsetting, isn't it?'

'I'm not upset. It isn't as if—'

Dora burst out, 'He's dead! You know he's dead! You're going mad!'

There was a silence. Laura turned her head away, looking out at the orchard, stark as dead fingers, burnt and twisted. She said, 'We didn't prune as we should. Michael wrote about it and I forgot. Can we do it now, do you think? We don't want to let the frost in.'

Dora said, 'Shall I get the doctor to come up? He's Polish and very good. I swear he saved my life '

'I'm not ill,' said Laura. 'It isn't illness to think differently from everyone else.'

'It is if you're wrong.'

Mary was lying in her cradle. Dora scooped her up in passing. Laura shouldn't have care of a child at a time like this. In the kitchen Marie was being haughty, eyeing Zwmskorski with a glacial stare. Dora said, 'Can you go up, Wojtyla? She's so odd. She says it can't be true.'

'It was the telegram,' said Marie. 'Missing, believed killed. So he's dead. Blown up. Gone.'

Zwmskorski chuckled. Dora felt her skin creep. They were such ghouls these continentals. Perhaps Europe was a blood-soaked continent these days, with bodies on every corner? Perhaps it made you like that?

Zwmskorski ran lightly up the stair. 'Mrs Cooper?' He went into the room with the open door. Laura still sat in the window.

She turned to look at him. 'I'm sorry. Have we met?'

He bowed, very formal. 'I believe so. Some years since. You were so young. The Rue de Claret.'

Her vague stare seemed to focus a little. 'Really? You have the advantage of me. That was a very long time ago.'

'Indeed.'

423

He took her hand, but she took it back and said, 'I am in no need of a doctor, I can assure you. It's just that my husband isn't dead.'

'But you know he is. They sent a telegram. He has been blown up, I think. They have no body.'

'It doesn't mean that! He's – he's missing. That's all.'

'He is dead, Mrs Cooper. Exploded. Gone.'

She closed her eyes. A brief tremor shook her. The doctor said musingly, 'I had forgotten how you were. So beautiful. So expensive. I saw you once out walking and I wanted you but I was too poor.'

She stared at him, wondering if she had indeed known this man. But all she could see was Michael. There was a knife in her heart. It had been there for hours now, and only by stillness could she ward off the pain. But now it was twisting all by itself, stirring like an animal waking from sleep. Images flashed across her mind, men all of them, naked men, cruel men, Michael – Michael. He was blown quite to pieces. That was what it meant. So little was left it was impossible to find.

She turned wildly to the doctor. 'I knew it would come to this! I told him. He didn't care!'

'Lie down. Come, lie down.'

'No!' She was shaking uncontrollably.

'You're tired. You must rest.'

'Don't touch me!'

After a moment Zwmskorski went down. 'Why was she screaming?' asked Dora fearfully.

'She believes it now. She's hysterical. She's that sort.'

'You know nothing!' spat Marie. 'She can take this.'

Something crashed on the floor above. Zwmskorski said, 'Come, Dora.'

She stood by the pony in the yard, looking up at Laura's window. Three women seemed to be wrestling with each other. 'She'll kill herself,' said Dora in amazement.

'They'll give her opium. She'll sleep.'

'Poor Laura,' said Dora wonderingly.

Zwmskorski climbed into the trap, putting down a peremptory hand for Dora. There was nothing to do but go.

Chapter Eight

Gabriel took a mouthful of whisky. It tasted of peat and heather. 'Not an island malt,' he said carefully. 'One of the glens.'

'Ah, but which?' Philip tapped the glass quizzically. 'You'll never be a master of scotch at this rate.'

'I'll have you know it isn't exactly my life's ambition.'

'Have you a better? No? I thought not. Have another.'

Gabriel sampled the second glass. 'Blend. Too easy. Any word on the new boy yet?'

Philip glanced round. 'No. Unless – ah, everyone's looking worried. Have another and don't ask.'

But Gabriel got to his feet and went across. 'Did he make it?'

'Yes, but he buggered the crate. Some of these kids can barely fly. When he gets back, will you take him as your wingman, Cooper? Put in some practice. Teach him how to fly.'

'You know he can't shoot, either?'

'Well, teach him that, as well! By the way, yours was confirmed. Someone saw it and rang in. Keep this up and they'll give you a gong.'

Gabriel went back to his friend. 'I've got to babysit Green.'

'Well. I suppose you asked for it.'

'For God's sake, Phil, someone's got to! I know how I was.'

'But we had time. They haven't, and it's nobody's fault but Jerry's. It does no good to go down with them, you know. It doesn't help.'

Gabriel knew he was right. But his other self, nervous, slow to learn, seemed still so very close. Sometimes, when he was halfway through a sequence of moves, he would imagine himself back with his confusion, unsure whether to do this or that first, not knowing why any of it mattered. When he broke away from a dogfight and found himself lost, the map aligning itself automatically in his head, he couldn't help but recall his map-reading ineptitude of the very recent past.

He said to Philip, 'You know, it horrifies me to look back at how I used to be. I keep wondering if I'll look back at my present perfection and feel just as much horror. If I get to look back, that is.'

Philip reclined musingly in his chair. 'Perhaps we'll gaze down from a greater elevation than we anticipated? Just imagine all the dead blokes looking down now and thinking, "Silly buggers. They'll feel like death in the morning."'

Gabriel chuckled. 'We'll get a feel for it, anyway. Oh, look. Here's Green. They've posted him back smartish.'

A short young man with dark hair and a nervous expression came into the mess. A few heads turned towards him, but no one called him over. He looked around unhappily, his shyness horribly apparent.

'Oh God,' groaned Philip. 'I hate the ones you feel sorry for. Give me the cocky buggers you're glad to see go.'

Gabriel put up a hand. 'Over here, Green. Come and have a drink.'

The boy dashed across with worrying enthusiasm. 'I thought – it wouldn't surprise me – I lost the plane, after all.'

'Nobody minds too much,' said Philip. 'People don't want to get to know you, that's all. Not until they're sure you're going to stay with the squadron, if you understand me?'

'Yes.' The boy looked greener than his name.

Gabriel said, 'Cheer up. You're to be my wingman. Do what I do, no questions asked.'

'I get the feeling – everyone sees me as a bit of a liability.'

'Well, everyone is, at the start. Just watch my tail for me. You'll be OK.'

Green took a gulp of malt whisky and choked. Philip turned his gaze skywards and sighed ostentatiously. 'Rather you than me,' he murmured, watching Gabriel lean forward and give his charge a firm slap on the back.

They scrambled before dawn the next day. Gabriel had hoped for an hour or two's tuition before the real thing, but it was not to be. He asked permission to move away from the main formation, watching the stubby little plane sticking like glue, twitching when he twitched, following instructions to the letter.

426

He could see now how Green had passed out of training – he was wonderfully obedient. Sadly, obedience was a quality not much needed in a dog fight.

They were trying to intercept an enemy formation heading for London. For some unfathomable reason attention had moved from attacks on airfields to blanket bombing of cities, which, Gabriel was ashamed to admit, was a great relief. Instead of a mad panic to take to the skies before you were blasted out of existence, there was now a leisurely journey to work. Then of course it was murder – he used the term literally – knocking out fighter escort, trying to get at the bombers. Sometimes, if you hung on until they reached London, you were in real danger from ack-ack as well. Sometimes it was a relief to know the gunners were notoriously inaccurate.

Dawn was coming up over the horizon, a soft glow that in a moment turned into blinding orange light. The R/T crackled, and Gabriel listened while automatically scanning the sky. If the heading was correct they should be in sight by now. He peered into the sun and sure enough, there they were – he could see them dead ahead. Bombers like fat bluebottles, the fighters like gnats above. He spoke tersely. 'Bandits. Twelve o'clock.'

'Confirm. Engage at will.'

He peeled away, gunning the engine, clawing for extra height. Green was at his wingtip still, that was good. The fighters were Focke Wulfs, he could see that from here, and he felt a certain relaxation. He had the legs of them, which he didn't with one of the souped-up Messerschmitts. Someone was firing, which was bloody ridiculous at this range. Look at them, scattering like pigeons. Which would he have for dinner today?

His lips peeled back in a rictus of a smile, he thumbed the triggers of the guns affectionately and kicked the rudder. He was on a tail, firing now, watching the shells slam into the engine. Smoke streamed back at him as he pulled the stick and left it, sure it was finished. Where was Green? Still there. He craned his neck, searching the sky, watching someone's tracer miss by a mile. Far below a bomber was turning, one propeller idling in the slipstream. Engine failure and running for home. This was one for the pot.

He dived, his mind automatically calculating deflection at relative speeds. He must talk to Green about that; the boy shot as if everything was standing still. Gabriel had been like that once. To the job in hand; come in dead astern, a small target was bound to be too much for the rear gunner. Thumb the trigger – he was gone. Next hit the engine and watch them go down. Work of a moment, really. Home now for bacon and eggs, while the crew of the bomber had a swim.

He felt a rising wave of exhilaration as he tootled home in the early-morning sun. Two down and Green still alive, not a bad morning's work. Gabriel let his mind wander for a while. He thought of Laura standing at the kitchen range, flushed pink and her hair coming down.

He caught himself up, conjuring instead the image of Dora before his eyes. Why not her? She was a nice girl, dammit, a really nice girl! She'd sent him a picture of the baby last week, a nice enough child although he couldn't bring himself to believe he had any connection with it. It was just a child.

His mood dimmed a little. The airfield was below him, and the clouds were gathering. If Jerry had any sense he'd stop these dawn raids altogether and stick to bombing at night. He was too high and glanced at his altimeter to confirm it. Reacting as always, he automatically side-slipped. A sudden squawk came over the R/T, Green playing the fool. He looked to his wing, only to see an absence of Green. He looked up. Green was rushing about the sky looking for him. Poor bloody fool. He went into land, waiting by the hangar until Green should see fit to join him.

The CO came across. Gabriel reached in his pocket for a cigarette, but the CO reached first and gave him one of his. Balkan Sobranie, where the devil did he get those? 'Bit of bad news, I'm afraid,' said the CO.

Gabriel's mind did a somersault. Who'd bought it? Philip? He hadn't been up. 'It's your brother,' went on the CO. 'Posted missing, but I gather it's definite. You're wanted at home.'

Green was landing. He emerged from his cockpit looking flustered and upset. He came across to Gabriel saying, 'Sorry, sir. You lost me, I don't know how.'

Gabriel waved him away. The boy was an unbearable irritation. The CO said, 'Get off straight away if I were you. The family's bound to want you around. I really am most dreadfully sorry.'

The ride home was unreal. He thought of Michael all the way, but the only image he could recall was of him ploughing. He could walk miles behind those horses, each furrow as straight as the one before. He could hear him calling: 'Whoa, Blossom. Get up, Banner. Go on, go on, go on!'

The car was waiting at the station. His mother was in the back seat, looking woebegone. 'Darling! Thank God.'

'I'm not the one that's dead, Mother.'

'Somehow I never thought it might be Michael.'

He felt a spurt of anger at her, because she had thought so little of Michael, hadn't thought him worth even anxiety. Perhaps he was angry at himself too. He hadn't appreciated his brother, he could see that now. Somehow he'd imagined he'd have years and years in which to repair the damage caused by a brother taking on a father's role. He'd resented Michael so. And now he was gone.

His mother said, 'Laura's impossible, of course. That foolish girl.'

'What do you mean – impossible?'

'Well, at first she refused to accept it, and then when she did we had to dope her. The screaming and crying! And now she just lies in bed and cries. Everything's in uproar, of course, all the visitors, Rosalind, everyone. And Laura just cries.'

'I suppose she thinks housework can wait,' said Gabriel sardonically.

'The farm can't. She would take over everything, and now no one knows what to do. Thank goodness you're home, darling.'

The sight of Gunthwaite's familiar walls did little to soothe him tonight. Rosalind came running out to meet him. 'Gabriel, darling! It's all so dreadful, isn't it? We don't know what to do.'

He pulled his bag out of the car, noting the straw in the yard, the rusting ploughshare, the lowing of a bullock from the barn. 'How's Laura?'

'Dreadful. In bed all day. While I wrestle with Father and the boys and everything.'

He grinned. Rosalind hadn't changed. She had never been domesticated. 'I'll go up and see her. Obviously she can't be permitted a day or two to grieve.'

Rosalind said, 'It isn't that, and you know it. She isn't right,

Gabe. We're worried for her own sake, not ours.'

He took the stairs two at a time, knocking perfunctorily on the bedroom door. No one answered. He hesitated on the threshold, suddenly thinking of all the years when Michael had come purposefully out of this very door, rolling his sleeves, getting on with the day, as like as not taking Gabriel to task for the latest misdemeanour. Tears welled up inside him. He stood, trying to gather himself, but there were people in the hall, people everywhere. He had to go in.

Laura was looking at the door. As he entered she sank back against the pillows, as if she had been expecting someone else. He needn't ask who. 'Oh my dear,' said Gabriel hoarsely.

She was blotched with crying. Her nose was swollen and her eyes almost closed. She was crying still.

'Do you believe it? Everyone says I must. They say he was blown to bits.'

'Perhaps he wasn't.'

'How then?'

'I don't know.'

She turned her face back to the pillow. He sat on the edge of the bed and rested his hand against her shoulder. She felt thin beneath the nightdress, as if she'd been starving. He felt an agony of emotion welling inside him, so much grief, so much tenderness, so much love. He put his face down to hers, kissing the tears as they ran in slow trickles from her eyes. 'You're not alone. Don't think you are. I'll never desert you.'

She turned her face to his. 'I needed him, you see.'

'I know.'

'He was my rock. My safe foundation.'

'I know. Oh, I know.'

'What can I do without him?'

He drew her up in the bed and held her close. Her breasts were soft against his arm, but the touch was bland, like that of a child. He had never seen her so helpless, he thought. Someone had taken away her steel.

He said, 'The house is in chaos. People everywhere and nothing done.'

'I don't care. I don't have to care any more.'

'I know. But there's a sick bullock in the barn. I can hear it bawling. I'll have to go and see.'

'What's the matter with it?'

'I don't know. Why on earth did Michael have to go to war? He had no business leaving you. What a pointless, worthless mess!'

She pulled back a little and looked into his face. 'What will happen to me now? Will I have to leave?'

'No! Of course not. The farm's yours.'

'I thought it might go to you now.'

He closed his eyes briefly. She might be right. The farm descended through the male line, and Michael had no male heir. He said, 'This is your home. Always. You're Michael's wife, Laura!'

She nodded, trying to smile. 'Not any more. And I never felt it, you know. He should have had someone better. More worthy than me.' Tears began welling again. 'Oh Gabriel, I don't know what I'm going to do!'

Her sobs were wrenched from somewhere deep within her soul. What had Michael done, staid predictable Michael, to inspire all this? He didn't even know the woman he had married! He didn't even satisfy her! But he was her rock, and on him she had built her house.

'Come on, then,' said Gabriel, shaking her a little. 'Let's look at this beast.'

'I can't! I can't.'

'We can't let Michael down, you know. He'd not leave it bawling.'

He shook her again, and her head rolled on to his shoulder. 'I wish you'd leave me here.'

'But I can't. Come on, my dear. Up with you. Michael's gone but Gunthwaite hasn't. You can't let it go.'

He helped her into a dressing gown. She stood before a mirror looking at her own, unrecognised face. 'I'm glad I look so bad,' she said wonderingly. 'I'd hate to look pretty. I don't ever want to look pretty again.'

Talking ceased in the kitchen as Laura came in. She ignored them all, and went to the door. Rosalind said, 'It's freezing out there. At least wear a coat,' but Laura took no notice. She meandered aimlessly across the yard, stopping halfway, as if too weak to continue. She straightened her back and went on.

The bullock was standing by the manger, saliva dripping

from its mouth. It was sweating and miserable, every now and then uttering its long, painful call. Laura contemplated it for a moment. Then she shouted, 'Bill! Bill, are you there? What's the matter with this beast?'

He appeared around the straw stack, a cigarette hanging from his mouth. 'I'll thank you not to smoke in the straw,' snapped Laura. 'Why is this beast like this? Has it got a wire?'

He took the cigarette out of his mouth. Less insolence now that the Missus was in charge. 'Could be. Don't rightly know.'

'How long has it been? Days? I won't have it suffer like this. Get the butcher to it.'

'We can't do that, Missus! The beast's half grown!'

She fixed him with an icy stare. 'I can do what I like, Bill Mayes. I'll not have it suffer. Get the butcher. And after that we'll see about some work.'

She started back to the house but Gabriel didn't follow. He felt so heavy and grim. He could see what would happen now. Laura turning like milk going sour, closing off the joyous source of her exuberant love of life. Like his mother, he thought bitterly. She must have been radiant once. But she had turned, and there was no going back.

It was at dinner that Gabriel suddenly remembered Dora. Rosalind and the Frenchwomen had between them concocted something out of smoked fish, and as he toyed with bones hidden in glutinous mashed potato his thoughts drifted to Mrs Fitzalan-Howard's fish mousse. It was of course her cook's fish mousse, but it had been a byword for culinary excellence hereabouts. Dora had once promised to steal the recipe for him.

He jerked upright. 'Dora!'

'What?' Laura looked bemusedly up from her untouched plate.

Rosalind gasped. 'My God. Gabriel, haven't you spoken to her? Pray she doesn't know you're here.'

'I called on my way to the station,' said Mrs Cooper who had joined them unannounced for dinner. 'I told her I was collecting you. Of course she knows you're here.'

'I'll have to get over there.' He grabbed his jacket and a lamp, snatching the car keys from the hook by the door.

'You can't take the car,' said his mother, almost smugly. 'The petrol's all gone. They'll bring some more out from Bainfield on Thursday.'

Gabriel felt as if mighty forces were opposed to him. He abandoned the lamp and searched instead for a torch, at last finding one that seemed to work. It would have to illuminate a long dark cycle ride.

He arrived at Fairlands just before ten. The bike had sustained a puncture two miles back, and he'd spent a futile ten minutes trying to pump some life back into the thing. The house was well blacked out and his torch was failing, so he fell up the front steps and cannoned against the door. Recovering, he knocked just as forcefully. Mr Fitzalan-Howard's voice called out, 'Who the devil's that?'

'Gabriel Cooper, sir.'

The door was flung wide. 'Thank God,' said Mr Fitzalan-Howard fervently. 'Dora's in quite a state. I can see that you wanted to get home and all that, but she's taken it hard. Sorry about your brother, of course. Michael was a good man.'

Gabriel nodded. He didn't want to hear tributes, they unmanned him. He went through to the drawing room where Dora was standing rigidly by the fire. 'I'm sorry about Michael,' she said stiffly.

Gabriel heard the door close behind him. It seemed they were to be left alone. He said, 'I meant to come earlier but Gunthwaite's in turmoil, you've no idea. Rosalind's swanning around in Whitehall clothes failing to cope.'

'You could have asked me to help,' said Dora. 'He was my brother-in-law, you know. It isn't as if I'm not involved.'

'I suppose we all thought the baby was keeping you very busy.'

She flung herself into a chair. 'He's only a baby! Anyone could look after him, he sleeps half the day. You might have come, Gabriel. After last time, too! I thought you were sorry.'

'I was. I am. Oh God, Dora, I had to go straight to Gunthwaite, you must see that.'

'Well, actually, I don't.'

She was looking sulky. He felt a rush of irritation. As if he hadn't had enough to contend with today! His brother was dead, and all she cared about was being paid some attention. She's young, he told himself. What's more she was bored and lonely,

433

stuck out here. Girls today didn't sit at home with folded hands, they joined up and did their bit. But here was Dora, condemned to sit in this house and play at motherhood, and be forgotten.

He knelt by her chair and put his lips to her cheek. She turned her face away and he nuzzled her neck, and suddenly she flung her arms around him and cried, 'Oh, darling Gabriel! I do love you so.' Her mouth fastened to his. He tried to lose himself in kissing her, but all the time he thought of her parents, waiting anxiously outside. He must go and speak to them and make his peace. When he thought of going to bed with Dora, in this house, he felt unspeakably embarrassed.

At length, social pleasantries over and a glass of whisky drunk, he and Dora retired to bed. He had never been in her bedroom before. It was frilly and cluttered, with pretty blue hangings round the new double bed. 'Mother thought we should have this,' said Dora breathily. 'She's very good about things like that.'

Gabriel was conscious of a great weariness. It was the very opposite to the adrenalin rush that sent him so easily into the arms of the nearest available girl when he was flying. Thoughts of Michael kept pursuing him, thoughts of Laura as she had been that day. He couldn't escape the image of her grim, unhappy face. It wasn't like Michael to let people down, he thought, and suddenly he was fighting tears.

Dora said, 'It's so lovely having you home, Gabriel. You've no idea.'

She sat on the edge of the bed, arranging herself in film star fashion. He said, 'Where's the baby?'

'In the nursery. Mother will listen for him, he doesn't often wake. We've got the whole night to ourselves.' She lay back, stretching out her arms to him, and he wanted nothing so much as to be at Gunthwaite, amidst Michael's things, Michael's memories, in Michael's home. He had no place amidst these blue frills with this girl he hardly knew.

'Kiss me, Gabriel.'

That was surely out of a film. His face must have revealed something because she sat up and said crossly, 'What is it? What are you thinking of?'

He sighed. 'Nothing. Look, let's get undressed, shall we? It's been a long day.'

'Are you too tired, then? Too tired to make love to me after all this time?'

'No! No, of course not. Look, I'll undress in the bathroom if you don't mind.'

When he came back, attired in Mr Fitzalan-Howard's voluminous pyjamas, Dora was lying mutinously between the sheets. He got in beside her, reaching across at once. She was naked. He ran his hand over her stomach, reaching beyond her hip to explore the soft furrow of her buttocks. Dora whispered, 'Say you love me.'

'I love you,' repeated Gabriel.

'You've got to tell me if I'm different. Since the baby. Your mother said I wouldn't be the same. But Dr Zwmskorski examined me and said I was tight as a good new sock.'

'The doctor said that?'

'Yes. He's quite naughty when he examines me, actually. He puts his fingers into me. It isn't very medical at all.'

It was easy to see what she wanted. He slid his hand between her legs, searching for the place. She turned on her back and as he found her let out a gasp. If she was a little less keen they wouldn't now be in this mess, he thought irritably, stroking her soft folds with his thumb. Her hands closed around his wrist, holding him into her. The gasps were coming rhythmically, she must have been aching for this. He pulled away to see to things. One child conceived carelessly was more than enough.

He could see her eyes shining in the gloom. This wasn't a shared experience, he thought, moving to cover her. All they were doing was selfishly taking satisfaction. He went up into her, cautiously in case she flinched, but she only grunted. She held on to his hips regulating his thrusts, suddenly stiffening in orgasm. Thoughts prevented his own release. Laura wasn't like this. She had been gentle, refusing to go where he could not follow. She had taken him with her on a voyage of delights.

Dora's nails were marking his buttocks, even through cloth. He was fully engorged, teetering on the brink, but the woman who held him began to shudder once more. Suddenly she opened her eyes and cried out, and he discharged himself, feeling the outrush with a sense of grim relief.

At some time in the night he was aware of her again. He was amazed. On honeymoon they'd been restrained, because of

Dora's pregnancy, but all that was gone. She lay beneath him, eyes closed, her pelvic thrusts urgent and direct. When she came on him, again with that guttural cry, he knew that he could have been anybody. There was something animal about her, a woman in her season, fully on heat.

He got up early in the morning and went into the bathroom to shave before Dora was awake. When he returned to the bedroom she was lying against the pillows, the sheet pulled up beneath her breasts. She was full of milk, swollen and oozing a little from her nipples. He said, 'Shouldn't you feed the baby first?'

'Mother said she'd give him a bottle.'

He touched her, finding the skin tight and hot. She grunted again. He was getting to know that grunt, it was of eagerness and expectation. He thought, if she wants it so much she can work for her pleasure, and he pulled back the bedclothes to lie down beside her.

'Come on then,' he said, lying back. 'You might as well learn a variation.'

She didn't hesitate. She climbed astride him, taking him up to the hilt, her breasts swinging in his face. Sexual excitement gripped him once again. He had never known anything so impersonal, so basic. We are married, he thought, as the surge began. This is my wife! But where was the tenderness?

He cycled back to Gunthwaite later that morning. He told Dora there were formalities to be attended to, although he could think of none. Without a body there was no funeral, and life would simply continue as before. But he couldn't stay away.

He found Laura up against the high field walls, marking the farthest boundary of Gunthwaite land. She was wearing a wool skirt, the one she used to wear on the farm when Michael was here. She had given up her trousers, renouncing them now Michael was gone.

He said, 'I was worried for you. Don't go out without leaving a message. It isn't fair.'

'I'm not going to kill myself,' she said sourly.

'But I worry. You know that.'

'I can't think about you just now.'

She wrapped her arms around herself. The wind was biting,

sending even the heavy-fleeced sheep into the dip behind the wall. Gabriel pulled Laura down there too, and they sat for a moment out of the gale. Her skin was blue, thin enough to see through. He said, 'You're not eating. You should.'

She looked at him briefly. 'I can't. It won't go down.'

'You're starting to look ill.'

'Am I? So are you.'

He made a sound, half laugh, half sob. 'It isn't because of Michael,' he managed. 'God! Dora doesn't give a damn about my dead brother, she just wants sex. At any other time I'd think, wow, just my luck to marry a girl who likes nothing better than a good roger. Not now, though.'

'It isn't her fault,' said Laura mildly. 'Women have needs.'

'Everybody does. Right now my needs aren't entirely sexual, though. I want to think and I can't when I'm stuck up Dora.'

Laura sighed. 'I wish I could stop thinking. Just for a moment. Even when I sleep I see him.'

The lapwings were swirling in a cloud across the high, bare fields. The landscape was beautiful here, its harshness serving to remind them that their tragedies would come and go, while this remained.

'I can only think of him ploughing,' said Gabriel. 'It's better when I'm in the house. I get flashes of how he used to look, scowling at me down the table when I was about thirteen.'

'Did he scowl at you?'

'You know he did.'

'Not so much a scowl, perhaps. A look of – exasperation!'

She smiled to herself, glad to have found the right word. Her eyes closed for a moment or two, and the sight of her blue-veined lids made him fearful suddenly, that she would fade to nothing and be gone.

'Come back and eat something,' he said determinedly. 'I've had barely a thing today. We can eat together.'

'Doesn't Dora even feed you?' enquired Laura.

'Neither me nor the baby. It's a bit alarming, really.'

Laura got wearily to her feet. 'She'll get over it. Her body excites her. She likes it. She's never learned to hate her sexual needs.'

Gabriel caught her hand. 'You don't hate yours, do you? Not now?'

'Now more than ever,' said Laura. She pulled away and walked back to the farm.

A pattern emerged in the coming days. Gabriel stayed at Gunthwaite all day, and returned to Fairlands every night. He was exchanged on the cart for Alan and David each morning and afternoon. More often than not he saw Laura walking again in the fields, heading up towards the high ground, exhausting herself. On the third day, as he climbed down at Fairlands, David commented, 'Poor Auntie Laura's out walking already. I know she's sad, but I wish she'd get right again. Mum says the house is a nightmare, and only Laura can manage it, and if she doesn't get well we'll have to be properly evacuated to someone we don't know.'

'She didn't eat her breakfast again,' added Alan, who liked his food. They ran off towards the schoolroom.

Gabriel waved automatic farewell to Dora. He was weary. They always did it in the mornings, a last quick thrill after the serious excitement of the night. She was so different to what he had imagined, he almost thought she wasn't Dora at all. Was she ever sweet? Or innocent? If not, he'd been more than a fool. But he wasn't about to complain. The frilly bedroom was a pleasure house, far removed from the real world. He no longer thought about Dora's parents, or indeed about anything except physical satisfaction. It was an antidote to the anxieties of the day.

His leave was almost over. In two days he'd be back at the base. He imagined telling Philip that his wife was the hottest thing he'd ever known. But he felt unsettled. What would a woman like that do while he was gone?

He slid off the cart at Gunthwaite and went at once into the house. The Frenchwomen were in the kitchen, one of them writing a letter amidst the remains of breakfast, the other spooning some sort of porridge into his father's obedient mouth. At this rate it would be lunchtime before breakfast was finished. There was no routine any more, he thought. It might be that routine didn't matter, but in a house like this its absence meant nothing got done. He would go out in a moment and talk to Bill Mayes, get him to gather the sheep at least, but the farm was a mystery to him, he'd been away too long. The many tasks that needed doing were a jumble in his head.

He felt a weight of depression gathering. He went in search of Rosalind and found her in the morning room, arranging some winter grasses in a vase. 'Isn't there something more important you ought to do?' he asked wearily.

She glanced at him. 'Not at all. I've cooked the breakfast and fed Mary and the boys and struggled for half an hour to light the copper, and in a moment I shall go out and see what on earth that stupid foreman is trying to avoid doing today. But in the meantime I need to calm my nerves. I don't know what we're going to do.'

Gabriel slumped on to the sofa. 'Father. The boys. The farm. The house. Even the baby. We can't leave unless Laura can cope.'

'She can't!' Rosalind threw up her hands. 'Of course, it's unfair to ask her to, but if she doesn't, it's all such a mess. I can't take the boys back to London, not with the raids, and I simply can't give up my job.'

'I'm sure you could,' said Gabriel.

'No.' She returned to her arrangement. 'It's rather important, actually. People depend on me. I only got the job because of Howard, and I may be a small cog, but it's a jolly important wheel. Intelligence and all that. I can't say more.'

Gabriel laughed incredulously. 'You haven't become a mandarin, have you? Negotiating America's entry to the war?'

'Of course not.' She finished the arrangement and stood back to admire her handiwork. 'It's to do with France. That's all I can say.'

Gabriel was nonplussed. Eventually he said, 'Well, good for you, Sis. I didn't know you had it in you.'

'Neither did I. But Howard seems to have had a good idea. Anyway, if the worst really does come to the worst, we'll have to hire someone. Several someones perhaps, since Mother's moved out so conclusively. And none of this is fair on Laura, but I do so wish she'd pull herself together and get on with things!'

She looked distracted and somewhat overwrought. Rosalind's forte had always been people, thought Gabriel. Domestication was beyond her. As a diplomatic wife she had excelled, remembering names and titles, tripping lightly from party to party with her husband's interests always in mind. She wasn't suited to Gunthwaite. But then, he thought, neither should

Laura be. It was an amazement to him that someone so sophisticated could be at ease here too. Laura took on the colour of her surroundings much as her eyes reflected the colour of her clothes, and it was sometimes possible to wonder if she was in fact colourless, an invisible person. She seemed at this moment to be about to disappear into thin air.

He went into the hall, picking up one of the old, heavy overcoats which they kept for work in the fields. He had to find Laura and talk to her.

He had walked for twenty minutes before he saw her. She was sitting on a rock, looking down the valley, her hair blowing back from her face. He called her name when he saw her but she didn't respond, and as he came up to her he saw that her lips were almost white with cold.

'Are you trying to freeze to death, Laura?'

She looked up at him. 'I don't know. I was going to come down in the end.'

'But why are you here? What use is it? We need you at the farm with us.'

She sighed. His heart went out to her, sitting on her rock, filled with a sadness that nothing could assuage. He reached out and took her in his arms, holding her. 'How can I help you? There has to be something I can do.'

'You can't give me Michael back.'

'Damn Michael! To hell with Michael! He should never have bloody gone!'

His breath was warm on her cheek. She hadn't realised how cold she was, chilled to the marrow. At least it stopped the pain, she thought, drinking deep of the clear cold air. But she was empty still. She was as hollow as an old tree, a space which used to contain life and now was dead. Gabriel's warmth touched her. She stirred in his arms, aware of a need to turn away from sterility and move towards the sun. His lips touched hers, a moth's breath of a kiss. It was like a burn, stinging her flesh. It would be easier to die than go on living, she thought. But she didn't want to die. Michael had left work for her to do.

'Kiss me again,' she murmured. 'It warms me.'

His lips were sore from Dora's kisses. He was sated, beyond desire. He bent his head to kiss her once more, softly, tenderly, feeling her mouth open beneath his. Their tongues met like

440

furtive friends. He opened his coat and enfolded her, holding her frozen body close. At the touch of his thighs on hers, she felt stirring in her belly. She wasn't surprised. Life is never stronger than at the moment when death seems most near. Her body fought to survive, her soul forbade all surrender. She was a woman, and she was empty. He must fill her up.

'I need you to make love to me,' she said.

He took in his breath. 'You're upset. You don't mean that.'

She said, 'It doesn't matter, does it? Michael's gone.'

'Dora—'

'Do you care about that? I thought you didn't. I thought you slept with other women all the time.'

'How do you know that?'

'Your letters. It's what you don't say, not what you do.'

She was a whore after all, so businesslike. He'd had his fill of women, he couldn't satisfy her. But all at once her hardness seemed to fall from her. 'Please don't turn away,' she said plaintively. 'I feel as if I'm dead. Bring me to life again, Gabriel. Make me better.'

She pressed against him, skin and bone, her breasts no longer luscious, two barely feminine additions to her rib cage. She wasn't desirable, he thought, this waif, this bereaved woman. But he knew then, and knew absolutely, that he loved her.

He kissed her again, holding her head, forcing his tongue into her in mimicry of his sex. She groaned and he pulled her down to the cold earth, the coat enveloping them like a tent. He unfastened her thin cardigan, pulled open her blouse, discovered those thin little breasts. He put his mouth to each one, the nipples like ice against his tongue. As he held each stalk between his teeth she cried out in real pain. He knew he had not hurt her. It was the pain of returning life.

He was almost ready. He knelt to pull off her underwear, stiffened by the sight of her stockinged legs, meeting in a moist, dark forest. She was crying again, and he thought of Michael. Damn Michael, he was gone, he held no rights here. The wind was blowing hard, thickened with rain. He pulled himself free of his clothes and went down to her. Her cold body closed around him, his head was spinning, his heart was thundering. He thought he hovered between heaven and hell.

Laura stared up at him, her eyes open wide. Her teeth were

clenched tight. He began to move in her and she felt as if the bow of a violin was being drawn across her senses, back and forth, back and forth, an agony of feeling. Her head sank back and her eyes began to close. She could trust Gabriel. No need to hide her pleasure or her pain. Her orgasm was building, a swelling balloon of tension that he, with his sword, must explode. Colours flashed across her closed eyes, blues, reds, a vivid emerald green. Michael was dead, she thought in anguish, dead, dead, dead! But her body, that lifetime rebel, opened the floodgates of pleasure.

She cried out, choking it back at once. No one liked a screaming whore. Gabriel was propped up on his elbows, staring anxiously down at her. She knew he hadn't come. She was very aware of him, locked in her body. She moved gently, purposefully, whispering, 'It's all right. You were good. You can let go.'

His face contorted, he let out a sound more sob than laugh. This is the act that shares everything, thought Laura, sorrows, pleasures, secrets of the heart. But she couldn't know what Gabriel was thinking. It was like a shout in his head. Why in God's name did I ever marry Dora?

Chapter Nine

The Italians were babbling again. There was some problem over food, he didn't understand it, they seemed to live on cheese and Chianti. They very decently included him in all meals, sometimes apologising, he thought, for the condition of the wine. It made him chuckle. He'd been living for months on bully beef and oily water, and now this.

It was clear that they didn't know where he should go. These boys hadn't been in the desert long, and they appeared to be in constant dispute. Should they go here, should they go there? Should they put some of their tanks forward or keep them back? Yesterday a German officer had turned up in an armoured car and made representations of some sort, but they hadn't been well received. Michael had kept his head down. Once the Germans got him he'd have no chance of sliding back over the line.

He wished he knew where he might be. It had taken him an entire day to find this little lot, by which time he'd been almost delirious from dehydration and heat exhaustion. They'd stuck him under a tank for a day or two until he felt better, making him sit on top whenever they had to move. In consequence he was completely disorientated, possibly as were they all.

God, but the sun was hot. He screwed up his eyes against the glare, trying to sort out a series of dots on the horizon. But he was imagining things again. Nothing there except flies. He wasn't used to this sort of idleness, he longed for something to happen.

One of the officers was walking past. Michael got up, automatically reaching for the scrap of paper on which he had written his name, rank and serial number, to be passed to the Red Cross to reassure the people at home. The man looked at it, smiled politely and moved on.

Michael felt a gathering sense of helplessness, of complete and utter futility. No one knew he was here. No one cared. He could pass the whole bloody war as the pet of an Italian tank unit obsessed with Chianti and cheese. 'Doesn't anyone speak English?' he roared. 'Doesn't anyone at all?'

One of the men leaned out of his tank. He was offering another cylinder of the bloody smoked cheese.

Laura was well again. She had come down from the hill with energy enough to relight the copper, send the men for the sheep and provide a nourishing lunch. Rosalind was bemused, but she couldn't ask Gabriel what had gone on. He was off back to Fairlands on foot, in the wind and the rain. *'Oh, là là!'* said Sophie mysteriously in French. 'He had it coming, that one. He's taken his time.'

Rosalind, who was fluent, asked her what she meant. But Sophie merely rolled her eyes.

They didn't see Gabriel again until his leave was over. He called in, dressed in uniform, on his way to the station with Dora. His mother was to accompany them, cadging a ride on Fairlands petrol. 'But I must talk to Laura first,' explained Gabriel. 'We've got to decide about the farm.'

'You won't decide anything,' snapped his mother. 'Whatever you say, she'll have her own way. You know what she's doing now? Moving those land girls into the cottage next to mine. All extravagance. Now Michael's gone, there'll be nothing to stop her.'

He left her moaning to Dora, took Laura into the study and closed the door. She gave him a slight smile. 'She never stops, does she?'

'No.' He stood in silence, looking at her.

At last Laura said, 'I'm all right, you know. You don't have to worry.'

'But I do. I always will. I wanted you to know – to understand – the other day was important to me.'

She said, 'You were very kind. I shouldn't have made you do it.'

'Any time!' He tried to joke, but it didn't come off. 'Any time,' he said again.

444

After a moment she said, 'I feel so old, now. Quite grown up. I'll take care of everything for you here. We won't sleep together again.'

'Because of Dora?'

She nodded.

He said, 'But you need someone. She wouldn't be hurt, she'd never know.'

She lifted her shoulders in a shrug. 'Possibly. I don't know. I can't tell what's going to happen any more.'

'We'll be careful. Just now and then. It's something we both need, after all.'

'You've got Dora. You don't need me.'

He reached out and took her hand. 'My God. If you only knew.'

The touch was like a spark to tinder. Their blood caught fire. In a moment she was in his arms. His tongue searched her mouth, brutal, unforgiving. But they hadn't any time.

'Come and see me at the base,' he murmured. 'You must.'

'Yes. If I can. But there's so much to do.'

'I know. My darling girl, I never wanted this for you! It shouldn't be.'

'It wasn't your fault. I keep telling myself it wasn't Michael's either. But I'm angry still.'

'Yes. This helps, doesn't it?'

'Yes. Oh, yes!'

They kissed again. She was urgent, and couldn't be satisfied. He had to go. She pulled away, going to the window to compose herself. He could hear Dora's voice in the kitchen, knew he should feel guilt, but there was nothing there at all. He was owed this, wasn't he? He gave Dora what she wanted. He could please himself in return.

His mind was distracted, he was already thinking of flying again. He'd be on patrol tomorrow, could be dead by tomorrow night. If something had to be said, he would say it now. 'I love you.'

She glanced at him, gave her head a little shake. 'No, Gabriel.'

'But yes. Don't worry, I don't expect anything. I just want you to know.'

He went out of the room. Laura stood at the window, waiting. Soon she saw him leave with Dora and his mother, saw him glance back once to where he knew she must be. She lifted her hand in a tiny wave.

The days settled into something of a routine. Laura felt as if she was living in a dream, although really nothing had changed. But inside her everything had. There was no Michael to expect, no Michael even to write to, for whom she must save the incidents of her days like nuggets of gold. In the mornings Mary looked up from her crib with such innocence that her mother's heart was tormented. Her daughter didn't deserve a childhood crippled by sadness. But where could she ever find joy?

There was only Gabriel. She held to him like a talisman, the only person who knew anything of her, the only person who understood. There was no need to feel guilty. Michael was dead, and Dora under no threat. She was a whore again, thought Laura philosophically. It wasn't strange for a man to stay with his wife because of his mistress.

Dora visited most weeks, bringing her baby, Piers, and sometimes fruit from the Fairlands' glasshouse. She was bored, thought Laura, who had no time to be bored. But she well understood the bleakness of heart that could waylay someone. She made an effort with Dora. They made a pram cover together, each corner filled with French embroidery stitches. But all too often Laura sat and sewed while Dora smoked a cigarette and paced the room, saying, 'Doesn't it kill you, living here? Everything's so dull.'

She stood at the window one day, watching Sophie guide old Mr Cooper across the yard. 'They look as doddery as each other,' she remarked.

Laura glanced up. 'Do they? Sophie shouldn't go out in the wind, she has a weak chest.'

'She's stopping, actually. You're right, she has a cough. Now look, the old boy's wandering off. He's getting worse, Laura. He's impossible.'

Laura put down the sewing and got up to see. Mr Cooper was taking slow but purposeful steps down the drive and Sophie, caught by a coughing fit, was trotting to catch up. All at once she stopped, put her hands to her ample bosom, and fell.

'My God! Sophie!' Laura flew from the house and out to the yard. The wind blew her hair across her face. She scratched at it, crouching over Sophie's still form. The yellow hair was streaked with iron grey. The make-up seemed like a mask put on after death. But she lived still. Her breathing sounded like a bellows.

'Do you need a doctor?' Dora had old Mr Cooper firmly by the arm. 'I'll put him in the house and cycle into Gunthwaite. I'll get a blanket. She'll have to stay here, we can't lift her by ourselves.'

'The men are in Long Meadow—'

'She needs the doctor most.'

So Dora wasn't helpless, thought Laura ruefully. Like most of the British, she rose to a challenge. As for herself, there was a great weight of tears in her breast. She couldn't bear to lose Sophie now. Fat, vulgar, silly Sophie, generous to a fault. Her eyes weren't quite closed. Laura put her fingers against Sophie's pallid cheek.

'Don't worry,' she whispered. 'I'll take care of you. Like always. I promise.'

Dora brought blankets and a pillow, and cycled off at speed. Suppose the children woke? thought Laura. Suppose Sophie died. She wondered where Marie might be. Probably taking tea with Mrs Cooper. They liked to spar now and then.

Time passed. No one came. Old Mr Cooper stood at the window and watched the odd tableau in the yard. Sophie was snuffling as if her nose needed blowing, Laura searched for a handkerchief. There was one in Sophie's pocket. Just then she heard a car. Thank God. The doctor.

But it wasn't Dr Hendon. Dora sat in the front seat and called through the open window, 'I brought the Polish doctor, he was visiting in the village. I was so lucky. Is she all right?'

'The same, I think. Go into the house, Dora, and see to the children.'

The doctor strode across the cobbles. 'At your service, Madame.' He clicked his heels and bowed.

'Dr Zwmskorski.' He looked quite inappropriate, nothing like the rumpled Dr Hendon.

He surveyed the yard. 'How this reminds me,' he said mournfully. 'So much like my much-loved home. Such beauty!' He touched his fingers to Laura's cheek.

She stared up at him. 'Sophie's very ill,' she said after a moment.

'Indeed.' He turned almost reluctantly to the patient. 'A

447

stroke, I imagine. We must fetch her inside.'

'There's no one to help—'

'I am very strong. Support her, please.'

Laura pushed Sophie's inert body into a sitting position. Zwmskorski bent down and took her across his shoulders, standing up with a deep exhalation of breath. He swayed under the weight, then walked steadily into the house. Sophie's stertorous breathing hiccuped and went on.

They put her on the sofa in the morning room. The doctor listened to her chest. 'So. It is all quite plain. The coughing strained her, causing the stroke. Not severe. She may get better.'

'What can we do?' Laura hovered unhappily.

'Nothing. Nurse her and wait.'

Dora brought more blankets. How were they to manage? thought Laura. It was one thing upon another. The doctor said to Dora, 'You are useful as well as charming. I shall visit every day.'

Dora said, 'I'll come each day too, Laura. You can't nurse her by yourself.'

'Could you? Oh, Dora, that's so kind!' Laura thought woefully how much she had misjudged her. Dora was proof that silly girls grew up into sensible women. She deserved Gabriel after all.

The doctor was to give Dora and Piers a lift back to Fairlands. Dora went to fetch the baby while Zwmskorski gave Sophie a last inspection. He said, 'These women don't live long. The life takes its toll. You were sensible. A woman should always give up while her cheeks still bloom.'

She took in her breath. Blood pounded in her ears, like drums. She said slowly, 'I don't believe we've ever met, sir. Although I understand you had – connections – with Marie at one time. She did have a period of misfortune in Paris, I know.'

'I was the one suffering misfortune. I could not afford the divine Laura, the toast of all Paris. I was told she made love like a goddess.'

'That wasn't me,' whispered Laura.

'No?' His fingers touched her neck in the suspicion of a caress. 'I saw you there. I dreamed of what we would do together. I longed to sleep with you.'

Suddenly she was back in her room, the customer eager and expectant and she gently probing to discover his true desires. She looked up into the doctor's face. He said, 'I am now a little more wealthy.'

'I don't – I really don't—'

'You're a widow now. Perhaps you need some money of your own?' They stood looking at each other. He had a thin, unsmiling face for all his charm.

'Will you tell Dora?' she asked.

'I don't know. The English are so odd about these things. Believe me, your skills shouldn't go to waste.'

Some nuance in his voice alerted her. 'My – skills?'

'Those lovely cherry lips. Their fame spread through Paris. It could spread here.'

In a high, strangled voice she said, 'I can't! Please. I don't do that any more.'

There was a step in the hall. It was Marie. She saw Sophie, paled and sank into a chair. *'Mon Dieu.* When?'

'Two hours since. A stroke. She may get well.'

Marie put her fist to her mouth. 'Sophie. May Christ preserve her, she's a good woman, despite it all.'

Dora was ready to leave. Zwmskorski bowed to Laura. 'Madame. Remember what I said. I'll call again tomorrow.'

She turned aside, looking down at Sophie, adjusting her pillows. Marie eased her friend's heavy body into a more comfortable position. They heard the car driving away. Now there was nothing but the harsh note of Sophie's breathing.

Marie said, 'He should not have come. What does he want?'

Laura shrugged. 'You know. A good long suck.'

'Why not give it him? Keep him quiet.'

'I don't think he's going to talk. Besides, I don't do it any more.'

'Don't get respectable! You do it with the pilot.'

Laura gasped. She should have known. There were no secrets of that sort between women of her kind. 'I didn't do that! I needed him. I had nothing else.'

Marie let out a bitter laugh. 'I know, *chérie!* There's always a good reason. And you've reason enough to take this one in the barn and work him over. You don't want people talking.'

'Michael's dead. I don't care.'

'Your daughter lives. Think of her, once in a while.'

Laura went to sit beside Sophie, looking down into her raddled, unconscious face. Look what she had become. Fat, frowsy and old before her time. It wouldn't help anyone to give in to someone like Zwmskorski. She hadn't come this far to slide back again. She thought of how polite he would be to Dora, when he had been so blunt with her. If it all came out no one would treat her as they did now. There would be leers and sideways glances. But, of course, it didn't matter any more. Michael was gone.

Michael sat in the truck, feet braced against the side. Travelling like this across the desert pummelled you black and blue. He tried to think of something, anything, that wasn't this endless shaking. They couldn't even look out, since every time he lifted a corner of the canopy the guard yelled at him and waved a gun. All Italians were not sloppy soldiers, it seemed.

He considered his fellow prisoners; one pilot, a South African with concussion and a broken arm; two privates who had failed to wake up when their unit moved off; and the surviving member of a tank crew who had made it out of the turret seconds before the explosion. Silent, glum, resigned human beings.

Michael considered the guard. He had shown no sign so far of speaking English. He said to the guard, 'Is it all right if we talk?'

The man looked blank. Michael repeated the question. One of the privates said, 'What the bloody hell do you want to say?'

'I thought we'd try and escape,' said Michael.

The South African groaned and turned his head aside. He was in no state to try anything. But the tank survivor said, 'OK by me. Are we near the line?'

'I've no idea. It's a month since I was picked up.'

'Well then,' said the private. 'Bit of a bloody waste of time then, ain't it? I don't want to die in the desert.'

'But we might discover where we are, if we keep our eyes and ears open. This is the first time I've been moved back, I think. So far I've been shuffled up and down the line.'

The tank survivor said, 'We've all been up and down this bloody desert more times than I can count. Who wants a desert? I'm for anything gets us back to some decent beer and a chance of going home, that's me.'

Michael grinned. 'So we'll try it? We're agreed? Let's all do our best to find out just where we are.'

He tried to lean a little more comfortably against the steel side of the truck. The guard was glowering at him, as well he might. It was so hot in here. He tried to think of something cool, clean and still. The sheets of his bed, that Laura scented with lavender in the wash. Laura. She wouldn't come near him now, stinking as he must. He settled his mind on her. She must know by now that he was a prisoner. An officer had at last taken details to be transferred to the Red Cross. With a little luck and a lot more planning, he could get out of this. What would be the first thing to do when he got back to the unit? Read her letters, of course. He could endure anything knowing that she was there.

Laura looked from the window and saw Dora cycling up the drive. The baby was strapped on to her back, and when Dora saw her she waved and wobbled precariously. Why wasn't she like Dora? The girl was so simply constructed, not a complication in her. Laura imagined the murky pool of her own, tangled soul. Thoughts lurked in the weeds like hunting pike.

Dora came in laughing, and Laura helped her unfasten the baby. 'He was so good! How's Sophie?'

'Better. She's coming round, but she stills sleeps a lot. And her speech is slurred.'

'Wojtyla said it might be. Is he coming today?'

'Yes. I don't like him much, actually. He's very forward.'

Dora giggled. 'Don't be such a prude! He likes women, that's all. I'm sure he likes you.'

'What does he say?' Her heart shuddered, despite herself.

'Only that you're very pretty and very brave.'

Marie was sitting with Sophie. She was reading some book out loud that made Sophie's downdrawn face almost woebegone. 'It's rubbish!' she said to Laura. 'Stop her.'

'No wonder you took to the streets,' snapped Marie, and banged the book closed.

Not for the first time, Laura thanked her stars that Dora had never acquired any French. She wondered why she had come, since she didn't after all nurse Sophie. After a ritual exchange of pleasantries, she retired to the kitchen, getting under Dinah's feet and watching Laura make Sophie a tisane. But the babies were happy enough. Seated together on a rug, they stared at each other with thoughtful eyes.

Mary, months the older, reached out and took Piers' rattle. He let it go without complaint.

'They get on so well,' said Dora. 'Wojtyla can give us a lift back.'

'I wish you wouldn't,' said Laura. 'You know what people will say.'

'I don't care,' said Dora bravely. 'It isn't as if I'd do anything. I don't want to be staid and boring all my life. Some of the wives live near the aerodromes, and so should I. I'm so out of everything here.'

'You couldn't take Piers, though.'

'Mother would look after Piers. She loves him. She wouldn't care if I wasn't there at all.'

Laura said nothing. She was more than a little shocked. Good women didn't leave their babies with barely a moment's thought. She couldn't leave Mary, she thought. To wake up and not see her would be torment.

'Have you heard from Gabriel?' she asked jerkily.

'What? Oh. Yes, a note. All's well. They'll be resting soon. He may move on to bomber escort, he says. And they stooge about doing reconnaissance and that sort of thing.'

'Will he come home?'

'I don't know.' Dora turned her innocent eyes to Laura's. 'Mother says if he does come home, we should go off by ourselves for a few days. I thought we should open up another of the cottages, perhaps?'

'Come here?' Laura blinked. She should have expected this. Michael was dead and the farm wasn't hers any more. Gabriel might not claim it, but Dora would. If Dora wanted to take over a cottage, there was nothing anyone could do to stop her.

She was conscious of a great reluctance. 'Do you want Mrs Cooper at your window every day? Gabriel won't like it.'

Dora shrugged. 'If it was Meadowside, it's half a mile from her. And there's the ford. I began to wonder – to imagine – what it might be like. A little house. All mine. Home is full of schoolchildren, you've no idea!'

She began to expand upon her theme. 'We'd have to repair

the roof. And rebuild the garden wall and keep the sheep out. Now the men aren't here we can do what we want, can't we? Make everything just as we like. We could even put a bathroom in.'

'What? Here?' The idea seemed revolutionary.

'Actually – I meant in the cottage.'

A bitter vision rose before Laura's eyes; Dora, reclining in scented water at Meadowside, while she still struggled upstairs with cans. The depression she had been warding off for days descended on her once more. She felt so tired and dispirited. Everyone needed so much from her and she had nothing left to give.

This was a bad day, she told herself. Tomorrow might be good. There was no way of telling. It was just that sometimes she woke and felt incapable of going on. With all these people around her, with her child, with her home, she felt alone.

Dora went off to look at Meadowside and make out a list of improvements. Laura made an excuse and stayed behind. The postman was wandering down the drive. He was impossibly late and no doubt full of gossip, but today she didn't want to know. She went out into the hall while Dinah spoke to him. She didn't want to be added to his tales at the next farm along: 'Young Mrs Cooper. Fair cut up she is. After all this time. And Dora Fitzalan-Howard queening it on the farm. Well, it's hers, of course. By rights. That's Gunthwaite for you and always has been.'

Dinah was calling her. 'Laura! Letters. One from Mr Gabriel, one with the regimental stamp. And one from Rosalind, by the look of it.'

Laura's heart leaped. She ran into the kitchen, ignoring the postman, and seized the envelopes. Gabriel's could wait, and Rosalind's even more so. Had they found Michael? Was he really not dead? Her fingers trembled as they spread the pages.

My Dear Mrs Cooper,
As your husband's commanding officer, I feel compelled to write and offer you my condolences on his sad demise . . .

She looked up woefully. 'It isn't anything. A letter of condolence.'

'It won't just be that,' said Dinah, and took the letter. 'They're sending his things back. And you'll get a pension. Should bloody well think so, too.'

Tom the postman said, 'Sad days, Mrs Cooper. Sad days.'

'Yes.' She fingered the other envelopes.

'Tell us what Rosalind says,' encouraged Dinah.

'We won't like it.'

'She's all right, is Rosalind. Clever. Some women aren't domestic, that's all.'

'Some women know which side their bread's buttered,' said Laura unkindly. She opened the letter, scanned it and tossed it down. 'As I thought. She's checking up on me. She's coming to stay.'

'Well, won't that be nice?' said the postman with false enthusiasm.

'Don't you go spreading our business all about,' warned Dinah. 'This family's had a lot of trouble these last weeks.'

'Sad times. Sad times,' said the postman again. 'And how's Mr Gabriel doing, then?'

'I shall read it later,' said Laura, putting the envelope in her pocket. 'Don't tell Dora he wrote, will you? It's only farm business, but she doesn't like to think she's not included.'

'Aye. Stands to reason,' said Tom, storing up yet another delicious morsel for later regurgitation.

He left at long last and Laura went up to her room. She sat on the bed and smoothed Gabriel's letter. He had a distinctive hand, large and scrawling, and he wrote in strong dark ink. He should have been the elder brother, she thought irrelevantly. He would have blossomed so much sooner.

My darling Laura,

We're in the middle of everything here – escort duties, Channel patrols, you name it. I can't tell you too much, of course, but it's all rather safer than what we were doing. No dog fights, at least none in the last week or so. We shall all be getting out of practice.

I've been given a section to lead, which is jolly good of them. I'm finding it quite hard to adjust to being one of the good pilots, although some of the kids we get nowadays give you goosepimples, they're so green. One of them is

454

called Green actually. He was a disaster at the start but he's improving.

I think of you all the time. I know you don't want to hear this, but quite honestly if I didn't have you to think about I don't know what I'd do. I've made enquiries in a village not far from here and you could come and stay at the pub. I thought you could tell everyone you had to get away for a few days. It wouldn't be surprising after all. I'd take some leave and disappear, and that would be that.

You're taking nothing away from Dora, you know. I don't mean to let her down. It's simply that I need to be with you, and I know you need me, for whatever reason. Please, Laura.

All love,
 Gabriel

She folded the letter carefully and put it away in a drawer. She felt a slow drumming of excitement. She and Gabriel in a pub, pretending to be – what? Man and wife? Pilot and short-time girl? There were enough of those, surely. There'd be no need to fuss. She could set down her burden for days on end, forget it all.

Plans began to form in her head. Rosalind could take over, and Dora could help. It amused her to think of Dora making it possible for her to sleep with Gabriel. But Dora deserved it, coming here and taking over Meadowside. Laura had no illusions. Soon she'd be in Gunthwaite itself.

Dora returned to the house full of plans. But Laura felt better now, after Gabriel's letter. Dora couldn't evict her without Gabriel's permission, she felt sure. And after all, the cottages needed to be refurbished. People needed homes, with the bombing as it was and nothing ever being built. The war that had been so sure to end by Christmas seemed likely to last for ever.

The women began to take an interest in their project. Laura decided to modernise not only Meadowside, but the pair of cottages housing Mrs Cooper and the land girls. Materials were hard to come by, and workmen harder still. Nonetheless the old men remained, used to lath and plaster and good wood. Laura scrabbled around on the farm, finding some oak in a shed, a piece of teak propping up a hay rack in the byre. Grudgingly work was begun, and in the absence of something they made do. One old man even mixed scarce plaster with straw, and plastered a good rough kitchen wall.

'I've never heard anything like it,' fumed Mrs Cooper. 'Everything will have to be redone!'

'I don't see why,' Laura demurred. 'The walls are sound enough. And the roof doesn't leak, as it did before.'

Mrs Cooper changed her tack. 'But it's all so disruptive. I don't mind for Gabriel, naturally, but what about work on the farm? Those land girls do nothing but fuss around here. No better than they should be. Mark my words.'

But somehow the old wood and rough plaster sat more easily on the cottages than anything new. With the stone slates once again lying snug instead of slithering about on rotten pegs, the dwellings seemed to regain their composure. They nestled back into themselves, smart with paint and varnish, secure for another fifty years or so of Yorkshire weather. But then came the bathroom fittings, and everyone sat up.

It was Dora who obtained them. She was determined that neither she nor Gabriel should be subjected to a privy and a tin bath. Her father knew a man who knew a man, and Dora telephoned and bribed until one day a van drove to the meadow gate, as near as it could get to Meadowside, and there was a bright white bath and basin and lavatory, complete with chain.

The land girls glared at Laura. 'For Meadowside? But no one's going to be there most of the time! And our privy stinks worse than that. It isn't fair.'

Bill Mayes said gloomily, 'You're going to need a cess pit, that you are. Brick-lined and all. Who's going to dig that then?'

And Mrs Cooper added, 'Didn't anyone consider that I might find a bathroom convenient? At my time of life?'

'There isn't room in the other cottages,' said Laura feebly.

'There is downstairs,' said Paula heatedly. 'You could build on at the back.'

'Yes, indeed!' agreed Mrs Cooper. 'A small extension to both. The girls can cart the stone from one of the fields, it's lying everywhere. And you, Laura, can exert yourself on someone else's behalf for once in your life.'

456

Laura felt a tightness in her chest. She was going to cry! She said, 'As a matter of fact, I'd like proper plumbing in Gunthwaite. If anyone should have it, then it's me.'

There was a silence. Then, to Laura's surprise, Mrs Cooper said, 'You're right, of course, Laura. Michael would want that. The big house comes first. I shall ask Dora to get another three complete sets of sanitaryware instead of two.'

Bill Mayes, purple now, said, 'And who's going to dig that bloody cess pit, then? Another bloody cess pit, just so's a few women can stick their arses in a pot! And where's the money coming? Right quick to spend when the gaffer's gone, that's what you are!'

But Laura, fortified by Mrs Cooper's unexpected support, said, 'We'll find the money. It won't be so much. And prices are up in wartime, we're making a profit. If Dora gets the stuff, we'll all help dig the pits. That's fair.'

'Fair?' Bill Mayes wagged a gnarled finger in her face. 'You'll get what's coming, that you will. You'll be sorry you thought of nothing but your pleasure. Too much water makes a woman loose, that it do!'

They stood silent while he stamped away down the track. Laura began to giggle and found she couldn't stop. She clung to the side of the shiny new bath, giggling and giggling, and the girls began, and Mrs Cooper, until they were doubled with laughter over the new white porcelain. Bill Mayes, storming off, muttered curses.

Chapter Ten

A group of twenty or so prisoners was gathered around a fire.
'So,' said Michael in a low voice, 'where do you think we are?'

'A good forty miles from our line,' whispered a voice. 'And
there are minefields, ours and theirs.'

Michael struck his fist into his palm. 'Too far.'

'We were moving up,' said someone. 'Getting ready for the
big push.'

'They've been getting ready for that for months,' said the first
voice, sourly. 'If you ask me, we're stuck here. The only reason
they haven't shipped us out is because they don't want to spare
the men.'

Beyond the firelight the young Italian guards leaned on their
rifles, smoking and talking. No one really cared if they escaped,
that was the thing. Prisoners were an encumbrance. They were
being moved back, little by little, gathering a man here and a
couple there. Most were wounded and disappeared off in
ambulances. The rest, the healthy ones, simply hung around
until someone decided to truck them out.

It would be easy of course if they were prepared to kill.
Michael had a blade hidden in the sole of his shoe. But somehow
he couldn't imagine using it on the boy who so liberally handed
out cigarettes and Chianti, let alone the truck driver who sang
arias from favourite operas before breakfast. He wasn't suited to
war, he thought. He found it hard to take it seriously. At
Gunthwaite, imagining the enemy, he had felt warlike enough.
Here, facing his enemy's human face, it was different.

Rosalind was laden with parcels. She swept into the kitchen on a
tide of perfume, embracing the boys, insisting on kissing Laura,
recoiling only a little at the sight of the lop-sided Sophie making
a pair with her father by the fire.

458

'Your mother wants you to go across for tea,' said Laura. 'She wants to complain about the building.'

'Oh God!' Rosalind groaned. 'I'll go later. I've been so worried about you all. But everything looks quite back to normal.'

'Almost,' said Laura tightly. 'Dora visits rather a lot. She seems to think Gunthwaite's more or less hers.'

'Yes. I suppose she might.' Rosalind paused. 'You haven't heard anything, I suppose?'

'About Michael? A letter from his commanding officer. They're sending his things. Nothing about how it happened, nothing at all.'

'No. Perhaps it's best.'

The boys were clamouring for their presents. There was a toy car and a set of toy aeroplanes, a Spitfire, a Hurricane and a Wellington bomber. They at once began to squabble over them and Rosalind looked perplexed. She knew nothing about children, thought Laura. At least, she knew nothing about her boys. She should have bought two sets of planes.

She was restless and unable to settle. She wanted to tell Rosalind she was going away for a few days, but the moment eluded her. After dinner, Dora came across in the car, much to Laura's surprise. 'Where did you get the petrol?' she asked, more sharply than she intended.

Dora made a face. 'Can't you guess? The black market. Wojtyla knows someone. And really, I can't believe the entire war effort will crumble because I use the car. Don't look so po-faced, Laura, you're such a prude!'

Laura blushed. She went to walk outside, knowing that Dora would imagine she was offended. It was guilt, of course. She was ashamed. But even if she had been ten times as guilty, she would still be doing this, she thought. Why? Because there is nothing else, said a voice in her head. She wasn't strong enough to stand quite alone.

'Laura!' It was Rosalind. She had come to find her.

'I'm here,' called Laura. She was hidden by the apple trees.

When she emerged Rosalind said, 'Good heavens. You look like a ghost. Really, you mustn't mind Dora. She's very young.'

'I'm not upset.'

'You are a little.'

Laura let the lie stand.

'You must be very tired of staying here,' said Rosalind. 'Especially with no electricity. Michael ought to have bought a generator or something. He was terribly old fashioned.'

'It wasn't that. Gunthwaite doesn't suit change.'

After a moment Rosalind said, 'I didn't mean to criticise, you know.'

Laura's teeth flashed in a smile. 'No. I'm sure you didn't.'

She took a deep breath and seized her moment. 'As a matter of fact, I was planning on a few days' away. I thought you might hold the fort.'

'Me?' Rosalind was taken aback.

'You did so well before.'

It was demurely said, but Rosalind burst into laughter. 'My dear girl! What a consummate lie. I'm hoist by my own petard. I was going to suggest that you go away, but I wasn't intending to take your place. I thought Dinah could come to stay.'

Laura was bemused. 'Where did you think I should go?'

Rosalind linked arms with her. 'Now that is a difficult question. I've been thinking how I might answer it and still be truthful. But I've decided I can be blunt with you. I thought you might visit France.'

Thoughts clicked in Laura's head. Rosalind's husband, Howard, was in the diplomatic corps. He had come back to a very secret job. And what did Rosalind do that required a glamorous, cosmopolitan woman of the world? 'You recruit agents?' she remarked.

'How clever of you, my dear. I noticed from the first that you had brains. When I find someone who would suit, I have to decide a lot of things. Would they be obvious? Can they take the pressure? Are they clever enough to make their own decisions, even if we can't tell them what to do?'

First the flattery, thought Laura. But all she said was, 'And then?'

'Then we ask them. At least, I ask them. It isn't all up to me, of course. After that there's a training period, and some people fail. You need courage, you see. And motivation. I thought now that Michael was gone you might have more than enough.'

Laura pulled free of her arm and turned on her. 'You thought

I might have nothing left to live for. I still have my daughter!'

'Of course. Of course you do. But if we don't win this war, what will your daughter have? What will any of our children have? A nightmare world.'

Rosalind's face was set. Underneath her smiles and affectations she was strong as steel. Laura said, 'What would I have to do?'

'I can't tell you that, I'm afraid. I don't know. Live in France as a Frenchwoman, that's all I can say. For a few weeks, a few months possibly.'

'I can't decide. I'll have to think.'

'Of course.' The coaxing, understanding Rosalind was showing now.

'Why don't you go away for those few days you mentioned?' she went on. 'You might as well. You can let me know what you've decided when you get back.'

Laura took in her breath. It was too easy, too pat. Something was bound to go wrong. She thought of Gabriel, and felt a fugitive warmth. She was so tired of cold and loneliness.

The room was small and dark. They could hear glasses clinking in the bar below. 'Sorry,' said Gabriel. 'It was the best they could do. You should have given me some notice.'

'I know. But the chance came and I couldn't turn it down.' She put her hat and coat on the bed.

'I'm so glad you didn't.'

He took her in his arms. They didn't at once kiss but stood looking at each other, taking in all the differences, and all the remembered things. Laura felt her spirits begin to rise, felt her lungs inflate with optimism once again. She was so sick of misery and work. For these few days she was set free.

Gabriel said, 'There's a strand of grey in your hair.'

She studied him in return. 'There is in yours too. Not so plain in blond hair, but I can see it.'

'I love you,' he said. 'I can't help it. It's like breathing.'

'And I need you to love me. It makes me feel safe.'

He bent his head to hers. The kiss was soft and exploratory. They had three days, there was no hurry. But it seemed to open a trapdoor in Laura's soul, letting loose all the thoughts and emotions that she could never express. She could talk, she thought wonderingly. She had lived for years now watching every word that was uttered and here, with Gabriel, nothing need be kept back. But suddenly there was nothing she wanted to say. There was just his mouth on hers, his hands on her breasts, his body that must join to hers.

She put her arms around his neck and turned her face from him. Their bodies seemed to yearn for each other, their skins seemed to burn for each other's touch. Gabriel ran his hands up her thighs and held her buttocks, rolling himself against her, and she murmured, 'Why don't you want this to be Dora instead of me?'

'Because you excite me more than any woman I will ever know,' he said. 'It can't be wrong to feel like this!' He lifted her skirt, discovering the bare flesh at the top of her thighs like a secret garden. She was wearing respectable cotton drawers, and he eased them down. 'These would never have done in the Rue de Claret.'

She leaned back to look at him. 'I don't believe I ever let a client do it standing up.'

He pulled himself free of his clothes. She leaned against him, exciting him with the ease of long practice, tempting him with gentle, pressing thrusts. But he couldn't wait. He put his hands behind her, pulling her thighs apart, bending his knees to aim himself into her, finding the place. As he straightened, and he filled her up, the sounds of evening became like clarion calls.

She clung to him, caught on a pinnacle of feeling, his smallest movement like a dart deep inside. Control was her habit, but it was lost to her. Not since Henri had a man excited her so without her willing it. She was coming before him, clinging to his shoulders, her feet barely touching the floor, and he was holding her, loving her, comforted by the very act of giving her comfort. She hung back from him, held by his arms, linked at the groin, a woman lost in abandonment. As the pulses ran through her, emptying her, taking away all her pain, she let out small, animal gasps.

When she subsided, crying a little, against him, he said, 'There then. That's better.' And he held her to him while he laid her down, and satisfied himself.

There was an odd feeling about the next days. They were uniquely, unexpectedly happy. Day and night, planes roared in the skies above them, and sirens wailed distantly. The war was with them, they couldn't ignore it, but somehow it was just the setting for these stolen hours. War was desperate, without rules. And so were they.

Once or twice, strolling down the street in the twilight after a poor dinner, they would see one of Gabriel's squadron coming towards them. They would dive into a doorway, or down an alley, anything to get away. 'How will they know I'm not Dora?' Laura asked.

'They won't know anything. But I won't say you're her. It would be horrible.'

'Are you ashamed then?'

He looked at her in amazement. 'What? Of you? My God, Laura, what a thing to say! If I'm ashamed of anything it's making such a mess of things. We should have married.'

But her face became sombre. 'Don't be silly, Gabriel. Neither of us wanted it. We weren't the same people then.'

Of course it was true. He had been too young, she too unsure of herself. The moment for this was now, when Gabriel might not have time to wait for happiness, when Laura was lost and afraid. At night, when they came together in the lumpy bed, they might have been the only two people in whirling black space. They felt as if they understood everything about each other. Just as they owned each other's bodies, with the right to do with them as they wished, so with their minds.

Now and then an oddly disloyal thought intruded. Laura caught herself thinking that she would never have known this, if Michael had not died. She and Gabriel would have remained at that level of detached physical interest, and no more. They could never have progressed to a time when they would lie together, he in her, talking softly, honestly, not wanting to go on because then they must part. And when the end came, it was the more exquisite because they knew they couldn't wait to do it again.

But she was only staying for three days. On the last morning, absorbed in each other, breakfasting late, they didn't notice the man by the bar until he said, 'Hello, Gabriel.'

It was Philip Lansbury. Gabriel said, 'Hello, Phil,' and then, stiffly, 'I think you know Laura.'

'Yes. Of course. Mrs Cooper.'

She could feel her cheeks start to flame. He would think so badly of her. She was stealing Dora's husband, now she had none of her own. Gabriel said, 'I'm sorry, Phil. I couldn't tell you.'

'I can see that. But you're wanted back. We lost Green last night, we're under strength.'

'Christ! What happened?'

'Flak. Never had a chance. Just when he was getting to be some use.'

'Yes. Poor bastard.'

Laura drew back a little. She felt as if someone had whisked back the covers from her lovely warm bed. The world was with them again, making demands, taking sacrifices, always asking more than she could reasonably give. She thought of Gunthwaite, and Mary. She thought of Rosalind, and what she had asked. Why hadn't she talked of that with Gabriel? They had spoken of everything except that. Now there was no time, she didn't know what to say.

Back in their room, watching him throw clothes into a suitcase, she felt shaky and afraid. 'Philip disapproves, doesn't he?' she managed. 'And he's right. We ought to be ashamed.'

'Are you?' He looked up at her, dragging the straps of the case tight. She shook her head.

'But I'm no judge,' she added. 'I was a prostitute. My body was for sale.'

He said fiercely, 'But I was different for you. I *am* different. We'll do the right thing despite this, so Philip doesn't matter. What anyone thinks doesn't matter. This feels like a miracle to me. If we turned our backs on it, we'd be turning our backs on heaven.'

She said, 'We won't get to heaven. Not after what we've done.'

He took her by the waist and pulled her close to him. 'Does it feel so wrong to you?'

She said nothing. But she came against him, easing her body into his, putting her hands behind his head and drawing him down to her. They stood without moving, letting their bodies say what they could not.

'I love you. I can't bear to say goodbye.'

* * *

The night was very clear. They lay in their tent, only six of them now, a scrap of paper spread on the ground by the door. They could barely see it in the moonlight. 'It's about ten miles,' said Michael softly. 'Provided you're correct, Smythe, and the line hasn't moved again. It's the best chance yet.'

'But the minefields!'

'We know the way through this one, we've watched them drive it a dozen times. As for any others, we'll have to take our chance. They're obviously getting ready to ship us out, we've got to go!'

'They might be arranging a prisoner swap. Bit bloody silly to have blown ourselves up then.'

'They just said that to keep us quiet. It won't happen. We either go tonight or resign ourselves to seeing out the war in a prison camp. I know which I'd prefer.'

The faces around him were grim. They weren't all that sure of the route through this minefield. They'd only watched from a distance. And dying was one thing, but lying maimed and helpless in the sand was something else. The flies devoured raw flesh. Michael turned his mind away from the thought, saying, 'It's a clear night. Ten miles is nothing.'

'They'll watch us for two hundred yards. And we can't run!'

'The guard's drunk, they won't care. I tell you, I'm going, with or without anyone else.'

He began to gather up his little hoard of things; some biscuits saved from their meagre meals, a Chianti bottle filled with water, the tattered little map. 'I'll give it a go,' said Smythe abruptly.

Michael was surprised. He'd expected him to stay if anyone. The others dropped their eyes. But a youngster, Matthews, suddenly said, 'I'm game. At least it's doing something.'

The others said nothing at all.

It was impossible to know if on this of all nights the guard was awake and alert. The three of them eased silently from the tent, their faces and hands smeared with carefully mixed mud. It was very quiet. Tents stood next to tanks and lorries. They could thread their way through a comfortable maze of cover. Then the notices, put up to stop the camp straying into the mines. Now they would be visible for two hundred yards at least, until they could creep behind a dune. But they dared not run.

In places lorries had left tracks, but on this hard, stony ground there was usually nothing. That was the clue, thought Michael. Keep to the stones, the mines were laid in sand. But a gasp from Smythe brought him up short. He'd been about to step on one. The detonator glinted in the moonlight, as unassuming as a bottle top. Mines could be anywhere, it seemed. And he was too far to the left.

Step by step they continued. They didn't dare look back. Michael began to imagine that his captors were lined up behind him, rifles at the ready, just in case he got through the mines. The others were following exactly in his footsteps. It was his idea, after all. When they were through this they'd set a course by the stars, those alien stars, and head for home!

It was over. He looked back at the camp, and it was already hard to see. They must have been invisible after the first fifty yards. He looked up at the spangled sky, feeling the beginnings of a dangerous exultation. It wasn't done yet, by a long chalk.

Matthews said, 'Let's get going! If we're still out here when the sun comes up, we've had it.'

Michael thought affectionately of Gabriel. He was just as impatient. He realised he'd hardly dared think of his family since he was first captured. Now, they filled his mind. Concentrate, said his conscience sternly. It all depends on getting this done. He touched his water bottle as if it were a talisman and stepped briskly out.

There was a brawling, rumbustious feel to Gunthwaite when Laura got home. Alan and David were playing noisily in the yard, and a newly weaned calf was in the stable, shouting its head off. Rosalind and Dinah were struggling with dinner in the kitchen, while Mary played on the floor and Marie sat at the table smoking a cigarette and leafing through a fashion magazine. Laura felt enfolded again; safe. Between leaving Gabriel and arriving here, she had wobbled inside herself.

Rosalind said, 'Ah, the wanderer! It's done you good, I can tell. You look calm again.'

Laura picked up her little girl and blew kisses on her neck. 'I am better. I needed a change.'

'It's good for us all. Challenge and change, that's what we need. We can't sit in comfort all our lives.'

Laura picked up the veiled reference. Rosalind wasn't going to let it drop, then. She had half expected that she might, now that in her own mind Laura was decided. She couldn't neglect Gunthwaite for some half-baked jaunt over to France. This family had given enough to the war.

So positive did she feel that she exerted herself to make a velouté sauce for dinner. She thought of the unpleasant food she and Gabriel had consumed these last few days, and giggled to herself. Perhaps the British were right and food didn't matter? At least when love was on your mind. At other times she begged to differ.

Dora drove over after dinner. 'Where does she get the petrol?' demanded Rosalind in a low voice, taking off her apron and smoothing her hair. 'I swear I'll report her, and if not her that Pole. He must have his own oil well, at least.'

Dora came in without knocking, arms full of boxes, pushing the door aside with her hip. 'Hello, Laura, are you back? I've got curtains for Meadowside. They only need cutting down.'

Laura said nothing. Did Dora think that she would make the curtains?

Rosalind said, 'Did you want to borrow the sewing machine, Dora? It's out of the Ark. I should have thought the one at Fairlands was far more advanced.'

Dora looked from one to the other. 'But I thought Laura and I could make them. In our sewing afternoons.'

'Laura hasn't time,' said Rosalind sharply.

She took a deep breath. It was time to be clear about things, which she always hated. Far better the mists of incomprehension than the brutal clarity of truth. 'I will have time, Rosalind,' she said firmly. 'I've had my weekend rest, after all. I'm not going away again.'

Rosalind said briskly, 'Nonsense! Everything's different now. No need to lock yourself away here. If Dora wants curtains she can make them herself.'

'But I'm the better seamstress. I shall start straight away.'

Dora bent to place a smacking kiss on Laura's cheek. 'Darling Laura! I knew you'd come up trumps.'

Rosalind went to the sink and clattered dishes hard enough to shatter.

They spread the material on the kitchen table. Old Mr Cooper came and patted it, and Dora said, 'Don't touch it, please. You might have greasy hands.'

'I'm sure he hasn't,' said Laura mildly. 'Don't be sharp with him, Dora. This is still his house. He means no harm.'

Dora said nothing. They each knew that when the old man died this house would be Dora's. Make these curtains well, she seemed to say. You could be living in the cottage before long, and I will be here, changing things. Laura thought of Gunthwaite under her sister-in-law's hand. Everything new and shiny. Except that it was vanity to imagine no one else could love this house as she did. Dora might be an admirable chatelaine.

As Laura cut the fabric Dora began to prattle about Gabriel and the cottage. 'I've taken the cabinet from his room. He'll want familiar things around him. And it does look splendid in the sitting room, whereas here it's quite lost.'

Rosalind snapped, 'Do help yourself, Dora. After all, this house has enjoyed its furniture for several hundred years. I'm sure it must be tired of it by now.'

Dora blinked. She didn't understand Rosalind's sudden bad temper. She said, 'I thought it was Gabriel's. No one said.'

Rosalind turned an unforgiving shoulder.

Laura was amused. Dora's innocence was reducing Rosalind to girlish spite. She finished cutting the curtain, folded it, and began thinking of bedtimes, Mary, the boys, Sophie and Mr Cooper, all to be despatched. No wonder Rosalind was frazzled, she thought idly. She must be dying to get back to London and the bombs.

There was a hammering on the door. Dora jumped and said, 'Something's happened. Oh my God!'

'It's bound to be Bill,' said Laura unconvincingly. 'A cow may be calving.'

'There isn't one due. He's gone home,' said Rosalind. Taking a deep breath she opened the door.

'Telegram,' said the postman quietly. 'I brought it up special.' They stood white-faced and stared. It had to be Gabriel. There was no one else. Dora let out a low moan. But Rosalind said vaguely, 'Look who it's for. Mrs Michael Cooper.'

'You open it,' said Laura. There was a tightness in her chest, like a hand closing around her heart. She didn't want this knowledge, she thought. Whatever it was would change things. She had struggled so hard to come to this.

Rosalind opened the envelope. Even the postman was agog. She read:

DELIGHTED INFORM LIEUTENANT MICHAEL COOPER ALIVE AND WELL STOP TAKEN PRISONER STOP ESCAPED AND RETURNED TO DUTY STOP LETTER FOLLOWS STOP

Laura closed her eyes. Rosalind read the telegram again, in a wondering voice. 'I'll have to tell Mother,' she added. 'I can't take it in. Michael's alive. He's really alive.'

She became aware of a low, sobbing moan. It was Laura, doubled over at the sink, vomiting up her supper. 'My dear,' she said at once. 'You poor dear. It's the shock, I'll make you a cup of tea.'

Laura let herself be led to a chair. She sank into it, her legs like jelly. 'I knew he wasn't dead,' she whispered. 'But I let you all persuade me. And now this! This!'

'You'd think she'd be happier,' snapped Dora, folding her arms around herself.

'It's the shock,' said Rosalind. 'It's bound to be a shock.'

'Do you want I should go over to Mrs Cooper?' enquired the postman, because he was, after all, intimately involved with all this.

'I'll go,' said Dora grimly. She wanted to be alone for a moment. It was hard to be joyous when a prize has been snatched quite away.

Laura sat shaking in the chair. What would she do now? Michael was alive and she had betrayed him. She had taken the love that was his and given it to someone else. Could she now take it back? How did you manage such a thing? She thought of Michael, and nothing was there. She remembered the people on the train when she was small, warning Sophie that orphans were a bad bargain. They were right, more right than they could know. There was no one less worthy of Michael's love than she. Promising to be constant, she had forgotten him. Promising to be faithful, she had sinned. Promising to love him, she had turned away. She put her face in her hands and sobbed.

Chapter Eleven

A head stuck itself round the door. 'Get a move on, chaps! You're wanted in the ops room.'

Gabriel sighed. He and Philip had been sitting down for barely ten minutes, taking in the rare peace. They had spent the morning on an abortive sortie over the Channel, looking for a stricken tanker. They had seen nothing, discovering on landing that it had been sunk by fighter bombers a scant half-hour before they arrived. No survivors. It was dispiriting to say the least.

They abandoned their tea and cigarettes and got up. Gabriel felt relieved that they were both wanted; this time at least it couldn't be Michael. He would never have believed that the day could come when news of his brother's survival would stun him into horrified silence. Philip had said, 'Christ, Gabriel. Now what?' Now what indeed.

He hadn't been home since. He'd had the opportunity – if you were on constant ops they liked to see the back of you every few weeks – but he couldn't face it. Not yet. Instead he'd gone to Philip's home in the borders, and tramped heather until he was dizzy. He'd tried to write a dozen times. But what could he say? Laura knew what was in his heart, and she knew too that she was lost to him. He could never take Michael's wife, even if she would come.

So there was work, work and only work. Sometimes the wry thought came to him that he didn't care any more if he died, that in fact it would remove a great inconvenience to a great many people's lives. But the recklessness that came when you no longer valued survival brought a surprising by-product; he flew like a dream. Now he was Section Leader, soon no doubt to be made up to leading the squadron. So much for justice, he thought.

He and Philip wandered off down the corridor. They had been in the Air Force long enough to know when something was up. When they arrived, everyone smiled at them, which had to be alarming. The CO motioned them both to chairs, sat at the table and linked his fingers.

'We're looking for good navigators,' he said, 'who have also spent time in France. We've got a little taxi job to do. How long since you flew a two-seater, Cooper?'

'Training, I think, sir. Not since.'

Phil said the same, but the man gestured irritably, as if troubled by a fly. 'No matter, you'll soon get the hang of it. Look at this as a way of getting off early for some leave. You can start the moment you get back.'

'From France?' said Gabriel slowly. His mouth felt dry. Was he frightened or excited? He couldn't tell.

'Of course France. I said so, didn't I? Two agents have to land there tonight. Have a shufti at the map, why don't you?'

No way they could refuse. Did they want to refuse? He glanced at Philip, noting the telltale twitch at the corner of his eye. Tension. But someone had to do these jobs. They wouldn't say no.

The plane was flown from the rear cockpit. Gabriel remembered the model from training days, slow but reliable. He took it up for a circuit or two during the afternoon, and found he had what seemed endless time to look about him as the ground passed beneath. He thought how easily enemy fighters could destroy him – but they had to find him first. At night, hedge-hopping in France, he'd be very unlucky to be seen.

Philip was unusually silent when he too returned from practice.

Gabriel said, 'Nothing to worry about, you know. Just a night's work, and then leave. OK if I come back with you again?'

'Yes. Of course.' Philip shivered, although the day was warm. 'I feel uneasy, for some reason. Stupid.'

'I suppose it is a bit unusual. Taxi rides to France. Tell you what, let's have a drink when we get back. With the wind behind us, it should be four at the latest. Celebrate surviving this tour.'

Philip brightened. 'Good idea. I'll get out my best malt. And

471

heaven help anyone who has a sip before I get back.'

At ten they were back in the ops room, once again looking at the map. The building was quiet in the evening. Deserted corridors felt almost alien. Gabriel found himself longing for the familiarity of the air. He was used to flying at night, a cold, noisy cradle in which he could think.

Two strangers came in, small, rather shabbily dressed men with bitten nails and nicotine-stained fingers. They didn't look at the pilots or each other, but gazed into the middle distance as if waiting for a bus. They each had a briefcase, of different design. Gabriel's man had his tied around the middle with string. If he'd had to guess he would have said that here was a French clerk, underpaid and disillusioned, off to his job in the Mairie of a provincial town. Which perhaps, among other things, he was.

They went out to the planes. 'OK?' asked Gabriel, as the man climbed awkwardly into his seat.

'*Merci*.' Perhaps he was really French. Like Laura. Although not like Laura, who was more English than the English sometimes. It was only when she spoke French and the Englishness fell away that you realised she wasn't what she seemed. This man could be the same.

'Got plans have you, for when you arrive?'

The man turned and fixed him with a glacial stare. Gabriel stopped chatting and got busy.

The flight across was uneventful. Gabriel was three minutes ahead of Philip, flying on a compass heading across a sea lit only by a sliver of moon. The waves glinted like gunmetal and near the French coast he saw ships at anchor, no more than shadows amid shadows, far below. He marked the coast and altered his heading, and the intercom crackled.

'What are you doing? What's wrong?'

'Nothing. We're following our course. Relax.'

As if the poor blighter could. Gabriel flicked on his torch and checked the map strapped to his knee, and then dipped a wing to see if he could spot the railway line. Sure enough, there it was. He dropped height and began to follow it, the little plane bobbing up and down in the disturbed air over trees. Another five minutes and they must change course again, to look for a single field in this carpet of fields. He saw a light, moved to investigate and came quickly back on course. It was a searchlight, raking the sky.

'Do they know about you?' he asked over the intercom.

The man said, 'I don't know. Possibly. How much longer?'

'About three minutes, I think.'

Now, to the left, a bonfire. He swung in a circle, checking the reference and compass bearing. It was right. It had to be. He dipped the nose for the approach, remembering the sluggish response of this old plane, and came easily to land on the rough grass. Within seconds his passenger was out, dusting himself off, putting his hat straight, adjusting the strap on his briefcase. Two men ran out from the hedge towards them, Gabriel heard a jabber of French and they were gone. All of them. He was alone. So much for thanks. He taxied to the end of the field, turned the plane and rose like a moth into the empty sky. As he flew home, following his new heading, he thought he glimpsed Phil above the trees, preparing to land. He went home thinking of the whisky they would share.

He had landed by half past three. He went to Phil's room and saw the whisky waiting, just as he had promised. Gabriel found two glasses and put them ready, and set a record on the gramophone, something soft and soothing, an American crooner. An hour passed. He got up and went to the window, his mouth aching for a drink. The moon had slipped down in the sky. Clouds were drifting in a high altitude wind, so perhaps Philip was blown off course and had landed elsewhere. They would hear soon. Another hour. Another. Wearily, heavily, like an old, old man, he rose and walked to the ops room. When he entered no one looked at him. And he knew, as he had known for hours, that he and Philip would never again drink whisky together.

Dora stood on Bainfield station, wearing her mother's coat with the fur collar. Her cheeks were flushed and her eyes very bright. She was pretty enough to be conspicuous. One or two people nudged each other and said, 'Isn't that the Fitzalan-Howard girl from Fairlands? Her husband must be coming home.'

When the train came in at last she saw him at once, pilot's uniform, top button unfastened. Seeing it, an elderly man offered to carry his bag. Gabriel looked taken aback and refused, but the old man stuck at his elbow, congratulating him on the work he was doing. 'Darling!' Dora ran forward and Gabriel sank thankfully into her arms. A small crowd looked on appreciatively. It was a fitting welcome for a hero.

Dora chattered non-stop as she drove him home. 'It's black market petrol, our ration goes nowhere. I had to plead with Daddy to let me have the car but I couldn't bear to have the taxi and that terrible man listening to everything we said. Are you tired? Are you hungry? It must be so odd everyone staring at you wherever you go.'

'I didn't sleep last night,' managed Gabriel.

'Didn't you? I suppose you were excited, you've been away so long! I didn't bring Piers, he's with Mother, I thought we'd collect him and then go on home.'

'Home?' He was bewildered. 'We're going to Fairlands, aren't we?'

Dora said, 'But you must have read my letters. We're going to Meadowside, to the cottage. I've worked so terribly hard on it. I persuaded Laura to make some lovely bedroom curtains, a sort of floral print, so different, I was so lucky to find it—'

The voice went on and on. Gabriel felt a dull pounding in his head, an echo of the aero engine that had roared all through last night. The familiar lanes and fields ran past his gaze, like a film he'd once seen. Everything seemed very distant and unreal.

He said, 'I'd much rather not go to Gunthwaite, you know.'

'Because it's so uncomfortable? The cottage isn't going to be like that. I mean, there's nothing we can do about electricity, but everything else is fine. A proper loo for once. I promise you, the height of luxury!' She laughed in delight, and he thought, She doesn't understand. She can't understand. He should never have come home.

They were in Gunthwaite village. Someone was standing at the kerb, waving. The vicar. Dora drew the car to a careful halt beside him, showing off a little, wondering why Gabriel hadn't congratulated her on her skill. The vicar leaned in and mouthed at Gabriel, the usual stuff, good work, good luck, good show. Gabriel said, 'Don't you think God minds that I'm murdering Germans?'

The vicar withdrew his head.

They drove on, Dora at last shocked into silence. Eventually she managed, 'That was very rude, you know. He was only being kind.'

Gabriel said viciously, 'If he thinks the war's such a bloody good idea, why doesn't he take off his dog collar and fight? There's something rather disgusting about a priest congratulating someone for the murders they've committed. The man's a hypocrite.'

'It isn't murder,' said Dora faintly. 'It can't be.'

'I can assure you, it is.'

He got out a cigarette and fumbled for his lighter. Dora said, 'Daddy doesn't like anyone to smoke in the car.'

'Then can you stop a minute? I'll smoke outside.'

He leaned on a gate, his back to her. Birds fluttered in the hedgerows, busily nest-building, and the scent of wild thyme drifted on the breeze from a nearby copse. It touched the solid lump of melancholy that was lodged in Gabriel's chest, causing it to burn and swell within him. He clenched his teeth until they ached and felt desperation rise up. He was at odds with everything in the universe. What was he going to do?

He tried to pull himself together. Finishing his cigarette, he ground it to nothing on the road. Turning to Dora, he said, 'I'm sorry, darling. I'm being a pig. It's just so difficult turning from one thing to another so quickly.'

'From fighting you mean?'

'Yes. Let's go and see Piers, shall we?'

But Fairlands was in the middle of playtime. Children of all shapes and sizes shrieked through the gardens, hiding behind bushes, climbing up trees, making hurried exits from the forbidden territory of the potting shed. Mrs Fitzalan-Howard came out with Piers in her arms, and he was one more infant that Gabriel didn't know. When he looked at his tall, imposing father, he turned his face to his grandmother's neck and howled.

'He's nervous of strangers,' said Mrs Fitzalan-Howard.

Dora snapped, 'Gabriel's hardly a stranger, Mother. Let me have him.'

Piers grizzled on, while Gabriel eyed him with equal lack of enthusiasm. What was he supposed to do with this child? One could hardly engage it in sensible conversation.

Two boys came whirling out of the crowd playing football on the lawn.

'Hello, Uncle Gabriel! Hello!'

He looked at them in bemusement. Two strapping, brown-kneed little country boys, pockets full of stones and string. 'Alan. David.' He couldn't remember which was which.

'Have you got a medal yet?'

'Yes. They're giving me a DFC.'

'Really? Whizzo!'

They were gone, back into the throng with a triumph to report. Dora said, 'Are they really giving you the DFC? How super. Darling, how like you to be modest.'

And Mrs Fitzalan-Howard said, 'That is good news. Congratulations, Gabriel.'

Mr Fitzalan-Howard emerged from his study. 'Gabriel. Good to see you. Fancy a whisky?'

He felt his gorge rise. Whisky. Why whisky? He swallowed hard, and said in a strained and unnatural voice, 'Yes. Thanks. A large one, if you don't mind.'

After a while, as the whiskies followed one another, he began to feel better. He let Dora drive him off to Meadowside.

'They've come,' said Paula, kneeling at the window as the car passed Gunthwaite Hall. 'She's brought the car, I'll swear that doctor gets her the petrol, they say he's got everything. I love that RAF uniform. What's a bloke like him going to think of her pretty little cottage then?'

'Don't be mean,' said Laura distractedly. She was at the table sorting through bills. Incredible though it seemed, they were making twice as much on barley this year as last. She kept her thoughts chained to the mundane, she would think of nothing else. Every day was the same, crammed full of things, until two or three in the morning, when at last she might sleep. But the nights were the worst. The dreams.

'What's going to happen if they flush the lav too often?' remarked Ruth. She and Paula chuckled reflectively, and even Laura had to smile. The final cess pit bricks had been laid only two days before, and no one was sure if they were set. Somehow, the thought of Dora's perfection coming to grief in a collapsing cess pit was rather delicious. Laura lifted her head from the bills. 'How does he look?' she asked. 'Is he well?'

'Fine,' said Ruth. 'As far as I can see. It must be awful,

mustn't it? Wondering when you're going to get killed. I bet there are some days you'd almost like to get it over with.'

'Don't be horrible,' said Paula.

The afternoon passed slowly. In the little cottage, so trim and neat, Gabriel was sitting in 'his' armchair, his feet on a stool, a bunch of flowers tickling his ear and a cup of weak tea in his hand. Dora was fussing, the baby was fretting and the cottage seemed grossly over furnished. What was his chest doing here? It looked horribly out of place.

He wondered if Dora wanted him to take her upstairs and make love to her. He could think of nothing he wanted less. Weariness and drink had brought him to a state of apathetic calm, in which he repeated phrases over and over again: 'Wonderful, darling. You've worked so hard. It's a delight. Really. A delight.'

All he wanted was to fall into that frilly little bed and go to sleep. He wanted out of it, oblivion, an end. Last night had changed him. It was as if something physical had happened, as if an arm had been lost, exposing the tattered raw ends of his nerves. Everything hurt. He realised suddenly that he couldn't go on like this, mouthing platitudes. He had to say it.

He blurted, 'Dora. I wanted to tell you – a friend of mine was killed last night.'

She blinked at him. She had been telling him about the tea service, a present from an aunt. 'Oh.'

There was a long, reproachful silence. I've ruined her day, he thought. She'll think I meant to do it. Why did I have to say it? He tried again. 'It doesn't matter, really, except – well, obviously it put me a bit down.'

'Yes. It must be horrid.'

'Yes.'

He wanted to scream. Why did he have to endure this, why couldn't he be alone, for a day or so only, until he was back on an even keel? It was intolerable. Unbearable. A knock came on the door. Dora rushed to open it, saying, 'Our first visitors. Who can it be? Oh, look, darling, it's your mother.'

Mrs Cooper made her stately way into the room. She kissed him. 'Darling! Darling, you must be exhausted. But I can't tell you the time we've had, Laura's been impossible. Such a fuss about Michael, such a mess with the building – I'm so glad you're home. I just wish you'd take charge again, things run so well when you're here . . .'

On and on and on. He said, at the wrong moment, because they both looked surprised, 'Tell Laura to come and see me. I need to speak to her.'

'Well, yes. Obviously.' His mother looked somewhat put out. 'If the girl had any breeding of course she'd know she should visit, but I shall have to give her the hint, I suppose. Let me tell you, she was unpleasant to Dora last week. It was quite uncalled for.'

He should ask what was said. The trouble was, he knew the words, he just couldn't say them. He'd been all right while Philip was alive. Philip had filled the gap, provided routine in place of pain, looked sensibly on these mad events. He hadn't changed things, simply made them bearable. And now he was gone, there was nothing between Gabriel and the truth. He had never felt so utterly alone.

His mother drank tea, asked questions, ignored the answers. Had his father lost his senses in retreat from her? He had lived so long with the myth of his father's love for his wife. It might never have been true.

But then again, perhaps part of her bitterness was the same as his. Whoever she had loved, they hadn't loved in return.

When she left, Dora said, 'You were rude, Gabriel. You didn't listen to anything she said.'

He didn't reply. After a moment she said, 'Piers is asleep, you know. We could go to bed.'

He thought, that as well? Yet he wanted a woman, wanted to be held in soft and loving arms. There'd be nothing like that with Dora. He was here to give it to her good and hard, she'd accept nothing less. The house seemed to close around his head, tightening, tightening. He said, 'I'll go for a walk, if you don't mind. I could do with some fresh air.'

Dora stood at the window and watched him go. Fresh air! In his letters he'd said he longed for the comforts of home, he was sick of a draughty airfield in the middle of nowhere. Was he sick of her? Everything she said seemed to annoy him. He didn't say anything but she could see. And she needed to talk to him, about Laura and the farm, about Michael's sudden miraculous resurrection. She wished he had stayed dead. It wasn't the same as wishing him dead, after all, and who could blame her? They would have had Gunthwaite! No one could have said then she'd been married for her money. Had she been? If Piers had been coming and there'd been no money, would he have turned aside? She put her hands over her mouth, silencing the whispered words. 'He doesn't love me. It isn't just now, it's always. He just doesn't.'

Gabriel tramped up to the high pasture. The cold air burned his lungs, stripped away the pain. He remembered Laura here, thought of her peacefully, happily. It was a curse to be denied peaceful remembrance. They had made love here, in this dell, sheltered from the gale that always blew on the tops, freezing the grass, letting the bracken take hold. The pasture was better this year. Laura was a good farmer, she had it in her soul.

She was climbing the hill towards him. He looked out from the dell and saw her, knew if she saw him she would retreat. He crouched down, waiting for her, listening to his breathing. Soon he could hear hers, she was panting from the climb, a long exhalation as she stepped into the dell. She saw him and froze.

He said, 'It's no good, you know. We can't escape one another.'

'Your mother told me I had to go and visit you. So I had to go out.' She sat down on a rock, her skirt folded around her legs. Still the same, pale now, her lips colourless, but hair like night and eyes like water. Just as he remembered.

'I shall never face Michael,' she said. 'I don't know how.'

'You didn't know he was alive!'

'Yes, I did. I knew I'd feel different if he was dead. But I was persuaded. I let him down, Gabriel, I promised so much and I let him down.'

'What about letting *me* down? I need you, Laura. You don't know what it's like with Dora and her stupid chattering. I could bear it if I had you. I could bear everything. Philip died last night.'

Her face became very still. 'Philip?' she whispered. 'Poor Philip. Did anyone love him?'

'He had a girl at home. Parents. Kind people, a bit distant. Not really your sort.'

'Why not?'

'You know what you're like. They'd intimidate you and you'd pretend.'

She turned aside, saying again, 'Poor Philip. You're going to be lonely without him.'

Gabriel came up behind her and caught her shoulders. 'I'm lonely without you! Philip knew that. What do you want to happen to me, Laura? Do you want me to go mad?'

'No! No. If it wasn't for Michael then I don't know. Dora's different, I don't know why. But I gave myself to Michael. It was for ever. I can't take myself back.'

'But you and Michael aren't meant to be. And we are.'

She turned again, in his arms, putting her lips almost to his. 'I promised,' she whispered. 'Would you really take me from him?'

'No.'

He held her close, feeling her arms enfold him in return, sad and joyous at one and the same time. He knew she loved him. Perhaps this was how it had to be, fulfilled only in the past, their present selves the closest, most intimate of friends. He shouted to the wind, 'God help me, I love you so much!'

And Dora, standing on the edge of the dell, let out a terrible shriek.

Chapter Twelve

Mrs Fitzalan-Howard looked from the window to see Dora running with the baby from the car. She felt her heart sink to the depths of her sensible shoes. 'Oh, Geoffrey,' she said miserably. 'Dora's back.'

'Already? My God.'

They waited in silence until she burst in on them, mud on her shoes, hair everywhere, the baby grizzling. 'I've left him!' she declared, and stood waiting for her parents' shocked response.

'Dear me,' said her mother.

Mr Fitzalan-Howard said, 'I think we'd better have a drink, don't you? You're upsetting that baby, Dora. Go and find someone to put him to bed.'

It was all much less dramatic than Dora had expected. She subsided into a chair and began to pour out the tale. Her parents listened in silence, all the while thinking, She should never have married. She's far too young. At last her mother said, 'I don't think you're right about Laura, darling. She and Gabriel are friends. And if his friend did die last night, then he was bound to be under strain. I thought myself he seemed very tense.'

'He's always tense with me,' said Dora.

'And he's always just come home from active service!' expostulated her father. 'Don't you understand anything, Dora? Last night he was in fear of his life and today you expect him to talk about – about curtains! He doesn't care about houses and new sofas, his whole mind is taken up with life and death and the meaning of it all. The point of it. He's mourning his friend.'

'I heard him say he loved her!'

'He was probably saying that he loved his friend. You were eavesdropping, dear.'

Dora screwed her handkerchief into a ball. 'You're on his side, aren't you? You don't care what it's been like for me, all alone here, trying to manage.'

'I wasn't aware that you were,' said her mother tartly. 'You seemed far too busy playing dolls' houses with that cottage.' Dora burst into angry sobs and Mr Fitzalan-Howard looked at his wife.

'That wasn't entirely fair,' he murmured.

She sighed. 'I know. I'm sorry, darling. But really, you won't get on any better with Gabriel by imagining things about Laura.'

'I'm not imagining,' said Dora dully. 'They're in love.'

After a moment, in which Mr Fitzalan-Howard privately admitted to himself that for a lonely young man to fall for a woman like Laura was not in the least unlikely, he said, 'Gabriel's a gentleman, Dora. When he's pulled himself together I'm sure he'll come calling and want to talk. Off to bed with you now. An early night will do you more good than anything.'

When she was gone, like an obedient child, her parents looked at each other. 'I wouldn't be surprised,' said Mrs Fitzalan-Howard.

Her husband got out his pipe. 'I was thinking much the same thing. Laura understands him and Dora doesn't. It's hardly surprising if he prefers an understanding woman to our green girl.'

'She won't always be green! If she could only grow up a little! It's my fault, isn't it, protecting her too much? If they can only last out until the war's done, then they might make something of this marriage.'

'Suppose we look after the child? She could go into Bainfield and do some war work. Get some experience.' He tapped out his pipe into his hand and threw the ash messily into the fireplace. His wife nodded, too distracted to complain.

Gabriel called the next day, in time for tea. In twill trousers and an open-necked shirt he was much less dashing than before. He seemed calmer, too, his nerves no longer like steel wire under strain. He put his hands in his pockets and said apologetically to Mrs Fitzalan-Howard, 'Is Dora in? We had rather a tiff

482

yesterday and I left it 'til now to let us both cool down. I wasn't fair on her. I was in rather a state.'

'She told us your friend had been killed.'

'Yes. But that's no excuse, is it? I know Dora doesn't understand.'

She ushered him in, past a column of children off for a nature walk, which in practice meant running about chasing birds. Mr Fitzalan-Howard was already drinking tea and eating seed cake, and he got up to welcome Gabriel in a flurry of crumbs. 'Sit down, my boy, do. Dora's gone to Bainfield. We've sent her to join up.'

'Join up?' Gabriel looked at him in amazement.

'The WVS,' said Mrs Fitzalan-Howard. 'We thought it was time she found out what's happening in the world. There doesn't seem much point in you two trying to get on right now, with everything upside down. So we're looking after Piers.'

Gabriel was almost speechless. He had come here today with gritted teeth, intending to persuade Dora to come back. He was prepared to promise anything if she would only not write to Michael. But she was gone.

He looked at his in-laws, deciding that everything had to be said.

'She was going to write to Michael. About me and Laura. But that must definitely be stopped. We can't know what he's going through, he can't possibly see that sort of tittle-tattle in its true light. Laura's a good wife to him. She's got the farm, my parents, everything to take care of. She can't be worried over this.'

Dora's mother said, 'She never mentioned anything to me about writing. I'm sure she wouldn't. People say things they don't mean, in arguments.'

Gabriel sat down and accepted tea and cake. He should have come home before, talked with Laura, settled things in his mind.

He said, 'Will Dora mind if I stay at the cottage? She's done it out wonderfully.'

'A little bit too feminine for you, I would have thought,' said Mrs Fitzalan-Howard. 'It's Laura's cottage, it's her you should ask. But I think you should stay. If you're on leave for a few weeks you can pop into Bainfield from time to time and take Dora out to dinner. Start again.'

He laughed incredulously. 'But we're married!'

His father-in-law snorted. 'Neither of you knows the least thing about marriage. This on-off stuff isn't the way, you know. Wait a while. Try again when things calm down.'

Gabriel let out a sigh of exquisite relief. 'That's a very good idea, sir. I'm sure Dora and I can make a go of things in the end. We've got to, haven't we? For Piers.'

Mrs Fitzalan-Howard looked at him fiercely. 'I'm glad you see that. You're both so very young.'

He rode back to Gunthwaite on his bicycle. He felt liberated, joyful. Two weeks' leave and no need to spend it doing anything he didn't wish.

His loins were stirring. Laura could say what she liked, but he would persuade her. She was Michael's, but Michael wasn't here. And he needed her. He imagined her naked against him, her breasts warm and soft. The remembered heat of the depths of her body sent a surge of blood through his veins.

There was no one in the yard. He propped his bike against the wall and went into the kitchen, but there was only Sophie, gabbling in lisping French, and his father, who didn't know him. When he asked where Laura was Sophie made a face, and he didn't like to persist. He went out into the yard and met Dinah, coming from the byre with a pail of milk.

'I was meaning to come and see you,' she said. 'The missus said to tell everyone she was going to London to see Miss Rosalind. I'm to see to everything while she's away.'

Gabriel felt the slow, mournful draining of all his good spirits. 'Did she say how long she'd be gone?' he asked.

Dinah shrugged. 'Didn't say. We'll get by, I dare say, but one of them land girls has had to come into the house, and she hasn't been gone five minutes and Bill Mayes tells me the cows need moving and he don't know which field she wants next. He knows, you can count on it, but he won't put them there. He'd ruin a crop rather than help out, that man.'

'I'll talk to him,' said Gabriel vaguely. 'I might as well run the farm while I'm here. I wish she'd told me.'

'Just decided, she did. And went.'

He walked slowly down to the meadow. The spring flush of wild flowers was gone now. Seed heads waved in the evening breeze. He could never hold her, never keep her, not even for a day. She slipped like thistledown from his grasp.

Laura looked in bewilderment about her. She had arrived in London very late at night, alighting from a train that had stopped for two hours in a tunnel. Now, seeing the city for the first time, she was appalled. Everywhere she looked there were signs of fire or explosion, a roof gone here, windows there, and across the road a great gap in a line of buildings. Rubble was heaped up where a house had stood, only its wallpaper left on the outsides of the walls still standing. Pink roses.

A policeman was standing by the kerb. She touched his arm. 'Was anyone killed in there?'

He looked. 'Couldn't say, love. Visiting, are you?'

She nodded. 'I haven't seen it since the war started. It's so—'

'Go and get yourself a cup of tea,' he advised. 'Got your gas mask? Good. You ladies from the country don't always remember, do you?'

So, her country habits clung, like dung to her shoes. Once she had been a city girl, but no more. The traffic swirled and snarled around her, and the people pushed past, intent on their day. It was hard to imagine that ordinary life could go on in this smashed and dying place. Every shop with a window intact had strips of paper taped to the inside, and shops which were less lucky had 'Business as Usual' notices pinned up on plywood. She looked surreptitiously at the dresses still displayed, ashamed to be so frivolous. Skirts were very much shorter, nowadays. And those lovely little hats!

She walked on, becoming used to the gap-toothed architecture and the holes in the road. The city was bustling, full of uniforms. A Wren tripped past, and Laura found herself envious. Women her age were up to their ears in war, with no thought for anything but that. It seemed easy for them.

She went into a Lyons café and had strong tea and an unpleasant cake. A tall man in naval uniform stopped at her table and asked if he could sit there. She agreed, only then realising that there were vacant tables elsewhere. He smiled at her. 'Best get something down us before the raid,' he said.

485

'What raid?'

'They always come in around dusk. Then they can get a second wave in around midnight.'

'Oh.' She finished her tea. She had better call on Rosalind.

'Can I take you on somewhere? There's a bar near here, never closes. I'm sure you'd like a drink.'

She gathered her gloves. 'No, thank you. I have to get back.'

'Are you sure? You could be blown up tonight. You're a long time dead.'

She fixed him with an icy stare. 'How kind of you to remind me. Good day.'

He stood up as she left. Really! Was everyone at it nowadays? Now she began to take notice she began to think they were. It seemed that London was full of soldiers and sailors with only one thing on their minds. Gabriel was just another airman, wanting a good time. She was right to have left.

The siren went as she was crossing Piccadilly. All at once the crowds began as one body to move towards the underground, and Laura went with them, urged on by wardens blowing whistles and being self-important.

'Come along, ladies and gentlemen. Sooner they get here, the sooner we can all get home.'

Somewhere near at hand guns were firing. Laura felt her stomach turn over. 'What is that?' she asked an old man, cautiously descending the station steps.

'Hyde Park anti-aircraft battery,' he remarked. 'If you ask me, they can't see a thing, but they bang away regardless. Listen to that, now.' He cocked his head for a distinctive series of faint thuds.

'Docks. Like a bit of light for the docks, they do. We won't get it yet.'

The station was packed, people everywhere. Tea was being served. Laura was given a seat on a suitcase by an airman who asked her out to dinner. She refused, more politely this time. They were all at it. Down here there was little to be heard except the chatter of people who seemed singularly calm about the raid. A woman was eating tomatoes. And then, quite suddenly, there was a mighty thud, and the air was full of dust. There was a brief moment of silence, and then someone said, 'Blast. That's ruined my hair.'

Laura got up. She couldn't bear to sit there and wait to be killed. She struggled to the stairs, guarded by a warden. 'What was that, please?'

'A bomb, Madam,' he said blankly.

'Yes, but where? How close?'

'At least a hundred yards, I should imagine. Come from the country, have you? You can't go up and have a look just yet, you know. Wait for the All Clear.'

Everyone looked at her with amused tolerance. She blushed and fidgeted, feeling that she was making an idiot of herself. Just then came the long wail of the All Clear, and people at once got up and began doing whatever they had been doing before. Laura struggled gratefully up into the open air.

Another building had gone. Firemen were hosing smoking piles of rubble. Laura felt tears pricking her eyes. If she had been standing there, she would have been killed! Perhaps someone was. She would never know. Walking quickly through the streets, she hurried to Rosalind's flat.

It was in a block served by a rickety lift. As she ascended, Laura wondered what would happen if a bomb fell. The lift would plummet to the ground and she would die in an instant. You could die anywhere. Nowhere was safe.

She knocked at Rosalind's door, wondering what she would do if she wasn't home. But when she answered and said, 'Good heavens! Laura. What on earth are you doing here?' she couldn't say.

The flat was large and well polished. A gas fire popped in the grate, and Rosalind went to the cupboard and poured two brandies.

'Isn't Howard home?' asked Laura.

'Not until midnight,' said Rosalind. 'A working dinner. Were you caught in the raid?'

'Yes. I made an idiot of myself. No one else is scared.'

'Everyone else is used to it,' said Rosalind. 'Give it a week and you won't turn a hair.'

'I think I'm a natural coward.'

Rosalind looked at her. 'Are you? Are you really?'

Laura went and sat down by the fire. 'Being blown up frightens me,' she admitted.

'Not other things, though.' Rosalind came and sat opposite

her, the brandy glass cradled in her hand. She had long, elegant fingers, much like her mother's, and now she was in town again they were varnished and smooth. 'You've decided, haven't you?'

Laura nodded.

The idea had formed slowly in her mind. There was guilt in it, and bitterness; but also a longing to put herself to the test. She had failed Michael, failed him as badly as it was possible for her to do, and no excuses, no reasons, made it better. She hated herself for being such a fool! Perhaps she deserved to die. And perhaps not. The decision wasn't hers to make.

She should have known the tricks life can play. Hadn't she seen them, often enough? She was sick of shame, sick of regret, she wanted it decided once and for all. If she survived France then at least she would have given the fates a chance. If they wanted her, she was theirs. But if, miraculously, she survived, she would consider life again. The result of this gamble would be clear as day. Another chance.

Rosalind drained her glass. 'There's nothing to eat here, we'll have to go out. Let's go to the Café Royal. We'll have to dress up, I'll find you something.'

'I'm too tired,' complained Laura, who was feeling battered by her day.

'Nonsense! You do far more at Gunthwaite. Best bib and tucker and some bright lights, it's what you deserve.'

She led the way into the bedroom and began rifling through wardrobes.

The room seemed full of glittering light; a small dance band was playing and a man and woman, both in uniform, were doing the foxtrot. Laura wished she too was in uniform. In Rosalind's blue cocktail dress, a feather in her hair, she felt indelibly marked as a passenger. She wasn't doing her bit.

Rosalind, immaculate in black satin, picked up the thought. 'What birds of paradise we seem! I almost wish I was in khaki.' She smiled at the waiter, who clicked his heels and whisked them to a table by the dance floor. Laura felt a stirring of relish for this life; when all a woman need do was smile, look lovely and be responsible for no one but herself. Small thoughts kept nagging at the corners of her mind, anxieties about children, cows; Gabriel. A glass appeared before her and she drank. It was champagne.

They ordered and sat back, admiring the crowd. Men were looking speculative, but neither woman caught anyone's eye. Rosalind said, 'When did you last hear from Michael?'

'Not for a month,' said Laura breathily. 'I don't mind not hearing. As long as it's not telegrams.'

'Has he told you what happened?'

'He got left somehow, in the desert. He had to walk to the enemy lines. At least, that's what I think happened; the letter was so censored it hardly made sense.'

Rosalind said, 'It must be such a relief for you. Why go to France now? Wouldn't you rather wait for him at Gunthwaite?'

Laura looked away. 'I'm tired of waiting. I'm tired of being out of it. I need something to do.'

'A challenge,' said Rosalind, and banged her palms flat on the table. She motioned to the waiter for more champagne.

The wine was going to Laura's head. She looked around the room and gave a half smile to a man in a suit. He put out his cigarette and came across.

'May I?'

They were playing a quickstep. 'Thank you.'

The man danced well and so did she. Laura's spirits began to rise.

'Tell me,' asked her partner, 'are you married?'

She flashed him a smile. 'I'm only here to dance.'

'You dance beautifully. Shall we try the next?'

'Thank you. But I think not. You're very kind.'

She walked slowly back to her table. The first course had arrived and a waiter rushed forward to spread her napkin across her lap. Rosalind said, 'You're a constant surprise, Laura. You'll do very well in France.'

They were eating prawns of some kind, tinned in all likelihood, but good. The waiter came and took their plates. At that moment the warning sounded, followed seconds later by the whistle of falling bombs.

'Oughtn't we to go to a shelter?' asked Laura, wondering how she could fetch her coat.

'Get down, Laura, do!'

Everyone sat underneath the tables. Rosalind reached up and

fetched the champagne bottle, and Laura the two glasses. 'I do hope Howard's all right,' said Rosalind.

Across the room Laura's dancing partner was crouched beneath his table, lighting a cigarette. He waved to her and she waved back. Rosalind said, 'I think I've got a ladder. This sort of thing plays hell with your stockings.'

Laura said, 'I'm still hungry. Shall we finish dinner, do you think?'

'I should think so. Eventually.'

A platoon of kitchen staff dashed out of the building, clutching buckets of sand. An incendiary had fallen in the road, the only evidence of the raid. People began to emerge from their hiding places and dust themselves off. The band got up, reclaimed their instruments and began playing once more, and the customers resumed their places and their chatter. Laura's dancing partner asked if he might have the pleasure, and they slithered into a sinuous foxtrot together. Eventually, dinner arrived.

Despite everything, Dora was enjoying herself. Bainfield had changed since the war, turning from a sleepy market town into a bustling centre. There were land girls, troops in transit, Home Guard and troops on exercise swelling the population to twice its normal size. There were dances every night except Mondays, and on Mondays too if someone could think of an excuse, and the family Dora lodged with received parcels from America once a month. Dora was in possession of her first pair of real American nylons.

There were three cinemas in town now, and she and another girl usually went twice a week, Monday and Wednesday. On Saturdays, of course, Dora went home to see Piers. It seemed an odd interruption. Sometimes, in the middle of the week, she could forget he existed, forget she had ever been married at all. And when she went home he hardly seemed to remember her. It was to her mother he turned now.

The work with the WVS hadn't proved to be nearly as exciting as she'd hoped. Mostly they drove around the town trying to place evacuees, either new ones or those whose placements had broken down. Some people turned up time and time again, one elderly gentleman because he insisted on playing the violin late at night, and nothing would dissuade him. Even confirmed classicists got fed up after a while. Dora at last billeted him on the deafest old lady she could find, and all was well. But mostly it was complaints about nits and bed bugs and cooking smells, and nothing dangerous at all.

She was walking from the vicarage one day, clutching an armful of coats which needed to be distributed, when a long black car drew up beside her. 'Dora! My dear girl.'

'Wojtyla! How wonderful. I heard you'd left us.'

'Only for a little time. Someone complained about the black market, a misunderstanding. I am returned. Get in, where are you going?'

'Everywhere. I have to deliver these disgusting coats.'

'And I shall help.'

The car was very grand. She inspected everything openly as they drove, remarking that Wojtyla himself seemed to be flourishing nowadays. He wore a new suit, and on the back seat, tossed carelessly, was a camel hair overcoat with leather edging. He lit a cigarette from the car's lighter, and handed it to Dora, lighting another for himself. She had only lately begun to smoke and felt awkward. It tasted of his lips.

He took no notice of her directions at all. She fell silent, waiting to see where he would take her. When they stopped it was by the railway, an area of scrub and few houses, with rosebay willowherb as high as the windows of the car. He sat smoking silently, watching her. She began to blush.

'What's happened to your husband?' he asked.

She shrugged. 'Not much. We had a dreadful row on his last leave. I came and joined up, and he followed and we had a talk. We're going to forget about being married until the war's over. So I don't know what's going to happen. He writes to me now and then.'

Zwmskorski said, 'You must be very lonely.'

Dora giggled. 'Not really. Bainfield's fun, I didn't realise what I was missing. I go to the cinema, dances, everything. Being married was frightfully dull.'

Zwmskorski threw his cigarette from the window. 'Do you have someone to make love to you?'

'Wojtyla! Really!' Dora's cheeks flamed.

He kept his eyes on hers and she had to look away. It was as if he knew of the times she had lain in bed and imagined his long, lean body on hers. He put his hand to her burning cheek. 'Dora. We must go to my rooms.'

'I couldn't! Wojtyla, you know I couldn't!'

'But you're not a virgin. Your husband doesn't want you.'

'Someone might see. People will talk.'

'We shall be careful. It's time you had a man.'

Her heart was thundering against her ribs. Heat was spreading throughout her body, as if someone had turned her blood to fire. He began to unfasten the buttons of her uniform jacket.

'Please – you mustn't. People walk down here! Someone could come!'

'We should go to my rooms.' Now he was unbuttoning her blouse. She felt helpless, full of panic. He slid his hand under the heavy elastic of her brassiere and cupped her breast.

Dora fell back, her lips open. 'Oh, Wojtyla!'

He caressed her nipple, watching her eyelids flutter. He knew he'd been right about her, she wasn't going to make him struggle. When he had brought her to painful hardness he pulled away and started the car again. She whispered, 'What are you doing?'

'Taking you to my rooms. I want you very much.'

He lived on the top floor of a big old house, surrounded by wild gardens. Dora slipped from the car by the back gate and ran up the rusting fire escape. Standing at the top, waiting for him to come and open the door, she didn't know why she was there. She was married; a mother; she ought at this moment to be delivering coats.

When the door opened she said quickly, 'Honestly, Wojtyla, I don't think this is such a good idea.'

He pulled her into the room, shutting the door firmly behind her. 'Really, Wojtyla—' she began again. But the look on his face made her trail into silence.

'Take off your clothes,' he said. 'Quickly. Now.'

He almost frightened her. There was nothing she could do, she told herself. He was going to insist. She slipped off her jacket and unfastened her blouse once again, but she must have taken too long, because as soon as it was open he dragged that off too, and pulled her brassiere down to her waist. He held her by it, kissing her violently, pushing his tongue far into her mouth. She had never been kissed in such a way.

When his mouth left hers she was gasping, aware that he was pulling and sucking at her breasts. Exquisite shards of pleasure seemed to stab her. She tangled loving fingers in his hair. Then, deliberately, he took her nipple and its aureole into his mouth and bit her. She let out a long, guttural cry of pain. He lifted his head and his lips were stained with blood.

He let her go and she fell away from him, whimpering, to crouch against the wall. Her breast was encircled with bloody indentations. 'Now, Dora,' he said softly. 'You see what I am. You must be faithful to me, and go with no one else.'

She watched him, amazed. What was she doing here, bleeding and still wanting him? Half an hour before she'd been delivering coats. He stood over her, taking off his clothes. He had a pale, hard body, and his back was scarred as if by a bullet. When he was naked she looked away, unable to confront what she desired. He took hold of her wrists and pulled her upright against him, forcing himself against her last defence, the serge of her uniform skirt. Something animal was rising in her, something beyond her control. She stared into his face, her own teeth bared in almost a snarl.

He pulled away and went to a drawer. Dora slipped off her skirt and knickers, leaving only her stockings. She was running with moisture, she ached to have him inside her. She went to press herself against his naked back, rubbing like a cat, nipples, belly, crotch. They were in clear view of the wild, untended garden, anyone there might see, but she didn't care.

He turned towards her, again taking control, holding her against him as he sank on to a hard kitchen chair. She didn't think, could no longer think, she went on to him with an instinct older than time. As he filled her, she felt the beginnings of liberation. He began to move in her, she gripped his shoulders with her nails and moved with him, consumed by the fire he had lit in her. Within seconds they were finished. They rolled together on to the floor.

After a while he said, 'You're quite a slut, aren't you?'

She flushed. 'I thought that was what you wanted. Do you mind?'

'Not at all. It leads to – possibilities.'

She looked at him doubtfully. 'What do you mean?'

He looked at her perfect rows of little white teeth, guarding her pink and waiting mouth. 'You should punish me,' he said, feeling the blood rush again into his groin. 'For biting you. I think I should like to be bitten – here.'

Dora laughed incredulously. He was a very bad man. And she was about to become a very bad girl indeed.

Chapter Thirteen

In the desert, the nights were blessedly cool. Michael liked to sit out under the stars, thinking of this and that, trying to remember a world that wasn't like this. They had buried eight men the day before, or at least, they had gathered up 'the remains' from the charred wrecks of their lorries. They had run into a Panzer division by all accounts, and that was that.

He tried to obliterate the memory of it. Surely someone who'd been slaughtering pigs since childhood need not choke over bodies of any kind, but there was somehow no training for this. A piece of a man, even a man you didn't know, struck with a peculiar kind of horror; and he'd known them all.

He felt suddenly angry. Eight men gone, for nothing. Why had the tanks been there? Lately Rommel's men had been running short of fuel. Perhaps they'd been taking the enemy's immobility for granted? There had been much talk and shaking of heads when it was realised that they were moving once again. Michael was becoming more and more convinced that this war would be won by the army best supplied. Some of the older men said it was the slogging, endless trenches all over again.

A soldier ran up to him and saluted. 'Major Cooper, sir. The Colonel wants you.'

'Thank you.'

He pulled his tunic straight and blew his nose. He was sure he was getting a cold. He walked briskly through the camp, hearing the distant throb of lorries pulling out on a run. Perhaps something was up.

The Colonel grunted when he entered. 'Cooper. Been waiting half an hour, you in the khazi or something? Got the trots?'

'No, sir. I went for a walk.'

'You'll stand on a mine one of these days, mark my words.

Now, your lot have got to get moving. We need the usual, fuel and ammo, up the line. Start now, work solid for the next ten days. Every unit must have sufficient to operate independently for at least a week. You understand me, I hope?'

'The big push,' said Michael.

'Looks like it. We've all had enough stooging around this Godforsaken place, about time we bloodied Rommel's nose. But it does no good if trucks go wandering off into the blue and get muddled up with tanks, like those blighters the other day. So we'll be watching you, Cooper. You've been a credit to us since that business of the escape and this is your chance!'

Michael muttered insincere thanks. The Colonel appeared to labour under the impression that everyone was as career-minded as himself, and thought nothing of danger so long as it presented an opportunity for promotion. The cynical view was that brave men got shot and cowards stepped neatly on to their rung on the ladder. With the possible exception of Montgomery, everyone got to the top that way, which accounted for much. But Monty wasn't a coward, thought Michael. He was every inch the professional soldier. Michael didn't doubt for a minute that Monty would sacrifice any number of men for a military objective, those very same men who now cheered him to the skies.

He walked to the sergeants' tent and rapped on the wooden pole by the door. His men turned out silently, wondering what was up, but Michael gave them only the bare bones; they were to get the crews together and start a run, he'd give them map references when they were ready to go.

Back in his tent, working out co-ordinates, he looked down at the ruler in his hand. It was of rosewood, half an inch thick, old fashioned even when he was a boy. He'd had it since school, had carved his name on it when he was twelve. This same ruler had helped him on the farm, marking out field boundaries, calculating yields. He'd killed a mouse with it once, throwing it across the room at Gunthwaite and making a lucky hit.

He grinned to himself. How good it was to know that Gunthwaite was still there, would always be there. When Laura's letters came, in a bunch, usually, he sorted them into order so that he could follow the way things were. Lambing, shearing, dipping, trimming, sending to market; ploughing, harrowing, seeding, weeding, harvest; the small disasters that were all Laura had to concern her, a fence down, a ewe dead, Gabriel fighting with Dora. He was here, in danger, so that Laura could be safe and secure, amidst his family, at Gunthwaite.

Laura crouched in the middle of a windy field and struggled with the wireless transmitter. She was useless with it, having no experience at all of electrical gadgets. The instructor sighed and moved forward, to show her once again how to tune to the correct frequency, adjust the volume, or the aerial, or whatever. Everyone else was deep in the intricacies of repairing the things, while Mrs Cooper couldn't tune into the BBC.

'It's just like your wireless at home,' he said encouragingly. He tried to smooth his hair back over his bald patch. 'We can't send you to France until you can transmit, you know.'

'If you could just show me again?'

But he was a poor teacher and her thoughts began to wander. She was miserable here, amidst fluffy downland sheep and fat cows. She wanted Gunthwaite, for all its harshness. She longed for her baby and her own things about her, even for old Mr Cooper on one of his bad days saying, 'Do I know you? Have we met?'

'So, you do it,' said the instructor.

'I'm sorry?'

He sighed, furiously. 'You realise your life could depend on this thing? If you want to get out, you have to call us. You could be in danger, terrible danger. Do you want to be tortured and sent to the gas chambers in a concentration camp?'

'What?' She blinked at him. 'What's a gas chamber?'

'According to our information, and I believe it to be correct, the Germans are exterminating thousands upon thousands of people in gas chambers. Jews, gypsies, and any agents they happen to find. You, Mrs Cooper. May I suggest you concentrate.'

She swallowed. 'Yes. Sorry. Yes, I will.'

She lay in bed that night and thought. What was she doing here? She had a baby, responsibilities. This was supposed to be a one-off trip, a few weeks in Paris, because she knew it so well, and then home. She hadn't imagined capture, or if she had, it was in terms of prison only. Torture, though – death. The trouble was, the more barbaric she knew the enemy to be, the more bound she was to oppose them. Sophie and Marie had talked of escaping the cattle trains. If Britain were ever to be invaded there would be trains here too, full of Jews and gypsies – and prostitutes.

In the morning, over breakfast, she said in French to one of the men, a Belgian only recently escaped, 'Have you heard about gas chambers? Do they exist?'

He glanced up from his single tough sausage. 'I don't know. There were pamphlets in the Jewish quarter. Very highly coloured. Hard to believe.'

'The wireless instructor said we'd be sent, if we were caught.'

He grunted. 'If we live that long. Personally, I'm taking the suicide pill. I don't want to be tortured.'

She smiled tremulously. 'I knew a lot of Germans before the war. They weren't so bad . . .'

He put his hand on her arm. 'It's bad now. Believe me, it is. I could tell you so many horrors, and no one's safe. They come in the night and take people, and they're never seen again. The torture is real, the camps are real. Who knows, maybe the gas chambers, too? Be frightened. It's the only way to stay alive.'

Instead of lunch that day, she wrote a letter in her neat, unforthcoming hand. When it was finished she folded the sheets, placed them in an envelope and sealed it, going to some lengths to find old-fashioned wax. She imprinted it carefully with a seal she found on the desk, a dove carrying a twig. And she wrote on the envelope 'To Mary. To be opened when you are twenty-five, or after my death, whichever is the later. Your loving Mother.'

Then she placed it in another, larger envelope, and thought. Who could take care of this? Rosalind? She might be bombed. Dinah? Her household was chaotic, someone would see it and be curious. She drew out another sheet of paper.

Dear Mrs Fitzalan-Howard,
I am sorry to burden you with this, but I hope you will oblige me. I enclose a letter for my daughter, which I should like you to retain. The inscription on the envelope

explains it. I am about to undertake something quite hazardous, which perhaps I should not be doing, with Mary so young. But I believe, and every day I believe it more strongly, that it is vital for us all to join in this struggle and win. So I entrust you with this letter. Thank you.

Yours very sincerely,
Laura Cooper

She sealed and addressed the packet. Then, because she was sure that their mail was censored, she walked into the garden, through the back hedge and two miles to the village to post it. She returned in the middle of a lesson on ciphers and was scowled at.

That night she was summoned to the commander's office. He was a small man, grey-haired, with a moustache still incongruously dark. He gave her a tight, unwelcoming smile. 'Mrs Cooper. Do sit down.'

She arranged herself carefully on a hard chair. Two other men stood by the wall, one of them the wireless instructor. The commander stared at her, in silence.

'Is there something about my appearance which unsettles you?' asked Laura innocently.

'You're memorable,' he replied.

She shrugged. 'A little, perhaps. I can change myself.'

'Yes.' He glanced down at a paper on his desk. 'So I believe. It says here you have a chameleon-like ability to take on the colour of your surroundings. Let's hope so, Mrs Cooper. Because, quite frankly, as an agent you're an absolute dead loss.'

She giggled. 'The wireless. I'm so sorry. I will try hard.'

He put his hands flat on the desk and said testily, 'Are you sure you're taking this seriously, Mrs Cooper?'

She considered him. 'You would like me to be frightened, I suppose? I am, of course. I don't want to die, or be the cause of others dying. But it seems to me the only way to be a good agent is to forget you're an agent at all. To be what you seem to be, through and through.' She gestured to the slim-skirted French suit they had given her, and the good leather shoes. 'It seems I'm to be a lady of some means. I'm not worried about the Germans. Why should I be?' She considered her neatly varnished fingernails. She had enjoyed her transformation, leaving behind the muck and mud of Gunthwaite, for at least a little while. She could still be a sophisticate, it seemed.

The commander said, 'We have a report on you – very little detail, of course. But I gather you have some friends in – let us say, a rather interesting profession?'

Laura's good humour fell quite away. She drew herself up. 'What?'

'Two ladies stay with you. Refugees. Your sister-in-law gave us to understand that they appear to have been prostitutes.'

'She can't know that! I didn't tell her a thing!'

'She's a very observant, very – intuitive lady. Perhaps you may have realised?'

'They – certainly led colourful lives,' Laura managed. 'I really don't know the details. What of it? I don't understand.'

'I'm sure you do, Mrs Cooper. Prostitution would be an ideal cover for our work. Odd hours, odd habits, men coming and going. Absolutely ideal.'

She drew in her breath. Rage was boiling up inside her. That was the reason for the suit, the silk underwear, the prosperity! They thought they could order her to do that? It was true, you could never shake it off. Once someone sensed the taint they had you labelled, packaged, boxed. You could never escape. She got to her feet, heading blindly for the door.

The wireless officer stood in her way. 'Please. There must be a way round this.'

'I will not lie on my back for England. I'll do nothing for you! Ever!'

'But perhaps you needn't sleep with anyone!'

The commander snorted. 'Really, Arthur! She wouldn't last five minutes.'

'But I've seen the girls in Paris, sir. Some of them are very high class. Just a few select customers.'

'We want her to be a drop for our agents. Half of them are butchers and plumbers, man! They wouldn't go to a girl like that. An ordinary, run of the mill tart's what we want.'

'Then ask your wife to do it,' snarled Laura.

Silence fell. The commander said stiffly, 'I'm sorry if we've offended you, Mrs Cooper.'

'Of course you're not.' She sat down again, and looked at him.

'Look. If you work in a big house, no one ever need know what you do. Madame, perhaps, and the doorman, if he does security as well. He'd know if there was a fight in your room or something. The other girls are in and out, in and out, it's all muddled. I should like someone to contact a Madame Bonacieux. I can give you the address. Say it's Lori, that Sophie's quite recovered after her very long illness, and she owes me a lot.'

The commander said, 'Can we trust you? We don't want you screaming if it gets out of hand.'

She gave him a sudden, blistering stare. 'I don't scream, Commander. I leave that to people like you.'

When she was gone the men looked at each other. 'More to her than meets the eye,' said the commander, throwing down his pen. 'Not the floozy we thought.'

'Devilish attractive, though,' said the wireless instructor. 'It's not something you notice immediately. Then she just looks at you and you realise she's an absolute sexpot. I'll swear she can turn it on and off.'

The third man pulled out a cigarette case and took out a Camel. 'She's made for it,' he said in a heavy French accent. 'I'll try to get her in by Sunday.'

The commander said, 'Then for God's sake teach her to work a wireless by then, will you, Arthur! And no looking up her skirt.'

Gabriel sat sunk into a deep leather chair, reading the newspaper. News from the desert was singularly lacking and he wondered what was up. The nation was so sick of failure and retreat, there had to be a victory there soon.

He looked over the pages at the men – boys, some of them – scattered about the room. Almost none of them had been here at the start. Old hands like him were few and far between and he supposed that as each day passed they grew fewer. Sooner or later the bloke you thought would always be there suddenly wasn't.

'Mr Cooper? You're wanted in the CO's office.'

Gabriel sighed. He was due to fly at nine and begin a series of night-fighting sweeps, in the hope of intercepting bombers. Someone had described it as trying to swat a fly in the Albert Hall by the light of a match, and he fully understood the analogy. But sometimes they got lucky, although all too often the ack-ack got them too. Ignominious, to be shot down by your own side.

The CO motioned him to a chair. 'Forget tonight's raid. We've got an agent going in. Rush job.'

'Where to?'

'North of Paris. Bound to be hairy, I'm afraid. But there's something to sugar the pill. You're making it to Squadron Leader this time, Gabriel. Richly deserved.'

Gabriel smiled ruefully. 'Thank you, sir. Let's hope I'm in for a long run.'

'If last week's anything to go by, your guardian angel's right on form. You're a lucky flyer, my boy. We only promote the lucky ones. Go and get briefed, will you? Good luck.'

Gabriel went out into the corridor. Only four days ago he'd had to parachute from his plane over woodland in Kent, only to be menaced by a detachment of Home Guard, intent on shooting him. He'd descended swearing vilely and singing snatches of 'Men of Harlech', which he hoped would verify his nationality, if not his geographical skills. He grinned. He had a sudden memory of Michael, at eighteen desperately shy, singing 'On Ilkley Moor Baht 'At' for someone's birthday, and blushing enough to set himself on fire. He'd try that next time he was floating down.

He was out on the airfield a good half-hour before take-off, checking the plane. His mechanic said, 'Nice clear night for you, sir. What is it this time?'

'Don't know. Wait and see, I suppose.'

A car began snaking towards them across the field, its lights very dim. They started the plane. No one ever wanted to sit about waiting at this stage. Gabriel was used to them by now, pale, tense, silent. They never wanted to talk. Two men and a woman got out of the car, and he went to shake hands, as he always did. 'Hello, Gabriel,' said Laura. 'I should have guessed it might be you.'

The blood seemed to drain from his face. He felt disorientated, couldn't at once understand why she was there. 'Has something happened? I mean – what are you doing here?'

'I'm going to France.'

She said it lightly, with a laugh, as if it was an adventure. One of her companions said, 'I didn't realise you might know each other. Pilot, you do understand that you can't talk about this?'

'Yes. Of course.' He replied automatically, as yet to take firm hold of the situation. Then he called, 'You can turn that engine off, now. We won't be going tonight.'

Laura caught his arm. 'Of course I'm going. It's all arranged, people are waiting.'

'And Michael wouldn't thank me for delivering you to your death! No wonder you haven't been writing. I rather thought you were angry with me.'

'With myself, more than you.'

The mechanic stood uncertainly, not sure what to do. Gabriel spun round on him. 'Turn that bloody thing off!'

'No!' Laura again contradicted him. 'Perhaps we should find another pilot? I have to go.'

One of the men said, 'We can't brief anyone else in the time. This is vital, Pilot. I can't tell you more. If necessary I'll have your commanding officer give you a direct order. You'll be court martialled if you disobey.'

Laura chuckled. 'Oh, Gabriel! Then I'd survive and you'd be shot. Really, it isn't as bad as you might think. I'll see some old friends. Who knows? They may even remember you.'

He said, 'You sound drunk.'

'Do I? It's only excitement. It's seeing you. And I've never flown before.'

In the faint light of the headlamps her eyes were like glass. Her lips were shining too, as if waiting to be kissed. He took her hands and held them, willing her to feel what he felt. She said softly, 'We'd better go now, Gabriel.'

'I didn't know you weren't at home. Why didn't anyone tell me?'

'They're managing. I've left a letter for Michael if the worst happens. Explaining.'

'What about me?'

'I don't have to explain things to you.'

He wanted so much to kiss her! If he made a scene now, what would happen? Nothing. She'd be late at her rendezvous and it might go wrong. Someone had to take her. At least if he saw danger he could fly her away. In the plane, alone, they could talk.

He turned away and got into the cockpit. Laura, helped by the mechanic, clambered awkwardly up too. 'Can you hear me?' asked Gabriel, through the intercom.

Her voice came back to him. 'You're shouting. I'm not deaf.'

Before the lid came down, someone leaned in and spoke to Laura. She nodded. The hatches closed. Gabriel turned the little plane, feeling the breeze tugging at its wings, set it face to wind and took off.

They soared into the dark, empty sky. Laura said timidly, 'Oh, Gabriel. It feels very unsafe.'

'Aren't you supposed to speak French now?'

'I'm supposed to do lots of things. Are you angry with me?'

'Yes. No. I'm not sure.'

She sighed noisily into the intercom. 'This is really for the best. I had to do something, had to dare, had to get away.'

'You're trying to get yourself killed.'

'I don't think so. I don't know. Let's say – I'm leaving it all up to fate.'

'It's my fault, then. If it wasn't for me you'd be safe at home.'

'If it wasn't for you I'd be half mad. We did it together, Gabriel. And sooner or later Michael's going to know.'

'Dora won't tell him. She didn't mean what she said.'

'He'll know just the same. I can't – I can't lie to him, Gabriel. You do see that, don't you?'

'No! No, I bloody do not. Telling him would be cruel and pointless and selfish.'

'Well then!' she flared. 'Will you be able to look him in the eye?'

He was silent. Then, slowly, 'I don't know.'

They flew on, through the night and the stars. After a while Gabriel said, 'I love you.'

'Don't say that. Please.'

'I'm allowed to love who I like. I knew you before Michael, I loved you before him!'

'You did not!' said Laura scornfully. 'All you wanted was to get me into bed.'

'Because I loved you,' said Gabriel. 'I just didn't know.'

He turned the little plane on to a new compass heading. Laura clutched at the straps that held her in her seat. There was so little between her and eternity, she felt so small. She thought back to the first time with Gabriel. It seemed funny now. But she'd been frantic with fear and revulsion, she'd known nothing of love. Somehow the years had changed them. Nothing now could frighten her as much as the sound of Jean's feet upon the stair. And nothing could warm her like a glimpse of Gabriel's shoulder, seen through a half-open door. Irrational feelings, but there for all that. She feared something that was not fearsome, and loved something that to another was nothing at all.

The sea was beneath them, a pewter plate dotted with white of egg. Once they saw a ship, no more than a shape, too big for a trawler, too small to be important. A light sparkled in the darkness, signalling up at them. Gabriel flew quickly away.

They passed the coast soon after, dipping low over cliffs. Gabriel said, 'Not long now. You must be terrified.'

'No. Not really. It doesn't seem real.'

'You will be careful? I mean, if you wanted, we could go back now. I could say it was engine failure, anything.'

'Then someone else would have to do it. And you know, I almost want to? It's a bit like a visit home.'

He could hear the lilt of excitement again. If she wasn't scared then he was, desperately fearful. Laura never took herself seriously enough, never took enough care! She had that sense of youthful invulnerability that he knew had long been shot out of him. But she had never known what it was to be faced by guns that meant to kill you. The ease with which death could claim you, and the pain of life's loss, were quite unknown.

He said, 'We'll be down in three minutes or so. There should be a fire.'

'I can't see anything.'

'You won't. They light it when they hear us. When we land you have to run, it's the most dangerous time.'

She tried to imagine it; landing, climbing out, running across the field. Her legs felt too weak to support her. There was a feeling of sickness in the pit of her stomach, that was also very like the need to pass water. An image came into her mind, suddenly clear and vivid; Michael's face. She felt her heart ache for him.

A flame appeared in the dark, small as a match. The little plane turned to it, slipping sickeningly to lose height. 'I forgot to ask,' said Gabriel. 'How will you get home?'

'I don't know,' said Laura. 'They didn't say.'

The plane's wheels were brushing the grass of a small, rough field. They touched, a teeth-jarring impact, he saw a bush too late, but it was whippy and went down under them. They juddered to a halt.

'Now,' said Gabriel. 'Get out and run.'

'I can't open this thing. How does it work?'

Good God, no one had shown her! He dragged back his own hood and clambered on to the wing. Men were running from the hedge, he wondered if they were German. It was always a chance. He pulled back the cockpit hood and saw Laura's face. She looked mildly concerned.

She said, 'I think I've broken my nail.'

'*Madame? C'est vous?*' A small, nervous man hovered by the plane.

'*Oui. Ça va?*'

'*Bien, merci. Vite, Madame, pour le bon Dieu!*'

She climbed carefully out, carrying her bulky case. The Frenchman took it, and stood politely while she shook creases from her skirt. She turned to Gabriel. 'Goodbye. Keep in touch with Gunthwaite, won't you?'

'Yes. Yes, if you want. You really must go!'

'Yes.' She stood, visibly reluctant. He thought, she doesn't want to leave me. Really, she doesn't. He bent and kissed her.

She pulled away. 'Goodbye, Gabriel,' she said briskly. 'Take care.'

'Laura—'

The men were running again, into the darkness by the hedge. She ran with them, careful in her skirt, not looking back. 'Laura!' he shouted. Dangerous, stupid. No reply. The field was silent, the fire extinguished. In the distance he could hear motors, a patrol perhaps, he or the fire had been seen. He stood uncertainly by the plane, gripped by a sudden, unreasonable urge to run for the hedge too. At least he'd be with her. It was madness. If he was caught he'd bring disaster on her head.

He climbed back into the plane, seeing too late that he hadn't shut the forward cockpit. He clambered out, dealt with it and got back in. The engine coughed into life again; he'd been a fool to stop it in the first place. The familiarity of the cockpit felt oddly reassuring, like home after a bad term at school.

Headlights were lighting the sky to his left. He gunned the engine, turned the plane, and raced back the way he had come, remembering this time about the bush. As he lifted into the air, skimming the trees, he heard the sound of fireworks. Something pinged off his wing, and he realised they were shooting at him. The little plane lifted, like a gnat threatened by a swatting hand, and he sped away to safety.

Laura ran across two fields, pausing at a hedge to catch her breath. 'How much further?'

'There is a barn, a mile away. We must hurry.'

'My stockings will be in shreds!' She turned her back and lifted her skirt, unfastening her suspenders. Each stocking was carefully removed, rolled up and put in her pocket.

'*Mon Dieu*,' said her escort.

'Now I can run,' she said, and set off. The man with the case ran at her elbow, smelling of garlic and truffles. She thought suddenly of Jean.

The barn was a tumbledown affair, hidden against some trees. They slipped inside, and someone lit a candle. Mice, or even rats, rustled in the dimness. Laura sat gingerly on a bale of musty hay.

'We didn't expect a girl,' one of the men said. 'So young!'

Laura said, 'It doesn't matter, does it? You can still get me to Paris?'

'Depends on your stockings.'

She smiled with them. 'I don't have so many I can afford to waste them, you know. I have to look smart.'

'Nothing smart about Robsart's old van.'

They pulled out a small packet of bread and cheese and began to munch. After a moment one of them offered her some cheese and she accepted. Then a wine bottle was produced and passed around. As she drank she had a sudden strong sense of recognition. This was the France of her childhood, sour wine, dark barns, men like old olive wood. Getting used to her, one of them grinned. 'Brave, aren't you? Coming into this?'

'No braver than you.'

'For a woman, though. And a pretty one. Remember, if the Gestapo get you—' he drew a finger expressively across his throat.

She drank some more wine. It seemed but a moment since she landed, but already there was light in the chink of the door. She got up and went to the back of the barn, putting her stockings back on. She combed her hair and applied fresh lipstick, brushing the mud from her shoes and the hay from her skirt. There was the sound of an engine outside.

'Robsart,' they said to each other, and peered out to check. They gestured to Laura. 'Get on with you. Good luck.'

'I can't go yet!'

They stared at her. 'Madame?'

She ran to her case. 'I'm not wearing my hat. I simply can't go without it.'

She pulled out a small velvet cloche and settled it carefully on her head. 'It's only an old van,' said one of the men awkwardly.

'But still. I've been visiting my sister. I wouldn't leave without my hat.'

The van was of rusting blue metal. The driver was thin, unshaven and bit his nails. Laura got in beside him, settling herself fastidiously amidst the ends of cigarettes and some pieces of skin from long-dead rabbits. She turned to say goodbye but there was no one there. The men had melted once more into the woods.

Laura said, 'My name is Louise Vorronceau. If anyone asks, I've been visiting my sister.'

'Robsart. I'm taking a load of game to Paris.'

'Where will you drop me?'

He shrugged. 'Out of town. You'll get a train, if your papers are good.'

Robsart chewed his nails as he drove. Suddenly, frightening her, he burst out laughing. 'Never had a beauty before! No one's going to believe this when I tell them.'

'Then you mustn't tell them,' said Laura. There was a tremor in her voice. Was she nervous after all? 'You must tell no one.'

'Wouldn't believe me. Whatever I said.'

He alarmed her, but there was nothing she could do. Besides, once out of his van he wouldn't know where she had gone. She looked out on flat countryside, with here and there the glint of a river. In a narrow lane they met a truck full of German soldiers. Robsart had to put his van almost in the ditch. 'Bastards,' he muttered.

There was a road block a mile further on. Laura wound down her window, feeling her heart begin to pound. She fastened her mind on her character; Louise Vorronceau, prostitute, visiting her sister. As the soldier advanced she tilted her head and boldly matched his stare.

'What can we do for you?'

'Papers. Where are you going?'

'Paris.' Laura handed him her papers and yawned delicately.

'What are you doing with him?'

'My sister said he was going. I didn't know he'd have the van full of dead bodies!'

'What?'

'Game. He's some sort of game dealer. It's disgusting.'

She made a face and the soldier laughed. His officer called out in German, and at once the soldier pulled his face straight. He went to the back of the van and opened it. He called to his officer, who came across. Out went four rabbits and six pheasant.

'Bloody thieves,' muttered Robsart beneath his breath. 'That's my livelihood!'

Laura leaned from her window. 'You don't need so much. Take half, that isn't fair.'

'Bloody hell!' muttered Robsart, and pulled his hat down.

The officer came to Laura's window. 'You're cheeky, aren't you? And who might you be?'

'My name's Louise.' She crossed her legs.

'Staying around here, are you?'

'Not any more. I live in Paris. Look, you can't take all that. This man has a living to earn.'

'And you don't, I suppose? Pretty girl like you.'

She grinned at him. 'I manage. Do you go to Paris much?'

'I do actually. Once in a while.'

'Put that lot back and I'll give you my address. You can look me up some time.'

He straightened and yelled at his men. Then he bent again to talk to Laura. His face was an inch from hers. 'I've got leave next month. What's the place?'

'Will you remember? I haven't a pen.'

'Oh, I'll remember all right.'

She whispered Sophie's old, squalid address. He'd have a

509

high old time trying to find her there. 'My name's Konrad,' he said. 'You can expect me.'

As they drove away, Laura blew Konrad a kiss.

When they reached the outskirts of Paris Robsart and Laura parted company. He said, 'You should be careful, you.'

'And you. Don't talk.'

He grinned. 'No use, is there? No one'd believe me. Good luck, sweetheart.'

She stood on the corner as he drove noisily away. He had given her a pheasant, in a damp paper bag. She passed it to her other hand and looked about her, seeing that Paris was just as it always was. A little drabber, perhaps. Full of German uniforms. She felt insecure suddenly, as if time had shifted, and she had lived here only yesterday and at Gunthwaite a century before. She shook herself and made her way quickly to the station.

Chapter Fourteen

Dora sat naked on Zwmskorski's bed. She was eating plums, putting each stone as it appeared in a small pile on his bare chest. He was smoking. 'Heard from the husband lately?'

She nodded. 'He's a Squadron Leader now. He wants to see me next month. He's got a weekend pass.'

Zwmskorski closed his hand on her thigh. 'Wants some stuffing, I suppose?'

Dora grinned. He was useless at English slang. 'I shouldn't think so. Would you be jealous, Wodgy? If I did?'

He looked at her. 'It is not something I would permit.'

Dora said nothing. She was a little afraid of him sometimes, she thought with good cause. He often liked to hurt her, never too much, but enough. If she couldn't see him, then the next time he was always rougher. And the things he did – she did – made her stand sometimes, in the middle of serving tea to old ladies, or evacuees, whatever, and blush scarlet.

Suddenly he got up, sending plum stones everywhere. Dora ignored them; this wasn't her flat, and she disregarded all hints that she should housekeep in it. He went to a box on the floor, saying, 'See what I got yesterday. You might want some.'

He pulled out yard upon yard of creamy silk. Dora said, 'That's a parachute, isn't it? Where did it come from?'

'Somewhere. I don't know. And in here, look. American nylons.'

He held them out to her, and she stretched full length on the bed. 'I don't need them, Wodgy. All the Americans give you stockings at dances. And I can't sew the silk, that's Laura's thing.'

'There are no Americans in Bainfield!'

'There are now. They're all at the training camp. And they've heard how desperately short of things we are and they're terribly generous. So you see, Wodgy, now I can even get chocolate.' She picked up a plum stone and tossed it at him. It bounced off his shoulder.

Suddenly, without a word, he was on her. His naked body straddled hers, he held her arms as if in a vice, his lips drawn back from his teeth in absolute rage. Dora screeched, 'It's all right! I didn't mean it, I was teasing! I can't get anything!'

'Are you sleeping with an American? Is he getting stuffed with you?'

'No! I promise – I love you. There's no one but you.'

He stared down into her face. The thought that he might kill her flitted across her mind. She lifted her hips and rubbed herself against him. 'Wodgy? Please?'

'You should be careful, Dora. My name is very old and very proud. I won't have you making me a fool.'

'I was only playing. Please, Wodgy.'

In answer, he closed his teeth on her breast.

When she went into her billet later, delivered from Zwmskorski's enormous car, her friend Edna said, 'That man! He's so rich!'

'He's a bastard,' said Dora flatly. She threw her bag down on the bed and went to the mirror. Her eyes were still puffy from crying.

'Had a row, have you? Probably for the best. I mean, I know your husband's away and everything—'

Dora turned to face her. 'We don't row, I don't dare. Tonight – he hurts me, Edna. I can't tell you how!'

She slumped on her bed.

Edna snorted. 'He looks the sort. Why don't you report him as a black marketeer? There are always rumours.'

Dora sighed. 'There'd be more than rumours after he spilled the beans. My parents would find out. The chief constable came to my wedding! I'm married to a hero, I've got a little boy! And here I am having it off three times a week with a blackmarketeer. You know what it's like round here, everyone would find out. I couldn't live here afterwards.'

'But your husband wouldn't mind. I mean, you don't see him or anything.'

Dora put her chin in her hands. 'I don't know what he'd think. I don't suppose he'd care if I was dead.'

'That's a bit strong, isn't it?'

Dora sat up, too restless to settle. 'I don't know. It's all a mess. I need time to think.'

When Saturday came she caught the early bus, to avoid Zwmskorski. Sometimes, in a show of power, he stopped her going home. Little by little he had increased his hold over her. She got off the bus at the end of the Fairlands' drive, and walked up through the banks of dark rhododendrons. The gravel was weedy now, and the flower beds ragged, which was hardly surprising with the gardeners gone. Would this war never end?

Her parents were breakfasting, enjoying the blessed peace of a day without the school. Piers was in his highchair, mashing egg into a pulp. 'Hello, darling,' said Dora, and bent to kiss his hair. He looked at her, perhaps in recognition, perhaps bewilderment.

Her mother said, 'Darling! We didn't expect you to be early. Piers is still in a mess.'

She got up, sweeping the baby into her arms and bearing him off. Dora felt a pang. Couldn't she do that, on her one day home? He wasn't her mother's baby. Her father, noting her expression, said, 'She enjoys it, you know. It's like having you all over again.'

Dora sat down and desultorily spread margarine on a piece of toast. There wasn't any decent jam, hadn't been any for years, but the bees on the estate provided honey. She munched, wondering why she always felt so trapped when she came home. Was it because nothing here, not even the baby, was really hers?

When her mother came back, she said, 'I thought I'd take Piers out on the bike later today.'

'Good heavens.' Mrs Fitzalan-Howard sat down again. 'You are feeling energetic. I thought after a week distributing pyjamas and tins of corned beef, you'd be ready for a rest.'

'A rest from that, perhaps. I'll go and put Piers in his coat.'

Her mother looked up from the tea pot. 'He's got a new one.

It was one of yours, I found it in the attic. It's quite suitable, it's blue.'

But Dora hated the coat. Despite the colour, it was all too feminine. She had seen a smart sailorsuit in Bainfield and imagined dressing Piers in that, when she had saved enough for it. She wouldn't ask her parents for the money, but she could ask Zwmskorski. What would Gabriel say to see his son dressed up like this?

Without a word to her parents she put Piers in his seat on the bicycle and pedalled off to Gunthwaite. The Fitzalan-Howards looked at one another. 'She really is the most moody girl,' said her mother. 'She hated looking after him when she had him to herself.'

'Since we were hoping that would change, we can't complain when it does,' said Mr Fitzalan-Howard. 'Remember, dear, he isn't really yours.'

She sent him a look like daggers.

When Dora pedalled into Gunthwaite's yard she was surprised. Fairlands' untidiness was one thing, but this was a muddy, neglected farm. Tools stood around rusting against the walls, and an old harrow lay in pieces, just where a horse could entangle itself. She had never seen Gunthwaite in such disorder. Even the creeper that shrouded the barn had been allowed to droop across the door. She felt nervous suddenly. Had Laura been taken ill? She might have gone to Gabriel, it might all be too late. But she had come, and there was nothing for it but to brave the kitchen door.

The two Frenchwomen were sitting at the table, nonchalantly shelling peas and tossing odd ones now and then to Mary, who sat on the mud-spattered floor. Old Mr Cooper was as usual mumbling by the fire, the stubble of several days on his wizened old cheeks. From the noise upstairs it appeared that Alan and David were killing each other.

'Where's Laura? What's going on?'

Sophie and Marie turned their eyes towards her for a moment before resuming their shelling of peas. 'She's away,' said Marie. 'She went to London, she won't be back for weeks. And Dinah's had to go, her son's been wounded. So you see, it is us.'

A thousand questions stormed into Dora's head. But the noise upstairs was untenable. She put Piers next to Mary and went to investigate. Alan and David, in a room full of clothes and books and chaos, were having a pillow fight. Feathers from a casualty covered everything, and their faces were wild, like slum children. They were turning into little savages.

'You naughty boys! Stop it at once. And – and clear this up. It's dreadful.'

'What are you doing here?' asked David. 'Is Auntie Laura coming back?'

'I didn't know she'd gone away. Who's looking after you? Not Sophie and Marie?'

The boys nodded. They didn't care, they could do more or less as they pleased provided they spoke French and wiped Sophie's dribble. 'Paula takes us to school. There isn't any today. It's Saturday.'

'But where has Laura gone? Is she with Uncle Gabriel?'

David picked up the torn pillow, letting the remaining feathers cascade over his head. 'She's in London. Mummy wrote and said she has some war work to do now and won't be back for a bit. She's probably a spy.'

'Don't be silly,' said Dora automatically. She made them begin tidying up.

She went back downstairs. Mary had smeared peas all over Piers' smart blue coat. Dora felt pleased, for the first time that day, and put the kettle on the fire. Through the window she could see piles of bricks left over from building the cess pits, and thought how odd Gunthwaite felt without Laura. The place lacked its heart.

She had brought coffee, a gift from Zwmskorski, and poured cups for Marie, Sophie and herself. She sat at the table without being asked and said, 'What is Laura doing, exactly?'

Marie shrugged. 'We don't know. It is all very mysterious. She goes off, pouff! A moment's notice. Your husband was here then.'

Dora stiffened. 'Was it something to do with Gabriel? I know he likes her.'

'She's good with men. She always was.'

Dora sipped her coffee. It was strong, it made her heart race, she almost felt dizzy. She said, 'I wanted to talk to her. To find out – about her and Gabriel. There's another man – I'm having trouble.'

'Not the Pole?' said Marie.

'Yes. The Pole. He's – being difficult. Unkind.'

Marie turned her gaze upon the girl. Dora coloured, unused to being contemplated in just such a way by a lined old woman with dyed hair and stained teeth who nonetheless made her feel a foolish innocent.

'I could have told you not to sleep with him,' said Marie in a matter-of-fact voice. 'I had him in Paris. He wanted everything, this way, that way. His sort uses a woman up.'

Dora tried not to look startled. Even allowing for a few years, Marie must have been old then. Why had she slept with Wojtyla? Why had he slept with her? She said, 'You must have been good friends with him.'

Marie chuckled. She had spoken loosely, forgetting Dora didn't know. 'Oh, yes. Very good friends. But not after that.'

Dora said, 'Did he – bite you?'

'Bite?' Marie threw up her hands. 'Does he do that? Well! You want to watch him, it always leads on. A girl can get killed by a man like that.'

In a low voice Dora said, 'I want to stop seeing him, but I daren't. I'm scared to tell, my parents might find out. And he frightens me.'

Sophie said something in rapid French which Dora couldn't catch. She must have understood. Marie said, 'She's right. It's best to go away. Or get a lover who'll see this one off, and even then you have to be careful. I've known girls slashed, you know?'

Dora shuddered. Could she go away? She looked down at Piers eating peas, and wondered if she could move back home. It wouldn't work, not now, and he'd still come and see her. But if she asked for a transfer she'd never see Piers. Or Gabriel perhaps.

Marie said, 'You can try to stand up to him. It sometimes works. Sometimes men go on until they are stopped.'

'But how could I stop him?'

Marie leaned on her hand. 'What is it that he likes you to do?

Do it badly or not at all. What do you call it in England? A man's part. The cock. Tame the cock like a naughty dog. The master has to follow.'

Dora finished her coffee. She got up, wondering if she had been terribly unwise. Marie might talk, and Sophie certainly would, to anyone who spoke French. All the same, they'd listened. She imagined what her mother would have said to the news that her daughter was in the grip of a sadistic lover. They'd confine her to a lunatic asylum before night.

She got up and wandered around the room. Ought she to take charge here? Ought she to go and see Mrs Cooper and the land girls? Three envelopes on the mantelshelf caught her eye, all addressed to Laura. Two were probably from Michael, they bore regimental stamps, but one was in Gabriel's distinctive hand. The women at the table were talking, not looking at her. She took the letter and slipped it into her pocket.

My Beloved Girl,
I am writing this within hours of getting back. Since you stayed away throughout my leave, I can only conclude you really don't want to see me, but perhaps you've come back now I've gone? Please, give me a little of your time and read this letter.

I know there's no future between us. There can't be, with Michael still living, and neither of us would ever wish him dead. I know you feel ashamed of what happened between us. But you can't blame yourself. If anyone's guilty then it's me, with a wife and child, knowingly committing adultery.

So now what are you going to do? I have an uneasy feeling about you, that you're going to punish yourself, and end up making everyone needlessly unhappy. Michael doesn't need to know what happened. You don't need to suffer. Don't make yourself a victim of your own guilt.

I know that when Michael comes home things can't go on exactly as they used to do. That would be unrealistic. But if you love me even a tenth as much as I love you, you'll try. Even if not for me, then for Mary and Michael. I see everything as a chain, all leading from the one false link –

517

you should never have married Michael. The thing with Dora was because of that, and everything afterwards. Because of it I'm a poor husband to a sweet girl, a lousy father, a treacherous brother. But I'm constant in loving you.

Yours, ever,
Gabriel

Dora leaned back against her bicycle. Piers, minus the detestable coat, played on the grass at her side. Curlews called over the dipping hills, and the fugitive sun, oddly warm on this autumn day, struck fire from a pond.

She got up and leaned on the fence, wondering what she should do. Her parents blamed her for its failure, but her marriage had never stood a chance. Gabriel had slept with her because he couldn't have Laura, and she had been too young and silly to see. Once Michael was gone Gabriel couldn't resist, he wanted Laura or nothing. And got her, it seemed. She had been right.

She felt angry, suddenly. Why should she feel shame about Zwmskorski when Gabriel had for years been chasing his brother's wife? Why not tell Gabriel, admit it, put her cards on the table? It was time they stopped deceiving each other. She wasn't sweet young Dora any more, and he wasn't the dashing hero. They were just people, who needed love.

She picked Piers up and held him close. He smiled at her, she had struck some chord in his memory perhaps, a remembered smell or gesture. She felt a surge of love for him, and at the same time her heart ached. If Gabriel had loved her just a little it would have been all right. She must have seemed to him like a child herself, understanding nothing. She knew much more now. She had reason after all to be grateful to Zwmskorski, for those lessons in lust and power and terror. She would do as Marie said, and subdue her lover's body. At least until Gabriel came home.

A barrage had been raging half the night. Michael lay under the truck, uncomfortable and headachey. Every few seconds one of the Bofors guns would fire, the sequence punctuated now and then by the distinctive whine of a mortar. It was unsettling,

518

despite the fact that it was aimed at the enemy and not at them. Only the day before a mortar, calibrated wrongly, killed four men leaning on a British Crusader tank.

It was almost dawn. Soon a squadron of Crusaders was to advance on the enemy positions, followed at a discreet distance by trucks. Michael and his men would ferry prisoners and wounded back behind the line, and take fuel and food on to it. Restless, and unable to lie still a moment longer, he sat up and fumbled in his rucksack for a pot of American jam. He had a hunger for unalloyed sweetness. He ate it, in the dark, with a spoon.

He wondered if he was afraid. He was certainly nervous, but that wasn't the same as fear. There was something thrilling, too, about this concerted assault on the foe, after years of sand dune spats that always ended messily. Time enough by now to know that he didn't flinch at the sound of gunfire.

Why then, this uncertainty? Not since he first joined up had he felt quite so dubious about the next day's happenings. It wasn't that he doubted them, he realised, but that he couldn't imagine them. It was as if, for him, the world was to end shortly after they pulled out that morning.

One of the nearby tanks was showing a turret light, they were probably making a brew. By its dim glow he could see his hands, his watch, the shine of his dipping spoon. He felt a rush of affection for his body, for each and every part, wondering which he would spare if he must. A hand? A leg? A finger? He might not mind losing a toe. If he was to burn, let it not be his face. He couldn't bear it if Laura could not look at him.

He went to his haversack and took out a small pile of envelopes. They were Laura's letters, carrying with them the breath of home. He sometimes thought it uncanny that she knew so exactly what he would like to hear, of the dead lamb as well as the live one, the poor crop as well as the good. But lately he had realised that she wrote to him almost as if he were a diary, in which she could record the daily happenings on the farm. There was so little that was personal. Almost nothing, in fact.

He found himself thinking of the Italian guards. Why think of them now? Young faces, young minds. The Bofors gun fired again. He imagined death, and felt sick suddenly, and put down the jam.

There was a clatter in the lorry. Stephens swung down, his weasel face more than usually discontented. He began to swear. 'Fucking lorry. Fucking battlefield. Fucking war.'

'Less of that, Stephens.'

For a moment he thought the man was going to add 'Fucking Major Cooper' and Stephens would be back in the glasshouse, whence he had so recently emerged, but the man thought better of it. As he watched him scratch and grumble, and relieve himself against orders by the wheel of the neighbouring lorry, Michael felt his nightmares recede a little. No one could know what the day might bring. To imagine that you did was just indulgence.

The barrage had ceased. With just the briefest of dawns, the sun came flooding over the horizon, the signal for the tanks to roar into life. The radio was crackling and men were everywhere making their last-minute preparations. To the rear the guns were limbering up, ready to advance in the wake of the assault. Michael slung his gear on the truck and yelled at Stephens to get a move on. He lifted his arm in signal to his men, and received the answering wave. They were all ready to go.

The Crusaders were pulling out, long, low shapes across the sand. In a few minutes the trucks would follow. Over the radio the commander, nicknamed Swansea Sam, for his lilting accent, was rapping out commands to the tanks to close up. They were moving quickly; the trucks, without tracks, would be hard put to follow. When they were almost at the horizon Michael lifted his arm again. His vehicles began to pull out.

It was a day of stop and start. The radio was full of confusion: this tank was firing, that fired upon, someone was tangled in wire and a track had come off. Michael's men moved slowly, through the shattered remains of infantry pits in which German and Italian corpses were all that was to be seen. There were many cardboard chocolate wrappers, and now and then the familiar straw-covered bottles of Chianti. Sometimes a truck would stop and garner what it could. No reason to stop them.

Grinding on, through the haze, he was suddenly aware that something had changed. His thoughts, dulled by gunfire and the drone of engines, struggled to evaluate what he saw. Tanks were moving over the ridge to his right, which should have been B Division, but which seemed, unaccountably, to be Panzers.

520

He looked away and then back, but those were German tanks. No doubt of it. Michael's trucks had somehow slipped through the line.

He rapped orders over the radio. 'All units. Retreat. Retreat without delay.'

Stephens looked at him with his usual foxy stare, which on this occasion meant he didn't know what was happening. 'Those are Germans!' yelled Michael. 'Get the fuck out of here!'

Stephen spun the wheel like a man demented. The truck lurched and swung, but just as they began to think they were escaping, one of the tanks opened fire. The shot struck one of the lorries, a vast explosion. Ammo, of course. Michael yelled to Stephens to stop, and when he didn't, grabbed the wheel and wrenched it from his grasp. They careered across the sand towards a body, that of Reynolds, the conchie, who had wanted to join the Medical Corps. He was groaning and Michael scrambled out, dragging him to the rear of the vehicle and pushing him bodily inside. He was burned down one arm, but Michael could see no other injury. Stephens was howling about tanks, and Michael was barely aboard before they were away again, racing towards safety. The bastard had nearly left him again!

They met a medical echelon an hour later, and transferred Reynolds. 'Pot shot from a Panzer,' explained Michael. 'They didn't stop to finish us, they were after tanks themselves.'

'Will you be going on? We had a message back that it was pretty hot up there.'

'Is it? Actually, I don't think we've got much choice.'

He gathered his drivers and told them to keep careful lookout from now on. If they couldn't tell one tank from another by now then it was a poor show. A few faces looked sardonic, no doubt remembering the incident a few days before when one of the new Churchill tanks had been mistakenly shot up because someone thought it must be the enemy. Out here, in the battle, confusion was the order of the day.

They started off again, following compass bearings. Soon they saw signs of war once again, burning trucks, deserted infantry pits, a body lying huddled on the sand. It was an Italian soldier, quite young. A canister of water lay open beside him, and towels were spread across his wounds. Not a quick death then, nor an easy one. Michael felt again the creep of nightmare.

Guns were firing ahead. There was the rattle of small arms fire, and the smell of burning fuel. 'Speed up, man!' said Michael, for Stephens was crawling forward.

'We're a supply truck,' said Stephens belligerently. 'We ain't got no guns!'

Topping the rise they saw the battle – tanks wheeling and firing, raked by mortars. One was claimed by a ditch, losing its track, and lay there, firing furiously, until at last they got the range and hit the emplacement. There was a gradual hush, broken by the moans and cries of men. Soldiers began to appear from the earth, hands raised in surrender, and Michael waved his men slowly forward.

Two trucks were assigned to prisoners, two to wounded. The crew of the disabled tank began mending their track, while the rest of the command moved on. The machine gun nests were full of bottles of beer, and Michael set his men to collecting some of it. The bottles Stephens brought in were sticky. 'What's this?' said Michael, touching it.

'Bits of German,' said Stephens, grinning. 'They was spread all over the place. Like jam.'

Michael wouldn't let him see that he was revolted. 'Throw it away, damn you!' he snapped. 'We'll have no more of that.'

He moved towards the gun emplacement, thinking that there might be water where he could wash his hands. In two minutes or so they must move off, it was almost noon. The sun, very high and strong, bleached colour from the landscape, turning even blood to nothing. Michael put his hand on the concrete balustrade of the bunker. Without warning, with no remembered sound, a great wind seemed to take him, carry him, and let him go.

Laura stood again in the high, domed hall of the house in the Rue de Claret. She looked about her, noting that the carpet was worn and the mirrors dusty. Essentially, though, it was the same. She had changed, she was utterly different, but here it was all the same.

A couple of the girls stopped on their way into the salon. 'And who might you be?'

'I'm here to see Madame. I'm expected.'

They laughed. 'You don't want a job here, *chérie*. We never stop! It's all those Germans.'

They swung their hips in the way Laura had half forgotten, conscious of themselves. No one else walked like a French prostitute, she thought. When the doorman came back and said that Madame would see her, she walked to the study in exactly the old way. The doorman said, 'I remember you. Little Lori.'

Laura glanced at him. 'That's not my name any more. I'm Louise Vorronceau. I like it better.' As so often before, she knocked and opened the study door.

Madame was reclining on the sofa. Once she had been statuesque, now she was monumental. As Laura entered she struggled into a sitting position, her face cracking into her little used smile.

'Lori! My angel! I couldn't believe it when I heard.'

Laura bent to brush her powdered cheek with her own less fragrant one.

'I'm not surprised, Madame. I myself found it hard to believe that Sophie left hospital after barely a month. I couldn't believe ill of kind Madame, I thought. Not after all she did for me.'

Madame made a face. 'You know how these things happen. A misunderstanding.'

'Of course.' Laura sat down opposite the sofa, letting Madame retain and pat one of her hands.

She wondered how much Madame guessed. Everything probably, she was an intelligent woman. Laura met her gaze frankly. 'It's kind of you to receive me, Madame. A lot has changed. You know my new name, of course. I shall only be here a few weeks, I won't have many callers.'

'Some of your old customers are still here,' said Madame slyly. 'Not everyone's gone. Remember Raimond? And Charles. They had to go for a time, but they're back now.'

'I shall see,' said Laura diplomatically. 'There's a lot for me to do. Can I – rely on you?'

Madame sighed and released Laura's hand. She scratched her head irritably. 'I don't know. It's an imposition, of course. I don't like to be involved in all this, we have many Germans here, many. I run a good, quiet house. But you grew up here. We're old friends. If you want to play games then the least I can do is rent you a room. Payment in francs please, weekly.'

Laura almost laughed. 'I think our debt must cancel out rent,' she said.

'You think so? Sophie was ill for months. Months! The expense was terrible. I was out of pocket. No wonder I didn't tell you she was well until my own costs were covered. A little rent, what's that? Don't they pay you for this?'

The woman was incorrigible. Laura threw up her hands in mock surrender. 'All right! I'll pay rent. But please, don't talk. It's my life, Madame.'

'And mine,' said Madame. She looked suddenly a little grim. 'They don't like Resistance. I do it for you and old times. And also for the girl they took. She was half Jewish, and looked it, but the German lads liked her well enough. Then an SS man was in and the next thing they've taken her. We heard she was on a train, going God knows where. And she'd had enough suffering in her life. She didn't deserve that.'

Laura made soothing noises. She had decided not to listen to any more tales. Where was the use, when all they did was frighten her? Madame was making efforts to rise from her couch, and Laura helped her. They stood for a few moments for her to regain her breath, and then strolled out into the hall.

Some of the girls stood about, their curiosity obvious. Madame surveyed them with a chilly eye. 'This is Louise Vorronceau,' she announced. 'She was one of my girls before the war. She was always a friend of mine. She's down on her luck and has asked me to take her on, but as I've said to her, I have enough girls. But I'm renting her a room and she can do a little business on her own account. If one of you is slow, or decides to be ill, then Louise can work the salon.'

The girls drew in their breath and glared furiously at Madame. Laura looked humbly down, hoping that they would take against Madame and not her. One of them said, 'That's not fair, Madame. If we're ill we shouldn't be forced to work. We all do our best.'

Madame shrugged, massively. 'We shall see. Some of you may perhaps do better. Go up to your room, Louise. And don't bring riff-raff here. You know my standards, like the rest.'

'Yes, Madame.'

Laura went upstairs, running up the first flight, panting up the second, her case bumping against her knees. She was in the room she had used as a child, right at the top of the house, its small window looking out over the street. It was just as she remembered, a narrow bed, a painted chest, a wardrobe with drawers. When she opened them she smelled dust and Sophie's perfume, the very essence of childhood. Here she was, back again, and nothing had changed. Except that now she was an agent. She giggled to herself. The world had gone mad.

There was a knock on the door, but before she could answer a girl came in. 'I'm Tatine,' she said aggressively, pushing back dark hair with a strong, mobile hand. 'Are you really Madame's old friend?'

Laura made a face. 'I'm not sure. You know Madame, it's all one way with her. If I upset her, I know she'll kick me out.'

'Couldn't you work one of the other houses? I know places that need girls.'

Turning her shoulder, Laura said abruptly, 'I don't want to do that. It's only for a while. I'm married now, I've got a little girl – I just need to save a little. I can't manage, with the war and everything! My husband – he wouldn't understand.'

'Where is he?' Tatine wasn't softening yet.

'He's away.'

Tatine took in her breath. 'You mean – the Resistance? Is he with the Resistance?'

'I don't know. He went months ago and I haven't heard. He might be dead. Sometimes I think he must be dead, I hear nothing! He sends nothing. I won't see my little girl starve.'

Tatine began pacing the small space of floor, waving her long arms. 'I see it all now. We must help. I'll get you customers, tell people, put out the word. If the girls put a little aside each night, you could have that, get your kid here, everything.'

'No. No, please don't do anything.' Laura's lie was cartwheeling out of control. 'I've got someone helping me. He's very strong.'

'A pimp, you mean? Don't let Madame find out. Or your husband! Would he kill him?'

'I think so,' said Laura. 'But a woman needs someone, don't you think?'

Tatine sniffed. 'If you're that sort.'

She went away and Laura sank on to the bed. She was exhausted, and longed to sleep, she had barely closed her eyes in thirty-six hours. She longed to escape into sleep and forget about all this. But it was almost four, and she had to call in. She pulled her bag from under the bed and unwrapped the heavy radio from its blanket of clothes. Sitting on the bed, ready at any moment to leap up, she laboriously sent her message in coded Morse. 'Arrived. Ready. Work can begin.'

Chapter Fifteen

The world was an odd shade of grey, shot through with red and sometimes black. Michael lay very still, wondering what was happening, if indeed he might be dead. He lifted a hand and felt his arm, rough khaki, as always, and across his tunic, noting the buttons. Stephens' voice, in his ear, said, 'Fuck me. Old Cowmuck's waking up.'

'Don't try to move, sir.' An educated voice. Endon, probably, the ex-convict done for fraud. It was comforting though to have someone other than Stephens in charge.

Michael said, 'What's happened? Why can't I see?'

'You took some shrapnel in the head, sir. Booby trap. We're taking you back.'

'Back where? Where's the line?'

'I should think you'll be sent to Alexandria, sir. Eventually. We've got them running, we're nearly through.'

'Good. Good show.'

He felt helpless and stupid. He didn't know what was going on. He wondered about tomorrow and the day after, wondered when he'd be able to see. Was this the thing that had been tugging at him? He thought of corpses he had seen and put his hand up to see if he still had the top of his head. Everything was there, but on one side was a bandage, matted with blood. What a sight he must look, he thought, lying there in the wagon. He reached out and touched bottles. 'I hope you slung that beer, Stephens,' he said warningly.

Stephens laughed. 'Don't you just?'

Thank God for Endon, thought Michael. He wouldn't want a dog at Stephens' mercy. He lay back, feeling a headache begin, watching the flashes of red and black spark like lightning across a grey and vacant sky.

* * *

Dora slipped from the house and ran across to Zwmskorski's waiting car. It was raining and she brushed the droplets from her hair as he drove. 'Where are we going?'

'Leeds. A place I know.'

'Can we dance? I can't bear it if I have to watch you getting drunk all night.'

He looked annoyed but said, 'There's dancing.'

He drove too fast, as always. He was the sort of man who took risks in everything, leaving disasters in his wake. There'd be a deal of some kind in Leeds, they weren't going just to dance. And sure enough, as the dark bulk of the city came upon them, he stopped the car and went into a huge, unlit warehouse. 'Lock the doors,' he told her. 'If someone comes, drive away.'

She almost hoped someone would come. She'd drive back to Bainfield and wait until Wodgy came hotfoot to claim his car.

She moved restlessly in her seat. Her thighs were damp, she wore nothing but stockings beneath her dress. She thought again of her plan for the evening, feeling her nipples tense with excitement. If she was a man, she thought suddenly, she'd never be faithful. She'd do everything, all the time. She'd go as far as she could.

He was coming back, carrying a box. She unlocked the door and he pushed it on to the back seat, covering it at once with a mac. She turned in her seat, kneeling to peek inside.

'Don't you touch that!'

She looked at him. 'I'll touch what I like. And you'll let me. If you want something good tonight.'

He caught her wrist and gripped it, almost crushing the bones. Dora forced her head up and met his eyes. 'I know you like hurting me. But there's something you like more. If you're kind, I'll do it to you. I'll do everything.'

He laughed. 'You'll do it anyway. You're scared enough.'

'It's no good if I'm scared. I can't relax. I can't – take my time.'

With her free hand she unbuttoned his fly. He was hard, he always was. He seemed to live in permanent eagerness for sex, so why had this taken her so long? She held him in her palm, gently squeezing and letting go. His hold on her relaxed. She slid from his grasp and lifted the cover on the box. It was full of guns.

'Who are they for? Can you sell them?'

He said nothing. His eyes were half closed. She at once let go. 'Why have you stopped?'

'I don't want you to finish yet. Who are the guns for? Not the Germans?'

He laughed. 'They're German guns. Looted from German troops in the desert. They're going to Palestine, for the Jews.'

'Oh. Oh, I see.'

She sat back in her seat. She said, 'I want to go dancing.'

'I don't want to do that any more.'

She dropped her eyelids. 'Oh, yes, you do. Come on, Wodgy. If we do it now there won't be anything to look forward to.'

He said nothing. But he started the car and drove to the club, a narrow doorway in a dark and narrow street. They were playing American music, and a woman was singing. Everyone was drinking Jack Daniels whisky and no one wore uniform.

They had a drink and began to dance. Dora pressed close, letting her breasts roll against his chest. 'Don't you like it? Isn't it good?'

He said, 'You're getting clever, Dora.'

'It was about time. You won't hurt me again.'

He laughed in her face. She felt her nerve shake, but knew he mustn't see it. He must think she was sure of herself, and of him. It was like training a dangerous dog.

He drank four more whiskies, but showed no sign of being drunk. When they danced Dora found herself staggering, and clung to him. 'We can go now,' she murmured. 'We can do it in the car.'

They drove away fast, almost colliding with a lorry parked in the road. He was very drunk, she realised, watching the walls rush past as if in a dream. As soon as the town was behind them he pulled off the road, into a wood. Dora got out at once, throwing her coat on to the front seat and climbing into the back. The box of guns was on the seat and she pushed it on to the floor. She slipped her dress to her waist and put her hands behind her head, letting Zwmskorski see the full glory of her breasts. 'Kneel on the box,' she murmured. 'I know what you want.'

He knelt, one arm around the front seat, the other entwined in a leather strap. There was something utterly obscene about him, his sex protruding like another limb, his face half smiling, waiting for her. She slid to the floor, putting her arms around him, rubbing him against her face, her breasts. He began to moan and mutter in Polish, but Dora took her time. At last, when he was sobbing her name, she opened her mouth and took him in.

He tasted of sour fish, neither pleasant nor unpleasant. He was bucking against her face, pushing himself into her, forcing her almost to choke. She kept control, digging her nails into his thighs, holding him just as she wanted. At his moment of climax, suddenly gagging, she pulled away, lifting herself up. He exploded against her breasts.

Their eyes met in the gloom. She said, 'That was for being good. Well done, Wodgy.'

He touched her breasts, feeling his own fluid, panting a little. 'And you were the good little girl.'

'It's your fault. You taught me to be bad.'

She lifted her skirt and knelt with him on the box, her thighs against his, her nakedness matching his. 'I can't do it,' he said. 'Not so soon.'

'Try. Come on, Wodgy. I want it. Try.'

He was an instrument, no more than that. Coaxing him into her, she held him until she was satisfied. Then, panting, she slipped away, leaving him to subside on to the seat. She stood beside the car for a while, listening to him snore. She wouldn't do this often, she resolved. He must long for it before she would give in. As for this evening, she would drive back to Bainfield and hope to God no one had noticed she wasn't in.

Michael lay wakeful in bed. He could hear the doctor approaching, the tap of his feet down the ward, the long pauses at each patient, the murmur of voices. Suppose he went by? Should he cry out, and perhaps look a fool? He blinked furiously, trying to see past the grey curtain that cloaked his vision. He had to know why.

Eventually the feet came to him. 'Ah. Major Cooper. Well, you'll be going home, so that's one good thing, isn't it?'

'Why can't I see?' asked Michael grimly. 'No one seems to know.'

'Really? I can't imagine why not. It's perfectly simple, old chap. A piece of shrapnel hit you in the head. It's a miracle you're still with us, actually. The only perceptible damage is to your optic nerve and I have to tell you that I very much doubt you will ever see again.'

He heard all the nurses draw breath. He said, 'Thank you, doctor. I suspected as much.'

'No need for total pessimism, of course,' added the doctor, now that the worst was over. 'Training's first class for the blind these days. And the rest of you's hale and hearty, no bits missing. What did you do in civvy street?'

'I'm a farmer.'

'Really? Well, that's all to the good then. You can produce a dozen sons to run the farm while you enjoy the roses. A good life, farming. Lots of fresh air. You can't shoot any more of course, but you might still fish.'

The sister was gently urging him on to the next bed. Michael was left like flotsam on the tide, part of the messy wreckage of a storm. He heard the curtains being drawn around his bed and a nurse said, 'No one can see you now, Major Cooper. Would you like a cup of tea?'

He shook his head, watching the red and black flashes gyrate. He imagined himself blundering amidst a rose garden, or stranded in a trout pool, unable to move without help. And he only had a daughter, who would never know her father as an upright man. And Laura. What would Laura say?

He heard someone come through the curtains with a swish. 'I'm glad you're bearing up,' said the sister, bracingly. 'There's a transport home tomorrow, we'll put you on it if we can. It's a long voyage and there's no point hanging around here when you could be at home. There's at least a dozen blind, so you won't be alone.'

He almost laughed. What did twelve recently blinded men have to say to each other? How would they find each other, for that matter? His head hurt, as if his thoughts were protruding through his brain. A voice kept repeating itself, This cannot be, it must not be. Nothing so terrible as this can happen! He thought of Laura, and tried to imagine her face. There was nothing, just hair and eyes, and when he forced himself to think, the features were those of the Italian corpse. She was lost to him, he thought in panic. He would never again see his wife! Tears began pouring down his cheeks.

'Hello, Gabriel.' Dora rose from a bench and put out her hand for him to shake. He took it, but then bent and hastily pecked her cheek. She accepted it, like a queen accepting tribute. He felt quite at a loss.

When she hadn't appeared at the station he'd supposed he'd have to call at her billet or something. And then he'd seen her, sitting on this bench, her uniform hat set firm against the wind. She looked very calm and very pretty, he thought. He wondered if she giggled any more.

'Shall we have a drink?' he asked. 'Is it too early? I thought we'd lunch, but I don't know where.'

Dora said, 'I booked somewhere. It's a pub, but quite pleasant. I ordered grouse, I hope you like it. And they're bound to give us a drink.'

'Right. Jolly good show.'

He sounded like a caricature of a Squadron Leader, which he supposed must be nerves. Dora was suddenly so self-possessed. A group of Americans was walking towards them, very tall, in rationed England looking a little too well fed, and as they came near two of them touched their caps and said, 'Hi, Dora. How you doing?'

'Carlton. Bill.' She smiled, nodded and kept on walking.

'How do you know Americans?' asked Gabriel in bewilderment.

She lifted an eyebrow. 'I know lots of men.'

The pub was small and full of old wood. Two chintz armchairs were drawn up before a blazing fire, and Dora asked if they might drink sherry there, since they were early. She drifted away to powder her nose, leaving Gabriel to the publican's admiration of a flyer.

Once in the powder room, she slumped in a chair. Her heart was pounding, she thought she might be sick. It was so hard to be self-possessed and charming when you had decided to tell your husband about an affair. But she wouldn't apologise. Oh, no. Why should she?

When she looked at her face she saw a thin, white-faced girl with bags beneath her eyes. She looked old, she thought. If Gabriel had ever found her attractive he wouldn't any more. She reapplied her lipstick and pinched her cheeks to make them glow. But it was only the thought of the sherry that drew her back to face him.

The publican withdrew as she arrived. Gabriel whispered, 'Thank God. I thought he was never going to go. He thinks I'm a hero.'

'Aren't you?'

Gabriel made a face. 'Dora, please! There's nothing heroic about trying to survive. You shoot the other guy because otherwise he'll shoot you. I don't want to die.'

They sipped at their sherry. He said, 'I suppose Laura's still not back?'

'No. No one seems to know what she's doing, and Gunthwaite's in a mess. You'll be sad, not seeing her—'

Gabriel said, 'Dora! I thought you'd got over that silliness.'

'Not in the least.' She met her husband's eyes. 'I read a letter you wrote to her. I knew I was right. You were having an affair.'

There was a silence. He said, 'You had no right to read her letter.'

'If we're talking rights—' said Dora, and Gabriel dropped his gaze. Dora went on, 'I'm not going to make a fuss, if that's what you're worried about. I was very young, wasn't I? And very silly. I thought if you wanted to sleep with me you must want to marry me, which wasn't very sensible. But I was just a stopgap, I see that now. You wanted Laura, and failing her you had me.'

Gabriel said, 'That isn't quite how it was, you know.'

'Are you sure? I'm not. But actually, I've got a confession for you as it happens. I've been having an affair too. With the Polish doctor.'

Gabriel looked at her for a moment. Then he said, 'Good God.'

'Why are you surprised? You know yourself I'm not cold. I needed someone and he was there. But – it's got rather out of hand.'

'Does he want to marry you? Do you want a divorce?'

Dora laughed. 'I wouldn't marry him if he was the last man on earth! He's a brute. He – he hurts me. If I break it off I'm frightened of what he'll do and what he'll say. He's got nothing here, nothing anywhere; he doesn't care about wrecking my life. I'm scared.'

Gabriel took her glass and his own, and went to the bar. He

ordered two more sherries and brought them back to the fire. Dora turned her face aside. Gabriel said, 'Don't. I don't mind, you know. I can't blame you.'

She smiled tremulously. 'He deals on the black market, everything you can think of. That attracted me at first, he had so many lovely things. But it wasn't really that. It was the sex.'

'Where do you—'

'We go to his rooms. Or in the car. I should be grateful to him really, I know far more than I did. I must have bored you so, on that honeymoon, asking all the time if you loved me. And the house – and everything!'

To her embarrassment she was crying. Gabriel pulled out his handkerchief. 'I wasn't bored! You never bored me, Dora. I was irritated sometimes perhaps, but that's all. It's just – I can't explain. When you're in daily fear of your life you don't act well. And you were so very young.'

'I feel a hundred years old,' she said mistily.

'You look about eighteen.'

She smiled at him. The publican came across to tell them that lunch was served in the dining room, if they'd care to come through, and he'd taken the liberty of providing a bottle of good claret, since it was a rare treat to meet a Battle of Britain pilot in the flesh so to speak, not to mention his good lady. An honour, it was. And not to take any notice of Sarah, who was waiting on, she was a silly girl who blushed at nothing. Liked flyers, she did. Like all the girls.

Gabriel thanked him sincerely. In an odd way he was enjoying himself, here in this pub with Dora. As they drank their soup he said, 'You know, about Piers. I know he's my son and everything, but I don't feel very – connected. I'm sorry, I know that sounds callous.'

'Why should you feel connected? You didn't feel connected to me. Not like Laura.'

He sighed. 'You don't understand about her. No one does.'

'What is there to understand? She won't leave Michael.'

'I know. I only hope she doesn't tell him. It would be so cruel.'

The grouse appeared. They were small, flavoursome birds, redolent of the years before the war. Gabriel felt comfortable with Dora as he never had before. He wanted to tell her about

Laura going to France; the words seemed to lodge at the back of his throat, ready to emerge. He wanted to stop being alone with his anxiety. He said, 'Have you heard from Michael at all?'

Dora gestured. 'There are some letters at Gunthwaite. I didn't read them, only yours. You see, I'm not quite without shame.'

He grinned. 'What a pair we make! I hope Piers can forgive us for some of it, at least. What should I do about this Pole of yours? Inform on him?'

'He'd know it was me. Bound to.'

'Not necessarily. I could talk to the police. You know, being a Squadron Leader has its advantages.'

'He'd be sure to go away? I couldn't bear it if he came back in six months.'

'I think you'd be safe. I'm almost sure, in fact. I'll let you know when, so you can get away. But then what?'

She shrugged. 'What indeed? I'll find someone else, I think. Maybe an American, someone good for Piers. You won't mind, of course?'

'No.'

They looked at each other. If this was the start of everything, thought Gabriel, it would have been better. And Dora thought, If I didn't know him I'd be just like that blushing young girl. But the gathering wind sent leaves rattling against the shutters, and Gabriel's mind turned to Paris. Did the same wind blow there? He felt his heart lurch at the thought of Laura, alone in the wind. He cast his love to her, sent it flying like a lure through the ether, to catch her and hold her safe.

The salon was busy tonight. Laura paused on her way out to glance inside. Germans to a man. As she stood there one of the officers got up and came across. In bad French he said, 'You look a tasty piece. Come and have a drink.'

'I regret. I'm already engaged for this evening.'

She gave him her cool smile, but he was drunk and caught her arm.

'Don't pretend. Got something against us, haven't you? Won't do it except with a dirty Frenchman. Or a dirty Jew.'

'Monsieur! Please.' She tried to shake herself free but he hung on.

Why had she stopped even to look?

But another man was on his feet. He came across and said something to his friend. To Laura he said, 'I'm sorry. He's homesick, he had a letter today. His girlfriend's given him up.'

'For a dirty Frenchman? Or a dirty Jew?' She couldn't resist the dangerous taunt.

'I'm sorry,' the man repeated. 'We don't all think like that. Even he doesn't. He's just drunk.'

'Yes.' She relaxed a little. The danger was gone. 'Thank you. Good night.'

Once in the street she hurried. The city was pitch dark and her memory played tricks. Twice she passed a turning she thought she knew. But this part of town was still the same, lots of girls, lots of men. Once someone grabbed her, saying, '*Chérie!* The one I've been waiting for!'

'Not if my pimp hears about it,' she replied, and slipped away.

She arrived, panting, five minutes before the rendezvous.

Was this the place? Girls stood about in the gloom, talking and smoking. As Laura stopped and stood, unsure of herself, one of them came over. 'You can't work here. It's full.'

'I'm not working. I'm meeting someone.'

'And I'm the Queen of Sheba! Get out of here. Go on, get!'

'I told you, I'm waiting for someone. He's rough. If I'm not here he'll come after me.'

One of the other girls, a redhead, sauntered across. 'He isn't Big Ishmael, is he? I'd heard he had a new girl.'

Laura cast her eyes down. 'I can't tell you. He gets nasty if I talk.'

'Does he now? Well, let's wait and see.'

Laura stood apart, waiting. Men were appearing in ones and twos, and Laura leaned against a wall. She was wearing high heels and an ankle chain with a rabbit charm. The men who had sent her had thought it a whimsical touch.

A big Lebanese came out of a café opposite. He yawned, drawing deep of the cool night air. Was this Ishmael? Laura felt her heart quicken its rhythm. What would she do if he approached her? If a pimp thought another was encroaching on his patch, he wouldn't rest until his rival was dead.

He wore soft moccasins and seemed to creep across the flags.

The girls fluttered like doves with a cat on the prowl, and flashed him worried little smiles. Laura kept her head down, watching the same piece of pavement. The moccasins moved into vision.

'So. It's you. About time.'

'I'm not late. I hurried.'

'Time you hurried a little more. Come with me. Quick, quick, I don't wait all night!'

Was it him? She wasn't sure. But there was nothing to do but follow. A buzz of conversation rose up as she left. She was indeed Ishmael's new girl.

He stopped at the corner. 'You have it?'

'I don't know you. I'm not sure.'

'Snow White.'

It was the password. She smiled at him, her teeth flashing, and said in relief, 'I didn't know what to think. I've got it here, there'll be another on Friday.'

'Good. This is for you.' He pressed a piece of paper into her hand, the return message that she must transmit. He said, 'Tomorrow night a man will call on you. Keep him two days. After that we'll be in touch. He's one of us. The Germans know about him. He has to get out.'

Laura was taken aback. She said, 'No one said I was to harbour fugitives! Is it worth getting caught for? I've hardly started.'

'He's a good man. He doesn't deserve to die.' She looked into Ishmael's bland face. Who was he to judge? He was a pimp. But she had no choice. He could send whoever he chose.

'I'll expect him,' she murmured. She walked away, glancing behind only once to watch him make his silent way back.

The house was rowdy by the time she returned. Men were crowding the doorstep, trying to get in. They grabbed at her, putting their hands up her skirt. She felt hysterical suddenly, as if she was truly respectable Mrs Michael Cooper. But she smiled and pushed past them saying, 'Steady, boys. You don't get anything unless you pay.'

Their faces loomed at her, drunken, flushed, some very young. She thought of Gabriel.

She didn't linger in the hall. In her room it was blessedly peaceful, the row downstairs no more than distant thunder. She looked at the paper Ishmael had given her, the usual rubbish.

Letters and numbers to be transmitted without understanding. It could mean anything. She lay on her bed, still in her clothes, unwilling to make herself vulnerable by undressing. The house threatened her, the atmosphere weighed so heavy. She had never noticed it before. But now she thought of Jean and his heavy hands, and Gabriel, in his ignorance hurting her, and the man who beat her and made her pregnant. Every girl downstairs had a story much the same. Why had she ever come back?

She wondered where she could hide Ishmael's man. There was a room next door, used for old furniture and rubbish. It would have to do. She'd filch food if she could, if not he'd go hungry. She knew Ishmael was exceeding himself, this wasn't her job. Except here she couldn't complain.

A body fell against her door. Men were laughing drunkenly on the landing outside. She eyed the frail lock and crept off the bed, moving towards the radio, hidden beneath a pile of magazines. There was nowhere to hide in here! She moved silently to the door and clicked off the light. A voice outside said, 'We know you're in there! We've come to talk to you!'

'Talk?' said another voice, and they muffled their laughter again. She stood in the darkness behind the door as they knocked and called. Soon they grew rowdy. Someone's shoulder hit the door and it shuddered. They began to organise themselves for a concerted assault.

Laura called out, 'Go away. I'm sick. That's why I'm not working.'

'Oh! She's sick! She didn't look sick to me. A bit of all right, that's what I thought.'

They were the men from earlier in the evening. The reasonable one, drunk now, mumbled, 'It might be catching. What do you think it is?'

'What is it, *chérie*?' called a voice.

If she claimed something horrible they might report her. Thoughts whirled madly, until inspiration struck. 'I was pregnant. I had an operation. I'm still not well.'

They began to mutter amongst themselves. Boots sounded on the stair. 'Our apologies, *Mam'selle*,' someone called. 'Our apologies.'

She sank to the floor, listening to the blessed sound of the retreat. What if they'd entered? They'd have had her, each of them, and thought it reasonable because they paid. The thought of it sickened her, and she was amazed. She'd done this for years, she was used to it, there was no more to care about than keeping well. Look at Sophie or Marie. To them having a man was no more than a cup of coffee.

But a face intruded. Gabriel's face. Her mind moved from the first time to the last. The same act, the same function, but nothing about it was similar. Laura's heart seemed to swell in her breast. The difference was love.

She took off her clothes and lay between the sheets, gazing wide-eyed into the dark. What about Michael? She had never wanted to betray him, had never willingly done so. It was all something that happened, like a spilled store of apples rolling down a stair. The barrels were knocked and the apples fell, nothing could stop them. And she had fallen, bumping, into love.

She had forgotten to call in. She got out of bed and crouched naked over the radio, twiddling knobs. She gave her call sign and the answer came crackling back. They were waiting, fearing the worst, when she had only forgotten. She sent Ishmael's message, making mistakes, declaring errors, sending again. When she had finished she waited, they might have something for her. But there was nothing.

Now she was thoroughly cold. She thought of the radio, reciting to herself the codes, trying to stuff dull reason into her head. But little by little she found herself imagining again; she and Gabriel, naked and warm. Lying beneath him, joined to him, feeling him pierce her soul. Dora didn't deserve him, and with Michael it wasn't the same. Why not she and Gabriel, why not the dream?

She had tried, before God she had tried. All her life she had struggled to be different, someone better, someone good. But it was all confused now. Perhaps, after all, it didn't matter what people thought of you. It mattered what you thought of yourself.

The man arrived early next morning. Laura was waiting anxiously in the hall, watching the maids clear up the wreckage of the night before. She could almost imagine herself ten years old, begging nuts or raisins or a leftover bon-bon as a morning

539

treat, getting in everyone's way. Days of innocence? There had been no innocence in her life.

The doorman called, 'Visitor. For Mam'selle Vorronceau.'

Laura hurried forward. The man was grey and unassuming, dressed in workman's overalls. He carried a tool bag, but held it like a briefcase. Although the day was cool, tiny beads of sweat covered his upper lip.

Laura took his hand and shook it. He murmured, 'I shouldn't be here, I might have been followed. I'll go, this is all too dangerous.'

She had been intending to be cool and businesslike. Instead she said, 'I'm sure you took care. Are you hungry? I see there's some food left over from last night. I'll make some coffee. It isn't real coffee but it does.'

'I ought not to be here!'

She hesitated. 'You mean – you don't wish to stay in a brothel?'

She saw realisation dawn on him. 'Forgive me. Is this a brothel? I've never seen one before.' His anxiety was momentarily forgotten. He looked around.

He breakfasted on leftovers in her room. Laura asked discreet questions about his activities, but he told her nothing. He was from a village, he said, he had worked there for many years.

'What as?' she demanded. 'You're not a workman. Look at your trousers, they're not a workman's. And your shirt's too good. Were you an official of some kind?'

'I was a priest.'

She covered her mouth and laughed. After a moment, so did he.

The house was beginning to stir, soon there would be girls everywhere. Laura took her visitor into the next room and showed him an old sofa he could lie on. 'You can wedge the door shut, but it doesn't lock,' she told him. 'How long will you stay?'

'I don't know. Two or three days, I think. Someone will come.'

She nodded, feeling doubtful. Secrets in this house were very hard to keep.

In the afternoon she went out, to try and buy a shirt and trousers more in keeping with the priest's disguise. She went to the market in Les Halles, but there wasn't much there, so she wandered the back streets, looking in the second-hand shops. She found a pair of blue farm overalls, and a checked shirt. She haggled, although she had more than enough money. As she left, parcel in hand, she caught sight of a face she knew. A German officer was browsing in the curio shop next door. He looked up and caught her eye. At once she moved away.

It was Konrad, the German from the road block. What foul, impossible luck! Someone called, then feet began to run. She darted into the nearest shop, full of knitting wool and linen, saying to the woman behind the counter, *'Pardon, Madame.'* She dived into the back, looking for the door, and heard the woman calmly deter her pursuer. 'A girl? We don't have girls. I'm sorry, you must be mistaken.' She slipped through a door, into an alley and away.

The encounter disturbed her a little. It seemed that the longer she stayed in Paris the more complex her lies must become. She went downstairs only once in the evening, to fetch mutton stew for her dinner, sharing it with the priest. She took a bottle of wine as well, and they sat on the sagging old sofa, drinking red wine and playing cards. But at last she sighed and gave up playing. 'I must go. If someone finds you, say you're a workman who got drunk. I'll try and get you out.'

He took her hand and held it. He was very warm. 'You're a good girl,' he said. For some reason she didn't understand tears pricked her eyelids. She turned quickly away.

The radio was difficult that night. The signal kept fading. She had a mental image of the instructor, telling her again and again what she should do, but the words were no more than a drone. A long, coded message was coming out. She crouched by the set scribbling everything down. But the signal was weak, and when she asked them to repeat she got several quite different configurations. She signed off, and took out her book, trying to decide what they were saying to her. She wished she had drunk less of the red wine.

They wanted her to leave. Whichever way she looked at it, back came the answer. She was to make her way to the coast by tomorrow night, when a boat would come for her. She was to leave at once.

Her surprise was complete. She had hardly arrived, she had done nothing! One contact, only one, and an escapee. It was as if she had begun to read a book, only to have it snatched from her with the first chapter half completed.

But then her thoughts moved on. Something had happened. Was it at home, or here? Was her visitor what he seemed, or an informer? Was Ishmael, in fact, a spy? She decided to hide the radio, something she should have done the moment she arrived. She took up the rug and inspected the floorboards, but they were all well nailed down. So she went out on to the landing and looked around. At the end, in a cupboard, were water tanks. Next to them, in a rickety box, was a stack of electric wiring. She went and fetched the radio, pushing it on top of the wires, but it wouldn't go down. Looking though, she could see more. Behind the box, beneath a cistern, was a narrow space. She slotted the radio carefully inside, sliding the code book into a mousehole nearby.

They were singing in the salon below. One of the girls screamed. Laura stood at the top of the stair, listening to the disturbance, shouting, it was probably a fight. The singing died away.

Someone was hurrying up the stairs. Heavy steps. She put her back to the wall, in the shadow, and saw Madame's head appear in the well.

'Lori!' she hissed.

'What is it?' She hung above Madame, while the old woman fought for breath. Her face was purple with exertion.

'They've come,' she managed. 'Get out. They're looking for you. Don't stand there like a fish, girl! Get out!'

Chapter Sixteen

Rosalind stared at her little boys in disbelief. Gone were the well-dressed, well-behaved young gentlemen she had last seen. In their place were two tousled, mucky, defiant little ruffians who had almost killed little Mary. Not a scant half hour before, she had arrived to find them sending the child on a helter-skelter run down the hilly field, strapped tightly into her pram. She was shrieking fit to bust.

'She didn't mind,' said Alan in belligerent explanation. 'Every time we stopped she started blubbering, so we did it again.'

'She was too scared to cry while you were doing it,' expostulated his mother. 'And you, David. As the elder I expect you to have some sense of responsibility! I don't know what's happened since your aunt left. You've gone to pieces!'

'We speak good French,' said David to placate her. 'Marie says we could hold our own with a Parisian ratcatcher any day.'

'I don't want you to hold your own with ratcatchers! I want you in polite society, as civilised boys!'

She turned away. She was losing her temper and that would never do. It was the strain of everything: the job, the bombs, Laura with the Gestapo on her trail, and then a telephone call in broken English from Sophie, summoning her here. If Marie had called then at least she might have understood. As it was she was here, quite unprepared for the chaos.

'Tell me, boys.' She struggled for composure. 'Do those women drink?'

Alan piped up, 'Tisane at breakfast, wine at lunch, although Marie always complains it costs too much, and cognac in the evening. We have lemonade in ours.'

'You – have cognac?'

'It's good for our hearts,' said David. He thought his mother looked rather pale, as if she could do with some cognac too. He decided to try and explain that their game really hadn't been all that bad.

'You know, Mother, when Piers comes to see Mary we send him down the slope too, and he shouts even louder than she does. And did you see, we've got a rope on the handle? That way they don't go into the stream.'

'That's – very sensible of you, David,' said Rosalind weakly. She moved like a sleepwalker back to the house.

The table was laid with a feast. Patties, pastries, sugar-topped custards – food such as Rosalind hadn't seen in years. The tablecloth was snowy white, as the boys' shirts might once have been, but the floor was thick with mud and chicken feathers. Rosalind's father sat as he always did by the fire, smelling of old clothes and unwashed skin. He looked like a tramp, she thought despairingly. But he was mumbling on a cake, and as Sophie passed him she patted his head with her good hand and said something in French. Rosalind felt mounting despair. They were good-hearted, these women, but why did they never clean?

Marie, her thick accent making her difficult to understand, said, 'Eat, *Madame*. We are pleased you could make so long a journey.'

Rosalind chose her words carefully. 'Did you know the boys were terrifying Mary? Sending her down the hill?'

'She cries when they stop,' said Marie. 'She likes it.'

'She could have been killed!'

'I think she is still alive. Come. Eat.'

Rosalind allowed herself to be plied with food. Gradually everyone assembled, even the land girls, who had been promised a special treat.

Mary and the boys had perfunctory clean patches in the general grime, and looked, Rosalind had to admit, as happy as could be.

Ruth said, 'We've had to buy a new linkage for the tractor. I hope Mrs Cooper won't mind. We saved money by fitting it ourselves.'

'You can fit a linkage?' Rosalind blinked at her.

'My boyfriend showed me.'

'And I can shoe,' said Paula. 'If there was a forge on this place we could make all our own ironwork. Mr Mayes won't hear of it, but then he won't hear of a lot of things.'

'I did think the place was looking rather untidy,' ventured Rosalind.

'Well.' The girls looked grim. 'Mr Mayes won't have it any other way but his.'

It was time to broach the matter in hand. Rosalind folded her hands and looked around the table. 'Is that why you called me? Because of Mr Mayes?'

'That man!' Marie looked scornful and Sophie burst into a torrent of French, too fast for Rosalind to understand. The boys sniggered knowingly, causing their mother to stare at them in surprise. Everything was different without Laura! Marie got up from the table and went to the dresser. She fetched a piece of paper. 'It is this.'

The letter was addressed to Laura:

Dear Mrs Cooper,
I regret to inform you that your husband, Major Michael Cooper, has suffered injury during the current conflict. He was struck by shrapnel whilst gallantly leading a supply echelon directly to the rear of tanks, and sustained a head wound. This has resulted in loss of vision.

We are repatriating him with effect from today, to enable him to receive appropriate medical assistance. You will be notified at once of his arrival. Please accept our sincere best wishes for both you and Major Cooper, whose courageous and determined conduct throughout this campaign has merited nothing but praise.

Yours sincerely,
Lieutenant-Colonel S. Llewellyn

Rosalind read the letter again, unable at first to take everything in.

'Uncle Michael's gone blind, hasn't he, Mother?' piped up David. 'I told Marie that was what it meant.'

'How long have you had this letter? When is he coming home?'

Like a conjuror performing his next trick, Marie produced a telegram.

MAJOR MICHAEL COOPER DISEMBARKED LIVERPOOL
ADMITTED SHELBURNE MILITARY HOSPITAL STOP

She was speechless. At last she managed, 'He's in hospital, here, and no one knows? Why wasn't I informed? What were you thinking of?'

Marie said, 'It is not good news for the telephone. Better face to face.'

'My God. Oh, my God. Poor Michael.' She half rose, then sat down again. Gunthwaite's isolation was a curse sometimes, urgent action was impossible! She turned to Ruth. 'Is the car going?'

'No petrol. Mrs Cooper uses all the ration.'

'Damn Mother! Doesn't she ever think?' A thought occurred to her. 'Has anyone told her?'

'Pouff!' Marie threw up her hands. 'A thousand times no! She and I have quarrelled. We do not speak.'

Rosalind knew that she was in no condition to face her mother either. She turned to Ruth again. 'We'll take the tractor to Fairlands and borrow their car. I can telephone from there. If I call my husband he can get in touch with the hospital and find out what's going on. At least then Michael can have a message. He won't think we've entirely forgotten him.'

'I bet he really wants Auntie Laura,' said David. 'Can't she come back now, Mother? We promise we'll be good.'

'She'll be back soon,' said Rosalind vaguely. 'Very soon, I hope.'

There was the tramp of boots in the downstairs rooms. Laura felt like crying, like running to her bed and hiding beneath the pillow. It was like the moment when a child fell, and you thought they were badly hurt; for a second you didn't want to know. She pulled herself together. She couldn't leave the priest. He had to go too.

She rushed into his room, he hadn't even wedged the door. They were both so bad at this! 'We've got to go. They're searching the house.'

'Go? How?'

'Come with me.'

Not for nothing had she spent her childhood in this house.

546

She went out on the landing again and listened. They were still on the ground floor, searching, interrogating the girls. She began to tiptoe down to the first floor, the priest following, breathing hard. He was terrified, she realised. For her part she was suddenly calm, all the fear within her turned to resolve. This was a game she could win.

The big room that used to be Thelma's was empty. The bed was covered with white lace with a doll in a wedding dress perched on it. Prostitutes often had dolls like that. The walls were covered with photographs of naked women in artistic poses, except for a curtain, hanging on the far wall. It concealed a door. 'In here,' said Laura. 'It leads to the next house.'

She drew bolts stiff with disuse. As she knew from her childhood explorations, the door led into the back of a cupboard, which in turn led into a bedroom. She and the priest stepped inside, closing the door behind them. It would be found no doubt, soon enough. The space was cramped and dark, Laura reached out in memory as well as the present, and pushed the cupboard door.

A girl was on the bed astride a man. He was groaning, his eyes closed, muttering in German. As the cupboard door creaked the girl looked up, her eyes widening in disbelief. Laura put her finger to her lips. Without once disrupting her rhythm, the girl drew a pillow over the man's eyes, nodding her head towards the chair. The uniform of a German officer. Without a sound, Laura and the priest crept away.

They took a train out of town, and spent the night under a hedge. In the morning the priest was sneezing, but he began to trudge along. The coast was some fifteen kilometres still, if Laura had guessed right. She dared not ask anyone. The priest seemed to trust her without question, doing everything just as she said. But his soft feet in their unfamiliar shoes began to trouble him and by midday he was limping badly. Laura felt exasperated. What had he done all his life? Why should she have to bear the burden of someone like this?

They stopped at a pond. She bathed his feet and put leaves in his shoes. He seemed quite helpless, almost a child. Her own feet were hot and sore. She put them in the water, stockings and all. A memory of Michael caught her, bare-legged in the trout stream, and suddenly she wanted to cry.

'We've got to get on,' she said brusquely.

The priest said, 'It's good of you to help me. You'd be there now without me.'

'Yes.'

She was unforgiving. Because of him she was risking her life. But as they walked on, and the priest sneezed but did not complain, she softened. 'Are you hungry? Perhaps, at a village, we could stop.'

'I'm not so hungry.' Yet she was famished. Her head began to swim and she took long breaths to clear it. Vaguely, at a distance, she heard the priest say, 'I thought at first you were one of the women who work in that house. But of course you're not.'

'Would it matter if I was?'

'It's a sin. Obviously, it's a sin.' Laura made a noise, half laugh half snort. He added, 'For myself, I don't think it would matter.'

'Well, now? Isn't that kind?'

Her irony was lost on him. But anger was good for her, she felt a new charge of strength. She walked more quickly.

The countryside was very flat just here. Laura felt conspicuous, two upright figures in a world of horizontal lines. They could not yet see the sea, except as a faint blue haze in the distance, punctuated by the black humps of fortifications. A woman was cycling towards them, they could see her coming for at least a kilometre. When she reached them she said, 'They patrol this road. They'll be here any time. You should get in the ditch.'

'Thank you.'

They scrambled down the embankment. A pipe ran beneath the road, taking water from the stream. It was the only place and they crouched in it, soaking in floating ice. After a while a car ran over the road above them, and they crawled out to look after it. The patrol.

'God be thanked,' whispered the priest. 'And the old woman too.'

'She might have given us some bread,' said Laura, frozen and irritable. 'Her basket was full of it.'

'How much further is it?'

She shook her head. 'I don't know. They showed me a map

548

before I left with lots of things marked on it, but I can't remember it all that well. The place is somewhere down here.'

She should have taken more notice, of course. If she survived this she would take notice of everything they said. She would practise morse code night and day, she would study maps until the world was as familiar as her own hand. But of course, if she ever survived this, she wasn't coming back. She'd done enough.

They were very tired by the time they reached the coast. Pillbox gun emplacements were everywhere, they didn't know how many had troops in them. They sat behind a sand dune while they massaged their miserable feet, and wondered about mines. The sea lapped grey and inhospitable, and it was growing dark. 'Where do you think the boat might come?' asked the priest. But she didn't know.

The chances of being rescued seemed remote. Instead they would be caught by a German patrol, it was only a matter of time. Laura decided they would wait until two in the morning, and then give up. They must find a farmhouse to give them food and shelter, and she would get back to Paris and her wireless. The fuss would be over by now and the priest could help himself, she didn't know how to help him any more.

It was very dark now. The wind was increasing, sending sand like wasps against her face. Safe from the pillboxes they stood up and went out into the gloom, looking at the rolling white crests collapsing against the shore.

A light flashed. Laura stared in disbelief, the steady pulses registering despite herself. 'That's for me,' she said. 'We need a light. I haven't a light.'

'I've a match,' said the priest.

Laura took the box, struck, and watched the flame die. It was no good, the priest must strike the match in the shelter of his hands, and she would move her hands in front of his, giving the signal. Three, four matches, and they were still struggling. The light out to sea disappeared. 'Oh,' said Laura.

It was like a death. She didn't know how much she had longed for rescue until she was sure it wouldn't come. Her lips were trembling, she wanted to rush to the waves, run through them, calling, 'Come back! Come back! Wait for me!' Didn't they know that home awaited her? For all its difficulties and confusions, her life there was the life she longed to live. It was the place where she belonged.

The priest said, 'We could find a farmhouse, I suppose. They might be kind.'

'I don't want a farmhouse! I want to go home!' She was sobbing a little and he patted her shoulder. After a moment he said, 'They've sent a boat. Look. Over there.'

A small rowing boat was bumping into the shore. Laura's heart leaped, she was running, hardly able to breathe. She spoke in French first, and then in English, when she realised they didn't understand. 'Have you come for me? Really?'

A burly seaman grinned at her. 'Should think so. If you're Snow White then we're the Seven Dwarfs. Let's be having you.'

Gabriel climbed over the door of the sports car and stood in the road, waiting until it had driven off. Everyone had been fearfully decent. When they realised his brother was in hospital here someone found a transport that was going, and when he arrived one of the Americans on the base gave him a lift. So here he was. The last place in the world that he ever wanted to be.

He turned to look at the hospital. It was a country house of some sort, one of the many commandeered for the care of injured servicemen. A paddock to the side of the drive had been ploughed up and sown with vegetables, giving the place a lopsided air. There were holes in the lawns where metal railings had been sent to be melted down to make planes, or whatever it was they did with the stuff. Whole suburbs in London, once neat with iron balustrades, now had nothing but sawn off stumps.

The war had wrecked everything, thought Gabriel. People, places, everything was changed, and once he would have delighted in it. The grim, poor, misery of the people needed to be turned on its head and shaken into something better. But in place of all that there were men like Zwmskorski, fat as a seagull feeding on refuse and scum. When all this was over, it wouldn't be the fighting men that came out on top, he thought bitterly. It would be the seagulls, stateless, voracious, suddenly made bold.

He found himself at the front door. A notice said 'All Visitors Report To Matron's Office'. He pushed open the door and wandered the marble hall, looking for a sign. An old woman came out of a room and snapped, 'Can't you read, young man?'

'I'm a visitor. I was looking—'

'The side door. This hall is for my personal use and for emergencies.'

Gabriel retreated.

The Matron's Office, discovered through the side door, was filled not with the matron but a pretty young nurse. She was delighted to see him. 'For Major Cooper? I'm so glad. He's had no one you know, and everyone else has been deluged, what with being away so long.'

'We didn't know. The telegram was misdirected.'

'Really? You'd think they'd be careful, wouldn't you, in war time? I mean, people could think anything.'

She led the way along polished wood floors, Gabriel following, his breathing suddenly short. Would Michael be scarred? What would he say? How in God's name could he begin to explain everything?

A figure was sitting by the window. As they entered he turned a little, catching the sound of their step. 'Hello, Major,' said the nurse. 'You've a visitor.'

And as Gabriel saw the leap of hope in Michael's face, he said quickly, 'Sorry, Mike. It's only me.'

'Gabriel! Gabriel. Oh, come here, old chap. At least let me shake your hand.'

Michael's hands were burned the colour of teak. Once he had been enormous, a giant to the small boy who was his brother. Now they gripped equally, two big men. But one of them was blind.

'Can you see anything?' asked Gabriel. 'You look so well, just as you always did.'

'There's some light. No more than that. Shrapnel, pressing on the nerve.'

'But they could operate. Surely—'

'Apparently no one wants to try.'

Gabriel took a long, steadying breath. Michael said, 'I find it's best not to think about it. There's nothing anyone can do. I try and keep my mind busy, and people read to me and so on. Out there you know, in the desert, thousands of blokes are far worse off. You've no idea, the carnage. I'd rather be like this than blown to pieces.'

'Yes. Of course.' Privately Gabriel thought, I'd rather die.

Michael smiled uncertainly, as if he sensed that Gabriel might not be with him. His head was tilted, striving to catch every sound. He looked like a blind man, thought Gabriel, and tears closed his throat. He made a strangled sound and Michael said quickly, 'Did you know we're all blind in here? They think it's nice for us, but it's a bloody farce. Nobody at all can see a bloody thing. Fifty blokes, blundering about knocking things over. The old girl who owns this place thinks we do it on purpose. She puts up notices which obviously we can't read and then we fall over them and that's that.'

Gabriel laughed awkwardly. He felt a strong sense of unreality, sitting here. Some basic rule of life was being turned on its head. He was the younger brother, spoiled, wayward, never permitted in the grown-up world. He had entered that world now. My God, he had.

Michael said, 'Where's Laura? I've been waiting—'

'We only heard yesterday. Some mix-up with the telegram. She'll come as soon as she can.'

'But you're here. Is it Mary, is she ill? Or the boys—' His hand went up to his face, in a gesture suddenly familiar; Michael's old, boyhood habit, nervously smoothing his chin. Gabriel felt desperate suddenly. Michael's invincibility had only ever been a myth. He had taken from his brother all that he held most dear, when all Michael had ever done was to be older. He saw that now. So much resentment, so much jealousy, all because of something that neither of them could change.

'No one's ill,' he said grimly. 'It isn't that.' He took a very deep breath. 'Laura isn't at Gunthwaite. She's in France.'

'France! Why? I mean – Good God!'

Gabriel said, 'It's something Rosalind and Howard are involved with. Resistance. And you have to admit, Laura's ideal. Clever, resourceful, brave. And as French as they come.'

'And – and you let her go?'

'I couldn't stop her! At least – she did what she wanted, Mike. She wanted to do her bit.'

Michael blundered to his feet, half tripping over the rug, standing stranded and helpless. 'But it isn't possible! I won't permit it! My wife, MY WIFE, going off from her home and her child, into danger! It's not women's work, Gabriel. None of this is!'

Gabriel caught his arm. 'It wasn't women's work looking after Gunthwaite, but you left her with that! And don't say you left Bill Mayes in charge. But for Laura, you'd be bankrupt by now.'

'I'll speak to Howard. I won't have it. I left Laura at home, that's her place, it's where she should be. We're fighting this war so that women like Laura need not grow hard and vulgar, need not know what it all means!'

'She's not a child. She isn't simple, either. Perhaps she doesn't want to be preserved in her innocent little world. She might want to fight for freedom. Even women have principles, Michael.'

After a moment, and more quietly, Michael felt for his chair. He said, 'Is she all right? Do you know?'

'I don't know anything. I don't suppose anyone does. She's only been gone a few weeks, no one knew about you. We haven't told Mother yet. I didn't think you'd want her coming here. Better at home, perhaps.'

'Yes.'

Michael touched his chin again. The gesture soothed him. He couldn't think straight, trapped behind this mist. Was Gabriel lying, was Laura dead, why couldn't he see? All at once he felt exhausted. It was shock, and anxiety, and the endless, unremitting weight of being blind. He said, 'I don't suppose you'd go, would you? I'm sorry. It's so hard to take in. Laura's gentle. Sensitive. She can be easily upset.'

Gabriel's hand closed on his shoulder, not in comfort but in rage. Michael flinched instinctively, bewildered. 'Do you believe that?' Gabriel was almost spitting in his face. 'Do you honestly believe that? I'll swear to God that you've never looked at your wife properly, never seen what she is! She's sensitive, all right. You wanted a soft little pet, and she pretended, just for you! You don't know her anger, you don't know her passion, you don't know her steel! Before God, Michael, I swear you don't know her at all!'

There was silence. Deprived of sight, seeing now what he had never seen before, Michael said, 'And you do, I suppose?'

'Yes,' said Gabriel softly. 'I do.'

He had said what he had vowed never to say. But Michael was his brother, they were of the same blood, the same rearing, the same history. Those unsaid words would have lived forever between them.

Michael sat very still. After a moment he said, 'I asked you to go. I don't know why you came.'

'I can stay in the village, I can come back. We've got to talk. We've got to make arrangements.'

'I'll make them with Rosalind, thank you.'

Gabriel looked at his brother's closed, set face, the unseeing eyes. He didn't know what he was thinking. 'I'm glad you're home,' said Gabriel, thickly. And he left.

Hours later, Michael rose and made his stumbling way to his room. He needed to sleep, needed to blot out thought, memory, most of all imagination. Faces lived before his eyes, Laura, Gabriel – more than faces. Bodies locked together, moving together, him and her. A nurse found him blundering around the landing and led him to his room. He closed the door, leaning on it, letting his face contort with anguish. This, as well as everything? In God's name, why? What had he done?

He fell on the bed, misjudging and hitting his head on his locker. He didn't care, he welcomed pain, blood, destruction. Let Laura die, and Gabriel too, let the three of them sink into a swamp of dying flesh. There was nothing left in the world that was clean and good, it was all putrefaction.

The tears burned his sightless eyes. He had believed in life, he thought wonderingly. He had placed his faith in goodness and love. He had been an utter fool.

Laura stood on the quay in the wind. Dawn was breaking, turning the iron dark to steel morning. Fine rain was soaking everything, and a crane was whining. She put her shoulders back. They were surprisingly stiff, as if all the time in France she had crouched a little. It was the fear, falling away like unwanted baggage, letting her stand tall in this cold free air. The priest said, 'I must thank you. You did so much.'

'It was nothing. I'm not a very good spy.'

He shrugged, seeming so Gallic amidst the sturdy figures of the crew. 'Who is a good spy? None of us intended so to be.

When all this is done we shall go back to being what we once were and try to be good at that.' Laura smiled. She might have liked him, she thought, if there had been time. If he'd been a bit less feeble. She said, 'I must go now. They've sent a car.'

'So soon? I am to wait, they say. An interpreter is needed.'

They shook hands. The priest took her case and carried it for her along the dock, looking about him too much and tripping over ropes and wires. Laura took hold of his coat and guided him, until they came to the car. He said, 'So. You take care of me to the end. I wonder why?'

Laura said, 'A priest was kind to me once, when I was very small. He did more than was necessary.'

He said, 'It was the Christ in him. When we have the Christ in us we can be very strong.' He moved his hands in blessing.

She got into the car. The priest waved to her, and continued waving, a silly flap of the wrist. She turned in the seat to stare back at him, wanting to press her hands to the glass, wanting to cry out to him, a man she almost despised: 'Am I forgiven? Is it done? What must I do now?'

They took her straight to her training centre once more. As the car passed along the avenue of beech trees she saw faces at the windows and as she approached the front door it opened to reveal a welcoming party. Foremost among them was the wireless instructor.

'Well done, Mrs Cooper! We're all thrilled.'

'Thank you.'

'If you'd like to come through? A glass of sherry perhaps?'

'You're very kind.'

It was all a front, of course. She was to report as fully as she knew how. Warmed by the sherry and a roaring fire, she began to talk, to tell them everything. It was a relief, an expurgation, letting them decide if Ishmael had helped her or not. 'He could have been an informer,' she said. 'I don't know.'

'He was picked up,' said the commander. 'That could be a front too, of course.'

'I don't know why he sent me the priest. He must have had others he could go to.'

'Perhaps he knew he was threatened. You were known only to him. You had to be safe.'

She twirled her glass. 'Any of the street girls could have guessed about me. Or the radio might have been picked up, or someone guessed in Madame's. But still, I think Ishmael.'

They were looking at her intently. 'Now,' said the commander. 'What about next time?'

'Thank you. No.'

'Perhaps you'd like a little time to think? We were impressed, you know. Very impressed. But such a short stay, so little done—'

She looked directly into the commander's cold blue eyes. 'Do you have news of my husband, please? And my daughter? I don't really want to discuss any more of this until I know if they are well.'

There was a brief pause. The men shuffled a little. The commander touched a bell, the door opened and Rosalind's husband came in. Laura got to her feet, suddenly afraid. 'Howard? What's happened, what is it?'

'It's all right, my dear.' Tall, very thin and grey, he rested his veined hands on her shoulders. 'It's Michael. They've sent him home. I'm afraid he's blind.'

Everything seemed to become very still. Like the night her mother died, time frozen to nothing. She saw how tired Howard looked, she thought of the priest, she thought how odd it was that she knew the wireless instructor was thinking about taking her to bed. And then she thought of Michael, sightless, blind, and the world began again.

'I must go to him. How dare you keep me here!'

'We had to debrief you, Mrs Cooper. We were as quick as we could be.'

'I have to go. Howard, where is he?'

'Rosalind's taking him to Gunthwaite. Please, Laura, try and be calm. You never know, there may be something they can do.'

Not since infancy had she believed in happy endings. When the foot comes on the stair and keeps on coming, despite your prayers and wishes and rabbits' feet, then you understand. You know you're cursed.

Chapter Seventeen

Michael was sitting at the window, where his father sat in summer, watching the hens in the yard. But he saw no hens, just the clouds, reflected in a shimmer of altered light. Now and then there were voices, Rosalind, the Frenchwomen, his own infant daughter or the boys. He felt remote from them. They touched him but he lived elsewhere. They might all of them have known what was going on.

He heard the car that brought her. He knew the instant it pulled into the yard. All those months without her, all those years longing for her, all those nights when he couldn't remember her face! He would never see her now. She could come as close to him as his own skin and she was still a mile away. He felt disordered, his mind in turmoil, he wished only that Gabriel had made sure that he never, never knew!

'Michael.' That cool, utterly English voice. How easily she lied. 'Michael, darling.'

'Laura!' Everything in him rose up and betrayed him. His hands reached for her. She put her arms around his neck, her face against his. She smelled French, of French perfume, and her skin was like silk. He put his nose into her hair, if he could he would die entangled in those strands. He wanted to die. 'I love you,' he said, as if surprised at himself. 'After all of it, I still do.'

'Do you? Really? Oh Michael, I'm so glad!'

She sounded as if she meant it. What a liar she was, what a trickster! She was French but sounded English, she was strong but seemed so weak, she was faithless when he'd thought her pure! He put her away from him, feeling tears fall from his helpless, useless eyes. 'Gabriel told me,' he said.

Her shock was tangible. He could feel her stiffen in his hands. She said in a high, strained voice, 'What did he say?'

'Do you think you might still get out of it? He said he knew you better than me. It seems he does.'

'You don't understand. There wasn't – I couldn't – Michael, I love you!'

'Do you? Do you really? And what about Gabriel?'

In a desperate, infant voice she said, 'That isn't the same. We thought you were dead. Please, Michael. Don't be unkind.'

'You betrayed me.'

She gasped, as if he had struck her. 'No! No. Never in my heart.'

He heard her get up and walk to the table. He knew that she was leaning on it, head down, trying to steady herself. She was near to fainting. He said, 'Is there brandy? Drink that.'

'But you must need something. You're ill.'

'I'm blind, you mean. Perhaps it's as well. I'm no use to you now.'

She said, 'I didn't marry you because you were of use! I needed you. I need you now. But you left me, and I was different on my own! I'll be different again, I swear it. I won't wear trousers or ride astride, I won't drive the tractor. I won't – I won't.'

The tears were rising again. Shameful, impossible tears. He fought with them, holding them down. 'Did I really ask so much?' he whispered hoarsely.

'No! You asked nothing I wasn't happy to give.'

She was close to him again. He knew her fingers were touching the merest tips of his hair. He said, 'I shall sleep in the chimney room. I think that's best.'

'It's a bathroom now,' said Laura. 'The house is full. I can't bear it if you stay away. Please, Michael.'

'I don't want you near me!'

'You're angry. You have a right. It's because you don't understand.'

She was confusing him. She should be offering to leave. To her this was the same as wearing trousers or driving a tractor, a little, unfeminine misdemeanor that she felt sure he would soon overlook. He turned his sightless eyes on her, feeling his world collapse and disintegrate, knowing that finally he was dust and ashes in the desert of his life. 'Don't you want him?' he asked. 'If you could have what you want, wouldn't it be him?'

'No,' she replied without thinking, without needing to think. Michael was here, hurting, a body and a soul with no comfort but her. She would give him what she had, as she had always given, without stint, without thought for tomorrow. She wrapped her arms around him, holding him again whether he wanted it or not. 'I'm here where I want to be,' she whispered. 'I'm with my husband.'

People came. A procession of people spoke and shook hands and wished him well. Well! Michael sat in his chair, wondering who knew, who was laughing at him, not even bothering to hide their smiles. A blind man could so easily be deceived. And a sighted man as easily perhaps.

At last, when the kitchen seemed quiet, he said, 'Laura?'

'I'm here.'

So close to him. He was surprised. He said, 'It started before, didn't it? You were always his.'

'No.'

Did she hesitate? Was she too quick? He felt the anger again, fighting against his grief. 'I should have known, of course. You're just a tart. A French tart.'

He heard her gasp, felt her draw back. He knew her so well, he could almost see the shock on her face. 'That hurts, doesn't it?' he snarled. 'If the cap fits!'

'I'm your wife,' she whispered. 'You can't – I'm not – I've tried so hard to be what you wanted!'

'What? You went with my brother the moment I was out of the way! For all I know you were doing it with him right under my nose!'

After a long silence she said, 'You're not my Michael. He would never say such things. I expected better. Because that's the measure of someone, that's the test! To endure, to suffer, and still to be kind.'

She was leaving him. She was walking away. He put out his hand, trying to hold her, stop her, and caught the hem of her skirt.

'I can't forgive,' he said helplessly. 'I don't have the strength for it any more.'

Her fingers fluttered about him, like butterflies. She dared not touch. 'But in time perhaps? Don't you think?'

'You don't know how much it hurts.'

She drew in her breath. He knew then that she suffered too. He wanted to reach out to her, hold her, take away her pain. But he was blind and helpless. What could he give to her? He was no longer an upright man.

That night, they slept in the same old bed, separated by six inches of sheet that could have been half the world. Michael imagined he could hear his wife's thoughts. Gabriel, of course. Or not? He didn't recognise this creature she seemed to have become. The Laura he knew, the Laura he loved, wasn't a faithless woman. But she must be. She had slept with his brother.

In the morning, they rose like strangers, walled off from each other by Michael's sightless eyes. They could each be naked and it meant nothing. She helped him dress, took him downstairs and helped him eat, placed the baby on his helpless knee. She knew that he hated himself as much as her. As she shaved him, tidying the inept and bloody mess he had made himself, she could sense that he despised himself for blindness, weakness, even for love.

His mother stopped by during the morning. When she saw Michael's face she said, 'Don't tell me you tried to shave yourself! You have to accept, Michael, these things are beyond you. Get Laura to do it.'

Laura said tightly, 'He'll learn how to do it. It only takes time.'

'You don't want to do it, that's all! I suppose you're too grand for mundane tasks after London. Michael, you've no idea the state of this place while you were away. Laura isn't up to the mark, I'm afraid. And I don't know how we shall manage now, I really don't. I'm thinking of writing to Gabriel, he'll have to come home and farm.'

'You'll do no such thing,' snapped Michael.

'But really! Someone has to see to things.'

'Michael will,' said Laura grimly. 'He knows the farm well enough.'

Mrs Cooper leaned conspiratorially towards her son. 'What did I tell you? The girl hasn't the faintest grasp of reality. Of course you can't farm.'

When she was gone, Laura said, 'She's so stupid! You won't listen to her, will you? I'll tell you what you can't feel or smell. We all will. You can farm.'

Suddenly Michael got up and blundered to the window. 'I don't want to exist on the instructions of my faithless wife! I want to see!'

Quietly Laura said, 'I'd still be faithless.'

He turned away from her. 'But I wouldn't need you so. How I hate it.'

She stood in the middle of the kitchen, a cloth twisted tight in her hands. Her heart was breaking into a million pieces, collapsing into dust. She had thought her care was building something once again, when each touch of her hands revolted him. She should never have loved, she thought desperately. First her mother, and now this. Such pain could barely be endured.

The days were grey and formless. Mrs Cooper, enraged by this turn of events, was looking for someone to blame. She went to the vicar and berated him, and he came to see Michael and depressed him for days. He should be sent away, people muttered, to learn Braille and to tell the time. Michael knew what they were thinking. He thought it himself. How much better for everyone if he had never come back at all.

Gabriel had returned to his squadron, but Howard and Rosalind stayed on. They felt it the least they could do, they said, unaware that Laura longed for them to go. She wanted rid of them all, Sophie, Marie, Mr Cooper, the boys. If it was just she and Michael and Mary, she thought wistfully, then things might go right. As it was, everything was going wrong. In the second week, she felt panic rising in her. Was this what it would always be? Was she to be her husband's nurse, his unwanted drudge, and nothing more?

She stood on the upstairs landing, watching him creep like a snail down the worm-eaten stair, clinging to the banister. Flashes of memory sparked in her brain, like a light turning on and off: Madame, warning her of the soldiers; Gabriel, laughing from below; Michael running down these same stairs, rushing to get on with his day.

She felt restless and afraid. She couldn't live like this, she thought miserably. Michael had turned from her. She had killed his faith in her. She had done everything, she wanted to scream, she had kept faith in all but this one little thing. Didn't he know, couldn't he see, that the sex meant nothing? If she counted it as vital, something you could never slough off, was she then to be crushed beneath the burden of all those thousands of other times with other men?

Was it she who was wrong? Or did the respectable people merely build false walls of sin to keep everything neat and nice? It was so easy to judge when you had never been tried. If the Germans had caught her in France she knew only too well that she would have killed to be free. And when she came home? Such congratulations, such praise of her courage! So much less courage than that required of a young prostitute, to face drunk men she didn't know, to keep from screaming, keep from crying, keep from sliding down and down until she too was drowned by it all. When your world will turn and smile on you, there is no courage required, she thought.

Michael reached the bottom of the stair. She said, 'I have to give the children breakfast. But you'll want to get out to the sheep.'

'There's no point. I can't do anything.'

'Trimming feet, perhaps. You could do that by feel.'

'Another day.'

He didn't want to do anything. If it was her or the blindness she didn't know, and after all, it didn't matter. He would sit, day after day, watching with sightless eyes.

Howard and Rosalind came in from the yard. They were flushed with fresh country air, and Rosalind's hands were full of winter grasses. 'I thought I'd make an arrangement, Laura. Something fashionable, they're quite the thing in London nowadays. No one can get hothouse flowers any more.'

'Lovely.' She came halfway down the stair, following Michael, ready to catch and steer him at each and every turn.

Howard said, 'Come into the kitchen, both of you. We've something we want to discuss.'

The kettle was singing on the range. Two empty bowls stood testament to the boys' breakfast, and Mary sat in her playpen, sucking on a rusk. Laura went and gathered her up. While she was gone the child had become a waif, passed from hand to hand, fed by anyone. She wanted to reclaim her and didn't know how. The baby didn't seem to mind.

Howard said, 'We're buying a house. Near London. Rosalind and I saw it some time ago and it really is ideal. We're taking the boys home. We think it's time.'

Laura said, 'Is it safe? The raids—'

'It's much better than it was,' said Rosalind. 'And it's going to get better still. We shall certainly win this war, even if it does take years. And the house is in a village; we'd have to be very unlucky to be hit.'

Laura looked at Michael. Did he know what his sister was really saying? She would rather the boys risked bombs than went on like this. She felt angry suddenly. Rosalind and Howard had all the arrogance of sophisticated people, they never thought that the needs of others counted for much at all. If she was unfair, then she had reason, thought Laura. But for them she would never have gone to France. The boys would be sensible, the house would be clean – and Michael need never have known. Gabriel had been wrong, she would never have told him. What was one more secret in the box? She would have done anything to spare herself this.

Howard looked at Michael too. 'We wanted to thank you,' he said. 'Both of you. Laura took the boys, she kept everything going.'

Michael said, 'It was nothing to do with me. Laura did as she wanted.'

'You were happy for the boys to come,' said Laura. 'Michael, you know you were.'

Howard continued smoothly on. 'And now this thing with your eyes, Michael. Rotten bad luck. Rosalind and I want to pay for a good farm manager, someone qualified, who can bring in the latest methods. He could help both of you, really ease the load. It's time Gunthwaite was dragged into the twentieth century, you know. What do you say?'

Once Laura and Michael would have exchanged glances. Now there was nothing, just space, a silent void. No two people had ever been so distant, thought Laura despairingly. Unable to touch him, unable to guess at his response, she spoke instinctively.

'We don't want Gunthwaite in the twentieth century. And Michael can still run the farm. He can't see but he can still think.'

Rosalind said diffidently, 'I understand your loyalty, Laura – but remember, the farm wasn't doing very well before the war. It's done much better since modern methods were introduced.'

'Are you saying Michael's a bad farmer? Are you saying that?' Her voice was rising hysterically. Michael simply sat there, looking out at nothing, as if he was in the wrong place and knew no one in the room. She went on hectically, 'There was a slump before. Grain wouldn't sell and neither would sheep. We did what we could with milk but we're too far away to have much of a market. If things have changed it's the war that's changed them. No more imported corn, for one thing. And as for modern methods – it would break my heart to see the horses go.'

There was a silence. Then to everyone's surprise, Michael chuckled. He said, 'You sound like my father, Laura, the day I suggested we should buy a horsedrawn binder and stop stacking the corn by hand. He said it would put men out of work. He was right.'

'There you are then,' said Laura shakily. It was the first spontaneous comment Michael had addressed to her since his first day home.

But Howard said, 'You have to realise, Michael, that things are bound to progress still more once the war's finished. The whole country's changing. There'll be better education, fewer class divisions, in all probability fewer people willing to work the land. All those men who used to work for a pittance won't come back from the war and start again where they left off! They've seen the world. They'll expect more.'

'You're telling me Gunthwaite's finished,' said Michael flatly. 'The old ways won't do, and it's new ones or nothing.'

'We're going to help you,' said Rosalind, moving to take his hand. 'A new trained man with new ideas. Then it won't matter that you can't see; you can relax, enjoy life.'

'The scrap heap,' said Laura. 'That's what you want for him. But Michael knows this land, he loves it. He could farm it blindfold, so he can certainly farm it blind!'

No one said anything. Rosalind patted Michael's hand, just as if he was her father and out of his mind. Howard said,

'Why don't you think about it? No need to make a decision now, or even a few months from now. Shall we say, by this time next year? Give us all time to adjust to things. So much has changed.' He and Rosalind stood smiling at them. Two benefactors, kind, well-meaning people stamping on their souls.

There was a disturbance that afternoon. Rosalind was packing the boys' clothes, making faces at darned sweaters, promising dozens of new shirts and socks. From time to time Marie or Sophie would pass her and sniff contemptuously. 'That woman!' said Marie to Laura. 'The first time she takes notice of those children in years.'

'She's had more to concern her,' said Laura, although she too felt like throwing something at Rosalind. How dare she stand in judgment? It was as if Gunthwaite had been good enough for years, but was now shabby and unnecessary once again.

She stood at the landing window, feeling disconnected from everything. The gander was stalking the yard, hot rage in his eyes, hissing at nothing. That meant the goose was laying again, the first sign of the end of winter. She saw Sophie and old Mr Cooper come out of the house, taking their afternoon walk together. Blowsy, good-natured Sophie, who had always thought too little of herself to take care. She was limping on her bad leg. She had never pretended to be other than she was. Laura felt an odd stirring in her battered heart. Not quite smashed, then. Dear Sophie.

The gander saw them. He hissed and flapped his wings, trying to deflect them from their course, in case they should happen upon his treasured nest. Sophie flapped back, too tentative to deter him, and the bird began running, wings spread, feet absurdly paddling, honking like a train. Sophie shrieked, old Mr Cooper dithered, and then even he took fright. Sophie and the old man began a heavy run towards the orchard, while the gander flapped in their wake, victorious. Laura laughed at the spectacle, thinking that soon it would be spring, soon there would be no war, soon Michael would warm to her again. She was still laughing when the old man stopped, swayed and collapsed to the ground. The gander stopped too, disconcerted, and paddled back the way he had come. In the seconds before Sophie's wail, the yard was suddenly very still.

Everyone came to the funeral. Mrs Cooper called it a travesty. 'He was dead in his mind ten years or more ago.'

Laura stood beside Michael before the service, introducing those who didn't introduce themselves, hearing the awkward condolences on more than his father's death. 'Danged shame about them eyes, Michael. Mind, you've still got your balls. Get a good few sons and let them do t'work, that's my advice.'

In a lull Michael said, 'I'm sorry they're so coarse. My father's side are plain farming folk, they don't mean offence.'

'I don't take offence at a bit of honesty,' said Laura tartly. 'Besides, they're probably right.'

In a voice like a stiletto, Michael said, 'We both know I won't soil myself with my brother's leavings, Laura.'

The shock was complete. She had thought herself beyond pain, beyond this ghastly sickness. She thought she might faint, she almost wished she could. A dark curtain rose across her vision, stopping at her chin. Above it, approaching, she saw Gabriel.

Fire seemed to scorch her breast. She wanted to scream, tear her hair, fall to the floor and lie twitching, at last driven mad. Gabriel was looking at her, his face full of concern. She must look strange, embarrassingly so. She turned her back, which meant turning to Michael, but he couldn't see. At least he need not know that Gabriel had come. She said in a breathless, bitter voice, 'We'd better go in. At least, we sinners should. You perfect people might not need to.'

Everyone was looking. She took Michael's arm, feeling herself shake with anger at the lie, suddenly filled with more hate and rage than she had ever known. She had warned him against marrying her, and he'd insisted. She'd begged him not to go to war, but he would. If he had tried to know her, tried to understand, she might never have failed him in this way!

The church was full, a sea of black. The vicar, at his most sonorous, began: 'I am the resurrection and the life.' Michael had been her life. He had rescued her from the swamp.

'I know that my Redeemer liveth.' So why could she never be redeemed? It was denied to her, she bore the taint that could never wash away.

'We brought nothing into this world and it is certain we can carry nothing out.' But some were born into softness, and some on to hard stony ground. She had taken what she had and made of it what she could, knowing no other.

The tears were pouring down her cheeks. She looked at Michael, willing him to see, to sense her distress. He looked ahead still. She couldn't stand another minute and scrambled out of the pew, pushing past Rosalind, Howard, her mother-in-law, out into the miserable afternoon.

It was Gabriel who came after her. She ran through the churchyard, past the waiting grave, the gravediggers standing chatting by the gate. Her heels slithered in the mud. She scrambled over the wall and into the vicarage pasture, laddering her stockings on the way. As she ran on, startling sheep heavy in lamb, Gabriel called after her: 'Laura! Laura, wait!'

But she couldn't wait. She had waited all her life, waited patiently for it all to come right. She had thought the years would be enough, leaving everything behind, only to find she had been cheated. Time looped back on itself, sending the past flying in your face, again and again. Why wouldn't it go? Why did yesterday haunt her, so that Jean could come again, night after night, to press down on her with his stinking, foul body? Sometimes she'd wake, breathing hard, and crouch in the dark. Was it him or another? The man who beat her, perhaps. Even the doctor who matter-of-factly scraped out of her another unwanted life.

She was in the willows, where their winter-brown hair touched the water still. The river ran slowly here. You could not drown. Even so, when Gabriel charged up he grabbed her, gasping, 'Don't! Don't jump!'

She looked at him. A tall, muscled, good-looking man with a nerve twitching near his eye. 'I hate you for telling him,' she said simply.

He sank on to a fallen tree, which would leave streaks of mould on his neat blue uniform. 'I know. I'm sorry, I couldn't not. We're not liars, are we? In the end we have to face the truth.'

'Michael likes to be deceived. He never wanted to know what I really was.'

'And what are you? A girl who fell on hard times once. A

567

woman who needed comfort. Not the greatest sins.'

She clung to the willow strands, tearing at them as if they were part of her. 'Nothing's what you think,' she said. 'Not even you know everything. I'm a bastard. My mother slept with the sons in the farm where we lived, she thought they might marry her. But she died and I was left. And Jean came up the stairs, so often – so often!'

She took a breath, and her eyes brimmed. 'I hated you. Madame thought she was being kind, giving me to you. But after that, she found a man to teach me. His name was Henri, and he taught me very well. I was a good whore, Gabriel. I learned that men can give as well as take. I loved it. Don't you think that's bad? I loved the clothes, and the way men looked at me, and making them do what I wanted!'

She swung on the bank, hanging by the willow strands, a demented, ranting child. Gabriel sat very still. She was holding to her sanity as much as to the willow. He said, 'But you gave up. Why?'

'One of the men.' She calmed suddenly, found her footing again on the slippery bank, and came and sat down by him. 'He wouldn't use the *préservatif*. I wouldn't let him do it, so he beat me up and raped me. I got pregnant. Madame sent me for an abortion, but I got infected and thought I should never have children. So, before the wedding, I didn't care. I loved you. I didn't know then, but it was true. I gave you what I could. And then I went to Michael.'

Gabriel felt the blood drain from his face. 'Mary—' he said feebly.

Laura nodded. 'Yours? It's possible. Who can tell?' She put her chin in her hands. 'It doesn't matter.'

He took a long, shaky breath. 'If I'd known you loved me I'd never have let him have you. He's a good man, a kind man, but he can be so bloody blinkered! Everything neat and right, that's Michael. Nothing in the least disturbing.'

Suddenly she turned to him, her black hair in wet strands across her face. 'I needed you, Gabriel. I need you now. I'm a bad woman, I need a man's love! Michael doesn't want me, he won't touch me any more. And before – it wasn't right. He takes something out of me, something I need. He leaves me empty. Gabriel, please.'

568

He felt a stab of pure lust for her. She wore a crisp white blouse, stained now with tears and rain, but within its neat revers her breasts swelled. And under that tight black skirt were soft-skinned thighs, sheltering a nest of pleasure. But suddenly the feeling changed within him. He looked into her pale eyes, and saw a woman in need. She might translate that need into lust, but he saw it now in its true light. The little child in her, the abandoned baby, needed to be held again.

He took her in his arms, moving this way and that, letting his warmth flow into her, his certainty comfort her distress. Her breathing began to slow. She whispered, 'Gabriel. Darling Gabriel. Don't you hate me too.'

'I couldn't ever hate you,' he murmured. 'You've done nothing wrong.'

'This is wrong.'

'You came to me when Michael wasn't there. He doesn't understand, Laura.'

'No.'

He rocked her like the child she used to be, that she still was. She opened her eyes and smiled at him. 'Thank you, Gabriel,' she said.

He took her back to Gunthwaite in his car. No one was there. The funeral tea that everyone had worked for days to prepare sat under cloths in the dining room, decanters of whisky and sherry standing guard. Laura sank into a chair, utterly spent. 'How shall I ever make it right with Michael?'

Gabriel said, 'That doesn't matter now. I'll find a place for you and Mary near the base. She's with Piers, isn't she? If you packed now we could go and pick her up. Michael won't be surprised. He must be expecting something of the sort.'

Laura's pale eyes looked at him blankly. 'But I'm not leaving him. Of course I'm not.'

'Darling, I know it's hard. But you can't stay just because he's blind! And you said yourself, Mary's my child. When we explain—'

'We won't.' Laura stood up and stared at him. 'That's something he will never know. She is what I believe her to be. Michael's.'

Gabriel said, 'Truth isn't what you want it to be. It's what is.'

'You don't know what is!'

'I know you love me and I love you. That's more than enough.'

She snorted. 'That isn't anything at all! We're of the same mould, you and I. We understand each other. We always have. So understand this, Gabriel. Loving you is too easy. You're as bad as me, and as good as me, no better. Michael's different. I love him because it makes me what I want to be. He's kind. He's loving. He'd never do what you and I have done!'

'Only because he's too narrow-minded to consider it! How loving is he now? How forgiving? You say yourself he doesn't know you, and if he did he wouldn't like it. What are you expecting, Laura? If you stayed with him for fifty years no one's going to give you a good behaviour prize.'

She turned her back on him. She couldn't bear to look into his face. Her heart was beating with dull, hard thuds, she imagined going with him now, to some hotel, a flat perhaps, looking at each other by the light of a dim bulb, still shackled by the memory of the people they had harmed. She couldn't leave Michael, let alone take his child. She couldn't leave Gunthwaite. What would happen if she couldn't be Michael's eyes? When Michael married her he had put his trust in her constancy and she had failed him. She couldn't leave him suffering as he was. If she left she could never redeem herself, could never be happy. It was all quite clear.

'You can't come here again,' she said to Gabriel.

He said incredulously, 'Laura! Laura, don't be silly. You know that you love me. My darling, we've waited so long!'

She glanced at him. 'I know you love Gunthwaite so it's bound to be hard. But you really mustn't come here again.'

'For God's sake, Laura! Sometimes I think you're deranged. I'm not some casual lover you can brush aside, not some client in for a short time! What will happen to me while you're saving Michael? I – I can't manage without you. You've had a hold on my life since you were thirteen years old!'

'I don't care,' she said dully. 'It's easy for you. Dora still loves you, and if not her, then someone else. You're easy to love. But me – I've got to make Michael love me again.'

He ran his hand through his hair. The twisted logic bemused him. It was like battering against a crumbling wall that should fall down and yet held. Michael was her calvary, her means of

570

redemption; Gabriel merely her occasion of sin.

He took a long breath. He hadn't given up, would never give up. Give it six months, he told himself. She doesn't know how implacable Mike can be. But he thought of his brother's sightless eyes turned after Laura that day, and felt sick suddenly. The power of helplessness.

There was the sound of vehicles in the yard. 'They're coming back,' said Gabriel.

'You'd better go,' said Laura. She went to the mirror over the fireplace to smooth her tangled hair and pinch colour into her cheeks. It wasn't possible that this was finished. Like tinder and spark, they only had to meet to ignite.

'I'll write,' he said. 'You'll change your mind, I know it.' He went out through the side door, to his car and away. The relatives, seeing him, muttered to each other. 'Trouble there. Treated his wife bad by all accounts. He and Michael will have had a falling out.'

Mrs Cooper, getting stiffly out of the car, saw her son driving past and called, 'Gabriel! Gabriel!' excitedly. He didn't once turn his head.

Chapter Eighteen

Mrs Fitzalan-Howard looked regretfully out on her lawn. Gone was the smooth green carpet of yesterday, and in its place a scarred, torn, muddy piece of field. The boys were playing football again this afternoon, some sort of tournament. She might take Piers to watch.

She went to take him from his playpen in the drawing room. Since Dora was expected later that day he was wearing an unattractive pair of dungarees. Dora seemed to like her son to look like an infant navvy, for some reason, and rejected out of hand the neat, smart clothes her mother thought suitable. It was hard not to resent Dora's interference. If she wanted the child, why didn't she come home again, or make some arrangements in town? Mrs Fitzalan-Howard fretted at the mere thought of it. Her husband was right. Something ought to be settled.

She took the child into the conservatory. Heating problems since the war began meant that it was no longer a charming refuge on a chill day, full of grapes and early peaches, but a damp jungle of profitless greenery. But Piers liked to toddle round the place, playing hide and seek amidst the giant pots. He was such a pretty child, with Gabriel's blue-eyed charm and all Dora's pinkness. She wondered what she would do when Piers was gone. How did she used to spend her days?

A car was coming up the drive. She got up from her sagging wicker chair and went to look. It was that man, the doctor, Zwmskorski. He hadn't been here in months. Shrinking back a little from the glass, she tried to remember what she had heard about him. Wasn't there some black market trouble? Hadn't he had to leave? She wished Geoffrey was home, instead of at some sheep sale. He ought to leave it to the men, he knew nothing about sheep anyway. It was an excuse, though, not to see Dora.

She picked up Piers again, although he struggled and complained, and went out to greet the visitor. His car was unbelievably shiny and well kept. There was a silk-lined overcoat thrown casually over the back seat. In contrast she felt again their own shabbiness.

Zwmskorski got out, smiling. 'Mrs Fitzalan-Howard! It's been too long.'

'Indeed. Do come in, doctor. I confess, I thought you'd left this area some time ago.'

He followed her into the drawing room, littered with Piers' things. She put the baby in his playpen once again, and swept some bibs off a chair. 'Do sit down. Some tea perhaps – or sherry?'

'Sherry. Thank you.'

She rang the bell, summoning Agnes from the upstairs cleaning, but it was better with someone like this to have the appearance of style. While they waited he admired the view of the muddy lawn, and the stopped clock that couldn't be mended until the clockmaker returned from the Far East. When Piers threw bricks from his pen, he said, 'It surprises me so much to see this child. To remember that I delivered him. Dora should remember it too.'

'I'm sure she does,' said Mrs Fitzalan-Howard awkwardly. It seemed bad taste to talk about childbirth in the middle of the morning, somehow. They were none of them ever likely to forget one moment of that night.

Agnes brought the sherry and poured two glasses, looking warily towards the visitor, taking in the expensive suit, the shiny shoes, the gold tiepin. As she withdrew Mrs Fitzalan-Howard said, 'Did you perhaps want to see Dora?'

'I have seen Dora.'

'Oh.'

After a moment she added, 'Was she pleased to see you?'

'Surprised.' He sipped his sherry. 'I was forced to leave Bainfield. I was threatened with arrest. Some foolishness about the black market, a misunderstanding.'

'But you've come back now.'

'Yes. I want Dora to come away with me.'

Mrs Fitzalan-Howard went cold. For a second she couldn't think, she simply wished that Geoffrey was here, instead of at some sheep sale, drinking beer and talking nonsense. Then she gathered her wits. 'You must realise that Dora is married?'

'She doesn't live as a married woman. She and I have been – intimate. You understand me?'

She took a painful breath. 'Yes. Yes, I do.'

'She refuses me because she fears what her parents will say. So I must tell you. This is a new age, a new time, we don't any longer cling to old superstitions! But Dora needs your blessing.'

Mrs Fitzalan-Howard got to her feet. 'I don't think I can ever condone immorality, however it's dressed up. I couldn't possibly give you and Dora my blessing. She's still a married woman! She has a child!'

He shrugged. 'You want the child, don't you? Of course. Give Dora your blessing and you can keep him. You have my word.'

She mouthed helplessly for a moment. 'You can't barter a child! Dr Zwmskorski, I really think you've taken leave of your wits. Where is Dora? I must speak to her.'

'She is in Bainfield. Where else should she be?'

He didn't know Dora was expected today. She was wary suddenly, sensing treacherous ground. Perhaps this wasn't some ghastly idea he and Dora had cooked up together. She had suspected for some time that Dora had men, but not that she intended to leave with anyone. It was all just too fishy.

'This has been rather a shock,' she managed. 'I have to talk to Dora. Please tell her – please explain that her father and I will be in touch. He's away at present. I can't decide anything without his support.'

He said impatiently. 'Of course you can! That is just humbug!'

Mrs Fitzalan-Howard drew herself up a little. 'Nonetheless,' she said coldly, 'I don't think we have anything further to discuss at present. I shall talk to my husband. Good day.'

He kissed her hand as he left, giving her his most charming smile. She didn't smile back. She was transfixed by the sight of his glittering shoes, tripping so neatly down the steps and into his equally glittering car. He had no right to be so smart in wartime! And he had no right to come here. She hurried to the telephone.

'Mrs Cooper, please. Mrs Dora Cooper. Oh – I see. This is her mother. I see. I'll expect her, then.'

She went back into the drawing room. Dora was taking the bus. Lifting Piers from his playpen she held him very close.

Dora trudged up the drive an hour later. She was wearing her mackintosh over a blue wool skirt and jumper. She looked wholesome and pretty, quite unlike Zwmskorski. Her mother put out her arms and embraced her. 'Oh, darling! I'm so glad to see you, I was worried. That man's been here. Zwmskorski.'

Dora's face paled. 'He hasn't! Why?' Her mother said nothing. 'Oh God,' said Dora.

They went into the house. Dora wanted Piers, but he was having his nap and she said angrily, 'He could have napped this morning! You do it on purpose, Mother.'

'I did today. I wanted to talk. Is it true? Have you been sleeping with that peculiar man?'

Dora said, 'I don't think that's any of your business, actually.'

'Perhaps it isn't. But – but, Dora, after Gabriel, and getting pregnant, and now this – I don't understand you. You know it isn't right.'

Her daughter reached into her bag for a cigarette and lit up expertly. 'Gabriel doesn't want me. The marriage is finished, it was never up to much. Sooner or later I suppose we'll get a divorce.'

'And then what? Not this man?'

Dora looked at her. 'No. Did he frighten you? He does me.'

Mrs Fitzalan-Howard was bemused. 'Frighten me? No, of course he didn't. Why should he?'

'I just wondered. He doesn't know, but it was Gabriel had him warned off. I told him he was becoming a nuisance and Gabriel had a word in a few ears. I wondered if he'd found out.'

'Gabriel! Gabriel knows about this?'

Dora nodded.

Her mother went to the cupboard and poured them both a large gin. She gulped a mouthful of hers and said, 'He wants me to give my blessing to you both. And to persuade me, he offered me Piers. I can keep him as long as I give you permission to go. I think he's mad.'

'Mad!' Dora put down her glass. 'He's the most arrogant, impertinent, conceited – I have to talk to Gabriel. I really do. This is too much.'

575

She went to telephone. Her mother stood beside her, anxiously hovering, wondering why it was that Dora complicated her life so needlessly. Dora turned her back.

'Squadron Leader Cooper, please – thank you – Gabriel? Gabriel, it's Dora. I'm having some trouble. It's Zwmskorski again, he's been to see Mother, left her in a terrible state. Yes. About a week ago, bold as brass. He does, actually. And he told Mother that if she gave her blessing he'd let her keep Piers. He thinks he's Rasputin, or something.'

Mrs Fitzalan-Howard waited with increasing impatience. 'Is he coming?' she hissed. 'Ask him to come home.'

Dora flapped at her. 'Mother says – Mother wants you to visit. I know you're short of leave, but if you could – well, why not here? I'll try and get the weekend off. It is time, isn't it? We ought to sort something out.'

'When? This weekend? Ask him which train?' interrupted her mother.

'Be quiet, Mother! All right. Thank you, darling. Thanks.'

She hung up, and her mother exploded. 'I don't know how you dare, Dora! Calling him darling. After having this affair!'

'We can still be polite to each other,' complained Dora mildly.

Her mother brandished a finger. 'The trouble with you, my girl, is you don't know the difference between politeness and immorality! And Piers is crying. I wish your father was here. But if he was I wouldn't want to tell him. Oh, Dora, what a mess.'

Dora felt tears pricking her eyelids. Her mother didn't know the half of it. For the past week Zwmskorski had been stalking her as if she was his prey, lurking in dark corners, catching her arm as she walked past. She'd had dinner with him once, and avoided more by pleading extra duty. She dared not tell him to go. She wasn't worried about what he might say any more, especially now that her mother knew, but his violence frightened her. He was letting property now, he said. If people didn't pay they knew what they'd get. And so did she.

'I'm going to stay for a few days,' she said suddenly. 'I'll tell everyone I'm ill. If he comes here again you can lie and say I've gone away, to Scotland or somewhere. At least until Gabriel comes.'

'The man's a criminal,' declared her mother. 'We should inform the police.'

'He must know they can't catch him,' said Dora resignedly. 'Otherwise he wouldn't dare come back.'

Her mother went to fetch the baby. He clung to her, catching her hair in his plump fists, smiling Gabriel's smile. When Dora put out her arms for him he stopped smiling and went solemnly, as if performing a duty. Dora felt helpless suddenly. Perhaps, like Piers, she ought not to resist? Zwmskorski was rich, wasn't he? And she knew how to handle him. When the war ended she would have to decide whether to come back here, and try and win Piers again, or to take him away and make a life on her own. She had no illusions about either course. Was Zwmskorski really worse?

Laura looked out of the upstairs window. 'Dora's here. She's brought Piers.'

Michael lifted his head. 'Why has she come? Were you expecting her?'

'Of course not. I tell you everything, I don't keep secrets.'

He said nothing. The silence was worse than a thousand angry words. She felt helpless against it, unable to speak or justify herself, unable to begin to reach him. What must it be like, locked in his darkness, thinking such terrible thoughts? If they could only begin to talk.

She went downstairs to greet her visitor. A light drizzle was falling; Dora's hair was beaded with tiny droplets of water. She shook herself like a dog. 'Goodness, what weather! It never stops.'

'Yes. Look, Piers, here's Mary.' The little girl toddled across, a doll in her hand. She lifted it up and thwacked Piers over the head with it.

'Oh, Mary!' both women cried. But Piers merely rubbed his head and toddled off to play.

'He's too tolerant,' said Laura tightly. 'He needs to learn.'

'To hit back? I suppose we all need to do that sometimes. Laura, I wanted to ask—'

But then Michael came slowly into the room. Dora at once asked if she might have a cup of tea.

Later, when the rain had stopped, they took the children to

the fields. They seemed to breathe more easily out of reach of Michael's silent, unseeing presence. It will be like this for always, thought Laura in a panic. I shall hate to be in my own home.

As soon as they were out of sight of the house, Dora said, 'I wanted to ask. Gabriel's coming at the weekend. Should he visit?'

Laura kept her eyes on the view. 'No. Neither Michael nor I wants to see him.'

'Are you sure? They're brothers, after all.'

Laura glanced at her. 'But that's why. I sometimes think that's really why it all happened. Gabriel wanted what Michael had.'

Dora said, 'I always thought Michael wanted what Gabriel had. His freedom. His looks. His mother's love.'

'Perhaps we only value the things we don't have.'

Dora looked at her obliquely. 'Are you talking about you and Gabriel? I think he loves you. I thought you loved him.'

'Did you?' Laura shrugged. 'A mistake. I was confused, I thought Michael was dead. It wasn't real love.'

'How can you tell? There's just love, isn't there?'

Laura turned on her heel and walked quickly on, making Dora hurry to catch up. The children ran across the grass, tripping sometimes over clumps of rough grass, picking themselves up and running on. The sky had lightened to a pale, soft blue, and an aeroplane glinted high up.

'It has to be ours,' said Dora. 'They wouldn't bomb here.'

But they moved closer to the children all the same.

Soon it was time to walk back. They followed the rutted farm track, past the hay ricks and the straw. Zwmskorski's car was in the yard.

'Oh, no.' Dora stopped and looked around for Piers. 'I can't see him.'

Laura said, 'I thought he'd gone away. I hate that man!'

'Yes. He's dangerous. Laura, tell him I'm not here!'

Laura assessed the situation. 'Take Piers in the dairy. I'll talk to him.' She approached the house with trepidation.

He was talking to Michael in the kitchen, making amusing conversation. Michael seemed awkward, turning his head this way and that. When Laura came in he looked suddenly hopeful, and her spirits lifted.

'Hello, Mr Zwmskorski,' she said evenly.

'Mrs Cooper! So beautiful. So charming.'

'Why have you come?'

'Do I need so much of a reason?'

Laura took a deep breath. 'There's no need to pretend that we're friends. My husband doesn't know why you left Bainfield in such a hurry, but I most certainly do. Black market, wasn't it? And a great deal more besides. Please tell me why you're here, and then go.'

The skin on his face seemed to thin over the harsh lines of his bones. Laura felt a shiver run through her. He said, 'Mr Cooper, do you permit your wife to address visitors in such terms? I do not mean to insult you, sir, but a woman like this, of such history, such morals—'

Michael said, 'Be careful what you say, please. I'll hear no words against my wife in this house or outside it.'

'Such devotion! If only she deserved it.'

Michael got slowly to his feet. Blind as he was, gentle as he had always been, he seemed suddenly menacing. 'State your business, Zwmskorski. Now.'

Things had gone too far. The Pole struggled to retrieve the situation, saying blandly, 'But we are distressing one another! I look only for Dora. Is she here? I understood she had come here. She was seen.'

'You must be spying on her,' said Laura. 'But she isn't here. She was, but she's gone.'

'And you, sir? You too say she is not here?' Zwmskorski put a long hand on Michael's arm.

The patronising touch inflamed him. He snapped, 'How dare you doubt my wife's word, sir? Take your hands off me and get out. You're not welcome here. If you come here again I'll take steps to have you removed.' He blundered towards the visitor, tripping over a chair, and Laura caught his arm.

'Michael, please. Michael, don't.'

Zwmskorski laughed. 'What a touching scene. The blind warrior defending the honour of a whore. My heart bleeds for you, Mr Cooper. The only person who doesn't know what she is is you.'

'Get out! Get out of my house!'

As he left Zwmskorski's soft laughter was like acid on raw nerves.

They listened to his car driving away. Laura said, 'Thank you. That was kind. He's a terrible man.'

'I won't have anyone insulting my wife,' said Michael. 'Much as she deserves it.'

Laura drew in her breath. 'That isn't fair. Truly, it isn't.'

'Don't talk to me about truth!'

She burst out, 'I thought you were dead! I thought you were never coming home! I didn't want to hurt you, I didn't want you ever to know! It didn't matter, can't you see that?'

His sightless eyes stared at her. 'I don't understand you. Sometimes I wonder if I ever did. Did I ever see you? Or was it a mirage? You were never really there.'

The kitchen door opened and Dora came in. She said, 'I heard him go. Was he awful?'

Laura nodded. Dora, misinterpreting their silence, burst out, 'I'm sorry. I should never have got involved with him, I know it was foolish. But everything's different in wartime, isn't it?'

After a moment, stiffly, Michael said, 'So it would seem.'

That evening, Michael went alone into the orchard. Hidden by leaves as damp as a tear-stained face, he moved from tree to tree, letting the rough bark scratch hands grown soft with idleness. He was so useless! He could do nothing, care for a baby, shear a sheep, even defend his own wife from the insults of a jumped-up, corrupt foreigner! What must she think of him? Useless, helpless lump of flesh.

He used to think of Gabriel as the useless one. It seemed so long ago. Days of health, strength, capability. What was it he hated most? Loss of his sight, or loss of his illusions? He had believed Laura to be different; special. But still, what he knew about her now vied with what he experienced day by day. She was still the calm, enduring, womanly person he remembered! Nothing outwardly had changed, while inside everything had.

How long before he gave up on all this? He was sick of life, sick of torment. What was he waiting for? He was blind, he was a burden and an embarrassment. It was as if fate had decided to take him out of the game, moving all the other pieces accordingly. But because of some slip, some slight failure in the

580

system, he had survived to disrupt the plan. Laura stayed with him because she pitied him. That was all it could be. And he couldn't even knock the smile off the face of that jumped-up Pole!

He ought to end it, of course. One day he would. But somehow the thought of a day without anything – knowledge, consciousness – was still impossible to accept. And he couldn't entirely lose the habit of optimism. He didn't believe life could continue to be this bad. There were good things still. The smell of Laura's hair, the sound of her singing to Mary, the touch of her hand as she straightened his collar. He took no pleasure in anything else, he thought ruefully. After all this, despite hating her sometimes so fiercely that it hurt, she was the centre and the focus of his life. He didn't know her; he might never know her. But in the end, if she was here, did it matter?

Gabriel threw down his parachute and stretched. 'That's it, then. Leave.'

'Orders for you.' Someone flicked an envelope towards him. He caught it, considered opening it, and put it in his pocket. Time enough to discover what joys were in store when he was safely on the train. Whatever it was, the orders had come too late.

'Must be a hot date.'

Gabriel grunted. 'My wife, actually.'

There was a silence. It had long been supposed that Squadron Leader Cooper's marriage was over.

On the train, still in that strange limbo that was neither operations nor complete freedom from them, he thought about Laura. In truth, he'd thought about nothing else for weeks. Every letter had been returned, sometimes two and three together. He imagined her waiting for the post, sorting through with brisk fingers, curling her lip when she came across his hand. Michael would say, 'Any post?' and she would reply, 'Only bills. And a catalogue. Nothing much.'

He closed his eyes. Sometimes he could hate her, positively hate her. She held out when she should give in, and gave in when she should hold out. Perversity was her middle name, as much part of her as those eyes, clear glass that seemed to reveal a simple and straightforward soul. Yet there was no one more convoluted. To understand Laura you had to know what had formed her. If he, who knew so much, struggled to make sense of her, how could Michael begin, who knew so little?

He had always been jealous of Michael. He acknowledged it, looked it in the face. From his very first memory he recalled Michael's calm, his good humour, his placid acceptance of all that he could not change. Gabriel had always known he couldn't match him. For all his mother's devotion, he had known that Michael would always stand above him, stronger, gentler, never bending to the whim of base desires. Gabriel was cursed with the need to take what he wanted, hold it, own it, defying everyone. It was Michael who had it in him to stand aside.

His cheeks were wet. He opened his eyes and saw that people in the carriage were looking at him. He took out his handkerchief and blew his nose vigorously. Perhaps they would think he had a cold.

He gazed out of the window at fields of cows, lying hunched against a cold wind. Everyone had a choice, he thought. He could have chosen to leave Laura to his brother. But he thought he had chosen to do that, he had believed the decision made. What chance did decisions have against love, against desire, against this hot, starved longing to be with the only person who ever made you feel whole? He loved Laura. He felt incomplete without her, lacking in some vital part. His brother might need her, blind as he was, might even deserve her, but if Gabriel looked upon the future and saw it empty of her he saw nothing at all. In a sense, they were both blind. Surely it was better that one of them should see?

The train was pulling in. He got up restlessly, thinking of the times he'd come home to find Michael waiting for him. His heart misgave him. To hurt Michael was almost to hurt himself, to crush whatever goodness lay in his own devious soul. Right from the moment their mother had turned from Michael to the younger, golden child, Gabriel had known she was mistaken in her preference. She saw nothing of what was within.

He found a message awaiting him at Dora's billet. The girl who gave it to him said, 'She'll be glad enough to see you. He's here every day, looking, asking. We've told him she's gone to Scotland.'

Gabriel turned Dora's note in his fingers. 'Did he believe you?'

The girl shook her head. 'Not him. Too clever by half.'

He went back to the station and hired a taxi to take him out to Fairlands, only to find he knew the driver. He made arduous conversation, about the war, about his brother. 'Bad do, him losing his sight like that. Fair makes you think. There's you, Battle of Britain and all, anyone'd think you'd cop it. But it's him. Just goes to show, don't it? Just goes to show.'

'Yes,' said Gabriel. But it should have been 'No.' He didn't know what was proved by all this, except that virtue was never rewarded.

When he arrived at Fairlands Mr Fitzalan-Howard came bustling out on to the steps. When he saw it was Gabriel he at once came to shake his hand. 'Glad to see you, my boy. We've had goodness knows what trouble with this Polish bounder. Dora says you'll know what to do.'

'I don't know about that,' said Gabriel. They went up the steps together, and Dora was in the hall, wearing her pale blue dress. He went to kiss her and she said, 'Dear Gabriel. I'm so glad you could come.'

They went into the drawing room. Mr Fitzalan-Howard said, 'I'll leave you to it, if you don't mind. Things to do and all that. Give the man a whisky and soda, Dora.'

She went and fiddled with the drinks. The room was cold, despite a small wood fire crackling in the grate. He said, 'That little house you did for us. It was pretty. I never said.'

She glanced at him. 'It was silly of me. I thought it would make things right between us, when I knew they were all wrong.'

'I'm sorry,' he said. 'All my fault.'

'It takes two to tango, as they say.'

She sat in a chair and crossed her legs. A sophisticated, desirable woman. 'He's back,' she said. 'I don't know what to do.'

Gabriel said, 'I made a mistake. He should have been prosecuted last time, it's all forgotten now. It seems he's out of the black market and into extortionate rents, every bit as crooked but quite legal. We can't chase him away. But if he doesn't see you for a while he's bound to get bored.'

'I don't think so,' said Dora, swirling her drink. 'I'm afraid he thinks I'm the answer to his prayers. It's my own fault. I took Marie's advice on how to enthral a man. And he's enthralled.'

Gabriel choked on his whisky. When he looked at Dora she met his gaze with a calm, worldly stare. 'You amaze me,' he said. 'You really do.'

She said, 'I went to see Laura. She doesn't want you to call.'

'That's what she says.'

'It might be what she means.' Dora leaned forward. 'It's possible, isn't it, that she means to stay married? She's so good to Michael. And he needs her so.'

Gabriel turned his face away. After a moment he said, 'How did she seem? With him. Is he kind to her?'

'It's hard to say. They don't talk much. But it's as if they don't have to.'

'You're trying to annoy me.'

'I don't think so. Unless the truth does annoy.'

She got up and went to the window. He remembered the old Dora, her sudden enthusiasms, her equally sudden huffs. Not everything about her had changed. He said, 'I don't mean to let her go on with him. She's staying because of duty, no more than that.'

'But if that's what she wants, you should leave her to it.'

'And let us both be miserable? No.'

She was silent. He had been wrong then, to think they had reached a new and better understanding. It was just the same, silences, not knowing what to say. But at least he could do one thing for her.

'I'll go and see your Pole, if you like. Warn him off, face to face.'

Dora said, 'You might get more than you bargained for. He isn't safe, you know.'

'Your mother's asked me to stay—'

She turned and said briskly, 'Yes. The blue room. You know the way, don't you? Excuse me. I have to see to Piers.'

He hadn't once asked after Piers. He felt the old dull heaviness, the sense of failure. In this house, in this world, he could do nothing right.

★ ★ ★

Dinner was awkward, a long silence punctuated with stilted conversation. Afterwards Gabriel and Dora's father sat with inferior brandy and talked about the war. 'What about when it's over, that's what I say?' said Mr Fitzalan-Howard. 'Too much is different. Too much has changed. Look at Gunthwaite. Bathrooms now. If Michael's got any sense he'll put in electricity, and what then? Convenient, I grant you, but where's the charm? The sense of timelessness. The peace.'

Gabriel got up and abruptly excused himself. 'I'm sorry, sir. Feeling a bit restless. Think I'll take a walk.'

He went out, aware that his host was sitting quite still.

It was nine-thirty, and the moon was full. As he walked he thought of Gunthwaite as it used to be, locked in primitive isolation. When he was a child the carrier came perhaps twice a month, and in winter not at all. Until they went away to school he and Michael hadn't understood that other people, in other places, lived differently. At first they had stood together in the school quadrangle, assailed by people and noise, utterly amazed. But that was all they shared. Michael had longed for Gunthwaite and its peace, but from that moment on Gabriel had known that the world awaited him. He had rushed to embrace it.

Clouds were racing across the moon, obscuring the path. But he knew it well enough. It would take him an hour, perhaps more, to walk across the shoulder of hill to Gunthwaite. He didn't care if it took all night, he couldn't sleep without seeing her. But when at last he rounded the bend and saw Gunthwaite's dark, unlit bulk he felt helpless before it. It was like flying again, outnumbered and outgunned, wondering if by some miracle you would see another day, or if it was all going to end. The same, fatalistic uncaring, that in a second would be transformed into caring more than you knew. He went up to the old oak door, lifted the knocker and let it fall with a thunderous bang.

Laura sat up in bed. It was Gabriel. Dora had said he was coming, she knew it must be him. Michael lay beside her, she didn't know if he had woken. Slowly, quietly, she crept from her bed and hurried downstairs. Marie's voice called: '*Chérie?* Is this expected?'

'Quite expected,' said Laura. She didn't care what Marie thought, or in that moment what anyone thought. She drew the

585

latch and saw Gabriel standing there, in his dinner jacket. She stood aside and let him come in.

The fire in the kitchen was banked for the night. She stirred the embers while Gabriel went to the dresser to light a candle. It was as if they had spoken only that day, as if all this was intended. She felt tearful suddenly. Gabriel felt so right, and Michael so wrong.

They stood apart from each other, the width of the table between them. Laura said, 'I said not to come. I told Dora.'

'I know. But you knew I wouldn't listen. I never do.'

'No. You never do.'

His hair was too long. He looked tired and dusty. She felt her heart melt towards him, felt herself yearn to embrace him. He said, 'Every time I see you, I think you can't be as beautiful as I remember. But you're more beautiful still. Every time.'

'I'm not beautiful at all. I never was. You see what you want to see.'

'I don't know. I always want to see you.'

'I know. Oh, Gabriel, I know.'

He came around the table for her. She went into his arms, her lips searching for his, uttering a small moan. It was as if she had been suffering a terrible pain which was suddenly assuaged. Such relief, such joy. Where there had been nothing but grey walls there was now a vista of ineffable beauty. She thought, I need not struggle. Things would happen as they must, it was all meant to be. They would go, she and Gabriel, forget everything, everyone, and be together.

'I love you,' he was whispering. 'Without you everything's grey.'

'I was thinking the same,' she replied.

'We always think the same.'

They kissed again. It was so peaceful. Laura let her thoughts float off into wonderment. And then the baby cried.

She stiffened in Gabriel's arms. 'Mary.'

'She's all right. She'll go back to sleep.'

'She has nightmares. I have to go and light a candle.'

'This damned house! You should have electric light. You could leave that burning.'

She went soundlessly from the room and up the stair. After a moment Gabriel followed, wanting to see her, watch her. She

586

slipped into her daughter's room, whispering endearments in French. He was surprised. He hadn't expected that. The baby murmured and Laura began a lullaby he didn't know, and he thought, I shall discover more about her each and every day. Even he, who knew her more than anyone, knew nothing.

A door opened behind him. He turned and saw Michael, and thought with relief that Michael couldn't see him. He edged towards the stair, but Michael said, 'Gabriel. I knew it was you.'

Gabriel felt his breath shorten. Stupid to be nervous now. 'How did you know?'

'You sense things. When you're blind. I want you to go.'

He looked at Michael's square, open face, the eyes looking so hopefully and seeing nothing. He felt a great pity welling up in him. He wanted to say, 'All right, yes, I'll go and leave you Laura.' Michael was his brother. The brother he loved. But it wasn't possible any more, too much had happened.

He said, 'I'm sorry. Laura and I have to be together. It's decided.'

'No. I won't have it.'

Gabriel put a hand on his brother's arm. 'It isn't up to you any more. We'll take Mary, of course.'

'No. I tell you, no!'

Michael shook him off, came forward angrily, striking at air. Laura came out of the bedroom, holding the baby. 'Don't!' she pleaded. 'You'll frighten her. Please, Michael, please.'

'Is it true?' he demanded. 'Are you leaving me?'

It seemed all at once very quiet. The baby was whimpering, and out in the yard something rattled in the wind. She said, 'I thought – the way you've been – you might want me to go?'

'No. No, never.'

'We can't go on as we have. You hate me.'

'You know I don't.'

She said desperately, 'I don't know anything! We were happy, we were safe, you were the one who ruined it! You left me alone.'

He said, 'It's not much of a marriage, is it, if you can't be left alone?'

Her shoulders drooped miserably. 'No. If I was different, perhaps. I was never a lady, you see, I never knew what a lady ought to do. I don't have your principles, Michael! I don't

587

understand them. If I'm honest, I don't believe that what I did was wrong.'

Gabriel said, 'It wasn't. We love each other, we always have. You two should never have married, that's all.'

Michael turned aside, as if someone had struck him. Laura said, 'Michael! Michael, don't.'

Gabriel went to her. 'It's time to go. There's no point in going over this. Your marriage is finished, you can't put it back together. Come. We must go.'

But she stood looking at her husband. She said, 'Why should I stay? Just to nurse you, is that it?'

Michael said, 'I can't talk to you. Not with him here.'

She turned to Gabriel. 'I think you'd better go downstairs.'

He looked at her face, and felt rising panic. She was slipping away! 'I won't go without you,' he said, and took her roughly by the arm, trying to hustle her down the stairs. She was holding the baby, she couldn't resist. She cried out and Michael lunged forward.

'Laura!' he shouted. 'Laura!'

She felt him brush past her arm, saw the look on his face, stood helpless as he plunged down the stairs. 'Michael!' She thrust the baby at Gabriel and ran down after him. At the bottom, arms outstretched, he lay quite still.

Chapter Nineteen

Laura sat next to the bed. Michael lay so very still, his breathing no more than a gentle lifting of the sheet that covered him. Gabriel stood in the doorway, watching them as he had watched for hours. He couldn't believe what had happened. Michael had once again won.

He said, 'You can't sit here for ever. If he was awake you wouldn't stay.'

'I never said I'd go.'

'There's no reason for any of this. I could almost believe he wanted this to happen.'

Laura got up. 'Go away, Gabriel,' she said. 'I don't want you here any more.'

He gaped at her. 'How can you say that? Last night you were going to run away with me!'

Closing her eyes for a moment she almost smiled. 'Run away. Yes. I was running away. I've been running away all my life, haven't I? Trying to leave myself behind. If I left with you now I'd be leaving another part of myself, though. The part that loves Michael. The part that loves this place. The part that hoped I might be better, in the end.'

'Better than what?' said Gabriel harshly. 'The little whore you so love to despise? You feel guilty because you slept with me and enjoyed it. But you're only guilty of loving me.'

She looked him full in the face. She felt very calm today, with none of the confusion of the night. Michael's fall had crystallised everything, shaping events into clear and intended patterns. What would have happened if he had died? The thought was impossible, a disaster barely escaped.

A car was drawing into the yard. She saw it was Dr Hendon again, bringing the specialist he had promised. She went calmly to the door and greeted them.

589

'No change?' asked the doctor, taking off his coat.

'Yes. A little. He mumbles now and then.'

'Good.' He glanced at his companion. 'As I told you, sir, a strong concussion. But with the old injury—' he stopped and looked at Laura. 'We may be some time, Mrs Cooper. Why don't you take yourself off for a walk?'

She glanced at Gabriel, standing silent by the door. 'Yes. Perhaps we should.'

Out in the meadow the wind was cold, and she shivered. She was only wearing the blouse and skirt she had flung on before dawn that day. Gabriel still wore his evening suit, minus the bow tie. He looked raffish, his chin covered in golden stubble, all except a small white scar. She touched it with a finger. 'What's this?'

'A bit of glass got me. The windows blew out when the field was bombed. I've had it years.'

And she had never noticed. He put his hands on her waist and pulled her to face him. She looked up at him, quite calm. He knew she loved him, knew she couldn't resist. He bent and kissed her, sliding his hand up to her breast, kneading and holding, urging her response. She stood quite still. He put his hands behind her thighs, pulling her against his sex, feeling up her skirt to the soft inner reaches of her body.

She stood so still, so unresponsive, that suddenly he couldn't bear it. He jabbed with his fingers and she cried out, vulnerable, and a little afraid. He felt a surge of hot desire, wanting to own her, subdue her, claim her once and for all. He pushed her down into the pasture, seeing her startled face, her disbelief. For once he didn't care.

She lay beneath him, quite unresisting. He was like a stranger, she thought, like anyone. But suddenly, he was no longer heavy. He leaned on his elbows, staring down into her face, unable to go on. She closed her eyes, not wanting to look at him, not wanting to remember.

'Laura. Laura, I love you!'

She looked up at the sky, grey clouds rushing to the coast. She thought of Michael, and knew that he could die. She thought, Without Michael there's nothing. He left her empty, she was a void to be filled up. And she had taken Gabriel, because she needed him.

She looked at him, his face an inch from hers, eyes wide open and fierce. Just like the first time, she thought. There might have been nothing in between.

He rolled away from her and groaned. She got up and began brushing herself down. 'You think you need me, Gabriel, but you don't. You'll make another life. But Michael – I think he loves me. I know he needs me. If I left him I couldn't be happy, knowing what I'd done.'

'But with Michael you'll be no more than a slave! A drudge, is that what you want, will it make you feel good? He won't forgive.'

'He might. If I left him I'd never know.'

Gabriel ran his hands through his hair. She was at one moment utterly malleable, and the next an implacable witch. 'Don't think you can come running when it all goes wrong,' he said bitterly. 'I won't wait on your pleasure, my girl. Do you like treating me like this, come here, go there, endlessly back and forth?'

'I don't want you to wait. I never did.'

'Well, I warn you! If Michael dies you'll be alone. I won't be there, I won't care!'

She hid a smile behind her hand. 'You don't grow up, do you, Gabriel?'

'Don't laugh at me! For God's sake, Laura, don't laugh!'

He turned his back on her, sure that if he looked at her a second more he'd smash his fist into her face. She stripped him of everything, all dignity, all restraint. She judged him by some weird standard of her own, and always found him wanting. She loved in him what she recognised in herself, he thought wearily. She loved in Michael what she thought she wanted. He didn't ever stand a chance.

When he looked at her he saw that she was far ahead, walking back to the house. He began to run after her, he moved his lips to call her name. But then he stopped and slowed. He had never owned her, never possessed her as he wished. He could never do so. Even when she seemed most his she was slipping, sliding away. He knew, with horrible certainty, that if she came to him she wouldn't stay. Michael had claimed her for ever.

* * *

591

Marie was in the kitchen when Laura returned. 'A tisane,' she said brightly. 'Everything's better with a tisane.'

'Better than what?'

Marie shrugged. With sudden horror, Laura ran to the bedroom. Both doctors looked up.

'What is it? He isn't dead? He was better, you can't have killed him!'

But the figure on the bed began to move. 'I'm all right!' said Michael in a blurred voice.

She fell into a chair. 'Marie said – I thought – oh my God!'

'It's bound to be a shock,' said Dr Hendon. 'These things are frequently unpredictable.'

'I thought he was dead,' she repeated.

The specialist gestured to Dr Hendon. 'We'll speak to you in a moment, Mrs Cooper. You have a talk to your husband.'

It was very quiet in the room. Michael's eyes blinked slowly, and he swallowed once or twice. 'Marie's making a tisane,' said Laura.

'Yes. The doctor said.'

The silence stretched again, like toffee on a nail, they couldn't get rid of it. Eventually, forcing herself, Laura said, 'You remember what happened, don't you?'

'Yes.'

'I'm not going. I told him so. I won't.'

The silence again. Cloying, sickening, silence. 'Don't stay because you pity me,' burst out Michael. 'If you love him as he says you do – if you wouldn't be happy otherwise – don't stay. But if you care – if you want to be as we used to be – it's worth a try, isn't it? I'd like to try to be happy again.'

She got up from her chair and went to kneel at the bed. She took his hand and kissed it, smoothing the hair from his face. 'Dear Michael. You're the kindest man, the sweetest man. I thought you didn't want me, I thought you didn't care. Gabriel said you wouldn't ever forgive, but I knew he was wrong, I knew it! Of course we'll be happy.'

He closed his eyes for a moment and sighed. She bent to touch his lips with her own, and in the middle of it thought of Gabriel. She trembled and Michael whispered, 'There's something I didn't say.'

'What is it? What?'

'Don't be afraid. It's good for once. I can see.'

She drew in her breath and pulled away a little. 'What? Can you see properly?'

'No. It's blurred, it comes and goes.'

'Will it get better? Are you cured?'

'They say they don't know.'

There was a knock on the door. Marie with the tisane. Laura got up and went to the mirror. She looked as pale as a ghost with violet shadows beneath her eyes. The doctors came back in, rubbing their hands and beaming. 'A great day,' said Dr Hendon. 'A great day.'

'Yes. Indeed. It's all too much.' Remembering her manners she said, 'Would you like sherry instead of tisane? We should celebrate, surely?' Without waiting for an answer she rushed from the room.

When she returned, with glasses and decanter on a tray, the specialist was standing at the window. 'I see the young man's walking off,' he said. 'Ought someone to go after him? He can't know the news, and besides, we could give him a lift wherever he's going.' Laura looked at once towards Michael. Could he see how she trembled?

She said evenly, 'I don't know where he's going. But I'm sure he'll be all right.'

The sherry tasted strong and rich. She hadn't eaten all day, even a mouthful made her head spin. She thought, Am I happy? Am I sad? But she knew it hardly mattered. She had held on to something for once, clung to it like a drowning man to a spar. Whatever her life would be, she would live it with Michael. She had won and she had lost, and if she wept for what must be she would do it in secret. After all, she was used to secrets.

Dora was in the garden. She saw Gabriel as he climbed the garden wall, his evening trousers ripped at the knee. He looked like a tramp, she thought. Or a gambler, down on his luck. The second image pleased her most.

'Oh dear,' she said, as he approached. 'You do look a mess.'

'And so I should.' He met her gaze frankly, his blue eyes hard as stones. 'Got any booze? I want to get drunk.'

'Turned you down, did she?'

'Yes. It's the last time. I've had just about bloody enough.'

She fetched whisky and glasses. He slumped on the balustrade at the edge of the terrace, cold now the sun was setting. Blackbirds twittered in the overgrown hedges, and the sky was shot through with purple and gold. Dora said, 'It's lovely, isn't it? I know you're miserable, but all the same.'

He took a gulp of the drink. 'Yes. It's lovely.'

The sun sank lower in the sky. He felt a strange sort of peace, part whisky, part release. If Laura was beside him it would all be to play for, he thought bemusedly. If she'd left with him he'd never have been sure she'd stay. At least with Dora he could sit in the twilight and drink whisky and expect nothing. They knew each other well enough to be frank, without the need to be sensitive to one another's souls. If you didn't understand someone through and through, you couldn't suffer for them, he thought hazily. You could live your life shallowly and in peace.

Dora said, 'You weren't good for her, you know. You're bad, and she wants to be good.'

'What a very profound remark.'

'Don't be surprised. I can be profound.'

'You never used to be. You seemed permanently too young.'

'No one's permanently young.' She chuckled. 'Zwmskorski would make anyone grow up.'

The sun sank finally behind the hill. Dora picked up the whisky bottle, saying, 'We can finish this indoors, you know. I think I'd like to get stinking drunk.'

But he sat on, looking at the dark horizon. At last he said, 'What are we going to do, Dora? I've lived so long expecting to be with her. From the moment I met her she's been part of me. And now she's not.'

'What if you'd never met her?' said Dora. 'Do you ever think of that?'

'I'd be worse than I am,' he said bleakly. 'And I'm no bloody good now, so think of that. It was only her, you know, that kept me going. I did it all for her.'

'What now? Will you do it all for you?'

His eyes glittered in the darkness. 'I'm damned if I know.'

The Fitzalan-Howards were seated in the drawing room, listening to the wireless. Dora and Gabriel headed for the conservatory, gloomy as it was. Dora sat in one of the old cane chairs and said, 'What a mess we've made. It's the fault of all

594

these foreigners. Without them we'd have made a very English mess, the sort we're used to.'

'It's the war,' said Gabriel. 'I don't know what I'll do when it's over. At least it stops you having to think.'

'Does it?' Dora poured them both more scotch. 'At least you're fighting. But me – all I do is think about Zwmskorski and Piers and my parents. And you. I think a lot about you and wish it had been different.'

Gabriel slid away from the turn of conversation. 'What about Zwmskorski?' he asked. 'Will he go?'

'Not before beating hell out of me, I shouldn't think,' remarked Dora. 'It seems to me that pleasing a man in bed is a very dangerous game. He's bound to want you to go on doing it, and when you don't, because you don't want to, or because he's got bored, then there isn't much left to entertain him. And what then? That's the question. If I leave with him now, will I be better or worse off in a year or two's time?'

Gabriel stared at her. 'You're not serious? You wouldn't go?'

'I don't know. Look at it this way. Either I stay in Bainfield, beating off other women's husbands and sweethearts, or I go with Zwmskorski, to live in brief but heady luxury. And I'm not very good at beating men off, so sooner or later it would all get difficult. And Mother wants to keep Piers, though she'd never say, and a girl can't keep hanging around at home. So you see, don't you? The problem?'

'But the man's a bastard, Dora!'

She put out a finger and brushed the tip of his nose. 'Spot the angel, Gabriel dear.'

She was rolling her glass against her cheek. In the dim light of the conservatory she was dark-eyed and thoughtful. He didn't love her, he thought. Whatever flame Laura had ignited did not burn for Dora, and he was glad. Now there could be reason and good sense. He would never again be such a fool.

He got up suddenly. 'I've got orders, you know. I haven't opened them. Shall I see what they are?'

'Of course. How can you bear not to know?'

'They might have cancelled my leave. Now we'll see what they're doing with me and go from there. It's all a game, isn't it? We've been forgetting. There's no need to take any of this seriously.'

595

He ran upstairs to fetch the envelope, crammed into a pocket of his uniform. The room moved unsteadily around him and he knew he was very drunk. It was the only way to be, he thought, the only way to endure it. Blur the edges, forget the dreams, pretend none of it mattered. He might then get through.

He went back to the conservatory and tossed the envelope to Dora. 'Go on then. Tell me the worst.'

She giggled. 'I don't think I can, I'm too drunk. Wait, wait – I'll do it. Oh, Gabriel – you're going to Canada. You're to be an instructor.'

'Oh, Christ.' He leaned back in his chair, chuckling to himself. 'Oh, Christ. She could have come to Canada with me.' Suddenly, to his surprise, he found he was crying. Tears ran unchecked down his face.

Dora said softly, 'She would never have gone. She belongs here, more than any of us.'

'Why should a French tart belong here more than us? I don't understand it. I don't understand anything any more.'

Dora came and sat on the arm of his chair. 'Shall I come to Canada with you? Would that be best?'

He looked up at her, bemused. 'Would it? You'd be rid of Zwmskorski. We needn't take Piers right away, we could come back for him once we were settled. Give us a chance to get to know each other. No more bloody Gunthwaite, no more bloody Laura – no more bloody misery!'

She put her hand on his chest, sliding it almost casually to his groin and holding him. He lay quite still, staring up at her. She murmured, 'I think it could even be fun. Don't you, Gabriel?'

The day was glorious, England at its best after a night of heavy rain. Tiny clouds, like suds in the wash, flew high across clear blue, and the trees in the orchard lifted their battered blossoms to the sun. Laura fiddled with the wireless to catch the news, but the battery was weak and nothing reached her. The lane was flooded, no one had cleared the drains on either side, so there'd be no new battery, or post for that matter, until it was seen to.

She went out into the stables and found the girls getting ready for the day. Bill Mayes was sitting on an old apple barrel, doing nothing, but he didn't get up, as he would if Michael had come in. He got no easier, thought Laura resignedly. 'The lane's flooded,' she said.

'Aye,' said Bill, who must know that it was. He lived in the village, he'd come by that way and must have been forced through the field.

'Who's digging out the drain? Mrs Cooper wants to go to Bainfield today, and the post won't come. We need a new battery for the wireless.'

'Dare say you do,' said Bill, and sat back a little more comfortably. He could make it no clearer, thought Laura, that now Michael was back she had no authority. She said tartly, 'Get yourself started, Bill. I want that drain cleared by mid-morning, no later. If Mrs Cooper takes the car and finds she can't get through, I'll tell her you were responsible. Then we'll see how energetic you feel.'

She turned on her heel and stalked out, her benign mood soured. Bill Mayes did nothing for her now that Michael was back. She wouldn't have it, she thought angrily. Things weren't as they used to be, and Bill would have to learn that both she and Michael had changed in these years. They couldn't step back into their pre-war boxes, as if nothing had happened.

But where was Michael? She went to the field gate and shielded her eyes from the sun. There he was. Out with the ewes, checking on the lambs. She hitched up her skirt, in itself a concession to Michael, and climbed over the fence. Halfway across Michael saw her and waved. She felt herself settle more securely into the day. Her heart lifted.

'Michael! What are you doing out here?'

He grinned at her, dark-haired, square-jawed, rejoicing in the day and in his health. She put a hand on his arm, and all of a sudden he caught her up in a great hug. 'Laura! Laura! Laura!' was all he could say.

She gasped until he let her go. Then they stood looking at each other. 'What have you to say that brings you out here?' he asked.

'Nothing,' she lied. She had intended to come at it more gently. Then she blushed. 'I've asked Sophie and Marie to move into Gabriel's cottage. We need more space in the house. I'm pregnant.'

She saw his face change. For a moment she felt afraid, and put up her fingers to silence the question she saw rising to his lips. 'Your baby,' she said urgently. 'Yours and mine.'

But he had to say it. She wished he need not. 'You didn't – with Gabriel—'

'No. It has to be yours. There's no one else.'

He put his arms around her again, holding her with infinite tenderness. 'I was thinking how lucky we are,' he said. 'We're both of us stronger than before. We've come through it all.'

Safe at last, she thought. She stood surrounded, protected by the fields, the trees, the sky. Sheep dotted the grass like fresh white pillows, and skylarks were singing, fluttering in the blue. Above the trees a hawk hung as if nailed, then swooped and was gone.

The land had reclaimed them, she thought. It had gathered them up, sure in the knowledge that they would care for it, love it, give it their all. Neither she nor Michael could ever be happy away from here. They were bound together with the land, like a hefted flock of sheep, that could not thrive on any but their own home pasture. She thought of all that had happened, all that still might be to come, changing everything, perhaps even taking from them this hard-won happiness. All she could do was hope, she thought. Those two pillars of her existence, Michael and the land, must stand firm through the years. There was nothing she would not do to sustain them.

She turned to him, the breeze tangling her hair across her eyes. He laughed and held her while she struggled with it, a big man, a strong man, who barely knew what kind of woman he held. She put up her face, childlike, trusting, for his kiss.

More Compelling Fiction from Headline:

MURDER IN THE COMMONS
A PARLIAMENTARY WHODUNNIT

NIGEL WEST

'A JOLLY, OLD-FASHIONED ROMP, WELL-CRAFTED AND FULL OF INSIDER INFO' *THE TIMES*

'MPs dread only one thing more than turning up in Nigel West's pastiche whodunnit – and that is being left out' *Today*

When an unpopular Labour MP is killed in front of the House of Commons, the Speaker asks Philip North, Conservative MP and the victim's pair, to liaise with the detectives in charge of the case. But even North is surprised when the apparent hit-and-run incident is revealed to be a complex murder investigation in which there are plenty of suspects: the jealous secretary, the ambitious ex-wife, the drunken back-bencher, the frightened mistress and the sinister constituency agent ...

As North digs deeper to expose carefully hidden secrets, the lobby correspondents smell corruption, the whips fear scandal and a government minister anticipates accusations of treason.

Praise for MURDER IN THE COMMONS:
'A fiendishly complicated murder story' *Sunday Express*
'He is at his convincing best' *Mail on Sunday*
'Solidly crafted plot, but main fascination lies in insider's exposure of parliamentary anachronisms and how 's your father' *The Sunday Times*

FICTION/CRIME   0 7472 4176 7

JOSEPHINE COX

JESSICA'S GIRL

In the grand tradition of Catherine Cookson

'Don't let him break you, child'

Despite her beloved mother's deathbed warning, Phoebe Mulligan has no choice but to throw herself on the mercy of her uncle, Edward. Wrenched from all she holds dear, the tragic young girl is delivered to Blackburn town, where she must live in a household terrorised by the cold, forbidding presence of her mother's brother.

Phoebe cannot understand why she is treated so harshly by Edward Dickens. She is not to know the guilty secret that lies in his past, a secret that casts its sinister shadow over his feelings for his lovely niece.

But Phoebe's spirit will not be broken. Her natural warmth and cheerfulness win her many friends and although she must endure horror and heartbreak, all the riches a woman can have come within her reach.

'Cox's driven and passionate book...stirs a pot spiced with incest, wife beating...and murder.'
The Sunday Times

More Enthralling Fiction from Headline:

HARRY BOWLING

Backstreet Child

The new Cockney saga from
the bestselling author of
THE GIRL FROM
COTTON LANE

Carrie Tanner's transport business in Salmon Lane is prospering by 1939 and
she has earned the grudging respect of her business rivals, even the Galloways,
father and son, who have played such a fateful role in the Tanner family's
fortunes. The years have been kind to Carrie and her deep love for Joe
Maitland has helped him through the darkest times of prison and his
alcoholism. But the scars she bears from the long-running feud with the
Galloway family are deepened by her daughter Rachel's blossoming love for
Geoffrey Galloway's illegitimate son.

Personal feuds though are overshadowed by the outbreak of the Second World
War, which brings the terrors of the Blitz to the Tanners' neighbours:
enterprising Maurice Salter, and his three daughters; publican Terry Gordon
with his guilty secret and his wife Pat, who has had her eye on Billy Sullivan
since his wife and children were evacuated; Josiah Dawson, out from the Moor,
and his wife, long-suffering Dolly, and simple son, Wallace.

Drawing on all their reserves of courage and humour the close-knit community
is determined to survive the difficulties of poverty, rationing and nightly air
raids. Even as, one by one, the men are called up, go missing in action or are
killed, and homes are bombed, their extraordinary spirit shines through.

Don't miss Harry Bowling's previous Cockney sagas, THE GIRL FROM
COTTON LANE, GASLIGHT IN PAGE STREET, PARAGON PLACE,
IRONMONGER'S DAUGHTER, TUPPENCE TO TOOLEY STREET and
CONNER STREET'S WAR, also available from Headline.

FICTION/GENERAL   0 7472 4180 5

A selection of non-fiction from Headline

THE DRACULA SYNDROME	Richard Monaco & William Burt	£5.99 ☐
DEADLY JEALOUSY	Martin Fido	£5.99 ☐
WHITE COLLAR KILLERS	Frank Jones	£4.99 ☐
THE MURDER YEARBOOK 1994	Brian Lane	£5.99 ☐
THE PLAYFAIR CRICKET ANNUAL	Bill Frindall	£3.99 ☐
ROD STEWART	Stafford Hildred & Tim Ewbank	£5.99 ☐
THE JACK THE RIPPER A–Z	Paul Begg, Martin Fido & Keith Skinner	£7.99 ☐
THE *DAILY EXPRESS* HOW TO WIN ON THE HORSES	Danny Hall	£4.99 ☐
COUPLE SEXUAL AWARENESS	Barry & Emily McCarthy	£5.99 ☐
GRAPEVINE: THE COMPLETE WINEBUYERS HANDBOOK	Anthony Rose & Tim Atkins	£5.99 ☐
ROBERT LOUIS STEVENSON: DREAMS OF EXILE	Ian Bell	£7.99 ☐

All Headline books are available at your local bookshop or newsagent, or can be ordered direct from the publisher. Just tick the titles you want and fill in the form below. Prices and availability subject to change without notice.

Headline Book Publishing, Cash Sales Department, Bookpoint, 39 Milton Park, Abingdon, OXON, OX14 4TD, UK. If you have a credit card you may order by telephone – 0235 400400.

Please enclose a cheque or postal order made payable to Bookpoint Ltd to the value of the cover price and allow the following for postage and packing:
UK & BFPO: £1.00 for the first book, 50p for the second book and 30p for each additional book ordered up to a maximum charge of £3.00.
OVERSEAS & EIRE: £2.00 for the first book, £1.00 for the second book and 50p for each additional book.

Name ....

Address ....

....

....

If you would prefer to pay by credit card, please complete:
Please debit my Visa/Access/Diner's Card/American Express (delete as applicable) card no:

Signature .... Expiry Date ....